THE KAT SEVERN CHRONICLES

ARDENT WARRIOR

Grosvenor House
Publishing Limited

PAUL E MASON

This book is published by
Grosvenor House Publishing Ltd
Link House
140 The Broadway, Tolworth, Surrey, KT6 7HT.
www.grosvenorhousepublishing.co.uk

This book is a work of fiction. Any resemblance to
people or events, past or present, is purely coincidental.

A CIP record for this book
is available from the British Library

ISBN 978-1-80381-439-1

PART SIX

THE KAT SEVERN CHRONICLES

PART I

DEBUTANTE WARRIOR

PART II

CLANDESTINE WARRIOR

PART III

SALVATION WARRIOR

PART IV

SOLITARY WARRIOR

PART V

INSURGENT WARRIOR

PART VI

ARDENT WARRIOR

ARDENT:

"To eagerly peruse, enthusiastic, passionate, devoted."

WARRIOR:

"A person experienced in, or capable of engaging in combat or warfare."

By the beginning of the twenty-second century the World had changed. Climates, nations, politics, all were in a state of upheaval. Much of the Earth, devastated from years of nuclear conflict, was still a contaminated wilderness.

From this decay rose a new order, for those who had survived the conflict and their descendants, now built a new life, crowding into a few gigantic cities.

For the vast majority, just existing day-to-day was hard enough, but a twisted few, some living in highly privileged circumstances, privately desired to over-turn the new order and fragile peace, and return to a state of global conflict. Their reasoning defying any sane mind.

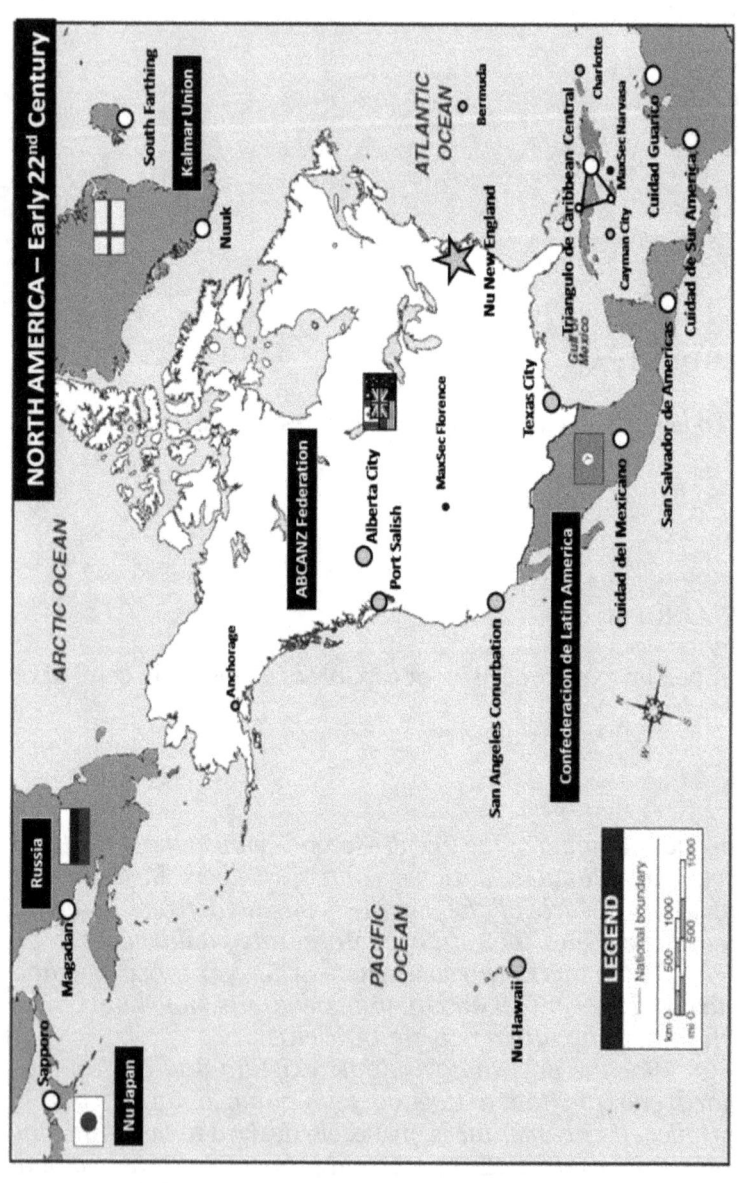

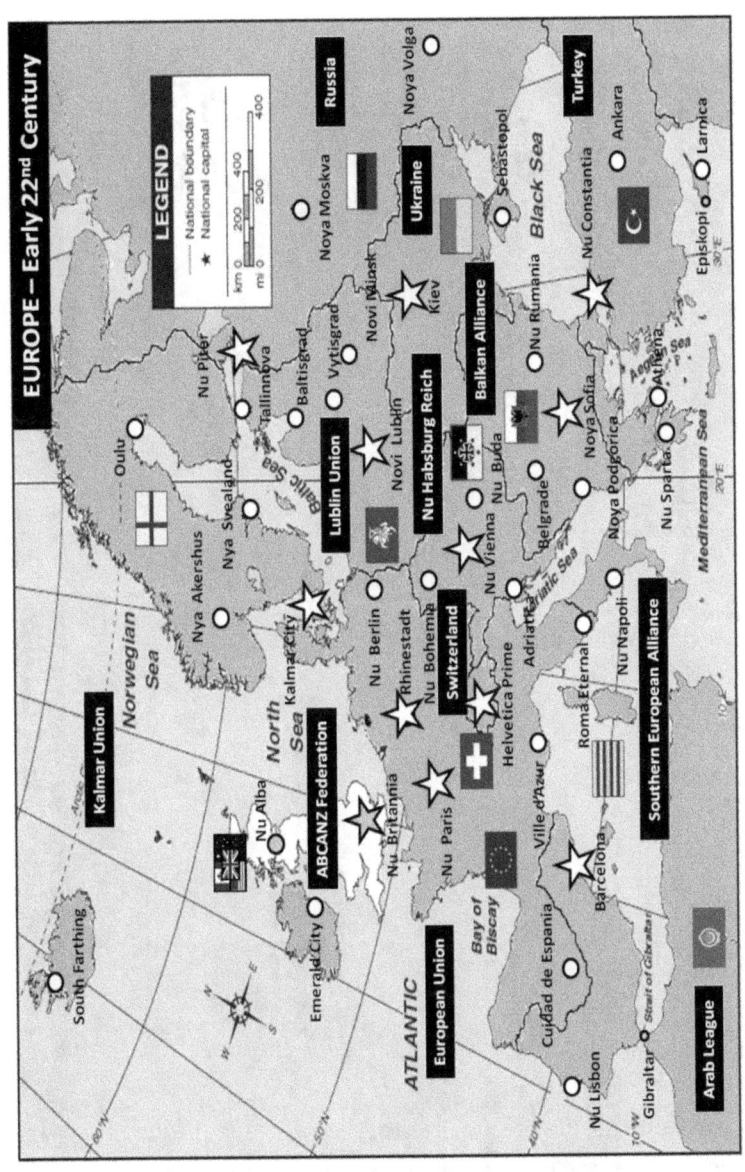

EUROPE – Early 22nd Century

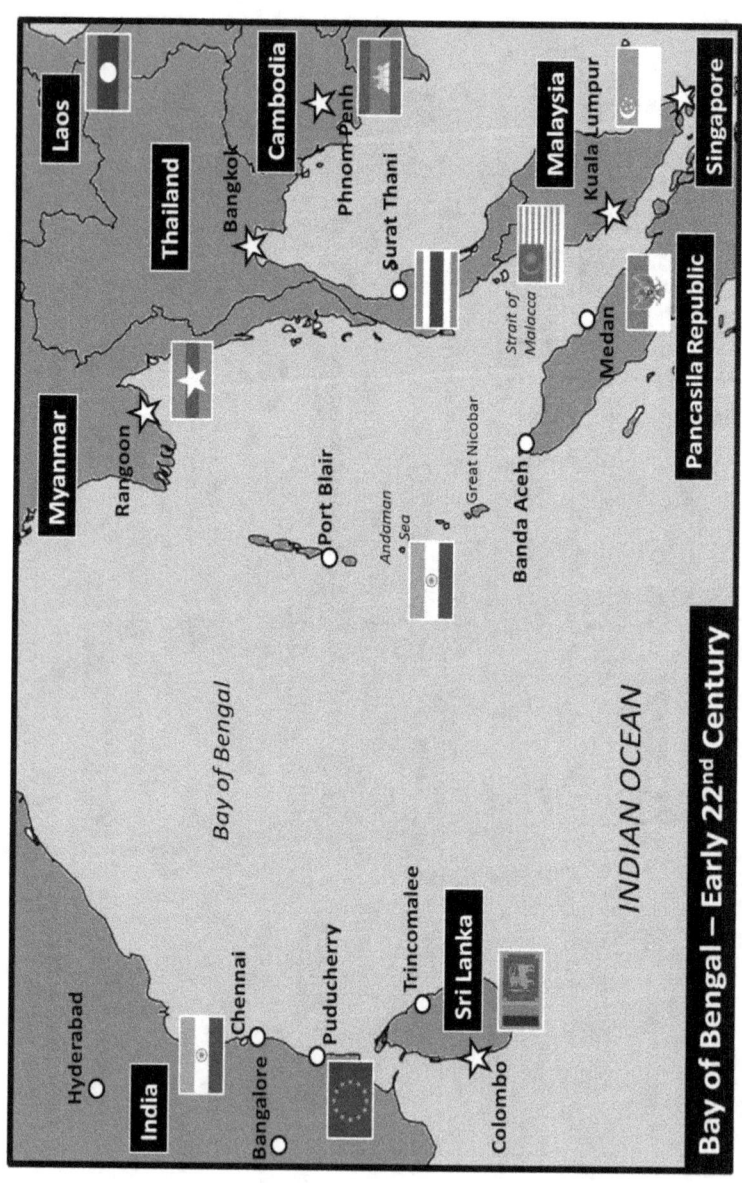

Bay of Bengal – Early 22nd Century

SIX : ONE

Lieutenant Kat Severn had been 'looking for a fight' for most of the last month. The 'pirates' who supposedly frequented these waters must be lying low, hiding.

It wasn't just the pirates who were avoiding her. She hadn't exchanged crossed swords, crossed gunfire, nor crossed words with anyone or anything.

This had to be a first.

She finished dressing, zipping up the front of her Fleet-issue dark grey shipsuit and turned to locate Anna, her Equerry, who was withdrawing to her own, adjoining cabin.

Kat quickly put an end to that. "We need to talk."

Conversation with Anna inevitably included crossed words, occasionally crossed knives and gunfire too.

Anna stopped, and without bending her always rigid spine a single millimetre, glanced over her shoulder. "I've never known you to have problems getting words out, ma'am. What's keeping you so quiet?"

"I'm not quiet," Kat shot back in her own defence, then realised that once again, Anna was counter-attacking before Kat had begun her own assault.

"All morning, from the moment you woke up, Lieutenant, Princess, Severn-ship, you've been as silent as a statue."

Kat's reply sounded weak, even to her. "Lost in thought."

"Well, when you find your way home, I'll be next door helping Grace with her schoolwork."

"It is progressing extremely well," Safi, Kat's self-learning personal computer, or HI (Heuristic Intellect) added from her usual position on Kat's left collarbone. The thought that Safi, after her latest ultra-expensive upgrade, was probably worth as much as a significant part of ship they were sailing in, and was now utilising her not insignificant abilities helping an eleven-year-old girl catch up on missed learning, was not what Kat wanted to hear.

"Thank you, Safi," Anna said.

"That is what we need to talk about. A warship is no place to raise a child."

"Agreed. It most certainly isn't. But the *Bella* isn't a warship," said Anna.

"It is. In all but name," Kat snapped right back, placing her hands on her hips. "The *Fires of Beltane* mounts a rack of Harlequin ASMs, has a rail-gun, and has AMAP hull enhancement in critical locations. And, we are out here, searching for piracy and other illegal activities."

"You may recall that it was Emma and I who were the contracting party in Fitzroy. I initiated the contract and now represent all the civilians currently on-board this ship. And there is nothing in the contract of this *Merchant Vessel* that makes her a warship. We might be considered 'DEMS,' to use the old, World War Two vernacular, a 'Defensively Equipped Merchant Ship' but, we are *not* a warship."

"We've got a troop-sized ship's detachment of Land Force Infantry."

"And a team of scientist and researchers, as well as all their equipment on-board. This ship has shipping containers almost everywhere that can take one."

"We have to look like a merchant ship if we're going to get a pirate to take a look at us. Any smart pirate would just sail on by or hide from a warship." Kat said, her voice rising.

"There you go, talking like a true Severn," Anna snapped. "No wonder Commodore Finklemeyer insisted I be the management representative of the civilians on the *Bella*. Captain Gillan and the original crew were very happy when they found out that you wouldn't be in their direct chain-of-command."

Kat started to point out they were civilians, so whatever relationship they might have with a Fleet Lieutenant, it wouldn't be hooked into any official chain-of-command. Certainly not any chain-of-command that an organisation might normally operate under. Under 'Special Circumstances' perhaps, but . . .

Kat heard the creak of the door opening between her cabin and Anna's. Grace stood there, her young eyes wide.

When Kat had first met Grace, she'd assumed the girl might be nine or ten. The ship's galley had been kind and she was filling out, but she still didn't look her full eleven years.

Except for those bright, limpid eyes. Eyes that had seen so much and lost so much more. Eyes so young they should not have that much 'old' in them.

"Are you arguing about me, Auntie Anna?"

"No honey. I often have these little 'chats' with the Princess."

"You're not going to lose your job, are you? We won't have to leave the ship, will we?" Grace struggled to say the words, her lip beginning to tremble.

"No Grace, you don't have to worry about that, not one bit. The Princess can't fire me even if she wanted to. Anna Sykes the civilian, the Equerry, was actually employed by the Princess's mother, so it is she who would have to fire me. And, the Princess wants to talk to her mother even less than you or I ever wanted to talk to Granny Jess."

The girl's eyes seemed to get even bigger. "Really?"

"Really," replied Anna. "And, *Captain* Anna Sykes of the ABCANZ Land Forces was given this posting by Manning and Records on the instructions of the Director of Fleet Intelligence, with the Chief of the Defence Staff and probably King James himself in collusion, so don't you worry yourself about that, my dear. Go and finish your schoolwork."

"Safi makes learning fun," Grace said and closed the door.

"I make learning fun," Safi said with more delight in her voice than a computer should ever have.

Kat sat down at the cabin's desk. Anna crossed the room to sit on Kat's bunk. Although Kat was a major shareholder in the Lennox Group, the *Bella* was fitted out as if she was warship. The facilities and interior decor of this ship were austere, functional and actually shouted nothing but 'warship.' However, her external paint job very deliberately suggested she remained a civilian merchant ship.

The accommodation for the scientists and researchers was another matter. Professor Brooks had taken for granted that the shipping containers were his to fill with gadgets, accommodation, recreation and any required technical support that he and his team might require.

The Land Force Troopers on-board were certainly making good use of the fitness equipment, which was good, as in recent weeks there had been no physical activity for them, other than their daily morning run around the top deck of the ship.

"I take it you are not happy with the current arrangements?" Anna said.

"When my Grandpa Jim conceded and gave me the *Bella*, it appeared to be just what I'd always dreamed of. An independent command to go and explore, a research team to study anything we stumbled across, and a detachment of Troopers and a rail-gun in case we needed to do something about what we'd found. What more could a girl ask for?"

Anna chuckled. "It might be nice if we were actually doing some of that."

"Exactly." Kat tried to smile, but it was more of a grimace.

The *Bella* had left 1st Fleet's Hampton Roads base, in Nu New England, crossed the Atlantic and entered the Mediterranean. She had then transited through the Suez Canal and Red Sea before reaching the Indian Ocean, using established 'green' coded STRs (Safe Transit Routes) the entire way. Almost three weeks had passed when they reached 4th Fleet's Thunder Cove base on the atoll of Diego Garcia to resupply, having maintained a steady eighteen knots throughout most of the voyage, a distance of more than eight thousand nautical miles. Once there, they had also embarked their absent Land Force Infantry Detachment and a number of additional scientists. That resupply had taken another week, and that was three, nearly four weeks ago. They had even taken an evening ashore to celebrate the news that Emma Pemberton-Byrne had given birth to a healthy three-point-five kilo baby girl. The infant's name was yet to be announced, but both mother and baby were apparently doing well. Kat had Safi arrange all the usual congratulatory gifts from herself, Mike, her dedicated close-protection security officer, and the crew of the *Bella*.

"When do you think that anyone will comment on your report?" Anna asked.

Kat said nothing, she just shook her head and shrugged.

In the decades that followed the war, those who survived the death and destruction built new lives, concentrated into a few gigantic cities. Much of the land outside of the cities was still uninhabitable with radiation, biological or chemical contamination.

A few opted to live outside these cities. Often it was individuals who had previously lived on the fringes of society, or those who didn't want laws and regulation, and therefore the imposed authority and order that city-life inevitably necessitated, for harmonious cohabitation. The option to live in small, isolated communities gave them their perceived ideal of 'freedom,' but at a price. Their lives were hard, with rising sea levels, contaminated land, occasional mutated creatures and the ever-present need for almost total self-sufficiency, that potentially turned their supposed 'dream' into a living nightmare.

It also cost money, significant amounts of money, to find a location and set-up a community. That meant significant unsecured loans or private sponsorship. If sponsored, that led to another, darker question . . . who, and why?

Questions that neither Kat's Grandpa Jim

nor her father William Severn, the Prime Minister of the ABCANZ Federation had answers for.

These 'settlers,' 'colonists' or whatever else they wanted to call themselves, on top of all their other hardships, also attracted pirates. Bad people who preyed on these often isolated and unprotected communities.

Independently owned merchant vessels made irregular calls among these dispersed settlements and communities, bringing essential medical supplies and trading any surplus crops or products the people had to sell. But these ships had started disappearing. Four vessels in as many months.

As much as the people in these communities really didn't want to see a uniformed Fleet Officer of the ABCANZ Federation, or any other nation for that matter . . . and especially not a Severn . . . many were secretly quite pleased to see the Fires of Beltane *and that someone with the authority of international law was finally taking an interest in them.*

Was Kat actually going to be appreciated by someone, even if it was by people who normally wanted to live unconventional lives? She certainly wasn't appreciated by her own team of scientists whose planned exploration was now on indefinite hold. Nor by the *Bella*'s crew, who didn't like waiting . . . waiting for the pirates, wherever they might be, to make their opening move.

"What's the matter, Kat," Anna asked her softly.

"Nothing," Kat insisted, then noticed that her right foot was tapping. She stopped it. Her stomach was still churning.

"I'm not stupid. I know you," her Equerry said, eyeing Kat. "You're all anxious because those nasty old pirates won't come out to play with you," she added in her best pre-school voice.

"No," Kat insisted.

"What's it been, three months . . . four, since someone took a shot at you? Since you terminated some very deserving low-life from any future existence?"

"Something like that," Kat admitted lamely.

"I think you're starting to enjoy all the fuss and feathers."

Kat had been warned by those who should know, experienced police or justice department operatives, private security agents, old Staff Sergeant Instructors, that the 'rush' could become as addictive as any drug. Was she really hooked on the adrenaline rush of being 'not quite' killed? Or was it doing the killing? She swallowed hard on that thought.

Anna shook her head. "Princess, get your head on straight. You've got nothing to worry about on the *Bella*. Don't you think we can't recognise those silly games your Grandpa Jim plays, that he thinks will keep you safe? Yes, they put me in the chain-of-command for the civilians, but when all hell is breaking loose, Captain Gillan is going to be looking your way for orders, not mine. Because you'll be there, at his elbow. And me? I'm going to be under my bunk, holding Grace safe."

That forced a laugh from Kat. Despite Anna's constant claims to being a very devout coward, Kat would more than likely be following Anna into conflict rather than leading her.

"Now, if you don't mind. I've got to go and help a little girl catch-up on a whole lot of missing education. I don't know what they were doing in those Sharjah schools, but it wasn't teaching."

"Any worse that when you were at those same schools?" Kat asked.

"Not me. Vicky and I had the very best education in Emirates City, paid for by our father's employers at the bank," replied Anna as she withdrew through the connecting door into the next cabin.

"You should chill out," said Safi into Kat's ear.

"What?" Kat exclaimed. "Go help teach the little girl.

And you are not my therapist," she snapped back at her HI. Maybe it was time to stop upgrading Safi every time something new came along. It seemed that every new addition to Safi, no matter what it was supposed to do, just gave her even more of an attitude, especially as she now had a real adolescent girl to learn from too!

Kat left her cabin and headed angrily towards the bridge. Hopefully she'd get some respect there.

She hadn't got halfway to the *Fire of Beltane*'s command deck when Professor Brooks apprehended her.

"When are we going to do some actual science?" he demanded.

"Good morning, Professor," said Kat politely, showing that she hadn't forgotten the customary exchange of pleasantries, even if he had. "I understand that pirates have a tendency to kill or enslave the crews of the ships they capture," Kat told him, as matter-of-factly as she could. "It's all in the Intel briefing we got from Fleet Command."

"Yes, I have read the file."

Kat gave him a thin smile, "Then you'll therefore understand why I might put a higher priority on neutralising the threat of pirates before we get down to any serious research. I'm very sorry Professor, but you may have to wait a little while longer."

"Regrettable. Understandable, but nevertheless most regrettable."

Kat managed to get another three paces nearer to the bridge, but the Professor stayed in step with her. "Is there any update from Marion Island?" He raised an eyebrow, as Kat came to a halt.

"Professor, I am as curious as you are to know what was going on down there. I'd honestly love to be there right now, believe me, but I've been *ordered* to stay away. Both of my mother's sisters, Dee and Philippa are currently there. I trust them both, implicitly. They know what they're doing, so I'm sure I'll get word if there's anything new."

"I too have been most curious, Professor," said Safi once Kat had finished speaking.

"As I would expect you to be, Miss Safi," Brooks said,

with a slight bow, certainly more than just a nod, towards Kat's collar bone where Safi was positioned. More respect than he'd ever offered Kat's 'Princess' status. "I have been given access to the recording you made when first opening the portal into the largest cylinder," he added. "Quite fascinating. We have to understand that technology."

"I agree, we do," Kat said and left it at that.

Professor Brooks mistook the following silence, and continued. "I know you saw weather maps, but did you see anything regarding ocean currents? We would need to run tests, but I have computer models that suggest the South Indian current brings cold Antarctic waters, that pass by Marion Island, eastwards then north, becoming the West Australia current. Twice a year, and if predicted correctly, when the South Asian Monsoon kicks in and then drops out, and reverses the gyre's overall direction, there are then a few days when this current won't be picked up by the warm South Equatorial current and carried back around. Instead, it continues north, up the eastern side of Sumatra and disperses in approximately our current location, amongst the islands of the Andaman and Nicobar Archipelagos."

"And your point is, Professor?" Kat asked, not really sure where this was going.

"I'm suggesting what *if* whatever the Chinese were doing down there involved the ocean's currents as well as the weather formations, then we may find evidence of it here."

"If you say so, Professor," Kat said.

"It is a possibility that I cannot begin to answer while you are busy hunting miscreants. But perhaps there is another way to do so."

What sort of trap was the scientist laying for her?

"If we could launch an automated beacon to monitor water temperature and current's direction, that then transmitted the data back to us, I think I could anticipate exactly when these windows will occur, and it won't impact on your other intended activities."

"Except that merchant vessels don't routinely launch automated beacons. If a pirate ship enters these waters, which is highly likely, and sees us and a beacon, it will be a dead giveaway that we are not what we are trying to appear to be."

"Unless you delayed deploying it until we were leaving and we used a sub-surface beacon."

"And as you have already prepared such a beacon . . ."

"Yes, there is that," the Professor admitted, his hands open, palms up, in polite supplication to Kat.

"I'll tell Captain Gillan that you want to launch a scientific beacon," Kat said.

"Thank you very much," Professor Brooks said and headed in the opposite direction to Kat.

Kat watched his retreating back. Was he mad? How could something from Marion Island possibly end up here if left to the currents of the ocean? He was the scientist, and theorising based on tiny specs of data was what they did. Then they applied further research to prove or dispel such a theory, one way or another.

"Good morning, Lieutenant," Captain Jensen Gillan said as she entered the *Bella*'s bridge, and stopped her having any further thought on that subject.

"Morning, Captain Gillan. Anything unusual overnight?"

"The answer this morning is the same as it's been for the last two mornings. No, ma'am. Nothing unusual. Nothing at all actually. Although there could be anything hiding in all these island's coves and inlets, especially if powered down, or deliberately running dark."

"Even with all the enhanced sensors we now have?" she asked him. "You really can't locate them?"

"That's more of a job for those unemployed boffins of yours than the likes of me. It's their equipment after all."

Kat looked around at the usual bridge crew of the *Bella*. They looked more like pirates themselves than respectable merchant sailors. No two were attired the same way. The Captain was his usual flamboyant self. Sato, the navigator looked like she was about to spend the day on the beach, in shorts and a modest bikini top. All a bit casual, if not decidedly reprobate, for Kat's liking, but actually not inappropriate for the weather conditions outside the air-conditioned environment of the ship's internal compartments.

The *Fires of Beltane*'s exact origins remained unclear, as did that of most of her crew. Apparently contracted in good faith by Anna and their former Intel analyst, Emma Pemberton-Byrne in Fitzroy on the Falkland Islands, it turned out that the lack of alternatives to select from was probably deliberately manipulated by the Director of Fleet Intelligence and her Grandpa Jim. The crew too, it seemed had a pedigree that suggested most were former military, if not actually still serving. Apparently, they were the best that Commodore Finklemeyer had ever contracted, knowing their jobs forwards, backwards and inside-out. Emma, Safi and Mike, had all run deep searches on the ship and her senior crew members for any discrepancies. But, with no search results of any consequence or concern, they continued to operate, as per the clauses of the stated contract.

"Professor Brooks tells me he wants to launch a beacon. Something about checking the origin of the currents in these waters. Way, way beyond me, I'm afraid. I have no idea what or where he's going with this. What do you think?" Kat asked Gillan.

"About what? His theory on the ocean currents or the launching a monitor beacon?"

"Launching of a scientific monitor beacon."

"I told him, if it was okay with you, then it was okay with me. It's already prepped and ready for deployment from the aft crane."

"I told him the same, but he didn't mention that he'd already spoken to you."

"He must have been an impossible child," Sato added from her usual seat at the navigation board. "Playing his parents off against each other until he got the answer he wanted."

"You're assuming he actually had parents and wasn't created in a laboratory somewhere. I've certainly not seen any evidence to support that he had them." Gillan muttered.

"Is there a problem with launching this beacon just before we leave here?" Kat asked, trying to stay 'on-topic.'

Despite the Professor's underhand approach to get their approval, if it didn't compromise the true intent of their mission, Kat conceded that the scientists did deserve some research.

Captain Gillan nodded. "I had my people check it out yesterday, when he asked me. We can safely deploy it and leave. It operates sub-surface, only popping up to transmit its data packet twice a day, then dropping back down again. Unless you're scanning for such devices, and it happens to be transmitting at the very same moment, rather than just collecting data, you'd never know it was there."

"We'd planned to get underway about in ten minutes," Sato added.

Kat nodded to the Captain in acceptance of the beacon's deployment, "Very well, proceed," then went to her station on his far left. From there she could keep one eye on the sensor board and the other on the weapons console.

"Stand by to launch scientific beacon," Gillan ordered.

"It's on the hook, Captain . . . deploying arm . . . ready to release on your order," came the report back from the crane operator further aft, overlooking the *Bella*'s rear hold.

There was a slight rumble through the stationary vessel as the arm of the crane extended, lifting the beacon up from the hold's floor, then swung it out, over the ship's side.

The operator nodded at the Captain. "Ready."

"Deploy the beacon," Captain Gillan ordered.

The beacon's outer-casing was of an old, outdated design, maybe from the war, exactly what a frugal merchant vessel's skipper might use and not damage his already slim profit margins.

The crane held it steady for a few moments while a test routine or two were checked, then once functioning as intended, the crane operator released the restraint on the hook.

The beacon sank beneath the waves. Almost a minute passed before it resurfaced. Data started to dance across the sensor operator's display, as water-jets activated and GPS sequences initiated to establish the beacon's location. Deployment complete, it disappeared back beneath the waves.

As soon as the crane's arm or boom, had retracted and was secured back into its 'travelling' configuration, Sato confirmed they were ready to get underway.

"Incoming vessel," the operator at the sensor board suddenly advised. "She's making ten knots, coming out of the passage between Nancowry and Trinkat Islands."

"Why didn't we detect her sooner." Kat immediately demanded.

"There's a natural basin or harbour between the islands of Nancowry and Camorta, ma'am. Dozens of inlets and hideaways on both sides. The eastern passage is only seventy metres wide and not particularly deep. The western passage is much wider, around two hundred and fifty metres, but is obscured by the bulk of Trinkat island, creating a sensor 'dark spot.'"

"Nancowry Harbour has been used by sailors since at least the seventeenth century and is considered as 'one of the safest natural harbours in the world.' It was often used as a base for piracy and in 1868 two ships of the Royal Navy's East India Squadron under the command of Captain Bedingfield on the screw sloop HMS Wasp accompanied by HMS Satellite, a screw corvette, entered the natural harbour, destroying ships and several huts ashore," advised Safi into Kat's ear.

"Nav, use the thrusters. Bring us about, so we are 'bow on bow' to the incoming vessel, ensure we present the minimum target profile."

"Aye, Captain, engaging thrusters, bow on bow, minimum target profile," Sato acknowledged.

As the *Bella* adjusted her profile to meet the incoming ship, Kat kept her eyes on the bridge's front windows.

A ship, easily twice the size of the *Fires of Beltane*, possibly even larger, approached them.

"Engineering, give me everything you've got for the thrusters," Gillan said into his comm-link. "Nav, back away from them, but maintain a 'bow-on' profile, I don't want them having a shot at our hull sides or stern."

"Aye, sir. Get us out of here, but protect the propulsion spaces."

As Captain Gillan handled his ship, Kat watched the other vessel. It appeared to be a medium sized freighter. *She's a bit big for a tramp freighter*, Kat decided. Tramp freighters were usually small, to enable access to the smaller and shallower ports and anchorages, and had no fixed schedule or published itinerary, being available for private charter. Its top deck was stacked high with containers. Its bridge was up-front along with accommodation for the crew and perhaps passengers. The propulsion spaces, the reactor and plasma tracts that provided the power, were located in the middle.

"Sensors, confirm her reactor signature," Kat ordered.

"Looks to be a single teapot, ma'am," said the crewman. "But, I'm still checking."

Kat replicated the sensor station's display onto her own board. He was only using a passive scan, deliberately not wanting to tell them anything that would inform the other vessel that the *Bella* was anything but a soft, defenceless, merchant freighter.

Then again, a pirate vessel would be doing its best to look as innocent as a lamb too, hiding the wolf concealed within. At the moment, both vessels were about even in the 'lamb' department. Or, the other vessel might actually be what she appeared to be, even if the *Bella* was most definitely not.

"She's a bit underpowered. Active reactor signature is a single Northrop-Sperry Mariner 150," the sensor crewmen commented, then adjusted the parameters on a couple of his sweeps. "I'm not one-hundred percent with these new gadgets the boffins have added ma'am, but the neutrino profile seems too high for a single reactor, and her engineering spaces look a bit big for just one unit. I think there's two, and the second is bigger than 150 mega-watts. That is definitely a wolf trying to slip by as a lamb, that's for sure."

Captain Gillan said the exact same expletive that Kat was thinking.

"Your orders, ma'am?"

Evidently Grandpa Jim and The Fink don't really know these people nearly half as well as I do! This crew had no problem following me into the jaws of hell. In a fast countdown to a fight, Gillan isn't discussing the best course of action with Anna, but requesting battle orders from me!

Kat swallowed the first thing that came to mind, which involved significant amounts of unfettered violence to their adversaries' persons, and instead said something much more fitting. "Let's make completely sure someone, like the Indians or the Malaysians, aren't also out here searching for pirates. Wouldn't want my Grandpa Jim facing a media frenzy because two allied nations shot each other's vessels up, now would we."

Someone snickered at Kat's irreverent familiarity with a man who everyone else referred to as 'King James of the ABCANZ Federation.'

"I do hope we're not going to put me in a situation whereby official military doctrine and standard operating procedures will be in direct conflict with your own orders, Princess?" Gillan asked. "We have come across a vessel that may, or may not, be up to anything good, but they haven't actually engaged us. However, your instinct, your gut, is telling you that things could go pear-shaped at any moment. Will you let the procedures laid out in official doctrine take precedence, overriding your own, highly-trained killer instincts, or is it to be *Primum impetum?* We strike first?" He was openly smiling, but his words carried no less weight.

"No, absolutely not. Only after the hostile, if that is what they really are, has engaged us, will we take any offensive measures," Kat told him.

"I do believe the regulations also state we have the right to take appropriate actions to defend ourselves. Hesitation could cost you . . . us . . . our lives."

"It could, but suspicion, gut, whatever you want to call it, Captain, isn't fact . . . it's fear. If we deliberately defy our own clearly defined Rules of Engagement . . .

we've already lost."

"Perhaps," Gillian said, not really convinced. "Does the morale high-ground really have any true value? To you, a politician's daughter, a Severn, a Fleet Officer, I'm sure it does, but me . . . I'd rather just be alive when the sun goes down this evening." His earlier smile was gone.

The other ship put an end to any further discussion when it beat them to the comm-channel.

"Unidentified vessel, this is the *Storm Cloud V* out of Singapore. Identify yourself and where you are bound."

Captain Gillan took the comm-link's handset. "This is the merchant freighter *Fires of Beltane* out of Fitzroy, Falkland Islands. I'll tell you where I'm bound when you tell me where you've been."

That elicited a laugh, much as Kat expected. Profits were super tight in these waters and a good way to go out of business was to follow in the wake of another ship, trying to sell your cargo in an already satisfied market or to buy-up cargo that had been shipped in by others.

Both Kat and Gillian . . . especially Gillan . . . had spent enough time in bars amongst merchant crews to learn that much about how trade was apparently conducted in these waters.

The laughing voice became serious. "You tell me something interesting, then I'll tell you something even more interesting."

"Sounds fair," Gillan said. "Our last stop was Hut Bay on Little Andaman." It really had been. "They took all our agricultural related cargo and wanted more, but they passed on our heavy machinery, as someone had been there before us."

"That festering rat hole's not growing anywhere near as fast as it should be. If they're not careful they'll get over-extended on their finances," the voice on the other end of the comm-link said disparagingly.

Kat let them waffle on, and systematically took the ship ahead of her apart, layer by layer, deck by deck, as much as a passive sensor-scan allowed anyway. If the ship did have weapons, it didn't appear to have any capacitors charged, thereby enabling them to be used quickly. It appeared that it's only source of power was a tiny pulse of hot plasma running from their reactor's racetrack, keeping the ship's main battery constantly trickle charging.

"Can you power weapon systems directly from a main storage battery?" Kat asked the crewman at the engineering monitor board. "Even if fully charged, is it enough? Or do you need the reactor fully operational for a surge like that?"

"Theoretically, no, ma'am," was the answer she expected. "You are correct, the power cables and couplings aren't designed for the surge. However, something small, a 'one shot wonder,' might be able to put something out, especially if the propulsion units were idling. Really depends what it was, but it probably wouldn't do very much damage, not against a true warship, but as we're just a delicate, thin-skinned merchant," he said with a grin.

A knife wasn't much use in a gun fight, but it could make all the difference if it was initially just fists being used.

"Where have you been?" Captain Gillan asked them.

"We're just coming back from Kolo-kak on Katchal," the other claimed.

"I thought Katchal was 'off limits,' has protected status from the Indian Government?" Gillan said.

"Exactly. What better place to hide away than somewhere that everyone else thinks is prohibited? It's meant to prevent the indigenous tribes from being exploited by passing visitors, but no one has seen any of these supposed local tribes in thirty odd years. There's not much at Kolo-kak, but they certainly have money. They bought everything I had. I'm hauling my containers back empty, except for some plants that the pharma boys pay the big money for. It's a good place to drop by. Where you heading?"

But whoever was doing the talking over there must have figured he'd done enough to distract the Captain of the *Fires of Beltane*.

On Kat's sensor display, a capacitor suddenly appeared on the schematic of the other vessel, moving quickly from a dormant red into a charging yellow as it took power directly from the ship's reactor.

"Evasive manoeuvres," Kat shouted, but Safi had already activated an evasive pattern and overridden the Helm. The *Bella*'s thrusters pushed her left, then right, as her main propulsion kicked in and increased their speed. Bursts of heavy-calibre small-arms fire, twelve-point-seven, perhaps twenty millimetre armour-piercing rounds, sought them out.

"What the f . . ." came from the other ship on the still open comms channel, then it went dead.

The green coding in the engineering compartments on the displayed schematic showed one, then a second reactor on the *Storm Cloud V,* coming up to full power, shattering whatever cover they had been hiding behind. The other ship surged forward, on a twisting, turning course of its own, that suddenly presented a solid targeting solution to the *Bella*, but as quickly as it came, it was gone.

More substantial weapons looked to be coming on-line as they powered up.

Then Kat's sensor board went black, flickered twice then came back on.

"They're trying to jam us," the crewmen at the comms station reported. He did something to his board and some of the interference went away.

"Blast shields," was Kat's next order.

Merchant ships didn't routinely have armoured shielding for their glazed bridge windows. Some had storm-shuttering, but the gauge of the metal was considerably different.

The protective panels came down and it took a moment for her eyes to adjust, as overhead lighting came on to replace direct sunlight. Several large screens powered up, giving exactly the same view that the windows previously had, just fed by camera.

"Sato, back us up, get some distance between us." Kat ordered.

"You ready to test that new rail-gun, your Highness?" Gillan asked her.

"I certainly am, Captain. Deploy the rail-gun."

Kat had never targeted a rail-gun in anger before. All

the previous Fleet assets she'd ever served on, the Fast-Attack Corvettes *Berserker* and *Comanche*, her first command, the Fast-Intercept-Boat *Osprey*, and then the Remote Operational Support Platform *3-Alpha-9*, had all been equipped with either Mk67 Marlin torpedoes, Harlequin Anti-Ship-Missiles, multi-barrel MPT-SD anti-air systems or 127mm guns that fired conventional ammunition. None had been equipped with a rail-gun.

She had trained on targeting a rail-gun as a Midshipman, back at OTA(F) in her third term as part of her specific-to-branch trade-training that had qualified her as a Warfare Systems Officer, but that was several years ago. This was the first time she'd actually do the targeting and fire such a weapon system for real.

The rail-gun was essentially a pair of parallel electrical conductors, or 'rails,' along which a sliding armature was accelerated by the electromagnetic effects of a current flowing down one rail, into the armature, that held the dart, and then back along the other rail. Apparently, it was based on principles similar to those of the homopolar motor, which was way too much information for Kat, as she had no idea what that was!

The ammunition it used was a high-velocity kinetic-energy projectile (APFSDS), containing no conventional explosive warhead or propellant at all. With a muzzle velocity that exceeded two kilometres per second, it could deliver the standard forty millimetre diameter x 800 millimetre long, shaped tungsten-alloy dart out to a distance of eighty-five kilometres with devastating effect.

The *Storm Cloud V* was still under way, partly exposing her hull sides as she came about.

The *Bella* continued to back up, still only using her thrusters. Kat's bridge station, now displaying a schematic of the *Bella*'s own on-board 'weapon systems,' showed that all four of their capacitors were starting to change from red into amber, rapidly heading towards green and being fully charged. Thanks to new science, new tech, and a recent repair and refit, the *Bella* was now able to convert extra power directly, and quickly, from the plasma flux in her reactors.

Times were changing, and this pirate vessel was about to discover exactly how much!

Then Kat got her own surprise. Extra sensors from the *Bella*'s own scientists suggested that The *Storm Cloud V* might have some kind of improvised protective shielding. But it didn't matter, the kinetic energy of the rail-gun's projectile at this range, probably less than two kilometres, would punch through anything.

"Ahoy there, *Storm Cloud V*, this is the ABCANZ Federation vessel *Fires of Beltane*. I am Lieutenant Severn of the ABCANZ Fleet. You just fired upon me. Flood your reactor and prepare to be boarded."

Several comments, mostly expletives, as well as a few suggestions that were biologically impossible, came back in reply.

The two ships circled each other. Whatever the *Storm Cloud V* did, Captain Gillan kept the *Bella* pivoting, always keeping them 'bow on' towards the other vessel. The *Storm Cloud V* was now trying to back up too, but the proximity of the surrounding islands was limiting her manoeuvring options.

The range was almost point-blank. If the other ship turned-tail and tried to run south, or turned to port and tried to slip back between the two nearby islands, Kat would have an unrestricted view of the *Storm Cloud V*'s side or stern. But, both these options involved manoeuvring before any speed could be applied. Or, the *Storm Cloud V* could keep her current course, heading north, and go to full power and try to move past by the *Bella* into open waters and get some distance between them before the *Bella* could turn about and give pursuit. Neither option was good for the *Storm Cloud V*.

"Hostile's weapons are fully operational," the crewman at the sensor board advised.

"Any idea what she has? Any obvious weapon profiles?" Kat said.

"Your Highness, what are your orders?" Gillan asked her again.

Kat though about that for a full second, maybe two or three. "She's not getting away from us, Captain. If she wants to dance, we dance, but she can't run."

"Yes ma'am. Rail-gun is fully deployed and powered up. It's yours when you're ready."

The exact detail of the *Fires of Beltane*'s registration might be subject to conjecture, but Captain Gillan and Kat had quickly agreed on her weapons policy. Targeting and pressing the 'fire' button would only be done by a serving ABCANZ Officer. They must respect international law. They couldn't dispense justice to those in need of it, if they didn't operate within it themselves!

SIX : TWO

Lieutenant Kat Severn of the ABCANZ Fleet aimed the *Bella*'s recently installed rail-gun at the *Storm Cloud V*'s bow-on profile, her point-of-aim was approximately at the mid-point below the bridge, but above the top line of the hull. She'd deliberatelaqy targeted the above-hull superstructure to avoid the reactors, plasma tracts and other machine spaces within the hull itself.

"*Storm Cloud V*, this is your one and only warning. Flood your reactor immediately or I will fire on you," Kat said, her voice was cold, without emotion, just factual.

Silence answered her.

"Prepare for an Evasive Assault Pattern," she announced.

Around her the bridge crew clicked home their restraint harnesses. "For what we are about to receive, may we be truly thankful," someone muttered sarcastically.

It was only a precaution, but Kat had to be ready to evade anything the hostile ship might throw back at them.

"*Storm Cloud V*, I will fire on you on the count of three."

Obscenities, in several languages, came back at her this time, one suggested she was bluffing.

"One," Kat said. "Safi, prepare to implement EAP on my mark."

"Ready," Safi advised.

"Two . . . three. Fire!" Kat said and flipped the switch that sent the dart down the rails.

It was all over before it had even begun. The tungsten-alloy dart punched effortlessly through the metal and interior of the *Storm Cloud V*'s superstructure. Travelling down the full length of the vessel.

"Safi, evaluate their movement, I want to know if it's deliberate, controlled manoeuvring or a result of the dart impact."

Kat waited for the 'ready' notification from the rail-gun's crew, confirming that a second dart sabot was loaded onto the launch rails, then took aim at the mid-point of the hostile vessel's bridge.

At the very last second, she held back from firing the second dart. Hopefully, the damage was already done.

"*Storm Cloud V*, you are hit. Flood your reactor and we will board and provide assistance." Kat advised them.

"Never," was the single word of reply.

Another fusillade of heavy-calibre small arms fire reached out for the *Fires of Beltane*. It was unlikely they'd inflict any significant damage, even at this relatively close range, but anyone outside, on the *Bella*'s external areas, such as those now crewing the rail-gun, were forced to seek cover. Then several shoulder-launched Rocket-Propelled-Grenades got added to the weapon fire being directed onto the *Bella*.

Two RPGs impacted amidships.

"Damage Control," Captain Gillan demanded.

"Couple of the shipping containers took the impact, sir. One's scrap, but the other can be salvaged."

Captain Gillan turned to Kat. "Can you please get this over with? I rather like my newly repaired ship the way she is, without any holes in her hull!"

Kat flipped up the safety cover of the rail-gun's firing switch. She realigned the cross hairs of the targeting array onto the *Storm Cloud V*'s bridge and as soon as the audible tone changed, confirming that she had target 'lock,' she fired.

Again, due to the extreme velocity of the dart, the short flight time and the damage the impact inflicted, it all happened in the blink of an eye. The *Storm Cloud V* appeared to be turning on her own axis.

"Flood your reactors and prepare to be boarded," Kat ordered them again.

"Leave us alone," came from the open comm-channel.

"Piss off, and leave us, or a lot of people are going to die."

"You are the ones who are going to die," Kat pointed out.

"We have the crews from two other ships on-board. If you shoot at us again, we'll kill them all."

"Not good," Captain Gillan said out-loud to nobody in particular.

"Surrender now or my next dart will target your propulsion," Kat told anyone who might be listening.

"What about those other crews?" Sato asked.

"We only have their word that they have them," Kat said, keeping her eyes on the targeting array.

"You're a hard woman," Gillan said. "I hope you're right."

So did Kat.

"They've flooded both of their reactors," announced Safi before the crew member monitoring the sensors could report it. "The *Storm Cloud V* now has only stored battery power. Her reactors are down."

"We surrender. You can board us. We won't fight you," was spoken by a new voice.

"I suggest, for your sake, that you do not," Kat answered. "My Land Force detachment could certainly use the exercise."

That got no reply.

"Ensign Steiger," Kat spoke into her personal comm-link.

"Standing by," he answered.

"Prepare to board the ship as soon as we come alongside and have matched their speed and course.

"Aye, ma'am. Understood."

"Captain Gillan, please place your ship alongside the *Storm Cloud V*."

"Yes, your Highness."

It took the best part of thirty minutes to come alongside the *Storm Cloud V*. Once in position, Mike launched two Rigid Inflatable Boats, or RIBs, each containing a Squad of Land Force Infanteers. One would attempt to board near the stern, the other towards the bow. Once secure they'd attempt to get a gangway or something solid into place that provided easier access than climbing up the other vessel's hull and over the safety rail.

At least that was their intention.

As Gillan manoeuvred the *Bella* into position, perfectly matching the speed and course of the two vessels, Kat released her restraint harness, left the bridge and dropped down several decks to join the Troopers of her Land Force Detachment. Third Squad would join their colleagues on the other vessel, just as soon as a gangway could be rigged.

She ran into Anna, holding a full set of chameleon body-armour.

"Thought you might need this, just the thing for a well-dressed Princess this season," her Equerry advised.

"I thought you'd be cowering under a bunk somewhere," Kat shot back, somewhat annoyed.

"I was, but I got bored down there on my own."

"Where's Grace?"

"Still engrossed in her homework. Confident that we'll all protect her."

Kat tried an alternative tack to side-step her 'Nannying' Equerry. "They surrendered."

"Right," Anna replied and continued to block Kat's passage through the *Bella* until the Princess did her own, reluctant surrender.

"Can't I put it on over the top?" said Kat, tugging at her shipsuit.

"You know full well that the thermal management system that modulates the suit's temperature and converts any excess heat into stored energy, won't function right if you wear that under it," Anna said with slight shake of her head.

"You're not very trusting," Kat said. She glanced left, then right, to check they were alone, then kicked off her boots and unzipped and wriggled out of her shipsuit. Taking the paramagnetic-coated base-layer of the protective armour from Anna, she fitted the padded crotch section in-between her legs and her Equerry then knelt to zip-up the fasters that ran from ankle to hip, up the outside of each of Kat's legs.

Anna then stood and silently handed Kat the parts of hard, armoured outer-shell that protected her knees, hips and thighs. Finally boots to improve grip, protect and support the lower leg, foot and ankle, and generally absorb the impact of a fully laden, fully armoured Ground Force soldier operating in a potentially hostile environment.

Only when Kat's lower-half was fully 'suited up,' did Anna respond. "No, not at all trusting. And, not unlike a certain Princess that I happen to know. Except that *I* do actually learn from my previous bad experiences and encounters."

Helped by Anna, Kat then zipped-up the top part of the base-layer suit to just beneath her chin and donned the armoured sections that protected her arms, elbows, shoulders and back, before finally clipping-in and tightening the breast plate.

Anna finally handed Kat the gloves and helmet. It was the Mk14, the open faced, pilot-like helmet with separate visor and breather. Kat knew that a new Mk15 helmet had recently been introduced, with a full-face visor and integral breather, but ship's detachments were never a priority when it came to new kit issue and would be way down on the list.

Kat didn't put either the gloves or the helmet on. She stooped down and retrieved her service pistol from its holster on the discarded shipsuit, then secured in into the built-in holster at her waist.

"The chameleon circuit is off," Anna told Kat. "So your base layer and helmet will stay at standard issue 'Fleet' grey, unless of course, you decide to activate it."

Satisfied, Anna now stepped aside and let Kat run to join the line of Troopers waiting to cross to the other vessel once the improvised gangway was rigged.

She arrived just as Mike concluded his initial assessment.

"Corporal Davis with First Squad advises that nothing much is working on the *Storm Cloud V*, ma'am. If I wasn't such an optimist, I'd think they were setting a trap for us," Mike advised. "Staff Freeman, your thoughts, please."

"Pirate vessels are not exactly known for their adherence to preventative maintenance schedules, sir," he growled. "It's pretty much what I had expected to find," came from Mike's comm-link.

"Okay, let's get that gangway secured, A-SAP, Staff."

"Sorry, sir. May have to disappoint on that. Not much to secure it onto at this end. All the usual ways are either missing or so badly corroded that I wouldn't want to put my trust in them to hold when loaded up with hairy-arsed Troopers."

"Understood, we'll go with Plan B then," advised Mike immediately, knowing not to question the Staff Sergeant's professional assessment. "RIBs are to return to the *Bella* and take Third Squad and the Command Team across amidships."

"Roger that," Staff Sergeant Freeman acknowledged.

Kat pulled on her gloves and helmet, then dropped her visor, following Third Squad's example. She followed them down the *Bella*'s starboard-side access-way to the RIB load-out point. By the time they reached it, the first of their two inflatable craft was waiting to receive them.

It took longer for them to climb up the scaling ladder, now thrown down the hull-side of the *Storm Cloud V*, than it had for the RIBs to cross the distance between the two vessels.

When Kat eventually reached the other ship's hand rail, Staff Sergeant Freeman was waiting. Like her, his helmet's visor was down, his breather-mask fitted.

He tapped it. "I think you might want to wait until we get a few more hatches open, your Highness, it smells pretty bad inside," he informed her.

All the Troopers who had initially boarded, at the bow and the stern of the *Storm Cloud V*, were also in full battle armour. Their visors were down, feeding their head-up-displays with data and protecting their eyes. Most had their breathers fitted too, filling their lungs with filtered, tanked air.

Kat, like Mike and every other Fleet Officer, had learned in her first couple of weeks at the Officer Training Academy (Fleet) to never argue with a senior NCO. She'd also seen ample evidence to substantiate that ideology since leaving OTA(F), so she waited.

"Corporal Davis, conduct another 'sniff test.'" Mike ordered over the comm-net.

A moment later, the Trooper that had been ordered by his Corporal to lift his visor and remove his mask, to test the air, reported back. "This boat freaking' stinks. It's real bad," He coughed hard, sniffed again. "That's evil . . . much worse than your usual tramp freighter." He re-checked his data tablet for several seconds. "Nothing's shows as being actually toxic, but it's ripe, sir. Enough to make you want to puke."

Kat nodded at the report, then retracted her own visor, and mask, exposing her face.

She had never been on a 'pirate' vessel before, recalling her time on-board *Das Furchtlos,* the mercenary-crewed ship they'd boarded and taken in southern African waters, and then the stinking crew-cabin she'd hidden in on the merchant vessel *Sekhmet*, when they'd apprehended that illegal arms shipment near Cape Town. Both had smelt decidedly unsavoury, concentrated by the vessel's confined spaces, especially on the lower decks where you couldn't simply 'open a window.' She vividly remembered the heady, vomit-inducing mix of stale sweat on unwashed bodies, ingrained tobacco smoke, rain-soaked dogs, propulsion drive lubricants and over-boiled vegetables.

As Kat worked her way through the vessel's interior, then down a deck, deeper into the *Storm Cloud V*'s hull, the stink grew much worse. Added to those usual smells was a whole different blend of filth . . . sewerage and death.

Mike and Staff Freeman followed close behind her.

The stench grew steadily as they reached the now open access hatch to the vessel's mid-ship cargo hold. The Lance Corporal coming through the hatch confirmed that the ladder access-well was clear of any potential booby traps.

Kat climbed through, into the ladder access-well, and very nearly threw up. The stench was unbelievably bad. She looked out, over the dark cargo bay, not actually that dissimilar in size and shape to that on the *Bella*, if you ignored the complete lack of any, even basic level, maintenance. In the gloom she couldn't see hold's floor and presumably the source of the unearthly smell.

Whilst Kat paused, to regain her composure and spit out the bile now in her throat, the Staff Sergeant moved swiftly past her, checking again for any bobby-traps in the well space and on the ladder down to the hold's floor. Thankfully he found nothing. He still had his visor down and breather fitted. Despite feeling ill, Kat decided not to follow his example, electing to keep her limited supply of filtered, tanked air for now. She might need it later.

"Are the propulsion spaces secure?" she asked Mike.

He nodded. "We're getting all the same excuses we got on the *Das Furchtlos*. Somehow the propulsion teams never seem to know what their Captain and his bridge crew are up to, they just 'tend reactors and plasma tracts.'"

"We'll soon see just how well that holds up in a court of law," Kat told him in reply.

"Staff, take the First Squad and begin a deck-by-deck sweep, every hatch, every cabin, anywhere someone could hide," Mike ordered.

"Yes, sir," Freeman advised, then started talking to his subordinate NCOs on his comm-link.

Kat turned to face the dark open space of the hold.

"Can we get some light down there? See what's creating all this stink?"

"Doesn't appear to be any internal lighting, ma'am. Except what's in this access-well," said the Lance Corporal whom she'd passed coming out when she went in, "And, the hold's top hatches look to have been welded shut."

Kat leaned over the edge, and dropped her visor. She cycled through the different display options her head-up-display offered, trying to gather more data as to what festered below in the darkness. Night-vision, thermal, electromagnetic emission. Every new image offered her

ARDENT WARRIOR

something, but actually, even when collectively combined and manipulated by Safi, it gave her little more.

"Can we maybe improvise?" Kat asked.

"Given the nature of the smell, there might be a methane build-up in there, ma'am, so we need to be real careful how we proceed," the Lance Corporal said. "It's a specialist's job, we need a combustible gas detector unit, a CGD, and I'm not sure we've actually got one with us."

"I can assist," advised Safi suddenly. "Methane or CH4, is colourless, odourless and heavier than air. Because of this, as the Lance Corporal rightly advises, it cannot be detected without specialist detection equipment. I have combustible gas sensors on my outer casing, enabling me to provide a warning to Kat of any such substance in her immediate vicinity, but they are somewhat limited in their range. I will need to reformat and recalibrate them to extend the coverage area. Methane is not poisonous, but it can replace oxygen when in a sufficiently high concentration. But, above everything else, it is extremely flammable and explosive, so I would therefore advise the utmost caution from everyone."

"Understood, Safi. Let me know when you're ready and what range you've achieved. We won't proceed until you're certain it's safe."

It took Safi all of the next fifteen minutes to recalibrate her sensors and double their effective range.

"Lance Corporal Jarvis, you take point, then you ma'am," ordered Mike, once Safi had confirmed she was ready to proceed.

This wasn't going to be easy. Mike and the Lance Corporal needed to sling their assault rifles across their backs, as the ladder required only one hand or one foot to be moved at a time, never both. Climbing up or down a ship's hold ladder wasn't something you did at speed, whatever the circumstances. It was a long way down if you fell, and nothing would arrest your fall, except the metal of the hold's floor when you hit the bottom.

Eventually Lance Corporal Jarvis reached the hold's

floor and he quickly returned his weapon into his shoulder to cover Kat as she began her descent.

Kat really didn't like climbing hand over hand, rung by rung, down into to stinking darkness, but just as the ladder gave them one restriction, the potential for methane gas provided another.

Finally she cleared the last three or four rungs of the ladder. Safi hadn't issued any gas warnings so Jarvis turned on the beam of the small flashlight, mounted on the same axis as his M37's barrel.

Sunken, blinking eyes, looked back at them from little more than skeletons wrapped in filthy rags. Most were restrained, with wire, rather than chains, to D shaped shackles welded into the hold's floor and sides. Many were surrounded by puddles of their own filth. A few were free and moved amongst the others, providing water and whatever care their two hands and gentle, almost whispered voices could. There was no obvious, visible source of water, but there were several brimming buckets that may have once served as latrines.

"Who did this?" Kat demanded.

Mike had now joined them on the hold floor. In the beam of his own weapon's flashlight he saw a man in what might once have been an officer's uniform from a civilian vessel, maybe a cruise liner or a ferry.

Lance Corporal Jarvis examined his restraints, but knew he couldn't try to cut the man free. Metal to metal or any type of cutting flame was going to have to wait.

In the flashlight's beam, the flesh under his restraints looked black and ugly.

Mike unclipped is breather. "Who are you?"

"Lyle Hutton, First Officer on the passenger ferry *Jessi Mauboy* that used to run from Darwin to Bali."

"You're the senior?"

The man looked around. "I am off the *Jessi*."

"Your Captain?" Kat asked him.

"Killed for resisting."

"Are all of you her crew and passengers?" Kat said, indicating the hold's other occupants.

"No," said an older man nearby. "Me Tulus Meljuto, Second Engineer on the Merchant Vessel *Dewa Ruci*, from Padang on Sumatra."

"Your Captain?"

"He dead. He surrender when they ask," the emaciated man told them in broken English, "but they kill him and all of the Officers right away."

"Who?" Kat asked. Her voice was low. She recognised its tone. So did Mike.

"I not know any names, Miss, but I remember their faces."

"Ensign Steiger, what say we get this man some faces to look at."

"My thoughts exactly, ma'am." Mike said and called Captain Gillan on his comm. "Captain Gillan, the Princess requests that you reduce the watch on the *Bella* to a minimum and get as many of your people over here as you can spare. Bring all the med packs and we need to get this ship's top hatches open. They've been welded shut and we can't risk using a cutting torch or a demolition charge as there may be a methane gas build up. We could certainly use some nano-mites or a metal corroding gel. Please ask Professor Brooks if his people have something suitable. We also need to cut off some wire restraints, but that can wait until the top hatch is opened up and anything combustible has been dissipated."

"Mike, send a Section of four Troopers back to the *Bella*," Kat ordered, "just in case the *Storm Cloud*'s crew try anything whilst we're distracted sorting this mess out."

"I'm getting image feeds from your and the Princess's helmet cameras," Gillan advised, "and even with the air scrubbers on full, I'm sure we're getting the odd whiff of what you're breathing. I'll get the *Bella*'s crew armed and looking for anyone you might miss."

"Can you accommodate this many people?" Mike asked him, panning his weapon's flashlight around the hold, now aware that Gillan was viewing the same scene that he was.

"Galley can prepare something hot that we can put

into thermal catering containers, along with some coffee," Captain Gillan said. "And some of the boffins are standing in line to help out too. They heard your request and apparently have an ultra-concentrated mix of nitric and hydrochloric acid in a paste application that should help get those hatches opened up again."

"Roger that. If you and yours could focus on the humanitarian aid, we'll do the other stuff."

"Will do. Give those scumbags a hard kick from me," Gillan said and terminated the link.

No sooner had Mike's comm-link gone dead that it came back to life again. It was Staff Freeman.

"First Squad has nearly finished searching the vessel, sir. We have all the *Storm Cloud*'s crew under guard in their mess hall. 'Mess' being and appropriate descriptor. We've photographed all those we've found. I can send you the files. I'll let them stew for a while, get them worried. I obviously don't want them to try anything, as all of them combined aren't worth a single one of my Trooper's lives. But, that doesn't mean I'd pass on an opportunity to dish out something a bit more than just harsh language to them."

"That's great Staff, send me over those image files as soon as you can," Mike told him.

Just as the last file containing the pirate crew's ugly faces finished downloading, from the Staff Sergeant to Mike, who then transferred it from his suit and helmet's central processor into his own TDT or Tactical Data Tablet, the crew and scientists from the *Bella* arrived to begin assisting them.

The *Storm Cloud V*'s propulsion space's engineering personnel continued to voice their innocence as they were added to the growing numbers of pirates detained inside the mess hall. More facial scans were taken, but full biometrics would have to wait, then their wrists were restrained behind their backs.

"Shut your freaking' mouths. Nobody's listening," the Staff Sergeant told them. His visor was now up, his breather down, exposing his face. There was anger in his eyes.

Kat's next dilemma was (a) what to do with the

pirates? And (b), what to do with their victims down in the stinking hold?

The *Storm Cloud V* had several powered life boats, so they could certainly get themselves to one of the nearer Andaman or Nicobari islands, which may or may not be inhabited. She doubted they had the range to cross the Andaman Sea to reach Malaysian or Thai territory on the mainland, but she immediately dismissed that idea. It just wasn't a viable option for either group. All of them needed urgent attention. The victims needed urgent medical care and the pirates needed an urgent date with a judge and whatever passed for justice in these parts.

The climb up and down the hold's ladder was a slow process for a fit and healthy person, so none of the former captives were about to make the climb up and out, anytime soon. They'd need an alternative, probably utilizing a 'personnel basket' on a crane or hoist to winch them up the eight or nine metres. Another Trooper, the Infantry detachment's medical technician, had joined Lance Corporal Jarvis and both were now moving methodically amongst the former crews of the *Jessi Mauboy* and the *Dewa Ruci*, assessing each individual's medical condition and confirming there were no concealed weapons or booby-traps amongst those who'd been held captive down in the hold.

"Ship's clear," Staff Freeman suddenly advised Kat via her suit's comm-link as she was halfway through her climb, up the hold's ladder. "Any and all crew we've found are now under guard in their mess hall, ma'am."

"I'm on my way to you, Staff. Hold them there," Kat told him.

"I am Lieutenant Severn of the ABCANZ Federation." Kat said when she entered the *Storm Cloud V*'s crowded mess hall. "Your time operating as pirates is now officially over. It is very simple ladies and gentlemen, you can survive the next few hours by fully obeying my orders, or you can resist. It really doesn't matter to me which you choose. Assuming you comply, you will stand trial in a recognised court of law for your actions."

Her speech raised a mumble of comments, most of which were in local languages. The few that were in English were mostly obscene.

"Why don't you bugger off and leave us alone?" One of the *Storm Cloud*'s detained crew shouted out in poor, Australian accented English.

"I have considered exactly that," Kat said.

That got positive comments from the detained pirates.

"But I'd have to leave this vessel adrift, as her reactors are flooded. Given their apparent poor maintenance, I'm not sure I want to restart them. Therefore, she'll be a hazard to other shipping, not to mention a potential environmental disaster, especially when her reactors do finally break up." There was also the matter of prize money for the *Bella*'s crew, although none of them had mentioned it. "I might get a line attached and tow you into port," Kat added.

There was a long silence at that comment. Around Kat a couple of Troopers had already followed that option to its obvious conclusion, and began to smirk.

"So, if you cast us adrift . . . what will happen to us?" Somebody finally asked.

"Nothing. I could simply leave you alone, until someone either rescues you, or you die of starvation. Considering your current location and past history, I suspect you'd probably be long dead before any passing vessel offered to come to the aid of *this* ship."

"You're going to hang us anyway," someone different shouted out.

Kat actually wasn't certain what she wanted to do, but it was irrelevant what she wanted anyway, as her personal preference definitely wasn't part of her official mandate. "I believe we are currently within India's jurisdiction, perhaps just into International Waters. The Pancasila Republic's island of Sumatra and their city of Banda Aceh is certainly an alternative, and both authorities have the death penalty, by hanging, for acts of high seas piracy." She paused, letting her words sink in. "As do Myanmar and Malaysia on the mainland. Thailand follows the same trend, but uses a machine gun instead, if that's what you'd prefer?"

"Which one are you taking us to?"

"I will take you to the nearest port with a recognized, secular court system. The Indian navy base in Port Blair, on Great Anderman is my preferred preference right now."

"Will they hang us?"

"I honestly don't know. I expect you to be given a fair and open trial by a civilian judge and jury."

Without a Captain or his or her second-in command, the crew of the *Storm Cloud V* seemed lost, without focus, or voice. After a bit of further discussion, they gave Kat their unconditional surrender.

By mid-afternoon the hold's top hatches had been opened and a personnel-basket had been rigged to an overhead crane. Lifting operations began soon after, moving the former prisoners directly out of the hold and across to the *Bella*.

"It would have been nice to have sent a few more of the scum who did this to meet their makers," muttered Mike as he and Kat watched the last transfer.

"I killed their Captain and First Mate with the rail-gun's second round into their bridge." Apparently, the *Storm Cloud V* had a bridge team of at least seven, maybe a few more. Only body parts from three individuals have been identified amongst the bridge wreckage.

All of their leaders, it hardly seemed appropriate to call them 'Officers,' except their Chief Engineer, had been killed when the bridge was destroyed.

Which left a certain young Fleet Lieutenant with what the instructors at OTA(F) euphemistically called a 'leadership challenge.'

If, as she'd been trained, she broke it down into its composite parts, (1) she had over sixty former captives that needed urgent medical attention. (2) She also had twenty-two prisoners, all of whom where loudly expounding their innocence, deluded that someone was actually listening to them, from the confines of a hastily adapted empty shipping container that would hopefully suffice as a makeshift detention brig. And (3) Kat had a very badly damaged *Storm Cloud V*, which it turned out, (4) had a rear hold full of very valuable looted cargo. Leaving her with lots of questions and not many answers.

Her first two problems could be solved. Get gone, and get gone as fast as the *Fires of Beltane* could manage, and she was a fast ship, a very fast ship, when she needed to be. As for the third problem, Kat was very reluctant to abandon the *Storm Cloud V*, but could she be towed? If the seas stayed calm, perhaps, but if the wind increased and sea conditions deteriorated, towing a damaged vessel twice their size, wasn't really a sensible option. There was also the problem that the ship itself was part of the physical forensic evidence in the crimes perpetrated against the crews of the two former merchant vessels so needed to be retained. And that still left the fourth problem of the pirate's 'treasures,' unresolved.

Kat was partially spared from her first problem. The health of the former prisoners improved considerably once they'd had a hot meal and the Land Force Detachment's med-tech, Trooper Layne, accompanied by the medical attendant from the *Bella*'s crew, had done their rounds, dished out antibiotics to almost everyone and performed a number of minor miracles. The *Fire of Beltane*'s civilian medic was surgically qualified and his professional opinion and prompt treatment would undoubtedly save several limbs from amputation.

Which led to the next 'challenge' that Kat really should have seen coming.

Second Engineer Tulus Meljuto of the *Dewa Ruci* somehow managed to 'borrow' a meat cleaver from the *Bella*'s galley and then tried to give an impromptu 'haircut' to one of the improvised brig's new occupants during an unscheduled ablution visit during the night.

Fortunately, the escorting Troopers managed to intervene.

Kat arrived only a second or two behind Mike while

two Troopers were struggling with a surprisingly strong and very distressed mariner.

"He kill my Captain," the man screamed at them.

"And he will pay for it," Mike assured him.

Outnumbered and overpowered, Meljuto broke down in tears, but still managed to curse them all for stopping him from taking revenge on his Captain's murderer.

Staff Freeman arrived to take him away. "We'll get him drunk on a few beers, then let him sleep. When he wakes up and sobers up, he'll be grateful that he's not added 'killer' to his profile. He's just traumatised and angry. I've seen situations like this before, ma'am."

"He showed a pretty solid commitment to making a go of it if you ask me," Kat observed, still trying to make sense of the old sailor's colourful curses.

"I'll increase the escort," Mike said. "I'll leave the Troopers keeping the pirates in the brig where they are, but I'll add a back-up Section to those on ablution escort duties."

Which left Kat wondering if she ought to do something about the pirates sooner rather than later.

Kat had guessed that the *Fires of Beltane* might be called on to pass quick and efficient justice on some minor matters, and had therefore requested that a judge to be part of the crew. However, high-seas piracy, murder and slavery on this scale went way beyond what she'd envisaged. *Am I being naive to think it would, could or should be otherwise?* She asked herself.

Somehow, in their hasty preparations to leave port, a judicial position hadn't been filled, it had been 'conveniently' omitted from the final ship's complement. Even if the position had of been filled, right now she really didn't want to use the services of an ABCANZ Fed's legal advocate. That meant they would be legally required to follow the statutes of International Law and those of the ABCANZ Federation with regards to an individual's human rights. And capital punishment had almost been abolished within the Federation.

Admittedly, not everywhere had signed that ordinance. Britain, Canada, Australia and New Zealand had all abolished such punishment during the 1960s and 70s, but more than half of the states within the USA had continued to have the death penalty on their statute's way into the twenty-first century. Kat's own father had almost lost his chance to be the ABCANZ Fed's Prime Minister when he used every stalling tactic in the politician's handbook to keep his signature off the document that would bring Nu New England, San Angeles and Texas City into line with the Federation's other member countries and cities. Nu Hawaii and Port Salish had already stopped such practices of their own volition. Predictably, Texas City, a fervent user of capital punishment, had immediately challenged the moratorium, citing the Texan Penal Code section 12-31, and continued executing all felons convicted of capital crimes. It remained the only ABCANZ Federation city that still regularly operated capital punishment, although Kat recalled that Cayman City had retained that option too. Theoretically, maybe some of the other, smaller Federation dependencies might have something similar, even if it wasn't regularly used. *I'll get Safi to check on that, but not now. Not exactly my priority!*

And, as Kat remembered it, Bill Severn's deliberate delay tactics hadn't been for ever, just long enough to see the punks, who had kidnapped and killed her little brother Louis, sentenced.

She and Safi had already checked out the capital punishment status of all the nations in this region, and all had retained it. And today that suited Kat just fine, Severns did not like kidnappers!

The next morning, while the medics continued to tend and mend those recently freed, and Mike kept alive those not yet sentenced to die, Kat led an improvised salvage and repair team through the dilapidated hull of the *Storm Cloud V*. Most of the team were borrowed from the *Bella*'s crew, but Professor Brooks's boffins had also provided a few technicians to assist. The Land Force detachment supplied a Trooper or two, those who had specialist skills. Even Kat donated Safi, in an attempt to get the *Storm Cloud*'s own computer back on-line.

Kat's well-targeted rail-gun bolt had made quite a mess of the *Storm Cloud*'s bridge. Even when the entry and exit holes were patched, it was still a scene of total devastation. Anything that needed electrical power, which was virtually everything, was fried, right down to the bulkhead lighting. Despite Kat's reservations, Safi assured her that the computer core could be accessed and recovered, and that she'd very much like to try.

"It's certainly a challenge, but I think there is something there," Safi advised her.

"Do what you can," Kat ordered.

An hour later Kat got her first sight of the 'loot' contained in the aft hold, and it certainly smelt a whole lot better that the front hold had.

Since all of the documentation that might explain the origin and circumstance was still in a non-operational computer, it left everyone to speculate as to how the pirates had come by such cargo.

"How did they transfer it into here from the vessels they boarded?" Myra Sato, the *Bella*'s navigator and second in command mused. "Unless they used an empty shipping container and stuffed it inside, then craned it across and pulled it out again?"

"Perhaps," said Mike. "How else would they have done it?"

"From what their engineering crew have said, it seems these 'pirates' started off as mutineers. So what happened to their own Officers?" Gillan added.

"They were pretty quick to murder the officers of the other ships they took," Kat reminded them.

"Someone needs to answer some questions," Mike said.

But any questions were met with a sullen silence. Even the propulsion space team who usually protested their innocence took to studying their finger nails, the overhead bulkhead, anything other than the person asking the question.

48

Neither Kat, Captain Gillan nor Mike objected when Staff Freeman suggested that, given that the security outside of the shipping container being used as the improvised brig, was becoming impractical to enforce, they should probably be restrained for the rest of their incarceration. A number of ex-pirates suddenly turned into 'barrack room lawyers' and demanded their human rights, but the looks and body language from the Land Force Troopers quickly put a stop to that.

"We need answers," Kat concluded.

With the *Storm Cloud V*'s bridge unable to command or control anything, the techs went looking for backups. As expected, the compartment immediately below the bridge had data and power plug-ins for an emergency, but like most merchant vessels, it had no actual stations. There should have been a bridge station or two in the 'spares locker,' but, to no one's great surprise, there were none. Two were salvaged from the bridge wreckage and reprogrammed to navigation and helm. Another was brought over from the *Bella*.

What had taken a fraction of a second to destroy, took all day to restore or replace. With a mixed crew from the *Fires of Beltane* and former captives, the following morning, both ships were ready to get under way.

The day of delay effecting repairs hadn't been a total waste of time on other fronts either.

Professor Brooks's technicians and boffins had already launched their sub-surface beacon, so once circumstances had calmed down, it was activated and data started to be received.

Brooks was delighted with the initial findings, as they apparently proved exactly what he had suspected. But rather than be satisfied, he pushed for more time, and Kat had to decline.

Sensing a mutiny rising amongst the scientists, and wanting to quell it without further discussion, Kat made concessions. "Professor, you have my word, we will return."

"When," he asked in reply.

"I don't know. Soon. As soon as circumstances permit, but surely you can see, right now, this really isn't my most pressing priority."

SIX : THREE

At a sedate and sensible ten knots, it took the *Fires of Beltane*, with the *Storm Cloud V* in tow, combined with near perfect weather and sea conditions, two full days to reach Port Blair, some five hundred nautical miles north of their encounter with the pirate vessel.

Of the eleven major ports in the Bay of Bengal that were linked by Safe-Transit-Routes, most ran from the north-west to the south-east, linking the major Indian ports of Kolkata and Chennai with Padang in Malaysia. None of them were in the direction the *Fires of Beltane* needed to head in.

Kat had seriously considered towing the pirate vessel to the 4th Fleet's Remote Operational Support Platform, *4-Foxtrot-6* which was a slightly shorter distance away, due east, towards Sri Lanka. But after careful consideration, and discussion with Mike, had decided not to. A ROSP's integral hospital and mess hall didn't have the peacetime capacity to process the additional numbers of people that had crewed or had been captive on-board the *Storm Cloud V*. It would also alert 4th Fleet, and the Admiral that commanded it, to Kat's activity in 'their patch.' At the moment, her operational mandate came from Fleet Command, or perhaps even the High Command in Nu New England. Commodore Finklemeyer, General Hanna and King James, had endorsed it, had helped facilitate it, although they'd never publicly admit it, and Kat decided, all things considered, she wanted to keep it like that.

Most of the crew of the *Fires of Beltane* had gone through the experience of capturing the *Das Furchtlos* from mercenaries and well-remembered the prize money the Cape Town court had duly awarded them when the vessel was sold off to become the *Chimera*.

For the forty-eight hours it took to reach Port Blair there had been little talk among the different factions aboard the *Bella* other than how they would spend their portion of the *Storm Cloud V*'s likely prize payment.

The crew of the *Fires of Beltane* held firmly to the notion that they had the main claim on any prize money. After all, they had fought the *Storm Cloud V* and captured her.

The Land Force Detachment initially followed the age-old military tenet of 'just doing our job' and weren't interested in anything as vulgar as 'prize money,' but once the potential sums involved started to circulate, they quickly pointed out that they too had made a *significant* contribution towards the capture of the pirate's ship. So advised, the *Bella*'s crew graciously, and sensibly, conceded that the Troopers did have a valid point.

Even the most stupid knew it wasn't wise to argue with Land Force Troopers!

But when the scientists and their tech staff waded in with their claim, things got heated. "Where were you when they were shooting at us?" Was a rather strong point in the crew and Trooper's favour.

"Our necks were as much on the line as yours when the pirates were shooting at us." And, "it was two of our containers and equipment within that took the RPG damage." And, "it was our enhanced sensors you were using for the rail-gun targeting."

Which did provide a certain counterbalance to the accusation that they were all cowering under their bunks.

By breakfast on the second day the atmosphere on the *Bella* was decidedly frosty, despite the unrelenting tropical heat. Eventually Kat called a meeting and let each faction choose three speakers to voice their perspective of how things should be. Well aware that harmony needed to be restored, she took the extra precaution of having Captain Gillan, Staff Sergeant Freeman and Professor Brooks included in each team of three. She met with them beforehand to establish the rules of how it would play out.

All three would let their most vocal hot-head have their say first, then carefully steer the stampede round in a circle with the second, with the final conclusion having a good measure of logic rather than impulsive emotion.

Clearly the *Bella*'s crew and the Troopers had put their necks on the line as the *Storm Cloud V* attacked and was subsequently boarded. And they had fought her until she was dead in the water and surrendered. There was also no question that the boffins had their necks on the chopping block when the pirates started shooting. Although not a totally unforeseen event, since they had all signed on with a ship that had one of those 'damn Severns,' if not actually at the helm, then certainly close enough to it for any degree of safety or longevity to be sensibly expected.

The final agreement reached would split any prize money paid out into the traditional eight portions the old law of the sea directed in such occurrences. Two portions to be split between the junior crew members, another between the seniors, then another by the ship's officers, which had previously included Mike and Anna and would now include Kat and the senior members of the scientific team. Gillan would get two portions as the vessel's Captain, and the chartering party, which was technically Fleet Command, would get the remaining two.

The *Bella*'s crew and the Land Force Detachment would each get a double allocation within their portion, the scientists a single. Problem amicably resolved, the crew were in a happy mood by the time they finally reached Indian Navy Station Jarawa on South Andaman.

Back in her cabin Kat discovered how far that happy mood went.

"And you will get part of that money too," Anna told Grace.

"Me?" said the girl. "But I didn't do anything."

"Everyone on-board will get a portion of the payment."

"I could get some money?" Grace let out a squeal of delight.

"For your university fund," Anna pointed out.

"I'm going to university?"

"Why not? I did," Anna said.

Kat listened closely. Any new detail about Anna's private life or past wasn't to be missed.

"But Granny Jess said I didn't need to fill my head with any more than she had needed."

"You're not with Granny Jess anymore, and you know what her way of living ended up doing to her and your mum."

That left Grace silent and reflective.

"I saved money and put myself through university, juggling my studies with a part-time job in a Brit City department store and reservist military training. Hopefully, you won't have to do that."

"The Duty Port Master of Indian Navy Station Jarawa, after his initial objections to accommodating an unscheduled port call, a matter that I have since educated him on," Captain Gillan began, "And, that how our apprehension of a pirate vessel therefore necessitates a certain amount of flexibility by all parties. He now *humbly* regrets to advise us that currently, he has only one quay available that is both long enough to take both vessels, in a 'towing' configuration and that also gives quayside crane access, should we need to discharge anything."

Kat nodded, assimilating what she was being told.

"I've accepted it, as there is currently no alternative option, but there is something else you should know, your Highness," Gillan finished.

"Is there a problem?" Kat replied, already knowing that the way Gillan was drawing this out, she was asking a needless question.

"Unfortunately, we'll be rather close to a visiting European Union Destroyer."

"They've got a European Union Destroyer in port!" Mike grinned, "I hope we're not interrupting anything." It didn't sound for one second that he meant it.

"What ship?" Kat asked.

"The Destroyer *Fenrir*," Gillan said.

"Who's in command?" Kat asked him.

Sato looked up from her navigation board. "Duty Port Master's log shows a Kapitän zur See Kurt Sörensen."

"Really?" Kat said, a grin forming on her lips to match Mike's. "I had several dances with him when we met in Cape Town, although he was still a Fregattenkapitän at the time. He's the father of several adolescent girls, the eldest of which was considering a naval career, just like her father, as I recall. I suggested that he and his daughters would have far more successful careers in the ABCANZ Fleet than perhaps they could in the European Union's Navy, and he accused me of sedition! I'm very much looking forward to continuing that conversation with him."

Mike rolled his eyes and shook his head.

Kat smiled warmly. "If the military can think of 'war as a continuation of politics by other means,'" she said, quoting the Prussian General and military theorist Carl von Clausewitz, "then surely a Princess can consider socializing as a continuation of politics by other means. No?"

The next morning Kat got her chance to socialise, or perhaps to politic, or maybe even fight a very small war.

A rather handsome, one might say 'dashing,' young European Union Navy Lieutenant, or Leutnant approached the *Bella*'s quarterdeck, and offered his Kapitän's compliments. There was an assumption by his superior, who recognised the name of the *Fires of Beltane*, that a certain Princess might therefore be on-board. If his assumption was indeed correct, he would like to request her company for dinner that very same evening.

Kat would have declined an invitation to the *Fenrir*'s wardroom as being way too risky, but you didn't get to command a Destroyer by being stupid. Sörensen was wise enough to have selected the restaurant of a relatively expensive . . . and neutral . . . hotel on the other side of Port Blair.

After only a single, brief and very one-sided argument with Mike, did Kat send her acceptance down to the waiting Lieutenant, and the 'deal' was done.

"I'm going with you," Mike muttered.

"Of course you are. You dance just as well as he does."

Kat chose not to hear Mike's mumbled reply.

"Please give me sufficient time to 'create a Princess,'" Anna said and headed towards the door to start preparing.

"No," said Kat. "Fleet Number One, Ceremonial and Mess Dress tonight. No swords, small medals. He has seen my ribbons before, and I've seen his too. We both know who we are dealing with," she said, with a slight smile. Then added, "Safi, do a quick check that I'm up to date in that regard."

"Yes Kat. The events off Cape Town, due to the relatively small number of Federation military personnel involved, will get the Armed Forces Expeditionary Service Medal. As you are already a holder of this award, you will only get the clasp 'Table Bay' that has recently been authorised for this action. This has been agreed in principle by the High Command's Honours and Awards Committee, but is yet to be authorised for actual wear. The more recent events in Emirates City will also, theoretically, be covered by the same award, primarily for those personnel of the Embassy's Protection Detachment, but you will also likely qualify. To date, the Committee has not sat to discuss the clasp wording or qualifying criteria, and I have no details as to when this might be scheduled for. The events in Nya Svealand, that even I am not privileged to know the details of," said Safi haughtily, "did not officially happen, so therefore there will be no recognition, officially or otherwise. Therefore, you are 'up to date' in all respects with regard to your honours and awards . . . ma'am."

By late afternoon Kat almost regretted going 'Fleet' for the evening's attire. The dark grey lancer pattern tunic, with its double thickness front plastron and high collar might look smart, but it was never comfortable, even in less humid, non-tropical climes.

Despite a long, cooling shower prior to putting it on, Kat now felt like she was melting. The accompanying white breeches were tight-fitting and just as uncomfortable as the tunic. Kat wondered if maybe the old dress or skirt and blouse combination, that her post-war female colleagues had eventually persuaded the Fleet Dress Committee to abolish, making their uniform the same as the men's, less the obvious accommodation for gender body-shape differences, would have been far more comfortable for dinner, in the hot and humid climate of the Indian Ocean. It didn't matter anyway. Fleet Dress Regulations were most definitely not up for any kind of negotiation or individual interpretation.

"Are you regretting going with the uniform?" Mike said as he joined her, tugging at his own tight collar.

"Personal Security details are not authorized to read my mind, no matter what the latest update to Fleet Regs might imply," Kat shot back as they moved towards the gangway leading down onto the quayside. Mike appeared to be unarmed too. Certainly, there was no sword hanging from his waist, but Kat knew his tunic would have the 'Embassy Detachment' modification to enable Mike to carry his service pistol unseen. Kat considered that she should probably get the same alteration done to her tunic, as the fall of the tunic's 'skirt' section, the material below the sash at her waistline, was not of sufficient length for her compact ceramic pistol to be secured unseen into its usual location, high up on her inner thigh.

The rented vehicle provided them with a short ride, as Port Blair, with a population of around two-hundred thousand people, was a medium-sized town. Its air-conditioning provided a welcome, but somewhat brief, respite from the heat as they travelled to the hotel, on the eastern side of the island. It overlooked a bay of green-blue waters and nearby Ross Island. The best hotels, charging up to five hundred ABCANZ dollars a night for the privileged, were on the 'resort' of Havelock Island, a ninety-minute boat transfer away. The hotels located within the town itself were somewhat more 'functional,' but provided a good standard of transit accommodation and formal dining to the Officers and Senior NCOs of the Indian Navy's nearby Jarawa Base as well as the more normal, less exclusive, tourist trade.

Kat had taken three steps into the Bayview Hotel's restaurant when she spotted Kapitän zur See Kurt Sörensen standing up from his table to welcome her. He was accompanied by a young woman whom Safi immediately confirmed as holding the rank of 'Fähnrich,' the European Union's equivalent of a 'Midshipman,' or an Officer Cadet, still in his or her training to become a commissioned naval Officer. She wore the European Union's formal Navy Mess Dress that managed the impossible. She looked even worse in it than Kat did in her military's equivalent uniform. Clearly the Dress Committee in their navy hadn't capitulated on feminine attire for such occasions. Dresses had been retained. The dress was black with a full-length skirt and showed off little cleavage. When Kat had seen it on the very few female Officers from the *Jarnsaxa* in Cape Town, they had worn it with a black, waist-length jacket. Tonight however, both the Kapitän and the accompanying Fähnrich had replaced it with a white version, far more suitable for tropical climes. The four gold braid rings and embroidered star that would have normally adorned Sörensen's black jacket cuffs were gone, replaced by an older, more traditional pattern of three plaited silver cords and two golden 'pips' on each of his shoulder epaulettes. Miniature medals, mostly for Long Service and Meritorious Conduct, adorned his left breast. The Fähnrich had two straight silver cords that came from the shoulder seam, looped around the epaulette's button and returned to the shoulder seam. First one, and then a second golden pip would be added as she successfully completed the second and third phases of her commissioning training. Unsurprisingly, no medals had been awarded to her at such an early stage of her career.

Momentarily distracted by their uniforms, and the career résumé they always provided, it took Kat an extra second or two to recognize the woman.

Kat almost faltered.

Beside her, Mike's nostrils flared, but he suppressed a snort or the need to reach for his concealed pistol.

Kat took a quick glance around the restaurant. It was early, still well-lit with natural light, and almost empty. Around Sörensen's table, four other tables were occupied. Although the diners were in civilian clothes, there was no mistaking the hair-cuts and hard bodies. The steely looks in their eyes.

Are any of them my people? Kat identified two female Troopers who she knew from their 'bathroom' escort duties. Four Land Force Infanteers. *And the other four?*

Sörensen had observed all the expected niceties.

Kat allowed herself one more second for another glance around the restaurant and out onto its external dining area. She wasn't taking in its pleasant décor, but checking for any other diners. There were a few seated outside, but they were clearly being kept separate from the military personnel inside.

Hopefully this would be a quiet dinner for all concerned.

Content that Mike and the four Land Force Troopers had her covered, Kat focussed her full attention on Sörensen. He maybe had a bit more grey at his temples since she'd last seen him, six months ago, but perhaps not. He certainly cut an impressive figure in his formal mess dress uniform.

Beside him, looking nothing but frumpy in a dress and jacket probably designed about century ago, no doubt to echo the formality of the men's equivalent that included a wing-collared shirt and bow-tie and had its own origins even further back into the Victorian era, stood Fähnrich Alexandra von Welf! Fähnrich, or Midshipman. *Midshipman?*

This didn't make any sense. Kat didn't know where to begin. She had so many questions.

Thankfully Sörensen started for her, giving her a full bow. "Your Highness."

Alexandra balked, but a tap to her elbow to make it clear that *She is a Princess, you are not, and as this is Navy business, we will do it my way,* left the Fähnrich in no doubt as to what was expected of her.

Alexandra performed a very quick and shallow curtsy. Kapitän Sörensen stayed in his full bow.

With a scowl, Alexandra von Welf curtsied again. Lower this time, and did not recover, but went a bit lower, and then some more, until her head was level with her Kapitän's.

Only then did Kat smile and give them a most regal nod of the royal head. "Thank you, Kapitän, Fähnrich, but we are in Indian waters, and I seriously doubt their government recognizes ABACNZ Federation patents of ennoblement."

"Perhaps, your Highness, but graciousness is recognized throughout the civilized world," the good Kapitän said, rising from his bow. "Your Highness, may I present to you my latest Trainee Watch Officer, Fähnrich Alexandra von Welf. She is currently undertaking the rather brief 'Sea Orientation' element of her Phase One, or as we call it 'Erste-Phase,' training, before returning to Das Mürwik."

"I'm glad that we are finally, formally introduced," Kat said, choosing to ignore, for now anyway, the several times that Alexandra had previously tried to arrange her demise.

"It is good to meet you," came from the Fähnrich, as if each word from her mouth was a snake or spider or some other grotesque creature from a fairytale, myth or legend.

As Mike pulled out Kat's chair for her, the Kapitän did the same for the young woman. She seemed startled by his chivalry.

You have an awful lot to learn, Alexandra, Kat thought to herself. *So do I, but at least I know that I do.*

Kat decided to start the conversation. "I cannot deny, I was rather surprised to see the *Fenrir* tied up when we came alongside, Kapitän Sörensen. If it's not a state secret, can I ask how you come to be here?"

"Some people might consider it to be so," Kapitän Sörensen said with a chuckle and a quick glance at the young woman he was escorting. "But a look at the vessel you towed in tells me that both our governments are likely concerned about the same matter. How did that freighter come to be so badly damaged that she needed a tow?"

"I'm afraid I did that," Kat said, not quite succeeding in looking coy. That only got her raised eyebrows from both the Kapitän and the Fähnrich. "It fired on the *Fires of Beltane* whilst we were operating as an unarmed merchant vessel, large calibre small arms and the odd RPG," she continued, in formal report mode. "I was on 'weapon systems' and returned their unwanted compliment. I targeted their bridge, and that was the end of the negotiation."

"Just like you did to my brother," Alexandra von Welf shot back.

"Fähnrich, we talked about that," the Kapitän said, giving warning.

Kat shook her head. "Excuse me, Kapitän, if you please," Kat said. "Fähnrich von Welf and I need to get this out in the open. She may never agree with me, but she needs to hear my side." Kat turned her full attention to Alexandra.

"You killed my brother just like you did that freighter's crew," Alexandra got in first.

"I cannot deny, I was involved in your brother's death, but it was not '*just like*' those people on that pirate vessel's bridge."

Alexandra's mouth was half open, another retort already coming, but with a glance at the glower on her Kapitän's face, she wisely swallowed it and shut her mouth.

"Your brother's ship had badly damaged my ship. A brand new, rather large, navy destroyer, against an old 'defensively equipped merchant ship.' Our old ROSP, sorry Remote Operational Support Platform 3-Alpha-9 was also badly damaged and cornered by the *Jarnsaxa*. My sensor board indicated that something was wrong on-board your brother's ship. Her reactor was overheating, and she was venting plasma to atmosphere. I pleaded with them to stand down, to flood their reactor. Eventually someone did, but it was too late." Kat paused for a few seconds, then continued. "On your brother's ship, every single crewman had an escape pod. On that pirate vessel we did not find a single such device. When I opened up her bridge, unbeknown to us, they were all doomed. Most were killed by the projectile's impact, so couldn't have accessed escape pods anyway, even if they'd actually had some, which they did not. But, on your brother's ship, they all activated their escape pods. Kapitän Sörensen here is living testament to that. With the exception of your brother's, they all worked. His did not." Kat paused again. She studied the deep blue eyes across from her. Tried to measure the acceptance, the comprehension in them. It didn't look like much, but hopefully there was something. "There is one more thing I can add, although I doubt if anyone back home will officially back me up."

"What is that?" Kapitän Sörensen asked.

"If it is not a state secret, could you tell me what were the makes and serial numbers of the escape pods on the *Jarnsaxa*?"

"The *Fenrir* was built about eighteen months before the *Jarnsaxa*. They both use the Nordsafe IEP19 model, serial sequences beginning 469 and 470."

Kat nodded. "The escape pods, none of which worked, on the unidentifiable Vulkana class Cruisers we fought off Nu Hawaii all had 660 serial sequenced pods. Do you know what the sequence number was on Gus's pod?"

Both Sörensen and Alexandra shook their heads in silence.

"I have video imagery of his pod. I could have my HI show it to you right now, but I won't." Gus's body was still in the pod. That was one picture Kat did not want to show Alexandra. There were still images from little Louis's kidnapping that Kat had never seen. Would never see.

"Do you know Gus's escape pod number?" Alexandra said.

"660-9473-175-golf, lima, delta," Kat said.

"Holy mother of god," Kapitän Sörensen muttered.

"That's impossible," Alexandra said dismissively.

Kat turned her hand, palm up, on the table. "My HI has all the imagery taken when the recovered pod of your brother was opened. I was there, as was Ensign Steiger and Kapitän Sörensen," Kat said pointing to each of them in turn. "Several of the video frames clearly show his escape pod number. Do you know the serial number of your escape pod on the *Fenrir*, Fähnrich von Welf?" Kat asked.

The woman looked at her Kapitän. "Yes, I do."

"I also know mine," the Kapitän said, and it is not a 660 serial."

"Why was I never told this?" Alexandra demanded.

Now it was her Kapitän's turn to roll his hands open, palms up. He shrugged his shoulders.

"Do you believe her?" Alexandra spat.

The Kapitän was silent for several seconds. "There is talk, late at night in the back rooms of private members clubs in Rhinestadt, Schleswig and Nu Paris," he said slowly. "Some in our Navy wonder, some in our Navy remember. They remember a significant number of former Officers and Senior SNCOs who are suddenly not around anymore. The military is not a big place, especially within a specific trade or discipline. Everyone knows everyone, either personally, by sight or even reputation, but it cannot be coincidence that the identities of those Vulkana Cruiser's crews you refer to, that were never confirmed, coincide with so many former navy colleagues, not a few, but hundreds, disappearing from the social and professional scene back home. They've been missed. So, yes Fähnrich von Welf, if I had to pick between the words of this woman, a professional naval Officer," he indicated Kat, "or the inherent deceit and complicit lies of the political class or social elite, I know who I would trust."

A waiter approached the table, but stopped until both sets of protection escorts waved him forward. He then took the food order from those seated at Kat's table, before withdrawing. He had been well briefed and left promptly.

"I don't believe you," Alexandra whispered once the waiter was gone.

"Care to tell me why?" Kat asked.

"Unknown warships, that may or may not, have a crewing connection back to the European Union, turn up and try to reduce one of your cities to rubble. You were decorated for stopping them," Alexandra said, pointing at Kat's medals. "How many friends did you lose?"

"A lot," Kat said evenly.

"And yet, here you are, sitting here, calmly talking to me, my Kapitän. Eating dinner with us. You are lying."

Kat nodded slowly. "How much history have you studied?"

"Quite a bit," Alexandra claimed.

"So you know what happens when two evenly matched adversaries resort to war?"

Alexandra von Welf didn't seem to know. After a glance at her Kapitän, he came to her rescue.

"When two nations of near equal strength go to war to resolve their differences, it is usually a disaster for both," the European Union Officer said. "The war is long, bitter and indecisive. Neither side can win, but neither side will give up. Entire generations may perish in the fighting. A nation's wealth may waste away, and nothing is actually proven. Is that what you are alluding to, your Highness?"

"That is what the wiser Admirals and Generals in our High Command told me when I went baying for vengeance . . . for blood."

"That is what the wiser heads in our Command Headquarters say too," Kapitän Sörensen advised. "So far, they have prevailed."

"That perhaps explains why we aren't at war with European Union right now. As I recall, you did open fire on an ABCANZ Federation military asset, and in the territorial waters of another nation, namely the Western Cape. That's pretty provocative, wouldn't you agree? How the diplomats have explained that away I can only guess at." Kat said, shaking her head. "Way, way above my pay grade!"

"We simply suggested that Kommodore Von Welf acted with good intentions, believing the vessel you were on, *Das Furchtlos*, but also known by several other identities, was the ship that had been harassing international shipping in the southern oceans. The Western Cape authorities had somehow overlooked declaring that the vessel in question was now in their custody."

"And as Gus wasn't about to argue these events as being anything otherwise . . ." Kat didn't finish the sentence, hoping someone else would.

"Nobody, not us, you, nor the Western Cape authorities wanted it to escalate any further . . . to get out of hand," said Sörensen. "So, the Western Cape apologised to all parties for not declaring they had the mercenary ship *Das Furchtlos* in their custody. The European Union then apologised for opening fire on it, and on the Platform you were on, as we believed it was under the hostile's control, it having suddenly and mysteriously, left it usual mooring location, and then your government apologised for damaging one of our warships, albeit in self-defence. Certainly, it's a bit of an ambiguous explanation, in several places, especially if you were actually there, but as not that many actually were, and as it will keep the peace between three 'allied' nations, it is probably best left there, don't you think?"

Before Kat could comment further, Alexandra spoke.

"Why are you telling her all this," she asked her Kapitän.

"You could just as easily ask the Princess the same question," Sörensen said.

Alexandra turned to Kat, her eyes asking the same, even if her lips did not.

Kat shrugged. "A war between the ABCANZ Federation and the European Union would be nothing but a bleeding ulcer. That is no state secret. Only a fool would want this. I am not asking your Kapitän how many warships you currently have under construction, nor is he asking the same of me. I could guess, so could he. We probably wouldn't be off by more than two or three. But that is irrelevant. Let me instead ask you something that I'd really like to know the answer to," she said turning her attention to Sörensen.

"I have four armed operatives at my back. I assume you will not ask me to commit treason within their hearing," he said through a broad, open smile.

"I will assume they have no better sense of humour than my own Troopers do," Kat said. There were chuckles from both groups of military security.

Kat refrained from saying anything more as their

starters were being brought to the table. She unfolded her napkin in defence of her uniform. The others did the same, waiting until all had food set before them and the waiters had withdrawn.

"Why are you here? Kat then asked Alexandra.

"My father was furious when I returned from Emirates City to Rhinestadt. I don't know what Jacob von Brühl had told him, but he put me here. I had no choice. I was under continual escort, even at night and in the bathroom, until reaching Das Mürwik. As you now know, I am currently in my Erste-Phase of Officer Training, and this, my temporary posting to the *Fenrir* for my 'Sea Orientation' element, is nothing but a coincidence. I could have been sent to any Frigate, or Destroyer in our Fleet, but somehow I am here, on the *Fenrir* . . . for the next three weeks anyway.

Alexandra had given her an answer. It sounded plausible. But how much did Alexandra really know? Kat wasn't sure she believed in coincidences. Maybe Sörensen knew more?

"Kurt," Kat said, staking a regal right to familiarity that a Junior Officer of her rank had no right to abuse. "How many European Union Military Officers have as great a love of their daughters as you have?"

The Kapitän had started to frown at her familiarity. After all, he was trying to re-educate one spoilt rich brat, and needed Kat's support, not her hindrance. But then he smiled. "I don't think there is another Officer in our Navy who has resigned himself to enjoying, maybe I should say enduring, *surviving*, feminine surroundings as much as I have."

"Your oldest daughter," Kat went on. "She would have graduated from university by now. Did she join your Navy?"

"Yes. She is also undertaking her Officer Training at Das Mürwik. She is part of the intake ahead of Fähnrich von Welf here, and is presently in her Zweite-Phase Officer Training."

"And she spent time on the *Fenrir* too?"

"No, unfortunately not. I would have gladly had her

on-board, but as a Doctor, and therefore a Professionally Qualified Officer her Sea Orientation Training was on a ship with a larger medical facility than the *Fenrir* has to offer. She did her sea training on one of our Littoral Warfare Ships, the *Raeder*. I believe there may be a young man involved too, another Fähnrich on her intake."

Kat remembered the friendship she'd made with Jack Byrne during her own training at the ABCANZ Fed's Officer Training Academy (Fleet), but that had never developed beyond the platonic, despite deep, heartfelt feelings of friendship for each other. A friendship that should have been life-long, but was ended prematurely, when Jack was killed in the fighting off Nu Hawaii.

"Do you trust him, this other Fähnrich?" Kat asked Sörensen.

The look she got from the Kapitän was something Kat couldn't easily fathom. He almost smiled.

"I will let you in on a little secret, Princess. Back in Rhinestadt, a loyal wife, be she wealthy or poor, should take nine months to present her husband with their first baby. An undisputed biological fact, no? However, a significant proportion of our blushing brides, in their eagerness to do this, somehow manage it in just six or seven months. Quite strange, don't you think?"

The *Fenrir*'s security detail, seated behind their Kapitän visibly relaxed. Kat had no doubts that if he had revealed any true secrets, they would have hauled him away, but from the smirks on their faces a few of them might be married and already beneficiaries of just such a bridal miracle.

"And your daughter?"

"She has been courted by him for several months, yet she still remains on active duty."

Kat's confused frown at Sörensen's reply brought a dry "Get pregnant, get discharged," from Alexandra.

That's medieval," Kat said.

"I mentioned that very notion to my father," Alexandra said, her voice without emotion. "Let's say we agreed to disagree. You would have thought birth control was difficult to come by!" She filled her mouth with a fork-full of her starter and said no more.

Kat decided to redirect the conversation. "When I asked you why you were here, Alexandra, I didn't mean in the Navy. What I was really asking was why you aren't back in Rhinestadt or Nu Paris. Your antics in Emirates City have potentially cost your father rather a lot. Somehow, I doubt your stay in the Navy will be any less expensive."

The way Kapitän Sörensen rolled his eyes confirmed Kat's supposition.

"But what I really wonder, girl to girl, is why you aren't quietly working directly with your father back home?"

"I don't do anything quietly, and working directly with my father has never proved to be productive previously. For either of us! He says that I need to develop self-discipline and understand how respect is earnt, not demanded." After a pause of a few seconds, but no break in eye contact, she added, "And I could ask you the same question. Why are you in the Navy? Why aren't you doing something back home with your father or grandfather in Nu New England?"

"Why am I not back in Nu New England?" Kat said, then took another fork of the food before her. "I don't want to be any nearer to my mother or father that I absolutely have to."

That got a snort from Alexandra. Derision or disbelief? It got a considered, thoughtful look from Sörensen.

"I am committed to a Fleet career and for some *strange* reason, Fleet Command can't find me a nice safe Staff Officer's position at a desk anywhere near my father, back in The Capitol. I refuse to become involved in his politics . . . but every time I get too near to Nu New England, I somehow get sucked into that mess, despite my best efforts not to. Then my father, mother or both, get mad at me. *Again!* Better for all parties concerned if I simply keep away!"

Alexandra used her napkin to hide her amusement.

Kapitän Sörensen looked at Mike and got a nod of validation. The Kapitän shook his head. "Your file is now starting to make more sense."

"And if you report all this," Kat said, "do you think it will make better sense to your Intel analysts?"

"They wouldn't believe a single word."

"Then let me add one more piece of wisdom . . . I was sent to Emirates City because my superiors thought I might be safe there."

"And you might have been, if I hadn't been there too," said Alexandra proudly.

"Hire better assassins next time. I didn't even work up a sweat doing my escape and evade from those useless idiots."

"I captured your aunt," Alexandra pointed out.

"A major mistake on your part. The Land Force Troopers in the Embassy Protection Detachment took that *personally*. You don't ever want Land Force infanteers to be *personally* mad at you."

"You realize she is critiquing you?" Kapitän Sörensen said.

"I thought she was just bragging."

"You might learn something if you listen to her. There have been so many attempts on her life in recent years, and yet here she is, still wrecking their plans."

"More often than not, the only reason I'm messing with another's plans is because someone is messing with me," Kat said with a sigh. "Honestly, I wish you'd all just leave me alone."

"Is that why you're out here?" Alexandra asked.

"I had actually hoped that I might find some peace and quiet out here. Less the odd pirate ship here and there that needed neutralizing."

Alexandra turned to her Kapitän and raised and expressive eyebrow.

"Strange, is it not," Sörensen said, "that you consider seeking out pirates as being a safer pastime than being back at home with your parents."

"Are we actually chasing pirates too, Kapitän?" Alexandra asked.

Kapitän Sörensen shrugged his shoulders. "How did

you get a shot at a pirate?" he asked Kat.

"Did you notice how the *Fires of Beltane* looks like a medium-sized, unarmed merchant freighter." Kat answered.

They both nodded.

"They attacked us. They took the first shot. I got the last one."

The main course of their dinner arrived and they all ate for several minutes before Kat threw out the next question.

"How bad is it being a Fähnrich in the European Union's Navy? My recollections of being a Midshipman are much more fondly remembered as they fade into distant memory."

"You started as a Fähnrich, or whatever you call it?" Alexandra asked.

"Yes," Kat said, "and I had a Commanding Officer who made my first posting after commissioning far more miserable that I suspect Kapitän Sörensen is making yours."

Alexandra von Welf raised her eyebrows as if to doubt that possibility.

"Making Fähnrichs and newly commissioned Leutnants lives miserable is one of the prime perks of a Kapitän's job," Sörensen insisted with a smirk.

"So how did I get handed this Fähnrich crap, when my brother started out as a Kommodore. He could boss Kapitän Sörensen around, yet little old me, I get bossed around by just about everybody. It's not fair," Alexandra said and scowled back at her Kapitän.

He said nothing, just took another fork of his dinner, chewed it for a moment, then waved his empty fork at Kat. "As a Lieutenant, two, significant promotions up from a lowly Midshipman, would you have any advice for my new Fähnrich here?"

Kat thought the question over for a moment before replying. "As a wise old Chief Petty Officer once told me, if you don't want to be Fleet, get out."

Alexandra scowled sideways at her superior officer.

He shook his head. "Presently, that is not an option

open to you."

"I see," Kat said and thought some more. "Your brother started his Navy career as a Kommodore. Part of your 'Tribune' initiative as I recall."

Alexandra nodded in confirmation.

"In my opinion, that was part of what killed him.

"What!" Alexandra almost shouted.

"Do you disagree with me, Kapitän Sörensen?" Kat asked.

The Kapitän patted his mouth with his napkin. "I can't say that I do."

Alexandra studied them both for a long minute.

Kat let the silence stretch. She was learning that more often than not, more was learned in the quiet between words than was ever conveyed by them. Now she waited for the young von Welf woman to show if she was learning . . . or not.

"Explain yourself. I would have thought that a Kommodore was much safer, much more powerful," Alexandra paused for a moment. "As a Fähnrich I don't feel any power or very safe."

Kat looked at Sörensen.

He shook his head. "Although I can offer advice, you have walked in her shoes and survived, and done so far more recently than I. You can speak to her from a more current and relevant perspective."

Kat put down her own napkin and pushed back from the table. Beside her Mike did the same. Around them the security teams turned their chairs to face out, giving them as much privacy as the risk factor allowed.

"A Kommodore does seem to have a lot of power . . . if he or she knows how to use it. Kapitän, did Gus know how to use the power of a Kommodore's rank?"

Sörensen shook his head. "Sadly, no. He played with the power, but he neither understood it, or how to wield it."

"That was my observation too," Kat said. "Kapitän, how long have you been preparing to take command of a Destroyer like the *Fenrir*?"

"Fähnrich to Kapitän sur Zee, a little over twenty

years," Sörensen said. "Including three years commanding a Frigate, your Highness."

"How long had Gus worn the uniform of a Kommodore?"

"Six or seven months when he died."

"That Alexandra, is what killed your brother. Power he didn't know how to use. You're a Fähnrich. Do you have any power?"

"Painfully little."

"And are you able to use it appropriately?"

Now Alexandra turned to face her Commanding Officer. "I am learning to be a competent Junior Watch Officer."

"That you are," Sörensen agreed.

Alexandra turned back to Kat. "Are you saying that it is better to do a job that you know how to do well, than to fake a job you can't handle?"

"I think so."

"I paid good money to get a copy of your personal file. It doesn't seem to me that you actually practice yourself what you now preach to me."

Beside Kat, Mike coughed, "Amen to that."

"Whose side are you on?" Kat asked, elbowing Mike.

"The side of me staying alive," he replied.

Kat got serious. "You purchased my file? Then I assume that you've read it? Did an analyst explain it to you?"

"No, I just got the file."

"Kapitän, as you have also seen 'my file,' albeit an official copy, perhaps you might take Fähnrich von Welf through it. Explain to her when I have been lucky, and where just maybe, I had a little help from others."

"Would you, sir?" Alexandra asked, sounding like a Fähnrich talking to her superior Officer for the first time that evening.

"My remit is to educate you. To help you stay alive and to learn. I think this could therefore, be considered part of such a remit. Though I warn you, your father will not consider Princess Katarina Sophie Louisa Severn as an appropriate role model for his daughter."

"I don't think any responsible father would consider me a good role model," Kat observed with a wry smile.

"Most certainly not for any of my daughters," Kapitän Sörensen agreed. "But I must remind you, Fähnrich von Welf, anyone without the luck of the Severns would have died a dozen times over, doing what is recorded in her file."

Alexandra looked very thoughtful and sensibly remained silent as she finished her meal.

"How is Kapitän Langer," Kat asked, changing the subject away from herself and enquiring after Sörensen's former Commanding Officer.

"He is well. I have not seen him in several months. He was acquitted of any wrong-doing in the inquiry that followed the events in Table Bay. He currently has a Senior Staff Officer's post in our Admiralty, a necessary and normal evil before assuming a Kommodore's rank, that I have no doubt he will, in time achieve."

"Good," acknowledged Kat with an open smile. She was pleased to get confirmation that Langer had not been made a scapegoat, taking the fall for Gus's own shortcomings and his refusal to heed Langer's wise words of wisdom that might have prevented the boy's unnecessary death.

"The data stored in the battle-board, comms log and other OpsCen equipment, combined with the testament of all the surviving senior officers, including myself, completely vindicated him, but I'd rather not go into any detail about that right now."

"Understood, Kapitän Sörensen, I completely agree, now is not the time."

"Talking of previous Commanding Officers, I do recall from reading your file that you served on the Corvette *Berserker* under a Commander Ellis. Is than not so?"

"Yes," Kat said, avoiding saying anything more.

"I believe that he is no longer serving in the ABCANZ Fleet."

"Not as far as I know," Kat said, trying not to sound too evasive.

"I know this, because I ran into him recently. He has

contracted to a merchant shipping line that provides an irregular service into the smaller ports of these Indo-Chinese waters. Are you aware of the illegal colonies?"

"We've visited a few, but haven't run into Ellis."

"Apparently, such shipping lines are the main prey of pirates. I hope nothing happens to your former Commander."

"So do I," Kat said, not sure exactly what she was being told or how she felt about it. *In the last 24 hours I've been advised that Kapitän Sörensen, then Alexandra von Welf, and now Commander Ellis are all present, right here, right now, in this remote little corner of the Indian Ocean? What's going on?* Kat thought to herself. She'd never believed in coincidences and wasn't about to start.

"And, there is one more thing, that I probably shouldn't mention," Sörensen said, glancing first at Kat's and then his own security team. "When the *Jarnsaxa* left your Platform for the first time, we sailed with a full ship's complement, or so we thought. The numbers added up and everyone was accounted for. Then we returned, under Kommodore von Welf's personal direction, and engaged your platform and two defensively armed merchant vessels."

"I am very aware of who and what you engaged, Kapitän," Kat said.

"Yes, I'm sure you are. When we compiled a casualty list, it appeared that one of our very few female NCOs, a Matrosenfeldwebel Aleyna Gürsel had been lost in the engagement, as her body could not be located."

"I'm very sorry to hear that," said Kat. "Genuinely, I am sorry for all loss of life, especially when it was all so completely avoidable," she added, staring hard at Alexandra.

"However, a day or two after we reached our base in Saint-Denis, on Réunion, we were advised by our Embassy in Cape Town that Matrosenfeldwebel Gürsel had been attacked whilst ashore in the city and was in one of their hospitals."

"She had somehow managed to swim ashore after the

Jarnsaxa disengaged?" Kat asked.

"That is what we also initially thought. But, when Gürsel joined us in Saint Denis a week or so later, she said that she had never returned to the *Jarnsaxa*. She and another crewman had been attacked by a woman in Cape Town. The other crewman, who's name escapes me, was able to corroborate some elements of this encounter, before he was rendered unconscious."

"The Police Superintendent did advise you of such an incident in the Century City complex," added Safi into Kat's ear.

"Therefore, if your Petty Officer Gürsel was in a Cape Town hospital bed when the *Jarnsaxa* originally sailed, who had taken her place?" Kat asked the Kapitän.

"Initially we didn't know if the imposter had been killed during the ship-to-ship engagement or had managed to slip away once we reached Réunion, as for the first few days after we arrived, we were not aware we even had such a problem. Initially we thought it might be one of your people, after all, the only access to the *Jarnsaxa* was via *your* Platform."

Now it was Alexandra's turn to scowl back at Kat.

"That's a serious allegation, Kapitän. And one that, as far as I or any of my crew are concerned, is completely unfounded. I, have no knowledge of something of this nature. Not then, not now," Kat responded.

Although I wouldn't put it past some of our 'grey slim' field operatives, she thought to herself. It was exactly the sort of tactic that Colonel Leo Wood or his Fleet equivalent might cook up.

"Don't panic. Once we started to investigate, we found new biometrics had been uploaded against Matrosenfeldwebel Gürsel's identity. And the same biometrics had been used, albeit under yet another name, to fly out of Réunion the day after we'd docked."

"I thought biometric data was ultra-secure? You can't just hack-in and update it," said Mike. "Yes, you can wear high-resolution printed contact lenses, get false finger-prints and have your face-shape surgically altered to deliberately deceive the scanners and sensors, to assume another person's identity, but not the other way around. You can't just upload new reference data so that you then become the original identity that the scanner checks your identity against. It doesn't work like that."

"I thought the same," said Sörensen. "But, evidently not."

"So who was she, this stowaway?" Kat asked him.

"When we ran this new identity through all the usual databases it came up as being someone called 'Priya Devi,' Apparently she's a known terrorist and wanted by just about everyone," Sörensen advised.

"And this information is in public circulation?" Mike asked.

"No, but I'm advised that our Intel people had already exchanged it with yours, hence me being authorized to share it with you now."

"Well it's news to me. Nobody in our organisation has advised us of it. Do you think this Devi's is in any way connected to the defective operation of Commodore von Welf's escape pod?" Kat asked the Kapitän, deliberately not looking at Fähnrich von Welf seated beside him.

"Impossible to say," Sörensen said. "It would seem most unlikely that even your Federation would be employing such people to do its dirty work, so who was she working for?"

Kat sat back in her chair. She didn't know what to say. And evidently Alexandra didn't either.

For Kat, this didn't add up. It explained how Devi had extracted herself from Cape Town, when all the usual points of departure were being watched, but having a hand in Gus's death? Someone had tampered, or more likely replaced, Gus's escape pod with the one that malfunctioned. However, it seemed highly unlikely to Kat that Priya Devi, or whoever her paymasters ultimately were, might be behind it.

But, if it made Alexandra von Welf pause in her private vendetta against Kat to reassess the situation, then she certainly wasn't complaining.

Meal over, polite conversation evidently exhausted

and goodbyes exchanged, they left the hotel and were going down the steps to the rental car in the parking lot when Mike leaned close to Kat's ear. "How much do you want to bet me, that despite all that from Sörensen, you are still in pole position on Alexandra von Welf's hit list?"

That really wasn't a bet Kat was willing to take, whatever the revised odds might now be.

SIX : FOUR

Four hours with lawyers, supposedly experienced in what passed for maritime law in the Indian Ocean Territory of the Island Archipelago of Andaman and Nicobar, and Kat was missing Cape Town's somewhat more informal approach to justice.

Although Kat, with a bit of help from the *Bella*'s rail-gun, had blown the *Storm Cloud V*'s bridge and most of its 'Officers' into small pieces, along with the vessel's registration documentation, the remainder of the hull and the cargo held within it, told an important part of the tale. The reactors had serial numbers stamped on them by their manufacturers, Northrop-Sperry. Their database gave valuable information as to which vessel they had been installed in, and that was the *Nam Khanh*, registered in Saigon Mói. Her last officially logged port of call had been Singapore.

Communications with the Singaporean Port Authority and local agent provided a Bill of Lading, and suddenly the shipping containers and cargo on-board began matching up. Some of it, anyway.

Some shipping containers were missing, and others had been added. Evidently Singapore had not been the *Nam Khanh*'s last port visit.

The vessel's owners had been given notification that they now had had fourteen days to take possession of the vessel. Failure to do so would result in her being declared forfeit, and she would then be sold off, or more likely scrapped. The proceeds of which would then go anywhere other than to Kat and the interested parties on-board the *Bella*. And . . . to further compound matters, the owners obviously had the vessel insured, along with its cargo, with a multitude of insurance companies. Said insurance companies were now retaining local lawyers to represent them, which necessitated the proceedings of the Indian Republic versus the *Storm Cloud V* pirates to relocate into a larger courtroom.

Kat was taken aside by five or six men in suits and told that there would be a nominal monetary award or 'finder's fee' made to her and her crew. And, until the case was formally convened the Judge had agreed that she and her aforementioned crew could go back to doing whatever it was navy people did when decent citizens weren't interested in them.

Kat took one look at the pitiful sum of the awarded 'finder's fee' and had to leave before she laughed at, shouted at, punched, or did all three, to one or more of the 'suits.' Anna's grand plan to start a fund for Grace's university education would get a contribution that would cover about five, maybe six minutes of tuition fees!

However, Safi then pointed out, thankfully before the assembled lawyers and legal professionals did, and quietly into Kat's ear only, that "Serving ABCANZ military, government employees and directly contracted civilians were prohibited from receiving or profiteering from any activity whilst on active duty, or directly or indirectly from the proceeds of any profitable activity, as per the articles of the regulations that govern how the Armed Forces and it's personnel conducted their business." Apparently, "Cape Town and the incident surrounding the vessel *'Das Furchtlos'* is totally different, as the crew of the *Bella* are all officially civilian," despite Kat's suspicions to the contrary, "and they had not been contracted by the military at that time, but by you, Kat. Even if the same logic is applied here by the Indian court as that of the Western Cape's authorities, the *Fires of Beltane*'s and therefore her crew, are now under a contract direct from the ABCANZ High Command. Our Land Force Ship's Detachment are serving military personnel and Professor Brooks and his scientists are also directly contracted civilians. There's no prize money, Kat. The 'finder's fee,' paltry as it is, is about as good as it is going to get!"

"Thanks Safi. That's more than obvious, now that you've explained it. I can't believe I didn't work that out for myself. I wish you'd told me sooner."

"You didn't ask."

"Who's considered to be the best maritime lawyer in town? Get me in touch with them as soon as you can," Kat told her HI.

The sharpest law firm in Port Blair, that dealt with maritime related issues, already had several of their partners following the *Storm Cloud V* situation and were naturally most eager to become involved.

"Exactly what is your interest in the vessel currently known as the *Storm Cloud V*?" the most senior legal partner asked her in good English when his image appeared on Kat's comm-link.

"I, and the crew of the *Fires of Beltane*, captured the ship you refer to, that was then being operated by pirates. We have subsequently brought the ship and her crew here for summary justice and the repatriation of the cargo. Until formal proceedings officially commence, we have been released by the Judge to return to our intended activities. Therefore, I would like to retain your services to represent our interests in any pre-trial activities that may occur during our absence."

"Very well. Now then, about payment for our services. Are you putting us on a retainer or shall we take this on contingency?"

"What kind of contingency?" Kat asked.

"How about one half. No win, no fee."

"You get a half of it, no other hidden expenses?"

"You drive a hard bargain, but okay, agreed."

Their 'finder's fee' just got even smaller! "Let me talk with the other interested parties. I'll get back to you," said Kat and terminated the connection.

"So, how exactly do we do this?" Kat asked after laying out the situation to all on-board the *Bella* over the ship's internal comms. There was an explosion of responses, many of which expressed her own thoughts, but used language sufficiently colourful to be considered 'inappropriate for a Princess,' if not a Severn.

Captain Gillan spoke. "I'll get back to you once I've had a chance to talk with my people."

Professor Brooks nodded and agreed to do the same.

"We've got about a day, certainly no more, to decide," Kat told them both.

"As the Professor is here, can you both spare me a minute?" Gillan asked. "Maybe join me in my office in five. You too, Mike."

Now what? Kat thought, but said nothing.

When Mike, Professor Brooks, Kat, and somehow Anna, who had also joined them, were seated at the small table in the Captain's office, Gillan closed the door and sat down too.

"What do we intend to do next? he asked them. "Do we have to stay in port for the duration of the pre-trial court proceedings?"

"Not if we hire a legal firm," Brooks said.

"That is already in-hand gentlemen, and I want to get back out to sea as soon as possible," Kat advised them. "The authorities have confirmed that we can, at least until official proceedings begin."

"So, what do we do next?" Gillan asked again.

"Explore," Brooks said emphatically.

"Yes, yes," Gillan said, looking more like most people's idea of a pirate, and certainly more so than any of the real pirates they'd encountered actually did. "But where?"

"Something tells me you already have an answer to that question, Captain," Brooks said, looking somewhat unhappy.

"Perhaps. I may have a suggestion, but I also wanted to understand if we legally need to stay in port, or if we can get back to sea. And, if we could collectively agree between us, where to go next," Gillan said openly. "Myra and some of the *Bella*'s crew met a man in a local bar last night."

"If you produce a treasure map with an 'X marks the

ARDENT WARRIOR

spot' . . ." The Professor didn't finish his sentence.

"No, there's no map, I assure you. It's just a man. I've talked with him already this morning. He's from one of the illegal colonies. His problem is that he is here in Port Blair and he and the cargo he has arranged, need to get back to one of the other islands."

"He wants to start up a colony on one of the islands that has restricted or prohibited access, as there are already 'un-contacted people' on it? Tribes that have previously had little or no contact with global civilizations?" Kat asked Gillan.

"No, your Highness. Not a start-up colony. He was sent here to get things that an existing, established, colony needed. It's a settlement that was set up just after the war apparently, although yes, it is on the supposedly 'prohibited' island of North Sentinel. Is it for us to decide the legal status of these colonies? Anyway, he hitched a ride on a passing ship, but what with all the pirate activity in recent months, he hasn't been able to get back."

"And with the *Storm Cloud V*, or *Nam Khanh* and her crew waiting their day in court," Kat said, "that has now changed."

"Assuming that the *Storm Cloud* was the only pirate vessel operating these waters," Mike added.

That got shrugs of "Your guess is as good as mine," from several of those seated around the table.

"Anyway, the contract I have from Fleet Command, in the small print, states that I may offer passage and facilitate the transport of goods for a fee if it does not interfere with my principal duties."

"And who decides what they are?" Kat asked, wondering just who and how such wording had slipped into the Captain's contract. Apparently, her Grandpa Jim wasn't the only one trying to twist this voyage of discovery his or her way. "Our mission statement includes 'searching for pirates and illegal activities' and this may be exactly that."

"He wants our help! Not to be arrested for living in a colony that is possibly illegal," Gillan countered, then paused. "As the civilian crew's officially appointed representative, what do you think Miss Sykes?"

"Depends on what my cut is I suppose," Anna replied with a grin that would have made any pirate proud.

"This is not happening to me and my science team," Brooks said, standing up in protest.

Kat shook her head. "And, what crimes will I get subsequently accused of?"

"It's in my contract to undertake some commercial work," Gillan reminded. "It helps maintain our cover as a civilian freighter."

"No," Kat repeated, but was drowned out by an even louder "No," from the Professor.

"I suspect that 'cover' got blown the moment we hauled the *Storm Cloud* into port," said Mike.

"Would you at least talk to the man?" Gillan asked.

"Why?" came from several around the table.

"He's been stuck here a while and really wants to get back home, and I'd rather he be the one who enlightens you on some other aspects of when this colony was established. Better it comes directly from him."

"What other aspects?" Kat said.

"He's waiting outside," the Captain said. This had to be a first for Gillan.

"No. This is not acceptable," said Brooks, again.

"Would you keep a man from his family?"

"You're laying it a bit thick," Mike added.

"No, no, no!" said the Professor, but was sitting down with a resigned look on his face.

"No harm in talking to him," Anna said with a shrug.

As the room mulled that over, Gillan opened the door and invited a young man in.

He looked about Kat's own age, maybe a bit older, dressed in jeans and a t-shirt, and gave them a smile of pure innocence that only a pre-school child could normally deliver. He was tanned, but genetically looked to be of European origin. "Hi. I'm Shalk de Klerk of North Sentinel."

"The same North Sentinel Island that was awarded prohibited access due to 'un-contacted people' status in the mid twentieth century, that was then reaffirmed in the early twenty-first," said Kat, repeating what Safi was informing her via her earpiece.

"My grandpa always said he didn't want to roll out the welcome mat for just anyone," the man replied. "He thought the island's prohibited status would keep unwanted visitors away."

"And has it?"

"Yes. There was about twenty, twenty-five families originally, in the years after the war, but it's slowly grown."

"What about the indigenous tribes?" Kat asked him.

"I don't know the detail, I wasn't born back then, you'll have to ask my dad, but as far as I know, the native people were all long dead. I believe Grandpa said there were these canisters, washed up on the south-side beach. We still have a few of them somewhere. Apparently, whatever was in them took down the natives a long time before we arrived."

"Do the Indian Authorities know you're there?" Mike asked him.

"Not sure. If they do, they've never come visiting or asked us to leave."

"How do you survive?" enquired Kat.

"We have just about everything we need. Anything we can't farm or fish for ourselves we buy from the passing traders who have the right comms-frequency to call on. In the early years my Grandpa's contacts helped pay for the start up . . . we became self-sufficient for food pretty quick, but we can't do everything. Then the pirate activity increased and the passing merchant traders we relied on . . . they stopped calling in."

"Maybe because they'd become the actual pirates," said Brooks cynically.

Kat was trying to place the young man's accent. Most of the English speakers in this region had an Australian twang to their words, but he sounded more like the South African's she'd met in Cape Town?

"He has five shipping containers to load," Gillan added. We have the space to take them."

"Why not take a look?" said Anna.

"You're the boss," Gillan told Kat.

She laughed. "Hardly."

"Leave these people alone," Brooks said.

"Too many people think we all need to live together in the mega-cities, to play by the rules, especially as the planet's 'nature' is just *way* too hostile . . . which it evidently isn't. Granted, the bits we've screwed up with chemicals and radiation are, but there's a fair bit out there that's not. Going self-sufficient is a hard way of life, no easy options, and I respect that. I remember the folks back in Alaska, in Elmendorf and out on the remote farms. They had it hard. But it's also empowering. They can make their own rules and live the way they want to. And, I respect that too. I don't think it will do any harm to check this out," decided Kat.

"Seems logical enough," Mike said, with only a slight scowl on his face, "but are you sure it's not just a Severn thing? Something horribly dangerous needs doing, and of course, you've got to be the one to do it, and without the right resources or back-up."

Brooks was nodding in agreement.

"It could be, but who do you think is the best person to check up on them? A merchant vessel's captain or a pirate ship's crew who are actually both only interested in various degrees of personal gain, or perhaps the Indian Authorities who may try to arrest or remove them, or one of those damn Severn's? I've got no interest in any form of personal gain at their expense and I have no authority to enforce Indian laws."

The young man turned to Gillan. "Hold on," he said. "You never said that there was a *Severn* involved."

"I distinctly remember that you didn't actually ask."

"Of all the ships on the ocean," the man groaned, "and I have to pick this one!"

It took another two days to get away from Port Blair. Kat found it frustratingly slow, but Captain Gillan assured her they were actually making good time, all things considered.

Those two days included sworn statements from everyone involved in the capture of the *Storm Cloud V*, detailing exactly what they personally did to capture said vessel. Luckily the crew of the *Bella* managed to account for every pirate on-board and their statements comprehensively corroborated each other's actions first time around.

Mike, assisted by Safi, used the time to do a deep search on 'Shalk de Klerk of North Sentinel' and turned up exactly nothing. Predictably there was no on-line presence and he and his fellow colonists paid cash, something they didn't seem to be short off, for anything they couldn't grow or make themselves. Large over-payments for goods and services, with the caveat of 'no questions asked' seemed to be the way they had always operated, even back in the early days of the colony's existence. Shalk was open, friendly and talked freely, answering all their questions, but only when he knew the answer, which wasn't often. He had no idea where the cash came from, as he too, it seemed, 'asked no questions' of the islands 'elders' or ruling council, just obediently doing whatever as he was told.

There was also the matter of loading five more shipping containers, those destined for North Sentinel island, onto the *Bella* and removing the ruined pair, as well as re-stowing the salvageable cargo that the damaged two had contained elsewhere on-board.

Two of Shalk's new containers then had to be repacked, as one had a combined weight of container and contents, that although easily within the lift capability of the port's quayside crane, exceeded the maximum lift capacity of the *Bella's* own Number Two crane. This meant she wouldn't be able to unload it herself when they reached the island. Shalk then asked Gillan why her two front cranes couldn't be used together, to lift in a 'tandem' configuration, which could then easily lift the heavy container, it being well within the capacity of the two cranes, once combined.

This was a question that Gillan really didn't want to answer. The *Fire of Beltane*'s new crane configuration was no longer standard. Usually, a vessel of her type would have two, identical cranes or 'gears' installed on the 'port side' of the vessel. This enabled the ship to load and unload herself, mooring the port-side against the quay. This reduced the distance, or 'boom' the crane arm needed to extend, as the further it extended, the less weight it could lift. The *Bella*'s Number Two crane still operated exactly in this way. Her Number Three crane, the smaller of the three, used for loading and discharging the small aft hold, cum floodable dock, did too. However, what had once been the rotatable turret mounting of the Number One crane was now the turntable of the *Bella*'s railgun. The telescopic 'rails' had been disguised with false triangular lattice and cabling along their length and a civilian paint job and appropriate signage added, so that when stowed in its non-operational position the railgun looked convincingly like a ship's integral crane to an untrained eye.

Kat didn't find many opportunities to do what she wanted, and there was always somebody requiring her to be somewhere, but when the first opening presented itself, she quickly updated Anna with regard to what Kapitän Sörensen had said about Priya Devi. Devi had taken Anna hostage, then extensively tortured her in Cape Town, leaving Kat's Equerry to die in a stinking slum apartment block. Anna listened quietly as Kat updated her, making no comment.

"I don't know what to tell you," Anna finally said. "I don't want revenge, I don't want anything, I don't feel anything towards her."

"Really?" Kat replied.

"Yes. That doesn't mean I forgive her, and it doesn't mean that I wouldn't want payback if I ever have the pleasure of her company again, but . . . until the star's align and such circumstances occur, it's 'parked.' Stored away, for another day. It's just the way I've come to deal with it."

"It was only six months ago, Anna. Do you think you perhaps returned to duty too soon?" Kat asked her.

"Maybe, but if I hadn't . . . you'd still have been posted to Emirates City . . . von Brühl would still have staged his coup d'etat, or whatever it was, but would Grace still be alive? No way to tell, but given the antics of my mother . . . I'd rather not speculate," Anna said. She seemed uncharacteristically dejected, even melancholy.

"Fair point," Kat conceded and decided to leave any

continuation of that conversation for another day.

Finally, the mooring cables were retracted and the *Fires of Beltane*, without the *Storm Cloud V* in tow, made her way out of the Indian Navy's base. Only then did Kat breathe a deep sigh of relief.

Mike caught her doing it. "You spend a couple of days with lawyers, port operators and local police, doing things where all you risk is breaking a fingernail, yet you sigh like Jack's old Irish grandmother probably did! We're heading for a bunch of unwelcoming, illegal settlers, armed with who knows what, and you look decidedly delighted at the prospect. Lady, you are certifiably crazy."

Kat thought for a moment, then gave her Close Protection Officer her best imitation of one of Anna's disapproving sniffs. "Sorry, Mike, who's crazy exactly? Me, or maybe you are, for following me?"

Mike turned away, muttering to himself.

Kat chose not to challenge him further and watched silently as Port Blair passed by the Bella's bridge windows.

"I see that the *Fenrir* is still here. What do you think they're really up to?" Mike suddenly asked aloud.

Kat glanced over at the navigation board, and then at the display of the port's layout. "The Indian Ocean is a big old place Mike, so who knows what they're really doing here. The Indian Navy is relatively capable, I'm sure they can hold their own against a single warship."

"It's not the ship that bothers me, it's the young harridan on it, a certain Alexandra von Welf," he added.

"You mean *Fähnrich* von Welf," Kat corrected. "Last I heard, she was learning how to stand a *Junior* Duty Officer's watch. If you keep your new Midshipmen and Ensigns suitably busy, then even she is going to have trouble scheduling enough free time just to do the essentials, like eat, sleep and crap, let alone conquer the universe!"

"If you say so," was Mike's response.

Kat let him have the last word. Unless you'd actually been a sleep-deprived midshipman yourself, it was virtually impossible to describe just how much trouble you had juggling all the 'must-be-done-now' minutiae that those more senior, deliberately dumped onto new Junior Officers.

Kat was on the bridge the following morning when they began their approach towards North Sentinel Island. Scans and sweeps from various sensors were all negative. "Get de Klerk up here," she ordered.

Two minutes later he joined them on the bridge. "Is this the correct island?" Kat asked him, pointing at the tropical island ahead of them.

"Are you picking anything up on your sensors?" He replied.

"Not a thing," the crewman manning that bridge position reported back.

"Then I guess it might be. The vessel Captain I went to Port Blair with, said he wouldn't have believed an island with that many people on it, could appear so quiet."

"I guess if I was afraid of being found, I wouldn't be sending out the 'hellos' either," Mike commented.

"There is a small inlet on the south-east corner. If you can come in there, but stop in the actual mouth, rather than inside, you can hoist the containers onto the right-side promontory," he said, pointing to a location on the navigation board's display.

It showed a jungle-covered island, approximately square, about seven-kilometres wide and the same in length.

"Take us in closer. Real slow," Gillan advised the Helm.

As the *Bella* nosed slowly closer, the island was still as silent as an ancient tomb. "There are no transmissions," the crewman at the sensor board advised. "Either there is nobody on this island, or every one of our sensors has malfunctioned at the same time," he said scowling at the display.

"Or it's the wrong island?" Mike suggested.

"Or someone has dug a very deep hole that's better than my old grandpa ever dreamed it would be," the young man suggested with a smile.

"Professor Brooks," Kat said into her comm-unit,

"You and your colleagues have about an hour to set up whatever equipment you might want, and tell me where the inhabitants are hiding on this island. Let me know when you find them."

"I'll call you when we do," he said, accepting the challenge without any further questions.

"Thank you," Kat replied, terminated the comm-link, then turned to the bridge crew. "Shall we start a pool? See how long it will take our resident boffins to find those settlers? I want a straight three hours."

"Not fair," Mike said. "I wanted that."

"Me too" said Gillan.

"Oh ye of little faith," Sato, who was sat intensely studying the nav board, said. "Even if you aren't operating broadcasting tech, there's always still some kind of signature." She looked up from her displays. "There has to be something."

Despite giving him an hour to provide a result, it was past three and approaching four when Professor Brooks started his update in Captain Gillan's rather cramped office. With a sigh he began, "These settlers, colonists, call them what you will, do not want to be found."

"So we've been advised," Captain Gillan said. "Does that mean you didn't find them?"

"I didn't say that, but I want you to know that any team less than the superb one I put together would still be looking."

Gillan raised an eyebrow, but said nothing. Sato had finally found the settlers with the aid of the *Bella*'s bridge crew and their regular equipment about an hour ago.

"How did you find them," Kat asked Brooks.

"They might be able to hide, but they can't make their witness marks in the terrain completely vanish. And, the laws of thermodynamics apply even to settlers who don't want to be found."

That was the flaw that Sato had spotted too.

"The temperature here is a steady thirty-one degrees, plus or minus two degrees all year round," said the professor activating the office's display screen. "So, if you constantly mimic that, your signature should disappear. Usually, you can spot habitation by areas of plowed or fallow fields. Not here. Apart from the beaches, virtually solid jungle. No corn, no potatoes, no rice, no wheat. I don't know what they're growing, but it's some kind of perennial that they can harvest calories from but leave the roots in place."

"I've heard about that," Kat said. "The drier areas of San Angeles and Texas City are planted with something like that for soil conservation."

"But would you want just bread, or whatever it is they are growing, meal after meal, after meal?" Brooks asked.

"Could they have bio-engineered other crops to have similar root systems?" Mike asked.

"Enough, no more agri-farming!" Kat said. "How did you find them?"

"Their structures, 'houses' if you prefer are buried deep into the soil, so are their barns and equipment sheds, everything is underground. but using an aerial drone with the latest three-dimensional, canopy penetrating, LiDaR, electrical resistivity tomography and high-resolution terrain mapping and analytics, we eventually located them. We also spotted trails where wheeled vehicles or equipment have been operating. And, right where you'd expect to find a settlement, there was one. Two actually. All warm and cozy," the professor said, finishing with a flourish. "All the buildings are subterranean and above them, to disguise the backfill, they're planted up. All the crops grown are at ground level and must be able to grow in the reduced light under the forest canopy. They certainly get enough rain to make some specific crops viable. There's one structure there that appears to be significantly bigger than all the rest but I cannot discern its function. The other settlement is smaller, nearer the coastline, and nearer the inlet we've been heading for."

"It would appear that you've found what we're looking for."

Mike was shaking his head. "They are clearly very security conscious, to go to such extraordinary lengths . . .

that definitely isn't the 'low-cost' option!"

"Do we have enough to make contact?" Anna asked.

"I think we know just about all we are going to from afar, without committing considerably more time and resource. Professor, I'm assuming that all your clever tech didn't find any concealed antenna or dishes for receiving or making broadcasts?"

"We haven't identified anything like that, no power plants or power lines either. They must be very well shielded."

"Anything military, or that could be considered defensive?" Mike asked.

"Nothing of that nature either," the Professor confirmed.

"I strongly suggest we don't make any multi-band or broad-width comm broadcasts yet. (a) The Indian Navy isn't that far away, and they might not appreciate what we're up to. And (b) it's futile. Any settlement that is going to these elaborate lengths to hide is hardy likely to answer a "hello, is anybody there," Mike added.

"Agreed," said Kat with a nod. "Have we asked de Klerk for the welcome frequency or any identification protocols we need to follow?"

"Not yet. We wanted to have this meeting first," said Gillan.

"Well let's ask him. He must have a return protocol or procedure to follow."

Fifteen minutes later, a tight, nano-burst message, on a very specific frequency was sent. "Greetings, this is the Fitzroy registered Merchant Vessel, *Fires of Beltane*. We have your colleague Mr Shalk de Klerk, and a number of full shipping containers that we are returning to you. Please acknowledge."

The message was followed by a long silence.

Kat shrugged. Waited another thirty seconds, then ordered it to be sent again.

"I heard you the first time." The speaker sounded very irritated.

Kat grabbed the comm-board's microphone. "This is Katarina Severn on the MV *Fires of Beltane*. We are going to begin discharging containers onto the promontory advised by Mister de Klerk. If you want to remain undetected, I suggest you send personnel to unload the containers so we can take them back to Port Blair, otherwise you will have several empty shipping containers sitting on your shoreline. Hardly inconspicuous I think you'll find. We will commence discharging in approximately one hour. Please don't try anything stupid. We have come here in good faith. Any hostility on your part will be met with force."

There was a burst of static, the kind you might get if the headset was being disconnected and passed to another.

"Miss Severn," came over the speakers. It was an older and more thoughtful voice. Voice only, no imagery. "Are you one of *those* Severns?"

"I do have the honour of being King James of the ABCANZ Federation's only granddaughter."

"So that would make you a Princess of some sort? I can't understand why your Federation is falling back on those failed titles of the ruling classes."

"I prefer to think we are trying a new twist on an old way of looking at things."

"We will permit you to offload the containers. Please do not put any more of your people ashore that you absolutely have to." The transmission light went red.

"Are all links closed?" Kat asked the crewman at the board.

"Aye, ma'am."

"So," Mike said, "How many people, my risk-taking Princess, should we 'absolutely have to' put ashore to facilitate this container discharge?"

"Captain Gillan, I'm assuming you'll need a team down on the promontory, in full comms with the crane operator, to act as his eyes on the landside during the discharge?" Kat asked.

"You assume correctly, ma'am."

"And that team will need protecting whilst they're working. So, Mike, put the First and Second Squads onto the promontory where the containers are going, to establish a defensive perimeter, and put the Third Squad ashore on the portside promontory. Get both to push out to the maximum range of a rocket-propelled-grenade, or at the very least the tree-line, so the ship doesn't get fired on."

"Ma'am," said Mike with a salute.

Forty-five minutes later both RIBs, fully laden with 'chameleon' battle-suited Troopers, left the *Bella* and began deploying onto the promontories on either side of the ship that was now stationary. The Captain had not dropped anchors and had the helm holding her position using her bow and stern thrusters.

Once Staff Freeman confirmed the protective picket lines were established the RIBs took some of the *Bella*'s crew ashore to begin preparation to receive the shipping containers.

The only members of the Federation military not in battle rig were Kat and Mike. Both were in a standard, dark grey, Fleet issue, shipsuit. Both had taken the sensible precaution of wearing a Kevlar-titanium weave bodysuit beneath it.

It was Anna that got raised eyebrows from everyone. She too was now attired in a Fleet issue shipsuit. Technically wrong, as she was Land Forces, not Fleet. On her left upper arm she had vertical stripes, in dark green, the colour of the Land Force Infantry Branch, and the fact that there were two, identified her as being an Officer. Enlisted personnel had only one and Brigadiers and Generals got three, although their centre one was only half the width of the outer two. Anna, although nearly as tall as Kat, was a lot 'curvier' and her suit was stretched tight in several places, not that anyone was about to make comment. Deliberate? It had to be. Anna never did anything 'by accident.' Her right upper arm, where her rank should have been, was tactfully devoid of anything. She was actually senior to both Kat and Mike, but that wasn't something she needed to be advertised. The winged dagger of 'special operations' at the top of her right arm said enough. Nobody was about to challenge her on any aspect of her 'uniform' and she was now complying with a request Kat had made a several months back, despite not initially wanting to.

Grace naturally wanted to go ashore too. "Isn't meeting new and strange cultures a great way to enhance my education?"

That got a "no," from Kat, Anna and Safi in rapid succession. The girl locked herself in her cabin to stomp, sulk and pout. Kat sincerely hoped her discussions with the settlers would go better that they had with this eleven-year-old!

"De Klerk and the two on the comms earlier, their accent sounded South African to me, well sort of, any ideas?" Kat asked Safi.

"The Afrikaans population, particularly on the eastern side of South Africa, in the old provinces of Transvaal and Natal, considered that they had been treated badly by both the British in the nineteenth and early twentieth centuries and the successive African National Congress governments of a hundred years later. The vast majority of South Africans of European descent had migrated into Western Cape in the years before the war, but some of the Afrikaans chose to defiantly remain on their farms and homesteads. But, when the brutal President Kwashaka had confiscated their lands, that was the final insult, and those that hadn't been indiscriminately slaughtered finally fled. Where they all went, nobody knew. Although a significant number did go to other African countries, such as Zambia, Namibia and Botswana, some went further afield to Australia, but . . . about twenty percent . . . completely disappeared."

"Are you suggesting that this might be one of those missing communities?" Kat asked.

"Certainly sounds like it could be," Mike said.

"There was no hint in the media at the time that they had come this far," continued Safi. "They were considered an argumentative bunch, even amongst themselves, and many only got out with little more than the clothes on their backs."

The RIB slowed as it neared the shoreline and two of the *Bella*'s crew jumped out and hauled the boat further in as the motor was shipped to prevent it fouling in the sand.

Mike went first, then offered Kat a hand so she might half-step, half-jump, from the RIB to dry land at no risk of getting wet. Then came de Klerk and finally Anna.

Half a dozen men and women approached, then waited as the first container was hoisted up and over the *Bella*'s side. All were dressed in the drab greens and browns usually used by the military. Was this just simple and sensible camouflage to reduce detection when above ground, or did this mean the settlement had a paramilitary culture?

A vehicle slowly and silently approached. It was open topped, with a driver in the front and a man in the back. It was flanked on both sides by an escort of four of Kat's Trooper's. The vehicle stopped and the man in the rear stood.

"I am Princess Katarina Severn," she advised him.

"I am Zebub. We talked earlier. My driver is Morax, my son."

Strange names, Kat thought. As if predicting Kat's deliberations, Safi explained into her earpiece. "When the Afrikaner people trekked east from Western Cape in the eighteen-thirties, they were deeply religious, and believed that Natal to the east was the 'Promised Land' because of the large swathes of land suited for farming. When these settlers had children, they were often named after Biblical characters. Nearly three centuries later, when they were forced to leave or die, by Kwashaka's policy of harassment, many believed they had been 'cast out of the Promised Land,' and therefore gave their first generation of children the names of fallen angels that may, due to popular fiction, seem unusual or even demonic to us."

Zebub, or more correctly, Beelzebub, unlatched the side of the vehicle's rear compartment. It folded down to form steps. "I brought this vehicle to help take the cargo home. I obviously should have brought something bigger, but unfortunately, we have nothing larger." He gave her a bit of an awkward smile. "Would you like to come with me for refreshment? We can walk, or take the vehicle, entirely up to you."

"Where are we going?" Kat asked him.

"To the Great Hall. That is the hub of our community. Our leaders will meet with you there."

"If it is no inconvenience, I've been on-board ship for a while and would rather walk. And, your vehicle can be utilized as intended, for cargo rather than passengers."

"Acceptable. And, it will give us more time to prepare. Your arrival is more than a little surprise. It is many months since Shalk left the island. We feared that he too, was lost to us, like so many who have gone before."

"Most settlements have sensors that can detect a ship's arrivals. Those settlements that are officially sanctioned and not on prohibited islands."

"Then you will surely understand why we have no such devices. We just want to be left alone."

Staff Freeman got the Land Force Detachment moving in the direction Mike indicated and called for a RIB to take the Third Squad from their left flank and to follow the main party as a rear guard. Half of First Squad, along with Sergeant Varko, would remain to protect the *Bella*'s crew who continued discharging the shipping containers.

Kat, with Mike, Anna and Shalk following, falling into step with the Troopers of Second Squad who flanked their progress on either side at a distance of maybe fifty metres, advanced into the vegetation of North Sentinel Island. The terrain was easy going, rising to only sixty metres above sea-level in the first kilometre.

Staff Freeman gave his people strict instructions to "Tread lightly ladies. And try not to break anything!"

"Your settlement is totally underground?" Kat asked Zebub, trying to get him talking.

"Yes, cut from the rock of the island. Our leaders, 'The Elders,' thought that the effort and hardship in creating such a place would bind us together against anything the outside world could throw at us, and it surely did. No person who helped to build our home has ever left. Morax tells me his generation need a similar project to bind them to this island too, as some of them *do* want to leave."

"Anything that builds community spirit is always good," Kat said.

"Would it be too impolite of me to ask how you found us?" Zebub asked.

"Your colleague, Mr de Klerk gave us the frequency to send our message on. After all, he was the one who contracted with us to bring himself and the supplies he had obtained, here." Kat saw no reason to admit they had done a full Intel gathering reconnoiter and a terrain-mapping scan before committing to any shore activity. "We scanned for tech, broadcasting or receiving, anything with an electro-magnetic signature, as well as infrared, all the usual stuff, but found nothing. If Mr de Klerk hadn't been on-board I think we would have sailed right on by."

"That is good to know. We installed thermal shielding on all power lines and heat regulators to store any heat we generate and then release it to mimic the outside temperature. We send nothing internally as a wireless broadcast, everything between our homes is with old-style fiber-optics. During the storm season the sandy soil of the island gets blown around. Our crops help to stabilize it, but we often have to top it up over some of our structures."

"What happened to the people that lived here originally?" Kat asked him.

"They were gone. When we arrived, we looked for them. We didn't want to hurt them. We wanted to live harmoniously, side by side with nature. We found their villages, but no people. All dead. There were canisters in the villages and some more had washed up on the beach, mixed in with all the other plastic contaminants that unfortunately pollute our oceans," he said angrily. "No idea what was in them. Most of the canister markings had been washed away or faded in the sunlight, and what little remained was in Chinese or one of the other eastern pictogram languages. I guess the primitive folk who lived here before didn't understand that any more than we did."

"Can I get one of my scientists to take a look?" Kat

asked.

Before the man could answer Kat, they approached a junction in the track. It was well worn, but was unpaved. Atop a nearby stone sat a man reading aloud from an old-fashioned paper-paged book. He didn't see or hear their approach, either in love with his own voice, or the message he preached, perhaps both. But some of the people tending the crops did and turned to watch the approach of Kat's party and the protective cordon of Troopers.

"The unbelievers will be eternally damned, and boil in their own blood. Then the Chosen People will take their land and cherish it. Woe unto those who ignore the words of the Angels of Light . . . those who do not to follow their teachings. Joy shall come to all those the Elders meet and who then give themselves over to the Angels of Light, for they are now enlightened, and shall rise up into the one true Heaven. Great is the reward of those who have done everything that was asked of them. Death and eternal damnation shall find those who have not."

The man reading from the book finally looked up from the pages to Kat and her escort, but it was not her that he spoke to.

"Woe unto you Beelzebub. What abomination is it that you bring amongst us? More outsiders. The damned, fit only for consumption by demons. Why do you waste your time and the fruits of our labour on the likes of these, those with hate filled hearts and deaf ears? Smite them all down. They must give up their lives of comfort and plenty and join those who know the truth about what is to come."

"Dear brother Astaroth, I do whatever the Angels of Light tell me, as I know you do what they tell you too. Please continue with your daily lesson. I assure you all, that any the Angels have put within my reach, now open their ears so they may listen to the wisdom of the Elders too."

That made quite a disturbance with the field workers. Kat caught the muttered words "may they be blessed," after his reference to 'The Elders.'

"May they bless your efforts more than they have ever blessed them before," Astaroth said, not willing to let Zebub have the last word.

The Land Force Troopers marched on. Maybe Astaroth did his preaching slightly more softly. His noise fell into the distance.

"I wasn't aware you still had faith in the old religions?"

"We have always been Christian, mostly mainstream NGK, the Dutch Reformed Church of South Africa. Many of our forebearers then joined the Afrikaans Reformed Church in the late twentieth century, but . . . after a few years of Kwashaka's barbaric rule there was revised doctrine. New scripture that no longer forgave those who persecuted us. It grew in popularity. It was the divine intervention of the Angels of Light, may they be blessed, that saved our forebearer's lives and guided them to this island that we now call home, and where we have lived in peace for over thirty years. Some of the more err . . . simple minded . . . like Astaroth are easily confused by such scripture and ignore the more subtle, finer points that The Elders have highlighted to us."

"So not everyone sees matters in the same way?"

"Astaroth's son left the island, and he has never forgiven me. My son, Morax, he preaches among the young for a need to have another great project to bring the younger members of the community together, but Astaroth's son boarded a vessel to procure supplies, just like Shalk has just done, and never returned, and is now lost to us forever. It is a heavy burden for Astaroth to bear and he eases this by blaming it upon me."

Kat let the rest of their walk pass in reflective silence.

SIX : FIVE

Kat had been in large 'halls' or barn-like spaces before, but this 'Great Hall' was not like anything she had ever seen previously. From the outside there was nothing obviously there, just a flight of fifteen to twenty steps that led down into a well-lit subterranean tunnel. After a hundred metres and a pair of heavy timber doors, they reached a space where other tunnels connected at right-angles on both sides to the tunnel they were in. Another tunnel of perhaps fifty metres and then they reached the underground space these people referred to as their 'Great Hall.'

The 'Hall,' like the tunnels, was of a hybrid construction that effortlessly mixed old with new, traditional with modern. The wall supports and roof spans were in a bright, chromed metal, combining improved durability in the island's tropical climate, but also adding to the overall grand spectacle and impressiveness of the building. The gaps in-between the metal frame, that formed the actual walls and ceiling were either timber, but in polished planks that were too wide to have originated on this island, or from thin stone slabs, that looked to be local rock, but put together without any obvious cement. The quality of workmanship, combined with the overall design and contrast of materials and colours was highly impressive.

Kat shook that feeling away. *I am a Severn, a Fleet Officer, a freakin' Princess!*

She had one final thought. There was a whole lot of rocks and dirt piled up there above their heads. Hopefully these 'Elders' had been better structural engineers than they were theologians!

There were no Troopers deployed ahead of Kat. Deliberate, (a) to avoid them getting so close that they might be considered intimidating to their hosts, and (b) to spread out their force, so they didn't bunch together into opportune targets. Mike had the Staff Sergeant deploy the Troopers in an extended line around the walls of this open space, so as to cover their route of withdrawal, back down the tunnel they'd entered from, should the need arise. It was just Kat, Mike and Anna making the walk towards the central area, set lower than the surrounding floor. Zebub and Shalk followed along at a respectful distance, maybe ten metres behind them.

Kat slowed as she reached the 'pit' in the centre of the floor. It was a good two, maybe three, metres lower than the surrounding level and there was no obvious way down.

Then suddenly, just like the side panel on the vehicle had folded over to create steps, a section of floor opened up, and folded over to make steps that went down to the lower level.

"You are honoured. The Elders have deigned to receive you," Zebub said.

Kat did indeed feel honoured, if not delighted, and knew she was being manipulated. Was that music she could hear?

"Safi, do a stimulant check. I think we might be getting the 'happy' and 'I believe whatever you say' varieties."

"You are correct. There are small traces of nitrous oxide and scopolamine gas as well as low harmonics reinforcing them," Safi confirmed in Kat's ear.

Kat tapped a wrist band that she'd had the med-tech prepare for exactly these circumstances, and the antidotes to multiple stimulants were being instantly absorbed through her skin into her bloodstream. She nodded to Mike, who informed everyone else to do the same. Behind her Zebub and Shalk came down the stairs in near beatific joy.

Once they had cleared the bottom step, the stairs folded silently up and away. A chromed metal rail then rose from the floor, forming a barrier, and marking the limit of their permitted advance. Kat reached it and stopped, looked around, but could see nothing. She turned around to face the others, waiting until whoever was choreographing the show caught up.

She looked up. Her Troopers still flanked three sides of the room. Staff Freeman stood above them, ready if necessary to help them up and out. His Corporals checked their individual Squads, making sure everyone stayed attentive, even though nothing seemed to be happening.

"Safi, talk to me," Kat said.

"I am not finding any electronic activity. Everything appears to be either hydraulic or mechanical."

Which was helpful, but it wasn't.

With a hiss of what looked like steam rather than smoke, that made Kat turn back to face the rail, the music suddenly seemed to get louder and more pounding, reminding her of a few dodgy concerts she'd attended whilst at university.

Like now, she had attended them 'drug free,' and hadn't enjoyed that show quite as much as some of her fellow students who had been 'under the influence.'

A section of the opposite wall slid aside and a procession of ten white-haired men and women entered the space on the other side of the metal rail. A second group followed them, dressed exactly as the workers had been on the surface and placed chairs behind each of the 'Elders.'

Kat was well aware that politics could quickly deteriorate into a blood sport. Her father tried very hard to keep it otherwise . . . most of the time. Hopefully their 'Angels of Light' wouldn't be talking directly to these 'Elders' any time soon. If they did, or at least the 'Elders' believed that they did, then this had the potential to go bad, and quickly.

The steam dissipated, but before anyone could speak, Kat took the lead. "Hi. I'm very grateful that you could find time in your busy schedule to meet with me today. I represent King James of the ABCANZ Federation."

Nothing happened. The man in the middle of the row of old persons studied Kat for a long moment through small, beady little eyes.

"You do not speak to us," he growled. "We speak to

you. And then you answer, and only when we wish it."

"I'm sure you've noticed my colleagues around the perimeter of the room?" Kat asked him.

"I could order them to leave, and they would obey me," the old man told her.

"You might want to double-check that. I do believe your 'I believe anything you say' gas, is somewhat 'old school.' Scopolamine is it not?"

"You there," he said, waving up at Staff Freeman. "Leave us."

The Staff Sergeant's grip on his assault rifle changed as he brought it up into his shoulder, sending a very clear message. He shook his head. "Sorry, not going to happen, sir."

"Let me tell you what *is* going to happen," Kat said casually, settling into a half sitting position on the dividing rail. "Humanity is currently at peace with itself, but let's be honest, it's all a bit fragile. You're not too far from China, especially if they do another expansion to 'regain lost realms,' like they did at the beginning of the last war. If that happens, it's not going to be very long before there's going to be a lot of warships in these waters. And sooner or later you're going to be found out."

"I told you we should have picked somewhere nearer the old country," said an old woman three seats away.

"China was expanding, growing like a rapacious weed, even before we came here," a man on the opposite end said.

"They began their filthy expansion forty years ago. It's too late to stop it now," said another beside him.

"Enough," said the one with the beady eyes.

Kat spoke into the sudden quiet. "You really don't have a lot of options. You can try to stay hidden, but it's only a matter of time before the Indian Authorities, or perhaps more pirates, find you."

"So, you stand here and demand that we join your Federation?" the woman asked.

"Oh no, you very much misunderstand me on that," Kat moved quickly to correct. "No new territory may join the ABCANZ Federation that is not acceptable to any of the five nation states. And, no territory without a democratically elected government would even be considered. So there's no question of you joining the ABCANZ Federation, not even as a Dependency, but we also cannot allow you to operate as a rogue entity or a resource for terrorism or piracy, enabling them to further prey upon the commercial shipping lanes. We have no intention of denouncing you to the Indian Authorities, but we will need certain assurances from you with regard to your future intentions."

"And if we choose to have nothing to do with you?" The lead 'Elder' said, his voice brimming with a belligerent defiance.

Before Kat could answer him, "I think that maybe we should reflect on this . . . carefully consider all the options," said another of the Elders.

"We only do the bidding of the Angels of Light. We will not become your instruments too . . . to play, to manipulate.

"I wasn't asking you to. I'd be very glad to leave this with you, for a week or two," Kat said lightly. "To enable you to discuss . . . to reflect . . . to contemplate . . . to think through your future intentions."

"Then we will have an answer for you in a week or two," the lead Elder snapped.

Kat stood from the rail and gave them a regal nod. The staircase lowered and she marched her people swiftly from the 'Great Hall.' The Troopers performed a smooth withdrawal, and in only a few minutes she was walking back down the jungle path, towards the *Bella*.

Zebub was evidently uncomfortable and quickly detached himself, leaving Kat with even more questions than answers. This visit had answered absolutely nothing, and Kat wasn't interested in hanging around a single moment longer than they had to.

Casper van de Rey, the old man who had spoken with Kat, asked the other 'Elders' on either side of him, for silence. They had learned the hard way before, being 'bugged' by visitors leaving behind remote listening devices. The Great Hall was being 'cleansed,' as were their persons.

"There are no hidden devices on you," the man with a very rudimentary 'cleansing device,' advised them.

"What about the Great Hall?"

The man consulted with a colleague."

"We have found nothing there either."

"I don't like this," said one of the other 'Elders.' "Outsiders always have bugs. If we cannot find them, it means they have gained an advantage over us."

"Or that this woman simply didn't bug us. How can I persuade you that we are not bugged?" One of the women amongst them said.

"You cannot," he snapped in reply.

"Shall we leave a monitor buoy?" Captain Gillan asked, as the *Bella* prepared to get under way.

"We don't routinely leave monitor buoys," Kat said. She hadn't wanted to make the 'Elders' angry before she had talked with them. Fat lot of good that had done. "I gave them a week, maybe two. We can wait. Captain, get us out of here."

"Aye, your Highness. Myra, take us out."

The *Bella*'s Navigator skillfully used the freighter's maneuvering thrusters to get them back out to open waters, then engaged the main propulsion and pushed them up to a steady ten knots in an approximate direction towards the open waters of the Indian Ocean.

"Where to next?" Kat asked the bridge team aloud.

It was the *Fires of Beltane*'s passive sensors that gave the first indication of trouble.

"There are two vessels of more than three thousand tonnes, one out in the roads, off the main habitation," the sensor crewman said. "Another against a jetty in the town."

"No chatter on any comms channel," added the crewman on the comms station, right after the crewman on the sensor's had finished his report.

"Hail them. All frequencies. Standard, 'identify yourself' messaging," Kat ordered.

Eventually the main screen on the bridge came on. Kat knew at first glance the situation was not good. Staring at her in the impeccably tailored uniform of a merchant sea captain was Samuel Ellis, the former Commander of the ABCANZ Fleet's Fast Attack Corvette *Berserker*, who when given a choice between early retirement or a court martial had chosen the former.

What is he doing here? was Kat's first question.

Nothing good had to be the only possible answer.

"Unidentified Merchant Freighter, there is no business here for you. Do not approach Elahi-Heya."

Kat thumped the button to close the screen image.

"Elahi-Heya?" Gillan said, looking at Sato with a frown. "I've never heard of anywhere with that name"

"You have now," Kat said, and brought them up to speed on who Ellis was.

Captain Gillan didn't seem surprised, but he did want to make sure he got the facts right. "He was the skipper of your first ship out of OTA(F), yes?"

Kat agreed that he was.

"And he ended up retiring out of the Fleet in lieu of a full court-martial,"

Kat agreed that he did.

"That might explain why I get such interesting looks in a bar when I admit to being your skipper," Gillan said, rubbing his chin.

"Then stay on my good side," Kat suggested.

"What happened?" Gillan asked her, suddenly very serious.

"Unfortunately you are not authorized for that information," Mike told him.

"I'd like to hear the story too," Anna added.

"If she told you, I'd then have to kill you," Mike said.

"In you freakin' dreams," Anna said with a wide grin, if not a laugh.

It might be interesting to see who would be the victor. Kat thought, then said, "Children, please, I think we have a rather full list of things that need doing. Could we perhaps put the fighting off until we're a little less busy?"

"We never get any real down time," Anna complained.

"Considering what you'd likely do with it, is that any

wonder? Perhaps I might deliberately keep you busy!" Kat said.

"Err . . . excuse me Princess, but what do we tell this former associate of yours?" Gillan asked. "If we don't comply, he'll threaten us again, or perhaps even put a warning shot our way, confirming his surprise at once more 'crossing paths' with his err . . . . well-remembered subordinate."

"You're the Captain," Kat noted.

"I suddenly feel a very sore throat coming on. Laryngitis probably," Gillan said.

"Send for a med-tech," Kat said.

The Captain shook his head. "Sorry Princess, but this is not the part I signed up for. I and my crew will support you fully, but not this." He said with an expressive shrug. "This is definitely a matter for one of those damn Severns I hear so much about."

Well . . . you did want to have all the fun, didn't you, said that nagging little voice in the back of her head. *I was so looking forward to exploring, who'd have thought that Ellis, of all freakin' people, would beat me to it! Afraid to face him? Scared he might hoodwink you, like he did last time?* Kat took a deep breath. Yes, he'd run her ragged, but she was the one still serving. He was the one who no longer did so.

Kat stood and moved in front of the main screen and its camera unit.

She squared her back, schooled her face to something approximately neutral, then nodded to Gillan. "Put me on."

She instantly found herself staring at Captain Ellis's confident smile.

"Long time no see, Ensign. No, sorry, it's Lieutenant now, my apologies. So tell me, what could possibly bring you all the way out here, so far from the nearest debutant ball?"

"This is Lieutenant Katarina Severn of the ABCANZ Federation, on the exploration vessel *Fires of Beltane*. We are on a scientific and survey mission of uncharted colonies and settlements and have this location recorded as being Campbell Bay, also known as Tenlaa, Captain Ellis. We have no hostile intent and wish you no harm."

Kat kept her voice even, allowing no inflection to either 'Captain' or 'Ellis.'

He said Elahi-Heya, yet we say Campbell Bay. With luck he'll explain the discrepancy.

Before Ellis could say anything more, Gillan suddenly cut the transmission again, both audio and vision.

"Excuse me ma'am, but I'm getting something from that vessel in the town," the comms crewmen immediately reported.

"What kind of something," Mike said.

The crewman's face looked pained, embarrassed. "Just a bit of backscatter from a very tight comms burst. Likely acting as a re-bro station from somewhere ashore, sir. Perhaps the Princess's HI might assist, maybe help make something of it?"

Safi didn't need asking twice.

"It is very weak, and very scattered. We are only picking up small, reflected fragments of the re-broadcasted transmission. It is also encrypted, so I will need more transmission sequences to crack it," Safi announced with confidence after only a few seconds.

"Quick as you can please, Safi."

The crewman at the sensors shook his head. "There's nothing obvious ashore. No power distribution pylons or huge generators."

"There was nothing detectable on North Sentinel either," Mike reminded them.

"Agreed, sir, but North Sentinel was meant to have nothing. Campbell Bay is meant to have several thousand people living there. Or at least it *did* have," the sensor crewman responded.

"Put the Land Force Detachment on sixty minutes 'Notice to Deploy,' Mike. Just in case," Kat decided.

"Aye ma'am, with pleasure. Sixty minutes 'Notice to Deploy' it is," Mike acknowledged, with another smart salute and an about face.

"And tell the Professor's people I want a full LiDaR, ERT, terrain mapping and analysis scan. Get our Troopers some Intel that is a bit more substantial that the 'nothing' we currently have."

Kat then turned back to Captain Gillan. "Run immediate checks on all our weapons and warfare systems and their associated power relays, we need to be ready for anything he might throw our way. Myra, hold position here, ideally without running us into anything hidden below the water."

"I was about to suggest exactly that myself," Gillan said. "Do it, Myra."

"And what other type of approach do you think I'd make on a former Fast Attack Corvette Commander's currently unidentified vessel?" Sato said. "Just because I didn't go to OTA(F) like you lot, it doesn't make me stupid!"

There were laughs and chuckles from the *Bella*'s crew at their Navigator's outburst. It was also the first inkling Kat had ever had that Gillan, as well as her and Mike, might have been to the Fleet's Officer Training Academy, at some point in his somewhat murky past.

Kat walked towards the crewman on the sensor board. "Talk to me. Tell me everything you have on those two ships. They and therefore you, have been way to quiet for my tastes," she said, pulling out a secondary, and far less comfortable, 'seat' to perch on and review the screens and the various scans and sweeps that got pulsed out and reflected or bounced back.

"Sorry ma'am. But there isn't very much to see or talk about," the crewman said, uncomfortable with having his 'boss's boss' in such close proximity.

Thirty minutes later, the comms crewman reported, "Incoming transmission."

Kat stood and took a moment as she moved to be in front of the video pick up to check she was correctly dressed. Her shipsuit was zipped right up and not creased. She would not allow her former Commander to critique or scold her in front of her own team.

Satisfied, she nodded to the crewman at the comms board. "Put me on."

Once again, Captain Ellis's image filled the screen, but it was actually the bridge behind him that Kat studied. The bridge and the crew on it.

Although Ellis's merchant marine uniform was predictably immaculate, those behind him wore a very un-uniform mix of civilian clothing. No two were the same. There was one other 'Officer' similarly attired to Ellis.

His bridge looked about as 'Fleet' as Kat's probably did. *But what is the actual reality?* Another good question, but she didn't see any immediate answers.

One thing was very apparent. To the left and right of Ellis there were two extra bridge stations. Navigation and Helm were usually in-front of the Captain. Comms, Sensors and Engineering to the rear. That likely meant both 'weapon systems' and 'warfare systems' were installed.

There was a distinct difference in the ANCANZ Fleet and most other world navies, between these two disciplines, or branches.

Warfare Systems, Kat's old branch-of-service before she had taken 'command' of the Fast Intercept Boat Osprey, was the specific sensors and other equipment used in detecting and then targeting the enemy. All ships had navigational equipment that used various different technologies to tell them where they were, but Warfare Systems often used the same tech, and other innovations, like radar, sonar, thermal, and optical to search out and locate the enemy, or 'Find and Fix' as the Fleet preferred to call it. Helm and Navigation were usually part of this branch to, due to their 'operational' functions on the bridge. The ABCANZ Military's Branch identity colour was yellow. It's insignia, also used by the Land Force's Armoured Branch, was a pair of crossed knights swords, both held by an armoured gauntlet, ('delivering the strike') within a weapon's sighting aperture, as they provided 'targeting' data.

Whereas, 'Weapon Systems' was the branch-of-service who crewed, programmed, operated and reloaded the actual guns, missiles, torpedoes and other offensive systems on-board the ship and manned the bridge station that displayed their fighting capability once a target was engaged. Their branch colour was red and their insignia, a pair of diagonally crossed gun or cannon barrels from history, with a more modern missile superimposed in-between. This identifier was also used by the Land Force Artillery branch.

Whatever these extra bridge stations were, there were certainly too many display boards on Ellis's ship for an honest, merchant freighter.

There was no doubt in Kat's mind that Ellis would have done his own check around the *Fire of Beltane*'s bridge too, and come to the same conclusion. She also had too many bridge stations for a true exploration vessel.

"Well now, Princess," he said. Twisting her royal status into some kind of crime, "As you can see, this is not the Campbell Bay settlement that you are looking for, but the start-up scientific station of Elahi-Heya, dutifully registered with the Indian authorities. You have no business here, so I suggest you leave forthwith. If you now approach this island, I will assume it is a deliberate act, and therefore hostile, and be assured, I will take appropriate offensive action. You are duly advised . . . that this ship is armed," he finished speaking, then gave Kat the same stern scowl that she long remembered from her time on the *Berserker*.

The connection was terminated and the screen went dark. Apparently, his sensors had not yet advised him of the weapon systems the *Bella* had installed. Kat saw no reason to hold back. She nodded at the crewman on the Weapon Systems board and he flicked the switch to activate everything. Kat wished she could see the reaction on Ellis's face when he realized what he was up against. From the way the crewman on the Warfare Systems board was working the incoming data, Kat would soon have a report on what capability Ellis's vessel had to respond with. She could wait. That wasn't her immediate priority.

"Safi, check out his claim about Elahi-Heya."

"I am already searching the Indian Government's on-line database. Yes, there is an Elahi-Heya. But it's several hours from here, on the next island north, Little Nicobar. The pharmaceutical consortium that made the registration for a scientific research station have no other claims anywhere nearby."

Safi opened a small window in the corner of the bridge's main screen. It showed a map-satellite hybrid image of Great Nicobar Island, and to its north was Little Nicobar, as well as Campbell Bay, and Elahi-Heya in its recently registered position.

Kat allowed herself a deep scowl. "Captain Ellis," she said aloud, even though the comms transmission was no longer active, "Not for the first time, you seem to have a problem telling me the truth. Maybe even to your own crew. Elahi-Heya is a fair way from here."

She paused to let that sink in with those listening. The ship's clock showed a time of almost thirteen-hundred-hours and she was hungry. "Keep backing us away, nice and slowly. I'm going for lunch. Captain Gillan, please call me if we get anything new from my old associate."

Putting on her best smile, Kat headed for the *Bella*'s mess hall.

The revised dining arrangements on board the *Fires of Beltane* since her recent repair and refit were the same as most other ABCANZ Fleet ships and shore facilities. The food came from the same galley, but the Officers, which often included the Senior NCOs on the very small ships and shore establishments, dined separately to the Junior Ranks. Captain Gillan evidently didn't like that arrangement and often sat with his crew on the other side of the partition. When Staff Freeman attempted to discuss the matter with him, the Senior NCO was quickly reminded as to who was the Captain of the ship, and that therefore he could do whatever he so wanted!

Kat did draw the line when Professor Brooks insisted that he and his boffins needed their own space too.

She settled herself at an empty table with a light lunch. It didn't stay empty for very long.

Gillan soon took the seat opposite her. "What do you really think is going on?" he asked her in a quiet voice.

Kat poked her lunch with a fork. They were still on fresh rations obtained in Port Blair, but they wouldn't last indefinitely.

"I can only guess," she said. "If Ellis is involved, I doubt it's anything good, but I think we need way more Intel before we get too carried away with speculation."

"He was very clear that he does not want us poking around . . . going ashore. There was nothing ambiguous about his intent. He was openly hostile. Do you think this might be a 'filibuster' expedition?" asked Safi.

Kat laughed. "As I have no idea what that is Safi, I can't really accuse someone else of being one, can I?"

"Didn't they make the fireworks in that old 'boy wizard' series they made us all read at school?" said Captain Gillan with a grin.

"I found it in my research," Safi said. "A 'filibuster expedition,' back in the nineteenth century, was when rich individuals engaged in an unauthorized, private military expedition into a foreign country or territory with the purpose to incite or support a revolution. Several United States citizens encouraged insurrections during that century in places such as Texas, California, Cuba, Nicaragua and Colombia. Such expeditions have also occasionally been used as 'cover' for government-approved deniable operations."

"A team of mercenaries from a wealthy country heads off to a poor one . . . and takes it over . . . looting it of anything valuable along the way . . . then either leaves, or if viable and sufficiently lucrative, perhaps keeps it operational for a return visit in the future. Can that really be what Captain Ellis and his associates are doing here?" Gillan said, his summary as much for himself, as for Kat or Safi. "Sounds a bit far-fetched."

"Good research, Safi," Kat said, knowing full well that her HI was going way beyond what usually passed for a data search, and doing it after setting up the search parameters herself. Safi was a 'growing girl.'

Has all this really come from tutoring an eleven-year-old?

No way to tell.

"They've got an ex-ABCANZ Fleet Officer running it," Captain Gillan said. "And I'd bet money that the tight-beamed message was to more 'trigger pullers' ashore."

Kat nodded. Perhaps those pieces did fit nicely into the puzzle as to why Campbell Bay was suddenly Elahi-Heya. *Too nicely? Too easily?*

Campbell Bay had tried to rebrand itself as 'Tenlaa' in the early twenty-first century, to give it an 'Indian' rather than a 'colonial' name, but it had only been a partial success. Maybe they were trying that again? Perhaps 'Elahi-Heya' really was another attempt at rebranding? Safi hadn't been able to give a definitive translation at to what 'Elahi-Heya' might mean. It wasn't any of the Indian languages of Bengali, Punjabi or Tamil, spoken by at least two-thirds of the island's population. The HI's best 'guess' was that its origins were the native language of Nicobarese or Shompen, and approximately translated it as 'Heavenly Haven.'

"Do we have a report on Ellis's vessel's capabilities?" Kat asked her Captain.

"We certainly do," said Gillan. "He's dropped anchor and his propulsion units are inactive. He's only running a trickle of plasma from his reactors. He has two, but he's trying very hard to make it look like there is only one."

"And weapons?" Kat said, her patience starting to wane. "Is anything charged and ready to engage a target?"

"The lumps and bumps on the hull might suggest a concealed ASM launcher, but can't tell if they're Ahabs, Harlequins, Cetus IIIs or something else at the moment. He also has concealed fore and aft guns. Unlikely to be 127mm, as their housing seems too small, so our best guess is 75mm auto-cannons."

Kat pushed back in her chair.

"Your former Commander sounds like someone eager to do unto others *before* they can do unto him. That's a lot of punch for such a small, supposedly civilian, vessel. I do hope you don't want us to fight our way in there." Gillan said.

"Way too early to tell, Captain. Please launch a couple of sea-skimming UAVs. Load onto them a full report of what we have encountered. Make them anonymous, so nothing is traceable back to us. Send one to transmit its data in the vicinity of Port Blair, for the Indian Navy Base's Commander. Send the other to Banda Aceh, message transmission for the Pancasila Republic's state governor."

"Sneaky, just like a Severn," Gillan said and started tapping at his comm-unit.

"Just what exactly is our 'sneaky little Severn' up to now?" Mike asked as he joined them at the table, taking the space immediately to Kat's right.

Kat quickly updated Mike on the offensive ability of Ellis's ship.

"Any tubes?" Mike asked.

"Don't know. Can't be a hundred percent sure, but doesn't look like it," Gillan said.

"Don't ever under-estimate Ellis. I wouldn't put anything past him," Kat added.

"So he's hot and loaded. Can't we put in a call to 4th Fleet Headquarters . . . wait this out until reinforcements arrive?"

"This isn't our patch, Mike. We need India's civilian authorities to deal with it. And believe me, they do love their procedural bureaucracy and are likely to find more objections about us turning up with half of 4th Fleet as back up, than whatever it is that Ellis and co are getting up to!"

"Could this be why the *Fenrir* is really here?" suggested Mike.

"As back up?" Gillan asked. "For who?"

"Good question . . . but it was Kapitän Sörensen who advised me that Ellis was operating in these waters. Why would he do that if the *Fenrir* is here to support Ellis's activities?"

"Do you trust him?" Gillan asked.

"Who? Sörensen or Ellis?"

"Sörensen of course. You'd hardly trust Ellis."

Kat reflected on that for a moment, then looked at Mike. "Yes, I think I do trust him."

Mike nodded. "I agree. He has always behaved most courteously towards you, Princess. He seems genuine . . . even honourable. I see no reason to distrust him."

"What about the von Welf girl?" Gillan asked.

Kat laughed. "She's from the same pit of snakes as Ellis, but I think Sörensen has her way too busy to try anything foolish."

Gillan nodded, accepting Kat's assessment.

"Oh yes, Safi has found a word I've never heard of," she told Mike.

"Nor me," laughed Gillan.

"What does 'filibuster' mean to you?"

Mike took a mouthful of his lunch, evidently thinking as he chewed it. "In politics, it's a little used, but legitimate delay tactic, which the minority parties can use to slow down or even prevent new legislation. When your old man wants to get something through, and the Opposition doesn't, they might deliberately over-debate it, thereby ensuring that they eventually run out of parliamentary time, so can't take a vote on it. They tinkered with the legislation to try and stop it happening back in the 2020s, I think, but don't quote me on that."

"How come you know so much about Parliamentary procedures, and *me*, the Prime Minister's very own daughter, doesn't?" she asked him.

"You work and hang out in The Capitol district as long as I have, and being trained to eavesdrop and gather Intel, well . . ." he shrugged. "Oh, and there was that Intern that I briefly dated . . . until I found out what she was, and that was against several Civil Service protocols . . . so I had to end it."

Kat glared at him, but said nothing.

"But . . . in the nineteenth century," Mike continued,

"I believe it was when 'entrepreneurs' with way too much time, money and firepower, helped the poor to stay poor by looting their country of anything valuable." He took another mouthful. "You're thinking that the latter might apply here?"

Gillan shook his head. "This Elahi-Heya thing, it's apparently a real place, but meant to be on the other side of the adjacent island. Are they planning on stripping out Campbell Bay and then relocating the other settlement here instead?

Kat shrugged. "If they want to rename Campbell Bay to Elahi-Heya and say 'oops, sorry, we took a wrong turn,' well . . . honestly, that's all a bit academic to me. I really don't care. However, to relocate or forcibly evict the local population . . . that's not going to be much fun for anyone. And, it doesn't answer the far bigger question . . . why?"

"My thoughts exactly," agreed Mike.

"So . . . what are you going to do," Gillan asked.

"That is something we'll have to think about carefully before we get any nearer," Kat said. "The real question right now is 'what can we realistically achieve without getting a lot of innocent people killed in the process?'"

"If we go for help, and the local authorities are as bureaucratic as you say, then by the time we've convinced them that they really need to do something, there may not be anyone left alive by the time we get back," Gillan said.

"True," Mike said, but it was a reluctant admission.

Kat considered all that she had learned so far. Then added in all she'd done to complicate her former Commander's own tactical situation . . . and decided it was still too soon to make any decisions of her own.

"What does this 'Campbell Bay' or whatever name it's going by now, look like? Have the boffins added anything new to the archived satellite imagery we can download?" Kat asked.

"The data from their LiDaR scan is still coming in. Would you like me to show you what we have so far?" Safi asked.

Kat pulled down the zipper of her shipsuit enabling a

telescoping, flexible appendage from Safi to project a three-dimensional image of Great Nicobar Island. It was almost entirely rain-forest covered, approximately fifty-five kilometres long, north to south and twenty-two klicks wide. Rolling hills, gently climbed to a maximum elevation of over six-hundred metres. The northern half of the island was designated a 'biosphere reserve' with access being strictly controlled. It was home to several unique species of plants and birds. Campbell Bay on the south-east corner was the only significant human settlement. There had once been other, smaller settlements, towards the southern tip, but successive tsunamis and the death and destruction they had left in their wake, eventually necessitated them being abandoned. The scan showed dilapidated remains in several locations, even through the jungle had done its best to reclaim them.

"That's Campbell Bay," Kat said as the buildings started to populate the projection.

"Most of the island is dense rain-forest, that's hard going on foot. What about the rivers?"

"They all flow south, or south-westerly following the general terrain profile," commented Gillan studying the projection.

Mike nodded in agreement, his lips tight and thin. "There's nowhere obvious to put troops ashore that doesn't involve a very long trek over multiple hills, through the jungle, or down a river. Except, sailing directly into the settlement itself."

"And that's right under Ellis's guns."

"We need another way in."

"There," said Kat, looking at the display. "Bananga Bay. It looks like some sort of overgrown plantation. We could put the Land Force Detachment ashore there, in RIBs, directly onto the beach at night. It's out of sight of any vessels in Campbell Bay as that headland is in the way. There's still a partial road that links the two locations. It's probably overgrown and around a ten-klick hike, but it has to be better than trying to cut our way over a hill and through the forest."

"Full Detachment deployment or just a couple of recon teams?" Mike asked her.

Kat decided lunch was over. She folded her napkin and stood. For the questions she now had, the bridge was the place to find the answers, not the Mess Hall.

Back on the bridge, Kat was pleasantly surprised by the minor miracle that Sato had performed. She had slowly backed them off until they were out of visual range of Ellis's ship and anyone ashore in Campbell Bay settlement. Yes, they would still show on his sensor equipment, but there was something satisfactory about being outside of visual range.

"I was going to swing us about, then get us lost in the radar clutter created by the higher terrain of the island," Sato explained.

"It will be reciprocal though," the crewman and the sensor board added. "He'll have a harder time seeing us, once the bulk of the island is between us, especially if we add in some ECM, but we'll lose some of our own capability too."

"I need 'eyes' on what he's up to," Kat reminded them.

Within the hour a tiny recon UAV, with another to act as a relay platform, bouncing the surveillance imagery around the island and back to the *Bella*, were operational. Both could fly at almost seventy kilometres-an-hour in perfect weather conditions, so were soon in their designated positions.

Ellis was no fool and predictably had a jammer operating for just such an eventuality, but that had been anticipated. Kat's team was doing exactly the same. Their recon UAV continued to do its reporting, changing location and hopping transmission frequencies for the data, but also flying about at unpredictable speeds and directions.

Anna had provided the transmission codes with only a slight arm twist from Kat. "These are from my own personal supply, from Commodore Finklemeyer," the Equerry pointed out.

"I'm sure they are," Kat said, "and with all these codes

up your sleeve, you can rotate them to the bottom of the deck and bring them out sometime when they'll be long forgotten, or even ask The Fink for some new ones. Give."

Anna gave in, grumbled a bit and said she needed to attend to Grace's education. Grace however was much more interested in staying, watching the comings and goings of the bridge crew and the *Bella*'s passage around the western side of the island. Neither her Equerry nor the eleven-year-old girl managed to stay entirely out of Kat's peripheral vision.

The island and Ellis stayed silent as the afternoon turned into evening and then into night. The *Fires of Beltane* stayed 'comms silent' and continued running dark, as did the island. Nothing, not even a flickering camp fire ashore, lit up the all-enveloping darkness.

Captain Ellis was 'running dark' and in 'comms silent' mode too. Uncharacteristically, he thankfully stayed at anchor in Campbell Bay's harbour. Which left Kat to wonder just what exactly was he up to, and why hadn't he given chase? This is not what she would have predicted him to do. Was the answer to that question actually the other vessel anchored in the harbour?

"It appears to be an underpowered merchant vessel, ma'am," the crewman at the board reported. "Reactor probably could only make ten, twelve knots at best, especially if fully laden."

Kat's elder brother Edward had asked her opinion when he got the assignment in Parliament of reviewing and updating the safety regulations that governed the ABCANZ Fed's registered merchant ships. The 'less ship' and 'more cargo' that a merchant hull moved, the better the profit margin. Unnecessarily over-powered propulsion drives and reactors, exactly like the *Bella* had installed, ate into the bottom line of profitability for any commercial operation.

Her Grandpa George, the CEO of the Lennox Group had pushed for reducing the standards. He had been challenged, but his retort back to the politicians was typically direct and forthright. "What do you know? Please don't tell a successful businessman how to run his business."

Kat now found herself looking at the updated data feed of imagery coming in from their recon UAV. The second vessel was a small merchant transport. More of a passenger ferry than a freighter. *Was Ellis going to load it with the citizens of Campbell Bay and haul them away? Or has he brought in a boat load of mercenaries, renamed the settlement Elahi-Heya and then notified the local inhabitants as to who now owns the sweat that dripped from their brows?*

Whichever it was, it was clear to Kat she potentially had two separate battles on her hands. One on the island for her Land Force Troopers and one out at sea for the *Fires of Beltane*.

Question? Which has the strongest call for a Severn?

And where did she put a dozen scientists and an eleven-year-old girl? Kat didn't see any easy answers, so she settled on asking questions. "Myra, what are your thoughts for a final approach?"

"Funny you should ask," the Navigator said, with a happy grin. "I do have an idea."

Kat had hardly got, "Enlighten me," past her lips before Sato was displaying her intentions on the main screen.

"Assuming your former Commander doesn't do anything, and stays within the roads or harbour, and we continue on our current heading towards the northern end of this island," the screen graphic showed exactly that. Sato advanced the display. "We continue on, to Little Nicobar, perhaps to check on the registered location of Elahi-Heya, to see what's actually there, or is not. We might then stop there for a few hours, like good predictable folks, and wait for him to give chase, perhaps even turn 'stern-on,' and make ourselves into a target that even a saint might struggle to resist. Is your old boss any kind of saint?"

Kat shook her head.

"I thought as much. What we'll really do when we get there, is launch another buoy. It will emit the same signature profile as our reactors and propulsion units. Whilst it won't fool all their sensors, all of the time, it may fool some of them, some of the time. We could put a three-dimensional projector onto the buoy too. That will generate an image of this vessel to deceive long range visual scans like satellite recon. Not perfect, but it will make them waste time validating the imagery."

Kat nodded.

"Meanwhile, we'll do a smart 'about-face' and at full speed, we dash back towards Campbell Bay, slowing down a bit where the other old settlements once were. We also turn off our ID transponder and come in dark," Sato continued.

"No," said Kat. "I am not about to break the rules by turning off our transponder. That's what those Vulkana's in Nu Hawaii did. We are not about to lower ourselves to their level."

"Would you consider encrypting it? So we're not actually turning it off, just making it not immediately readable?"

"Perhaps," said Kat. But didn't concede.

"We can then get troops ashore *and* be ready to engage when he realises that he's been duped and comes rushing back round that headland. Not perfect, I know, but I can't think of anything else."

The screen now showed all of what the Navigator had just described.

"Do we have to dash back at full speed?" Gillan asked.

"No," Sato replied.

"Yes," Kat said.

"Okay," the Captain sighed. "I take it that Myra thinks we could do things as slow as I might want to do. You, my Princess, no doubt want to go for the fast attack that gives poor Captain Ellis as little time to think and react as possible."

"If we're intending to come back fast, then I need to do a full sonar scan when we're going up slow. There are no STRs anywhere around here, so I don't want us colliding with any unwanted surprises when we're coming back at full speed," Sato told them.

"Agreed," Kat said, "And, I would also like to suggest

that some of us go to bed," she said looking straight at Mike. "We'll need to be well rested before deploying ashore."

"We, your Highness?" Mike asked.

"We," Kat told him.

"Oh wonderful." The Captain commented sarcastically. "Does that mean I get my ship all to myself in this battle? A battle, all on my own, against a former Fast-Attack Corvette Commander! Oh, such joy!"

"Don't worry, I'll be looking over your shoulder," Kat insisted, "But with the comfort of having dirt under my feet for a change."

"Who is going to provide you an Intel feed? Anna asked.

"You are. Stay here, look after Grace, and work Intel for us, and run co-ord with Brooks and his boffins."

SIX : SIX

"What do you mean, taking me and my team into gun fight?" Brooks roared as he banged hard on the door to Kat's cabin.

Evidently, she wasn't about to get any sleep until this was resolved. Somehow, she'd been half expecting this. In a movement that was half twist, half crunch, she swung herself out of her bunk, pulled on a t-shirt and had Safi release the door.

"Professor, you did not complain all that much when we encountered the pirate vessel," she said, facing the upset scientist.

"I honestly didn't expect the pirates to bite back. None of us did. We had a pool running, only two thought we'd end up in a full-on fight. Now you are evidently gunning for a confrontation, and with this Ellis individual, who I am advised, is a former Fleet Commander, and has weapon systems concealed aboard his vessel!"

"Have your technicians identified exactly what he has ashore?" Kat asked him.

"Not just yet."

"I assume you're working with the *Bella*'s bridge crew on that?"

"Of course. It's our lives too!"

"I'm glad you see it that way," Kat said. A small smile was all she could manage.

"But see here, this really is too much. We haven't gotten any real scientific research done at all!"

"You didn't object too strongly when Captain Gillan took on the containers for delivery to North Sentinel."

"He promised to upgrade our cabins with some of his ill-gotten gains," Brooks said, looking at the wall like a three-year-old who had been caught with his hand in the cookie jar.

Kat swallowed her smile. She'd never have thought the ebony skinned professor could look so embarrassed. She was tempted to let the conversation go on, but she found herself stifling a yawn. She really did need to sleep.

"Ensign Brooks, I suggest you and the other Defence Science and Technology staff review the small-print of the contracts you signed before boarding."

Brooks twisted his face into something not quite ugly, but it certainly wasn't radiating sunshine. "So, I'm an Ensign now, am I? We've been 'drafted' just like you did to Mr Steiger?"

Kat ignored his underhand comment about being drafted.

"You and your team are rank-ranged from Petty Officer, through Chief, up to a Fleet Chief, with you as their Officer in Command." Kat advised him. "Defence Science and Technology Specialists in the ABCANZ Fleet's Reserve, entitled to all the obligations, protections and fun that such a position duly permits. That includes facing my old Commander, who loves to give Ensigns a hard time. Believe me . . . I know. Your pay, seeing as you are all 'Professionally Qualified,' is significantly higher than those in the same military rank." She tried hard not to sound too patronising as she apprised Brooks of his team's situation.

The Professor and, by the commission he now held, Officer, and therefore a gentleman, took in a huge breath, followed it with a deep sigh. "Doctor Razafindra warned me those documents we signed were not standard, never could be with a Severn on-board, but I foolishly ignored her. She will have more than a few words to say to me over dinner tonight, and I will be reduced to hanging my head and conceding that an anthropologist just might be wiser than an oceanographer. How the world has evolved!"

"Now, I'd really like to get some sleep," Kat said, "if you don't mind, Professor." Kat was careful to use his civilian title. It was more appropriate. He and his team should have actually been given military ranks somewhat higher than those they had been allocated, but Kat had wanted to ensure that nobody was more 'senior' to her whilst on-board. She didn't want anyone 'pulling rank.' Captain Gillan, as the master of the vessel outranked her in that respect, but that hadn't caused any problems so far, as he was contracted by Fleet Command, who had then placed him, his vessel and his crew at Kat's disposal. Anna technically outranked Kat too, but as she fulfilled the position of Equerry, someone who attends and assists their primary, her seniority had never been a problem previously. Furthermore, she hadn't actually revealed that she held any current military rank until quite recently.

"Yes, I will withdraw in abject defeat," Professor Brooks said. "But I wonder how well you will sleep . . . as that little girl in the next cabin . . . did not sign herself into the Fleet, did she?"

The door closed, and Kat manually turned off the light, leaving her standing alone in the darkness. She was sleepy, but Brook's words had hit home.

The situation on the island was full of unknowns. And if Captain Ellis was involved in cooking it up, whatever 'it' might be, it would not be an easy one to figure out, or to make evolve in any way other than exactly how Ellis wanted it to be. Kat should be concentrating on how to solve that issue.

But Ellis was not her only problem. The list of dead at Kat's hands never seemed to stop growing. Originally, they had been the 'bad' people and had deservedly died so that good might prevail, at least that was how she reconciled it to keep her sanity. But after Hawaii, the list of those who had died in her list of previous commands had gotten so much longer than she would have ever liked and now seemed unavoidably destined to grow once again.

And now she was risking an eleven-year-old! And an eleven-year-old was too young to volunteer for anything.

Kat woke without any of her numerous questions being any closer to an answer.

She cleaned her teeth, splashed some water onto her face, pulled her hair back into something close to what Fleet regulations prescribed, then wriggled herself into a fresh shipsuit.

She headed for the bridge, fully aware they were still several hours away from their intended RIB insertion into Bananga Bay, something Kat hoped would be a big surprise for Ellis and hopefully knock him off his game, or whatever it was he was up to.

Unfortunately, her own game plan was not developing all that well either. "Have we found any evidence of the island's original population," Kat asked.

"No, ma'am," the crewmen at both the comms and the sensor boards answered in close succession.

"Nothing at all?"

"Nothing significant, several 'occurrences' to speculate on, but nothing definitive. We've encountered no vehicle or pedestrian movements," Mike said. He was standing behind the two crewmen. One of Professor Brook's team was also huddled with them and nodded in agreement.

"Can we send up anything better or different to try to locate them?"

"We did, while you were having your beauty sleep, err ... ma'am," the scientist advised. "They are either (a) hiding, or (b) they're not there, or (c) we're too late and they're all already dead."

"What's your money on?" she asked Mike.

"Hiding, but don't ask me why. If they were already gone or if they had been killed, executed, massacred ... whatever you want to call it ... we'd surely find some kind of evidence. We might have identified a dead body on the beach, but it's only one, not multiple, and we're not a hundred percent certain it's human, it could easily be a washed-up gibbon or macaque."

Kat nodded and considered the problem herself. "I can think of several other scenarios, but if we assume that the locals know there's a couple of ships out there somewhere, hostile ships, loaded with sensors and weapons, and that they probably have 'bad guys' on the ground too, then it's a reasonable assumption that the locals will be hiding from them. And, if they're hiding from the hostiles, they're not going to be rolling out the red carpet for us now, are they? Am I usually this slow in putting it all together?"

"No, your Highness," Captain Gillan said, "you are not normally slow in 'putting it all together,' or on anything else for that matter. My crew, along with Anna or Emma's help, are usually able to work their magic and give you more or better Intel than the bad guys normally have. But on this occasion, and despite the valuable support of our specialist colleagues from the science and tech disciplines, we can't do any better than what we have already offered."

"Maybe, when we get closer," Mike offered.

"And maybe not," Gillan added.

"I don't like it," said Kat. "I'm sending my Land Force assets into one huge question mark. Do we have a soil analysis yet?"

"Mostly coral sand in the coastal areas, but these islands have sandstone and limestone cores. Barren Island, about one-hundred and forty kilometres northeast of Port Blair, is the last active volcano is this island chain," Mike offered.

"It will be easy to dig in the margins between the soil types, but the sand is too soft, and the limestone to hard. There are often caves within limestone. And that would shield anything inside from our sensors," the scientist added.

"And that's where you think the local population could be hiding out?" Mike asked him.

"Seems logical," said Kat.

"And the bad boys?" Mike left that hanging

"They got a hot message from my old buddy Captain Ellis to do their own vanishing act as soon as he found out I was leading the team that had come knocking at their door."

"Oh that's just freakin' wonderful, a game of blind man's bluff. Going blind into a battle against a bunch of hostiles, potentially as professionally competent as our own Troopers, and in this environment! The terrain and the weather here are hostile too. This does *not* fill me with confidence, Princess," Mike said.

Kat let their conversations cascade around in her

brain for a moment. She evaluated what they had told her, and found that she still didn't know nearly as much as she wanted to before she took strong men and women into battle. But she'd asked for this job, this was what she wanted to do!

"Sensors, look for military vehicles, trucks, buses, armour. Any kind of transportation. Hunt for their tracks if you can't find their metalwork's retained heat in the night environment. Campbell Bay was home to several thousand people, its footprint is too large for an occupying formation to cover on foot. They had to bring in, or have commandeered, local vehicles. Where you find vehicles, you'll likely find the guys holding the guns too."

"Doing it, your Highness," said the crewman with a grin.

"If you can find a cave, you hide inside. We've got to accept that. So we don't look for the cat, we start looking for the tail on the cat, anything that they forgot to pull into the cave. Look, boys and girls, look."

The return leg of their voyage down the western coastline of Great Nicobar island had been undertaken at a steady thirty-five knots. No sooner had the deception buoy been launched and its data transmission checked, including the three-dimensional projection of an image that approximated the *Bella*, than they had turned about and were on their way back down to the opposite end of the adjacent island. Up close, the projection really wasn't up to much, but as they pulled away and put distance between them, Kat conceded that it did look pretty convincing.

The thirty-five knots they now travelled at was nowhere near the *Bella*'s full capability, but it would hopefully be enough to make Ellis's sensor personnel reject the approaching vessel as the freighter they had seen the previous morning. Freighters of that size simply did not do this kind of speed! Not normally anyway. Sato had their second reactor on-line, deliberately giving them a different profile to any searching sensors. And the encrypted transponder . . . Kat just hoped it would be enough. But . . .

she doubted it. Not against Ellis.

Captain Ellis held his face in a rigid mask as everything he'd done in the last three days shattered into numerous questions.

"What does the Severn girl think she's doing?" Mr Badali shouted. "She could spoil everything." As one of the financial backers of this operation, he considered it his divine right to shout at everyone. The man would benefit from trading in his fine Emirates City hand-made suit for a midshipman's uniform at OTA(F). Fifteen minutes under Ellis's command and he would learn a lot more about leadership.

Unfortunately, the man already considered himself a leader. He had the money. Did that not make him a leader? Not for the first time, Ellis wondered if taking this contract had been such a good idea.

But it had inadvertently put that Severn brat, the girl who had ruined his Fleet career, in the sights of his weapon systems, and that made up for a lot!

"Shall we see what the Severn girl is actually doing at the moment," Ellis said, his voice even, controlled. Around the bridge his crew responded to his voice. His calm orders, not the other man's screaming and ranting.

"She is stationary on the north side of Little Nicobar Island. At the location formally registered as Elahi-Heya, sir." The operator projected a sensor drone's image onto their main screen to confirm the equipment's findings to her senior officers.

"Do you think she has done something logical, sensible, heeded your words?" Badali asked. "Is she returning north?"

Ellis shook his head even before the fool civilian got his question out. "Severns don't run," he snapped, "Warfare, project a revised course. Assume best possible speed for that freighter she's operating on, as eighteen, maybe twenty knots."

"Working revised calculations sir, please wait a moment." The crewman on the Warfare Systems board advised.

"Warfare, have you found what I asked you to look for?" Ellis asked, his impatience growing. The young woman on the warfare board was good. Not as well trained as a Fleet Officer, but certainly more trustworthy than that Severn bitch ever had been.

"There is a conflict sir. There is a vessel signature on the western side of the island. Its transponder is operational, but encrypted. The reactor profile does not match that of the freighter with Miss Severn on-board and it is making thirty-five knots. I cannot get a firm fix due to the islands profile being between us. I don't believe it to be the same vessel."

"Very good," Ellis said, and allowed himself a smile. "Very, very good."

"What do you mean?" Badali asked.

"Just a moment . . . kind benefactor," Ellis said.

Badali seemed to preen on the title. Most of the crew knew it for what it was. Contempt. Ellis's utter contempt for a man who was foolish enough to think gold could motivate a true warrior.

"Weapons, do you have a firing solution?" Ellis asked.

"I have a solution being calculated . . . Just a moment, sir. Putting it onto main screen."

An old style "howitzer format" high ballistic arc, or parabolic trajectory filled the display.

"That's using a ten-round burst from both 75mm guns. Dumb munitions. Can't be jammed. Or, if you prefer I can target them with an ASM, but that obviously risks jamming."

"You can predict that ship's course?" Ellis asked her.

"I can, sir. But there is still a vessel matching the profile of the original ship we scanned, at full-stop in Elahi-Heya."

"I want all options open to us." Ellis snapped and turned to face Badali.

"Are you sure a vessel like that freighter can move at speeds of thirty-five knots, Captain Ellis?"

"Normally I would agree with you, it cannot. But when

a Severn is part of the mix, nothing is ever what it might seem when they become involved. You are, I hope familiar with the concept of a 'wolf in sheep's clothing?'"

Badali fancied himself as an expert in military matters because he has read several data-files and watched numerous on-line videos, a real 'armchair general' who had never actually served or undertaken any military training himself.

Ellis curtly shook his head. "That Severn brat once served on my Corvette, the *Berserker*, and has since commanded one of those ridiculous fast-intercept patrol boats. Despite what it might appear, I think *that*," he said pointing as the display, "is actually an ABCANZ Fleet warship messing in our activities. I know an ABCANZ warship when I see one."

Badali eyed the upper-left-hand corner of the forward screen skeptically. There was the best image they'd obtained of the other vessel. A somewhat insignificant merchant freighter. It was undeniably the *Fires of Beltane*. Ellis told everyone to get familiar with the target. To memorize it.

Badali wasn't able to bite his tongue, to say nothing. "It looks like a merchant freighter to me. And there appears to be shipping containers amidships."

"Mr Badali, walk with me, please," Ellis said, his teeth clenched.

Badali looked like a rabbit caught in a vehicle's headlights. Ellis steered him towards his day cabin.

Once inside and the door closed, the man shrank as if from a white-hot rage that poured from a maddened fiend. "If you ever question me in front of my bridge crew again Mr Badali, I will kill you." Ellis spoke in a voice that was so low, so cold as to freeze the tropically humid air. "Never again will you raise a doubt about any order I issue. Do you understand me?"

Badali tried to step back, but found himself against the bulkhead. Ellis was close, hemming him against the cabin's wall. "You . . . you can't issue orders to me. I'm not one of your crew," Badali insisted.

"No, you are not. You are not as useful as the junior

cook's most junior pot washer. All the other financiers stayed back where it was safe . . . comfortable. What exactly are you doing here Mr Badali?"

"Someone had to look after our financial investments."

"And you think I couldn't? That I or Major Melnik would be cavalier with your money if you weren't here to nursemaid us?"

"No, Captain. No."

Ellis shook his head, showing no belief in his financial master's words. "Badali, understand me. One more display like that last one and I will have you killed. Are we clear on that?"

"You can't do that. None of the crew would turn against their paymaster."

Ellis laughed, and the smile he gave Badali was an ancient one. The kind that tigers give just before they tear their prey's throat out.

"Badali, these men and women will march with me and the Major to the very gates of hell, go through them, and into whatever lies beyond. They will do this, because they know we will lead them out again. You are way outside your comfort zone. People with your soft hands and doughy bellies should not trifle in the affairs of true fighting men. I would hate to report to your associates, those safe at home, that while we were defeating this Katarina Severn brat, most regretfully, she killed you. Think about that for a moment Mr Badali."

Ellis turned to go, then turned back again. "And stay off my bridge. I could suffer your idiotic comments when I only had unarmed locals to deal with, but not now. Severn might be a spoiled brat, but she is no fool. She *is* capable. Killing her will be a fight. A real fight. And a real fight is no place for the likes of *you*. Do we understand each other?"

Badali already suspected that he would never understand the likes of Ellis. Actually, he never wanted to. But even a lifelong civilian could understand when he'd been given an order as blunt and as threatening as this one. "Yes," he said. "I understand."

Ellis activated the cabin's door and went back to the command chair on his bridge. Badali tried to smooth out his suit, and turned aft, towards the exit.

"Are you going to stop or just slow down to get the RIBs away?" Kat asked Sato.

"When we finally clear the head-land I want to present the smallest possible profile to Ellis. I want to maintain this speed for another hour, then start to ease off. Therefore, it will be an "underway" launch for both RIBs ma'am, if that's alright with you? But that does mean you can't come back for a second loadout."

Kat nodded. *What else?* She needed that eleven-year-old off her boat! It wasn't personal, it was just the reality. Warships didn't have families or, even more so, children on-board. Plain and simple.

"Ellis's vessel is still at anchor in the roads off Campbell Bay. His sensors must have detected us, but is he sure it's the same ship that he spoke to you on yesterday? Will he shoot first and ask questions later?" Gillan offered.

"Yes," said Kat. "Ellis will shoot first. Without doubt. I don't have to think about that for a single second."

"Then I need to think of a Plan B," said Sato with a grin.

Captain Ellis was livid for the second time in an hour. He had all his weapons charged and hot, but had no target. "Where's my target?" he accused the crewmember manning that board.

"There is no longer any ship along the plotted trajectory, sir," the operator said. "Nothing to lock onto."

"There has to be a target," Ellis snapped, searching the display. "There has to be."

"Sir," the weapons operator asked, "Could she have done an emergency brake and ducked into the shallows, or pushed up to fifty plus knots and arced around and back out into the ocean?"

"Not possible, or at least not probable," Ellis said, forcing his mind to adjust to what he was being told.

"Sir," the crewman on sensors reported. "I do have a dissipating trail of reactor ions."

"Show me," Ellis growled.

A faint cloud showed on one of the displays.

"Can you estimate the speed and vector that would be needed, referenced against the ship we briefly saw yesterday, to create such a signature?"

"Err . . . considering that it got them from the tip of the island and back out to sea before we could get a firm lock on them, I'd say they must have pulled at least fifty if not sixty knots, sir. But she's surely far too heavy for that?"

Someone on the bridge began a soft whistle. Ellis whipped his head around and the noise instantly died.

"They appear to be carrying containers, but perhaps they're really empty. Maybe they actually are an unarmed exploration ship and decided to make a run for it? But at that kind of speed?"

Heads around him nodded in acknowledgement rather than agreement. Nobody dare offer an alternative suggestion, or imply their Captain was misguided in his assumptions.

"Sensors, widen your settings, increase their range. Find me that damn ship, find me Katarina Severn!"

"Yes, sir."

"Sir, if I may, as there are no Safe-Transit-Routings in this area. A vessel of that size, and moving at that speed, is taking a huge risk. I think they're making for STR-PD04 that runs in a north-westerly direction from Padang to Chennai. It can't be anything else, sir," the crewman at the Helm timidly suggested to his superior.

Ellis didn't respond.

Kat had done an "underway" launch during her training at OTA(F) like every other Midshipman on every intake did, but she hadn't done one since, and certainly hadn't done one at this kind of speed, or at night. Being dropped, freefall, from the winch when the vessel you were deploying from was stationary was bad enough when you hit the water, sending a jolt through every bone in your body, but at speed, it hurt even more and wasn't advised for anyone not encased in fully protective, shock-absorbing battle armour.

The med-tech on the *Bella*, by the light of a red-filtered head-torch, had set up his 'shop' amidships between the two RIB launch bays.

When Kat had approached, she was handed two pills to take. "What are these for?" she immediately demanded. She had stopped taking whatever she was handed about the age of twelve or thirteen . . . and was much the better for it.

"Just a pain reliever. The speed Myra wants to drop you guys off at is going to hurt. (a) Immediately," he said holding up one pill, "and again, (b) several hours later." He held up a second.

Kat took the pills with a swig from her suit's integral filtered water reservoir, then surveyed the organised chaos of each launch station. She, and all of her people, had been issued with two additional components to their battle armour. Beneath her para-magnetic under-suit she now had a wide belt-like brace that fitted snuggly around her lower spine and pelvis. Fixed about her neck was another brace to prevent whiplash and her head from being thrown forward or back when the RIB impacted with the water.

Mike had managed to cram two equipment capsules full of everything except their M37 assault rifles, so they could get extra bodies into each of the RIBs. The Troopers stoically climbed aboard and improvised ways to strap themselves down.

"Port or starboard, ma'am?" Mike asked her.

"No preference," Kat said smoothly, not giving Mike any opening to debate again the proper place for a Princess in the ensuing deployment.

"I've assigned Staff Freeman to you. Now before you change your mind about leading the Detachment ashore, please excuse me while I look over my half of this improvised lash-up." Without waiting for a reply, Mike threw her what might pass for a salute and left. Since chameleon battle armour wasn't really intended for parade and ceremonial occasions, Kat attributed his lame effort to the equipment and not a deliberate act of insubordination.

Not that Kat and any right to complain about a little insubordination here and there.

She turned to the Staff Sergeant. "Let's do this Staff."

"Yes ma'am," he said, but there was no salute with the words. He reached for Kat's suit and began tightening 'this' and moving 'that' to where it belonged. "Don't want the drop to dislodge anything," he muttered.

Kat had an immediate flash back to the launch bay of the *Berserker*. To her now deceased friend Jack Byrne, doing exactly the same checking process before she inserted by SCIF onto Cayman Brac. *Not now* she thought. She willed it away, standing patiently throughout the Staff Sergeant's inspection and corrections. Officially she should be doing the same to him. She did an eyeball check, and just as she expected, there wasn't a single item of equipment out of place on him.

It wouldn't dare.

Finally, she met the Staff Sergeant's high standards. Kat turned to the two Land Force Squads that would ride in with her. Maybe he had already reviewed the Troopers, or perhaps Sergeant Varko had, but Kat found nothing amiss.

Accepting the offered hand of assistance, she climbed onto the RIB, taking one of the regular, rather than the newly improvised seats and strapped herself in.

She made a mental note that the *Bella* needed a couple or four, SCIFs, or 'Scuba-Craft-Insertion-Fast' to be added to the ship's inventory. They'd be much more suitable for this kind of operation.

Silently Kat, Staff Freeman, four junior NCOs and twelve Troopers waited in their assigned RIB. Someone muttered a prayer in a language that wasn't English.

"Standby," called Staff Freeman in the darkness.

On Sato's signal the winch operators simultaneously released both craft. The 'free-fall' was only seconds yet it seemed much longer, like everything was happening in slow-motion. With a thud that felt like being struck by a high-speed train, they hit the water. It took another twenty, painfully slow seconds, for the craft to right itself in the water and clear the *Bella*'s churning wake.

A quick set of calls and responses initiated by the helmsman was enough to establish they had no major issues and their equipment pod was still attached. He immediately started-up the out-board propulsion units, checked they were firmly set for "quiet mode" and took the tiller.

Despite the pain, Kat was hurting in almost every muscle of her body, she smiled. "What a great way to start a fight," she muttered to herself as the RIB powered its way towards the shoreline.

The *Bella*, having dropped the two RIBs, barely gave them time to get clear, before she rapidly increased her speed. Exceeding fifty knots, she came around in a tight arc to starboard and headed back towards open ocean, rather than continue with their original plan of rounding the headland and confronting Ellis. Evidently this was Sato's 'Plan B.'

The shore element's 'mission brief' or 'Orders,' given to the Detachment had been painfully concise. Their mission was essentially to search for a needle in a haystack, a needle that didn't want to be found, oh and there was also a gunboat in the next bay that would open fire on them if it could get a target-lock, not to mention a hostile ground force, of an unknown size and composition ready to 'neutralise' anything that Ellis's auto-cannon might happen to miss.

The Troopers had taken their orders with their usual nonchalant bearing. "Better than hanging around the boat with nothing to do but wait for the next chow call," one of them had said.

Kat decided it felt good to be back with people who made life simple, rather than complicated. Who broke everything down to its basic composite components and tackled each issue as it came, rather than worrying about the whole.

Her own job however, was somewhat more complicated than that of the Troopers riding in with her. She was concerned about the quantity and sophistication of sensors they'd find ashore and what they had to counter them, or more to the point, what they didn't have to counter them. She knew that if she'd been running the show ashore, she'd want as much tech as possible backing her up. And weapon systems slaved to them as well.

Some might consider that nasty of her, but she didn't. It was just a sensible precaution. And it was definitely something that a certain Captain Ellis's twisted mind would consider. She had to think like him, get inside his head.

Their approach towards the beach was no more than two or three nautical miles. Already the sky was beginning to transition from black into lavender, then orange, as the dawn approached. It got light early and fast in this part of the world.

They were reducing speed, which meant they were nearing the shore. The helmsman knew to keep the cover of the headland between them, the next bay, and Ellis. The RIBs limited sensor equipment stayed silent, as did their comms.

For now, Kat would just have to bite her nails. Metaphorically if not actually, as Anna would never approve, and wait. Wait to find out if this part of her plan worked, failed or headed for points unknown.

When they hit the shoreline the Land Force's 'amphibious operations' training kicked in and the Troopers disembarked the RIBs with supreme professionalism, each boat about a hundred metres apart, on the white sands of Bananga Bay.

Once it was apparent that their arrival was not about to be challenged, the RIBs were quickly hauled off the beach and into the rainforest that started when the sand stopped. They would be recovered later, when this was over. The trailing equipment capsules were pulled ashore, opened, emptied, then followed the same route of the RIBs into the tree-line. There were evidently no mercenaries hiding, watching from the rainforest and Ellis's ship hadn't rounded the headland guns blazing. But that didn't mean there weren't electronic snoopers and sniffers at work, trying hard to detect their presence.

Kat watched whilst the Troopers hauled the second

equipment capsule up the beach. "Safi, test everything. Water, air, temperature, anything you can think of."

"Everything is within accepted tolerances for the seasonal norm," Safi advised a few seconds later.

Kat then waited until Staff Freeman confirmed there was no evidence of them having ever been on that beach. Nothing but a few footprints that would soon be washed away by the incoming tide.

The old road, that twisted its way north, from Bananga towards Campbell Bay was soon located and although heavily overgrown, its once tarmac road was still sufficiently intact to make the initial few kilometres relatively easy going. The first two klicks went briefly eastwards, then north, through the remains of the plantation workers accommodation, then began to climb steeply.

In a 'patrol' formation, each of the Detachment's three, eight-man Squads moved along the road.

The Squads were spaced at approximately three hundred metre intervals. Between the First and Second Squads was half of the Command Squad, consisting of Kat, Staff Freeman, the Detachment's sniper, and their UHF signaler. The signaler's 'Dolos' equipment didn't really give Kat any significant enhancement of capability over Safi, except a far greater range without needing to piggy-back onto other systems and platforms, and it also gave them fast access directly into the military network, having integrated IFF 'handshakes' as standard.

Between the Second and Third Squads was Mike, Sergeant Varko and their med-tech. Mike also had the two armoured vehicle drivers with him. Both of their troop carrying 'Spartan' combat vehicles remained secured in the rear hold of the *Bella* and would continue to do so on this insertion. Whilst fully amphibious, Kat had decided against their use. The Staff Sergeant had supported her decision. There was nothing quiet about them. The power needed to propel a heavy 'metal box' ashore was considerable and 'stealth' wasn't something an armoured vehicle did very well. Both drivers had reverted to their first and foremost

skill-set,
that of infanteer.

Lance Corporal Jarvis in the Second Squad had the tech scanner and he confirmed that as far as the ABCANZ Fed's finest technology told him, they were currently not under any kind of surveillance, but he believed at least one aerial sensor drone was operating. Hopefully their armour would do exactly what the manufacturers claimed . . . keep them concealed.

The latest generation of 'Chameleon' combat armour worked well, and was tried and tested, as long as you didn't fully immerse it water for a prolonged period.

'Chameleon,' like any effective dynamic camouflage system, managed to provide concealment at a varying range of distances, by automatically adapting as the surrounding terrain, vegetation and ambient light changed. It used rapid visual scans to evaluate colour, contrast, likely enemy engagement/concealment range, and spatial sizing, to create an effective disruptive effect.

The suits integral GPS unit knew exactly where the wearer was on the planet, so automatically selected which of the seven distinct biome zones of polar, tundra, temperate, Mediterranean, arid, steppe or tropical, they were operating in. As it also knew the date and time, it made further adjustments to accommodate the time-of-day, prolonged or reduced daylight hours and any seasonal variance in any climate zones that had distinct winters or summers.

Each biome zone came in three distinct camouflage options, 'splinter,' 'mottled' and 'digital' or 'large,' 'medium' and 'small,' to accommodate the differing spatial sizes of terrain composition and vegetation elements.

'Splinter' and 'mottled' were the usual preference in biome zones that has tree coverage, such as temperate, tropical and tundra. 'Digital' provided poor concealment in all of these zones, except perhaps in the reduced light of dawn or dusk, but got selected a bit more frequently in the 'open' landscapes of arid deserts and polar snows. The suit's integral scanning sensor detected even slight changes in the wearer's immediate vicinity and automatically adapted the suit's exterior camouflage.

The paramagnetic molecules within the exterior finish of the wearer's under-suit and helmet could be made to change colour by applying a small electrical charge that varied the spacing between each molecule, thereby making it appear to look like a different hue. To make the suit's analysis and data processing faster, the pallet has been limited to just thirteen distinct colours, with each biome zone having a four colour combination drawn from those thirteen.

The colours all had official names, reference numbers and red-green-blue separation ratios, so that precise information could be passed from military procurement out to the various component manufactures.

Two of the four colours in each biome zone were also used by the adjacent biome zone. This was deliberate, to facilitate fast and smooth transitions.

Polar – All year:
> I : Icelandic Blue (15-3908)
> J : Snow White (11-0602)
> K : Spa Blue (12-4305)
> L : Frozen Fjord (15-3917)

Tundra —All year:
(Including mountain ranges with continuous snow cover and
Boreal Forest during winter months only)

> A : Olive Grey (16-1110)
> C: Winter Moss (18-0523)
> I : Icelandic Blue (15-3908)
> J : Snow White (11-0602)

Temperate – All year:
(Including Boreal Forest during summer months only)

> A : Olive Grey (16-1110)
> B: Golden Cypress (18-0537)
> C: Winter Moss (18-0523)
> D: Phantom (19-4205)

Mediterranean – All year:

> B: Golden Cypress (18-0547)
> C: Winter Moss (18-0523)
> F : Alabaster Gleam (12-0812)
> G : Golden Apricot (14-1041)

Arid – All year:

> E : Roasted Pecan (17-1052)
> F : Alabaster Gleam (12-0812)
> G : Golden Apricot (14-1041)
> H: Desert Mist (14-1127)

Steppe – All year:

> B: Golden Cypress (18-0537)
> E : Roasted Pecan (17-1052)
> H: Desert Mist (14-1127)
> I: Olive Oil (16-0847)

Tropical – All year:

> B: Golden Cypress (18-0537)
> C: Winter Moss (18-0523)
> D: Phantom (19-4205)
> E : Roasted Pecan (17-1052)

After another hour of patrolling along the old road they reached the crest of the hill. The road tracked left along the ridge. When the surrounding rainforest briefly stopped, it gave them their first view over Campbell Bay.

To their right, the rainforest covered hillside sloped gently away, over some seven hundred and fifty metres, before dropping suddenly off a limestone cliff edge to the waters of the harbour. After a kilometre of open water there was a solitary quay, like a long thin island that had a single port-crane at one end, for unloading ships that didn't have their own ability to do so. The quay was connected to the settlement by a narrow jetty of six to seven hundred metres. The ferry, or passenger vessel was moored against this quay. Ellis's own ship was maybe a kilometre, perhaps a bit more, further out, in open water of the 'roads' or approaches to the bay, and thankfully remained stationary.

What was she heading into? Orders passed by age-old hand signals or whispered voices, a map with nothing on it. All she needed was for the hiding settlers to be riding about on horses, and they'd be firmly back in the nineteenth century! Would she end up riding into battle too?

But there were no horses evident. Goats however were in abundance, used by the locals for meat, milk and keeping the vegetation down. And there was no way Kat or any of her people were going to ride in on a goat!

"There has been a scientific breading program here for the last hundred years," Safi advised. "Probably best not to tell the Professor you came across something scientific and didn't include him."

Kat briefly smiled at Safi's attempt at humour. "Agreed."

Her priority right now was to find some of the island's inhabitants. They had to be around here somewhere. Unless of course they were too late, and Ellis's people had already removed, or worse, 'disposed' of them. But that didn't make any sense. You always needed someone to do the manual work. They were probably hiding near to the town, not too far away, but not too close either, but how to spot them?

Behind Kat, Staff Freeman ordered those with tech-equipment to check for surveillance again.

Kat continued to reflect on her main problem. How to make contact with people who didn't want to say "Hi, hello, how are you?"

Assuming they had gone to ground, even moles needed air. Air was one of the weaknesses of any hidden existence.

But before Kat could begin to say "Hi" to anyone, she had to get past or deceive any sensors Ellis's people must have deployed.

This was being played out like a chess game. Kat had made her move. Now she waited for Ellis to make his.

Their progress was slow, cautious, as they constantly checked for static sensors, overhead drones, hidden defences and booby-traps.

Ahead of them, as the road began to head down, towards the settlement, was a clearing in the rainforest. It was fenced off and full of goats in various colours and sizes. A large, evil looking ram wandered over to inspect these invaders of his domain.

"They're a lot bigger that I thought they'd be," said the team's sniper to Kat. "You sure they're not dangerous, ma'am?"

"I think we've found something that actually smells worse than you lot after a week deployed in the field," Freeman said with a slight smirk.

"Looks like they spend all their time outside, can't see any shelters. 'Wet goat' is certainly a step up from 'wet dog,' and that's bad enough."

Once the tail-end Trooper of the Third Squad had cleared the track-side goat enclosure, Kat ordered a halt and told them to take an hour of rest.

Around her there were nods of acknowledgement, but no actual sound as they moved off the track and into the roadside rainforest. They were a good, professional team.

SIX : SEVEN

"Where is she?" Ellis demanded. "You can't fool me with that pathetic holo-projection, girl. You're a Severn. You can do better than that!"

"Our sensor drone flying over Bananga Bay was briefly transmitting static but it's back now and shows nothing that it shouldn't do," the crewman on sensors reported.

"Did it pick up anything in the seconds before it cut to static?"

"Something coming in fast, way too fast for that freighter, but it was partly masked by the islands profile for all but a brief second. Major Melnik's people report no hostile activity ashore."

"Our investors obviously should have provided us with better ground and aerial sensors than the outdated crap they chose to procure," Ellis said with a scowl towards Mr Badali. The man was back on the bridge, but sensibly kept his distance and his mouth closed. "A single aerial drone is not enough. If that goes down, we are effectively blind."

Badali was however, one of the few eternal optimists among the investors, who had been supremely confident that they'd be facing nothing but local goat herders and agri-farmers, without any sophisticated weaponry, so considered that the sensors they'd procured were suitably appropriate for the task. But he wasn't stupid either, and kept his mouth firmly shut, wisely opting not to respond to Ellis's comment.

"Sensors, re-task that drone, if anything came ashore, I want to know where. I'm sure Major Melnik and his gravel-crunchers would be most happy if they had something to shoot at."

Two minutes later, and with no response from the crewman at the sensor board, Ellis was ready to pull his hair out.

"They have to be out there somewhere," he said, glaring at his bridge crew.

"Yes sir. But like the local inhabitants, the problem is, where?"

"We seem not to have surprised them," Ellis said.

"The few that the Major has encountered and detained claim not to have been warned. Apparently, because of increased pirate activity, they haven't had a large ship visit the island in several months."

"We can have this conversation later," Ellis snapped. "I want Severn. I want her now. She's just put someone or something ashore. I want to know where."

"There are only two ways ashore, sir. Either by marine craft, or by air. We've searched every square metre of the beaches on the southern end of the island. There is no evidence of any boat or sub-surface craft on any beach."

"She's a champion skif racer. Check the tree-line. That's what she did on Cayman Brac."

"Already doing so, sir. Nothing so far. As for an air insertion, that merchant freighter had no VTOL pad or hanger in evidence from the brief imagery we obtained yesterday. The Major reports no aircraft activity over the settlement, although there has been the occasional small UAV."

"Let's stick to what's likely, shall we," Ellis said. "Severn will insert by boat. Military SCIF, or civilian skif, or perhaps a RIB, at least that was her preference when I was her Commanding Officer. Have you checked all the river mouths and estuaries?"

"There are five rivers on the island, sir, but all except one, the Galathia River, have their estuaries a considerable distance from this settlement. I'm using infrared, but picking up nothing at this location. If she did come ashore there, I can't tell you where. They've disappeared."

"Like the rest of these damn people," Ellis muttered. He was tired of hearing that response.

"There is one thing sir," the crewman at the weapons board said.

"What?" Ellis demanded.

"Well sir, any craft that she came ashore in, if hidden in the tree-line will have a different heat profile to the surrounding, natural signature. If I recalibrate the sensors to exclude anything within 'natural' parameters, then I am left with two anomalies."

"Anomalies?" Ellis repeated.

"Anomalies yes, but actual targets? They can easily be explained by natural causes," the sensor crewman responded.

"Two, you say?" Ellis said.

"Two sir. As if she'd split her forces, about a hundred metres apart in the tree-line of Bananga Bay. Maybe a strike force and a reserve, or perhaps a couple of recon teams?"

"You're inventing an enemy to fit nothing but a bit of unexpected sensor data," another crewman said.

"Where?" Ellis demanded. "Show me."

The forward screen was replaced with a map of the southern half of Great Nicobar Island. Campbell Bay, Bananga Bay, Galathia Bay, the river estuary and Indira Point were all displayed. The image then changed from the regular feed, as an infrared filter was applied. "Now if I take out anything within 'natural' seasonal parameters," the crewman said, "There."

"It's less than half of a degree outside of your parameters," the sensors crewman pointed out. "It could be anything."

"They're Fleet-issue equipment capsules. I recognize their profile. Weapons, two targets if you please. Target both locations with a ten-round salvo of seventy-five millimetre." Ellis ordered.

After a pause of maybe a minute, "Weapon systems are now deployed. I have the target coordinates locked sir. Auto-cannons are loaded and ready to engage. At your command, sir."

"Fire," confirmed Ellis.

Ten rounds from an auto-cannon took around twenty-five seconds to discharge. Flight time was short, despite the high, parabolic arc, with the first round landing before the last had been fired.

Ellis watched as the fore and aft gun platforms of his ship, the *Hyperion*, drew more power from its operational reactor. Now his only regret was that he'd have to wait for confirmation. Confirmation that he'd finally nailed the Severn brat.

Dumb munitions were old school. Warships of World War Two vintage, especially the big German, American and British battleships, had turret-mounted multiple-barrel, large-calibre guns. But, by the end of the twentieth century, 'smart' programmable munitions and associated delivery systems had effectively rendered ships guns to an almost obsolete status. Most warships still mounted a single 127mm gun, but nothing more.

But being 'dumb' was sometimes an advantage on the technology dominated battlefields of the twenty-second century. The gun system was largely mechanical, its recoil pneumatic, and the rounds were based on the explosive force of a chemical reaction, so nothing could be electronically 'jammed.' Although the targeting, that calculated the bearing, elevation and propellant charge needed to achieve the target, were calculated by technology for speed and accuracy, these could all, should the need arise, revert back to a pre-technology state, using old-fashioned manual 'firing-tables' and coordinates plucked from a map or nautical chart.

Kat doubted that the Staff Officer who had so casually dismissed the effectiveness of a ship's gun had ever been on the receiving end of it.

Without warning, the tree-line back on the beach

erupted. It came apart in a hurricane of destruction as shrapnel tore into anything in its path.

They hadn't been looking skyward, so had missed the contrails that the hot shells made in the dawn sky overhead, but nobody could miss the unmistakable bark of the auto-cannons opening up, or the 'crump' of the rounds as they impacted into the rainforest.

"We have three jackhammers with us, ma'am. If we can get nearer to Ellis's ship, maybe we could try to take his weapons systems out?" Staff Freeman suggested.

"Understood Staff, I'll do my very best to get you a target within jackhammer range, then it's all yours," Kat assured him. "Safi, can you fabricate me some nano-UAVs that can sniff out exhaled CO_2? People, even hiding people, still have to breathe. Somewhere around here, air is being sucked in, so extra CO_2 must be coming back out. It's probably concealed, scrubbed, masked from sensors."

They needed another plan B. Maybe they were already on plan B and needed a C?

"I have launched two nanos," Safi advised. "Damn, one has already been burned," the HI added only a minute or two later.

"Safi, please don't use such language, remember who you work for."

"Yes, ma'am. I am sorry," And she did actually sound it, well as much as a computer ever could.

"You are picking up bad habits, Safi. Habits I suspect you are getting from the company you now keep. If you want me to let you continue working with Grace, you need to watch yourself. You might let Grace know that she needs to clean up her act too. She is, after all, no longer living in Sharjah or Emirates City, but is residing 'next door' to a Princess."

If an HI and an eleven-year-old really wanted to stay together, maybe Kat could at least get some leverage in this child-adult relationship. Little things like pirates and filibuster expeditions aside, Kat had the odd feeling that all the other adults currently on the *Bella* were out-numbered by one little girl, a little girl and a Heuristic Intellect, top-end self-learning personal computer that had somehow forgotten exactly who wore it across her collarbone.

"Kat, I will be more decorous, and I will teach Grace to be more appropriate too," Safi conceded. "And, my remaining nanoUAV has found a vent and is now exploring it. The airflow is either subterranean or from a cave-system, or a combination of both. Shall I build more nanos and send them in? The vent or shaft is currently just a single path, but it may branch at any time."

Kat was once more back to juggling that which could merely kill her, rather that which really bothered her.

A question for later consideration, she suddenly thought. *And, is Safi also taking lessons from Anna on how to avoid being questioned on her actions by changing the subject?*

Enough. Stay focused on the current mission.

"Mike, Staff Freeman, Safi's UAV might have found evidence of the local's hiding place." It felt strange to be giving orders verbally, rather than over a comms net, but it had been good for military commanders since the beginning of time, so why shouldn't it be good enough for her too?

"Do you want the Detachment to form on you, ma'am?" the Staff Sergeant asked. "New Orders?"

"No, stay dispersed. Safi has located an air shaft and has a nanoUAV inside it right now. I don't know where it will lead, but I suspect it will be nearer to Campbell Bay."

Kat studied the map display on her TDT. Its reference point was archived data, as no live satellite feed that might give their ground position away was being accessed. She took another long look at the terrain before them. The road dropped over the next kilometre down to sea level, then another kilometre across an exposed causeway. Once, the causeway had been at the water's edge, but a hundred years of silt and shifting sands had redefined the coastline and it was now inshore by several hundred metres. The old road then tracked around in a gentle, clockwise arc for another two kilometres, past the airfield, before reaching the outlying buildings of Campbell Bay, or 'Tenlaa' as the locals apparently preferred.

Visibility, at least until they reached the causeway, on either side of the old track was no more than a few metres, as the rainforest became dense extremely quickly. Here and there the jungle plants bloomed with beautiful exotic flowers. Long-tailed macaques constantly called to each other, but they were yet to see one. Kat reminded herself not to become distracted. She had to stay focused. This was perfect ambush territory.

It had been a while since Kat had operated in full combat armour, a backpack full of additional ammunition and field rations, and with an assault rifle. She gritted her teeth and dug deep, calling up a rarely used part of her physical stamina. *Have I really let my fitness slip this much?* She couldn't afford to be unable to keep up with her team. And it was still early morning, the sun had only risen in the last hour or so! What would it be like by late afternoon?

"I have a location from my remaining nanoUAV. It is exiting a vent."

"Where?" Kat snapped, signalling a halt and powering up her TDT again.

Safi provided a direct, cabled interface, rather than a potentially detectable transmission, and a small green pea begin to flash on the display. "They are in a cave system."

"Mike, Staff Freeman," she called, then tapped her right upper-arm with four fingers, and then the top of her head, indicating that those with Staff Sergeant rank or higher should form on her location.

"I know it's a long shot," she began when they arrived, "but do we have anyone in the Detachment who might pass as a local? We might be making contact soon, and I don't want them thinking that we're with any of the hostiles ashore."

Staff Freeman nodded, immediately comprehending what he was being asked. "Trooper Kumar." He pointed at the indicated soldier, then tapped the top of his own helmet twice.

Trooper Kumar double-timed in towards the command team, arriving only a few seconds after being summoned. With his helmet on and visor down, he looked just like any other Trooper.

"Take your helmet off," Staff Freeman ordered.

The young Trooper complied, slinging his M37 at his side, then lifting his visor. Using both hands he pulled off his helmet. He was evidently of Indian extraction. He ran his gloved right hand through the black hair that was stuck to his forehead from hours of wearing his helmet, trying to make himself look more presentable.

Kat had deliberated long and hard about the use of camouflage face-paint. Staff Freeman had argued that it reduced the effectiveness of their 'chameleon' armour, if they didn't then disrupt the shape, shine and colour of their faces too. Kat agreed with him, but countered his viewpoint with the fact that (a) the top half of their face was obscured by the helmet's visor, and (b) she wanted to present as 'friendly' a face as possible when the time came to make contact with the locals.

"It's a good start," she said, "but I don't suppose you speak the local language too?"

"No ma'am. My family have lived in Nu Britannia for at least the last hundred years, probably more," he said in perfect English without any trace of an Indian accent.

"Do you know any of the Indian languages?" Freeman asked him.

"A few works of Hindi, but not enough for a proper conversation, and I don't think they speak that here."

"Enough to say, 'Hi, we're the good guys, we're here to help?"

"Just about," he confirmed.

"Good, Safi can help you translate. Keep your helmet off, and stay with me," Kat ordered as she removed her own headgear and fixed it to the equipment running around her waist.

It took them almost another hour to get into position. Safely across the causeway, and approaching the perimeter of the airfield, Safi's identified location was inland, over a kilometre from the beach and separated from the shoreline by a two-way road and then the airfield's single runway. The rainforest started again on the other side of the airfield's security fence. A wide, sandy track snaked its way inland, and four hundred metres along it, another track merged with it from the right. At the intersection there was a lone outcrop of limestone. Perhaps a dozen metres in diameter and maybe forty or fifty in height. A flight of spiralling steps had been cut into the bluff's side, and from its flat top it probably offered a most picturesque vantage point. In different circumstances, maybe somewhere to sit of an evening and watch the sun go down.

"There is an access vent by the base of that outcrop," Safi advised. "And there is also someone on watch in its immediate vicinity."

Kat got down onto one knee and took out her binoculars.

Clearly you didn't dig a tunnel under a lone outcrop of rock, not unless you wanted it to potentially fall on you after heavy rain. *If the top of this stack has such a good view, why doesn't Ellis have someone or something on top of it?*

The base of the outcrop was overgrown with bushes and rainforest plants. Only the ground directly in-front of the steps was clear of vegetation.

Kat thought she saw movement, but maybe she imagined it.

"Is anybody getting anything hostile? Any hostile sensors operating."

"No ma'am. Nothing," Freeman confirmed. He was kneeling next to her, using his own equipment to confirm what Kat's eyes and Safi's nano were providing.

"Kumar, you're with me. Staff, keep us covered."

Kat jumped up, and with Kumar covering her back they moved cautiously towards the vegetation at the base of the stone stack, a third Trooper soon joined them.

Kneeling down again, Kat pushed the vegetation aside and revealed a stone-cut slot about the size of an old-fashioned letter box, from a time when people still actually sent physical mail to each other. Behind it she could see a young man, approximately her own age.

He was clearly very startled to find himself face to face with Kat, but wasn't slow to react. He jammed a long-barrelled hunting rifle through the vent into her face.

She raised her hands.

"Slow down. We're the good guys," Trooper Kumar quickly told him. "Sorry, I don't speak any of the local languages. I hope you can understand me?"

"You are with these people?" the man asked him.

"No, no these are not the men from the boats. This is Princess Katarina from the ABCANZ Federation. She's come to help you."

"A Severn. You know what our Mahaapaur says about the Severns?"

"I can probably guess, but this one is on your side."

"If the stories I have heard are true, they usually are," the man said, but the rifle barrel was removed from Kat's face, so perhaps her Grandpa Jim hadn't come off too bad in the local stories.

"She needs to talk with the town's leaders. Can you take us to them?"

"Yes, but not from here. Take that track into the rainforest," he said pointing with the rifle. "At the big narra tree, where the track forks, take the right side. Go another kilometre. When the track runs alongside the cliff, there is a cave and we will find you once inside."

The man was gone, crawling backwards into the darkness.

Kat did her best to rearrange the vegetation to conceal the slot, then got back onto her feet.

Standing up, she took a brief moment to re-evaluate her situation. Kumar was already moving towards the indicated track, eager to get into better cover and move towards the inland cliff-face a kilometre or two along the track. Kat was equally eager to be off, but she couldn't simply ignore the apparent lack of interference from Ellis.

Freeman joined her. "Staff, move our Third Squad into defensive positions around this location, I want them covering our rear, then get the First and Second Squads to follow us. It would seem that there is an entrance to a cave under these hills, a bit further down that track."

"I used to have a friend who believed in the little people, who lived under the hills, swore by them a lot of the time, as I recall," the Staff Sergeant said, "or maybe it was *at* them."

"I had a friend like that too, once upon a time," Kat said. "Word is, the people under these hills are the inhabitants of Campbell Bay, so potentially they're our friends. Let's hope they stay that way. See what you can do about getting our Troopers into position without leaving anything obvious as to where we went."

"You know that this is all way too easy, ma'am? How did we find these people so quickly, when it would appear the hostiles haven't? And, why haven't they found us either? Something's not right."

"I agree, Staff. But we've assumed that they're looking for us, and for the Campbell Bay inhabitants. Maybe they're simply not looking. Maybe there aren't any troops ashore. Perhaps we've assumed way, way too much, thinking they would operate like we would in such circumstances . . . but perhaps they haven't. We mustn't lower out tactical awareness, not yet anyway."

A nod, and "ma'am," was his only reply.

Trooper Kumar took point and led off, down the track.

Behind Kat, the Staff Sergeant went silently about the business of getting the Detachment back into a patrol formation and having Lance Corporal Jarvis and his tech-scanner double-time it after Kat.

The last Troopers in the file used tree branches to sweep away any evidence that they'd been there, such as their footprints, in the sand of the track.

The patrolling file of soldiers soon reached the big narra tree and took the right fork as instructed. A limestone cliff loomed out of the rainforest and the track ran along the cliff's base for several hundred metres. Once, probably thousands of years before, this had been the island's shoreline.

There was an opening in the cliff wall and although it was good to get out of the morning sunshine, the interior stank of goats and their accumulated bodily functions.

The cave was large and went back at least fifty metres. The smell got progressively worse the further Kat moved inside. It was soft underfoot and she hoped it was sand rather than anything else. Kumar activated the flashlight fitted to his assault rifle, giving everything a pale blue glow.

Moving cautiously, in a far corner, tucked deep within the shadows, was a doorway. Thankfully it was square, confirming that this wasn't some strange fantasy adventure, but it was low, maybe a metre square, and disguised to look exactly like the surrounding rock.

Because Kat had removed her helmet, as the 'hearts and minds' doctrine said that making friends went easier if you presented a human face and not one encased in battle armour, she unfortunately couldn't breathe the 'tanked' filtered air that her suit provided. The odour of age-old goat urine and excrement in the confined space of the cave was overpowering . . . nauseating. And probably deliberate. Great place to hide an entrance, in the shadows of a cave that most people wouldn't venture too deeply into because of the appalling, gut-wrenching, eye-watering odour.

Nasty smells were becoming a too regular occurrence. First the *Storm Cloud V*'s hold, and now this cave!

The doorway was already partly open and showing a small white light. Kumar went through first. Kat followed him.

The first man she saw caused her to quickly reassess that the door definitely wasn't round. He was short, rotund, with an excess of bushy black hair coving his head and face, and did look as though he'd be quite at home in a fantasy movie. By contrast the woman beside him was tall, thin, had an aquiline nose and high cheekbones. If she suddenly offered Kat an apple, she wasn't about to accept it! Instead, the woman eyed Kat as if sizing her up for a cauldron but did nothing to obstruct her passage.

Kat's journey down the 'rabbit hole' was then brought to an abrupt halt. The doorway was closed behind Lance Corporal Jarvis and as the overhead lighting flickered into life, a young woman, wrapped in swirl of multi-coloured silks, raced out of the next-door Kat was being directed towards. She had a bushy mane of black hair too.

A small child then came from the open doorway, calling after the woman a word that Kat assumed must be 'mummy' in the local language. An older woman, her hair grey and also wrapped in bright silks, swept the child up into her arms. The child wriggled, trying to escape from what Kat assumed was her grandmother and was eventually put down and promptly toddled off, after the first woman, calling out for her as she went.

The rotund man led the way, through the second door and down a short flight of rock cut stairs. The ceiling height was uneven and Kat managed to scrape her head. At the bottom of the steps was a short corridor. Then they climbed up a metal ladder, along a gantry, turned once, then a second time and finally a third, only going a short distance in each direction. In the rock-cut room they ended up in, was a large, roughly made wooden table and a dozen or so seats around it.

At the end of the table, eyeing Kat warily, was a man easily her Grandpa Jim's age. His skin was dark, from living a life outside, rather than inside, behind a desk. His hands were large, his knuckles red with arthritis. Beside him sat the tall, enchantress-like woman.

Kat stood waiting for formal introductions.

A few more people squeezed into the room. It was dimly lit by a single light unit in the flat, man-made, rather than natural rock, ceiling above their heads, and the large display screen fixed to the far wall.

The old man waited until the other people had seated themselves at the table before he spoke. Kat remained standing.

"So, we drew a Severn. I thought I'd seen the last of your family when James didn't manage to get me killed fighting in Malaysia," he said in accented English.

"But you've saved your way of life here. The Chinese haven't made any territorial demands in the last thirty-five years."

The man snorted in derision, but then softened it with

a slight grin. "Yes, we certainly did. His hand reached over for that of the woman seated beside him. "*We* certainly did."

"Those of us that survived all those butchers passing themselves of as Colonels and Brigadiers," the old woman hissed. Her teeth must have been replacements. They were far too white and perfect for someone of her age. Her right eye had a cataract or a similar looking defect. Something that would have been easily rectified with laser eye surgery in the ABCANZ Fed or European Union for the last hundred years.

Kat schooled her face into a genteel neutrality and waited patiently to see where this was going.

"We haven't needed your help for over thirty years," came from another seated man. The others nodded and agreed among themselves that he was right.

"I completely agree. You certainly haven't," Kat said into their wave of self-affirmation. It died down after a while.

The old man shook his head and actually smiled at Kat. "Nice of you *not* to point out that we are hiding down here like a bunch of rats just now."

"I thought you'd explain that to me when you were good and ready," Kat said. "If you don't mind me asking, this is quite a set up you have. I hardly think you created all this in the last few weeks. This is a well-prepared defence, and has undoubtedly thrown a spanner into *their* plans, whatever *they* might be? How did you come by all of this?"

The old man's smile deepened. He took the praise for what it was, a pat on the back, well earned. Around the table, some congratulated each other as if they had won the war.

"The Indian military once had an airbase here. During the war it was expanded, and this complex was dug in total secrecy, preparations for it going 'nuclear' in this region apparently. Thankfully it didn't, at least not here anyway, and about ten years after the war ended, and in the financial pressures that always follow a conflict, INS Baaz Airbase was closed down, although the civilian part still operates for the few flights that go through here. We were given access to this complex about ten years after that, and then enhanced it as a refuge for the island's citizens when a tsunami threatens us. Honestly though, I never envisaged using it like we are now."

"So, you're planning on staying in here until they leave?" Staff Freeman asked. Whilst they had talked a second group of Kat's team had been permitted entrance and now joined them in the 'conference' room."

"Are you some kind of Sergeant?" the old man asked him, pointing to the rank insignia on his right arm."

"Yes, some kind of Sergeant. I do work for a living, sir" Staff Freeman admitted, as he removed his helmet.

"Back in the war I had some exceedingly good Commanders. Some exceedingly bad ones too. Some men. A few women. Is this one any good, 'some kind of Sergeant?'" he asked, nodding towards Kat.

"I've only been with her a couple of months, sir, but so far, she's not half bad."

Kat tried to show no reaction to the low level of praise the Staff Sergeant passed her way. Then again, laying it on thick would hardly impress these locals.

"Not half bad, you say. Hard to believe that of a Severn," the old man said.

"Usually they're all bad," the woman beside him added.

"That depends on what you want them for, ma'am," Staff Freeman fired right back. "I've seen her come to the aid of folks that most definitely needed it, but had no right or claim for it. So what are you planning to do in here, sir? Sit it out?"

"I hoped we could," the old man admitted.

"Have they landed any ground troops? That other vessel on the quay in the bay looks like a short-range transport," Staff Freeman continued. "Not much more than an island-hopping ferry. I'm evidently no sailor, sir, but in my humble opinion, you don't bring that type of vessel into somewhere if you're then intending to strip out its assets. They don't have enough hold space to do that. Therefore, I don't think your 'infestation' is going away any time soon." He paused for a few seconds, looking at those seated around the table "My Troopers are pretty good at dealing with unwanted 'infestations,' sir. And, this here Officer," he said, with a nod towards Kat, "she knows her stuff. She's exactly who you'd want in a situation like this."

The old man eyed Kat. "I never thought I would be pleased to see a Severn," he finally said.

"And I cannot believe you are pleased to see one now," the old woman said. She stood, and stormed out of the room, her black sari swirling behind her. There was silence in the room for a long moment after her exit. Kat listened to the sound of her departure, her footsteps growing more distant. Nobody said a word until her footfalls were out of earshot.

"Her husband died in the war, fighting on the mainland. My sister never remarried. She never forgot . . . or forgave."

"I'm sorry," Kat said, wondering if some of those who died under her command would be remembered for so long. So bitterly. Was that an unavoidable legacy of her chosen career? If she ever found some slack time to herself, she might have to think on that some more.

The old man shook himself, as if to break loose of a memory that would never let go. "Tell me young Severn, what would you have us do? Grab our hunting rifles and seek out these unwanted visitors?"

Kat managed to stifle a frown, and then swallowed a question. *Just what exactly did my Grandpa Jim do to you?* Instead, she switched her face to the cold, steely battle one, and said, "Let's see what Ellis does next. He seems to be a main player, if not *the* main player, in all of this."

That got raised eyebrows from the old man, and silence from the others seated around the table.

Staff Freeman smiled. Smiled like a wolf catching the first glimpse of his next meal.

Captain Ellis waited a full thirty seconds after the *Hyperion*'s auto-cannons had both completed their ten round salvos. He considered himself to be the very epitome of patience, giving his subordinates sufficient time to gather and interpret the data their display boards and screens provided.

"What have you got?" he said, honing his voice, to smooth, supportive, but eager to confirm a kill.

"Several things, sir," the young crewman at the warfare systems board advised.

"Give me your best assessment."

"Both salvos hit and destroyed their intended targets."

"Good, but I doubt they were a critical element of Miss Severn's intended withdrawal plan. Have you passed this information along to Major Melnik?" Ellis asked his comms operative.

"Yes, sir," the communications operative advised. "He is on the net now, and laughing."

Ellis might enjoy a laugh later, when he had confirmation that Severn was dead. "Tell me more, Major," Ellis said, indicating to the crewman to put the net onto speaker.

"Your aerial sensor drone has detected a partial heat trace, moving along the old road between the abandoned settlement at Bananga, towards Campbell Bay."

"Ignore it. She will have put that there deliberately, to distract us."

"I guessed she might," Melnik said. "But, according to the drone's sensor feed we're getting a fair bit of new activity towards the rear of the settlement, by the airfield. Nothing solid, mostly isolated small-scale motion sensor activation and background electronic signatures, but certainly more activity than we've had in the last twenty-four hours. Something is definitely happening, just not sure what. I've sent out patrols to take a closer look."

Ellis pursed his lips. "Which suggests that either the natives are finally getting restless, or . . . perhaps my young apprentice is up to something. I thought she was smarter, wiser than that. What do you think, Andrev?"

"I could suggest that your 'apprentice' should have paid more attention in class, but like you, I too have crossed swords with Miss Severn before. In Emirates City about six months ago. She foiled a plan that had been years, over a decade, in preparation. I lost a lot of good men in that fight.

She should not be underestimated. Most definitely not."

"Has she really come ashore, Major? Or is it just a ruse?" Ellis asked, thoughtfully.

"Who knows? The two equipment capsules might suggest a platoon strength formation, but it could easily be scientific equipment, as per her official remit. Maybe we should have sent that transport ship away, as it does rather give away our less than impressive troop numbers," Melnik said.

"You no doubt recall Major, that I couldn't send it away because our financiers wanted an immediate return on their investment. You're supposed to stuff it full of any money, gold, gemstones, fine wine, pretty girls, *pretty boys* and any other good stuff that you might find and send it to them, despite it being totally the wrong vessel to do that with!"

"Fine wine! You must be joking. You haven't tasted the goat piss that passes for beer on this island, have you? Maybe I should load up the boat with that swill for them! This place is poor! Agri-farmers and goat herders scratching a living. It hasn't got anything like the riches they suggest. It's a first class shit-hole. It stinks."

"So what's your current tactical situation?" Ellis asked him.

"Unclear. Exactly the same as it's has been since we first arrived. I've just sent the Third Platoon of the PSCs out on a patrol, to check out this new sensor activity on the back end of town. I obviously want my own people here for the moment, so I've sent Two Platoon of the PSCs out to do a search and destroy sweep along the old road and all the goat farms and coconut plantations between here and Bananga, just in case that heat trace we picked up isn't a ruse. I currently have One Platoon back here, acting as my reserve. As for commandeering local vehicles as we'd intended, I have no idea how they keep this junk moving, but fifty percent are broken at any one time and 'awaiting spares' and the other half belong in a museum. I've never seen so much 'vintage' in one place before."

"I get the impression that our financiers' expectation

of this island might have been somewhat optimistic?" Ellis said eyeing Badali, who was standing in the bridge access stairwell.

The money-man wisely didn't enter the bridge, but went elsewhere.

"Andrev, do you see any new targets worth using the auto-cannons on?"

"No, nothing, not a single thing. You could shell this shit-hole all damn day and be forgiven for not noticing the difference."

"Roger that, and I agree, Severn is far from stupid, to underestimate her would be foolish, an error," Ellis said.

"I know. So . . . if your lost 'apprentice' is now ashore and getting ready to party, who is commanding her ship? I know the calibre of the ship commander *I'm* working with, but how good is the one she hired? What kind of person would be willing to work with her after what she did to you?"

"A most interesting question, Andrev, but the situation is not clear. Her vessel looks like a merchant freighter, and there is something trying to mimic exactly that off the north side of Little Nicobar. However, another vessel tracked down the western side of this island during last night at high speed, before turning for open ocean. It did not fully match her freighter's profile, but is *has* to be it."

"We haven't intercepted any comms chatter between them," Melnik advised. "Have you?"

"No, nothing. Perhaps you might try to draw her into a contact situation, to make a force-strength evaluation, but take extreme care."

"I will, Captain Ellis. You do the same. I shall endeavour to bring you the head of *Princess* Severn."

"Roger. Out," Ellis said. He leaned back in his command chair and studied the main screen and what his sensor team had displayed. It was a hazy collection of question marks, maybes and possibilities. Was this the fog of war?

This is no way for professional military to fight, Ellis decided. Still, it was the fight he currently had. Damn the Campbell Bay residents for running away. They were little more than the stinking animals that they tended. If it was up to Ellis he would happily turn wherever it was that they were hiding, into their graves. But the financiers wanted a return on their money. Badali was always whining on about that. Ellis really didn't care. He considered himself a warrior. He wanted another warrior to fight with.

This Katarina Severn claimed a warrior's name. And she had certainly shown some talent at it, even if you only believed half of what the media reported.

Ellis dismissed almost everything he saw on the news broadcasts of the numerous media channels. His own experience of media reporters had never been satisfactory. They saw or were told one thing, yet managed to twist these facts in their actual broadcasts into something that only vaguely resembled the truth. As the wealthy and powerful owned most of the media, they broadcasted whatever they wanted the rest of humanity to see, to think. Even the few, supposedly impartial organisations, were run by 'liberal luvies' who presented the information just as twisted, suiting their own agendas and bias. If it suited the Severns to think they'd spawned another war hero from their weak bloodline, then they'd also know exactly who to pay to write the required supporting fiction!

Ellis decided he would enjoy testing this Severn brat. She'd been a half decent, newly commissioned Ensign once upon a time. *Let's see how long you survive when I know you're coming.*

SIX : EIGHT

Kat spent the time waiting for Ellis's next move with the Campbell Bay elders going over a local map and the three-dimensional projection provided by Safi. It was amazing what Intel she could glean from someone who'd lived, administered and walked this island for most of his life. There was a lot of information being offered that wasn't in any database or satellite imagery.

The local population had invested heavily in time and resources to turn the former subterranean bunker into a suitable habitat for them to survive a tsunami in. Thankfully they didn't get them too often, but when they did, they were devastating. The Indian authorities seemed for the most part, to leave these people to their own devices. Tourist cruise ships had once been a regular occurrence, but with the increase in pirate activity, they had become much less frequent. Once, not that long ago, it wasn't unheard of to have two medium sized cruise-liners anchored in the bay at the same time. But now, it was decidedly unusual. When the current pair of ships arrived, nobody thought that legitimate 'business' from tourism had returned. Some people went immediately into the shelter, but most appeared to continue their lives as normal, but were discretely moving their families and valuables into the hidden subterranean sanctuary.

Kat studied the plan of the tunnels. It would be difficult to get from here to where she wanted to be by the waterfront, to give her line-of-sight on both the vessels. A vehicle, through the town's twisting streets would certainly be quicker that walking.

Kat also learnt what resources, scientists, doctors and other important skills they had, and what offensive paramilitary capabilities the local population could potentially offer. After two hours, Safi's projection was 'busy' with plotted information.

She probably had more relevant information on Great Nicobar than Ellis had ever had. With only one or two ships arriving each month, that not only meant that little was arriving, it also meant that not a lot of current Intel about this place went out. *Just an idea, not yet an assumption, but ... know thy enemy! That might not be your strongest trait Captain Ellis!* Kat decided to herself.

He probably figures all he had to do is intimidate some unarmed goat farmers out of their livelihood. He doesn't know these people!

Kat still didn't understand the full-extent of her mission here, but 'start a rebellion against a hostile occupation,' was fast moving up her list of potential options.

"Want to meet the guy you're up against?" the old man suddenly asked her.

"Unfortunately, I already know the one commanding the ship," Kat told him.

"I mean the one on the island."

On the wall to Kat's left, ignored during her 'inquisition,' by the islanders, was a wall-mounted monitor screen. She'd noticed it earlier, but it showed only a blue screen with a small rotating white logo. Closer examination showed it to be an official looking seal or insignia. Now someone called up imagery from its connected data-storage. It was a bit hazy and bounced around at first. It showed heavily armed, battle-suited troops dismounting from the transport ship.

"Can you pause there, please?" Kat asked.

The picture froze. Hazy at first, the monitor cleaned it up, then Safi worked her magic. Kat, Staff Freeman, and Mike, who had now joined them, all leaned in close to get a good look at what it showed.

"Mark XI Andrac battle suit," Freeman said. "No, perhaps a Mark XII. Not bad. Someone with reasonable resources, that lot isn't cheap. And G58 assault rifles, that are as good as ours."

"Maybe. Wait and see what comes off next," the old man said with a sour grimace.

There was another, much larger file of troops all clothed and equipped with what could only be described as war-time surplus. Old AK12 assault rifles armed every individual.

"Maybe the initial thirty or so are professional, but this lot look more 'bargain basement' to me," the old man said.

The soldiers formed ranks and marched down the jetty that connected the quay to the land, three abreast. Whoever was in charge didn't know that it was wise to break step when crossing structures that might not take the synchronised pounding of marching feet. Sadly the jetty held, but if this was meant to instil fear in the observer, they missed their mark with Kat.

"They're heads are bobbling like a bunch of raw recruits," the Staff Sergeant growled.

"I was thinking the very same thing, Staff," Kat said. "Is their weapon training as rudimentary as their foot drill evidently is?"

"My thoughts exactly, ma'am. Somebody just unloaded a bunch of half trained recruits."

"This is familiar," said Mike. "Professional mercenaries at the core, even sporting the same pattern of body armour and weapons we saw that night out in the Emirati dessert. Recruiting teenagers and local gang members who don't know one end of an assault rifle from another. Either we are experiencing standard mercenary operating procedure, or could this be the remnants that got away that evening in Emirates City, after that gunfight we had at The Pavilion, or whatever it was called?"

"I guess that when it comes time for us to take back what was rightly ours, we start with this larger bunch," the old man said, "but I do have to admit, I'm only too glad to share the honours with you."

"There," said Mike, pointing as the screen, "on their shoulders, there's a badge."

"Safi, do what you can to get us a clean image of that."

"Yes, Kat."

It took the HI only a few seconds to show a circular embroidered badge of a red on black design that depicted the head and upper body of a large monitor lizard. The text wrapped around the edge wasn't anything Kat recognised.

"It is Thai script," the old man informed them, "but I couldn't tell you what it means."

"Safi, start a search. Find out who this lot are," she ordered. "You said I could meet the man in charge?" Kat reminded the old man.

"That's coming in a minute," he told her.

A moment later the picture wobbled some more, showed the ground for a few seconds, then the sky, and then a close-up of somebody's armour. The Andrac Mark XII was serious protection.

When the image zoomed out, it was focussed on one man's face. He looked European, or at least his ancestry was of European extraction. His blue eyes gave the camera a hard, measured look. "Are you live?" he demanded in English. It was hard to place his accent. Russian? Maybe German?

"Yes, Major."

"Then broadcast this to whoever is watching. I am Major Andrev Melnik. I and my troops have come to restore law and order in Great Nicobar. All terrorists who surrender their weapons in the next twenty-four hours will be allowed to live. Anyone seen carrying any weaponry one minute after that will be shot on sight. Further orders will be issued, and their nature will depend on the cooperation we have received." He paused. "Did you send that?"

"Yes, sir."

"Give me that." The image recording and broadcasting device ended up being dropped on the ground. The last picture it sent was someone's armoured boot.

"Andrev Melnik," Kat said softly.

"Safi, do another search. Anything at all?"

"Isn't that the same excuse the European Union uses when it parks one of its warships in your front yard, a fictional claim that you're apparently harbouring terrorists and that they have come to restore law and order, whether the locals like or want it," suggested Mike.

"You're back to suspecting the *Fenrir* is somehow involved in all this again, aren't you?" Kat replied. "Maybe to provide Ellis and this Melnik character with backup if it doesn't go to plan?"

"Pure speculation on my part I admit, but perhaps the noble Kapitän Sörensen privately doesn't approve of his Lords' and Masters' orders, but can't do anything about that, not officially anyway, but has instead tipped you off, so that maybe you could help him out?"

"Perhaps," Kat said, "but they've never done it with mercenaries before. Not as far as I know, anyway. Remember how it was in Cape Town? Bands playing, flags flying, troops marching. Their own troops."

"Maybe they've just skipped directly to the end bit, 'troops marching,'" suggested Mike.

"Maybe, but it still doesn't answer the question, why? What has this island got that is so damn valuable? Can't imagine it's going to be the goats!"

"If I may interrupt your deliberations," the old man, referred to by his people as 'Mahaapaur,' said.

Kat didn't know if that was his name or his title until Safi advised into her ear that a 'mahaapaur' was the equivalent of a town mayor.

"The pharmaceutical properties of many of our unique plants are incredibly lucrative. A unique plant equals a unique drug patent, and a unique patent equals big, big money."

"The consortium that registered Elahi-Heya listed their principal business interest as being pharmaceutical development," Safi reminded them all.

Before Kat, Mike or Safi could make any further comment, Sergeant Varko joined them. "There's an underground garage inside this complex, ma'am. There are five good-sized 4x4 utility vehicles, three with trailers. They're a bit old, but we could mount up and go for a little reconnaissance drive downtown, if you so wish?"

Kat nodded. They weren't going to get any

reconnaissance and intelligence gathering done by hiding down here and speculating, and if possible, they needed to get 'eyes on' Ellis's ships. "Could we maybe use a couple of your vehicles?" Kat asked the old man.

A young man, around Kat's age, spoke "As her soldier just advised, we have five vehicles ready to go, my most honorable Mahaapaur and a dozen of us are armed with hunting rifles and could go with them."

"Let Venuji and Tirath go. It needs people that the residents will instantly recognize as not being hostile, and we still need some good shooters to stay back here to defend this place."

"We'll get going within the hour," Kat told him. "Do you have any suggestions for a location where we might observe, without being observed ourselves, somewhere along the waterfront?"

"Try the Suruchi Hotel. Its family run, by the Lakheras. It's not a big place, but the rooms on the upper levels should give you a view right across the bay. I can't think of anywhere else."

"Why are the owners not here, with you?"

"Mrs Lakhera is err . . . how shall I put it . . . independent. Yes, she is most independent. She really doesn't like other people making decisions on her behalf."

Kat nodded, acknowledging what she was being told.

"Are we going dressed like this? Staff Freeman said tapping the hard armour over his chest, "Or are we going to borrow some civvies?"

"Good point. I don't know. What do you think?" Kat asked them all.

"Nothing says 'Hostile Intent' like full battle armour, even with our helmets off, and our best, most friendly smiles," Staff Freeman said.

"Exactly like Melnik's people when they came ashore," Kat agreed. "So, we go into town in civvies, yes? Mahaapaur, do you think you could find us some civilian clothes to borrow for a few hours too?" she asked the old man.

"I am sure we can find you something," he replied. "But, will that not then change your status? Will you not then be considered 'spies' and can therefore be legitimately shot . . . executed if captured?"

Both Kat and Mike smiled. This was a mandatory series of lectures, on the complexities of the Geneva Convention, that everyone attended during their time at OTA(F).

"Shooting spies at dawn is all a bit 'Hollywood,' said Mike. "Usually, it's better to interrogate them for any information they might have, then trade them back. That way, you get something for the spy. And, if you start executing enemy spies, it's highly likely to become reciprocal."

"Theoretically, we are uniformed soldiers, part of our nation's military forces, and when operating as such in a foreign country during an armed conflict, we have certain protections. We can be held as prisoners-of-war, but we cannot be put on trial and we cannot be executed. However, not every country is a signatory to the convention," the Staff Sergeant explained. "If we are operating as civilians in a foreign country, as we are now considering doing, we are then subject to the laws of that country. If you litter, and the punishment for littering is to be shot, you can be shot. If they say you are a spy, you can only be punished as per that country's laws regarding spies."

"But we are not at war, and technically you should not be here any more so than our other 'visitors' should. And, you have no authority here. I can assure you that espionage is very much illegal in India, but as we are not *actually* at war, it is that technicality that *might* save you from being shot, by our authorities. You'll just be locked up for a very long time, and then maybe exchanged" the old man told them. "But, if you were here 'officially,' with the appropriate type of visa, as a research scientist, a journalist or even a tourist, then as the Mahaapaur, I must officially stamp your permit. Will that give you any form of legitimacy?"

"Before this discussion gets too deep gentlemen, may I remind you that Ellis, Melnik and their people are probably mercenaries, private security contractors or both and are not signatories to any kind of rules or conventions. Ellis will not hesitate to shoot, I can assure you of that, regardless of what we are wearing. We are only considering this because we want to present a 'friendly face' to the island's local population," Kat told them all. "But, if his Private Security Contractors do stop us, rather than simply 'shoot first,' then I suppose some kind of credible 'back story' might be a sensible precaution . . . buy us some time?"

Kat, Staff Freeman and six Troopers, all in loaned civilian clothes, false visitor IDents and augmented by an islander behind the wheel, started their journey into the 'downtown' area of Campbell Bay, and perhaps into battle.

Kat's borrowed backpack contained a mid-range professional camera that captured still and moving imagery. As they travelled through the town, she deliberately added more images to those already on the equipment's internal data storage that Safi had hastily created. As back-stories went, it would never stand up to a deep e-forensic investigation, but it should be convincing enough for any superficial check. If they were caught, and the hostiles didn't just shoot first and ask questions second, they needed to have a credible back story as to what they were up to.

Katya Strömstad, according to the IDent was apparently from the Kalmar Union. Kalmaran documents were a safe bet. Nobody was ever angry with the Scandinavians. With a trans-Atlantic accent, Kat would need to explain that she'd grown up in Nu New England, but her father was from Nya Svealand or perhaps Kalmar City.

Freelance media journalists were certainly not uncommon. Young men and women trying to make their fortune with footage that might be good enough to get globally syndicated. Staff Freeman was now supposedly her producer, and the Troopers with cased 'equipment,' acting as her camera crew.

They had been on the road maybe fifteen minutes when the *Fires of Beltane* suddenly came back on-line. Kat immediately had Safi send a condensed, tight-beam encrypted report giving Gillan their present status and what they'd found out from the island's local population.

Captain Gillan appeared on Kat's enhanced contact lens a moment later. "Satellite imagery suggests that there is increased activity in the town. A number of commandeered vehicles are suddenly on the move. Looks like it might be a patrol."

"So they're making no attempt to hide their vehicle movements?"

"Anna assesses that they are trying to do exactly that, but things aren't going all their way. Lots of young men in outdated uniforms are walking around kicking at the tires or peering at the propulsion units of equally old looking vehicles."

One of the locals riding with Kat who could hear her responses added, "In all honestly Miss, we've got a lot of old stuff here. Some of it has been operational since the Mahaapaur was a boy. It's old, some might say temperamental, but if you know how to treat it right, its fine, but you can't select the drive control and expect it to work like your modern vehicles do. Every truck on this island has its own way of looking at you."

"And that's going to be to Melnik's detriment. They should have thought a bit harder about what they'd need," Gillan added.

"Why? Why bring what you need when you can commandeer it. And besides, it also confirms my supposition, that this entire operation appears to be on a very tight budget indeed," Kat said.

"A tight budget that didn't include a contingency for a Severn showing up," said Gillan.

"Let's not read too much into that," Kat told him. "If they were planning on running, they'd have done so when we first showed up. They've stayed, so they aren't going anywhere without a fight."

"Don't you just hate it when things are like that," said Gillan.

"Ellis doing anything?" Kat asked him.

"Nope. It looks as though he's just sitting there."

Kat thought for a moment. "Us keeping them in the dark is one thing, but I don't like it when it's working both ways."

"So, what do you have in mind?"

"How about our own broadcast? Send me your imagery of broken-down trucks. We'll share it with everyone in the Campbell Bay area. All channels, let everyone know about their difficulties. Also, we'll resend the footage of them disembarking, but highlight a few issues, help reassure the locals that the people they're facing might not be all that much to worry about."

Which then gave her another idea. "And while we're at it, maybe we should add in some of the conversation I've had with Ellis. Let anyone listening on an open channel know that the times, they are a changing! How long will you need to put something suitable for broadcast together Safi?"

"Thirty minutes, maybe a little bit longer."

"Anything else?" Gillan asked her.

"Not at the moment. For now, keep the *Bella* away, well out of range. Call into Banda Aceh if it gives you a plausible cover story and protection from his long-range weapons. Even Ellis isn't crazy enough to open fire on you there," she said, then terminated the link.

Concentrating on the road ahead of them, Kat swayed from side to side, with the momentum of the 4x4, as the driver avoided numerous pot-holes, as she considered what to do next.

The local residents 'disappearing' must have seriously screwed up their plans, she thought.

But now their 'absence' was helping the invaders as much as it had initially hindered them. So long as the residents hid and did nothing, they could hardly be considered a resistance. Not an effective one anyway. That might need to change.

Sooner or later Melnik and Ellis would start ferreting out those in hiding. If the residents did nothing to support each other, they'd go down, one by one. Granted, Kat and her Detachment were an unexpected element, but the big question for Kat was . . . what to do next . . . and when?

Part of that was perhaps already solving itself. Her two 'borrowed' vehicles now moved deeper into the town. If

Melnik directed his people to attempt an interdict, then there would be a meeting, an 'engagement,' and soon.

Kat's people would engage whatever Melnik threw at them, intentionally or otherwise, but Melnik was no fool and might sensibly try to avoid contact, at least until he had better Intel.

Kat wanted one thing, and Melnik potentially another. That was usually when battles often occurred . . . or elections. Kat's chosen profession did the battle thing. Despite her father's strong opinion on the matter, she still considered that she had chosen more wisely than he had.

Safi made the broadcast. It got no immediate reaction from Melnik. Kat had figured him to be like Ellis, a 'shoot from the hip' type, so had anticipated some form of direct challenge or response, but he kept silent, made no 'knee-jerk' reply.

"Safi, make a note of the time of our broadcast."

"Yes ma'am. Can I ask why?"

"Because sooner or later, someone is going to say something about our loud and blunt declaration. It would therefore be useful Intel to see how long the 'decision cycle' is that the other side are operating to."

"I see," Safi said. "I should therefore start timers on everything of this nature. That way, I can answer your questions faster."

Another lesson for the jumble of smart circuitry around Kat's collarbone.

The Suruchi Hotel eventually came into view. Two local men in their early twenties, both armed with bolt-action hunting rifles, immediately recognised the men riding with Kat, and waved the small convoy towards the building's rear entrance.

Kat was out of the vehicle and into the building within a second of the vehicle stopping, avoiding any potential for overhead surveillance by keeping firmly to the shadows.

"And she broadcast *that* on an open comms channel! To

everyone?" Ellis said, struggling to keep his voice under control.

"Yes," Major Melnik replied. "I think she was trying to appeal to the local population. Get some kind of resistance or rebellion underway."

"Then we must execute some of these locals, to ensure that we are feared . . . maintain a proper level of control over them. Do you have any problems with getting the apprehended townspeople organised into groups, of say ten or twelve, Major? If they kill one of our people, you may respond by killing ten of theirs," Ellis said. "Or, if you'd prefer . . . I can get Mr Sobhraj to take care of it!"

Before Melnik could respond, "No, you will not," came as a shout, almost a scream over the comm-channel.

"Who said that?" came from both Ellis and Melnik.

"I did, Kamal Badali. We will need this town's population to support our ongoing operation. Don't go killing the very people we're going to need to keep this place returning a profit. Do you have any idea how expensive it will be to bring new workers in?"

"Who gave you access to this comms frequency?" Ellis asked, his voice low and cold. Ellis hit the mute on his comm-link. "Don't hurt him. Just bring him up here. *Now.*"

Two crewmen left their bridge stations and headed down to Mr Badali's cabin.

Finger off the mute button, Ellis continued his talk with Melnik. "Did you see the way the images in her broadcast had been processed? It's the original feed from your disembarkation," he said. "Re-run it," he ordered the crewman at the comms board.

The footage of Melnik's people marching ashore reappeared. Now there was commentary over it. "Note, that these troops have minimal protection," followed at the end of the piece with, "and, they can't march straight. So . . . can they shoot straight?"

"That looks like an incitement to rebellion to me, Andrev."

"That's exactly what I'm thinking," the Major said.

"The Severn girl enjoys yanking a true warrior's chain.

We therefore . . . need to give her a good solid yank back."

"Like a short noose over a tall tree." That gave them both a chuckle.

"Exactly," said Ellis, but his mirth was gone when his crew dragged Badali onto the bridge. Whilst not restraining him or hitting him, he wasn't being handled with any servility, and bounced hard off the door frame. The two crewman seemed to be experts in moving uncooperative sailors, probably inebriated crewmates, around the ship.

Badali seemed to bounce off of anything that happened to be in their way. It was a bit pathetic to see a grown man offer them zero resistance.

The two crewmen manoeuvred him until he stood, unsupported in the centre of the bridge. Any half-trained sailor would have braced up, faced his Captain. Taken his dressing down like a fighting man.

Not Badali.

"Please explain what you are doing listening in on my command net?" Ellis demanded.

"I represent the money. Therefore, we listen in on anything we damn well want to." His comment would have been more effective if he'd maintained defiant eye contact with Ellis. Did he have any idea how ridiculous he looked? Could he hear the bridge team snickering at his empty claims?

As much as Ellis hated playing to his crew, this civilian was challenging his authority, challenging him as the vessel's Commander, and that could not be permitted. He stood and approached Badali until they were almost nose to nose with each other. "While you are on my ship, you follow my orders. It's that simple. Do you understand me?" he said in a deadly serious, low voice.

"I represent the money that got you this ship," the business man said defiantly, but the power in his voice was neutralised by the tears forming in his eyes, the blubbering of his mouth.

Ellis glanced at his two crewman and they both took a step forward and each grabbed one of Badali's arms.

Badali gave a yowl. "You can't do this to me."

"You are on my ship, therefore you are under my discipline. You, and every other sailor or soldier here. The assumptions you predicated this investment on have been shown to be more than a little inaccurate. I am, at present, attempting to resolve this conflict of expectations with reality. This is a matter that can only be handled by Officers like Major Melnik and myself. You are interfering with our work."

Ellis turned and went back to his command chair. He settled back into it. "Now then, *you* . . . Mr Badali, will return to your cabin and stay there. Comms, please accompany Mr Badali and remove any unauthorised communication equipment you might find there."

"Yes, sir."

"You aren't going to start shooting hostages are you?" Baladi's voice cracked as he pleaded. Not for the sake of the hostages lives, but the knock-on effect it would potentially have on his bottom line of profitability.

"Not yet. But not because of you. But because *I* don't want to. Major, have you been listening?"

"Every word."

"You've detained a few of the local population?"

"Yes, Captain. About fifty, perhaps a few more."

"Organise them into groups of ten as I suggested. If you have to shoot them, start with the least valuable, those that contribute little to the community, the old, the ill. Those with the brains will submit long before you get to anyone our employers might weep for at his or her funeral."

"I'm not a big fan of massacring civilians, sir. Oberst von Brühle had us do exactly that at The Pavilion in Emirates City. Hundreds of them. Not the work of skilled, professional soldiers in my humble opinion. So, yes, perhaps you should get your Mr Sobhraj to facilitate."

"Understood Major. I'll get Sobhraj and some of his crew to do it, as you and your men evidently don't haven't the stomach for it."

"That's *not* what I said, Ellis. I said we'd *rather not* . . . not that we *wouldn't* do it."

"Noted, Major. Leave it with me," Ellis ordered his

subordinate. "Now, do you think it prudent to broadcast a martial-law decree, Major?"

"I've already recorded one, just as a precaution. I'll send it to you now, sir."

About the same time Melnik's martial law announcement finished downloading, the comms crewman returned, several pieces of equipment in his hands, all trailing wires and connectors that showed they'd been removed with little regard to reinstallation.

"Is he still snivelling?" Ellis asked.

"No sir. He actually seemed quite happy. I think he's convinced himself that he had something to do with the outcome."

Ellis scowled as he shook his head. "How do such naive fools survive to become adults?"

"I wonder why he was the only financial backer who insisted on coming with us?" The crewman at the weapons board added.

Ellis ignored the comment. "Comms, show me Melnik's declaration of martial law. It would be most satisfactory to send something out that didn't involve dilapidated trucks or non-armoured troops.

Melnik's face snarled into the lens, threatening the islanders. Promising disproportionate retaliation if even one of his men were attacked. That should get the attention of these damn locals!

Ellis glanced at the time shown in the corner of the main screen. *Somehow the Severn brat and her team have produced a better product . . . and in less time. Probably that damn interfering HI of hers!*

Then again, she doesn't have to deal with that idiot Badali. And . . . once the fighting starts . . . neither will I.

Ellis shook his head. Let Severn think she'd won some small victory. When the rounds started flying, she'd soon discover that she couldn't count on a slow decision. Not from Major Melnik, and not from her old Commander!

"Broadcast the declaration," Ellis ordered, then settled back in his chair to study the main screen. It showed all that he'd learned from the latest drone scans. East of

Severn's two landing sites, on the edge of the town there was a nebulous cloud of something, but it wasn't immediately obvious what. Melnik's ground troops would deal with it, whatever it was.

For a brief moment he considered targeting the location with his ship's auto-cannons, then rejected it. He needed to conserve ammunition, needed to be ready to engage Severn's vessel when it eventually returned.

Briefly he reflected on his own ship. He had to wonder where the financiers had found such a vessel. Under-powered with two weak reactors, yet over-gunned with two seventy-five millimetre auto-cannons, but with limited reloads, and a single rack of Ahab anti-ship-missiles. Likely designed for defensive, rather than in any kind of offensive action.

But I took this command. Jumped at it, because anything was better than being ashore unemployed. I'd have chewed my own arm off to get back to sea.

"Does Severn still have access to their military satellites?" Ellis asked the crewman at the comms board.

"Potentially sir, yes, she does. There are two currently overhead. They frequently adjust their orbit parameters to prevent us or others jamming them. Not that we have anything to do such jamming with. But she doesn't seem to be accessing them. If she did I could maybe pin-point her location."

"A rich brat like 'Princess Katarina' could have access to privately owned satellites if her own military can't provide what she needs," Ellis said. Thanks to the frugality of those funding this endeavour, he had nothing like that. He swore inwardly to himself, but kept a confident face for his crew and waited to see what the Severn girl's next move would be.

"Comms, get me Bavi Sobhraj, I have some work for him ashore."

Kat viewed Melnik's martial law declaration with Mrs Lakhera in the Suruchi Hotel's back office. She was evidently the matriarch of her extended family. The Mahaapaur had diplomatically described her as being 'independent' which Kat now understood to be a polite synonym for a somewhat opinionated and obstinate lady. She might have been about the same age as her mother's older sister, Aunty Dee, but it was difficult to tell. All the islanders seemed to look much younger than their actual years.

Mrs Lakhera may have aged well, but she certainly didn't lack any fortitude in her resolve.

"One of my boys went down to the waterfront when they came ashore. We haven't heard from him since. I told him he was stupid to go and see what all the fuss was about, but there's this girl you see. He said he'd talk her into coming back here to stay with us," she told Kat in good, but accented English.

"Mrs Lakhera, we didn't come here to start a war, only to find out what is happening," Kat told the woman.

"I've heard that about you Severns. You say you never start a fight, but by the ghosts of my ancestors, they certainly find you. You want to reassure an old woman? Then tell me what you are really planning on doing, especially as half-a-dozen of her family now want to go along with you and your soldiers?"

Kat shook her head. "It's not that I know . . . and won't tell you. . . It's simply that right here and now, I don't know what is going to happen. It looks like many of these unwanted visitors are second-rate soldiers, but I can't begin to tell you what they're really here for. Your Mahaapaur thinks it is to do with lucrative pharmaceutical patents, because of your unique plants and wildlife, but so far, we've seen nothing to confirm this."

The hotel owner moved her head, but Kat wasn't sure if that meant she understood, agreed or was simply just listening.

"So, you will take my boys, my older grandchildren on your journey to provoke confrontation. Use them as . . . what is it you call them? 'Cannon fodder.' I believe that is the term. I heard from the Mahaapaur's sister that in the war James Severn used up a lot of this 'cannon fodder.' No?"

That wasn't what Kat had read in the history files, but

then again, she had less and less trust in what the supposedly learned scholars and media reported as being the truth. She silently considered several replies and eventually chose her first, as it seemed the most honest. "Mrs Lakhera, I'd like to promise you, but I won't. If it would make you more willing to let them come and do what I order, then I guess I could raise my right hand and swear any oath you want, but the truth is that what we're heading into won't be easy to do, and therefore, it's even harder to foretell." She paused, looked the woman directly in the eyes. "I certainly don't plan to use anyone as 'cannon fodder.' I suspect that my Grandpa James didn't think he was using all that many, certainly not as many as you've been led to believe. However, what a fighting man says he used after the battle and what he'd anticipated may not come out sounding anything alike."

The old woman snorted. "I've had a few partners, business and personal, go that way too. To hear some men talk, you would not think we had been in the same city, much less the same bed! I appreciate your honesty young lady. I will trust you with my boys. And two of the girls want to come along too. They are good with the hunting rifles. As good as any of the boys. Are you okay with that?"

"My mother wouldn't be, but as almost a third of my Detachment are female, as well as me, I'd be a bit of a hypocrite if I didn't take them!"

"What are you going to do about this martial law thing?" Mrs Lakhera asked, changing the subject.

"What would you do?" Kat asked her right back.

"I'd tell our people not to provoke or kill any of those rascals right now. Not now, not until the time comes. They are looking to provoke a fight, but we must not give it to them. Don't get in their way. When we are ready, we will take the fight to them, on our terms. Then there will be more than enough dying and suffering. Maybe there will be enough that they will not be all that interested in killing unarmed people again." The old lady closed her eyes for a few seconds. "I know that's probably not what you wanted to hear, but that is what I would tell them."

"Safi, did you record what Mrs Lakhera just said?" Kat asked her HI.

"Yes, I have a record of your conversation."

"Prepare another message for all frequency broadcast. Add my voice and take a still image of Mrs Lakhera. 'I strongly advise the people of Tenlaa to follow Mrs Lakhera's good advice. A time of reckoning will come, but that time is not now. Don't do something that causes these perpetrators to hurt your families and friends.'"

"Do whatever you need to, Safi. Prepare it for transmission. Advise me when you're ready. How long did it take Ellis to respond to our first broadcast?"

"One hour, twenty-four minutes. He sent the martial law declaration as a response."

"Let's get our reply out as fast as we can."

Staff Freeman returned from the upper level of the hotel. "Do you want the good news or the bad, ma'am?"

"As it comes, Staff," Kat told him.

"The good news, is that I have line-of-sight on both ships. One is on the quay, the other out in the roads."

Kat nodded.

"The bad news, ma'am, is that only the nearer one, on the quay, the passenger transport, is within range of our Jackhammer launchers."

"Okay, so we'll leave the M504 Halberd teams from First and Second Squad here," ordered Kat, using the weapon system's correct military designation rather than how it was universally known amongst the infantry. "They can establish an OP, keeping 'eyes on,' and if required, take out the transport ship."

"Roger that," the Staff Sergeant acknowledged, then added, "I could potentially modify the designator from one 504's aimer unit, ma'am. Use it to "paint-up" Ellis's ship for a Harlequin ASM fired from the *Bella* to lock onto. It's simple enough; I just need the Harlequin missile's transmission codes. Alternatively, someone back on the *Bella* changes the Harlequin's transmission codes to that of a Jackhammer's. But . . . honestly, the current approach vector of a ship launched missile, searching for a laser 'splash' initiated from this hotel, is almost three-two hundred mils out, so it might not work, as the Harlequin doesn't have a sustainer motor, so will lose velocity with every course correction it undertakes, and a full three-two-hundred u-turn is quite a bit of adjustment."

"Don't worry about that, Staff. Just concentrate on taking out their transport ship with a standard 504 projectile should we need to."

"Understood ma'am," Freeman said and stomped off to update the weapon system's crew with the 'good news' that they'd be 'checking-in' to the Suruchi Hotel for the next night or two.

"Let me come with you," Mrs Lakhera suddenly told Kat. "The people of this town will feel reassured if they see me riding with you."

"Very well, if you think that prudent, Mrs Lakhera." Kat said and headed out of the back door of the hotel. Another two vehicles promptly joined their improvised 'convoy.'

Safi got the message responding to the declaration of martial law ready and transmitted in less than ten minutes. Useful Intel continued to be thin. There were always two sides of a coin. Telling the local people to do nothing was one side, a side that would hopefully save their lives. But the flipside was it gave Melnik more time. Time to deploy his full force.

Kat just hoped that by giving more time to Melnik she was also giving more time to Mike, who she hoped was drawing Melnik's forces into the ambush that they'd planned.

Actually, it was two ambushes.

Kat sat in the rear seat of the ageing 4x4 utility vehicle on the way back to the subterranean shelter, letting one of the locals sit up front with the driver. She studied the town as they drove through it.

Mrs Lakhera's vehicle was now in the lead position, taking them a different way back from the route they'd used on the way out. A wise precaution.

The side windows of the vehicle were powered down.

Her M37 assault rifle was also down, between her legs, not visible from outside the vehicle, as she maintained an intense over-watch. But it was the occupants of the other vehicles that gave her most concern. These locals might be willing volunteers, but how would they react when they saw the targets in their sights fall. When the men and women beside them fell, their friends and family fell, with half their head missing. What could Kat expect from these amateurs? Yes, they were fighting for their freedom, if not their very lives, but had they had enough time to realize this, to understand exactly what was at stake here? Could they find it in the pit of their stomachs when they needed to go on, when everything that was natural, human nature, screamed 'run.'

Kat sat there considering her latest issue. How did she train these civilians to become fighters in the short time she now had? A very short time indeed. She remembered the indentured workers, minor criminals, back in the snows of Alaska several years before, who when starving had turned against the farmstead owners. They had nothing more that hunting rifles. She also recalled the competency of the Fleet and handful of Land Force Troopers that she'd resolved that little issue with!

The vehicle convoy was coming to a stop. There was what appeared to be an old woman and a teenage girl up ahead. Mrs Lakhera was talking with them.

Kat got out and joined them at the roadside. They looked dirty, dishevelled.

The younger of the two said hello in English. Kat asked if she could take their photograph, giving more substance to her supposed back-story.

The teenager smiled shyly and told Kat her name was Nishi.

"Where are you going?" Kat asked them.

Mrs Lakhera translated.

The girl pointed down the road. "Home."

What could Kat tell them? The streets of Campbell Bay were not a safe place to be.

"We have come from the shelter. We need to get more

clothes and blankets and the medicine needed by my grandmother," the teenage girl told Kat.

The older woman was wearing a traditional Indian sari that covered her greying hair. Once it had been brightly patterned in a swirling turquoise blue and orange design, but was now dishevelled and dirty. The woman's face was barely visible through the folds of grubby material, but in her eyes, Kat could see the old lady was dying.

"I like your hair," the teenager who was dressed more like a tourist from Europe or Australia in shorts and a vest top, suddenly told Kat, reaching out to touch it.

Like the teenager, Kat had her hair down, something she didn't normally do. Military regulations liked it up and out of the way. Wearing it down for this trip into town was another part of the deception that would maybe prevent her from being instantly recognised.

Kat gave them the two ration bars she had in the pocket of her shorts. It was all she had to offer them.

The girl thanked Kat profusely for her kindness. Then, as if she had forgotten their predicament for a few seconds, she struck a pose, right shoulder towards Kat's camera, head flicked to the side, her hands on her hips. "I would make a good model, no?"

Kat brought the camera up to her eye, but couldn't bring herself to press the 'image capture' button. Tears were suddenly streaming from the teenage girl's eyes and down her cheeks as she came back to the reality of their predicament.

SIX : NINE

Major Melnik did not like the smell of what lay ahead. The ground was low, waterlogged and smelt of stagnant water and rotting vegetation.

If he hadn't already issued orders to put a stop to the bitching about 'Why not let the islanders keep this damn shit-hole,' he would have muttered something very similar himself.

Melnik searched the terrain ahead with his binoculars. The mapping and imagery that Ellis had sent him showed low-lying coastal wetlands. Ahead was the causeway, a grass sided, flat topped dyke, maybe four or five metres higher than the wetlands on both sides, with the old road to Bananga running atop. The causeway didn't have a hard gravel or tarmac road surface but had been planted with some form of bamboo, each stalk about four or five centimetres in diameter. It was then cut down, leaving just the last few centimetres that protruded from the sandy soil. The thousands of sliced-through, densely packed shafts providing an ecologically-friendly form of hardened road surface.

One of the Private Security Company's 'officers' had a couple of local hostages, wading along through the water at the base of the dyke. They were up past their waists.

"It gets deep in some places," one of the locals shouted, that nobody could avoid hearing. "And there are saltwater crocs in these waters that like to do more than just nibble on your toes."

Andrev Melnik didn't know how much to believe of that last claim, but it got a lot of the security contractors around him muttering and eyeing the murky waters. All visibility in the water ended after only a few centimetres.

"What do you make of it, sir?" Kapten Sarikan asked as he climbed aboard Melnik's command vehicle. The only purpose-built military transport they'd brought with them.

Melnik shook his head. "This is where I would ambush us, if I had anything resembling a proper fighting force. My people could lurk out there in the water and only surface to shoot us into a bloody pulp. Is that not so, Sarikan?"

"Yes sir. Just so," the Kapten said, with an expressive sigh. Sarikan had been sent along on this 'joyride' by the Private Security Contractor's senior management. He was to ensure that nothing untoward happened to their people and they returned home in good shape. Some actual battle experience might be gained, which was good, especially as someone else was paying the bill, but to ensure there was no significant damage to company property was his management's primary objective.

Melnik had wanted to hire a much larger formation, but the penny-pinching financiers of this ridiculous expedition had cited hard learnt lessons about 'minimizing losses,' using the destruction of that unidentified squadron of cruisers that had suddenly arrived off of Nu Hawaii, while the ANCANZ Fed's 2nd Fleet was elsewhere, as an example of using excessive force to achieve the objective. So, all Melnik got was a single Company formation, with a Platoon of his own 'professional' people as back up. And the financiers had been 'most appreciative' of the saving.

Major Melnik turned to the Kapten. "Does the pioneer Squad attached to your Company have sensors that would enable me to see any warm bodies in that muddy water, or pick up the electrical impulses of a sniper's heartbeat if he or she is a klick away, where that rain-forest starts?"

"Certainly sir. We have a fully capable team of pioneers back in Bangkok," the Kapten said with tight smile. "But, 'we don't need any pioneer or engineering support on Nicobar.' That is, as I recall, what your investors told you and Captain Ellis when you asked them to rent such resources from my employer."

"That's because your employer set such an outrageously high price for eight or ten pioneers."

Kapten Sarikan snorted. "The gear my people are wearing is twenty, perhaps even thirty years old. And yet, it is a lot newer than anything we've seen on this island."

"Except, we don't actually know what we're facing," Melnik shot back.

"They've done pretty well on the march here. Do you have any estimate of what the Severn woman has?"

"No. Ellis isn't telling me much about her. Rants on about her plenty. How she ended his military career, but there's not a lot of hard fact behind all the noise."

"I did a search, but couldn't find anything on Ellis and her, but one of my Junior NCOs found this article on-line from Emirates City."

Sarikan produced an ageing document reader. There was a still image of a very curvy young lady attired in an ivory-coloured dress that looked as though it had been painted on. Next to her was a taller, much less buxom woman in a more modest, pale blue number.

"Severn's the one in blue," Melnik said. "The other is Alexandra von Welf, the daughter of Ernst Augustus, the seventh of that name."

Sarikan nodded. "You've met them? Do you know them?"

"No. But I know the venue," Melnik said. "That's Delavigne's house in Emirates City. We considered using it for something we had planned, but only 'B' list celebrities ever turned up to her events. Not the real political movers and shakers we needed to target. What's your NCO's interest?"

"I don't think he ever expected to meet either of them personally, except perhaps in his dreams. He's good . . . ambitious, so was doing his own 'threat assessment.' Check out the rest of the article."

"'Guilty of many sins for which both harlots will burn, deep within the worst fires of hell.' And this matters to me because?"

Sarikan scrolled down and pointed at the second to last paragraph.

"'Miss Severn committed many licentious acts in

Emirates City, including riding in cars with men she was not related or married to, masquerading as a military officer, violating the city's data censorship laws, associating with illegal gangs of the worst sort.' Sorry Kapten, this does not leave me quaking in my boots."

"Keep reading, Major, the last sentence."

Melnik scrolled down to the end. 'After a significant disturbance of the peace, an occurrence that left thousands dead from gunshot wounds and explosives, Miss Severn was escorted from the city by ABCANZ Federation Ground Forces, only moments before she would have been arrested to face judgement for her sins.' He looked up as he finished reading.

Sarikan raised an eyebrow. "How many Troopers does it take to escort a debutante, and how heavily armed were they? Are they still with her?"

Melnik read through the last paragraph again, slowly, looking for anything not actually stated in the words, but implied by them instead. Nothing. "I don't know," he said slowly. "Ellis sent me images of the ship she supposedly arrived on. A medium-sized merchant freighter."

"What is a Severn doing on a merchant vessel?"

"What is a Severn doing interfering with our operation here?"

Sarikan removed his helmet and swiped the sweat running down his face. "What is a Severn doing here?" He put his helmet back on. "What are *we* about to do here, sir?"

"I'm reluctant to run this collection of local vintage vehicles along that mound of dirt out there, as I can't see anywhere to turn them around."

"So we march across instead?"

"And leave our spare ammunition and heavy weapons behind? I think not, Kapten."

Kapten Sarikan made no further attempts to answer his own question. He paused, an expectant expression on his face. The smarter junior Officers of the 'Hai' Private Security Corporation learned quickly.

"We will wait for my own people to join us, and for Ellis's sensor drone to provide another update. Then we will take the Company across, with plenty of local hostages out in front."

"So that Severn thinks twice about opening fire," Kapten Sarikan said.

"Precisely, Kapten. And, while we're waiting, and before we go any further, get the hostages down on their knees, with knives, and get them checking for concealed mines or trip-wires."

Kat was back in her armoured battle-suit, less the neck and pelvic brace, and had just finished putting her hair back into a tidy pony-tail when Safi received a new data package from Captain Gillan. She wasn't the least bit surprised by the imagery it contained. The hostile's formation was sat where the track on the causeway crossed the wetlands on the western extremity of the town, a kilometre or two past the end of the airport's runway.

Melnik was being sensibly cautious. He was letting his mercenary Platoon, those in full combat armour, who had protected the other three Platoon's rear as they'd moved out from the settlement, catch up with his main formation. Smart move. So much for Kat's wish for a brash stupid one. Safi had not been able to find out anything about a former military officer called Melnik, but she had identified the Private Security Company. Bangkok registered, the 'Hai' Private Security Corporation or Hai PSC were the largest privately owned security provider in the region. There were other organisations, such as the ubiquitous Clearwater, who had a larger global presence, but not in these parts.

As further proof that Melnik wasn't stupid, he had some of the captured islanders on their hands and knees, whilst he waited for his mercenary Troopers to reach his location.

Safi enhanced the imagery. The kneeling islanders had something in their hands. Knives. The blades glinting in the afternoon sun.

Kat smiled. More evidence that they'd saved money by skipping on proper mine detection equipment.

Mike's orders didn't specifically say he couldn't mine

the causeway, and the dems-tech in each Squad could undoubtedly improvise something with the plastic explosive charges they carried, but it wasn't in their immediate plans to do so. Then again, she hadn't given him explicit instructions not to.

Kat suddenly hoped that Mike hadn't put IEDs out, as things would start getting bloody somewhat sooner than she wanted. Not that she wanted them to get bloody at all.

These developments were something Kat would like to talk over with Mike and both her Senior NCOs. However, only Staff Freeman was with her. Mike and Sergeant Varko were busy setting up the 'obstacle' elements of the impending 'advance to contact' that would inevitably follow their first 'encounter.'

Right now, Staff Freeman was also busy, talking with the locals, telling them the bare necessities of soldiering that might somehow keep them alive. From what she could see, it looked like he held their rapt attention.

Kat assessed the hostile's progress, then worked out where she wanted to be by first light tomorrow. The two elements seemed to balance.

If only she didn't hate waiting quite so much.

"The situation ahead of you has not changed in the last ninety minutes," said Ellis in his open comms with Melnik. "Stop wasting time and get that show of yours on the road," the former Fleet Commander, now merchant ship Captain, ordered curtly.

Easy for him to say, his neck isn't about to head into a potential ambush, thought Melnik. He had never worked with Ellis before, so took communications like this on a private, encrypted frequency.

"Do you have any information on the Land Force Detachment who escorted her from Emirates City," Melnik asked him.

The comms feed from the *Hyperion* went on 'hold.'

"Land Force Detachment . . .?" Ellis said when the link was restored.

"One of the Private Security Company's NCOs came

across an article about Katarina Severn getting into trouble in Emirates City recently. Something that I can confirm."

Ellis interrupted. "That woman is always in trouble, or creating it."

"So it would seem," Melnik said, but did not allow his line of conversation to be dismissed. "According to this article Miss Severn was escorted from the city one step ahead of the law. The article does not detail the size of that Land Force formation or if they were an Embassy Protection Detachment, a full Expeditionary Force or a four-man recon team. Nor did it say if she still had them with her."

"ABCANZ Federation Land Forces," Ellis said slowly.

"Potentially, if the media hasn't taken its usual liberties with the truth and accuracy. Admittedly, it is in the 'gossip' articles of a tabloid publication."

"The kind of people who read, or believe the contents of those kind of sites never care or understand anything about the military," replied Ellis.

"I agree, but Severn and Land Force Troopers. A bad combination. They gave a good account against my people in Emirates City, forced us to withdraw."

"Why would ANCANZ Fed Troopers want to waste time being with her? Once they got her out of Emirates City, if indeed they actually did, they would have wanted her gone, out of their hair."

"I would certainly think that is the case, however, there is the little matter of just what exactly is she doing here? We did not expect her. No Intel source suggested we might encounter her here, but . . . here she is, claiming to command an ABCANZ Fed survey and science vessel."

"And she did ignore my orders not to persist and to withdraw."

"Matters are becoming most unclear."

"She's good at that," Ellis snorted. "Are you going soft on me, Andrev? Did she give your oh-so professional mercenaries such a pounding in Emirates City that she's got you running scared? You want to cut and run because of this . . . this . . . rich and privileged brat?"

"No Captain, not at all," Melnik exploded. If Ellis had

made such a comment to his face, and not via a comm-link it might well have been his last. Melnik had certainly killed lesser men for such insolence. "I know ground operations are not your forte, being a naval man, but please understand, my forces are currently concentrating into a location that is exactly where I would have prepared an ambush. Before I stick my head into it, I'd like to know as much about the situation as possible. Intelligence Preparation is critical and I do not like what I have learned. Do you know anything that I should?" Melnik managed with effort to turn his last remark into a question.

Ellis heard everything that Melnik had said and inferred. He took a long moment to reply. When it came, his words were deceptively soft. "Major, you have your orders. We have good reason to believe that whatever forces Severn has landed with may well be to train and equip the local population in armed resistance. Therefore, you and your men will advance and destroy them. All of them. Show no mercy!"

"Yes, Captain."

"*Execute* your orders."

The link went dead. Melnik shook his head in disbelief. He evidently had his orders. Now all he had to do was make them happen!

As Melnik climbed from his command vehicle, Sarikan approached him, but did not salute. Considerate of him, as there may be snipers out in the tree line.

Ten paces away, and waiting, were the three Hai PSC Platoon Commanders. Melnik motioned for them to join him. Leftenan Akarathit was the only one in uniform and equipment over and above the bear minimum their company had provided. His record was impressive enough, except it lacked any actual combat experience. If he survived the coming battle, he would be far ahead of his peers in the race for promotion. The young man's enthusiastic grin showed he knew that too, and was eager for it to begin.

The second of the three lieutenant's or 'leftenan' uniforms showed where the usual bright metal accoutrements and insignia of officer entitlement, that would have made them targets, had been hastily removed. He seemed ready to challenge his superiors. Did they not know how hard he'd worked to reach and then hold on to this rank?

Promotion was apparently a hard-won entitlement in the 'Hai' Private Security Corporation, but it wasn't necessarily by military ability. This man has not spent enough time in the field getting dirty as far as Melnik was concerned.

The Major watched, with considerably more interest, the approach of the third Leftenan. He was older, perhaps 'passed over for promotion.' Melnik had insisted that he got to select at least one of the PSC's officers. He'd placed his bet on Leftenan Suvit Diskul and given him Three Platoon. With luck, the man might leave the world of private security contracting and sign up with Melnik's mercenaries after this sorry little affair was a long distant memory. Then again, Officers of the Hai Private Security Corporation were notoriously loyal, even sentimental about their monthly pay parade, symbolically held in-front of a temple in Bangkok, where they also reaffirmed their loyalty to the corporation's CEO. If Leftenan Diskul couldn't break that habit, then he'd probably retire on a Lieutenant's pay grade in twenty years time!

As Leftenan Akarathit and the second Officer approached, they both halted in quick succession and smartly saluted Melnik.

"No more saluting," Melnik seethed. The two Lieutenants pailed as they hurriedly got their offending hands down. Leftenan Diskul came to a halt, no sign that he had ever intended to salute, but perhaps it was just down to timing.

"Are you trying to get me killed, you freakin' clowns?" Melnik growled in a harsh whisper.

Leftenan Akarathit didn't relax his posture any, but his face did show, if only for a second, an unhealthy curiosity about Melnik's future. The Major moved forward to stand nose to nose with the Leftenan. He pointed to the swamp ahead. "Out there, that terrain, has the perfect ambush profile. Do you see it?"

"Yes, sir," said all three of the Junior Officers. Leftenan Diskul studied the ground, blinked, then nodded ever so slightly.

"There may be snipers sighting on us right now. Snipers who can put a bullet into your brain from over a thousand metres. Who do you think those snipers most want to kill?"

The three Leftenans stood speechless. This was apparently not part of their doctrine.

"Officers," Leftenan Diskul observed.

At that moment, one of Melnik's Feldwebels or Sergeants, and another who'd been in The Pavilion when all hell had broken loose, came past. He nodded briefly towards the Major as he escorted another ten locals towards the front of the column.

"Correct," Melnik began, stepping back from the Leftenan who right now probably wanted to identify Melnik to any passing snipers. "Quick march Two Platoon up to where the mine clearance detail is on the causeway. You are now the vanguard. Advance your men, keep watch for anything in the water beside the road or in the trees at the edge of the water. Is that understood?"

"Yes, sir!" the Hai PSC Leftenan said, and only just managed to suppress another salute.

When he did nothing further, Melnik gave him a long stare.

"Err . . . you, err . . . want me to go now?" The Leftenan stuttered. Excitement or confusion?

"If I wanted you to do it tomorrow, I would have told you tomorrow."

"Yes, sir," he said bracing up and only just stopping himself from saluting again, before running off for his command.

"Do you think he'll remember his orders, sir?" Sarikan asked Melnik.

"They are simple enough, but I'm sure as a good XO you will drop by and help him to remember. Is than not so?"

"Definitely, sir."

"Three Platoon. You, along with my men, will provide the main force. Mount half your people into the available local transport. Have them keep their rifles ready and their eyes searching for anything concealed in the shallow waters on the right of the causeway or the sand banks between us and the sea. Understand?"

"Yes, sir," came from Diskul.

"I will keep my command vehicle with you."

"Yes sir, my men will lay down their lives for you," came in reply.

Melnik did much care for such comment. It certainly wasn't reciprocal. He had no intention of dying for these amateurs. He let it go with a dismissive wave of his hand.

"Leftenan Akarathit, your platoon will take the rear guard. Keep well back. If there is an ambush waiting for us out there, I don't want us to make it easy for them to get all of us in it. If they spring an ambush on us, you are to spread out and take them on whatever flank they are attacking from. If there is no attack, then when we get across, I will 'about-face' and do the same, covering you whilst your Platoon come across the causeway."

The Leftenan eyed Melnik to assess the true prospect of the Major coming to his rescue, but let his conclusion pass unsaid and just nodded. "Stay spread out, eyes open, and assault rifles ready, sir. No problem."

"Good. Then let's do it."

Akarathit turned to go about his duty. Then stopped. "Aren't we going to have a prayer?" he stammered.

"May God help the poor fool that tries to take a bite out of us. Good enough for you Leftenan?" Melnik said. "Because it's about all we have time for."

Eyes wide, the young Officer hastened to catch up with Diskul.

With his Officers sent on their way to do his bidding, Melnik climbed back inside his command vehicle. Once seated comfortably, he studied the terrain ahead. After two minutes, he decided that the disorganised milling about outside did not meet with his satisfaction. He had only to shout once to get Two Platoon trotting out to reinforce the mine-clearance detail as they'd been ordered.

Five minutes later, Diskul's Third Platoon was ready to move out. The Unteroffizier, or Corporal driving Melnik's command vehicle slid it easily into the convoy of commandeered civilian transports.

Melnik flipped his helmet's visor down and *prepared* himself to receive whatever was coming their way.

Ensign Mike Steiger, only recently commissioned to the ABCANZ Fleet, sat on a small timber packing case and stared into to the darkness of the cave. The young boy of about ten who showed it to him had proudly introduced it as being his very own 'secret base.'

Before today, it had protected the lad from nothing worse than the afternoon sun, and his parents continual list of household chores. Its main advantage had been its closeness to a waterhole. Until this morning, that the cave's entrance was well hidden by the exposed root ball of a narra tree, had not been of any great concern.

It was now.

Mike wondered why so much of this island seemed to be about caves and subterranean living. Then the lad spotted something in the cave's darkness and picked it up with great reverence.

Mike initially thought it was a seed cone, like that of a pine tree, but from one of the local tree species, but no, it was something very different indeed.

> *The masked palm civet, also known as the 'racoon of south-east asia' was a nocturnal cat-like creature endemic to the region.*
>
> *Not unlike the coffee, or 'kopi luwak,' manufactured from the part-fermented coffee fruits eaten, then passed through the digestive system and defecated, by the palm civets on the neighbouring island of Sumatra in the Pancasila Republic, the Nicobar equivalent, that fed on the unique flora and fauna of the island, produced something that had become*

much more valuable.

The local boy became vague when Mike asked if it was the poo, vomit, snot, congealed sweat, or some other bodily secretion used by the animal for marking its territory. Maybe the boy simply didn't know.

"Black Gold, my father calls it. The drug and perfume companies pay us top dollar, *big* money, for this," the lad told him enthusiastically in reasonable English.

Strange that the Mahaapaur hadn't mentioned it as being of so much value? Mike thought. *Is this what Ellis is up to? Why he's really here?*

As a significant source of revenue, it might explain why so many of the locals spent time scratching about in the island's dirt, and what young boy didn't like messing about in the mud. Was the discovery of some of the larger caves that now housed their extensive underground infrastructure just a by-product of searching for this civet poo, or whatever it was?

Mike peered at the display of his TDT, as if it would somehow help him better understand the events now evolving. One of Safi's tiny nano-UAVs buzzed away on the far side of the swamp, relaying images via an even smaller relay UAV, that had at least for now, apparently passed unnoticed by the hostile troops at the far end of the causeway.

Princess Katarina and her self-learning personal computer, or Heuristic Intellect's incurable addiction for gadgets and the latest tech, were once again proving to be invaluable, giving him quality Intel on whatever was going on over there. The hostiles looked to be using nothing more sophisticated than the basic MkI human eyeball and ear, and whatever sighting enhancements were fitted to their ancient weapons.

Unfortunately, one set of those ears and eyes appeared to be connected to a human brain that was more advanced than the average. Major Melnik had identified this location's potential for an ambush, and had called a halt to his advance.

He hadn't done anything else, such as launching rocket propelled grenades at potential Land Force sniper nests, or deployed any kind of weapon system that delivered large-scale death and destruction. It appeared that neither Melnik's eyes, ears nor limited overhead sensors had given away Mike's defensive array. Melnik's training and experience meant he could sense danger in this place, but couldn't put his finger on any specific targets.

And fortunately for Mike and his troops, Melnik did not appear to have an abundance of spare ammunition to use blasting away at anything that looked like a potential target concealed within the periphery of the rainforest.

Not for the first time, Mike said a silent 'thank you' to whoever had sent these troops out to grab what they thought was an easy prey.

He remembered exactly where they'd hidden the RIBs and intended to get back there and off this island just as quickly as he possibly could, and he sincerely hoped Kat did not have other plans. Having been thrown, run or ushered out of half a dozen cities in the last few years, she should be used to the concept of helping folks out, then getting out of their way, and quickly. Very quickly.

They're starting to get organised, he thought, looking at the data feed on his TDT.

Mike hadn't really needed the idiot saluting what had to be the Officer Commanding. The man was standing next to the only modern looking, and camouflage painted military rig, that had enough height to its rear cargo space to be an effective command vehicle. He also wore the very latest combat armour from head to toe. If that wasn't Melnik it could only be a hologram of him.

Mike briefly considered changing the battle plan, now that he had a solid IDent on Major Andrev Melnik, but Kat had been firmly opposed to turning this into a bloodbath if it could possibly be avoided. Mike mentally conceded and held to Kat's plan. Melnik would live to see another evening's sunset, assuming that he didn't somehow slip off the causeway and break his neck.

Suddenly, from stationary and milling about,

everyone was now moving with purpose, running or jogging. Mike waited to see if Melnik had stayed within the decision cycle Kat was betting on.

A Platoon sized formation of around thirty to thirty-five uniformed figures moved onto the causeway in double-time. They halted where the crude attempts at mine detection were being enacted. More local hostages were now pushed ahead of them, doing mine clearance the 'old-fashioned' way, with human feet. Staff Freeman had warned them that this was a real possibility. War had never been civilised.

Mike unfastened a utility pouch on his belt and removed a little box with a red button. At present, it was safely protected by a hinged cover. Mike kept the cover's retaining pin in place. He wasn't going to need it for maybe another ten minutes.

The commandeered civilian vehicles in the main body of the convoy on the causeway had started moving. The Hai PSC personnel rode or walked alongside them, eyes and assault rifles focused mainly on the water or sandbanks on both sides of the causeway. A few studied the distant tree-line. There were no shouts of discovery, only the occasional yells of NCOs snapping at subordinates who weren't sufficiently attentive or engaged in their current task.

Mike momentarily ignored the human activity and switched his attention to the vehicles. In their open rear sections, there were more assault rifle wielding private security contractors. He saw multiple makes and models of transport, no two were the same. Maintenance would be a nightmare for that collection of clattering spare parts, and spare parts was exactly what they would be needing about thirty minutes from now.

Another five minutes passed. Bringing up the rear came another Platoon sized formation of Hai PSC. If Mike's command, with the support of eager, but untrained civilians had to shoot it out, matters could get ugly and quickly.

His TDT measured the distance from hunched-over hostages in the vanguard, to the last troop formation in the rear, just pulling onto the causeway. Just over one kilometre.

Mike was glad nothing in Kat's plan involved his force trying to engage that formation in its entirety. Melnik evidently knew he was going into terrain that screamed 'ambush,' and was offering anyone stupid enough to try what appeared to be a perfect opportunity.

Mike had somehow acquired a group of islanders, and their animals. Very eager, but mostly untrained. Half a Squad of his Land Force Troopers were now deployed in keeping them quiet, about a klick away from Mike's current position inside the young boy's 'secret base.'

Out on the causeway, the detained islanders in the vanguard shuffled across the midpoint of the swamp. They looked totally dejected. The sun was now high in the sky, past noon. The humidity, the heat and the insects had all helped to drain any and all energy from them.

Mike watched as the lead Platoon of Hai PSC troops followed the islanders across the causeway's midpoint. He removed the retaining pin of the protective cover on the firing device and the cover sprang open. He checked the power bulb was lit green, counted to five, then depressed the button.

"I'm picking up a nano-burst transmission," the comms-tech in the rear of Major Melnik's command vehicle advised.

Melnik extracted himself from his command position and moved into the vehicle's rear compartment, just as the driver slammed on the breaks.

"Don't stop, keep driving," Melnik shouted. He was with the PSC's Third Platoon, so there was a good hundred metres, maybe two, between the front of Third Platoon, and the rear of Second Platoon, up in the vanguard position at the front of the column.

The six over-size tyres spun in the compacted sand, mud and sectioned bamboo stalks that made up the causeway, then the rig lurched forward.

"Stop," Melnik suddenly shouted.

The explosion that ripped the causeway in two wasn't all that impressive. Most of the kinetic energy of the charge acted as intended, and was absorbed by the soil and sand, but the central concrete culvert that enabled the swirling water of the coastal mangroves and wetlands to move from one side of the causeway to the other, now collapsed. The mud, sand and bamboo of the causeway immediately above it, now moved, assisted by gravity, to fill in that space. A gap, four metres wide and two deep, now severed the causeway.

Melnik lept from his command vehicle, "Get back, you freakin' idiots," he called to the Third Platoon.

Whether it was the insults or the look on Melnik's face, the Hai PSC personnel quickly got the message and backed away from the gap in the causeway.

Melnik angrily thumbed his comm-link. "Sarikan, please tell me your people have something to bridge this gap for our vehicles."

"No, sir," the PSC Kapten said in a calm, calculating voice. "As I'm sure you'll recall, using the same tone as the financial backers had, 'such equipment is considered an unnecessary expense.'"

Melnik didn't know whom he wanted to shoot the most. Sarikan for reminding, almost mocking, him as to how they'd let a bunch of spineless civilians call the shots regarding equipment requirements, or perhaps the spineless civilians themselves. He'd never operated under such severe financial restrictions before. Certainly not when working for Herr von Welf, either directly or indirectly through former colleagues like Jacob von Brühl. If he survived this, he wouldn't be taking another low budget job ever again, whatever the potential return, which definitely wasn't enough to consider dying for. But, since the recent fiasco in Emirates City, the better paid and financed work had dried up. Oberst von Brühl, his former commander turned business executive, was dead. And Ernst Augustus von Welf didn't return his calls or reply to his messages.

Melnik hated the thought of being out here, exposed on the causeway, unable to go forward. Unable to turn. They'd have to reverse back off the causeway. The other alternative was to drive off the causeway and into the water, but putting an armoured vehicle of several tonnes into a water that was of uncertain depth and bottom composition without some kind of recon was foolish. And, it meant exposing the thinner top armour whilst going down the bank from the raised level of the causeway into the fetid, stagnant water below. He had limited options . . . which one exposed them to the fewest risks?

A shot rang out.

Not the usual sound of small-calibre assault weapons, 5.56 or 7.62 millimetre. This had the deep-throated bark of a larger calibre. Maybe 12.7 or even 20 millimetre.

Instinctively Melnik dropped down to his knees, trying to present a smaller target to the incoming round.

As his knees hit the trackway, he realised he wasn't the target. Behind him came the sharp gnashing of metal on metal, followed by the whirring propulsion unit of the vehicle becoming suddenly silent. The Major dropped onto his belly.

The steel louvers that allowed air to circulate around the vehicle's propulsion unit, as even electrical vehicles had motors whirring away, converting power into actual drive, were angled and spaced. But the large-calibre round had found its way inside. An ABCANZ Federation, Land Force, infantry branch sniper had aimed between the slats of the louver and found his mark. Once past the outer metal, despite losing momentum, the big round had punched though the internals. Major Melnik's command vehicle wasn't going anywhere soon, not until its propulsion unit could be evaluated.

The military usually exchanged vehicle propulsion units or 'packs' with a 'pack lift,' where the entire unit was swopped over with a replacement. That wasn't about to happen here anytime soon, if ever. They didn't have a spare pack to exchange it with, nor the crane to lift the old one out and the replacement in. And even if he had, such activity wasn't going to be carried out in the causeway. His vehicle would need to be winched back, off of it first!

Another bark from a sniper rifle. Ahead of him a civilian 'acquired' museum-vintage vehicle was consumed in flames as the old-style lithium battery pack caught fire and sent those Hai PSC personnel inside and around it running in all directions from the rapidly intensifying flames.

Melnik was back on his feet. "Stand in front of the vehicle's propulsion unit. Get your worthless bodies in front of them. They're not aiming at people, just the vehicles," he shouted.

The Hai PSC contractors just looked at each other, not comprehending Melnik's strange orders. Some of the men walking beside the trucks started to move in partial compliance, but it hardly seemed to matter. Eventually all the commandeered vehicles were silent and inoperable.

Angry and frustrated, Melnik lost his usual calm, controlled demeanour at the uselessness of his patched-together, second-rate command. He grabbed the nearest Private Security Contractor and shoved him back along the line. "Go . . . find a working vehicle and put your head in front of its propulsion unit."

The Major was furious. He struggled to control his raging temper, then the sniper rifle fired again.

"No, you don't!" shouted Melnik. "You don't take out the drive or battery compartments of my vehicles so carefully that I won't have an excuse to execute at least one damn local."

His command vehicle was rocked as one, then the other two tires on the left side were punctured. His vehicle might have 'run-flat' tires, but the locally acquired vehicles did not.

Private Security Contractors, who had been ordered only a few moments earlier to put their bodies in front of the propulsion units moved to kneel in front of the tires.

There was more incoming fire, aimed at the tires. "Look for the muzzle flash, watch for targets," he ordered. But even as he gave the orders, he knew he had a problem. Order . . . followed by counter-order . . . equalled disorder.

Melnik had learned this long ago, when he'd been at the Ryazan Academy. As a young Lieutenant he'd watched as Field and General ranked officers had foolishly proved the validity of that old adage. Now it was his turn.

Clueless Private Security Contractors began hunkering down in front of the tires. Some of them even laid prone, still not comprehending what was required of them.

The sniper fire stopped.

The silence that followed was pure. Only the chatter of birds, the calls of the macaques and the incessant cicadas. No moan of wounded, no calls for medical attention. Just a mesmerizing silence.

"Return fire," Melnik screamed.

"At what?" Someone dared to ask.

"Out there," Melnik shouted, waving his pistol over the murky waters of the wetlands. "Out there. They're withdrawing. Return fire. Shoot anything that moves, looks to be moving or might move."

The first shots were sporadic. Then, as the Private Security Contractors took up kneeling, prone, or even standing unsupported firing positions. The weapon fire grew. It grew into a deafening roar. Weapon magazines and ammunition belts were emptied and replaced. The 'mad minute' lengthened into two. The rainforest absorbed the fire. Nothing happened.

Melnik studied the unimpressive effects of the small-arms fire. Perhaps they'd hit something. Maybe some rounds had caught someone or something as they withdrew. Perhaps.

But Melnik saw no blood, no bodies, no effect at all. He raised his hand and shouted, "Hold your fire."

It took a moment for the Officers to see his raised hand, to implement his order. Another minute passed before the silence returned.

This time, the silence truly was deafening. He ignored his ears and stared to the left of the causeway, then the right. Here or there an occasional piece of rainforest, a damaged tree or a plant, unable to defy gravity any longer, toppled.

Melnik looked for any sign of movement. To his left a large bird, probably a Nicobar pigeon, squawked loudly and tried to fly away, but crashed headlong into the murky waters.

If there had been hostiles, concealed within the

rainforest, there was no sign of them now. No sign of any wounded or dead. No sign or evidence of anything at all.

"How will we get out of this mess?" It was the voice of one of the Private Security Contractors near the destroyed road culvert, who had spent the last few minutes face down in the dirt, trying hard not to get hit by the incoming or outgoing weapons fire.

Melnik turned back to his initial problem of oh, so long ago . . . maybe five minutes before. The Major's latest survey showed nothing more than his first glance had already told him. He continued to survey the wreckage now surrounding him.

SIX : TEN

So, thought Mike, *Melnik is a 'mad minute' soldier. And Kat owes me ten bucks.* Kat had assumed someone at the end of an extended supply line and now without effective transportation would want to conserve his ammunition and other resources.

But Mike considered that anyone stupid, *or maybe desperate*, enough to take this job would have a temper.

It had been a friendly bet, well as friendly as a Severn ever got about a live-fire encounter!

So, Mike made sure their sniper was ready to go to ground once his job was done. Last shot fired, then hide. The sniper had sensibly pre-prepared somewhere to hide from the likely retaliatory fire.

Despite Major Melnik's ear-splitting response, Mike neither saw nor heard any evidence that any of his people had been hit.

He had effectively debilitated Melnik's force. Proceeding or withdrawing on *foot* was now their only option.

Mike had allowed two hours for his sniper to withdraw from contact and extract himself north, to the temporary RV point.

With any luck, both he and Kat would be in that same location tonight, able to update each other. Gillan would hopefully keep the *Bella* out of weapon range, but continue to feed them much needed overview intelligence.

Would Melnik now use this 'pause' to cut and run? Get back to the transport ship and get out of town? Neither Mike nor Kat were willing to take that bet!

Both of them, in their hearts, genuinely wanted to see the end of this encounter as soon as possible, but to 'hope' for something to happen was not a recognised tactic or strategy. If Melnik withdrew, and headed back to town, he'd most likely go into a defensive formation, rather than embark his troops, and that would force Kat into the offensive action she really wanted to avoid.

So far, Mike was thoroughly enjoying the task Kat had given him. 'Exercise a strategic offensive by maintaining a tactical defence.' Let Melnik chase them until they had him exactly where they wanted him. It had worked this time. Unlikely that he'd be accommodating enough to let Kat and Mike do it again.

Time to get started. Mike activated his comm-link. "Sergeant Varko."

"Yes sir," came back a fraction of a second later.

"You can release the islanders."

"They'll be pleased to hear that. They haven't stopped moaning about it."

"Tell them to either go home, or stay and help us, but they must follow our orders. We need to dig in. So, if they're willing to dig, we'd love them to stay, as we need to prepare a new defensive position."

There was a bit of silence. "They say that if you will give them a chance to shoot back at the hostiles, they'll do some digging for you first."

"Good. Then let's get them digging. Assign Corporal Davis and a Section to escort any islanders who have brought their animals with them. Order them to head north, but to stay away from the wetlands by the causeway. They can shoot back, but only if compromised, otherwise, try to avoid all contact."

"Roger that sir, I'm on it." The link went dead.

Mike checked his UAV feed. On the causeway an occasional shot rattled the silence and sent winged creatures, large fruit bats, birds or both into flight. Mike doubted they were hitting anything, but he couldn't be sure. The capability of Safi's UAV was limited and had been programmed to detect human heat signatures and movement, not identify the local flora and fauna.

He studied the imagery of the swamp from the safety

of his borrowed 'base' one last time, then closed the Tactical-Data-Tablet down. At the back of the cave a newly dug exit tunnel quickly put him back outside among the rainforest plants and between a pair of ancient narra trees. He then had a three kilometre foot patrol back to a concealed vehicle.

Melnik wanted to get the first word in when Ellis called him, but "What are you doing parked on that causeway?" came from the speaker before the Major could get into his command vehicle. Melnik deliberately took the call on 'speaker' so that all his officers could hear it.

The Major considered several choice replies, *enjoying the view* being his first unvoiced answer. But Melnik swallowed them all and instead said, "Considering the best way to fill the gap that has halted my advance."

"Don't you have a fascine you could fill it with, or improvise one?"

"Not in the budget." That drew a snarl of responses from Kapten Sarikan and Leftenan Diskul, "You might want to take that up with Mr Badali. I know I would if he was within my reach."

Ellis took that under consideration for a moment, or maybe he was distracted by other matters. His next comment was, "I'm getting strange imagery from your transports."

"Not surprised. We've been attacked."

"Any casualties?"

Melnik failed to suppress a snort of contempt this time. "Do you see any hostage bodies in your imagery? No, not a single casualty."

"I don't see any dead attackers' bodies either."

"I suspect you're right, though I don't have the sensor array your ship has, or a direct feed from that drone. As I recall, I don't have any sensor equipment at all!"

"You must have seen something. You *were* actually attacked?"

"Yes, by sniper rounds whizzing past for a minute or three."

"Yet none killed any of you? And, you didn't get any of

them?" Ellis sounded incredulous.

"Nobody got hit. Those strange readings you're getting are from my transports?"

"Yes."

"Every vehicle is dead, even my command vehicle."

"Dead?"

"Propulsion unit, battery pack or both in every one of them is shot through, as is every tire that isn't 'run-flat,' so that's all of the civilian rigs. There are two reasons we're sitting here, Captain Ellis. (1) There is a gap in the causeway that is too wide to bridge without Combat Engineer or Pioneer support and (2) we now have nothing but our boots to take us anywhere.

"And you're calling it a day because of that?"

Major Melnik so wished he'd gotten out the general overview before Ellis had started talking. Surrounded as he was by Sarikan and Diskul and the senior NCOs from Third Platoon, his options for throwing a tantrum were somewhat limited. It was about forty minutes since the firefight, and now a former *Navy* Officer was accusing him and his command of cowardice! Oh, how Melnik wanted to scream, if not punch, or kill, someone.

Somehow, he held on to his rising temper and asked through gritted teeth, "What makes you think I'd do that?"

Captain Ellis must have sensed he was only millimetres away from crossing a line that should never be crossed among military professionals. He had the good sense to say nothing more explicit than "Ah . . ." then added, "You haven't suggested anything, Major."

"Then let me respectfully suggest that we hold a council of war between my Officers, you and the representative of our financiers. Is Mr Badali within hearing?"

"I'll get him. Wait out."

There was a long silence. Maybe Ellis was finally comprehending the magnitude of the mess they were now in. But . . . maybe he wasn't.

Then Badali squeaked. "Yes, you wanted to talk with me?"

Melnik quickly outlined what had happened to his command. Neither Badali nor Ellis interrupted, not even for clarification. A wise move.

"That does sound concerning," Mr Badali said when Melnik finished.

Was the man so damn stupid that he lacked any comprehension at all? "Our situation is certainly not hopeless, but it could be somewhat better," Melnik replied.

"What would you suggest? Badali asked him.

Not for the first time, Melnik wished this conversation was taking place in person, or at least with visual. It would be interesting to see how Ellis looked as he swallowed his silence.

"My options are rather simple, Mr Badali. I can continue to advance. To seek out and engage the forces under this Severn girl. So far, they have gone out of their way to avoid serious contact and inflict any casualties."

"They didn't take out any of your people while shooting up your trucks?" Ellis still couldn't seem to comprehend that fact.

"Nobody was hit . . . not a single PSC was even slightly wounded. I therefore seem bound to honour my word and do nothing as our broadcast was most clear on the terms for retaliation."

"Should we change it?" Badali asked.

"Perhaps, but I don't think we'd gain any advantage by doing it right now," Ellis said. "By the way, Major, I checked-in with the troops you left back in the town. They do not appear to be under any kind of threat. The locals seem to have totally disappeared."

"There are only eight personnel back at our 'base' in the town, Captain Ellis, and half of them are protecting the jetty. I will order them to appropriate more local transport, or perhaps locate replacement drive units that could be swopped out."

"No chance," someone said. Melnik turned to see a local old man sitting in a group of hostages. "We don't have 'spare' propulsion units in their entirety, just waiting around, 'just in case.' We repair things when they break.

You've effectively put all of us 'on foot' for the foreseeable future."

"Did you hear that," Melnik asked Ellis.

"Yes. You've been in the town a few days, did you see any garages with repair shops, or retailers of automotive spare parts?"

"No, nothing like that. I'm very open to alternative suggestions, gentlemen."

"If you withdraw, you'll have to do it on foot," said Ellis, stating the blindingly obvious.

"And if I try to advance," Melnik pointed out, "I'll also be doing it on foot."

"But you have to be close to making err . . . contact," Badali put in, reiterating his *huge* knowledge deficit of matters military.

"That is very true," Ellis agreed. "You've come too far, Major to just walk away from your attackers."

"You don't have a viable alternative option, Major," Badali put in. "I mean, what are the chances that this Severn girl has got her hands on some local transport? Could she use borrowed trucks to get about in too . . . to get around your . . . what do you call them . . . flanks, and be ahead of you no matter what direction you decide to move in?"

"It certainly does seem that the Major will be 'advancing to contact,' in whatever direction he chooses to go," Ellis agreed.

"But in one, I'll be getting closer to my base. In the other direction, I'll be going further into unknown terrain," Melnik said, but really wanted to scream '*you pair of freakin idiots, pull me back to our base. There's a chance we might hold Campbell Bay if I use these troops to defensively garrison it. Wandering about out here is futile. I'll be just the latest in a long line of commanders to have their people wiped out.*'

And if he said that, he'd be immediately labelled as defeatist, a coward, a loser. Was that what Ellis wanted to do? Label him? Relieve him of command and turn everything over to Kapten Sarikan? Melnik threw the Hai Private Security Company's senior man a hard glance.

Kapten Sarikan shook his head and took a step back. He waved both hands and mouthed, *No, not me. I don't want this mess.*

Melnik would have preferred a stronger vote of confidence, but a look around the causeway showed no reason for such optimism.

"I think you should keep going," Badali said. "There are no other settlements, just Campbell Bay, or whatever the locals now call it, and the occasional isolated coconut plantation. I assume you significantly outnumber the Severn girl's formation, given the size of the landing craft Captain Ellis identified earlier. Probably three or four to one, no? Maybe even a bit more. Therefore, it seems to me that you should attack them."

"That sounds like a good idea to me, too" Ellis agreed.

It would, you freakin fool. But Badali did have a point. It might work.

And, Melnik reflected, on the approach to the causeway, they had driven through plenty of places suitable for an effective ambush. There would no doubt be others. But this time, they would be waiting for them. Waiting to 'return the compliment.'

Sooner or later, Severn would no doubt do something to enable him to 'dispose' of his hostages, and then the gloves would really be off!

His armoured suit's control unit projected a map onto the ground in front of him. He scanned it quickly, looking for somewhere that could be used defensively. Ahead there was a coconut plantation, just before the rainforest swallowed everything, and it was only a quarter of the distance they needed to travel to get safely back to their improvised base in Campbell Bay. They'd head for the plantation's farm buildings.

If he could just find this Severn and fix her in place, his three Platoons, backed up by his own mercenaries, should be easily capable of taking her life away. "We will continue to advance, sir. In pursuance of your orders," Melnik advised.

"Very well, Major," Ellis replied, "Provide us with a

sit-rep every six hours."

Melnik made sure his comm unit was off before he said anything. "So, gentlemen, we throw the dice. Who knows what we might win."

"Yes, sir," Sarikan said, "But what should we do about our spare ammunition and rations? My men can't carry it all."

"Use the hostages. The locals, the islanders, they can carry it."

Leftenan Diskul put his hand to his pistol's grip and tugged it from its holster, but Melnik gave him a quick shake of the head.

"I don't trust them. Given an opportunity, they'll either run for it, or try to kill us, sir," Diskul said.

"And if and when they do, you can respond accordingly, but until then, we use appropriate force."

The sun was edging towards the horizon by the time all the rations, water and ammunition had been hauled across the gap made by the destroyed culvert and Melnik's people had reformed on the other side.

With a single Platoon delegated to protecting the rest of the formation, and once everyone and everything had eventually reached the other end of the causeway, Melnik called a halt and ordered his troops to dig 'shell scrapes' or 'fox holes' to spend the evening in.

The Platoon that pulled that night's Guard Duty got a serious talking to. "If anything moves within your arc of fire, you kill it." Grim faced, they took their orders.

The night was regularly broken by gunfire. Winged and four-legged creatures that caught the guard's attention died. Unsurprisingly not a single shot was returned. Sleep for just about everyone was therefore was not particularly plentiful, but when the dawn came the next day, their makeshift camp was still secure.

Kat finally got an opportunity to talk with Mike around sunset.

"How'd the first ambush go?" was her first question.

"Surprisingly close to plan," Mike answered happily. "In a couple of minutes our sniper took out every truck they had. They're all on foot now."

"Anyone get hurt?"

"Them, no. Our man got winged when Melnik rewarded us with one of the most ferocious 'mad minutes' I ever hope to encounter. The rainforest absorbed it all, the damage was actually minimal."

"Just as long as none of our people got taken out."

"As I said, our sniper took a nick in his left arm, but nothing more. How'd your trip into town go?" Mike asked Kat.

"I've got quite a collection of volunteers. Staff Freeman and Corporal Groucutt are busy training them in a few basics."

"Will they be any good?"

"Won't know until the shooting starts. On that same note, what's your evaluation of Melnik's people, Mike? Are they up to our Land Force's standards?"

"Don't let Staff Freeman even hear you *thinking* that question. From what I saw of them on the UAV imagery, that formation of troops in full combat armour aren't doing very much. The main formation is the Private Security Company, operating in three Platoons. They have little body-armour, only the Officers and SNCOs, and their weapons and equipment are decades old. They haven't done anything to impress me so far. I didn't take any of them out when we blew the IED in the culvert, as per your orders, but they still behaved like a bunch of amateurs. And they didn't comprehend what the sniper's target was until Melnik shouted at them, and even then, too many didn't really get what was going on. They're good for following orders, but lack any initiative to operate on their own. Give our NCOs a couple of weeks with your local recruits and I bet he'd have them in better shape than Ellis and Melnik's people."

"Except we don't have a couple of weeks. Staff and his NCOs are doing everything they can with them, but an hour or two isn't anywhere near a couple of weeks."

"Are you getting cold feet?" Mike asked her.

"I'm worried about our second ambush."

The pause between them was only for a few seconds before Mike came back. "It bothers me too. Looks all a bit obvious on the map, and I don't trust this Major Melnik with the obvious. Not after what we did to him in the last '*obvious*' ambush."

Ambush Two was a narrow section of the road north, where the ridgeline to the west reached almost down to the wetlands and mangroves on the east. Someone or something had dug up the area, probably looking for civet poo, leaving behind what looked like shallow craters in the UAV recon imagery. It looked like the perfect place to set up a second ambush.

Or did it?

Kat gave Mike her threat assessment. "He's going to be looking for us there. If we take up positions in that cratered area and he then deploys to flank us, we'll be seriously screwed. Ellis's ship has auto-cannons, but even a couple of small mortars could saturate that area, and we'll then be stuck, taking the incoming fire. These locals won't handle it. They'd run, and get shot down as they do."

"So, if we skip that location, where do we hit him next?" he asked, as soon as Kat stopped speaking.

"Don't laugh at me until I've finished, okay?" she said, perhaps a bit defensively. "I see you've been herding goats today. Goats, pigs, anything with four legs I believe? Well, I'm thinking of putting them at one of the locations where there's already been digging, then covering it sufficiently so that Melnik or Ellis can't get a clear visual on them, but can get a trace heat-signature. I bet you ten bucks that our Captain Ellis and his stalwart crew will look pretty stupid after launching a full-scale attack, maybe with naval gunfire in support, against a collection of farmyard animals!"

Mike chuckled. "That would certainly be humiliating. And if we did a little battlefield preparation here and there, he might have a casualty or two to show for his efforts."

"No, I'd rather not use explosives," Kat said. She wasn't ready for this next evolution to get deadly. Not yet anyway."

"Understood."

"I'm looking for an alternative location," said Kat. I see a couple of options, but we can get into the details tomorrow. I suggest we all get some rest."

"Hard to believe that we're actually following a plan and somehow its surviving *'contact with the enemy!'*" Mike said with a grin. "Sleep tight, Princess."

Kat nodded. Mike's words fresh in her ears. A plan that works. Freakin amazing! But further back in her head was the old von Clausewitz quote she'd learnt at OTA(F), 'No plan survives contact with the enemy.'

Well, this time, theirs had. Well, so far anyway!

Was that good? Or did it just mean that when everything did eventually fall apart, it would be an even bigger mess?

Now that Kat had so many local volunteers supplementing her Land Force Infantry, she might have to consider spreading them out, have small formations covering all of the nearby coconut plantations until it was more apparent as to what Melnik was truly intending.

Tonight, she had them sleeping rough in improvised shelters out in the rainforest. Although it significantly reduced the likelihood of multiple casualties if they got attacked, it also meant she couldn't talk to all her people easily. Their morale, mind-set and skill-set would all remain an 'unknown' for her to fathom in the morning, and unsurprisingly she didn't like that at all.

The alternative was to concentrate them together, and although that made communication considerably easier, it was much harder to conceal their combined movement, and it also intensified their thermal signature.

As for Ellis, he'd been very quiet since he'd fired that salvo of seventy-five millimetre auto-cannon just after dawn. Now she'd stopped for the evening, would he use that opportunity to engage her again, to send another fire mission in her direction?

New battle, but the same old worries. Kat rolled over, feeling the armour adjust around her, and tried to sleep.

She hadn't spent a night out under the stars in full body armour since Cayman Brac and OTA(F) before that. The Chameleon battle-suit had an internal body temperature regulator and once you hit the 'sleep' function on the control panel the 'night thermostat,' that stored the energy that her moving body generated during the day, kicked in and the graphene layering within the suit converted that same energy back into the optimal environment for sleep. Apparently, the hard armour that usually provided ballistic protection also softened and reformed into something more comfortable for lying down in.

Despite her scepticism of the suit's capability, combined with her growing anxiety of the evolving ground situation, sleep actually came to her quickly. There would be plenty of time for worrying in the morning.

Major Andrev Melnik mopped his forehead, then glanced up at the clear blue sky. It was only ten-hundred hours but the temperature was already into the low thirties and the humidity was intense.

"Medic!" came from his left flank.

That was the third time this morning. Melnik signalled the column to halt. Kapten Sarikan pointed to where a group of his men were gathered around one who was screaming like a child.

"Watch your step," Melnik snarlerd. "Break your legs and I'll leave you where you fall."

The islanders sensibly moved at a slower pace, their eyes fixed on the ground.

"This is ridiculous," Melnik said.

"I agree. The island itself is depleting our numbers, without any help from the Severn girl."

"Tell me something I don't know," Melnik snapped. He reviewed their formation. It was standard. Second Platoon was scattered in the vanguard about a kilometre ahead. Third Platoon was patrolling along their left flank about five-hundred metres away through the tall palm-trees of a coconut plantation. First Platoon covered their right, about the same distance out. His own people were now with him, escorting the islanders being held as hostages.

Casualties were already adding up amongst the Hai PSC personnel and the battle hadn't even started! Melnik didn't know much about the Severn girl, but from what he'd seen so far, she was good at driving competent officers to insanity!

Melnik squatted down in the limited shadow cast by a coconut palm and projected a three-dimensional map ahead of him. Kapten Sarikan, still standing, edged the toe of his boot in, indicating a location.

"Yes," Melnik nodded. "I agree. I would probably set up an ambush there too."

The projection showed a track twisting around the boundary of another coconut plantation several kilometres ahead, followed by yet more mangrove, wetlands and rainforest. The irrigation ditches running around the perimeter of the rows of palm-trees looked like ready-made trenches.

The excavations didn't look new. "I'll request a thermal scan of this area from Ellis," Melnik said.

"His thermal scans haven't been of very much use so far," Sarikan pointed out. "No hint as to where that Severn girl and her people are. No warning of that sniper fire at the causeway either. A blind man could have done better."

"Maybe she'll get lucky. Maybe we'll get lucky," Melnik answered, staring out across the plantation and thinking.

We got ambushed. Fact. We were subjected to highly accurate sniper fire. Fact. But no automatic fire. The vehicles were made inoperable by single shots. Automatic fire would have shredded the tires of the vehicles too, but it would also have put holes into the troops nearby. No holes in the trucks, other than the tires and propulsion units, and no holes in my troops. Some very good shooting. And no thermal heat sources picked up on Ellis's scanners. Who could shoot that fast, that accurately, and had battle-suits that didn't give off any heat signature?

Melnik pursed his lips. "ABCANZ Land Force

Infantry. Maybe their Special Ops," he whispered.

Kat watched as Mike's borrowed vehicle approached her after cresting the track running down from the top of the adjacent hill. At the base was a shallow stream, fed from the more distant rainforest covered peaks, that it easily splashed through.

His vehicle came to a halt. The window was already down. Its air-conditioning hadn't worked at any time in the last decade, perhaps longer.

"Where are your troops?" she asked him.

"I didn't see much point in bringing Sergeant Varko and Corporal Groucutt's Squad in here. They're out with the islanders, preparing defensive positions along those irrigation ditches."

Kat nodded at his explanation. Mike may have only been in the military for a short period, but he'd been at her side much longer and she trusted his judgement.

"They're moving their goats and other livestock up too."

Kat shook her head. "The locals are all up for a fight, but they don't have any concept at all as to how dear the cost might be."

"The likely 'butcher's bill' is rarely considered," Mike agreed.

"Well, they need to freakin' consider it!. Otherwise they won't stand. They'll run as soon as the first casualties are taken amongst them," Kat said. *Just once, I'd like to lead a real command with regular, professional, trained troops.*

How could she forget, she had occasionally done exactly that, just not very often. On Cayman Brac and more recently in Emirates City, although the latter had technically been Lieutenant Harb's command. And, they had been just as eager for the shooting to start. But none had run at the first casualty. Land Force Infantry would never do that. The islanders she now had, eagerly volunteering to assist her, were another matter entirely.

"Gillan's due to send an update any minute. Let's see what the good Captain has to offer us," Kat said, changing the topic of conversation.

Captain Gillan was right on schedule, and greeted them both cheerfully, as someone might who had slept in his own bed and eaten breakfast made with fresh produce from his very own galley. Kat tried hard not to grumble, her battle suit hadn't been all that bad. Her breakfast however had been the contents of an Individual Field Ration or IFR and some of the locally baked bread. She and Mike had dined exclusively on IFRs when moving the Remote Operational Support Platform 3-Alpha-9 from Tristan da Cunha to Cape Town after she'd taken command. That certainly wasn't something that her digestive system needed to repeat, not for a protracted period anyway, ever again.

That was one of several reasons why she had joined the ABCANZ Fleet and not their Ground Forces. Eating IFR, digging holes and sleeping in ditches wasn't Kat's idea of fun.

"Major Melnik appears to have spent the night at the far end of the causeway, opposite end to the airfield, and has since dawn, been moving westward," Gillan advised.

Mike ran his fingers over the imagery displayed on his TDT. "He's deploying his Private Security Contractors on the flanks and in the vanguard, with his own people in the centre. Looks like he's using the islanders for mules."

"Did you booby-trap that track?" Kat asked Mike.

"No. There are hundreds of small holes either side of it already, so plenty of options to trip up, twist an ankle, even break a leg. It will be hard going on foot if you're not on the actual track." Mike then waited for the image to refresh. "It doesn't seem like they're moving with any great urgency."

Kat nodded, satisfied that a certain Major wasn't having a good day, then switched her attention slightly further north.

It was easy to spot their defensive preparations where the irrigation ditches that enclosed the coconut plantations were, and the improvised fortifications that Sergeant Varko and Corporal Groucutt were helping the locals install. They were far more extensive that Kat had expected them to be.

"I've got them split into two groups. Corporal

Groucutt is supervising the ditch enhancements. Sergeant Varko is further down the track selecting a location to set up an OP, and an extraction route without becoming a casualty himself. There's a sensor drone that passes overhead approximately every two hours, so we have to take cover until it has passed by. Lance Corporal Jarvis's scanner tells us when it's approaching."

"Are you using that nearby farmstead to hide in when Ellis's drone is overhead?" Kat asked Mike.

"Yes, the main barn is plenty big enough. After the culvert's destruction in the swamp, Ellis and Melnik certainly know we have forces ashore, but not in what strength, and our local volunteers are still totally unknown to them."

"And, 'war hath no fury like a non-combatant.' I remember hearing that someplace. These islanders are carrying hunting rifles, but none of them have ever fired a shot at another person before." Kat wasn't sure where she was going with this, but knew she was getting tired of waiting.

"Some of my volunteers are naively talking about 'taking no prisoners' and 'fighting to the last man, or woman,'" said Mike.

Staff Freeman had reported similar talk amongst the locals he had done some basic tactics and weapon competency training with, following their trip into Campbell Bay. Kat hadn't heard it herself, at least not from the Mahaapaur and the older locals she'd talked to. "You've explained to them that's not the way we fight? Slaughtering prisoners is not only stupid, but against all the conventions that govern how war is fought?"

"Of course, but I'm not sure they're listening. They don't want this to happen again. So, they figure that by completely eradicating this bunch it will send a clear message, 'Don't mess with us.'"

Kat shook her head. "Don't they understand, most of these troops, the Private Security Contractors and the mercenaries, are 'rented.' If we send them back to Thailand and wherever else they've come from grumbling about the 'savages' that inhabit these islands, then what started as a low budget little excursion by some get-rich-quick entrepreneurs could quickly escalate into a full-scale bloody vendetta."

"I know that. You know that. But how do we make them understand that? I'm assuming you're trying to manoeuvre this into a well-managed surrender, the less blood spilt the better? Like you did against Gus in Cape Town?"

"I must admit, that's not an unattractive solution," Kat said.

One thing at a time.

"I've ordered the 'zoo' that the locals insisted on bringing with them, to take cover every time Ellis's sensor drone is due to pass by. My best guess is that they'll be at those irrigation ditches by noon."

"Okay, and no use of fragmentation grenades or explosives. Not yet."

"Ellis is going to regret the day he didn't load his people back onto that transport ship and make for open waters when you came to this island."

"Really? You don't know him like I do, Mike. He was never going to do that. That's not how he operates. I don't think he's ever had a single regret in his life, about anything, ever."

Mike took a deep sigh. "So that isn't something you'd take a bet on? Not at any odds."

"Nope. I wish it was. But not Ellis."

Ellis contacted Melnik directly, not waiting for the next scheduled sit-rep. "Major, what's taking you so long. "You've hardly moved more than a couple of kilometres since dawn."

"All things considered, I think we're doing well to have achieved that, actually Captain."

"Then you need to but a boot up the backsides of your troops," Ellis replied. "Get them moving faster, Major."

"I need them to look carefully where they plant their boots actually," Melnik answered, then enlightened the maritime element of their operation on what the land component was facing.

"The locals are digging those holes, so start shooting some hostages," Ellis said, with no regard for the morality of what he was suggesting. Ellis was always harping on about professionalism, being a true warrior, yet as far as Melnik was concerned, shooting civilian hostages was not the way a professional military operated. Von Brühl's antics in Emirates City had recently reminded him of that.

"I can't, as I haven't actually seen any locals digging the holes. Some islanders I have here insist its natural geology, whilst others are suggesting it's done by those cat-racoon things whose crap is so damn valuable."

Ellis scowled at Badali. He'd taken to summoning the businessman to the *Hyperion*'s bridge whenever he talked with Melnik.

"Those pharmaceutical extracts could still bail us out," Badali said. "The quantity we have already 'obtained' is approximately the equivalent of four years of harvesting, and it has been loaded into the transport ship. Even if we withdrew immediately, it will easily cover our costs here, perhaps with a small profit."

"I don't care about your damn profit," Ellis snapped. "I want to know if these creatures are digging the holes that are causing problems for our infantry. Did they dig the holes our people are stepping in?"

"How should I know," the representative of the expedition's financiers said with a dismissive shrug. "We buy whatever comes to market. We don't care how it came to get there or what it looks like in its native form or environment. Repulsive as this stuff so evidently is, Captain Ellis, it is quite irrelevant to me where it comes from or the behavioural habits of whatever creature might create it."

Again, Ellis noted how different a businessmen and a true warrior's perspective was. And how poorly prepared the intelligence had been for this operation. Next time he did something like this . . .

But before 'next time.' Ellis had to finish the current. He pounded his comm-link. "Mr Badali is, once again, a veritable fountain of ignorance. We'll widen our sensor parameters and see if we can identify who or what is doing the digging that is impeding your advance, Major."

"I've already looked ahead with what you've provided so far."

"It doesn't look like very much," the *Hyperion*'s Captain conceded.

There was a long pause before Melnik replied. "You're right, it isn't. Someone has to be in those hills watching us. I've studied all the feeds you're sending. I see the occasional thermal signature, under bushes and in the trees ahead of us, and on a parallel course, sometimes along the route of this track and in the surrounding fields and ditches."

"Agreed, Major. I see them too. Unfortunately, they are too spread out for an auto-cannon salvo," Ellis advised, deciding not to mention that he also wanted to conserve ammunition until he had a target significant enough to warrant its use.

"Maybe consider a rolling barrage?" Melnik offered.

"As soon as the sensor drone moves on, they probably start moving about again," Badali offered.

"You know that for certain, sir?" Melnik said.

"No, absolutely not. I don't know anything for certain," came back in his crestfallen voice.

"Thank you for you input, sir, but I really don't need any half-baked speculation from offshore," Melnik said. "They haven't moved onto the causeway, so aren't directly behind us. They seem to be skirting around the eastern side of the swamp, through the rainforest."

"But if they do move onto the track behind you, that will physically cut your withdrawal route, and they may then move in to attack your rear." Ellis knew he was stating the obvious, but wanted to assess the morale of his land component. Officers who lost the fighting spirit started looking over their shoulders for ghosts on their flanks and rear.

"Not a problem. My supplies of water, rations and ammo are being transported by the local hostages we have with us. Once I destroy Severn's main force I can easily sweep up any remnants on my way back into town. They'd still have to either cross the gap blown in the causeway, just as we had to, to intercept us, or advance through the open wetlands on either side, before they can effectively get at our rear."

"Assuming that her main force is actually the one ahead of us and not this other activity?" Sarikan added.

"True, there is that Kapten Sarikan, there is that," Melnik said to his subordinate. "Well Captain Ellis, if you don't have anything else, my latest fractured ankle case is now splinted and medicated and we are ready to move on again. I assume everything is quiet out at sea?"

"Yes, nothing is happening out here."

"Very well," said Melnik, then cut the link.

"They have no idea! Whining on about nothing!" Major Melnik growled as soon as he was sure his comm-link was silenced.

Ellis's dismissive and callous disregard towards the killing of the hostages was reckless. Melnik had initially suggested it to get leverage on the islanders, but had never intended to actually carry it out. Ellis, however, seemed to relish the idea.

This entire operation was balanced on a knife edge. Killing the locals would contribute nothing to winning this battle. And, if matters did not go as well as Ellis was so sure they would, Melnik would be the one trying very hard to remind this Lieutenant Severn that he respected and upheld the articles that made up the Geneva Convention, even if a certain Captain Ellis had not. It would not be easy to claim that, if he was standing there with his hands covered in the blood of the islanders, physically or metaphorically.

The contract between them was clear to him. If they killed one of his men, he would reluctantly execute some of them in retaliation. But so far, the Severn girl had gone out of her way to ensure his troops remained alive. Melnik decided that he would not be the one to change that tacit agreement between them. Not now. Not when things were, if anything, going her way more than his.

Kapten Sarikan brought Melnik back from his

thoughts. "And he insulted us. Suggesting that we were worried about that other group attacking our rear. He, who hasn't offered us a single baht of proof, that there is anything ahead of us," the Private Security Contractor's senior Officer spat angrily.

"Be careful what you say in front of your men, Kapten. You don't want them thinking that we don't know what we're doing."

Sarikan looked over his shoulder at his men. Their eyes might be looking elsewhere, but their ears?

"But we don't," he whispered to Melnik.

"I know that. You know that, but we must not have anyone else thinking that. Put you game face on," Melnik ordered, glancing up at the blue, cloudless sky. The sun continued to glare down at him.

He looked at the projected map again, then stabbed his finger at what he saw."

"There. There is heat. See Sarikan. See that . . . troops in trenches."

The Hai PSC Officer repositioned himself to look at the imagery from the same angle as his commander. "No visuals of people though, just more heat amongst the bushes and trees," he pointed out.

"But that is a linear feature. There are thermal traces here," Melnik said, waving at the projection, "and there are agricultural irrigation ditches all along here. But that particular one now has a linear thermal trace right along it."

"Do we attack them this afternoon?" Sarikan asked.

Melnik measured the distance, both cross-country, over the hills and through the rainforest and then using the winding track-way. Then he checked the weather. He shook his head.

"No, too far to go, and our troops are hot and tired. And, the faster we push them, the more likely they are to step into these damn 'rabbit holes' or whatever you want to call them. No, we will make camp around here tonight," he said pointing again at the image. "That's about four kilometres from them. We will get up early and patrol in under the cover and coolness of the early morning rain."

Sarikan grinned, then nodded. "It's high time we started dictating what the dance will be."

SIX : ELEVEN

As Kat spread her Detachment over two adjacent farmsteads for the evening, she also had two problems to consider. (1) How to get the most out of tomorrow's fire-fight at the newly enhanced irrigation ditches. And (2), the quality of the island volunteers and their actual behaviour in a real fire-fight. She was pretty certain that neither problem would be resolved tonight, however, tonight was all the time she had left to put a plan together.

She started with a small, informal orders group with Mike, Staff Freeman and Sergeant Varko.

As soon as she'd finished the final 'command and signal' section against the 'Service Support' heading, she asked if any of them had any bright ideas, given their somewhat limited resources, for achieving human 'eyes-on' command and control over the opening stages of the impending engagement.

Sergeant Varko immediately offered a suggestion. "Ma'am, if your HI would be kind enough to give me pair of nanoUAVs, I think I can make things happen the way you want it, when the hostiles eventually advance-to-contact. Nothing fancy, just an 'alarm' function when they sense something's coming."

"I can program a pair of nanos to squeak so that only someone listening for that precise squeak could tell it isn't part of the rainforest's background noise. What sort of range, both for sensing movement and for positioning in front of the trench lines do you think you need, Sergeant?" Safi asked him primly.

Mike failed to hide a grin. Kat just shook her head. Safi was developing yet another personality. Every time Kat now spoke with Safi she didn't know which one she was going to get! Some might consider that to be 'fun,' but did it mean that her Heuristic Intellect was becoming inconsistent? Inconsistency could easily mean 'unreliable' too!

But Sergeant Varko was having no such problem. "Five hundred metres for sensing movement, and the same for maximum distance in front of the trench, should do it. Include motion sensors, both for air and water, please. If I was attacking that improvised trench-line, I'd have their battle-suited infantry try to infiltrate in from the flanks, along the actual irrigation ditches themselves. And, I'd also like the ability to remotely set-off all the trip-flares we'll put out, even if their wires haven't actually been triggered. If I understand your intent correctly, your Highness, the objective is to undermine their Officer's credibility with their own troops. Any self-inflicted casualties they might take are just icing on the cake."

Mike looked at Kat, who was grinning happily.

"Yes, Sergeant," Mike said. "You have understood your Commander's Intent correctly."

"Safi, how long do you need to assemble these nanos?" Kat asked.

"Not long, the mechanical requirement is basic and the operating software is something we've used before, so I won't need time to create anything original."

As answers went, it wasn't precise enough for Kat. It was way too vague and didn't actually answer her question. Safi was picking up far too many bad habits from a certain eleven-year-old girl who now infested Kat's ship.

For a brief moment, she wondered how Grace was doing, with her principal teacher ashore and wrapped around Kat's collar-bone. The girl had probably spent the time wrapping Professor Brooks and his helpless boffins round her little finger instead. Children did not belong on warships. She would have to do something about that.

And she would, just as soon as she got Melnik and Ellis to leave Great Nicobar . . . and then decided what to do about the illegal settlers on North Sentinel Island!

She had come to these waters to explore and dispense justice, which she was doing, but she couldn't forget that particular crowd of deluded individuals. Something about their hidden existence just didn't feel right. Kat couldn't put her finger on exactly what right now, but hoped that by the time she paid them a return visit, she'd figured out just what that elusive 'something' was. And, hopefully a palatable solution for young Grace would present itself too. But . . . both of those conundrums were going on hold until the current 'distraction' in the rainforests of Great Nicobar was resolved.

"Sergeant Varko, could you hold out your TDT, please," Safi said a few minutes later.

The senior SNCO did as he'd been told.

"I've transmitted the operating sub-routines into your device. Please familiarise yourself with them, so you can operate the nanoUAVs once I have finished their assembly. I do wish the military procured more capable equipment."

"Safi!" Kat said.

"Yes, Kat. Maybe you should pay for enhancements, so your Officers and senior NCOs have more suitable equipment."

"Stand down," Kat ordered her HI.

"I am not in the Fleet, therefore you cannot order me around."

"Don't bet on that lasting indefinitely," Mike said, giving Kat an evil grin. "If she takes her mind to it, Kat might draft you too!"

"Advanced Heuristic Intellects such as myself do have some basic rights. Not Human Rights, but certainly Civil Rights," Safi said primly, then paused for several seconds. "Mike had Human Rights, yet you still managed to draft him. Although I have some basic Civil Rights, you still might be able to draft me. I need to ruminate on this matter again."

Safi's voice was back to the basic, the standard one she used when devoting considerable amounts of her processing capacity to something a mere human would find way beyond complicated.

"They'll be awarding 'Rights' to 'imaginary friends' before you know it!" muttered Kat to nobody in particular.

"Safi," Staff Freeman said, "you do know that you're

an important part of this team, and all of us, both Fleet and Land Force, we really respect and appreciate what you do for us?"

"You do?" It was still her basic voice.

"We certainly do. Now, does Sergeant Varko need any help with his nanos?"

At OTA(F) Kat had learned that senior NCOs were more like a deity than most humans who believed in such things, thought a deity was. And that NCOs made a point to look out, first and foremost, for their subordinate troops. Staff Freeman was more 'hands-on' than any recent apparition of a more traditional 'divine being' ever was. His attention was usually to the surprise and often the dismay of his minions.

Right now, Kat watched the Staff Sergeant in full transcendent concern for Sergeant Varko and all his trigger-pullers.

"No, Sergeant Varko is good to go," Safi said, starting to sound a bit more normal. "I'll need another ten minutes to finish the UAV assembly."

Sergeant Varko nodded. "I'll be waiting. I'll get my TDT to cycle them through a series of tests and check everything is working as soon as they're available."

As the Sergeant sat to wait for Safi to finish, Kat glanced around the large barn she expected to spend the night in. Like many of the other buildings she'd seen on the island, it was constructed from timber with a corrugated metal roof, a low-cost and efficient design that hadn't changed in several hundred years.

One of the last vehicles to arrive that evening had disgorged the Mahaapaur and Mrs Lakhera. Kat couldn't name the other grey-haired people that accompanied them, but she suspected someone had called a meeting of the town council or whatever name the local convening of those in authority went by. Evidently, they had forgotten to copy Kat in on the notification.

Bales of coir fibre, this island's equivalent of hay or straw, were being arranged into some kind of circle. Grey-haired heads were settling into their improvised seats. Kat had rejected politics as her chosen career, but she did have some experience of such proceedings.

Mrs Lakhera joined Kat. "I am very sorry about this. The Mahaapaur, he insisted. It has taken us most of the day to get here, now that the causeway is impassable, we had to go on a much longer journey, using the old way, to get around the wetlands."

"Let's get this over with," Kat said with a sigh and a shake of her head, and led the hotel owner to where the speaker's rostrum would be located, had this been a more conventional setting.

Kat stood at 'stand easy,' or 'parade rest,' and let her eyes rove across the people getting seated before her. Mrs Lakhera took a nearby bale to be seated on.

Clearing her throat, Kat then asked, "Do you have questions for me?"

The initial silence gave way to murmurs as heads turned to those seated each side of them. Not one of them stood to take the lead in the proceedings. *Have I made my move too soon? Before they are ready, or still have differing views that haven't yet coalesced into a common consensus?*

Maybe a 'common consensus' wasn't a concept they understood? Great Nicobar had no government in the conventional sense. Defined by the Indian Government as a 'Union Territory,' it therefore had no Federal Administration like the Indian states of the mainland. It was theoretically run directly from India's national capital, via this island chain's capital, Port Blair. However, the reality was that Campbell Bay, although only around three hundred nautical miles to the south of Port Blair, with a resident population of around five thousand people, was left . . . left to effectively govern itself.

Kat hoped she wasn't going to have to teach a whole lot of reluctant souls 'How to arrive at a common consensus and then make a decision 101.'

"We hear there is going to be a fight tomorrow, up the track from here," one of the other grey-haired individuals said in accented English. "Why out here? Why not back in town?"

"Yes, there will be a 'contact' with the hostile formations that have landed on this island," Kat informed him, "but we . . . you . . . aren't going to be part of it."

"It's quite a while since I wore a uniform," the Mahaapaur said, "but don't you need two adversarial participants for a 'contact.'"

Kat acknowledged him with a nod. "If you want to go down in the history files as a great conqueror, it certainly does help if some opposition turns up for the fight and duly gets their butts kicked in the process."

A second or two of laughter was the response Kat had hoped for. "Us turning up tomorrow serves nobody's benefit, except perhaps Major Melnik's. His dawn attack on a menagerie of farmyard animals should undermine his credibility with both his subordinates and his superiors, as well as a wider audience. Especially if it reaches the social media, don't you think?"

Many of the elders were nodding and smiling.

"You can't win a battle unless you fight one," the Mahaapaur said when Kat had finished speaking.

"I agree, sir, you can't. And depending on how fast Melnik regroups from our little joke, we should be engaged by late tomorrow or maybe early the day after," Kat told him.

Now she had everyone's attention.

"When are we going to kill them?" Another old man asked.

Kat didn't like the question. It presumed rather a lot. That they would be *able* to kill them, and that they would *want* to kill.

This old man evidently had no doubt about either.

Kat did not share his confidence.

Kat commanded about twenty assault rifles, plus a half-dozen squad support weapons, three jackhammer rocket launchers and a handful of other specialist 'toys,' but it was still only about a quarter of those Melnik could muster. His PSC's equipment might be old and there were no larger calibre support weapons evident, but his mercenary Platoon was just as well equipped and protected as Kat's detachment was.

If she had doubts about the capability of Melnik's PSCs, then Kat suspected that the Major probably had doubts about his private-security-contractors too. No question, Kat certainly had multiple doubts about the civilians who had attached themselves to her.

Like most civilians, Kat finished university 'knowing' that the military turned their troops into trained automatons who did exactly what they were ordered to.

It hadn't taken her very long at OTA(F) to unlearn that.

Soldiers and sailors had to be able to do their jobs without thought for one simple reason. They had to load, aim and fire without thought when their brains were numb, or shocked, or horrified, by what they saw. They had to keep doing it, until they'd brought themselves out of the hell that made thinking impossible. Trained, instinctive responses and actions were their only hope of survival in such an environment!

These civilians might have rifles, and they did have their homes to defend, if not liberate, but they had little or no training. They'd probably be good for their first shot. Maybe a second. Perhaps a third.

But sooner or later. They'd run. They'd want to run. In the noise and blood and screams, they'd forget why they came. They'd forget everything but their desire to be somewhere, anywhere, else.

Maybe not all. Maybe a few would find what it took. How many? Victory would go to whichever side held on for a second longer than the other.

Another factor to consider was that once they started "killing" they no longer had the 'moral high-ground.' That might not be important to the islanders, but it was to Kat.

Kat eyed the old man. He was so sure he knew what tomorrow would bring, but was actually so ignorant of it. She took a deep breath.

"We'll fight Melnik among the irrigation ditches of the location shown on the mapping as Pandit's farm," she said.

"So that's where we'll massacre them."

Kat chose to ignore that comment. "I'll have my people engage the Private-Security-Contractors with aimed shots at arms and legs. Those of you with hunting rifles can take on the professional mercenaries, all those in full battle-armour."

"But our old guns won't be enough to penetrate their armour," the old man jumped in exactly where Kat had expected him to. She ignored him for a moment to study the reaction of others around the barn. The old man had plenty who agreed with him. About half. But the other half looked more confused than actually siding with Kat.

"From painful personal experience," Kat said with a reinforcing wince, "I, and Ensign Steiger here, can tell you that bullets, even those that don't get through protective armour, can leave you black-and-blue underneath and quite disorientated. That is what I want. The Private Security Contractors with superficial wounds to their arms and legs, and those in body armour to be very much aware that they've been hit and both having a tough time finding something to shoot back at. Five minutes of that and Major Melnik should be ready to listen to any offer for his surrender."

"But I want them dead. All of them," the old man shouted.

"Evidently," said Kat.

"We don't want them coming back with reinforcements."

"This island is our home. We must defend it, so why not kill them for trying to take it," said another.

Kat said nothing for a long minute while the 'war' faction blew itself out. She looked for the Mahaapaur and Mrs Lakhera. They both looked puzzled, but not quite ready to join their colleague in shouting for blood. Finally, the Mahaapaur stood up and the room quickly went silent.

"When we were fighting the Chinese, back in the war, there wasn't a lot of prisoner taking. Not by us, not by them. So, I am most curious about this idea you have, Miss Severn. I recall your grandfather only being happy with dead

Chinese."

Kat nodded. "Maybe in that war there wasn't much room for anything but a lot of dead bodies. We all came close to being dead when it went nuclear." Even some of the hotheads nodded along with Kat on that.

The old man who wanted nothing but death to their unwanted visitors just scowled.

"Smart Commanders know that the easiest way to get an enemy off your patch of land is to threaten their line of withdrawal. Threaten to make it impossible for them to go home. A really smart Commander, when he or she fights, is careful to leave a hole somewhere so that the enemy can run away."

"So that's it," the old man hardly looked able to get his words out past his rage. "They've occupied our town, destroyed our property, killed anyone that resisted, and you want to let them run away?"

Kat shook her head. "Of course not. My intention is to have Major Melnik surrender to us. To have his troops lay down their arms and become our prisoners. That is what the Law of Armed Conflict requires of me."

"Of you?" this was the Mahaapaur's question.

"I am a serving Officer of the ANCANZ Fleet. Despite being rented mercenaries and hired-in Private-Security-Contractors, they are all in uniform. To date, in the current situation, they have followed the laws that govern how armed conflict is conducted. So therefore, they deserve to be treated appropriately under such laws, should they surrender, be taken prisoner, become wounded, or even die. I request that you too, abide by the same protocols. I have to take the moral high-ground, otherwise I am no better than they are. If I, if we, adhere to such laws, the international courts will support us."

"I want them dead," the old man said again.

"How high a price are you and this island's community willing to pay for that?" Kat asked softly.

"We kill them. That's the end of them. Simple," the old man snorted.

"Are you sure about that?" Kat asked.

"What do you mean? Dead is dead." But the old man wasn't sounding so sure anymore.

"What do you know that we don't?" the Mahaapaur asked Kat.

"Actually, it's what we both don't know," Kat replied. "What do you know about the latest alliances among the city states of northern India along the border with China?"

"I don't even know we had city states," admitted Mrs Lakhera. "What kind of alliances do they have?"

"Ever shifting ones. Officially they support your national leaders and government in Nay Dilli, but with such a powerful neighbour they don't want to appear openly hostile. I'm not all that up-to-date on who's sympathetic to whom right now. I don't have exact data as to who is trying to gain power, or who is afraid of losing it, as we are trying to keep our own data transmissions to a minimum, but, even if we weren't, monitoring the political situation along that border is a full-time job!"

That didn't help. Around the barn a lot more people frowned, not understanding the relevance of her example. It had been way too abstract for insular people who had lived their entire lives on a tiny tropical island. For a few, faced with the idea that a Severn might not know everything, it began to dawn on them that they might not know it all either.

And what they didn't know . . . might hurt them.

"So, here's the deal folks. Let's say that a story comes back to whoever hired these mercenaries and PSCs, that a bunch of godless, barbarians on this remote little island just slaughtered three platoons of Thailand's finest," Kat started.

To be interrupted by, "We are all god-fearing Hindus or Christians."

"Ah," Kat said, raising a finger to make her point, "But are you the right kind of believer? Especially to a Theravada Buddist."

Murmurs grew around the barn as the situation took on a different dimension.

"So probably not a good idea if we used the blood and bones of these invaders to fertilise our crops," the

Mahaapaur said.

"It might amount to nothing at all, Kat told him. "Only a fool tells you he or she knows *exactly* what anyone is going to do. And, Thailand has a population of what, about seventy million?" She shrugged. "Look at what someone had told Melnik about how easy it would be to take control of Campbell Bay. 'They're *only* agri-farmers.'"

The barn became very quiet.

Kat spoke her next words softly. The old people leaned forward to hear her better. "There are several patterns in history that repeat. The religious missionaries come. The missionaries get killed by an uncomprehending or resentful local population. A revengeful army gets sent. Houses and crops get burned. Native populations get killed. The flag . . . the ideals that it represents, that comes last. Suddenly the local population find themselves with an Empress, a Kaiser, or a President that they never voted for. And that's not as 'ancient history' as you might think. Territory appropriation, and to hell with what the local population might want, is still happening or at least being attempted." She paused, looking slowly around at the attentive faces. "And *their* idea of what an individual can or can't do . . . how they dress and how they behave . . . what they say, even think . . . might not be as unrestricted as what you currently enjoy."

The barn didn't stay quiet after that. Kat turned back to Mike and Staff Freeman, leaving the islanders to talk that out amongst themselves.

"How much of that did you make up?" Mike whispered from behind the hand over his mouth.

"None, I think," Kat said. "At university I did a paper on European colonialism in the eighteenth and nineteenth century."

"You studied all that, ma'am?" Freeman asked.

"Yes, a bit. It was background context to my main studies."

The barn was full of heated conversation and stayed that way until the Mahaapaur stood. He got silence.

"Thirty something years ago, I came home after

fighting in the war against the Chinese. I tried to build a life for myself and for my family. I did not like others telling me, especially those who had not put their lives on the line during the fighting, what to do. Eventually I became the Mahaapaur here and encouraged like-minded people to find a home here," he said, looking around at the people gathered in the barn, and was clearly proud of what he saw. "I thought we could handle anything that came along, either individually, or collectively. Well, it looks like something bigger than us has finally come our way and I want you to know that I'm most happy to have the help of this young Severn." He turned to face Kat. "But I am not sure that we will agree about when the most opportune moment will be for you to leave us when you are finished here."

Kat did her best at a dramatic sigh. "I'll be adding Great Nicobar to the list of places where I've been thanked but told not to return to."

"Yes," he said, deadly serious. "I imagine that is a hard way to live, but you are the one doing it, not me."

For a moment, Kat felt the loneliness of what life would be like for someone so rooted to the fields and dirt of a remote little island.

For a moment, she felt the emptiness of her own life.

She shook her head, willed away the emotions. Right now, people depended on her. That was enough.

"Okay, young Severn, tell us what you would have us do." And with those words, the old man sat back down.

The barn's occupants still held its collective breath.

Kat took a moment, to let all that she'd heard and felt, soak through her . . . and out again. Done, she squared her shoulders, and said, "I want all of you to accept the surrender of anyone willing to throw down his or her weapons and put their hands in the air. I want you to respect any white flag, calls for quarter or anything remotely close."

The old man who wanted nothing but total war was back on his feet. "And what do we do with them then. Wrap them up with a pretty bow and invite them home for dinner."

"No," Kat snapped. "Absolutely not," she added for

emphasis. Because this audience needed all the emphasis she could muster!

"Then what do we do?" The Mahaapaur asked, standing again.

The angry old man already had his mouth open, ready to exchange more cross words with Kat. Only the Mahaapaur could have gotten him to shut his mouth, and he did, sitting back down.

"They owe us young Severn, they owe us," the Mahaapaur repeated as he too took his seat.

Kat wanted to fire something back, Quick, effective. She found she didn't have the right words even close to hand.

"They do present a very real problem," came from behind Kat. It was Staff Sergeant Freeman. "If I and my Detachment find ourselves in a bad place, even if we surrender, our connection to the ANCANZ Fed can't be broken. Anyone who accepts our surrender knows that . . . and also knows they have the ABCANZ Federation to deal with about us," he paused. He had their attention. "But these hostiles, although they might wear the uniform of their employer, they are hired guns, whether that be professional mercenaries or Private-Security-Contractors, in the employ of a private individual or a commercial entity, not a recognised international state or government. And that gives the likes of us Senior NCOs, a difficult problem."

Kat tuned around to face the Staff Sergeant. He gave her a wink.

"It seems to me this is something that an Officer might need to think further on."

"Thanks Staff," she whispered full of sarcasm, but he had given her time to think and define some limits. Kat turned back to the old islanders feeling almost confident that she had a solution.

"One of the recurring issues I keep hearing amongst the communities, legal or otherwise, of these islands is the reliance on manual labour, either because using clever tech gives away your location with GPS and or EMP signatures, for the illegal colonies, or that the economy-of-scale doesn't justify large-scale mech or tech investment on the officially settled islands. Great Nicobar . . . Port Campbell, sorry Tenlaa, after Port Blair, is one of the biggest, but is it really any different here?"

"No," the Mahaapaur said and it was echoed by the others.

"Without seeing the Private-Security-Contractor's contracts and the small-print contained within, the circumstances of a 'contractor being captured' are not known to me. They might forfeit their pay, or might be abandoned by the company and be 'on their own,' with the PSC's company not paying any demand for their release. Or perhaps even using the individual's own accrued pay to secure their release. I therefore don't see any reason why you shouldn't feel free to offer any of them that want to stay a job. Some might actively want alternative employment. It might be better here than wherever they originated from in Thailand. Those that want to go home can do exactly that."

"With their weapons?" The angry old man was back on his feet.

"No, just the clothes on their backs," Kat snapped back, her tone suggesting 'are you really that stupid!' She had it going her way. She didn't want to lose them now. "Their military equipment is forfeit and is yours. You can sell it if you want. Personally, I'd keep it, use it to better equip yourselves."

The murmurs that filled the room sounded like they might be reaching an agreement.

"What about their officers? Those who have been giving the orders," the angry old man shouted as soon as the background noise let him. "Are we going to let them get off with just some hard labour?"

Kat had hoped that this question might get overlooked in the interest of getting a few things settled. She could get to really dislike this belligerent old man.

"No," Kat said, already reading which way the room was thinking. Damn it, if she'd wanted to live by popularity polls she'd have gone into politics like her father and brother. They did their best to follow the will of the people, as often as not, the people were right.

Kat let her political instincts loose. "Their Officers have committed crimes against humanity, by the raising of arms against a peaceful people. As my prisoners, I would see that they face such charges and pay the consequences."

"If you can do that, why can't we?" was the old man's comeback.

"Because these crimes were not planned here. They were planned elsewhere and whoever planned and financed them needs to understand the consequences . . . and think long and hard before they try something like this again. The legal mechanisms in numerous countries have failed to prevent this from happening, so they need a 'wake-up call' too. That's not to say you don't have a right to try them yourselves, although I think the Indian authorities, if they can ever fast-track this through their bureaucracy, may want to bring charges too and their authority will surpass yours, even you, most honourable Mahaapaur."

"That sounds more like a political solution that a legal one," the angry old man shot straight back.

"Maybe because it *is* partly a political problem," the Mahaapaur pointed out before Kat said anything. Having risen from his improvised chair again to speak, he continued to address those seated. "They got rid of the United Nations after the war, as it hadn't prevented another global conflict. Many of the good, humanitarian activity that it did was passed to NATO and that didn't work out too badly for the next thirty-two years, but when that also went, finding any kind of legislation that is legally binding in every country is now virtually non-existent. Political masters, particularly from countries that weren't members, wanted NATO to go, and eventually despite a long-argued resistance, it was disbanded a couple of years ago, as I recall. What has happened here is a direct result of that. Simple opportunism. A hostile action that the perpetrators knew would likely go unpunished, because there's nobody filling that policing or judicial role anymore."

"Exactly," replied Kat. Grateful that someone had finally understood where she was going with this discussion.

"You are not as isolated on this island as you may think. It turns out that most people don't like being told what to do, especially when it's by a non-elected quango thousands of kilometres away," Kat said.

That got a chuckle out of some.

"It gets lonely out here on our own, especially since the pirate activity stopped the other trading and tourist ships from calling in," the Mahaapaur said. "I guess that if you work hard to make a place good, others might notice, and then you need to be ready to protect it, or others may come to try and steal it from you."

The proud old Mahaapaur looked around, saw a sad kind of agreement in the eyes of his old friends looking back at him. He nodded before going on. "What is this ABCANZ Federation about, and how can we join it?"

"As far as I know, there is no membership fee," Kat said, and immediately knew she'd missed his point.

"Everything has a price, young Severn. We are learning our freedom has a price, and we are not paying our dues. Now we'll potentially pay the full price with our blood, our lives! What price is your old fart grandpa asking?"

Kat took a second to scratch her ear. *Think.* Then she gave her usual answer. "I don't think you can become a member. You're an Indian 'union' territory. Therefore, you are part of India, and that's that, unless being a 'union' territory gives you some sort of different rights? But somehow, I don't think the Admiral who commands the Indian Navy Station on Great Andaman, and is I believe, this territory's notional Governor, will be any too pleased."

"Then he needs to provide us with better protection," the Mahaapaur said.

"That is for you to discuss with him or her, not with me, not my grandpa."

"Then that is what I will have to do," the Mahaapaur said.

"Try to keep my name out of it, please. I'm in enough trouble with my masters, both military and political," Kat said. Hopefully the Mahaapaur could see by the look on her face that she was serious.

It was Staff Freeman who stepped forward. "Ladies, gentlemen, who is going to win tomorrow and who is going to surrender isn't something we can't work out tonight, but if we don't get some sleep, it isn't going to help us any."

"Spoken like a true Senior NCO," the Mahaapaur said, and followed the Staff Sergeant in heading for somewhere to bed down for the night.

"You find somewhere too, ma'am," Freeman whispered as he passed close by to Kat. "Tomorrow will come soon enough."

Kat was getting more and more familiar with circumstances such as these. Somehow, she actually did get some sleep!

Major Melnik waited until Ellis's sensor drone had flown on, continuing its scheduled overhead sweep, before he formed his troops. He'd woken them before the drone came over, but left most of them in their bedrolls, so its thermal scan would show exactly what Ellis, and anyone else who happened to be watching, would be expecting.

As the troops made their way out of the improvised overnight camp, the dozen stay-behinds, those with damaged ankles and calves, along with the islander hostages kept the camp fires burning.

Maybe that Severn brat won't get any warning that my little army is on the move until it's too late!

It would be nice to have the luck break his way for a change. But ultimately, he knew that luck and hope could never pass for sound strategy, tactics and training.

Melnik assigned Kapten Sarikan command of his own mercenary formation. They'd take the 'wet' route and come out of the rainforest on the left flank of the irrigation ditches. Their sudden appearance would be a major surprise for the locals.

The Hai PSC personnel would take a more direct route, but they'd have to stay spread out. No matter how much Melnik pushed them, he doubted he could have them ready to assault the ditches before the sun came up. He'd have to keep them spread out, moving slowly, staying cool, in the early morning darkness, and doing their very best to stay out of sight.

Nobody had ever told Melnik that soldiering was easy. He wouldn't have taken the job if they had.

He had a tough leadership challenge today, and if he was honest, he was enjoying it. That Severn girl had been calling the shots for way too long. Now he'd play a few tunes and see how she liked dancing to his music!

Sergeant Varko had already identified a solid clump of waterlogged mud and a couple of bushes and trees, for his observation post or OP. It wasn't much, but it would do.

The murky, stinking water that swirled around his little island haven was deep, giving him a good place to withdraw to if he needed to hide for a while. And it gave him a reasonable view if he was reduced to using his own, human senses for intelligence gathering.

For the moment, and the range and endurance limit on Safi's nanoUAVs, he chose to use the MKI eyeball, unless he saw something interesting. He'd keep the nanos perched on his TDT, conserving their power.

It would be most acceptable if Safi talked Kat into getting the Detachment some better equipment. Not that the TDT and his comm-unit didn't do everything the Infantry branch of the ANCANZ Land Forces required of it. But, what the Director of Infantry expected of his troops and what a certain Princess demanded were not even close.

He shook that thought away. He needed to concentrate on the here and now, studying what lay before him in the light of the quarter moon. The light was fine, and he could smell and hear.

What he heard were small animals making nice, if not familiar noises. They had fallen silent upon his arrival, but now they were back to full volume. The smell was something all its own, no hint of man or anything man-made. Varko liked that.

What he saw was marsh grass, mirror flat water, unbroken by the wind. No, something just flopped into the shallow water. There was some thrashing, then the silence returned. Some other creature had gotten its breakfast.

Varko smiled grimly. Some much larger predators would be making much more noise, and very soon too.

He lay flat on his stomach, under a bush, ready to fit his breather and drop his visor, then lower himself into the water at the first sign of business. The Sergeant waited like some primal beast at the water's edge. Varko was patient.

Events would get lively soon enough.

Kat's NCOs roused the Detachment and had them move out as soon as Ellis's sensor drone had moved out of range. Outside the barn it was still dark, and ahead lay the last pair of farms that would keep them concealed from Ellis's sensors. They just needed to reach them before his drone came around again on another sweep.

Only ninety more minutes to keep up the game of 'not here.' After that they'd be in the open, and the 'cat,' or was that 'Kat,' would be 'out of the bag.'

Kat had to shake her head as she watched her task force form up on both sides of her into two parallel columns. The vehicles, with their main lights off, had a hard job keeping the required spacing of a military convoy.

Maybe not all the drivers were fully awake.

A local woman, her hair in two plaited pig-tails almost hit the vehicle next to her. The verbal comments in the local language didn't need any translation, and were no better or worse than the ones a guy who actually bumped the rig next to him received. Maybe all the shouting and cursing would put an end to their sleepy driving. The convoy eventually moved out and the 'bumper-car' competition ended.

A few minutes later Captain Gillan came back on line. "What's the latest," Kat asked him, once the usual pleasantries were exchanged.

"Someone is trying to jam us, and they've got the fires jacked up at their overnight camp. If I didn't know better, I'd say the cooks are planning to deliberately burn their breakfast.

"Or 'burn' your sensor scans,"

"They'll have more success with their own breakfast,

my crew and the Professor's team are on the job. Anyway, some of their bedrolls are occupied . . . warm. Most are rapidly cooling and a few are already cold. Sending you the latest imagery now." Gillan paused before going on. "You know, if I didn't already know that your regal-ness's current opposition are all a bunch of lazy bums, I'd speculate that they've already broken camp and were now out causing mischief on this fine morning."

"They're professionals . . . they'd never do such a thing," Kat said, letting sarcasm flood her answer. "Can you tell me where they really are?"

There was a long pause at that question. "I'm not sure that I can," Gillan finally said. "There's a faint thermal trace on the trackway heading towards the irrigation ditches, but I'm not sure if I hadn't drawn a line between their camp and the ditches that I'd have noticed it. They've figured out a way to keep themselves concealed from our thermal sensors.

"Dig a hole, put a thermal shield over it, and you'd be hard to see. Simple enough," Kat said.

"Ah, and there you go using words no self-respecting sailor would ever use. 'Dig a hole,' hide in the dirt. Not our way."

Kat suppressed a chuckle at the weird looks her vessel's Captain was getting from the local farmers who were close enough to see or hear the conversation. "Well how about this. It's going to get decisive in the not-too-distant future. I want you to reposition the *Bella* nearer to the island, but stay out of visual range of Ellis for now. Get yourself into a position that he could get a visual on you within a minute or two."

"So, I can pop into his weapon sights all 'sudden and accidental' and he might take a shot at me, not with any malice or intent, just kind of 'accidental.'"

"I didn't think you wanted those of us ashore to have all the fun," Kat chided him.

"Whatever gave you that idea? Be my guest, go on and have it all," Gillan offered.

"I have a course laid in," the *Bella*'s navigator advised. "Do you want us coming in on his stern, or ahead of him?"

"Let's allow for a stern chase," Kat said.

"Very well," Captain Gillan said, now deadly serious. "Position us for a *very long-distance* stern chase."

"Let me know if your sensors pick up anything new."

"We will, Gillan out."

Kat found herself alone once more in the early morning darkness, soon to be driving into a day not yet begun to dawn. But, before the sun went down again, all the questions now set before her would be answered.

SIX : TWELVE

Major Andrev Melnik spat out the dirt he'd nearly eaten as he tossed aside the thermal shield he'd being hiding under as soon as his Unterofficer with the tech-tablet called "sky's clear."

"Everyone up. Get moving. You're wasting the darkness," he shouted.

"Don't dismantle your thermal shields, leave them assembled," Melnik shouted at a PSC Private who had begun to do exactly that. Melnik was very aware that Majors do not correct Privates, however the three NCOs in close proximity were standing about doing nothing as at least one PSC Private destroyed his ability to hide quickly from overhead sensors.

"Koperals," Leftenan Diskul said, climbing out of the 'shell-scrape' or 'fox hole' he'd dug just behind the Major's. "See that the men keep their thermal shields assembled. These may not be the last holes we need to hide in."

"Yes, sir," the three junior NCOs answered and began moving among their troops, turning rolled-up sheets back into kite-like thermal reflectors.

"My apologies, Major," Diskul said. "The men had been briefed on the use of thermal shields, but not since we deployed ashore." Which was a polite way of reminding the Major that perhaps he should have issued said reminder.

Melnik hadn't. Nothing could be done about that now.

"Leftenan Diskul, your Platoon is in the centre. I want you to hit those ditches fast and hard, using a 'bounding overwatch.' One and Two Platoons will do the same on your flanks," Melnik said, glancing around. If they weren't exactly fumbling around with their brains in neutral, they certainly weren't moving towards the enemy. "What do you think of the idea that Three Platoon challenges One and Two in a race to those irrigation ditches?"

The Leftenan grinned. "Yes, sir. Sarjan Rattakul, form the men on me."

With only the briefest of pauses, to check the bearing on his combined compass-cum-GPS navigation-device, "Follow me," Leftenan Diskul said, altering course slightly to his left.

Major Melnik trotted off further to the right and found the Lieutenant commanding One Platoon. "Three Platoon says they intend to beat you to the irrigation ditches."

The Officer glanced up from where he and his Sarjan were sharing a mug of tea. "In his dreams," he said. The tea went into the grass and the Sarjan dashed off, shouting at his subordinate NCOs. In a minute or two they were formed and trotting off after Three Platoon.

Except for a pair of young Privates. One had stepped into a hole. The second had stayed behind to render assistance. Melnik paid them no attention. He was already looking for Two Platoon.

Someone had their eyes open. Two Platoon, with their Leftenan in the lead, was already trotting after the other two Platoons of the Company.

Major Melnik swung himself around and followed in the wake of Three Platoon. It was good to get this bunch moving towards contact. It would be very bad if they just kept running until they ran head-long into the Severn girl and or the idiot islanders. Leftenan Diskul probably had the brains to halt his men at the last tree line before the irrigation ditches. Probably.

Melnik would be a lot happier if he was there to make sure. He increased his pace.

Sergeant Varko waited an extra ten minutes after his TDT had notified him that the sky above was clear of any surveillance drones before releasing Safi's nanos. The wind was coming from behind him and towards the irrigation ditches.

Safi had also programmed the nanoUAVs to look for

something to rest on. The one intended to cover the approaches at a low-level settled onto the grass, then reeds, even the scum covering the surface water of the ditches. It reported its final location and status on the display inside Varko's helmet visor, then went silent. It showed good coverage.

The other, high-level nano rode the wind, reaching out for the distant tree line. If he could set it down in the top of one of the narra trees, he'd then have a good view of all the surrounding approaches.

For the best part of an hour, Varko watched as nothing happened. Then his visor's display reminded him that the hostile's sensor drone would be overhead again soon. He fitted his breather mask, waited for the icon in his visor that confirmed there was a good seal between the mask and visor and that tanked air was now flowing to his lungs, then eased himself into the water. He surfaced, added a trailing antenna to a half-submerged tree-trunk then slipped himself under it.

Something was already there, under the tree. Something sharp and strong took an interest in the Sergeant's boot for a second or two. Varko pulled his foot up then smashed down hard. That settled that argument. Unless it returned with its big brother, Varko figured the underside of the log was now his. There were saltwater crocodiles in these islands. Varko tried hard not to dwell on that fact.

"Andrev, things are going well I see," Ellis said.

"We should have them neutralised before noon," Melnik replied.

"Major, you sound out of breath."

"I am running. My entire formation is running."

"Just as long as you are running towards the enemy," Mr Badali said, smiling. Ellis wondered if the idiot had any idea of the insult he'd just given to the land component of their operation.

Hopefully Major Melnik hadn't heard him.

If he had, the Major showed no interest in it. "Have

you got any new Intel you'd like to share?"

"No, nothing. Faint traces here and there, nothing significant. I'm not sure if they haven't all congregated at the area you refer to as the 'ditches.' Hard to tell from the drone data alone, and especially at night. There's no activity south of you, between your position and the town, so it doesn't look like she's trying to get around behind you. Wipe those insurgents out Major, and the rest of the island's population will do as their told."

"I'm glad you think so," Melnik said.

The Major's age was beginning to show. He was struggling a bit, but he had to lead by example.

"Since I have nothing else for you," Ellis advised, "I shall let you get on. We'll be waiting for the body count of killed and captured. And by the way, if you can capture the Severn girl, I hear some people are willing to pay a small fortune for her. More alive than dead unfortunately, but personally . . . dead suits me just fine."

"We will count whatever we have to count," Melnik said and the link went dead.

Kat took a long drink from her suit's filtered water reservoir.

Lance Corporal Jarvis looked up from his device. "We are out of sensor range of the hostile's drone, ma'am."

"Staff. Mount up and move out."

Others, encouraged by Staff Freeman, moved to obey her order. Drivers were more awake this time. The vehicles rolled out of the barn and other outbuildings and quickly formed into a column again. Within ten minutes, Mike's column, that had used another farm a klick or two away, had joined them and took up formation on Kat's left.

The sky was starting to change colour. The sun would soon rise, and the assault on the irrigation ditches would likely begin. If Kat was in command of that attack, she would try to get at least part of the way across the open ground before the increasing light made matters more deadly.

That was the right way to do it . . . and despite the miserable choices she'd given Melnik so far, he had always made the best of them.

The Major silently raised his left hand, signalling that his people should halt their advance.

The Platoon Commanders and the NCOs repeated the command down to the soldiers. Through the trees, Melnik watched as the other two Platoons halted and went to ground. He'd been half-afraid that some idiot would keep running, wanting to be first at the irrigation ditches.

He surveyed his target through his own night-vision filter. The moon had gone, along with any light it had provided. That left him studying the ditches by a few stars, but it was enough. The islanders were not likely to have any night-vision gear of their own.

Unless the Severn girl and her Land Force Troopers have shared their equipment . . .

Melnik shook that thought away and studied the target. He could see no guards, no patrolling, nothing that resembled normal overnight guard duty or security. There were no pickets or OPs anywhere in the hundred or so metres of flat ground between the tree-line of the rainforest and the first irrigation ditch. The crop they needed to cross, of a grass-like grain, had not been harvested and was above waist-height to an average person. Unbelievable . . . if this really was the Severn girl's idea of a defensive position . . . how had she lived so long?

In the ditches he could see one, maybe two heads, and from the noise he was now picking up, snoring seemed to be a popular pastime. The wind blew from the ditches, bringing with it a whiff of open latrines. Had they really fouled their own fighting positions? Melnik shook his head, then caught himself. Ellis had underestimated this girl, and look where he was. Melnik would not make the same mistake.

He checked the time, then the colour of the sky that was just starting to brighten behind the ditches. His formations would have the shadows with them for another five minutes, not much more.

Best to make good use of the time then. He flipped up the protective cover on his comm-link, pressed the send button for two seconds, then released it.

Kapten Sarikan responded with two clicks. The professional mercenaries were in position.

Melnik pointed at Leftenan Diskul, then tapped twice on the top of his head, indicating that the Lieutenant should come to his location.

"Leftenan Diskul, advance your Platoon at a low walk, by Squads, continue as a bounding overwatch," Melnik whispered. "Pass word to One and Two Platoon to do the same. Keep low and keep quiet."

Melnik gave Kapten Sarikan another single click on his send button. Around him, a Squad from Three Platoon began to advance at a stooped walk for fifteen to twenty metres, then went to ground. There was little to see.

Leftenan Diskul signalled his next Squad to do the same, to advance with him. He led them for another fifteen or so metres past the first squad Squad, then went to ground. When his last Squad started its advance, Melnik moved with them, leading them a further twenty metres past the furthest advance of the previous Squad, exactly as the platoon level tactics manual said a bounding overwatch, or 'leapfrogging' advance, should be executed.

And so it went on, the rear Squad would rise to a slow, stooped-over walk up to, then past the two Squads ahead of it. When Melnik wasn't moving forward with one of the Squads, he studied the ditches with his binoculars.

No movement, no action, no nothing.

The ditches might be empty for all he could see.

They were over halfway across the crop field, and Melnik was beginning to think he'd be able to get everyone up to the ditches before a single shot was fired, when things started to suddenly happen.

Somewhere in the ditches there was an explosion. Had one of his mercenaries thrown a grenade?

For a second there was silence as even those near to Melnik went to ground and held their breath. A flare ignited and turned the early morning gloom into day.

But there was only the occasional shot coming from the ditches and Melnik couldn't identify the weapon type from its bark.

To the Major's left and right, the PSC Privates returned fire enthusiastically, but at what they were aiming he had no idea. As he studied the ditches, trying to identify actual targets, there was another small explosion, then a second trip flare sent its parachute suspended phosphorous package skyward. It caused flaring on his night vision equipment and temporarily robbed him of any further night sight.

It was time for Three Platoon to advance again. Its Leftenan and Sarjan were now ordering, shouting at their men to move forward, as the need for a silent advance was gone. But that Platoon's advance had stalled.

Melnik stood. "Three Platoon, follow me," he shouted. Running low, he advanced, waving his arm to indicate that the others were to do the same. Most did.

About a third of his men adopted proper, standing-unsupported, firing positions and were ready to give effective covering fire from the tall grass. Melnik turned his attention to One Platoon.

They weren't moving forward either.

Melnik stood up to his full height, "One Platoon, advance. Come on, they're only a bunch of farmers."

The Squads of One Platoon were now up, their Lieutenant, Akarathit was leading them, calling for his Squad Commanders to follow him. He'd taken about four paces when he clutched his leg and went down, but his senior NCO was up, and kept them moving forward under the Major's watchful eye.

As they passed Three Platoon, Melnik fell into line with them, hustling them forward and kicking any who had tried to go to ground before covering the full distance to put them ahead of Three Platoon's lead elements.

Major Melnik turned as soon as One Platoon had completed its advance, ready to get Two Platoon moving, but their Leftenan was already up, moving that Platoon forward.

Melnik gave him a thumbs-up then dropped to one knee to assess the situation.

There were more flashes as additional pyrotechnic

devices triggered up and down the ditches. This time it was the more conventional trip flare, where the illumination pot remained on the ground. As he watched, a couple of them ignited amongst the forward Squads of Two Platoon, but as far as he could tell, neither produced any casualties amongst his men.

Melnik wondered where his professional, expensive mercenaries were? What he would give for a standard TDT or personal battle-board, but that meant having GPS data, Intel feeds and your commanders having them too. That was way beyond the budget of this ridiculous lash-up!

For a final time, he advanced his Platoons by 'leapfrogging' Squads. The two Platoons on the flanks weren't advancing as far as Three Platoon in the centre of the formation. Either he'd have to go and personally take over, getting one or two of their Squads to do an extra advance, or they'd have a lot more distance to run when he ordered the full attack.

Major Melnik scowled, then decided he'd funnel them into the ditches as reserves to support Three Platoon. Or, if the islanders broke and ran, the two flank Platoons would be in a better position to engage or pursue them.

Around the Major, troops fired and advanced, did their duty as they were trained. He looked at it, found it was good . . . and smiled.

And as he smiled, he realised it was time.

Three Platoon was less than twenty metres from the first irrigation ditch. The two flanking Platoons were about to move forward again. This would work out fine.

Melnik flipped up his comm-link's cover and pressed 'voice-only: send.'

"Sarikan, I'm about to order a general assault. Get ready to receive those that break and run. On a count of five, stand by, and hold your fire unless you have a clear target."

"You drive them to us and we'll take them down, sir."

Melnik stood and signalled to Three Platoon. "Up and at 'em," he shouted, and they obeyed.

"Come on, you heard the Major," Leftenan Diskul shouted in his native Thai.

With a roar, Three Platoon was on its feet and moving forward at a fast trot.

"Don't go too far out in front, keep in 'extended line' so we don't shoot each other in the back," their Sarjan shouted.

Their naive enthusiasm was quickly curbed.

In a moment, all three Platoons were up, on their feet and moving forward. Some stood to fire aimed shots, others waiting until they had cleared the crop in the field and opened up from the hip.

Here and there the odd PSC Private went down, mostly out on the flanks. If they had bullets in their backs from their own people . . .

Third Platoon was now shouting and roaring as it ran for the first irrigation ditch. Something in the ditch blew up, almost blinding Melnik. The noise was deafening, even though his mercenaries weren't engaging. Men fired, shouted, ran.

And Melnik was at the front, leading them.

He reached the parapet of the first ditch. He scanned left and right in the dim light of the dawning day.

And saw nothing.

He ran back a few metres, then ran forward and jumped the first ditch and raced for the second, across the trackway in-between. The second ditch was maybe five metres behind the first.

This ditch he jumped down into. Some revetment had been added on both sides. He fired his pistol into the gloom and heard a horrible scream. He whirled back to find something large charging him. He couldn't make it out in the shadowed light of the ditch, he just fired at it.

His target screamed in rage but kept on coming, if anything it increased its speed. Melnik pulled his trigger again. He was hitting the target, he hadn't missed, but the huge shadow kept coming at him.

Then, with a final roar it collapsed at his feet, white tusks gleaming in the darkness.

"What the hell is that?" a Private asked.

"Biggest boar I've ever seen," came from another

behind him.

"Look out, Major,"

The warning came too late to prevent Melnik from being slammed hard in the back and knocked forward onto the dying boar. He went down, feeling one of the tusks press hard into the armoured plate that protected his groin. He rolled off the pig into the wet mud beside it.

His pistol got a mud bath too.

Rolling onto his smarting back, Melnik faced something with two twisting and sharp-looking horns, long whiskers . . . and appalling breath.

It looked eager to butt those horns into his face.

Melnik swung his mud-caked pistol around and took aim, putting two rounds right between the eyes of the creature.

Its head exploded with a satisfactory "thack."

And Melnik noticed, as he wiped off the horned thing's gore, that matters had suddenly got very much quieter.

The battlefield wasn't totally silent, but it was considerably quieter.

Melnik struggled to his feet and was grateful for the hand one of the Hai PSC Privates offered him.

Out of the ditch, the Major took a second or two to survey the situation. There was no more weapons fire, no more explosions.

A dense cloud of acrid smoke hung over the two ditches. It didn't smell right, it wasn't the usual 'cordite' smell of battle. Only the slightly 'garlicy' smell of the burnt phosphorous was as he expected.

A glance along the ditch showed him, next to the body of the creature he'd shot, a row of flare pots, both conventional trip-initiated and the variety that sent up a white burning flare. Melnik eyed the PSC Privates beside him and realised that they were probably doing the same assessment as him.

No dead enemy, no fleeing enemy.

He turned to the Private who had identified the Nicobar pig. "What kind of animal is that?"

"It looks to be a goat, sir, but I don't know what kind. Bigger than anything I've ever seen before."

Melnik nodded, then turned, "Leftenan Diskul."

"Sir," the man said and this time saluted.

Melnik didn't chastise him, he returned the compliment. These soldiers needed to be steadied by routine, by rendered honour. They needed to be distracted . . . and fast . . . from their brilliant assault on a farmyard. It was evident there was no enemy around.

Melnik knew he'd been had. Could he prevent these PSC Privates from knowing that too? What a command challenge! To keep his troops from feeling like he did.

"Our fleeing islanders have been kind enough to leave behind some fine livestock," Melnik said. "Let's see what we can do about having a good barbecue for breakfast."

Leftenan Diskul was quick on the uptake and promptly began issuing orders. "Sarjan, get a fire pit dug."

One and Two Platoon consolidated on Three Platoon's position. One Platoon got picket duty and were ordered to send out patrolling sentries. Two Platoon got the detail of going back into the rainforest to gather wood or anything else that might burn, whilst Three Platoon continued to dig fire-pits large enough to take the two animals despatched by Melnik.

As Leftenan Diskul saw to the details of their breakfast, as evidently not all Buddhists were vegetarian, Melnik brought Kapten Sarikan quickly up-to-date.

"So, there are no islanders or any of Severn's people here, just farm animals?"

"No," Melnik snapped. "Not even the ever-innovative Severn could have put such accurately timed fuses onto those flares from several hours ago. There is someone out there, observing us. I want you to find them. Track them down. I want their head."

"Yes, Major," Sarikan said, and was gone.

Melnik turned his back on the preparations for breakfast, but was careful to keep a smile on his face and make it look as though everything was going exactly as planned.

Several of the Thai PSCs had experience in gutting and preparing the animals for roasting. They butchered the available breakfast, hacking it into the smaller parts that could be cooked quickly. It was all done with such a familiar panache that several of their colleagues looked decidedly queasy.

Melnik's rear party, those with ankle and leg injuries and the islanders being used as hostages eventually arrived at the irrigation trenches. In a bit more than an hour, the goat was sufficiently cooked to eat. The wild boar took longer.

Sarikan led a very wet mercenary formation in at about the same time the pig was declared fit to eat. He dropped a length of antenna wire in front of the Major.

"He hid under a log near the end of the ditches, right at the edge of the wetlands, and was long gone by the time we found his location. We didn't see it or him on our way in, but we must have passed reasonably close by."

Melnik scowled. He threw the portion of goat leg he'd stripped of all its edible flesh into the fire-pit, then stood.

In a low voice, so only the Kapten and his own mercenary Feldwebels could hear, he said, "This is the third time that the Severn girl has played me. She did at The Pavilion in Emirates City . . . then at the causeway across the swamp . . . and now here." He glanced around at his command. "Three times that girl has crossed swords with me and settled for nothing but a touch." Melnik shook his head. "She will not make a fool out of me again. Get some chow Sarikan, the pig is a bit tough, but tastes good. Get something in your stomach. It's been a crap morning. At noon we'll march."

"I assure you sir, the afternoon will be more to our liking."

Lieutenant Kat Severn stood just below the crest of the hill and surveyed the work going on below. She, Mike, Staff Freeman and the farmer who owned the land had come up to get a better feel of the terrain. For Kat it was her first look.

For the farmer, it was unnecessary. He or his father had built everything within sight with their own sweat. He fidgeted. His pride in ownership was now replaced with fear. "This battle you want to have, it is not going to destroy everything, is it?"

The Staff Sergeant looked at the farmer with an honest sadness. Mike looked away. It was left to Kat to admit, "I don't know. Only a fool will tell you in the morning how a battle will evolve in the afternoon."

The farmer shrugged. "As least you're honest."

Kat took a moment to survey what her people were up to. The 'battlefield' below them was roughly triangular. The two hills, locally known as 'poore' approximately to the east and 'pasha' to the west, formed a side each, rising gently several hundred metres from the narrow, tiered terrace that cut a winding ribbon in between the coconut plantation and the beginning of the rainforest that blanketed both hills. The triangular shape of the flat land between the terraces was sliced through its centre by a dirt track that passed by the farm's outbuildings, then multiple neat rows of palm trees. Before finally reaching the farm house at the far 'tip' of the 'triangle.' The track then continued, twisting its way further into the rainforest and the island's interior. On either side of the main track, a shallow gully moved the daily rain away, then rows and rows of equally spaced coconut palms, extending back towards the wetlands.

Although each tree would take six to ten years to begin producing a harvestable crop, a mature tree was then harvested every sixty to ninety days, producing a crop of between five and fifteen fruits. Acres of plantation covered the south eastern corner of the island, between Campbell Bay and the rolling hills of rainforest that eventually became more mountainous.

Started by the farmer's father, as their family grew, so did the expanse of land cleared and levelled and the number of coconut's being cultivated. On the flat tops of the stone-faced terraces, fruit trees had been planted.

As Kat had recently found out, most of the island's inhabitants tolerated the masked palm civets and their highly valuable droppings, but not this farmer and his family. Although preferring to eat rodents, lizards and snakes, the civets also feasted on the fruits and flowers of palms and other forest plants, including the mangos and figs growing along the tops of the terraces. The civets, despite looking a bit like cats, were actually nearer to rodents and whilst preferring a life up in the trees, could and did, burrow, destroying the roots of the cultivated crops. This farmer had no qualms about shooting them, and proudly showed-off the hunting rifle he used to do it.

"Wouldn't poisoning them be a easier?" Mike asked.

"Yes, most definitely, but how to control it so than only those damn creatures eat it? Great Nicobar has 'biosphere' status," the farmer explained. "Anything like poisoning, including using pesticides on our crops, is strictly banned. Anything we do here has to be approved as being in sync with the island's ecosystem. A unique problem often needs a unique solution. So, I am authorised to shoot them," he said patting the cradled weapon. "In Thailand they have trained macaques to climb up the trees and harvest the coconuts, but I am not permitted to do this. Almost everything we do on this farm is heavily regulated. If I do not comply, I cannot sell my produce."

Checking her M37's sights, Kat confirmed she had the open and flat expanse of the coconut plantation well within her weapon's maximum effective range on either side of the track. Anyone coming up the track could be engaged from within the relative safety of the farm buildings, or from atop the terraces. Between the palm trees there was absolutely no cover. Anybody foolish enough to come up that track would walk right into the sights of their weapons.

This had the potential to be a very one-sided slaughter.

"*If* they walk into it," Mike said, reading Kat's mind.

"You think maybe he's had enough of walking into things?"

"You've done a pretty good job of teaching him that lesson, ma'am," the Staff Sergeant said.

Kat laughed. "I have less trigger pullers than Melnik,

even with the help of the islanders, and except for our own people, I can't expect any of them to fire and manoeuvre once under hostile fire. Probably best if we deploy the locals into the farm buildings and terraces. They can just sit there and only engage when we tell them to."

"I don't remember anyone telling you battles were supposed to be easy," Mike said.

"If you put my fellow Nicobari inside the buildings," the farmer observed slowly, comprehending how the battle might unfold, "they won't be able to get away if things go wrong. What are those things you use . . . hand grenades? If a few of them get thrown inside . . ." He didn't finish the sentence.

Kat had to put an end to that thought. "The coconut plantations are cleared of ground-level vegetation. Those terraces are approximately parallel to each other and the road, so we can achieve mutual support with one shooter keeping the flanks of those opposite to him or her clear. My Troopers will act as a mobile reserve. They'll move in to engage anything unexpected."

"And just what exactly are you expecting?" the farmer asked her.

"That they are not going to march up that track in a nice long line, ready and waiting to be shot up," Kat said, glancing at Mike and Staff Freeman. The both nodded in agreement.

"He's not going to do anything the easy way anymore. He's going to be looking for us under every rock and behind every bush and tree. We'll need to conceal any defensive preparation as best we can."

As if to confirm Kat's words, Captain Gillan came on. The *Bella* was repositioning herself to be nearer to Ellis's *Hyperion*.

"It looks like Melnik has finished his morning barbeque," he reported. "They are breaking camp at the irrigation ditches and forming up on a nearby track."

"What kind of formation are they in?"

"Sending you the imagery now. It's very similar to yesterday. His PSCs are the vanguard and out covering the flanks, with his own people and the islanders in the centre, and they have a few of the Private Security Contractors herding along the animals they didn't kill and eat."

"It would have been hard to eat all of the animals we left there in one go," Mike said. "What's their casualty numbers looking like?"

"Wait out," said Gillan. He came back in less than a minute. "About fifteen maybe twenty are either injured or need helping with their mobility. That's an increase on yesterday morning," Gillan chuckled.

Kat didn't. The local farmer also looked more worried by the minute.

"And . . . Ellis has somehow intensified his efforts to jam our sensors. Not all our sweeps are coming back with anything useable," Gillan added.

"Just keep sending me updates on his location and troop formation. A still image is sufficient if that's the best we can do."

In a moment, more imagery was sent and downloaded.

"Safi, map these onto our three-dimensional terrain display."

A minute later Safi had projected the scientists' earlier LiDaR-based map of the island, then zoomed in on the south-eastern corner and their current location. Melnik and the Hai PSC personnel were scattered in an extended patrol column, along each side of the track, about six kilometres away from the farm. The track wound its way around the base of the numerous hills. Coming along the track itself was a professional looking formation of Melnik's own mercenaries. Trailing behind them were dejected looking islanders and then several more PSCs wielding long sticks and trying to keep the meandering livestock together.

"Do you think they'll stay this spread out? Mike asked.

"How will our people on the terraces engage without killing their colleagues on the opposite side?" the farmer then added, making it apparent that he hadn't understand her earlier explanation about providing mutual support, whereby one fire team protected another by engaging any targets that appeared on the flanks or behind their opposite fire-team, outside of their direct line-of sight.

"We need to make sure that every fire-team is sited so it can give mutual support to one other fire-team, ideally to two," Kat said, "But, not be within the arcs of another fire-team itself."

"Understood," Staff Freeman said and nodded. He knew that the sighting and engagement arcs of each fire team was critical and would need to be controlled and coordinated.

"But what about grenades?" the farmer said again.

"We need to create some kind of sangar for each of the fire teams amongst the fruit trees along the terraces, to limit the blast of a grenade," Freeman suggested.

"Use the bailed coir fibre. The farmer must have lots of it," Mike suggested.

"I do, but it will catch fire, no?" the farmer said.

"Agreed, but it will also help absorb the explosion blast and fragmentation," Freeman added.

"So will cut down on potential casualties," Kat explained to the farmer.

"Would a wall built of rice, it's in twenty-five kilo sacks, not be better?" the farmer suggested. "That won't burn like the coir does."

Kat also wanted to explore the best options for deploying her Land Force Troopers and their support weapons, but having a civilian agri-farmer in her current war council was not going as well as she'd hoped. Too many questions . . . not enough answers.

They began walking back down the hill, to get on with what needed doing. She'd talk with Mike and Staff Freeman later.

How many battles had she got herself into since she'd joined the Fleet?

Too many.

And none of them had been anything like the battles she had read about in the history files. Would some future professor, from the safety of his dusty ivory tower, match this battle up against some historical precedent and make its conclusion look easy and forgone?

Of course, he'd know what Kat and her assets had done. What had worked. And, what hadn't.

Matters weren't that easy under a hot sun with dust rising from digging shovels. Hindsight was easy. Foresight was not!

Melnik had come to despise his little updates with the *Hyperion*'s Captain, who sat so nonchalantly out at sea. The Major had cut Ellis off in mid-response when he requested an immediate sit-rep after they had assaulted the irrigation ditches. Ellis hadn't called him again while his formation ate their 'victory' breakfast.

But Melnik was moving into what could only become a 'contact.' Only after he asked Ellis for a sensor drone sweep of the next likely ambush location did the ship send him imagery and mapping.

Melnik studied the terrain and the plantations ahead of him. It was Leftenan Diskul who identified them as being coconut.

"So there will be no cover at ground level, only the trunks of the palms themselves, and that's not much wider than a man," Kapten Sarikan observed.

"And they can shoot down at us from these terraces and the overlooking hills," Melnik said.

"It's obviously a good place for an ambush," the Kapten agreed. "But, will this Severn girl do something so obvious? Will her Land Force commanders let her?"

"Valid questions," Melnik agreed. "That first ambush was an obvious one . . . and she got away with it. Our breakfast stop was obvious . . . and she passed on it. She's got to engage us sooner or later. Have you spotted any good sites further up this track, after this next farmstead?"

Sarikan shook his head. Diskul shrugged.

"So," Melnik concluded, "she either gives up the last good ambush site, or she doesn't. Either way, I intend to walk into her trap armed as a bear, but disguised as a fox." The Major studied his limited Intel for several more minutes. "We'll take a break here, establish a final RV. It's a good three kilometres away from them," he said pointing at the display. "Diskul, your Platoon handled the vanguard well enough, but I think it's time to replace you with another formation."

"Who, sir?" the Leftenan asked.

Melnik knew his grin was pure evil, but he savoured every second. "Why, the gift they so kindly gave us. What else?"

Kat licked her lips. The sun was up, the sky was clear. It was hot . . . and she was anxious. She'd done all she could. Now she waited. Waited for Melnik to show up.

Her Troopers had added a number of refinements to her plan. First Squad had been split up into four, two-man fire-teams to add control and discipline to the Nicobari volunteers, a pair every couple of hundred metres, along each side of the raised terraces. Improvised rice-bag sangars on the upper level, alternated with others on the lower, that had just been completed. Their orders were to concentrate on the un-armoured Private-Security-Contractors. Mike had positioned himself down on the terraces too.

The Second and Third Squad, less their support weapons, would be held as two mobile reserves. She'd use them to counter whatever surprises Melnik came up with, and she expected some good ones from him! Was she making a mistake in trying to fight this to a surrender? Only time would tell.

Kat's comm-link clicked, then clicked again.

Sergeant Varko had come in just after noon from his job orchestrating the fun and games at the irrigation ditches. He'd got a brief laugh and then been assigned another tough job. He was now in another concealed OP, well out in front of Kat's intended ambush.

Two clicks meant the Sergeant wanted to talk. Kat clicked once.

"I can see them. They're about fifteen hundred metres out," Varko advised. "Looks like someone's called a break. Their Officers are circulating among the men, giving final reminders. My bet is we've been spotted."

No surprise. Nothing would surprise her in this fight. Kat gave a single click, and the comm-link went silent.

That was the problem with fighting smart people. What looked good to you, looked good to them too. When she'd worked with Ellis, he hadn't been stupid, far from it, just driven. Therefore, she had no reason to think he'd have a stupid person running the landside element of this operation now.

Kat turned to the people within her improvised Command Post. "Pass the word, they're about klick and a half out from our OP and have stopped for a brew. We can expect them anytime."

Locals and Troopers went to pass the word. The time for waiting was officially over.

Kat stood in her improvised command post, hidden amongst a tangle of rocks, the roots of several large narra trees and the bushes that grew around their bases. It was at the extreme far end of the coconut plantation, past the farm house and outbuildings where the rainforest started, and the terracing stopped. Behind them, the terrain rose steeply.

Melnik it seemed, continued to march along the course of the main track. Kat laughed. His vanguard was now comprised of a small herd of goats and wild pigs!

At approximately one hundred metres before the pillars that marked the entrance to the plantation there was another culvert running under the main track. Once there had been gates, as the rusty hinges remained embedded into the pillars, but the gates themselves were long gone. At a nod from Kat, a chain of explosive charges detonated, dropping the culvert and destroying the track.

The pigs and goats were unperturbed and simply blinked away the dust and stomped, pranced or did whatever their natural inclination was, over the latest obstacle as if it didn't exist. Their hooves easily coping with the newly uneven terrain.

The herders, a few of the Private-Security-Contractors with long poles of bamboo in their hands and their rifles slung over their shoulders, kept pushing at the back of herd into the newly created obstacle, at least they did for a while. Soon they were losing control of the animals, and of their own situation.

Several of the animals were now over the other side. They were getting away from their handlers.

Beside Kat, the plantation owner shook his head. "I hope these animals don't get caught in the crossfire, it would be such a waste, and they should not suffer."

On the track a Hai PSC Sergeant came up to oversee the 'herders.' He activated a speaker unit. "You in the farm. Come out with your hands up and there will be no problem." He then repeated his message in another language.

The Sergeant only waited a quick thirty seconds. "You were warned," he added. Beside him the acting livestock herders now threw aside the sticks they'd been attempting to control the animals with and followed their senior NCO's example by un-slinging, then making 'ready' their assault rifles. At a signal from their Sergeant, they followed the livestock and climbed down, across, then back up the obstacle ditch the explosive charges had created and moved through the gateway, before fanning out. The man on each end moved off the track, jumping the shallow rain-gully that ran down each side. They moved swiftly into an 'arrow-head' formation, taking a route directly towards the nearest cluster of farm outbuildings a hundred metres ahead of them.

A second formation of PSC Troopers followed, taking up over-watch positions, covering their comrades as they entered the cluster of barns and equipment sheds. In a few minutes, the Sergeant was standing at an upstairs window. "Nobody home," he reported to his superiors, using the speaker unit.

That's one way to communicate, Kat thought, but he was only announcing what his opposition already knew.

Beside her, the Land Force Detachment's comms-tech said. "I'm getting action on several comm frequencies, ma'am, but it's all encrypted."

"Safi?"

"They are using a standard military narrow-band FM

frequency. I could decipher the encryption in about half an hour, perhaps a bit longer. Assuming they don't change the key-setting every thirty seconds."

Which could be a problem in a battle not likely to last more than an hour or two.

"Can you jam all military frequencies?" Kat asked her signaller.

"In the immediate vicinity, for three or four klicks maybe, yes, but it will obviously effect our own comms too, ma'am," he advised.

"I know," Kat said.

Jamming meant Kat could not talk to her people on their military communications network, either. But being on the defensive and on ground of her own choosing, Kat was prepared for just such an eventuality, well sort of.

"Visual Signal Set, ma'am?" Staff Freeman asked her via his comm link. "It's very limited, and slow, a bit crap actually, and that's why we don't often use it, and we'll need to get it set up and synced before you start jamming."

"Do it, Staff. Quick as you can," Kat ordered.

The Visual Signal Set was a series of five rectangular panels, arranged along their long edge, one above the other. The panels could each display one of three colours, (red, blue or green) at any given time, and could be illuminated at night. The colour combination, top to bottom, delivered a number, in roman numerals. Red was I, Blue V, and Green X. The sent number related to a pre-agreed message.

Each signal box needed to be visible, (direct line-of-sight) to the next, so even with enhanced, twenty-second century optics was only good for a few hundred metres. They were usually arranged to operate as a 'chain,' passing messages along a defensive line, or as a 'wheel' with the outlying 'rim' passing and receiving messages from a central hub.

Routine messaging was restricted to the

top four panels to save time and keep messaging simple, meaning that 18 (XVIII) and 23 (XXIII) that contained five components were only used when communicating a time, and 27 (XXVII) and 28 (XXVIII) were also not used.

"We'll just have to hope that Visual Signalling Set is enough, otherwise we'll be resorting to old-fashioned runners!" Kat commented.

"Visual message from Staff Freeman," the comms-tech advised Kat approximately twenty minutes later.

Using her own binoculars, Kat turned to the bearing she now knew the Staff Sergeant's signal box to be at, then looked up the hillside unit she located it. Three red rectangles were just about visible.

"III, Message 3, that's 'set-up complete.'" The comms-tech confirmed.

"Excellent. Start radio jamming," Kat ordered.

"Yes, ma'am."

An hour later the messages from Staff Freeman started to come in, in quick succession.

"Single red, that's I, 'enemy sighted.' Red over blue, that's IV, 'direction.' Green, green, blue, red, that's XXVI, 26, 'to the south east.' Green, blue, red, XVI, 16, 'distance.' Blue over red, VI, 6, so six-hundred metres.

Kat was looking as her display at the comms-tech deciphered the incoming messages. It was everything that Staff Sergeant Freeman had said it was . . . slow, limited and cumbersome, if not a bit crap, but it was better than nothing . . . just . . . maybe.

"Hostile activity, ma'am. On our left flank, at the end of the terraces," the comms-tech told her, evidently more accustomed to this kind of communication than Kat was.

"Two Squads of enemy are . . . Wait out." There was a pause of maybe thirty seconds. "They're splitting up, ma'am. One Squad is heading up, into the rainforest on 'poore' hill, the other is moving along the upper and lower levels of the adjacent terrace."

Staff Freeman's elevated location was to be their fall-back, reserve position, on the 'pasha' hillside behind the farm house. He was 'dug-in' just below the hill's crest. He would begin engaging long before anyone coming up that hill got anywhere near to his position, as he had four of their six Squad support weapons and the Detachment's sniper with him. All these weapon systems had effective ranges exceeding a kilometre, the sniper's rifle even further.

The comms-tech was looking in a different direction. "It's Ensign Steiger this time."

A quick glance out of her improvised Command Post told her why. A Hai PSC formation of almost Platoon strength, maybe a few less, was spreading out in a line, extending right across the palm plantations on either side of the main track.

So far, Kat's numerous firing positions and sangars amongst the fruit trees on the terraces hadn't been seen.

Using her binoculars, she scanned along the track. Yet another formation was advancing in a bounding over-watch to support those now deploying ahead, those that had already reached the neat rows of coconut palms. Melnik had committed about half of his troops.

Damn. When Kat gave orders to open fire, everyone she had would start shooting. Melnik would see exactly what she had. Or more to the point, what she did not!

"Can you tell Mike . . . sorry Ensign Steiger to hold his fire?

"Yes, ma'am." The comms-tech quickly adjusted his own signal box to show red over green, IX, or 9, which meant, 'hold your fire / break contact / do not engage.'

A green over two reds came back. "That's XII, ma'am, he affirms."

"Can you stop the jamming just long enough for me to send a transmission to all our Trooper's comms units?"

"No ma'am. They started jamming us as soon as I started jamming them."

Of course they would.

"Send that same message to all our locations, I don't want our people engaging unless I authorise it. I repeat, not to engage. Let's try not to give away all that we have."

"That's a bit of a challenge ma'am maybe it's already time for old-style runners."

"Then get them running," She turned to glance at the Staff Sergeant's location. "Tell Staff Freeman to give it one minute, then 'sniper only' to engage enemy advancing on the terraces."

"On-it," the comms-tech said and began adjusting the coloured rectangles on the visual signalling box.

Kat didn't need to tell Freeman that the time for arm or leg shots had passed. She'd tried so very hard not to endanger the islanders, by not killing any of Ellis's people ashore, but she wasn't a novice in such matters. Taunt a wild animal enough times and eventually it would bite you back and something told her that the time for restraint had now passed, it was kill, or at the very least, incapacitate, or be killed!

"He's affirmed the message, ma'am, Sniper to engage in sixty . . . fifty-nine . . ."

Kat turned back to Mike. "Prepare a message for Ensign Steiger. Tell him to engage, but only send it once our sniper has fired his first shot."

"Roger that, ma'am, that's a nice easy one."

Kat turned to the plantation owner. "Tell everyone here not to fire."

"Not to fire, got it," he said and began telling others in the local language.

The word was passed. Kat doubted it would get to everyone, but it should keep the fire down, and just maybe she'd have a few surprises left for their inevitable second assault.

A single shot rang out.

Fifteen seconds later the panorama before Kat erupted with small arms fire.

Her viewing aperture showed the full shock and intensity, and it's almost immediate impact.

Men dropped. People died.

The Platoon moving forward had their weapons at the ready. At the first sounds of rifle fire, they returned the compliment, but most of it was un-aimed, sprayed automatic.

Kat couldn't see any targets, they were just spraying rounds before them, and the unfortunate, untended, wandering farm animals took way too much of it.

Kat could hear single, aimed shots, mostly from her Troopers M37s or the deep bark of the sniper's rifle, but the occasional low-powered report of the hunting rifles and shotguns used by the farmers was definitely in the mix too. Thankfully, none of her M214 Squad support weapons had engaged.

Many of the Hai PSCs in the coconut plantation went down, most twitched, some called for medical assistance. Not many, but a few. Their advance faltered. They began to fall back.

The Hai PSC Platoon that had been advancing to support the colleagues in bounding over-watch was also trying hard to return fire, but couldn't see anything to fire at. The rapid-fire, automatic volleys of their colleagues ahead weren't going anywhere near to where Kat had actually positioned her people.

"The odd round is bound to get lucky if they spray enough of it about," Kat commented to one of the islanders standing beside her. It was the old man who'd challenged her intentions the night before. "Please put that gun down. Don't even think about firing it from here. I don't want this position being engaged just yet. If you fire at them we reveal our location."

Mrs Lakhera put out her hand and rested it on the old man's weapon. The barrel sank towards the floor. "Seems a cowardly way to fight a war," he growled.

"Melnik is just probing for us," Kat said. "I doubt this is his main attack."

The automatic fire from the Private Security Contractors reduced as their force withdrew.

Kat could make out more reports from her own Trooper's weapon systems as they continued firing, the unmistakeable report of the sniper's rifle discharging. That was from Staff Freeman's elevated position, taking down Melnik's armoured infantry that was still infiltrating the farm's left flanking terrace. One target, one shot.

"Staff," Kat called him without thinking on her comm-link.

"We're still jammed," Safi advised.

Kat returned her attention to the battle before her. One of the Hai PSC personnel in the plantation had noticed a rice-bag sangar on the nearby terrace.

Yanking a grenade from his belt, he pulled the pin, leapt up and sent it towards the structure, then dropped down into a shallow rain-gully, waiting for it to explode.

Multiple shots stopped him. Even before his grenade exploded, he was falling. From what Kat could see, he was still alive, but was flat on his back, unable to move.

This was battle, so unfortunately, people died.

"Message from Staff Freeman, ma'am. The enemy on the terraces of the 'poore' side, both upper and lower levels, are also withdrawing."

Kat nodded at her comms-tech's report.

The PSC Private in the rain-gulley wasn't going to be the only name on the butcher's bill for today's endeavours.

No, maybe not.

One of the PSC Troopers on the main track got to his feet. He had no weapon, and his hands were held up in the universal sign of surrender. He ran across to the gully to where his wounded comrade lay.

Kat held her breath and watched as the man pulled his colleague up, dragging him back to the main track, then arranged him so that he could attend his wounds. When the wounded man began to regain consciousness, his rescuer smiled.

A single shot rang out and the man fell forward, someone had put round into his back from his own lines, sending out a very clear message. Compassion obviously wasn't something their enemy wanted to encourage amongst its ranks.

SIX : THIRTEEN

Andrev Melnik scowled as he studied the terrain and the battle evolving before him. He'd watched a tableau of mercy through his binoculars. And a moment before that, he'd watched about half of a Private-Security-Contractor Platoon get neutralised by concealed defensive fire. Thus, Melnik's planned envelopment of what he'd mistaken as being a 'limited' position had come to a sudden halt.

"That is not a small force," Melnik growled to himself.

"It must be at least a company sized formation," Kapten Sarikan said. "Maybe larger."

"But, how many of them are ANCANZ Federation Land Force Infantry?" Melnik asked aloud, briefly biting his lower lip.

"If we believe that tabloid media article," Sarikan said, recalling it onto the screen of his reader, "All the Severn girl has with her is what's left of an Embassy Protection Detachment, those that didn't get killed in your last engagement with her in Emirates City."

"She'd had plenty of time to get it reinforced, or replaced," Leftenan Diskul pointed out with dismissive shake of his head.

"Enough speculation!" Melnik snapped. "We are here to either kill, or capture and evict her, so let's stop talking and start doing, shall we gentlemen? She's dispersed her forces to cover the entire front, but she can't be strong everywhere. If most of her firepower is just the local farmers, well . . . they can't 'fire and manoeuvre.' That takes training, practice."

Melnik gauged the reaction of his subordinate Officers. Diskul's face was a wolfish grin. Sarikan's eyes had narrowed. He was holding his judgement and therefore his opinion back. A wise XO.

"Diskul, Three Platoon is still at full strength, well more so than the other two. Take it right flanking, go wide, around all the palm plantations and the east-side hill. Stay low and use the rainforest as cover. Skirt around the base of the right hill, go on for another kilometre, then climb up and over that same hill. Continue over its crest and come back down into this valley. You'll then hold that right flank and the high ground. Once you're established up there, send a patrol down to infiltrate the rear of their positions along the terraces."

Diskul nodded. "Yes, sir. Understood."

"You," Melnik said, indicating the youngest of the three Lieutenants from the Hai PSC. "Take what remains of Two Platoon and move onto the terraces on our left flank, don't go too far along them, just enough to set up a fire lane that covers the open ground where your people got hit earlier. You must prevent the enemy from deploying a reserve or moving troops from one position over to reinforce another. Do you understand me?"

"Yes Major,"

"And don't just sit there once in position. Send out a reconnaissance patrol. I don't want you launching a full-scale attack, but don't let them ignore you either. Probe for their firing positions. I need to know where that damn sniper is. I won't be upset if you manage to take it out. Not at all. "

"Yes Major." The Leftenan looked both scared and excited. Melnik would need to keep an eye on his left flank. He didn't intend for this lad to do much more than hold Severn's troops there, but the young Officer might surprise him.

A good surprise or a bad one?

"Kapten Sarikan, you go with him." Melnik said, then studied the terrain before him again. The trees along the rainforest's edge were the only solid cover he could see.

He turned to Leftenan Akarathit. "What remains of One Platoon are to advance as quickly as possible, using fire and manoeuvre, through the plantation towards the farm house and outbuildings at the far end of this re-entrant," he said pointing. "Once you get there, your task Leftenan, is to keep whatever assets they've got deployed up there pinned down, to stop them from reinforcing their positions along those terraces."

He paused, looking at their faces for any signs of confusion. "I will take the remainder of my people and advance on the farm outbuildings that we have already taken control of, those just past the entrance, and establish a forward Command Post, and provide a reserve for the rest of you, should it be needed."

Melnik finished his orders.

As soon as they engaged Severn and her bunch of island farmhands with coordinated fire, they'd break and run. Yes, this would work well.

"Any questions?" he asked them.

There were none.

"Then good luck gentlemen."

Safi had somehow managed to get Kat a brief, tight-beamed conversation through the radio jamming to the *Bella* by piggy-backing onto the global distress frequency for emergency radio transmission's of 156.8 MHz, also known as 'Channel Sixteen' in the VHF network. More than a bit unorthodox, and probably illegal, but it had worked.

"I see you're both at each other's throats," Gillan said when the static cleared. He confirmed that the *Bella* was now in position, much nearer to and within sensor range of Ellis, but just outside of visual. "Do you need anything else from me?" he asked her.

"No, not at the moment. Ellis won't dare use his auto-cannons on us, not with his own people so close. Unless you're able to give me any new Intel on his troop positions?"

"I can send you a visual from our UAVs last overhead pass, but I'm no analyst, I have no idea what he's up to."

True to his word, Gillan's UAV imagery did give Kat a good update on what was happening. Melnik certainly wasn't withdrawing. He was clearly ordering his men into position for another attack. Adjusting his forces, sending some to the east to infiltrate the rear of Mike's position on the terraces, another to the west to engage with Staff Freeman's crew.

And, he still had enough men to deploy directly up the middle, towards Kat's location.

The force on the western side, those heading for Staff Freeman's 'pasha' hill looked to be the smallest, but was it just a feint?

Could this really be the opening of his main thrust? If Staff Freeman lost the high ground, then this could all come apart, and fast! Kat shook her head. This was always the problem with overhead imagery, yes it let you count heads, but what those heads were attached to, and how capable the brain inside was . . . well that didn't show up in an image taken from two or three kilometres up.

Kat looked for her comms-tech. "Update Staff Freeman, it looks like he's got company heading his way."

"I'm on it ma'am."

Kat then turned to Mrs Lakhera. "Send a runner to find me if anything interesting starts to develop," Kat said, then moved off to undertake a quick review of her nearby troop positions.

Close to her CP the islanders had received the word not to shoot. Some were none too happy to have missed out on the first contact, but they now liked what they saw. More than a dozen Hai PSCs lay in the dirt under the coconut palms. A few still called for medical assistance.

Kat's next place to visit was a large barn, a short distance away from the farm house on the other side of the main track. As she moved nearer, hostile fire found her.

"Hey," Kat called out, "You've got wounded lying out in the sun. White flag, no weapons. Do you want to attend to them?"

"Okay, but you stay inside the barn. You break cover and we'll open fire." It was a PSC Corporal who called back in broken English.

"Agreed."

Compassion aside, if they got a few of their wounded into cover, then perhaps they might be a bit more reluctant to throw grenades about. But the Corporal wasn't stupid, he'd worked that out too. "But only the conscious. Leave the dead and any that are unconscious where they are," he ordered his men.

Three PSCs slipped forward. Unarmed, nobody took a shot at them. They made several trips, pulling five of their people into cover.

Nobody objected from the hostile's main position either. Nobody else got shot in the back for showing compassion this time. Evidently, whilst they redeployed into their next attack positions, there was now somehow an opportunity for humanitarian care too. Or perhaps they were too preoccupied to even notice?

When the casualty evacuations had finished and running in a low stoop, Kat made her way into one of the sangars on the 'poore' side's upper terrace. Twenty-five kilo sacks of rice had been used to build fire positions and blast walls. It wasn't much, but was better than nothing at all. Despite these rapidly improvised defences, this position still had the potential to deteriorate into a blood-bath . . . for both sides.

A women moved past Kat, pushing another sack of rice along in a wheelbarrow. She seemed to know exactly where she was going. At the end of the sangar she upended the barrow and dumped the sack out. Two men hefted it up into position. They worked in a determined silence. Maybe Kat didn't need to worry about the islanders running after all.

Maybe. But, blood-baths often occurred when neither side recognised that it might be a good time to surrender.

Princess, you had better come up with a plausible reason for Melnik, if not Ellis, to call it a day, as it doesn't look like these islanders have any such intentions.

A skinny local girl, probably about fifteen, came to a breathless halt beside Kat. "Mrs Lakhera says that stuff is happening that you need to see," she said in good, but heavily accented English.

Kat followed the girl at a brisk, 'double-time' jog back to her improvised Command Post in the tree line.

A quick glance outside told her everything she needed to know. It was time.

Mike stood aside as a young farmhand pulled another rice-bag into position, then another. A woman then held the steel rod steady for him, forcing the man to be careful, accurate with the sledge-hammer.

The third swing of the hammer drove the steel construction rod in, trapping the rice-bags into position within the improvised defensive wall. When they'd finished, Mike got down behind it, checking the required engagement arcs weren't impeded by this latest enhancement.

He nodded. "That will do nicely," he told his eager assistants.

The young man picked up another bag of rice and headed towards the other end of the sangar to repeat the process.

Mike put his eye to his weapon-sight again and studied the coconut plantation in front of him.

He hoped Melnik's people wouldn't immediately spot where the weapons fire was coming from. Sooner or later though, Melnik would get his act together, and his troops would attack.

Mike stood and headed further along the terrace, moving at a brisk pace. The boy who'd shared his subterranean camp only a few days before was now acting as his 'runner,' following along behind. "Anything for from Lieutenant Severn, sir," he asked.

"You just keep watching her signal set," Mike told him.

"And you must keep your head down, sir. Or your mother's going to be real mad if you get yourself hurt. You do have a mother, don't you?"

Mike laughed, "Despite the tales my Troopers might tell you, I am not a reptile hatched from an egg or created in a laboratory young man, so yes, I do indeed have a mother!"

"I told you he did," said the boy, sticking his tongue out at a nearby Trooper.

"And you're going to take *his* word for it?" the soldier

shot back with a grin of his own.

"Come with me," Mike told him.

None too happy, fearing he may be in for a reprimand, the Trooper followed his Officer.

After another dash along the terrace, they reached a flight of several stone and concrete steps that linked the upper and lower levels of the terracing. Mike went down, M37 at the ready, constantly scanning his surroundings with his own eyes and the cluster of clever tech fixed into the left side of his helmet.

The accompanying Trooper did the same, following Mike's lead.

Mike stopped and dropped to one knee. He took out his binoculars and studied the ground across the other side of the plantation. There was almost no wind. The Trooper went into an over-watch stance, weapon tight into his shoulder, protecting Mike.

Sergeant Varko approached them silently. He knelt beside Mike.

The Sergeant had deployed into an OP at the furthest extent of the farm, nearest to its entrance.

"Anything out there?" Mike asked him, still moving his binoculars across the terrain ahead.

"I know they're out there somewhere, sir, but I haven't physically seen their second-wave formations yet. We should be able to easily detect any movement or thermal anomalies, but nothing so far."

"Unless they've got some kind of personal shielding operating?" the Trooper said. "It might not be the latest clever tech. Old-style, thermal kites could work just as well in this environment."

Mike raised an eyebrow. Low rank didn't mean small brain.

Changing body position, Mike reviewed the deployment of nearby assets. Two Troopers were inside the next sangar, keeping themselves concealed, along with a dozen or so islanders.

Whoever had orchestrated the initial assault had wrongly assumed that Kat lacked the manpower to cover such a wide front. Unfortunately, they wouldn't make that mistake again.

Mike studied the treeline, and blinked. A minute or two ago there had been nothing. But now his thermal filter showed a long file of Hai PSCs were moving into the rainforest on their opposite flank, heading towards Staff Freeman's position on the 'pasha' hillside. They moved as silently as the terrain allowed. They moved slowly, but with purpose. The more of the ground they covered in the relative safety of the rainforest, rather than the open ground beneath coconut palms, the better for their survival.

Mike stowed his binoculars and made 'ready' his rifle.

"Show time," Sergeant Varko grinned and went back to his concealed forward OP.

"Roger that," agreed the Trooper as he adjusted the magnification on his M37's sights.

"Remember, against the PSCs, target their arms and legs . . . if you can . . . but don't jeopardise your own life. Use lethal force only if you really need to."

"And the mercs?"

"Our 5.56 rounds won't have much effect at maximum range on their armour, so either go for head shots, or risk them getting much closer, probably 150 metres, maybe less. Your call."

"Roger that."

"Excuse me, sir," the young lad was now at his side, "New message from the Princess."

Mike glanced at the replicated coloured rectangles. Three green then a blue. XXXV, 35. His helmet did the rest. "She want's a sit-rep. Well . . . this ought to tell her everything she needs to know," he said, and fired the first shot of what would hopefully be Great Nicobar island's last battle.

As Kat waited for her two flank commander's rudimentary updates, then watched as events evolved in front of her. Armour encased infantry advanced through the farm's entrance pillars and continued on, towards the out-buildings a further hundred metres inside. On her far left, out of visual range, where the plantation stopped and the rainforest started, Sgt Varko advised that he now had the 'enemy in sight.'

Another long message containing directions, distances and enemy formation sizes came in from Staff Freeman. It took her comms-tech almost as long studying the map on his display screen as it had to receive and interpret the actual message before he made his report.

"Ma'am, Staff Freeman advises that he has two sections of enemy advancing on his position, although they're still about five hundred meters out. He also advised that a platoon size formation is cresting the ridge-line of the hill known as 'poore' opposite his position."

Kat consulted the display to get a better understanding of what she was being told.

"Tell him to engage both formations as soon as they are within range. The quicker that happens the less likely they'll be able to establish defensive positions."

"On it," the comms-tech simply said.

Minutes later Mike and Sergeant Varko both send the simple, single blue rectangle of signal V, 'Enemy engaged.'

Another extended volley of M37 fire came from that direction. A few hunting rifles joined in.

"That says it all," Kat decided. "Update all call-sign's, engage as targets present," she shouted, both at the comms-tech and to those around her.

The farm and the surrounding countryside came alive with small-arms fire within a minute of her order being given.

Armoured infantry on the main track stumbled and fell as they took several direct hits from sniper rounds. Only one picked himself up and ran to catch up with his still advancing colleagues. Hunting rifle ammunition didn't penetrate high grade military body armour.

Kat had command of the fire teams in and around her Command Post and the farm house, but she was also the personal owner of one of the few M37s in the immediate vicinity. She frowned, inwardly deciding between just observing, like the doctrine said a good commander did, or doing something about the adversaries advancing her way, their hostile intent now more than evident.

Kat 'made ready' her M37, then double-timed it from the CP to her nearest four-man Section or Fire Team. The four Troopers were holding back, not engaging.

"No point wasting ammo at this distance," Lance Corporal Vries told her, as if she might disagree.

"Did you pass that message along to the islanders?" Kat said.

"No ma'am," the junior NCO admitted. Then sent a Trooper running in each direction, spreading Kat's orders, but stayed around himself to watch as Kat took aim with her own weapon.

The sighting mechanism told her the advancing hostiles were now just within the weapon's effective range. She thumbed off the safety, controlled her breathing and took aim. Out in the sun, a sweating PSC, his uniform accoutrements suggesting he was at least a senior NCO, if not an actual Officer, was driving his men purposely forward.

She took a deep breath, partially exhaled, paused briefly and gently squeezed off a single round like she'd been taught.

The sighted PSC took the hit square in his right shoulder and crumpled immediately to the ground. Not a fatal shot if he received prompt medical attention.

Kat settled herself into a more comfortable firing position. Three shots later, and two more hostiles down, She dropped another PSC with a round into his centre of his visible mass. Predictably, his nearby colleagues went to ground, then sent a heavy hail of fire back in Kat's direction.

She countered by changing her own firing position and saw others around her do the same. "We have to keep them engaged. If we go silent, they'll charge us," she warned those within hearing distance.

"Understood," the old man beside her said, "but we don't have unlimited ammunition. It's not like we planned for this."

Kat swore inwardly to herself, why hadn't she taken a

detailed inventory of how much ammo the islanders and brought to this fight. The old man had a good point. Some islanders had hunting rifles, most farmers around the world did, but it was for vermin control, not to fight a war. But . . . if they didn't keep up their side of the ongoing exchange of small-arms fire, Melnik with all his mercenaries and PSCs, would walk right in and start shooting them at close, perhaps even hand to hand, range!

Note to self, next fight, bring along a Logistics branch supply specialist.

"Tell everyone to conserve their ammunition," Kat ordered, "but we have to keep up a minimum level of exchanges."

The old man nodded and headed off to spread the word.

Kat moved back to her Command Post. Even with no shooting coming from her immediate vicinity, there was still a sufficient volume of rounds flying about to confirm that the PSCs suppressing fire was effective, and that they were steadily advancing towards her position.

"They are seriously pissed at us," Mrs Lakhera commented to Kat when she arrived back inside the CP.

"We've not exactly been forgiving," Kat replied.

"If you invade people's homes," Mrs Lakhera continued, "You can't expect to then win a popularity contest."

"Are we winning?" Another of the islanders asked Kat.

"That depends on how much ammunition they brought," Kat said. "If they shoot themselves dry, then they've got a problem. But we could quite easily do exactly the same!"

"I was wondering when someone might consider that," another islander said, maybe only now realising that he'd not thought of it before. Supplies, be it food, fuel or ammunition all mattered in a fight.

Kat reconsidered her options. She could hunker down and wait to see who ran out of ammo first, or, err . . . she didn't have an alternative option. This was a battle she hadn't planned on, against a mercenary officer, who styled himself as 'Major,' and who had most probably never anticipated this level of defiance either. The outcome might come down to who had the last round remaining within their magazine.

Unless . . .

Kat needed to change her thinking. Evaluate the situation.

Then an idea occurred to her. She was certain that Captain Gillan and the rest of the *Bella*'s crew wouldn't appreciate her dropping this hot potato into their laps. Well, they'd voluntarily signed on with her, nobody had forced them. They admitted themselves, that being with her was 'never boring.'

"Safi, try to establish a secure link with the *Fires of Beltane*," again. Do whatever you did last time if necessary."

"Jamming is still in effect, from both us and them," Safi confirmed. "But I will try, despite it being illegal to piggy-back onto the emergency channel."

"I fully expected it to be, but I need to speak with Captain Gillan. It's rather urgent. Do whatever you can, *please* try to establish a comms channel."

Major Melnik did not like the way this battle was going.

Too many of his own people now lay in the dust in between the palm trees of this re-entrant. The intensity of enemy small-arms fire targeting his men had actually been pathetic, it was nothing like the ferocity he'd expected it to be, and it was already tapering off to almost nothing, but he hadn't given sufficient consideration to that damned sniper, a very skilled sniper. His MkXII armour provided good protection against 5.56 and 7.62 millimetre rounds, but not the 12.7 used by this sniper's high-velocity rifle. He considered sending out a runner, to give revised orders to Leftenan Akarathit, but then thought better of it.

Only a half dozen PSCs were now firing from his position in on the main trackway.

Sarikan had done a check of ammo after his last Orders Group. Several of the crates everyone thought were full of ammo had turned out to be otherwise, instead containing propaganda pamphlets. Apparently, part of their financier's strategy for subjugating Great Nicobar's unwilling inhabitants. Not at all what he needed right now!

Sarikan had sent a runner to advise him of this. That unfortunate individual had come under a hail of fire from the islanders a full three hundred metres out from the Major's position. Caught out in the open, with no cover or protection, the runner had nowhere to go and was mortally wounded, but somehow still managed to deliver his message.

Major Melnik might not be happy with the current 'ground,' nor the 'situation' or his overall 'mission.' Nor was he happy with the 'service support' and 'command and signal,' because neither of them existed, but he was a methodical thinker. He checked on his subordinate formations. First, his right flank. Then the centre, which was rapidly going nowhere. What did that leave him? He glanced to his left, where a few of his PSCs had gone to ground half way up the facing slope of the west-side hill.

Changing position, he used his voice, combined with age-old infantry hand signals, to attract the attention of his nearest Mercenary Sergeant or Feldwebel.

"Sir," the Senior NCO called in acknowledgement.

"Give me half of your men, Feldwebel Gant."

"Yes, Herr Major. What do you want me to do with the rest, sir?"

"Stay here and keep the islanders from retaking this position." Melnik looked around, spotted the Unteroffizier who usually drove his command vehicle, and motioned for him to get closer.

"When our men get here, check their ammo levels. We'll need to move fast."

"Yes, sir," the Unteroffizier confirmed with curt nod.

While the junior NCO did as he'd been ordered, checking the ammunition levels of his colleagues, Major Melnik went quickly down the list of other things he would need doing in the next fifteen to thirty minutes . . . assuming he'd guessed right.

*   *   *

It had taken a considerable amount of Safi's computing power and programming, but eventually the HI had managed to get a communication channel out to the *Bella*. "I am sorry it has taken me so long, Kat, but their EM jamming is not of a normal format. In simple terms, the obstacles to overcome are simple but the depth of them is extensive."

Kat didn't respond to Safi, instead choosing to concentrate on Captain Gillan.

"I see you're fully committed," was his first comment.

"Yes, we're up to our necks in shit and snakes once again! And, I have no idea how much ammunition the locals brought with them."

"Ahh, that's could be a problem," Gillan agreed.

"You think?" Kat replied sarcastically. "It's a 'big time' problem for us. Therefore Captain, I need *you* to settle this, or events may not go down as well as my growing reputation now requires them to."

"That bad. But how? Do I have any weapon systems on the *Bella* that could engage a target ashore?"

Kat could almost hear the frown growing on Gillan's face.

"I know I'm going to regret this, but what do you want me to do, Princess?"

A voice from somewhere on the *Bella*'s bridge could be heard saying, "That's something you should never ask a Severn, and especially not our one!"

It sounded like Myra. Kat chose to ignore it. "I need you to engage Ellis and the other ship in the bay. I don't care if you scare him out, chase him out, or blow him out of the water, but I need Melnik to think his ride out of here is gone."

Kat paused to glance out of her Command Post. The fire-fight hadn't slackened any. "Jensen, a whole lot of good people are going to die if we let this fight go the full distance. Right now, I can't think of any other way to stop it."

"How I hate it when you tell me I'm the only one who

can save the situation, and *you* as well!" Gillan sighed. "But then I should have known you hadn't actually got my ship into this position for fun."

Actually, Kat had done that long before she'd thought of this way out. To her, the two events weren't connected. *Or perhaps I was subconsciously planning for such an eventuality? Who knows?*

"Thank you, Captain Gillan, and please thank the whole crew. There are a lot of people here who are going to owe them their lives."

"Kat, only heroes respond to that kind of talk. Remember, we're just in it for the money."

"Of course, how could I possibly forget," she replied, hopefully it still sounded suitably sarcastic back on the *Bella*.

"If you'll excuse me, Lieutenant, I and my reprobate crew have a bit of manipulating to do. You said you wouldn't mind if we scare Ellis away? Did I hear that correctly?"

"Anything that makes him unavailable to give Melnik and his troops a ride out of here would be most appreciated, but he doesn't scare easy. He'll almost certainly fight back, don't forget that."

"Hmmm. Let me talk with Myra, I'm sure we'll come up with something."

"Whatever it is, do it soon."

Melnik led a 'strike-force' of his own mercenaries up the main track of the plantation as fast as he could push them. His Unterofficer was behind, collecting up any stragglers who couldn't maintain the pace. When the 'stragglers' became the larger group, the Major conceded and reduced the pace. Slightly.

He wanted to get ahead of Two Platoon and Kapten Sarikan on his left flank, and get ahead of them now, with whatever he could, rather than get there with a larger force in an hour or two.

Melnik knew only too well that he was in plain sight of that damn sniper, but also that he was probably out of range or effectiveness, or both, of every other weapon ranged against him. He had no artillery, not even a mortar, but as the Severn girl and her island farmers hadn't anything of that ilk either, he wasn't unduly concerned.

Not for the first time did the Major shake his head. The idiots who had put this escapade together were so certain this island occupation was just a 'walk in the park.' Just walk in, intimidate the locals, and start raking in the money from the islands valuable natural assets. How utterly wrong they had been!

Melnik suddenly wished the soldiers he was hustling along were the financiers of this screw up. No . . . no he didn't. They would have dropped dead from a collective heart attack a long time ago, and he wanted to get paid for this screw up.

He signalled a halt and his men went to ground. The cover was non-existent between the palm tree's trunks. Whilst his men rested he raised his binoculars, studying the ground situation.

To his left, Two Platoon and Kapten Sarikan still attempted to move through the rainforest and close with the enemy emplacements high up on that hillside. The defensive works looked hastily prepared, but professionally camouflaged and concealed. Except to his trained eyes. There didn't seem to be that many shooters, so why had his people made such little progress?

If he worked his way along the base of that hill, past the farm house to where the terracing stopped and the rainforest began, he could support Sarikan by drawing some of the enemy's fire away from Two Platoon . . .

Here and there, he saw the spit of flame, as rounds left a rifle's muzzle, easily visible along the terraces and in the treeline.

He smiled. These islanders must pack their own ammunition. They were farmers, not soldiers, so used the cheaper powder that created a smoke plume when fired. And that told him a lot. Each round would therefore be variable in both range and stopping power. They might not be hitting what they aimed at, and at what effective range? But, up close neither wouldn't matter, so he'd keep back for now, let them shoot. Hopefully Kapten Sarikan had worked that out too? *Who really has the worse ammunition situation here?*

Melnik turned, moving his focus to the opposite hillside, the taller of the two features and Leftenan Diskul and his Third Platoon.

He scoured the hill. Systematically searching for anything, but found nothing. Occasional fire came from concealed positions just below its crest.

The Major slowly put away his binoculars. He had a lot to think about.

Kat had run out of things to worry about. She really didn't like how that felt, not one little bit.

Gillan had his sailing orders. She just hoped that whatever it was he was going to attempt, was soon! She needed to know how Ellis would respond. In a few hours it would be getting dark. And once it was dark, the question would be, who would use the night to slink away?

Kat wondered how things had gone for Mike amongst the rice-sack sangars on the 'poore' side terraces. The attack there seemed to have stalled. As long as Mike had ammunition to keep them at bay, nobody seemed to be enfilading his position with any determination.

In front of Kat it didn't look any better for Melnik. His fire was steady, but he'd stopped his advance, no longer risking the open ground beneath the palms.

How long had it been since a simple, stand-up fight, just infantry against infantry, had occurred? She'd have to ask her Grandpa Jim next time she was on speaking terms with the old git.

Kat edged as far over as she dared without exposing herself to any hostile fire and squinted. Not much to see.

That wasn't a good development.

A local girl of perhaps ten or twelve, approximately Grace's age, ran in to the Command Post. She smiled at Kat. then turned to Mrs Lakhera. "My mum says you need to come quick," she explained in the local language. "Mum says she can see something that you can't, and you need to." The words came out in a garbled rush, the girl was out of breath.

Safi translated instantly into Kat's earpiece. She couldn't see anything new or developing from the CP so maybe a different view was indeed required.

"Keep an eye on things here," Kat told Mrs Lakhera. "Let me know if anything significantly changes." Then she followed the girl outside into the darkening evening.

Unlike most adults, who used flashlights, the girl had no difficulty seeing in the dwindling light. Kat followed her for a while, until they'd crossed the main track and were back inside the main barn. A floor level access-hatch had been pulled up. The plantation owner was standing nearby.

"Where does this go?" Kat asked him.

"Storm drain. When the monsoons come, this helps get the water away from the plantation before root damage to the palms can occur. Takes the rain away, into the wetlands you came through to get here."

Kat climbed down to the chamber below. Four circular, pipe tunnels, each at ninety degrees to each other led off from where she stood. She activated the flashlight fixed to the left side of her helmet, casting a blue hue over proceedings.

They took the tunnel to their right, then after ten, maybe fifteen metres it turned a sharp ninety degrees to the left.

"We're right under the main track," her young guide informed Kat, "The rain gullies on the surface feed into here."

This latest section of pipe they'd entered was long, with a numbered designation painted every dozen metres. There was no other light within. It seemed to go on forever, and evidently wasn't designed for someone of one-point-eight-two metre stature clad in full combat armour! The girl didn't stop and continued to scamper her way along it. Kat followed diligently along behind.

"Are you certain this is the right way?" Kat asked.

"You follow, you follow," the girl told her.

Another hundred metres and the girl suddenly stopped. Kat did the same, and found herself in an underground chamber hewn from the limestone bedrock of the island. The interior was well lit, so Kat flicked off her helmet's flashlight and took a look around.

The islanders inside the chamber obliged, and promptly turned off the overhead lighting, plunging the space into total, pitch-black, darkness. Then they pulled down a retractable ladder, exactly the same as the one she'd used in the barn, and proceeded to open the hatchway above.

In the very last of the evening light that now filtered down into the chamber Kat studied the faces of the islanders who surrounded her. It didn't look like these islanders had done much fighting so far. There were no spent cartridge cases, nor the acrid smell of propellant that went with it.

The girl was getting a hug from her mother and in an avalanche of words, repeating that she'd brought the Princess just like she was told to. The mother, an attractive woman somewhere in her late thirties, saw Kat glance at the hunting rifle and somehow felt she had to justify why it hadn't been used. "We haven't had anything in range to shoot at, well not with the bullets this thing puts out anyway."

"I doubt those in battle-armour would even break step even if you had hit them."

The woman smiled. "My thinking exactly. But, I think we'll be needing it real soon. You need to see what's happening."

Kat climbed the ladder and looked out, but couldn't see very much. She was further down the track. Not as far as the entrance pillars, but not too far from the cluster of outbuildings. If her improvised CP was at the 12 o'clock position, then she was now at the six, or perhaps the five or maybe the seven.

"You need to stick your head right out to see anything," the woman said, and promptly did. No helmet, no armour, the mother didn't seem to realise the danger she risked from a stray bullet. Or maybe she did.

Kat tapped the woman on the leg, indicating that she should come back inside. Kat took her place. She dropped her visor, hoping its numerous filters would give her something more significant that black to be looking at. If anyone got serious about shooting at them, they'd most likely be dead in a single volley.

Off to Kat's left, camouflaged from the casual observer, was Staff Freeman's position and the sniper team, along with four of their M214 machine gunners, occupying a trench line just below the crest of the hillside.

Suddenly Kat realised, her ammunition problem, at least for her own people was solved. The cycling multi-barrels of the M214 spat out a scything hail of destruction, and for that reason Kat had deliberately restricted their sighting and use. Aimed shots into arms and legs to reduce the number of casualties that ended up dead simply wasn't achievable with such a weapon system. But, the ammunition pack that each of the gunners had on their back took twelve hundred rounds. If they broke those open and took the rounds out of the linkage that enabled them to feed the rotating barrels, then she was back in business. Two of the M214s located with Staff Freeman could keep their ammunition packs intact. That was, after all, their final defensive position, so it might yet be needed for a 'last stand.' But the other two . . . .

An Officer of the Land Force's Infantry Branch would have known all of this, but she and Mike were Fleet, and this wasn't something covered in their training at OTA(F). Staff Freeman and Sergeant Varko obviously knew all about this too, and that's why they hadn't raised ammunition as being problem earlier, because it simply wasn't one. Issue resolved. Should she now try to recall Captain Gillan? Stop whatever he was about to try with the *Bella*? Providing that Safi could actually cut through all the comms jamming a third time!

In the valley between the two hills what looked like the survivors of the PSC's first attack, reorganised themselves. They'd probably try to out-flank the farmhouse. No fire came from them. Not yet anyway.

Using her binoculars, Kat looked further up the valley towards the farmhouse.

About three hundred metres ahead, a column of soldiers moved along in single file. They were the PSCs. Maybe the odd mercenary was in the mix too. Kat needed to think, to focus. What was their objective? It wasn't clear. It wasn't obvious.

Were they going to sweep back through the coconut palms and clear the barn and farmhouse of Kat's people and the local farmers? Or maybe move along the terraces and try to take her Command Post?

Kat turned back to Staff Freeman's position. She poked her head out a bit further and looked to see what level of defence his improvised ridge-line fortifications might offer them.

The term "broadside," came to her. Sailing ships with all their guns pointing out on either side. The weak spot was the unprotected stern.

She shook her head and ducked back down. "Is this the furthest we can get, just this single access point?" Kat asked the woman.

She nodded silently.

Kat stuck her head out again. Staff Freeman had been busy enhancing his position, digging more zigzagging trenches down from his improvised firing points near the hill's crest. He'd now be able to bring weapons down the hillside, to engage targets further along the valley in either direction, deterring anyone that might be trying to out-flank him, but also potentially get engaged himself from the fruit trees on the terrace directly below him, assuming that those particular PSCs had any fight left in them.

That wasn't a bet Kat was willing to take.

Damn it . . . Captain Gillan will hopefully get Ellis suitably distracted out at sea in another ninety minutes or so, but . . . what were the odds that this ground situation will still be evolving when the Bella *engages him?*

Kat risked another look around the valley in the rapidly dwindling evening light. The lead elements of the patrolling file of PSC personnel had appeared along the crest of the hillside opposite Staff Freemans position. They had stopped and then gone to ground.

Further down the valley, at ground level, a kneeling figure. His or her binoculars came up. Yes, most definitely an officer.

Kat adjusted the focus on her own optics and studied the figure.

Armour. MkXII armour. His only weapon was a pistol and he wore it at his hip. Old fashioned, traditional . . . maybe.

He turned and looked right at her. The two of them seemed to study each other for a long moment.

Kat briefly wondered if she was looking at Major Melnik when Safi confirmed that it was indeed him into her earpiece.

Am I watching him manoeuvre his formations, committing his reserves for a final throw of the dice? What is he playing at?

Could her own Troopers hold the advancing PSC infantry back?

Kat ducked back down inside. "I'm going to get you reinforcements. Until they get here, you have got to keep everyone out of this place."

"I know," the woman said solemnly.

"Can I take your girl as a guide?"

"Yes. She knows these tunnels very well."

"Good, when I get the reinforcements up here to replace you, you get out. As soon as the soldiers get here, you and your child, you both get out."

"I'll be out and running," the woman nodded.

"Maana, are we going to be alright?"

The woman knelt down to be eye to eye with her daughter. "Yes Shaharn, we'll be fine. You show the Princess back through the pipes. She is going to introduce you to good soldiers who have guns. The Mahaapaur might be there too. You bring the soldiers back here, then you and me, we're going to run and hide. Is that okay?"

"Yes, maana," the girl said bravely.

The woman tousled her daughter's hair. "Now, run."

The girl backed slowly away from her mother. Kat stooped and headed into the tunnel opening, moving as fast as the protective body-armour permitted.

Then she heard. "No, that's the wrong way, follow me."

Kat backed out of what looked like the right way and followed the kid for what seemed like an eternity, but was probably wasn't more that fifteen, or twenty minutes, before the tunnel opened up and Kat was finally able to stand again.

Then she was climbing up the ladder, back into the barn. No sooner had she cleared the ladder that the red beam of a sighting-laser splashed onto her breastplate.

"Hold your fire," she shouted.

Hardly a breath later, a helmet encased head ducked out of the shadows, maybe ten metres in front of her. Then a second armoured figure appeared behind the first. It was Corporal Ferro of Third Squad.

"That you, your Highness?"

"We've got problems," Kat informed them.

"Not back here, ma'am" the nearest of the two Troopers said.

"And it was all going so well," the other one added.

Kat stopped, resting her hands on her hips whilst she slowed her breathing. "I thought I'd brought a detachment of Land Force Infantry to this party, not a pair of second-rate stand-up comedians!"

They came towards her, assault rifles at the ready, their faces hard, serious.

"What's the problem, ma'am?"

Kat explained the situation. They didn't need to be told twice.

"That's so inconsiderate," the Trooper said.

"Don't worry, ma'am, we're on it," Corporal Ferro added. "We can split into two sections. I'll take mine to the location of the girl's mother, Lance Corporal Vries can set up a blocking position. Did you have a specific place in mind for that, ma'am?"

"This young lady will be your guide," Kat informed him.

"I'm a big girl, I'll be ten next birthday," The kid protested.

Kat had no idea when the child's 'next birthday' might be, but it was irrelevant, she just smiled at her.

"Her mother is holding another access chamber with little more than a hunting rifle. Get down there as quickly as you can, then get her, the kid and any other islanders, out. Maybe improvise a sangar from rice bags about halfway along the tunnel if time permits? Use that as your blocking position. Understood Corporal?"

"Yes, ma'am, one fire-team will hold the chamber, no withdrawal. The other section holds the blocking position. Again, no withdrawal, no retreat, no surrender. We fight to the last."

Kat knew she had just sentenced Third Squad to victory or death. Not an easy order to give, but there was no other way.

"I'll try to get more rice bags sent down. If you have time you might want to build a couple of fire positions within the tunnels."

"Don't worry ma'am," Corporal Ferro said. "We'll hold them." He turned to his subordinate. "Rob, bring the rest of the Squad to my location, double time. The Princess has a little job for us."

Within ten minutes the other members of Third Squad arrived. They took a few more minutes to prepare their equipment, relocate additional water, rations and ammunition from their back-packs onto their belts and into their suits. Then they followed the young girl down. into the tunnel network of the storm drains.

"Corporal," Kat began.

"I know, ma'am. If they get past us, the threat axis completely changes, and we're potentially all screwed."

"But, don't ignore any other hot-spots that might develop," Kat told him.

"That's why us Infantry NCO's have eyes in the backs of our heads as well as the front, ma'am. Any chance we could get a few more of our people to support?"

Kat's group in the middle were supposed to be the reserve and now she was committing most of them to a specific tasking too. She didn't really have any more assets to assign, to manoeuvre with.

"I'm sorry, Corporal, if I can I will, but don't count on it. Everything, everyone, is already committed elsewhere."

Ferro nodded in acceptance and returned to deploying his Squad.

Kat went in the other direction, returning to her improvised Command Post.

SIX : FOURTEEN

So, this is the infamous Princess Katarina! Melnik reflected. Apparently, Ellis had initially dismissed this woman as nothing but a spoilt brat, a rich debutante looking for her next social function. Jacob von Brühl hadn't given her more credibility either. Andrev Melnik would not be making that same mistake.

His face was hard. Determined.

"She has fought well, with intelligence. Not as a frightened little creature, trapped in the bewildering headlights of modern warfare," Melnik pondered to himself.

He returned his binoculars into their 'stowed position' in a purpose-made indentation of his breast-plate, then unholstered his pistol, waving is it air. He signalled his men to move forward.

"Death or Glory," ran up the line of nearby Hai PSC personnel.

Melnik stepped forward.

"Death or Glory," they shouted again.

Melnik dismissed their shouts as meaningless bravado. *Amateurs, they have no idea.*

"Death or Glory," came again from his un-armoured PSCs.

"Follow me," Melnik shouted before the following formation could shout out again, leading them forward in an extended line at a walking pace. All of his accompanying mercenaries followed him along with any nearby PSCs. He tried not to smile. This was like something out of ancient history. Men with assault rifles walking into battle. He was under a kilometre from the enemy position below the crest of the left hill. That left ridge seemed to have all their weapons aimed down, into the valley, nothing covering their own flanks.

That was something Melnik strongly suspected that a certain Lieutenant Severn of the ABCANZ Fleet was busy correcting. Melnik had troops infiltrating the terraces and they already held the farmstead's outbuildings near the entrance.

"Forward," Melnik shouted again, and increased their pace. No need to tarry here, whilst still out of range. They'd be at the double, running, soon enough when the bullets started flying.

"Anything from Staff Freeman?," Kat asked her comms-tech.

"No ma'am, nothing. Had nothing from him in the last thirty five minutes," was his reply.

"Ensign Steiger?" Kat enquired after instead, taking care that her face didn't show her growing concern.

"I spoke with the young lad who's acting as his runner, maybe ten minutes ago, but he reports the Ensign Steiger is somewhat busy. If you really want to talk with him, he'll go and give him a message, but honestly, it's not very safe to be moving about out there now.

Without radio comms, Kat's command had just reduced itself to those in her immediate vicinity.

"Okay folks, listen up. We've held Melnik back in most locations." That brought a small cheer from the locals standing around her. Her own people didn't join in. "But he evidently hasn't had enough." That stopped any further jubilation.

"I believe he is now advancing through the valley, the plantation, clearing out any of our remaining fire positions. He'll want to get his troops down, inside that storm drain too."

"No," and "we can't let that happen," or variations thereof, seemed to be a popular response to her words.

She didn't have time to wait until things quietened down. "I'm taking the few Troopers that I have in this location to try to stop that attack. If we fail, you will be the only thing left to stop them."

"Then I will see to it that we do exactly that," Mrs Lakara said with a confirmatory nod.

"Mahaapaur, do you or any of your people want to come with me?" Kat asked.

"Can't bear to have me out of your sight, is that it?" the old man said.

"No, I just thought you might like to use that rifle of yours." Kat said then looked around for the plantation's owner. "The hostiles that have occupied your outbuilding . . . that might become a problem . . . so we'll need to retake those buildings and neutralise their unwelcome 'visitors.' How hard and thick are the walls?

"They are made from local wood. From padauk . . . all the trees came from this part of the island. To do otherwise would create discord, an unhappy structure, as tree-spirits from different areas would not get along," the man told her with much sincerity. "My father built them maybe thirty-five years ago."

"Could you and your farm workers infiltrate those buildings? I need all of the enemy troops within to either be dead or to surrender."

"I understand. We will try."

"Safi, as soon as you can, get a message back to the *Bella*, even if it's only a nano data burst, get me another sit-rep on whatever Ellis is up to. If he runs . . . well, maybe we can use that to stop this bloodshed."

"Understood, Kat."

As Kat turned to leave, the old Mahaapaur came to stand beside her. "I am much too old for this, but two of my sons will stand alongside you."

"They're very welcome," Kat said. More than one political dynasty was evidently based on being in the right place for the right shoot-out. The Severn's weren't the only ones!

Corporal Davis appeared and Kat quickly updated him on the latest employment taskings she'd requested from the locals. She also enlightened him on her latest problem. They consulted Safi's projected three-dimensional map display for several minutes and agreed that the farmstead's outbuildings needed to be liberated first, to make Melnik's rear position vulnerable.

"You take three of your Squad and clear out those fruit trees along that terracing on the right side," Kat ordered. "Give me the other two and we'll help the locals take those outbuildings back."

"Ma'am, if you go and get yourself killed, the Staff Sergeant will kill me himself, not to mention Ensign Steiger, if not the King and the Prime Minister too!"

"Don't worry, Corporal. I promise not to get suddenly dead. And, you take care yourself too," she told him, moving towards the plantation owner, his relatives and workers were now waiting for her.

The dash back to the barn, into the access shaft and through the storm drain was uneventful. They squeezed over and around Lance Corporal Vries's rice bag fire position. Once Kat, her accompanying pair of Troopers, the plantation owner's workers and Mahaapaur's sons were all in the water intercept chamber with Corporal Ferro, and any and all flashlights had been extinguished, Kat slowly climbed up the ladder, opened the metal hatch and slipped out into the balmy night air.

She ran for the first outbuilding and made it, but the first of many enemy shots now came their way like a swarm of angry insects. Her accompanying Troopers were only halfway to the nearest outbuilding when the rounds sought them. The bullets missed the first infanteer, but the second Trooper had an incoming round take a deep gouge from her left shoulder pauldron, causing her to tumble, before regaining her feet and finding most-welcome cover.

Kat waived the plantation owner and his un-armoured workers back, then checked her rifle's safety-catch was off. She aimed a three-round burst into an upper window from which some of the incoming fire issued. Someone got hit. A weapon fell from the window and clattered down the steep pitch of the roof before dropping to the dusty ground below.

Kat and her two Troopers quickly neutralised anyone

foolish enough to present themselves at a window or door of the largest outbuilding. In the silence that followed, the plantation owner with a number of his workers, made a run for the largest outbuilding. Someone from within the building complex opened up on full-automatic, red tracer ammunition illuminating the evening darkness. One of the plantation workers was hit in the leg.

Kat returned the hostile fire with another burst from her own M37, then shouted to the farmer. "We," she said, indicating her two Troopers, "Are going to put that building under deliberate enfilading fire. When we do, you and your workers are to get across that courtyard, either individually or two at a time. Once you're all across, signal me. When we storm the building, you are to follow us inside. We can use grenades, but it will obviously increase the amount of internal damage."

"I'm sure my wife will object, but I think she'd rather lose the equipment we store there than me or one of the boys," the plantation owner replied.

"I'm not so sure about that," one of the others added, but it was accompanied with a wide grin.

Kat sighted on the target outbuilding. "Stand by . . . fire," she said and opened-up on the timber walls of the principal outbuilding's upper level. Their tungsten-cored 5.56 millimetre rounds punched effortlessly through the building's timber panels. Someone screamed. The two Troopers added their weapons capability to the attack, and the farmer and his accompanying workers, less the one with the leg wound, moved swiftly across the courtyard. One of the Mahaapaur's sons went down. Kat couldn't see how bad his injury was, but he didn't get up.

Her weapon clicked and she changed magazine, but when she put the sight back into her eye, she couldn't identify any weapon's fire emanating from the building. It took her a few seconds to realise it was coming from the terraces of fruit trees where Corporal Davis was now attacking.

The Trooper to her right loaded up his assault rifle's integral grenade launcher and after calling out the obligatory "fire in the hole" warning of a grenade going into a confined space, sent one, then a second high explosive fragmentation grenade on its way towards the largest outbuilding's open door and upper-level hatch.

For a slow count of around five or six seconds, nothing happened, then the first grenade detonated and fire belched from inside.

Training took over and within a few seconds of the second grenade exploding Kat her two Troopers were up and charging towards the blown-out doors. There were shouts in several languages as the farm workers followed them inside.

No shots were fired.

"Captain, sir, we have company," the crewman at the *Hyperion*'s sensor board advised.

"Cast your board onto the main screen," Ellis ordered.

"Aye, sir, on main screen."

"Is that it? Is that the best we can do?" Ellis already knew the answer from the data displayed around the screen's edges. It showed a ship, at extreme visual range, in a 'bow-on' configuration.

The image grew slightly and centred itself on the display.

"Sensors, anything else you can tell me?"

"Not a lot sir. It's putting out some kind of electronic counter-measure that we don't have the tech to even attempt cutting through. It has two large, military grade reactors, but there is no reading from its race-track, so it must be shielded."

"What kind of ship would have shielded plasma tracks," Ellis said aloud as he studied the image. He already knew the answer. "What's that?" He pulled a laser pointer from his chair. "There, what do you make of that? Is that AMAP? Has modular armour been added to this vessel?

Mr Badali looked blankly at Ellis. It meant nothing to him.

"Some warships have AMAP. It prevents some anti-ship missiles and torpedoes getting through, or at least reduces the damage that those that do might make." Ellis scowled at Badali. "Whoever sent Princess Severn out here . . . with a Detachment of Infantry . . . ECM capability . . . and a dual reactor configuration usually only found in warships . . . not to mention AMAP enhancement . . . do you somehow think they would have then overlooked her offensive capability? What do you think Mr Badali?"

"Err . . . no . . . that would seem unlikely" the man stuttered.

"Sensors, can you tell me anything about the weapons fit on that vessel? Anything at all?"

"Nothing, sir. Our sensors can't penetrate the ECM. I can speculate, given her apparent dimensions and hold configuration, but cannot substantiate anything. ASM missiles and or torpedo tubes would seem most likely. I see no evidence of any 127 or 155 millimetre guns or concealed auto-cannons, but with that much reactor power she could potentially have any number of experimental weapon systems fitted. Hypersonic strike missiles, laser anti-air defences or perhaps even a rail gun."

"So, they're just sitting there . . . patiently waiting for us to take a swing at Miss Severn ashore with our puny auto-cannons . . . and then they'll retaliate . . . and swat us like an annoying insect." Ellis finished speaking and drew a breath. It was full of anger, like he'd just expelled fire. He wanted that meddlesome girl so badly. She'd taken the *Berserker* away from him, and now this!

Only two choices immediately came to his mind. One was to attack, but that probably meant death for him and his ship. The other was to withdraw. *But that is effectively worse than death! A long, slow, agonising humiliation, the total loss of all honour.*

If it was up to Ellis, he knew exactly which one he'd take. He was certainly not a coward . . . but . . . he needed to remain professional. His duty was to his crew. His *civilian* crew. They had all signed up for a certain level of risk. Risk that may result in their death, but not for a suicide mission! Most of them were here for the money! Badali could take the blame for this, for underfinancing the entire expedition. Yes . . . Badali would make a fine scapegoat as far as Ellis was concerned.

Nevertheless, the words nearly choked him as he spoke them. "Helm, bring us slowly about, I don't care in what direction, just do it very slowly. Gradually withdraw us to a position outside the lethal range of their likely weapon systems. I need time to think."

Multiple, mixed emotions were now coursing through Ellis's veins. He needed to get off the bridge before the red mist of uncontrolled anger took over and he changed his mind and ordered an all-out attack. "I'll be in my cabin if you need me. XO you have the conn."

Ellis stood from his chair and walked towards the entry hatch and out into the passageway. He needed to work this through. Come up with a plan that didn't involve raw emotional reaction.

Once again the Severn brat has ruined my plans, my life. Twice she has done this to me! It will not happen a third time! Believe me, if we ever cross paths again Severn, I will kill you!

Then it occurred to him. He stopped, turned, and went back to the *Hyperion*'s bridge. Perhaps . . . just maybe . . . there was an achievable third option . . .

Lieutenant Kat Severn did not like what she saw. In the far distance, Hai Private Security Contractors in a well spread-out arrowhead formation moved through the neat rows of plantation palm trees. Individuals stopped here and there to shoot at any targets that had presented themselves, then hurried to get back into formation in the continuing advance.

Melnik was professional, he knew exactly what he was doing. Kat was tempted to start shooting into the rear of his troop formations from where she currently observed from the cluster of re-taken outbuildings.

Sergeant Varco had joined her and commented on the current wave of assailants ahead. "We've got some of them lying down and acting very dead, ma'am, but I'm not convinced that they really are, or that there's enough of them."

Kat now looked at the slumped PSC bodies through her binoculars. Further up the valley the armoured mercenaries were rapidly advancing. Some fell to sniper fire, but not many.

"Time to frustrate their advance, Sergeant Varko," Kat ordered.

"My thoughts exactly, ma'am," the Sergeant said and took Kat's two Troopers with him. "You follow up later, with the locals, ma'am," he said and was gone into the darkness before she could discuss anything with him. He moved deliberately, firing single, aimed shots when he spotted something worth the effort. On either side of him, a Trooper moved in perfectly trained synchronicity with their Sergeant.

Kat swopped her binoculars for the optics of her weapon, flipped on the thermal-imaging functionality and continued to watch the advance of Sergeant Varko and his escorting Troopers. Wounded PSCs that they encountered threw aside their weapons, putting their hands skyward.

One of her Troopers went down. The other responded with another grenade from his under-slung launcher. On the terrace a fruit tree came apart in an explosion of fire, dirt, mangled branches and body parts.

With an abrupt suddenness, that little corner of the battlefield fell silent. Sergeant Varko and the other Trooper still advanced, studying the wreckage before them through rifle optics, trigger fingers ready to respond, but nothing moved.

A few plantation workers came from the terraces, moving ahead of the Sergeant, moving amongst the wounded under the palm trees, identifying those that were still alive and had the strength to manage the words, "I surrender," through their parched lips.

A farm worker went down, shot in the arm, but the round hadn't come from the terraces, it had come from the hillside, on the left flank, or 'poore' side.

"Down, get down," Kat shouted. "There, on the left flank, on the hillside!"

Her people went to ground, in some cases using the

bodies of fallen PSCs as cover, as there was nothing else. Looking more than a bit confused, the islanders did the same, lying prone behind whatever protection they could find. Almost instantly, the sound of deliberate rifle fire filled the night air.

Up the 'poore' hillside the PSCs began to fall, but the armoured mercenaries in the plantation now advanced unchecked, their objective looked to be Kat's original Command Post beneath the large narra tree.

The range was extreme. Too extreme to risk her precious ammunition.

From the Command Post a Land Force Trooper appeared, but Kat couldn't identify exactly who in the darkness. Safi probably could, but it didn't matter. The figure crawled forward then dropped one, then another, then a third of the advancing adversaries as they moved ever closer.

A grenade flew towards him and before he could return, smother or deflect it, it detonated.

Kat knew she had to stop the hostile formation's advance. Despite the extreme range she took aim and fired.

Another of Kat's Troopers came out from the Command Post, firing in three-round bursts.

Up on the 'poore' hillside more PSCs went down as Staff Sergeant Freeman's M214 support weapons finally opened up and sent a hailstorm of 5.56mm ball and tracer scything through the night-sky, over the tops of the coconut palms and into the opposite hillside.

A mercenary stood with what looked like a single-use, short-range missile or rocket system on his shoulder and fired at the roots and rocks below the tree that concealed the Command Post.

The explosion was blinding. Kat felt her anger rise, and knew she could not lie there, holding her breath while she waited for the smoke, flame and dust to disperse. There were still hostiles throughout the plantation and flanking hillsides, and hostiles meant targets!

She stood and advanced. Identifying a target she fired, then another. Beside her the islanders did the same.

"I'm out of ammo," came a voice beside her after another ten metres. Kat ignored it. Then a second and a third, "Me too, I'm out," and she realised that these people needed a commander right now to direct them, not the 'shooter' she'd momentarily become.

The smoke and dust that had shrouded the Command Post had gone, taken away on the evening's breeze, and a gapping black hole was now visible directly beneath the narra tree's trunk, that somehow still stood defiantly against the attack.

Three mercenaries moved forward, only to be blown backwards by shots fired from within.

Kat screamed and ran forwards. All around her the islanders and her own Troopers moved with her. If the local inhabitants had possessed bayonets, she'd have ordered them fixed!

Private Security Contractors fell whenever encountered, either shot dead, or looking for their own leadership to give direction. They looked at the dead around them, ahead of them, and wisely put their faces into the dirt, their hands into the air and surrendered.

Any that got too close to the black maw beneath the tree were shot from inside. Someone inside evidently still lived.

The hostile's assault had stalled, it had lost momentum. It had failed.

Around Kat, rifles fell silent.

Up on the hillside Staff Freeman was ordering his people to "Check fire. Save it until we need it."

Finally, the valley, the plantation, grew silent.

Kat, her assault rifle before her at the ready, stopped running. She drew a breath. She lived. Unlike so many, she was still alive.

Ellis's little expedition, his private army had been stopped. She knew it was way too early to celebrate a victory, this battle certainly wasn't over. It could still be lost, but for now, Kat was alive, and Ellis . . . Melnik . . . they had been stopped.

She had barely caught her breath, much less celebrate

that she could actually still do so, when she spotted movement out of the corner of her eye. She watched as one of her Troopers made their way forward at a crouch.

For a brief moment anger flared in Kat, what was this individual doing?

It took Kat's battle-numbed brain several seconds to recognise her comms-tech.

No shots were fired. For a very long moment it seemed that the comms-tech was the only thing moving on the battlefield.

He came to a halt not too far from Kat, only slightly out of breath, and explained the wide grin across his face.

"I've just received a nano-burst message from Captain Jensen, ma'am. It was somehow piggy-backed onto our surveillance drone. Never seen that done before, must be some clever tech from the boffins. It's not that clear, lots of static and its one-way only, so we can't respond, but he sends his complements, and reports that Captain Ellis and the *Hyperion* have departed. Direction and, or destination unclear."

If Kat hadn't been hearing it from so reputable a source, she would never of believed it. *No way. Ellis would never run!*

This was a tale she wanted to hear from Gillan's own mouth, but evidently that would have to wait.

"I need something white. Bed linen, a towel, anything white?"

Nobody had anything.

"A big bandage? A hankerchief? Anything white? Anybody?" Her question drew blank stares from those around her.

A local woman came forward pointing at her t-shirt. It had a name and logo of some fictitious yacht club emblazoned across it, but the base material was white.

"Close enough," Kat said. "May I have it?"

The woman didn't hesitate, pulling it off and handing it to Kat. Another islander offered the woman his shirt to cover her exposed skin.

Kat turned the t-shirt inside out, so the logo was no

longer visible.

Sergeant Varko had joined them and stripped the flashlight from the fore-stock of his assault rifle, then used cable-ties to fix it to the rigid radio aerial the comms-tech was assembling to use as a flagstaff. More cable-ties helped prevent the t-shirt from sliding down when the ariel was held aloft.

The Sergeant only got as far as clearing his throat to begin objecting, when the comms-tech interjected.

"Ma'am, its part of my job to come up with the protocols that allow dissimilar systems to communicate," the comms-tech told her, looking around the battered coconut plantation. "This is my job."

Kat really wasn't sure if their improvised flag of parley would stay together if they began arguing or fighting for it.

The plantation owner settled the matter. "I took this from the dead soldier in my out-building," he said, producing the speaker unit the PSC Senior NCO had used to broadcast his demand for their surrender. He handed it to the comms-tech.

The Trooper took it, then turned on the flashlight, illuminating the white t-shirt further up the staff. Reluctantly, Kat would let this dangerous job of making 'dissimilar systems communicate' fall to this Trooper who had demanded it.

Sergeant Varko smiled.

Kat found that hard to believe, after this bloody battle, the Sergeant could smile contentedly over winning such a small thing in a battle of wills with a certain Princess.

Then again, she didn't have Staff Freeman and Ensign Steiger to report to in her chain-of-command, the comms-tech did!

Handing his assault rifle to Sergeant Varko, the comms-tech waved the improvised flag in the air. No shots came his way. He then began the slow process of walking forward. Kat listened for his footfalls, but the sandy soil was too soft. A bird, or perhaps a macaque called out into the night. Still no shots.

The comms-tech stopped about two hundred metres

ahead, about halfway between Kat and the rear positions of the PSCs. Raising the speaker unit, he called out, "My Commander requests a parley with your Commander."

A good, open, honest start thought Kat.

A PSC stood and came forward. "Perhaps my Commander will spare your Commander the time for a few words, if the subject is your surrender," he called back.

"It is not for subordinates like you and I to discuss such matters."

Kat had to suppress a smirk. She waited to see what the comeback might be, but a man in full combat armour was now standing.

He looked like the man Kat had seen in the footage of the mercenaries' arrival.

"As you were, Leftenan," the man said in a voice that needed no speaker unit to amplify it.

The PSC Officer physically flinched and went to stand beside his superior.

The figure that Kat now took to be Melnik, gave his pistol to the Leftenan. They exchanged a few words then the Leftenan promptly saluted his superior and shouted, "Yes, sir," before running off.

Melnik began to walk towards Kat's waiting comms-tech.

Handing over her own pistol and then her assault rifle to the Trooper with Sergeant Varko, Kat stood and she too began her own long walk.

As she walked, straining her senses, looking, smelling and listening with every step, she heard the moans and murmurs of multiple wounded, some of whom were yet to receive medical attention.

"Princess Katarina Severn of the ABCANZ Federation, I presume," said the man as he removed his helmet. The physical exhaustion that was starting to fatigue Kat's own movements didn't seem to be affecting him in any way at all. The rank insignia on his upper left arm was a dark green horizontal bar, perhaps a hundred and twenty millimetres long and twenty high, with a further pair of dark green, elongated and entwined oak-leaves, the same length and width as the bar, positioned above it. It wasn't a rank system Kat was familiar with, but presumably that identified him as a Major for those who needed to know. Safi would know, but Kat didn't ask.

"Major Andrev Melnik?" Kat enquired, offering her hand.

He shook it firmly. "Andrev is acceptable, if you'd prefer to keep it informal. Should I call you *Princess*?"

"I'd rather you didn't," she advised. "Kat will do fine."

"We are wasting time with unnecessary pleasantries," the Major said with a bit of a scowl. "You wanted to talk . . . I am here. I am listening . . . tell me what you want."

"Before I start," Kat said, keeping her voice light, calm, "Nothing I'm planning on saying will require us shooting at each other for the next thirty minutes or more. Therefore, as you have many wounded, would it not be appropriate to use this time to tend to them?"

The Major turned around, his scowl growing deeper as he surveyed the scene. "I'd like to tend them, but in truth, I don't have the necessary medical supplies to do so. Most of it is back on our incapacitated transport."

"I have a combat med-tech, and some of my local volunteers are doctors and nurses," Kat responded, choosing to ignore his point about 'incapacitated transport.'

"And you have sufficient medical supplies to spare?" he said, giving Kat a questioning glance.

She had no idea, but now was not the time to admit that, she needed to get this proud man comfortable with the idea that he was the supplicant and she the one dispensing benefits.

"Yes, seeing as we've been defending. Keeping our heads down."

"If we had engaged you sooner . . ." Melnik started.

Kat stopped him, 'But you didn't."

"But we didn't," he echoed. "Yes, I agree to a cease-fire for two hours. Does that satisfy you?"

"For the plantation and the two overlooking hillsides."

"How low are you and your farmers on ammunition?"

"Low on ammunition?" Kat repeated back. Her father,

a career politician, the ABCANZ Fed's current Prime Minister, would be so proud of his daughter's skill at lying with a straight face.

Major Melnik snorted. "So be it. A cease-fire between all my forces in this location, and those under your command. Can you guarantee the conduct of your irregular forces too, Lieutenant Severn?"

"They've followed my orders so far, Major," Kat said, then motioned her comms-tech to come forward. "Tell our volunteers that they are safe to render medical assistance to anyone willing to accept it."

"Yes, ma'am," the comms-tech said, then saluted, and passed Kat the white banner.

"I will personally execute any of my people who violate this cease-fire. But, don't concern yourself, as I doubt any of them would hit anything," Melnik advised Kat.

Kat was tempted to commiserate with him. Certainly her farmers had no better skills. Instead she said, "Now who's stalling?"

The Major nodded. "And you came out here to tell me what exactly . . ."

"Have you communicated with Captain Ellis recently? Kat began.

"No, I've been somewhat busy of late, and we weren't exactly on the best of terms after what you did to us yesterday and this morning."

"I'd like to say I sympathise with you, but honestly, I don't," Kat admitted.

"So what is it about that pompous, conceited . . . provocateur, you wish to enlighten me on?"

"He's no longer out in the roads off Campbell Bay," she said softly.

Melnik shook his head. "Ellis would never run from a fight. He'd never abandon us," the Major snapped, but his eyes perhaps showed a tiny flicker of doubt.

"I have it on good authority, that rather than fight my ship, he has powered up and withdrawn from these waters."

"You've talked with your Captain?"

"No, my comms-tech received a message."

"And you've conveniently just sent him off on an errand. I'd like to see him tell that lie to my face."

"What did Ellis's ship have?" Kat asked. "A pair of twin-barrel seventy-five millimetre auto-cannons. We heard the salvo yesterday. Anything else?"

"No, that's all the financiers would authorise." The Major looked like he'd gladly execute those persons too! But, it was clear, he was slowly being beaten down by the thought that he'd been abandoned, left holding the hot-potato for this whole affair.

"Be advised Major . . . my ship has a rail gun . . . AMAP enhancement . . . a Harlequin anti-ship missile rack . . . and the power needed to simultaneously operate it all. Do you really think Ellis would have stood a chance in a ship-on-ship engagement?"

Melnek started to say something, then swallowed it. All he got out was "You obviously realise, I will need to shut down our comms jamming, as will you, to verify that what you have told me is true. I must do this before I can even consider a formal Cessation of Hostilities between us."

Kat nodded. "That assumes he's still within comms range, of course. It wasn't clear how far he'd withdrawn."

A pair of Kat's Troopers ran by, one was Trooper Layne, the detachment's med-tech, his bag had a subdued variant of the serpent entwined sword over a short-armed cross that the medical branch used as its identifier. The usual shade of a pinkish 'raspberry' red, that often adorned ABCANZ medical branch uniforms, vehicles and equipment was absent. Kat and the Major watched as islanders followed, some carrying civilian first-aid kits, others with more professional civilian medical equipment.

"I don't know how you are feeling right now," Melnik finally said, "But if I don't sit down, I might fall down, and if anyone is watching that occurrence through a weapon sight . . . well, they may not act exactly as you'd like. If you get what I mean?"

Kat nodded and folded her legs beneath her. "I'm glad you offered Major, I was close to suggesting the same."

They sat there on the sandy soil beneath the coconut

palms, watching as Melnik's PSCs, Kat's Troopers and the local island inhabitants all rendered whatever medical aid and assistance they could to the wounded. Kat removed her own helmet.

After five minutes without any dialogue, the Major let out a deep sigh. "*If* . . . I was to agree to a Cessation of Hostilities between us . . . what would your terms be?"

Kat had no trouble recalling the terms that several elders had talked about last night. Melnik was careful not to use the actual word 'surrender,' preferring 'cessation of hostilities' and she knew that was deliberate. The Major knew his trade and would understand the nuances of one term over another. Kat was sure that lawyers could and would argue over the finer minutiae, the semantics that defined the differences, but right now, anything that prevented further death and bloodshed was acceptable to her. "You will hand-over your weapons, munitions and all equipment brought with you to this island. Any and all materials seized by you will be returned to the civilian population from which it came. Upon doing so, you will be treated and protected as Prisoners of War. All enlisted personnel will be provided transportation back to Thailand, or from wherever else they might have originated from."

"That's most considerate of you," Melnik said. "Is there a detail that I'm missing?"

"No. In addition, any enlisted personnel who might want to consider a new career, a new life, and stay here on Nicobar rather than return to Thailand . . . they will be considered for employment, paid at a rate comparable to locals, and accepted as part of the island community for as long they wish to do so."

The Major raised an eyebrow. "A most generous offer. Are the island's prospective employers are going to care for the wounded and pay medical, accommodation and subsistence costs for them whilst they recover?"

That caught Kat off-guard, she hadn't considered that scenario. "I'll have to get back to you on that," she said. "Somehow that's been overlooked."

"What about my Officers?" the Major asked.

"They too, will be given the option of remaining on Nicobar. If they decline, they are my prisoners and I will deliver them to a mature justice system, off island, so they can be tried for their crimes."

"And if they refuse both options?"

"I can easily let the local hot-heads string them up if that's what you'd prefer?"

"But they'll be your prisoners . . . your responsibility."

"And therefore, I will not permit it."

"Thank you, Lieutenant," he said with a gracious nod, and seemed to genuinely mean it. For a moment he sat, thinking. "Am I included with the Officers?"

"No, sir, you are not. In the absence of Captain Ellis, you are the senior man leading this hostile incursion, so you will be tried in a court of law for you and your people's actions."

"I think I saw that coming. You need at least one hanging to discourage others."

"Preying on small remote island territories cannot become a habit. You must understand that."

The Major rubbed his throat. "You must appreciate that I might view it somewhat differently from where I sit."

"I guess so." At that exact moment, Kat was seeing matters quite a bit differently from the way they had looked twenty-four hours ago.

"I should warn you . . . that whilst I can agree to a Cessation of Hostilities between us here," he said indicating the plantation, the overlooking hillsides, "The majority of assets back in the town are not under my control. Yes, I can order the handful of men I left back there to stand-down, but the transport vessel and her crew, as a 'maritime component' are under Ellis's direct authority. They are not disciplined men. Their commander is one Bavi Sobhraj. A particularly nasty individual. You may not know him by this name, as he is usually referred to as Ular Hebat, the Great Serpent by those who have had the, err . . . displeasure of his company, shall we say. He undertakes all of Ellis's 'dirty work' ashore. I would not suggest that you try to be subtle or negotiate with him."

The Major then glanced around. Some of his troops were being moved about on stretchers. After a few minutes he said, "You know . . . I always thought of the Severns as being all 'talk' and no 'action.' All horse, but no charge. If you understand what I mean?"

"I do," Kat confirmed with a whisper.

"So just my luck to run into a young one who has got a strong spine, a sharp eye, and knows how to use them."

"Your Captain Ellis always seemed to look at me and see my father William Severn, the politician. Never my grandfather, James Severn, the . . ." Kat paused.

"The legend," Melnik finished for her.

"Something like that. I'm still trying to figure out exactly what he is."

"Well, when you do, young lady, don't tell anyone!"

"Kat," Safi said aloud, "Our vessel is on-station. If the Major stopped his ECM jamming, it will make comms much easier for all parties."

"Agreed," Melnik muttered. "Don't need that anymore." He got to his feet, faced his waiting mercenaries and shouted "Close down the comms jammers."

An armoured-clad mercenary stood, acknowledged the Major with a clenched fist held aloft, then he turned away an began issuing orders to subordinates.

Kat signalled for Sergeant Varko to approach.

When he arrived she told him, "Find our comms-tech. Get the jamming turned off."

"So, you made Ellis run away," the Major said when the Sergeant had withdrawn.

Kat nodded.

"If I'd known what I was up against, I might have re-embarked the transport and sailed away myself. Isn't hindsight a wonderful thing!"

"Did you really think about doing that?"

He laughed. "No . . . absolutely not. Run my command away from a handful of farmers. Even if they did have an ABCANZ Land Force Infantry formation in support. There is no way I would ever run. That however, was the situation then. But now . . ." he paused. "Hindsight is always so much better than what you have at the time of going in. But . . . there are perhaps some other things that you should know . . ."

"Please . . . do enlighten me," Kat suggested.

"We . . . I . . . never came here for a fight. We didn't have the resources to fight. The ground elements of this deployment were only ever intended to intimidate the locals. Make them suitably compliant. Ellis was always content to have Sobhraj execute a few of them, to hasten their obedience, but a full-scale running battle . . . no, absolutely not. Ellis recruited me, and honestly, work has been a bit thin over recent months. The money isn't good for this job . . . not even close actually, but it's certainly better than nothing. It definitely isn't enough to go down in a blaze of glory for. Not for Ellis, not for me. Yes . . . we both have our professional pride, our reputations to uphold . . . so neither of us would ever 'run' . . . but this . . ." he indicated the plantation again, the island, "Is most definitely not worth dying for. However. . . Ellis's focus has become rather, err . . . 'clouded' . . . in recent days. He hates you with a passion, wants revenge . . . that I do know. Apparently, you ruined his Fleet career . . ." Melnik let that hang, gauging Kat's response.

She said nothing initially. "But here we all are . . ." she finally replied.

"Yes. Ellis might be driven, but he isn't stupid. He's professional military, and like myself, he's in this for the money, nothing more. I say again Princess, *this* isn't worth dying for. Not me, not Ellis . . . and not you!"

Several minutes of silence then passed before Safi advised, "I have our vessel's 'handshake.' Putting her Captain on." Security protocols in her programming theoretically prevented Safi from mentioning the *Fires of Beltane* or Captain Gillan by name, thereby maintaining 'operational security,' but with Safi nothing should ever be assumed. Whilst it wouldn't be terribly difficult for Melnik to access such information, why give their adversaries something for nothing!

"Hi there. It looks to be somewhat quieter now than it

did earlier. How's it going?" He sounded annoyingly chipper.

"I'm having quite a pleasant little conversation with Major Melnik about him potentially agreeing to a Cessation of Hostilties. Whether we continue this conversation or go back to shooting at each other, rather depends on what you now say, Captain."

"Like the fact that Ellis has gone?"

"Did your vessel and his actually engage each other?" Melnik asked.

"No, Major. I activated all my weapon systems and highlighted my hull protection, and he folded without calling by to inspect it close up."

"This young lady advises me that you have a rail gun fitted?"

"We certainly do, but it's a bit of a secret, so please don't tell anyone!"

Kat knew that Gillan would have the very worst piratical grin spread right across his face after that last exchange!

Melnik's lips formed into a forlorn frown. "It would appear . . . that I now find myself in such circumstances whereby I have little choice, as a responsible commander, but to accept your previously outlined terms, and agree to a Cessation of Hostilities, Princess Katarina."

Kat held out her hand.

The Major took it. "If I had any weapons on me, I'd surrender them to you."

"Weapons aside Major, I'm quite sure you understand the conditions of any such parole and the implications if you should violate them."

"I may have been unlucky in recent months, but I think you have already established that I am not a fool . . . nor am I suicidal." Melnik said. He watched as Kat's people, seeing the hand-shake, now stood from their firing positions along the terraces.

Across the plantation, Hai PSCs and mercenaries stood too. This battle was over. For some it was lost, for others won. The conscious wounded pleaded for assistance.

The dead made no such demand.

This is way too easy, thought Kat to herself. *If Melnik is cut from the same cloth as Ellis, then this apparent cessation of hostilities . . . surrender, call it what you like . . . it just doesn't add up! It has to be a ruse . . . a trick. I expected vitriol fuelled defiance, bravado about fighting to the last man, the last breath, the last drop of blood! His explanation of 'not worth dying for,' does seem sincere . . . honest, but it just doesn't feel right . . . this doesn't add up!*

SIX : FIFTEEN

It has been Sir Arthur Wellesley, the 1st Duke of Wellington writing after the Battle of Waterloo in 1815, who had penned 'Believe me, nothing except a battle lost can be half so melancholy as a battle won." Kat found that she and Melnik shared the burden of both.

Melnik cooperated fully, organising his PSCs to gather up their wounded and bring them to the vicinity of the main barn and adjacent farmhouse. Although she was only scaled for one trained medical technician in her Detachment's composition, all ANCANZ military personnel undertook an annual Battlefield Casualty Procedures refresher and test. Half her uninjured Troopers now assisted, doing whatever their med-tech instructed them to.

The other half manned the patrolling picket Kat had set up around her captives. She'd seriously considered not doing so, as where could they realistically run to? Additionally, her people were exhausted, their apparent fatigue compounded as the adrenaline-high that had surged through their bodies during the fighting, now subsided.

Unfortunately, none of the locally trained doctors and nurses had any recent experience in treating the destructive power of modern military weapons. However, they all did their very best for the wounded of both sides.

Regrettably it was a long way away from being enough for some, as a few of the wounded couldn't hang on and died before the sun came up again, although Trooper Layne's medical kit thankfully contained enough pain-suppressant that nobody died screaming.

Whilst the medics fought their private battles with preventing further death, most of the islanders were overflowing with joy and gratitude, albeit tempered with exhaustion. The animals that had died became the beginnings of a planned victory celebration, despite a distinct lack of any alcohol. The casualties amongst the locals had been relatively light. Thirteen dead, forty-two wounded. Kat had lost two of her Detachment in the fighting to take her original Command Post, and another two, the pair who had held it to the bitter end were severely wounded and the first priority for surgery. Staff Freeman had lost one of his team up on the hillside and another one had wounds that needed attention before he could be moved. Mike's fire teams along the terraces had one killed and another pair that would need professional medical attention.

Kat's Detachment had just become considerably smaller. She'd lost a third of her people.

The sun had only just cleared the horizon when Kat was approached by the Mahaapaur, Mrs Lakhera and the plantation owner and shepherded to a long table that had been set up inside the barn. "We need to talk," they all told her.

"What do you think we should do with that?" the Mahaapaur said, indicating the stack of confiscated weapons. "We have custody of them now, but I'm pretty sure I don't want such things, in such numbers, on our island."

"You can offer employment to any of the Private Security Contractors and mercenaries that surrendered. Anyone except Major Melnik," Kat told them. Repeating what she'd told the Major when she'd outlined her terms. "You could do a lot worse than hiring the officers. They could train the local population. Maybe a senior NCO or two in the mix and you'd be much better prepared if anything like this ever happened again."

"Like we can trust them?" Mrs Lakhera said sarcastically. Clearly such a concept wasn't high on the list of things she wanted to do with them.

"It's entirely up to you," Kat said, "But, I wouldn't count on me being around if another lot turned up with similar objectives next month . . . next year."

That got the entire table talking. Normally, these

people couldn't agree on anything. They didn't normally need to. However today, knowing that they needed to do something, even if they couldn't agree specifically what that was, was a solid consensus.

"How long *are* you intending to stay?" the Mahaapaur asked her.

"I have a court case coming up in Port Blair that I need to attend, not that a date for it has been set yet, and then I need to pay North Sentinel another visit."

"It's true then?" the Mahaapaur asked. "There is an illegal settlement there? There have been rumours of such for many decades."

"It's really not something I want to do, I can assure you. They claim to want isolation . . . but their ideology is . . . highly questionable. They need to be monitored. Staying as an isolated 'hermit kingdom' just isn't an option anymore."

"I don't think they'll cooperate with you," the Mahaapaur told her, and the others echoed his sentiment. "I certainly wouldn't!"

Kat had just finished her early breakfast of two IFR bars and a mug of instant coffee when Sergeant Varco announced he was ready to leave, taking a road convoy back to Campbell Bay, travelling the 'long way round.' That meant a lengthy incursion through the rain-forest covered hills on dirt tracks towards the nature reserve at the very heart of the island. Eventually they'd partially turn back on themselves, entering the town from the northwest, rather than the much quicker southwest route that the damaged causeway now prohibited.

Rather predictably, Mike had objected at not being included, but Kat quickly explained that the continued detention of Melnik ideally required a 'Commissioned Officer' to be present, and that right now, she didn't have a lot of alternative options. Reluctantly, he conceded.

Kat and Mrs Lakhera joined the Sergeant. They took half-a-dozen local volunteers along with them too. They would initially go to the hospital for medical supplies, then a food retailer for water and provisions and finally check-in on their four-man 'jackhammer' team who theoretically still had 'eyes-on' from the top floor of Mrs Lakhera's hotel, observing the transport ship moored against the jetty. Hopefully they'd all be back at the plantation before nightfall, if not just after.

From where Kat was now concealed inside the hotel room, observing the jetty on the opposite side of Campbell Bay, the adjacent beach looked more like the old media footage she'd seen of the D-Day landings back in 1944. A long stretch of wave-lashed sand, entanglements of barbed wire and an occasional crater, filled with stinking water. Here and there a sand encrusted arm or hand clawed up at the sky, pleading for help. Help that had never arrived.

It was a dull, grey afternoon. Hot tropical rain poured unrelenting from the dark clouds overhead. It would pass, it always did, but for now it continued to tip down and showed no signs of ever stopping. The rain tried hard to wash the sand away from the half-buried corpses, and judging by their state of decomposition, Kat's best guess estimate was that some had been there for a week, but it was difficult to tell . . . in tropical climates organic matter decomposed much faster than elsewhere.

The full-height sliding windows of the budget hotel room opened onto a small glass-fronted balcony, giving Kat an uninterrupted view right across Campbell Bay. The gates to the jetty had been closed and chained, preventing the local inhabitants from getting access, unless restrained and being escorted at gunpoint by Ellis's people.

The small, foot-passenger sized ferry moored up against the external edge of jetty was in a poor condition, heavily pitted by rust and years of neglect. Black scorch marks suggested that she might once have sustained fire damage.

Kat had counted maybe four or five PSCs in addition to the ship's crew through her binoculars in the last hour, as they sheltered from the heavy tropical rain on the partially open-air main passenger deck. A thermal filter showed that the vessel was leaking heat from just about every hatch and opening it had. One of Melnik's armour-clad mercenaries patrolled along the jetty, with a second, an NCO, theoretically keeping an eye on the PSCs and ship's crew. Both were seemingly oblivious to the rain.

Kat could only guess that they were waiting for new orders. Orders that weren't coming any time soon. Melnik had agreed to a Cessation of Hostilities and was now her de-facto prisoner, and Ellis had run, yet somehow, it didn't look like these men were about to 'cease hostilities' against her or the islanders any time soon.

Kat remained encased within her own armoured suit, less the helmet. She had considered taking it all off, or at least some parts, but decided against doing so. Although quite bulky overall, it regulated her body heat, or tried hard to do so anyway, keeping her at a more comfortable temperature. She had sufficient IFRs and water remaining within her pack for two more meals, and hopefully the hotel's kitchens would rustle up something more palatable if she asked nicely. She had only one magazine for her M37, having given everything else she had to Sergeant Varko and the four Troopers he now had with him. And . . . unlike anybody currently outside, she was dry.

Kat raised her binoculars again and scanned along the jetty and beach.

The furniture inside the hotel room had been rearranged to conceal any movement within it from outside eyes. A sensible precaution against anyone doing the same as her, observing the taller buildings of the town, and therefore Kat, through image enhancing optics from the ship or buildings on the opposite side of the bay.

Kat adjusted her position slightly, then swapped her binoculars, making sure that the objective lens at the front end of the Jackhammer's laser designator had an unimpeded view of the target vessel. Once Sergeant Varco was in position, Kat then had a decision to make. But . . . until that time came, she needed to gather as much Intel as possible. Intel that would hopefully inform her as to which option she'd finally select.

Initially there had just been 'Option One' whereby Kat

would get the *Bella* to fire a Harlequin anti-ship missile in their general direction to disable the transport vessel. Sergeant Varko had already modified the Halberd's targeting unit, changing it from recognising the transmitted coding that guided M504 Halberd missiles to their targets, to the different code sequencing required to guide a Harlequin ASM. As the anti-ship missile approached, it would detect the laser splash that Kat would illuminate the transport vessel with, adjust its approach vector accordingly, then ride the laser beam in, to the targeted point. Or that was the theory anyway. And this time, the firing platform, the *Bella*, was approximately over her right shoulder, rather than in the exact opposite direction, so any in-flight course corrections and therefore velocity loss, would be minimal.

Their hastily added 'Option Two' involved Sergeant Varko and the section of Troopers who had originally been in the M504 equipped hotel room's 'Observation Post.' They'd storm along the jetty and onto the vessel. 'Option Two' had been devised when her Troopers reported that they'd seen several of the island's local inhabitants being led along the jetty and into the ship. Therefore, maybe blowing a hole in it wasn't such a good idea. Maybe, if islanders were being held onboard . . . they would need to be rescued first.

And, they need to sterilise this room to a forensic standard before they vacated it, just in case the Indian authorities wanted to make something of their unauthorised presence. Mrs Lakhera's valued opinion was that they most certainly would! The legality of their presence would be far more important to the bureaucrats than any lives they may have saved!

Kat looked through the target designator's sight again. The heavy rain hampered the display, despite Safi's best efforts to assist in manipulating and enhancing the image feed. The group of men that Kat assumed must be the vessel's crew were still visible. Smoking old-fashioned cigarettes, chatting with the PSCs, laughing and keeping out of the rain. No two had the same uniform. All wore a selection of sweat and dirt-streaked military surplus. It wasn't like that of the PSCs, that although old, was at least uniformly the same. And, a hundred years in the past when compared to the smart-armour and tech that Melnik's mercenaries wore. Actually, as far as Kat was concerned, this vessel's crew looked way too similar to the crew they'd apprehended on the *Storm Cloud V* for her liking. *More pirates? If they are . . . then blowing them out of the water will be my pleasure, an absolute honour!*

However, about an hour ago, just as Kat had taken over on her turn or 'stag' to provide 'over-watch,' two islanders, both male, one old, another perhaps his late twenties, their wrists bound, had been man-handled by the ship's crew along the jetty. Kat could not hear their shouts and screams from the distance she observed, but she could well imagine. After being savagely beaten the younger man was shot in the chest, double-tap, then his body tossed unceremoniously into waters of the harbour. No doubt his corpse would wash ashore on that evening's high-tide and join the other bodies now decomposing along the beach. The outcome of the older man she'd seen wasn't known.

Sergeant Varko had commented that executing a restrained captive with shots into the chest was strange, why not a single bullet to the back of the head? Certainly cheaper, as well as statistically a more proven outcome. Kat chose to ignore that her Sergeant had such 'specialist' knowledge and instead worked with him, putting together their 'Option Two' delivery with the limited resources they had immediately available.

When the tropical rain eventually stopped, the 'football' started. The ship's crew were the only side playing, using the open-air passenger deck as a pitch. Today's 'ball' was the head of the older man. His hair was matted with blood. Kat lowered the designator's sighting unit. She really didn't need to see this. She fully understood the psychology of that was happening here. This had been included in her 'political history' studies at university.

Just like the Gestapo of 1930s Nazi Germany, and a decade later in the territory they then occupied, establishing and enforcing a reputation of abject terror amongst the general population was a recognised way of keeping society obedient.

Kat quickly reconsidered her choices. 'Option One' was to disable the ship and as many of those onboard. And, there was no risk to her people. 'Option Two' involved considerable risk to Sergeant Varko and the four Troopers, but the islanders had to be saved. But . . . *what if I send my people in, and the islanders have already been executed?* Then she'd be putting her people at risk for no reason . . .

A convoy of three, locally acquired vehicles approached the gates at the end of the jetty. Kat watched as another nine or ten locals were man-handled out of the vehicles. Scared, bewildered, some wrapped in blankets, the children and women screamed and cried as they were separated. Kat knew what was coming next. Her Troopers had included this daily occurrence in their situation report or 'sitrep' when she and Sergeant Varko had first arrived back at the hotel. The men would be beaten, then shot, Followed by the older women and children. Why not shoot them wherever they were being held in the town? Why bring them all here? It had to be for the public spectacle! Public executions always helped promote the 'terror' tactic of 'comply or die!'

Anyone unfortunate enough to be female and between the ages of about fifteen and thirty would be isolated. They would be taken back to the ship. They would then be raped, potentially repeatedly and handed around the crew. Some of the women might get killed during these assaults, but ultimately most of them would be dead before the sun set, one way or another.

Kat knew there was an active sex trade in the Thai-Malay region, with young women being routinely exchanged for cash, drugs and other illicit substances. Women changed hands for as little as the equivalent of five hundred ABCANZ dollars!

The macabre match of football promptly stopped. There was now a new 'game' to participate in and the 'players' found their weapons and filed off of the boat and along the jetty after the PSCs. They left the bloody, mutilated head where it was.

Kat accessed the DTG, or Date-Time-Group app on the display and data interface mounted on her battle suit's left forearm. If they kept to their usual timings, according to her team's activity log, it would take the vessel's crew about fifteen minutes to process this latest group of islanders. If she ordered the *Fires of Beltane* to launch the Harlequin now, some of the locals might stand a chance, *if* they survived the blast when the anti-ship missile impacted. If she didn't do something they were almost certainly going to die in the next hour or two anyway.

The display pinged, getting her attention. A craft was inbound. It looked small. Probably a rigid-inflatable boat or RIB. It had to be, given the size and the extreme speed it was approaching at.

Kat had been ready to call the *Bella*, to give the missile launch order. Instead, she waited. Watched.

The extraction and separation of the islanders, three from each of the vehicles was almost complete. A child's mother was arguing with one of the crew who was trying to pull her boy away from her and put him with her husband. Kat couldn't hear her words, but she could read the body language through the designator's sight. The mother dropped to her knees and begged, pleaded, holding on to her child for dear life. The lad didn't look any older than Grace, maybe ten or eleven.

A new figure appeared along the jetty. He was tall and thin, clean-shaven and his clothes, whilst not an immediately recognisable uniform, were considerably cleaner and of better quality and style than any of the crew. He was striding purposefully towards the group. The woman's begging and arm waving stopped. The newcomer looked to be unarmed. He held his hands openly in front of him, nothing to hide. As soon as he cleared the unchained gates at the end of the jetty, and began to talk. Was this the 'infamous' Bavi Sobhraj that Melnik had warned her about?

Kat studied him through the sights. He looked to be in his mid-thirties. His body language was confident. The ship's crew, if not the PSCs, were most definitely subordinate to him. They stopped processing the islanders. The boy's mother stayed on her knees, clutching the child to her.

The crew looked like they'd been suitably reprimanded, but Kat couldn't help feeling that this family's reprieve was going to be short lived.

The man helped the woman back to her feet and took her and the boy back to the other women standing nearby. The crew even parted ranks to let them through.

Then there was the shot . . . a stunned silence followed . . . then another shot. The boy's father crumpled.

The islanders started to scream, to shout, to protest.

There was another pair of shots. Slow, methodical.

Kat had seen enough.

The RIB entered Campbell Bay on its western side and swept round in a wide arc, parallel to the shoreline, reducing speed as it did. The front half of the craft was enclosed, concealing the pilot and passengers. It was similar to the Launch she'd operated from the ROSP 3-Alpha-9 off Cape Town, just a decade or two newer! The rear of this RIB was open, with enough space to hoist in a pallet or two of equipment. There was also a substantial roll-bar that bristled with antenna, spotlights and a twelve-point-seven or maybe a twenty-millimetre machine-gun fitted in the central position. A pair of pods were bolted onto each bulwark amidships, although no actual missiles or rockets appeared to be loaded. The overall appearance and the way it was being handled, somehow said more 'playboy billionaire,' or at least the protection of such an individual, rather than being suitable for any kind of serious military operation. All it needed was to be pulsing out the repetitive beat of a rap or hip-hop music track to complete the overall look!

"It is transmitting something," Safi immediately advised.

"Transmitting what?" Kat asked.

"Unknown. I am running full diagnostics."

"Another comms jammer?" Kat asked her HI.

"Unlikely. Military communications use VHF or UHF. This is a low power radio frequency, in the L Band."

"Hello all stations, this is Zero-Alpha. Radio check, over," said Kat, not wanting to take any chances.

"Hello Zero-Alpha, this is Zero. Okay, over," came back Anna on the *Fires of Beltane*.

"Hello Zero-Alpha, this is Zero-Delta. Okay, over," responded Sergeant Varko.

"Send sit-rep, Zero-Delta."

"Still on-route. ETA one-zero mike," said the Sergeant, advising he wouldn't be in position for another ten minutes.

"Roger, Zero-Delta. Out."

The RIB coasted up to the inside edge of the jetty and auto-tie downs activated, securing it against the protective fenders, on the opposite side the transport ferry, the jetty itself separating the two craft.

The crew and PSCs at the end of the jetty, by the vehicles obviously knew exactly who was onboard and ran towards the RIB, forming themselves into ranks, coming up to an approximate resemblance of 'attention.'

An armoured clad figure climbed from the RIB, up a metal ladder and onto the jetty. The usual helmet wasn't worn, he had a peaked cap instead, and after an exchange of salutes with the individual Kat now assumed to be Sobhraj, and therefore the crew's ranking 'Officer,' a frank exchange of words followed between them. A second figure then climbed up the ladder. He was wearing what looked to be an expensive business suit, but it now looked somewhat dishevelled. When the second figure reached the quay, he followed the others towards the transport ship.

Although she couldn't see his face, Kat knew exactly who the armoured encased newcomer was. She'd spent enough time at the Warfare Systems board on the Fast Attack Corvette *Berserker*, staring at that very-same neck.

She contacted the *Bella*. "Hello Zero, this is Zero-Alpha. My . . . err . . . *Plus-one* has just detected some low-level RF transmissions. Working to identify their purpose, but comms and data appear unaffected. Stand by for

Harlequin launch, over."

"Acknowledged, Zero-Alpha. Do you have the target, over?" Anna asked.

"Target acquired. I confirm, Target acquired, over" Kat advised, but didn't elaborate as to what her 'target' might now include.

"Roger, Zero-Alpha. Standing by."

As per her agreement with Captain Gillan, only a serving ABCANZ Officer would target and fire the *Bella*'s offensive weapon systems. That was, in reality, meant to be exclusively Kat, without actually naming her, but given the current circumstances, Anna, or Mike would do just as well.

Back on the *Fires of Beltane* the Harlequin launcher would now be deployed, the rails loaded with missiles. The Harlequin certainly wasn't the best anti-shipping missile available, but it wasn't the worst either. There were about a dozen manufactures world-wide, but only three had established market dominance. The Ahab ASM was the preferred choice of those civilian ships that had concealed weapon systems. Very short-ranged, small warhead, defensive use only, and relatively cheap. The Harlequin, standard issue on ABCANZ Fleet warships and aircraft, was short-range with a large, effective warhead, suitable for both offensive and defensive engagements, and although many times more expensive that the Ahab, it was considered by the 'bean-counters' in Fleet Procurement to give good 'bang for the buck.' The Cetus III missile was by far the best ASM currently available, by whatever statistic you chose to measure it. Longest range, fastest speed, hard to jam or hack, most destructive, but also incredibly expensive.

Kat remained silent, waiting for the *Bella*'s own 'warfare' board to calculate the missile's 'time of flight' or 'time to target' from launch. She just needed Ellis to stay around long enough for her to kill 'two birds with one stone.'

Most of the crew and Private Security Contractors had followed Ellis, Sobhraj and the man in the suit towards the ship. A few helped unload equipment from the rear of the RIB. Kat couldn't see what the boxes contained, but if their external marking were accurate, it looked to be provisions from the 'gourmet' department or food hall of the high society retailer *Galeries Lafayette* in Nu Paris. Cuisine that was a very long way from the IFR bars that Kat now lived on.

Ellis stood at the bottom of the access-way onto the transport vessel, his hands on his hips, seemingly oblivious to the stench that the dismembered bodies on the beach must be giving off.

Anna came back on the comms net. "Hello Zero-Alpha, this is Zero, time to target . . . three mike ten. Acknowledge, over."

"Roger that Zero. Time to target, three minutes, ten seconds. Out."

Not long. With a bit of luck they'd just be sitting down to pre-dinner drinks before their 'gourmet' meal when Kat shoved a Harlequin ASM firmly up Ellis's backside.

She took aim on the side of the ship. Kat had no idea where the crew's dining might be located on a ship of this type, so went for the centre of visible mass, about half a metre above the concrete of the jetty. There was a margin of error with this missile system of under three metres, so Kat wanted to ensure that there was no chance it would drop short, piling into the sea. If it was a bit right or left, it wouldn't matter, she'd still get a hit.

Suddenly Ellis turned around and stomped off up the jetty towards the vehicles and the captive islanders. Sobhraj and the man in the suit followed.

There was nothing Kat could do now, but wait. She didn't want to order the ASM launched too soon, and right now Ellis seemed content to go for a little walk. There was no rush. This needed to be right.

The ship is the target, not Ellis, Kat reminded herself. But . . . it would be highly fortuitous if the very same missile strike actually dealt with both 'issues.'

Five minutes passed. Hopefully he'd seen enough rotting corpses and petrified living civilians to feed his inflated ego and would soon go onboard the ferry.

Another five minutes. No change. Kat took aim on the side of the ferry. "Zero, standby."

"Roger Zero-Alpha, Standing by. Do you have

designation?"

"Yes Zero, I have designation."

"Delayed fuse setting?"

"Yes, no change to attack profile." A few more seconds passed. "Zero Standby" Kat ordered. "Standby . . . fire!"

Anna came straight back. "Zero-Alpha, time-to-target, plus three mike ten. Five, four, three . . . missile away."

"Acknowledged Zero. Missile way."

That was it. In three minutes, ten seconds from now, the Harlequin would make contact. All that was left for Kat to do was switch on the laser designator in ninety seconds and splash the ship's hull.

Kat monetarily switched her focus back to Ellis. Sobhraj was busy chastising one of the crew. It looked heated. Ellis's face was contorted with uncontrolled anger. She remembered seeing that rage before!

Ellis pointed at the man in the suit, then prodded Sobhraj angrily in the chest. The man stood his ground. Calm and collected. It was Ellis who was the angry party. Kat watched, half expecting her former Commander to draw his pistol and begin executing the suited man and a few of his own for the misdemeanours they had apparently committed. Then she remembered . . . Ellis never did his own 'dirty-work,' he always got others to do the actual killing for him. It was always others being ordered to shoot people on his behalf. She remembered talking Sergeant Jones out of just such an occurrence back on the *Berserker* when Kat had relieved Ellis of command.

Ellis pushed Sobhraj back again, causing him to stumble and fall to the jetty. Days, perhaps weeks, of pent-up anger, frustration and aggression were now flowing freely and unchecked from Ellis.

If Sobhraj truly had the reputation as 'Ular Hebat' as Melnik had claimed, was Ellis not playing with fire? Poking the hornet's nest? Maybe this wasn't Sobhraj? The man took the assault from his superior completely calmly and picked himself up. Ellis was evidently very frustrated and continued hollering and shouting. Waving his arms, he pushed the man back again, then stood back, hands on his hips, glowering at his subordinate. Finally, he shouted something at the ship's crew, pointed at the RIB, then turned and stomped off, back down the jetty. The man in the suit seemed uncertain, should he follow Ellis or stay with the other man.

Bavi Sobhraj, or whoever he actually was, spoke quickly to his men who promptly herded the remaining civilians together by the same vehicles they'd arrived in. He then pulled his own pistol and put two rounds in rapid succession into the suited man's chest, a third into his head.

Kat wanted to send Sergeant Varko and her four Troopers in immediately, but she knew that the odds of them succeeding were somewhere between slim and non-existent. They'd be cut down long before they even reached the gates at the exposed jetty's entrance. Extreme odds of success had never stopped her before, but somehow this felt different. Her people had bled enough in recent days. She expected to see a hail of small-arms fire cutting into the forlorn islanders at any moment.

Instead, they were told to get back into the vehicles. Sobhraj stood nearby, waving for them to hurry up.

Kat checked the time again on her forearm comm unit. Whoever was driving those vehicles needed to hurry up. *Get those people away from here!*

She changed her point of aim back to the transport ship's hull and pulled the trigger. In the sighting aperture the laser 'splash' was clearly visible, although it wouldn't be to anyone who happened to be watching. Despite the best efforts of movie-makers for the last two hundred years, most lasers were invisible to the human eye.

Seventy-five seconds out. The Harlequin missile would be screaming in towards the transport ship.

Quickly Kat glanced back at the jetty gates. One of the vehicles was leaving. Two remained, one certainly wasn't needed. Its former passengers were now all dead. Their bodies remained exactly where they had fallen. Sobhraj was still by the gates, his gaze now watching something further down the jetty. Kat followed his line-of-sight.

The three young women had been kept behind. Their

arms were entwined, mutually supporting each other as they stumbled along. All three were sobbing.

Kat felt the surge of anger, of adrenaline. Her heart thumped painfully in her chest. She hadn't recognised the shorts and vest-top that the middle girl wore, but she did recall her face! It was Nishi, the teenage girl Kat had taken the photograph of whilst travelling back from her first visit to the Suruchi Hotel and Mrs Lakhera.

Sobhraj pointed at the women, then the suited man's corpse, shouted something at his men, before he too began walking back along the jetty. The three young women were quickly herded at gunpoint towards the transport ferry. The man in the suit was tossed unceremoniously off the side of the quay into the waters of the harbour.

Two of the young women, but not Nishi, were immediately taken up the access-way and onto the ship. Their legs slipped and buckled as they tried to resist.

Kat focused on Nishi. She had stopped crying. She didn't look frightened. She just stood there. Was she numb with fear, defiance perhaps . . . some new-found inner dignity? Whatever it was, she was momentarily blocking the beam of the laser designator, preventing the 'splash' from marking the hull of the ship.

The other two women were dragged up to the open-air deck that had previously been the 'football pitch.' One of the women, little older than a teenager, quickly had her back against the safety railing running around the deck edge. The top half of her body was roughly stripped naked, her arms flailing. She turned her head left and right, screaming, begging. Her body jerked as one of the crewman pushed himself hard against her. The other women was being stripped too.

Kat checked the countdown timer again. fifteen seconds to go. Just as she changed her point-of-aim to slightly further along the ship's hull, past where Nishi now stood, the first women fell, backwards over the rail, landing hard onto the surface of the jetty. She didn't move. Empty eyes just stared skyward.

The enraged Ellis pointed at the woman's body.

Two of the ferry's crew quickly rolled the body over to the jetty's edge, then off, into the water.

Ellis was shouting at Sobhraj again.

Three seconds to go. Kat started counting aloud. "Three . . . two . . . one," she braced herself.

Nothing happened. She counted another five seconds. She checked the counter on her wrist unit. She checked the laser designator. The 'splash' was still illuminating the target. Everything was exactly as it should be. The target was designated. Where was the damn missile?

Two minutes passed, but it felt like ten. Still nothing.

"Zero Alpha, comms check," enquired Anna.

Kat responded quietly, but didn't whisper. Whispering had never worked over a comms net. Better to keep her normal voice low and constant. "Zero, comms are good, I'm good, but no strike. I repeat, no strike."

"Roger that Zero Alpha, no strike. Understood. Wait out."

Anna evidently didn't know what was happening any more than Kat did, but Kat needed an answer. Should they try again, re-designate the target, launch another missile?

The silence was stretching for too long. It was three minutes since the missile should have impacted.

Something wasn't right.

"The L Band RF transmission that the RIB is putting out is effectively jamming the missile's global positioning functionality," Safi advised. "I can't counter it at this range."

"Zero-Delta, this is Zero-Alpha, proceed with Option Two, wet insertion. I repeat, wet insertion. over," Kat instructed Sergeant Varko.

"Roger that, Zero Alpha. Wet insertion. Zero-Delta out."

The crew on the transport ship were oblivious to the failed missile attack and the other woman was now the full focus of their collective attention.

Her screams of protest and pain must have galvanised Nishi's resolve. Suddenly she ran towards the jetty's edge and dived headfirst into the waters of Campbell Bay. The other woman continued to cry and scream, but several of the crew who were not actively taking part in her violation and defilement now laughed and nonchalantly removed their slung weapons from off their shoulders. The next part of their afternoon 'fun' was about to begin.

Silently Kat willed her absent Harlequin to come screeching out of the sky, to finish this. No such luck!

Nishi surfaced from her dive and began an erratic, panicked stroke through the water. She went under for a few seconds, then resurfaced and carried on swimming. She changed direction, making for the town, and directly towards where Sergeant Varko and his team, now also in the water, was moving in from.

The ship's crew hadn't fired a single shot. Maybe she was too close for them . . . not enough of a challenge. They were still laughing and joking, deciding who should have the first shot, maybe making a wager with each other.

The first shot rang out. It missed. Kat thought she saw it splash in front of the young woman.

Nishi kept on swimming. There was another shot. They'd missed again. Kat could see more laughter and cheering from the crew.

There was another shot, then another. The rounds zipped into the sea around Nishi. It was only a matter of time, but they hadn't gone automatic. Not yet.

Nishi was no more than ten metres from Sergeant Varko. She was down to five when she finally saw him. Confused she stopped swimming. She went under. When she came up again, gasping for breath, she started to swim again.

There was another shot. She took it in the back just as Sergeant Varko reached her. He pulled her arm around his shoulder. Her eyes were begging him for help.

He turned himself around in the water, using his body to shield hers. She whimpered her gratitude, but there was blood at the edge of her mouth. Blood that the sea washed away with every wave.

Automatic fire now sought them. The crew were angry, evidently someone hadn't won their bet.

Kat needed to do something. Then she realised, she

still had offensive capability. Pushing away the modified laser designator, she moved across the hotel room to the other M504 Halberd launcher.

Picking it up, she took it out onto the room's balcony. Going back inside, she located her suit's helmet and pulled it on, as the weapon system's sights worked better when integrated with her helmet's targeting systems, rather than her naked eye.

"Safi, do whatever you can to assist, but we need to make this count," she told her HI as she went out onto the balcony and hoisted the weapon up onto her shoulder.

It was at the extreme range of the Halberd's projectile's effectiveness, but she wasn't targeting an armoured vehicle with composite armour protection. She wasn't even targeting the hull of the vessel like she'd done for the absent Harlequin minutes before. This time she wanted to scour the vessel's open-aired passenger deck of human life.

The tone in her ears changed, the targeting lines inside her helmet's display changed from red to green, and she fired. Instantly the first projectile rocketed away. Called the 'jackhammer' by the infantry because of its 'double-tap' capability, Kat didn't wait to see the damage the first Halberd had inflicted, sending the second rocket along the same trajectory before the smoke and flame of the first had dissipated.

The double-shot launchers backblast was far from insignificant, making 'rather a mess' of the hotel room. Kat would need to apologise to Mrs Lakhera, but the need for a forensic clean might now be negated!

Ellis was still on the quayside. He was now running, back towards his RIB. Quickly Kat dropped the empty Halberd launcher from her shoulder and went inside to find a pair of reloads in the shattered room.

She found them easily enough, but quickly worked out whilst removing them from their protective transit-tubes, that she then had no idea what the procedure was for arming them, or 'making safe' the launcher unit whilst the replacement ordnance was inserted, or the start-up sequencing that did a systems check of the freshly inserted munitions. Safi could no-doubt provide a step-by-step guide, but Fleet Officers had no knowledge of the intimacies and operator drills required to operate Land Force Infantry weapon systems.

Kat swore, a word the Princesses definitely, and Fleet Lieutenants probably, shouldn't use. Ellis was going to get away, and there was nothing Kat could do to stop him. He was going to live.

Predictably, no sooner had Ellis and his RIB cleared the bay, the RF jamming transmission was gone. He'd outsmarted her. He'd survived this encounter. This time . . .

Sobhraj and his crew were thankfully dead, and if she ever crossed paths with her former Commander again . . . he'd be joining them!

The *Fires of Beltane* was under way thirty-six hours later at a rather sedate ten knots.

The passenger ferry had a composite crew drawn from the *Bella* and the Land Force detachment. Because of her under-powered propulsion and poor maintenance, she was still struggling to match the *Bella*'s ten knots. Kat intended to declare the vessel forfeit as soon as they got back to Port Blair. Any insurance pay-out would go to the people of Great Nicobar.

Aboard the *Fires of Beltane* there was only a single prisoner . . . Major Andrev Melnik. All of his officers, including Kapten Sarikan, had been offered varying forms of employment on Great Nicobar, some even had more than one option to choose from. Only a few had turned them down.

But first, Kat needed to see how the situation she'd provoked on North Sentinel was evolving.

Not eager to think too hard about that, and knowing she had some serious appeasement to undertake with her own scientific boffins, Kat spent all of her meals with the them for the first twenty-four hours after departing Campbell Bay.

"Yes," she promised, "Just as soon as we drop off

everything in Port Blair, we'll head out, go and do whatever it is you want to do." Which wasn't believed by all of the scientists, who then took turns in telling her just how important their particular piece of research was. She did a lot of listening. She didn't understand a significant percentage of what she was being told, but she listened nonetheless.

It was on the second day back at sea that Kat finally took a meal with her own Officers and Seniors.

And found Melnik in the spot she often occupied at the head of the table.

"Why exactly . . . are you not secured in the brig?" Kat demanded.

Melnik looked at Mike, and the Ensign stood. "Ah . . . err . . . Kat . . . err, as we were serving him the same food, and . . ." he glanced around the room, and Kat did too.

The Mess Hall was full. Captain Gillan was at the other end of the Officer's table with most of his bridge team scattered around the other tables. Staff Freeman and Sergeant Varko were at another table. Anna and Grace were sitting close to the Major. Grace was almost at his elbow!

"And . . . so . . .? Kat snapped, giving Mike the frown she'd learned from her father, about the age of three, when she'd been caught stealing snacks from Beth in the kitchen back home at Bagshot.

"And . . ." the Fleet Ensign said, after taking a deep breath, "We're having the . . . ah, well, some really interesting and informative discussions. I feel like I'm getting Command and Staff College lectures delivered through a fire-hose."

"Your prisoner really is quite a military historian," Captain Gillan added.

"And, it's not as though he can go anywhere," Anna pointed out.

"He's more fun to listen to that an old vid-file," Grace added.

The Major took a sip from his glass. "I do sleep in the brig. Having spent most of my adult life in ditches and camp-cots, sometimes with a sleeping bag, sometimes not, I can assure you, your brig is most comfortable.

Kat headed for the serving line and began loading a plate. "And the subject of tonight's debate is?" she snapped.

"Terrain analysis, your Highness. How water features, dense vegetation, urbanisation, steep inclines and depressions, they all dictate where and how your enemy might deploy . . . and, what you can do to counter their mobility."

"Then please do continue," Kat said, but her tone suggested she was clearly most unhappy.

First an adolescent schoolgirl, now a middle-aged Major, both doing their very best to wriggle their way into her good books. Maybe that might work for Grace, but not Melnik. Just as soon as Kat found someone to hand the Major over to, he'd be escorted from the *Bella* with his wrists restrained!

But . . . for now . . . he was interesting to listen to.

SIX : SIXTEEN

Later that day they reached North Sentinel . . . and unexpectedly, Kat found herself with not very much to do. The island was even quieter than before. There was no answer to their hail, not even to tell them to 'shut up.'

"Captain Gillan, slow to five knots," Kat ordered. "Sensors. Put together a team of magicians, use the science team and Safi, and do whatever you can to crack that silence. I want to know something before I stick my head into whatever noose they've prepared for me whilst we were away."

"They've dug themselves a hole and pulled the dirt back in on top of them," the Crewman at the sensor board reported on behalf of the team that had steadily grown to eventually include every boffin on-board who might have something to add to their findings.

"We can't find the thermal trace we used to locate them last time either, it's gone," he added.

Kat thanked them for their efforts then turned to her command team, which Major Melnik had somehow attached himself to.

"Any suggestions on what we do now?" she asked them.

Mike shook his head. "If there is no apparent threat, may I suggest we put the Detachment ashore and have a look around."

Melnik frowned.

"You have a problem with that?" Kat said.

"No, ma'am. It seems that you must do what you must do. However, I am reminded that both Cortez and Pizarro marched deep into the two empires they encountered. It was a trap. The native's intention was to kill them. Somehow, they got out of it alive and were hailed as conquerors, but that was never the intention of the local inhabitants."

That left everyone with cheery thoughts.

"Okay, we go ashore. I want hand-held sensors calibrated to report on any noise, squeak or squark."

"Ma'am," said Mike with an acknowledging nod.

Kat headed for her cabin and Anna, to get herself prepared.

With only a single RIB on board that was seaworthy, it took three circuits to get them all ashore. The two RIBs that had been used in their night insertion had been recovered from their hiding place in Bananga Bay, and the one that had sustained the most damage from Ellis's 75mm salvo against the nearby equipment pod had been sacrificed for parts as it was way beyond repair. 'Reclamation' Staff Freeman advised was apparently the preferred military term. The other RIB was still being worked on.

The *Bella*'s medical bay remained full of Land Force Infanteers, recuperating from their recent endeavours on Great Nicobar.

Today's insertion onto North Sentinel was well spaced out. Mike insisted that the occupants of the RIBs first circuit be deployed and covering all avenues of approach before the next rotation even approached the beach, much less the third circuit that included Kat.

Predictably Kat didn't approve, but Mike had authority over her in certain circumstances. He could, and did, order such precautions, and she had no choice but to obey her security chief's orders. It reminded her how much she didn't appreciate her Grandpa Jim messing with her life, even if his intentions were ultimately well meaning.

When Kat eventually knelt down at Mike's side at the edge of the beach his updating 'sitrep' still contained a whole lot of absolutely 'nothing.'

"There's no active electronic signatures, not even a beating heart, within two klicks," the Lance Corporal with the tech scanner reported. He took another device from a pouch on his armoured suit and connected it onto the hand-held device. A minute later he added, "No residue from cooking smoke either. Not even as much as a candle burning."

Kat looked up the track they'd previously walked to reach the subterranean hall. If she was going to find anything, it would most likely be up there. She was about to give 'orders' when the Lance Corporal spoke again.

"Hang on, I have a heartbeat. It's about three hundred metres away."

Kat held back on issuing new orders. Now might be a good time to let the ground situation evolve a little while longer. A figure climbed from a stairwell that was much closer that Kat recalled from their previous visit. Like the 'elders' she'd spoken with in their 'great hall' this individual was clothed only in white. The person made their way carefully towards Kat, arms outstretched, showing no hostile intent. It was a man. A man who looked back, over his shoulder, after every two or three steps.

He stopped around fifty metres from Kat's position, then started to run. He was middle-aged and no athlete. Kat and Mike headed towards him. Staff Freeman and a half-squad of four Troopers provided escort.

As they approached him, he shouted in a harsh, out-of-breath voice. "You have to get out of here, and take me with you. Please . . . take me with you."

"What's going on here," Kat demanded.

"There is no time to explain. You must leave."

"I'm getting heartbeats, certainly two, maybe more, about five-hundred metres away," the Lance Corporal advised.

"You have to leave. They'll kill you. Kill me," the man shouted as he reached them.

Kat recognised the man. It was Beelzebub. 'Zebub? Is that you?" She knew it was, but was the man under the influence of drugs or was he lucid?

"Yes . . . yes it's me. Please, get back to your ship and go. And please . . . take me with you. Do it now, before they kill all of you."

"Kill us?" Kat said. "I don't think you understand the fire-power we have at our disposal."

"They will kill you. And me too, now that I have spoken with you."

To add emphasis to his words a weapon fired. It missed the open visor of Kat's helmeted head, but only just.

"Down, all round defence," Staff Freeman shouted. The Troopers followed his orders instinctively. A second Section moved up to reinforce their colleagues.

Three more rifle rounds came in a fast succession. A Trooper went down, cursing, only to stand up and prise a rifle slug from the armour plate protecting his abdomen.

"Snipers," was Mike's only comment.

Four M37 assault rifles responded. Single, aimed rounds. The range was too far to hear the results, but no more shots came back at them.

"Get the RIB back in, we need to talk with this man before we talk to anyone else ashore," Mike ordered.

"You're assuming we'll do any talking at all with them," Kat added.

Predictably, the extraction from the beach was handled smartly and professionally by the Detachment. Kat ensured her new 'best friend' was safely secured into the first extraction the lone RIB made, then strapped herself in alongside him.

In good time, the *Bella* recovered the RIB itself and its occupants after the third rotation, then withdrew, getting distance between the ship and the island, putting them outside of the effective ranges of any RPGs or heavy-calibre small-arms fire. Apparently, that was a standard-operating-procedure for such an encounter.

But it wasn't required. Once Kat and Zebub had left the beach, the island went back to being as quiet as a tomb.

Kat let Mike and the sensor chief start Zebub's interrogation. "How did you mask your heartbeats? How did those snipers conceal themselves?" Mike demanded.

"You might think we're crazy, but we're not stupid," the man snapped back at Mike. "We've spent thirty years finding ways to make ourselves invisible to visitors. Do you think we're primitive? Couldn't handle a few obvious things like heartbeats? We have electromagnetic cardio-blockers that are evidently more sophisticated than your scanners."

The sensor chief didn't look as though he believed that for a single second, but with the recent evidence not in his favour, he chose not to challenge Zebub's comment.

"So why exactly do we have to take you with us?" Mike asked him.

"Isn't that obvious? I am now rogue, deemed worse than a non-believer to the Angels of Light. I have talked with you . . . you whom the Elders have placed under interdict. My life is now forfeit, to be terminated in the slowest and most painful ways possible. However, rather than let me escape and talk with you, they would instead, grant me the mercy of a quick death from the hands of a sniper. The lesser of two evils."

"And what exactly is it, that you are prohibited from telling us?"

There was no quick reply to Mike's question. He seemingly shrunk down, into his seat. When he finally spoke it was little more than a whisper. "I really don't know," he said, then made no effort to expand upon his words.

North Sentinel was a puzzle. It had been to start with, and it wasn't getting any better, just worse as they got deeper into it.

The *Fires of Beltane* wasn't equipped with an actual 'interrogation suite' and her single-celled brig already had Major Melnik 'in residence.' For the moment, Zebub was being held, unrestrained, in Captain Gillan's office, cum meeting room. Staff Freeman had posted Troopers on a guard detail both inside and out.

Kat had the Detachment's medical-tech go in next, to check Zebub over, both physically for signs of abuse, and mentally. A tablet for sea-sickness was prescribed as a precaution, which he accepted with a glass of water, but he declined any food or additional drink.

Kat settled into a chair, followed by Mike and Staff Freeman.

Anna, Captain Gillan and Professor Brooks sat around the other side of the table.

Kat was in no mood for bickering, vagueness or protracted discussions. She was busy replaying their last visit to North Sentinel in her head, trying to figure out why so much had apparently changed. Yes, in hindsight, she had probably played her cards a bit heavy-handed in the face of the Elders obstinate response. That probably accounted for their generally hostile reaction, but that didn't explain why this man was here? What had changed for him?

"When we last visited," Kat started slowly, "You and your son were our original contacts. "Where is he?" Kat asked.

"My son has gone," the man whispered.

"Gone where?" Kat asked.

The man looked at her, his eyes misting. "I do not know exactly. He's gone. Not just from the settlement, he has left the island."

"So? . . . We found Shalk de Klerk in Port Blair," Anna said.

The man shook his head. "You don't understand. Morax didn't run away. He left North Sentinel with the Blessings of the Elders. That doesn't happen. He left with all our other young men and women. All together. And all went with Blessings. Never have the Elders done this before. And they all took their burial shrouds with them. Shrouds and a handful of dirt from the island. They will not come back alive." He fixed Kat with a stare. "Not unless you can do something to save my son. Will you? Please don't tell me that I've thrown away everything I hold dear to save my son, and now you won't help me."

The temptation to just to agree with 'of course we will,' but throwaway words would be a travesty in the face of this father's begging. He'd given up everything he believed in to help his own flesh and blood. If Kat made him a promise of help, she knew that she'd better be willing to keep it.

Kat looked around the table. Mike's face mirrored what she was partially thinking too. Maybe Zebub wasn't all there. Something deeper than anxiety or depression had to be fueling his paranoia. Was he a certifiable crazy? He might have just run away from a whole bunch of other crazies, but exactly why was still not completely clear to Kat, and certainly not worth risking a single drop of any of her people's blood for.

That was the crux of it. Her Troopers had just paid a high price for an island's freedom. This man would have to trump that if he wanted them to take a bullet for him too.

Kat measured her next works carefully. "Mr Beelzebub, let me see if I understand you."

The man locked eyes with her. Kat had often held people's attention at political rallies, at military 'Orders' Groups, at command and staff briefings. She'd never held anyone's attention as tightly as she did this man's.

"Your son, Morax, he has left North Sentinel. Something that never normally happens."

He nodded.

"He did so with another thirty plus young people on an undisclosed mission for the islands 'Elders.' A mission that they all believe will likely be suicidal."

Again, the man nodded.

"But you have no idea what than mission is."

Zebub leaned back in his chair, took a deep breath and then let it out again . . . slowly. "Correct," he said, then added, "Except that my son told me that with just one death, they will send the nonbelievers into such a war amongst themselves, that the Angels of Light will not find a dozen left alive when it is over. He mentioned that to me only once, then he went quiet." The man's eyes lit up. "Does that help you?"

Mike shook his head. "Sir, globally there are currently dozens of powder-kegs, all waiting to explode. Her Highness here has personally yanked half-a-dozen sputtering fuses out of just as many kegs in the last few years."

The light went out of the eyes of the father.

"But," Kat put in, "We are in the habit of chasing fuses and putting them out. Remarkably, despite what you might think, that has not made us as many friends as it has new enemies," she said to a general chuckle from around the room. "If your son has just lit such a fuse, or has left a trail that will lead us to find such a fuse, I think you can count on us taking an interest."

"Can you save his life?"

Kat briefly reflected on the trail of death and destruction she'd left during her four years of Fleet service. That sent a shiver down her spine. "I can try, sir . . . but, I can't promise you anything."

She glanced around the table. None would tell this father that he had come to the right person to plead for someone's life. People died around Kat. Friends, enemies, she didn't discriminate. Kat was an 'equal-opportunity' totem of death. She hadn't set out to be, but there was certainly something about the name *Severn*!

People who got too close to a Severn often ended up dead.

"Captain Gillan, lay in a course for Port Blair," Kat ordered. "Let's see what the latest rumours are around town!"

"Maybe they've increased our share of the insurer's 'finder's fee' on the *Storm Cloud V*?" Gillan commented as he got to his feet.

"In your freakin' dreams!" Anna laughed at his sarcasm as she followed him out.

The *Fires of Beltane* docked in Port Blair just in time for a late meal. That seemed perfect, since the principal partner in the local legal practice that Kat had retained to represent their interests whilst away, insisted on giving her his update over dinner, rather than in his office the next morning.

Unfortunately, Kat took an immediate dislike to him. It wasn't an intense dislike, not yet, but it was early evening. Give it a couple of hours . . .

"You are not going without a security detail," Mike insisted.

"I'm going for dinner with a lawyer, Mike. Why would I need a security detail for such a meeting in Port Blair?"

"Princess, *you* weren't safe in Emirates City, the supposed weapon-control capital of the planet!" Mike reminded her.

She didn't take the bait. "Kapitan Sörensen and the *Fenrir* aren't in port are they?"

"No, so Miss Alexandra von Welf is probably elsewhere plotting misdemeanours we know nothing about!"

"And which need not concern us. Sorry Mike, the senior partner of a legal firm wants some private words with me. I want to hear what he has to say. I do not want him to hold back because he feels intimidated by a security detail. Understood?"

Mike growled. "I hear you."

"Good." She looked in the cabin's wall mounted mirror. Anna had outdone herself. Kat looked amazing. Even to her own super-critical eye. She had a bust, and the pads that created it didn't double as explosive charges! She'd checked on that. Clinched in at the waist, the white ensemble flared out nicely when she walked and give her plenty of movement if she needed to run, and locations to conceal Safi and her compact ceramic pistol.

Captain Gillan appeared at the door of her cabin. "There's a 'suited and booted' lawyer type waiting on the quarterdeck for you. Apparently, he's your 'date' for this evening?"

"He's what?" said Mike.

"His words, not mine," Gillan insisted.

"Kat, this is a bad idea."

"Mike, please . . . if anything gets out of hand, I'll break his arms and legs and walk home. Okay?"

"Why not simply shoot him?" Mike countered.

"That would leave an unnecessary mess for the waiters and waitresses to clean up. People bad mouth me enough as it is. I really don't want to add any substance to the rumours."

She moved toward the door, pausing only to give Mike a peck on his right cheek. *Why didn't you invite me out tonight instead?* she thought. "Don't worry about me, I'll be fine."

Anna handed Kat a shawl, positioning it across the

small of her back, supported by the crook of each arm.

"Wow, Princess you look real beautiful," came from Grace, now standing behind Captain Gillan.

"Anna, please teach young Grace here some grammatically correct appreciation for beauty, and also enlighten her how flattery doesn't ever work on me!"

"Well . . . you might not think of yourself as a beauty," said Anna, "but what I have done with you tonight certainly qualifies as such, well for us mere mortal types anyway."

Kat decided not to respond.

Mike did not follow Kat to the quarterdeck. Captain Gillan did, but only long enough to remind her . . . again . . . to look into the matter of the insurance 'finder's fee' for the pirate ship, the *Storm Cloud V*, that they'd apprehended several weeks before. And to report that the damaged transport ship from Great Nicobar would arrive in the morning.

"With us running at fifteen knots and them only making about six or seven, I'm amazed they aren't further behind."

"I'll also look into the legalities of that ship," Kat assured him.

"I just hope they don't tie her up in legal limbo too," the Captain said, "But somehow, I know they're going to do exactly that!"

"Most probably, it seems to be how they prefer to operate here. Someone owns her, but I'd assume that whoever the contracting party was, the same entity that hired Ellis and Melnik, well . . . they probably paid for the owner's discretion too, so I can't imagine this will be simple. And lawyers do like it complicated . . . justifies their exorbitant fees!"

The senior partner of the local legal firm wasn't *exactly* waiting for Kat on the quarterdeck as Captain Gillan had advised. He was talking to someone on a comm-unit, and quite forcefully. "Stand up to them, they're robbing us blind. You'll never become a partner if you can't deal with a simple situation like this!" His pacing took a turn when he reached the bulkhead, bringing Kat into view. "I'm about to have dinner with a rather attractive young lady. Talk to me in the morning, and bring me some good news!"

He blinked, slowly, deliberately, which may have been his way of terminating the connection. And with said blink he took on a totally different persona. The angry man was gone, a gracious host took his place. The biography that Safi had compiled from his on-line presence, put him six years older than Kat's father. If that were true, then his years had been much more kind. There was no grey in his black hair, and his figure was toned, not even the slightest hint of a middle-aged belly. Had he been genetically enhanced 'pre-birth?' Or was this the result of a surgeon's scalpel and chemical procedures. He looked half his alleged age. He was everything that Kat's father, the consummate career politician, despised. "How can you be seen as honest and sincere with the electorate if your public guise is so evidently artificial, false and manipulated?" It was more of a statement then a question.

The man smiled at her. It was a perfectly white, tooth affair that involved most of his face. If it was genuine, she should have felt some warmth.

She didn't.

Maybe it was the quick, and easy change from anger to smile, or perhaps how artificial and insincere it seemed to be. It might all change again, at any moment.

Kat offered a genuine, sincere smile that included teeth and shook his offered hand.

"There are so many quality establishments to dine at within Port Blair," he informed her. "This town has quite a reputation for fine food, you know."

"It's your patch," Kat said lightly. "Your choice."

"Well, I'm a simple man at heart," so there is this little place I know."

"Lead on."

The food was as good as promised, local flora and fauna that complemented each other with different flavours and then expanded on them. The lawyer dominated the conversation. He knew his business, and Kat suspected that this would have been a conversation better had by her Grandpa George, the CEO of Lennox Industries, rather than a mere Fleet Lieutenant.

When he did invite Kat to talk, she took the conversation in the direction of what her on-board science team wanted to do next on their continuing voyage of discovery. Kat really hadn't realised she'd captured so much of what the boffins had told her until she realised that she was boring the lawyer with way too much detail. He changed the conversation.

The lawyer's favourite subject was evidently himself, a topic he knew very well. There was a lot of egotistical, bumptious dross, but the occasional nugget of Intel 'gold' was forthcoming, if not actually given deliberately.

"You're not planning on visiting Puducherry on the mainland, are you?" he asked.

"Is there a problem?

"You might want to give it a miss. It has just been annexed by the European Union. Apparently, there was a terrorist cell operating within the city that needed to be apprehended, but their troops have now stayed and returned it to its pre-1954 status and a French Overseas Territory."

In much the same way that China had granted enclaves to the European powers in the name of 'trade' in the late nineteenth and early twentieth century, (Hong Kong to the British, Macau to the Portuguese and Guangzhou to the French, in addition to the conglomerated trading hub in Tianjin used by Austria-Hungary, Belgium, France, Germany, Italy, Japan, Russia, Britain and the United States,) a similar model was already in operation in India.

Although Britain took overall control of mainland India in the 1850s, it and the other European powers had already established trade enclaves for several hundred years prior to this. The Portuguese, primarily in Goa, but in other locations too, since 1510, the British in Surat (1610) Bombay (1668) and Calcutta (1670), the Dutch in Cochin and elsewhere from the 1650s, the French in Pondacherry during the 1670s and even the Danish in Tranquebar during the 1620s.

When India finally became an independent nation in 1947, Goa remained in the hands of the Portuguese until 1961 when it was forcibly taken in an operation by the Indian military. The Dutch and Danish operations had ceased in 1825 and 1850 respectively, having been sold off or ceded during the period of British dominance. France also retained her Indian enclaves (the coastal city of Pondacherry and three smaller locations) post-independence, until 1954 when they were peacefully transferred to the Indian government. (The name was changed to Puducherry in 2006).

The Spanish were notably absent from these activities as their Empire's 'modus operandi' was fundamentally different to the other European powers. 'Trade' or Capitalism was the main driver for the British, Dutch, and Portuguese. Territorial expansion was not their desired objective. However, it was sometimes necessary to engage in such activity to curtail the antics of other nations undertaking exactly that. The French territorial expansion in Canada in the 1750s and Russian activity, known as the 'Great Game' throughout the 1800s necessitated Britain taking reluctant military action to curtail such antics.

Spain however had a different, double-edged agenda. 'Trade' was certainly not their objective. The 'sword' was their preferred tool of empire, (a) seeking out and taking gold and *silver to fuel the economy of Spain and (b) to convert the local population to an extreme form of Catholicism, dominated by the church's much feared 'Inquisitors,' were their primary objectives. The Spanish exponents of empire, the likes of Cortés and Pizarro were referred to as the 'Conquistadors' for good reason.*

"A rather sudden arrangement," the lawyer explained. "One minute they were minding their own business, and the next a Cruiser or two arrived and 'suggested' they immediately revert to being a French, or more correctly, a European Union Overseas Territory."

"Unfortunately, it is a concept I am somewhat familiar with," Kat said, briefly recalling Gus's failed endeavours in Cape Town. "What was the Indian government's response?"

"They are still debating it! No surprise there, and I guess the EU knew that it would be weeks, if not months before there was any response, by which time they will have consolidated their 'acquisition' against any type of military response." He took a long drink, then continued. "Strange thing is, and perhaps it's just a coincidence, but I understand that Ernst Augustus von Welf, the seventh of that name, is rather excited about the new business opportunities this will bring him. Rumour is he plans to pay a visit next week, if not sooner."

"I'm told he travels a lot," Kat said almost dismissively, still assimilating what she'd just been told.

"Rather bizarrely, we had a group of young adults here a few days ago, thirty-four of them as I recall. All trying to book passage to Puducherry. Their travel documents were apparently South African, but there were numerous anomalies that initially prevented their onward journey, but we soon sorted that out for them, once the required fees had been forthcoming. You must understand how it is. We have a weekly Ro-Pax service that connects us with the other ports of Bengal. One ship goes nominally anti-clockwise, from here to Chittagong. The other, the one that these adolescents took, goes clockwise. They should be in Colombo by now, and from there they'll continue on to Puducherry. I can't fathom why they'd want to go there right now, but at least the monsoon season has finished. Apparently, it is some kind of pilgrimage to the Golden Temple at Matrimandir?"

Kat swallowed another fork of her meal and let the lawyer talk about anything he wanted to. She'd learned early on to ignore the noise. Noise couldn't physically hurt her. Unlike a bullet or a knife.

Somehow his six-pack stomach did not require him to pass on desert. While he ate, Kat got down to business.

"I assume you recall the matter of the pirate vessel we brought in under a prize crew last time I was in Port Blair?"

He chuckled. "I've done little else but deal with it since your last visit. Do you have any idea how ancient the Admiralty Rules of Prize are? They haven't been applied for centuries."

"I do believe they were applied within the last twelve months by the authorities in Western Cape."

"Yes. . . yes I know all about that," he said dismissively, "My admin staff had great difficulty in locating that case. Cape Town . . . Western Cape, they're hardly the centre of the universe for Maritime Law, you know. Not really the centre of anything actually. Their case law hardly sets an international precedent. Don't get me wrong, I'm not saying that to you, I'm just telling you what they lawyers of the half-dozen interested parties are telling me."

He then spent the next twenty minutes telling Kat things she really didn't want to hear.

"So when do you think all this might get settled?" she finally asked him.

"I have no idea, although a trial date is being suggested about six weeks from now. With so many interested parties, I think the best thing to do would be to sell the ship and distribute even portions from the sale to all the parties." He finished with a dazzling smile.

For the next ten minutes he expounded about the brilliance of his idea. One that, if Kat's approximation on the value of the vessel in question and the rates charged by lawyers, would probably yield them about enough to cover said lawyers fees and not much more!

As he talked, Kat began to review her options and modify her intended plans for the transport ferry she'd 'acquired' in Great Nicobar. That ship must not present its documentation to the Port Master in Port Blair. Between Anna and Captain Gillan, they ought to be able to reflag that ship in the next day or two. The new papers need not be perfect, just sufficient to get her replenished and on-course for ABCANZ Fed territory. Thunder Cove on Diego Garcia would do, if not Darwin or Black Swan City in Australia.

Major Melnik was another problem. She'd intended to hand him over to the military Governor of the Indian Union in Port Blair for trial, so when the senior lawyer before her paused for breath, she tentatively asked his advice.

"You crossed swords with a filibuster! And lived to sit here in that lovely dress and tell me all about it. Your troops must be most capable to handle such dirty work."

Kat saw no reason to claim that she'd gotten her 'oh so lovely' hands dirty too. Anna had said many bad words during the last few days, attempting to restore what this man might call her 'lovely skin.'

"Your Highness, I've naturally heard about these things. I've never drawn up a contract for such an endeavour, although I must say, for a contract to hold up amongst such disreputable types . . . it would be a work of legal art!"

Kat begged to differ, but said nothing. She was willing to bet money, good ANCANZ dollars, that the original outline contract for such an operation had indeed been prepared by the very lawyer who now sat before her, if not one of his associates!

Kat responded with one, simple question. "Do you think the Land Forces Commander of such an expedition would get a fair trial under Indian law here in Port Blair?"

The man didn't pause to reflect for a single second. "Of course, your Highness. They would get the fairest of trials. I'd even take it 'pro bono.' Assuming that they agreed to sign an exclusive contract to let us agent them once we had reduced any sentencing to parole and community service. I suspect there are many people who would pay handsomely for their 'advice' on what to do . . . and what not to do in such an operation. The successful ones never tell. They'd potentially be a highly lucrative, moneymaking asset."

Kat stood. This dinner was over. Indeed, if she didn't get this 'reptile' out of her sight, she might resort to punching his nose. Something that appealed to her right now.

The lawyer stood. "I was hoping that you and I might continue to enjoy the evening together. You've been on-board ship for a long time, and I understand that as its captain, you must set a certain standard, deny yourself the more pleasant aspects of adult life."

Kat was rapidly expanding her desire to inflict violence on this man from punching his nose to breaking his arms and legs. Thankfully she spotted Mike, in civilian clothing, seated with a female Trooper. Staff Freeman had similar company at another table.

The good guys had not let her out of their sight. And, knowing Mike, he'd probably feel obliged to help the waiters and waitresses clean up any 'mess' they might make too. No, she would control her anger, and leave this worthless 'maggot' behind her.

"Safi, make a note, we are never to do business with anyone working with, or for this lawyer or his associates in practice, ever again."

"Yes, your Highness. I will advise Lennox Group of your recommendation too."

Turning her back on the lawyer, she marched for the restaurant's door. Mike, Staff Sergeant Freeman and the pair of female Troopers formed around her.

Only when she was outside, far from the air sullied by that odious man, did she slow down.

Mike came up on one side, Staff Freeman the other. "I am so glad to see you two gentlemen," she said.

"That bad!" Staff Freeman said.

"Oh yes, and then some. I am so pleased to be sharing my life with the likes of you two." She almost rested her head on Mike's shoulder, but remembered who and where she was. They might be away from the ship, and all dressed up for a night on the town, but as Mike would no doubt remind her, 'standards' needed to be maintained.

There was a lot to dislike about her chosen career. The terror, the blood, the killing, the dying . . . but . . . there was a lot to like about it too. Sometimes she got to stop some really bad stuff from happening, and she got to do it with the likes of the men and women who now surrounded her.

Back on the *Fires of Beltane* there was 'no rest for the wicked.' Late as it was, Kat called a 'Staff Meeting' and immediately went to work.

Anna arrived in dressing gown and slippers.

"Looks like we may have a couple of problems, boys and girls," Kat said by way of a preamble. "And, both of them need our immediate attention." Then she filled them in on the legal mess surrounding the *Storm Cloud V*.

Captain Gillan muttered something containing multiple expletives under his breath.

"We can't dispose of the transport ferry here then, can we," Anna said.

"Exactly, Kat agreed. "We'll need to crew and provision her, but then get her away to ABCANZ Fed territory."

"I'll cut her a new set of docs," Anna said. "If they only have to stand up to routine scrutiny a couple of times . . . that's relatively easy."

"And, secondly, there's a potential, but rather large problem, evolving in Puducherry. This also needs our attention," Kat advised them.

"Puducherry?" Professor Brooks echoed. He'd just arrived. He looked worried. "Your Highness, need I remind you that you assured my colleagues and I that some scientific research would be our next priority, and it would last for a full two months."

"Yes Professor, I did, and I will not renege on that," Kat said, "But, this problem in Puducherry cannot be ignored." She then informed them all of the information she'd obtained from the lawyer over dinner.

"I see," Professor Brooks said with slow nod. "Yes, I

concur. A detour would seem prudent. It will delay us by a few days . . . but, what must be, must be."

Around the table, that seemed to represent the general feeling of all parties.

"Excuse me Professor," Kat said, "Perhaps you misunderstand me. We *are* going to Puducherry."

Silence filled the room. Nobody said anything.

Eventually Mike spoke. "Your Highness, please excuse my lack of respect, but are you freakin' crazy?"

"No more than usual," she replied.

"Yes, this is *way* more than usual!" Mike shot back. "Kat, Ernst-Augustus senior has been trying to kill you since . . . well, forever!"

"I am well aware of that Mike."

"And those cruisers at Nu Hawaii," Anna added. "He was probably behind that . . . and Louis's abduction when you were a kid . . ."

"I know, I know."

"And, if Ernst Augustus the seventh does finally go and get himself killed, we do not want a Severn within a couple of thousand klicks, or even the same continent. You do not want to go to Puducherry," said Mike slowly, like he was talking to a stubborn child.

"I don't *want* to go there. But, answer me this, where do you think Beelzebub's son and his nut-job mates are heading to right now?"

"Puducherry, by any chance?" Mike said. "I know you'd like to perform a miracle for that deluded old fool Zeebub, but Kat, you need to stay away on this one."

"I can't, Mike, because my fingerprints are already all over the future death of Enrst-Augustus von Welf . . . the seventh of that name."

That brought bland looks from most around the table. All except Anna. "Oh . . . I see."

"You explain it to them," Kat told her.

All eyes now turned to Anna. She spoke slowly. "Whether one of the deluded, adolescent servants of the Angels of Light actually manages to kill Mr von Welf, or not, it doesn't matter. They are bound to become part of the investigation before his body gets cold. That creates a direct line back to North Sentinel Island, and 'Princess' Katarina Severn has been on North Sentinel twice in the last month."

There was a long silence even after Anna had finished talking. As the mess they were in now dawned on those sitting around the table. Heads began to shake slowly.

"We are so screwed," Captain Gillan muttered, saying what everyone else was probably thinking.

"Couldn't you just send a warning?" Professor Brooks asked.

Kat shook her head. "Even if I did, it could be taken as us just trying to cover our tracks. At best, they might credit us with having had second thoughts on an operation after we'd turned it loose, and we're now trying to help them close it down. Either way, it still comes right back to us . . . me . . . killing von Welf. *I* have to go."

Mike was still shaking his head. "So, you're just going to sail in, broadcasting 'hey everyone, listen up, there's a plot to kill Herr von Welf,' and hope you'll be believed?"

"I have to try, Mike."

"I can have the ship underway in thirty minutes, your Highness," Gillan advised, standing from his chair.

"Make it so, Captain."

Gillan left to do exactly that.

"What other loose ends do I have?" Kat said and turned to Mike. "I had planned to turn Major Melnik over to the authorities here in Port Blair, but . . . change of plan. We will be keeping him on-board a little while longer."

That got a frown from Mike.

"It would seem, that the lawyer I've just had dinner with, is rather confident he can get Melnik off of any charges brought against him with just a 'slap on the wrist.' He's already planning a lucrative career for the Major, consulting on future filibuster expeditions, with an 'agents' fee added on for him, naturally."

"I think Melnik was expecting exactly that, or at least something very similar," Mike advised.

"Well not anymore! He will not be leaving the ship, at least not in Port Blair anyway."

Mike nodded.

Kat then tuned to Anna. "Captain Sykes, correct me if I'm wrong, but POWs can be put to work and get paid accordingly, can they not?"

"Yes, you are correct, ma'am" Anna confirmed.

"Very well. After you've re-documented the transport ferry, please prepare a contract of hire for the Major. As a 'consultant in military affairs.'"

"What kind of pay grade?" Anna asked.

"Something appropriate for a Major's rank. Check the published rates for an ABCANZ Federation Major or Commander with a Special Operations pedigree, do the same for the European Union and anyone else you want to add into the mix and split the difference. And, make it a short-term contract. I still want him gone as soon as practicably possible. Understood?"

"Ma'am," Anna said again with a confirmatory nod. "Maybe get rid of him wherever we dispose of the transport ferry? Cape Town perhaps?"

"No, not Cape Town. Gus tried to add that city to the EU's empire remember, and the locals somewhat objected, and that was before Gus got himself killed!"

"We're up to our necks in another croc of crap aren't we, Kat." Safi added.

Before Kat or anyone else could respond, the cabin's tannoy speaker came alive. It was Gillan. "All Hands, this is the Captain. Prepare for immediate departure. Department heads report when ready. Gillan out"

SIX : SEVENTEEN

The voyage to Puducherry was uneventful. Their inbound transport ferry was met at sea and the false documents enabling her to get her re-provisioned in Port Blair were provided. New orders were also issued, instructing her to make best speed to the nearest ABCANZ Fed port. Darwin was two thousand eight hundred nautical miles away and Black Swan City almost three thousand. Either destination, given the poor speed the vessel could currently manage, were going to take in excess of two weeks. The ROSP 4-Foxtrot-6 and Thunder Cove on Diego Garcia were both considerably nearer, but were military facilities, with no ability to process an 'appropriated' civilian vessel.

The only decision that now had to be made on the *Fires of Beltane* was what speed she should travel the eight hundred nautical miles to Puducherry at. She could be there in under twenty-four hours, if she maintained a steady forty-five knots, but it also blew their cover of being a typical civilian freighter, and it was more than a little dangerous, as there was no direct Safe-Transit-Route linking the two ports. The more usual fifteen knots the *Bella* operated at extended the journey to fifty-three hours. Kat had fully expected complaints from her scientists, but ended up facing Staff Sergeant Freeman instead.

"Ma'am, I assume you'd like as many Troopers as possible to be ready for Active Duty when we arrive?"

"Of course, Staff."

"Well, as you know ma'am, I have five in the med-bay. They've all started physio, and both our own, and the ship's med-tech tell me that reducing the speed down to around eight-point-five knots would be better for them."

"Noted, Staff. Let me coordinate with Captain Gillan.

I'll get back to you."

Twice a day, the ship reduced speed, from fifteen to eight-point-five-knots. As a result, Sato the ship's navigator, complained to Kat at every meal time they happen to cross-paths about the extra course adjustments this necessitated, but Kat countered it, citing it was prudent, for the multiple reasons they had all previously discussed.

The Troopers got their physiotherapy. Kat wanted every available 'trigger-puller' fit and healthy by the time they arrived in Puducherry.

No sooner had the *Fires of Beltane* began her approach into Puducherry's 'Karaikal' port they were hailed and told to 'hold position' out in the roads. Apparently, the port was now temporarily closed to all shipping. All shipping except European Union warships!

Captain Gillan once again proved himself to be the biggest teller of tall-tails that had ever sailed the seven seas and blagged them permission to enter for emergency repairs, on the condition that nobody disembarked or boarded the *Bella*. Absolutely nobody. And, armed security would be posted at the accessway to reinforce this requirement.

They fully complied. Nobody disembarked.

Naturally, Gillan forgot to mention that Princess Katarina Severn of the ABCANZ Federation, putative killer of von Welf scions, was currently residing on-board. Kat figured that once word of that little over-sight got out, the guards posted to keep the crew contained on the *Bella* would be given a new assignment. To forcibly board her, and take Kat into their immediate custody.

Kat was at her usual station on the bridge as Gillan began his ship's final approach into the port. The view from the bridge's windows showed multiple EU warships tied up against the numerous quays.

Kat might be at her usual station, but her usual attire of regulation ship-suit was absent. Instead, she wore clothing more appropriate for a civilian merchant vessel's crew.

Kat spotted only two quays with enough space to take the *Bella*, and watched as Gillan manoeuvred towards the one that he'd been allocated.

"You have a call, your Highness," the crewman manning the comms board advised.

"From who?" she asked, Kat had hoped her presence here might remain a secret a little bit longer.

"He asked me not to tell you. He said to trust him and take the call."

"Put it on speaker. Audio only, no visual," she agreed with a sigh.

"Good afternoon, your Highness. Kurt Sörensen here. I saw the *Fires of Beltane* had talked her way in and thought you might still be on-board."

"How are your daughters and trainee Watch Officer?"

"My daughters are well. Wedding bells for number two in the next year or so I think. A good lad. It will be a pleasure to see her marry. And . . . the trainee Watch Officer to which you refer put this call through. Her father wants her to join him later this week for a few days, but she's in no hurry to do so. Your file suggests you like to stay well away from your father too! I am very pleased that my own daughters don't share whatever affliction it is that you two have."

"Much as I love talking family, Kapitän, I don't think that is why you called?"

"No, you are quite correct. I thought I had better warn you. As soon as you are alongside you will be told to flood your reactor and discharge any stored power over and above the minimum to keep the ship habitable."

"What?" was Captain Gillan's immediate reaction.

"Yes," every civilian ship currently tied up is cold with empty capacitors. It's nothing personal. It's a security precaution issued by our Intelligence and Security Agency."

"What could possibly make us think it was personal!" muttered Gillan.

At that moment a harassed man in the rumpled uniform of Puducherry's Port Authority appeared on the right half of the main screen. Behind him Kat could clearly see a figure in the uniform of a European Union Fleet

Officer. He was armed, and the weapon wasn't in its holster. He also had the eight pointed 'star' of the 'Sicherheitsdienst,' the uniformed element of the 'Intelligence and Security Agency' on his right breast pocket.

"As soon as the auto-tie-downs have secured your vessel, you must flood your reactor. Both of them. If you do not wish to do this, then return to open water and find an alternative port to undertake your 'emergency repairs,' in." Kat was told in accented English.

"We won't make anywhere else," Gillan lied, "So will comply." After a short pause, "Engineering," he pushed a button in the arm of his chair, "Prepare to flood the reactors and discharge our stored energy."

"On your signal, boss," came back.

The man on the right side of the screen disappeared.

"Thank you Kapitän Sörensen, for the warning," Kat said.

"I thought you might like a bit of advanced warning. Your file suggests that paranoia is a long-established family trait."

"Understandable, seeing as someone seems to be out to get us most of the time, don't you think?"

"I wouldn't know anything about that."

"I didn't think you would. But you are no doubt, just a little curious as to why we are here?"

"It had crossed my mind," the Kapitän said dryly.

"There is a plot to kill Herr von Welf."

"Do tell, there has already been one attempt, yesterday morning. The perpetrators either died during the attempt or during their subsequent interrogation. None of that is public knowledge by the way. Let's keep it so."

"Yesterday morning?" Kat said, and glanced around the *Bella*'s bridge. The clanking sound of the first auto-tie-downs activating, resonated through the ship's hull. A hissing followed and the lighting in the overhead bulkhead briefly flickered.

They were committed to Puducherry. No escape now!

"Kapitän Sörensen, were any of these would-be assassins connected to North Sentinel Island or the Angels of Light religious sect?"

"Good grief, does that lot still exist? But no, it was locals, objecting to the new regime change. At least that's the official story. There might be more to it, but as dead men tell no tails . . . as I am sure you are well aware."

"North Sentinel has a hidden, non-indigenous population of more than a hundred people. I know this as I've visited it twice within the last month. It appears that a 'tactical team' of around thirty young . . . err . . . 'enthusiasts' . . . has been sent to do the bidding of the 'Angels of Light.' Their mission is to somehow start a 'new war.' Our threat assessment suggests that this may involve an attempt on the life of Herr von Welf."

"The Angels of Light . . ." there was a short pause as the Kapitän consulted with someone else. "They were . . . are . . . on our watch-lists as being fundamentalist, known religious extremists, but are not identified as a terror risk."

"Things may have changed."

"Understood, it's a logical evolution for some . . . fundamentalist to extremist . . . to terrorist. But how will assassinating Herr von Welf precipitate another war?"

"As I said, sir, I've been to North Sentinel twice in the last four weeks. I have Intel that suggests a group of them are now either already here or on-route to Puducherry. I suspect this whole plot has been contrived at very short notice. Opportunistic, so as to have 'Severn' fingerprints all over it."

The Kapitän nodded. "I need to talk with our Intelligence and Security Agency. Will you be available to talk later?"

"I'm confined to my ship, Kapitän. We all are."

"My apologies, of course you are, you're confined under the port's lockdown protocols. Give me an hour. I expect our Sicherheitsdienst agents will want to talk with you. I'm also going to share what you've just told me with my trainee Watch Officer too. We may need a direct link to the old man himself."

"I think we will."

The second auto-lockdown engaged, winching the

Bella hard against the rubber fenders protecting the quayside. The sounds resonated through the ship's hull and just for a second Kat thought they sounded like a prison door slamming shut. She'd been in some desperate situations before, but never had she felt so vulnerable. Then came the order to flood both of the *Bella*'s reactors and purge her energy storage cells. She'd spent most of the last four years, her entire Fleet career, if not the last fifteen of her life, doing her very best to stay out of the long reach of the von Welfs!

Now she was totally at their mercy. Her stomach was sour, she felt quite sick. It couldn't get any worse . . . could it?

Six men, all in the uniform of the Sicherheitsdienst, the Intelligence and Security Agency of the European Union's military arrived on the quayside next to the accessway onto the *Fires of Beltane.*

They dismounted from their transport, splashing into the puddles that the rain was creating along the quay. All were armed, four with assault rifles. The only saving grace was that Kapitän sur Zee Kurt Sörensen was with them. And, he had a certain Fähnrich in tow.

From the window of Captain Gillan's office Kat watched as events evolved.

It got interesting when they came up the accessway onto the *Bella*'s quarterdeck. Six ANCANZ Federation Land Force Troopers, all encased in battle-scarred chameleon armour, their weapons at the ready, blocked the interloper's way.

Staff Freeman stepped forward to greet them. He saluted, paying the appropriate respects, then asked, "Do you have business on-board this ship, sir?"

"I am Fregattenkapitän Kaltenbrun, here to see the Severn girl."

"You request an audience with Princess Katarina of the ABCANZ Federation?" the Staff Sergeant corrected him.

"May I remind you that you are now in a European Union Protected Territory. We do not recognise your archaic notions of royalty."

"I am very aware of where I am, sir," Staff Freeman said with a gentle voice. "May I also point out that you are on an ABCANZ Federation military requisitioned vessel bearing the granddaughter of King James."

The two men glared at each other. The Fregattenkapitän's was that of a snarling dog. Staff Freeman's was open and friendly. Despite the rain it was hot and humid. Staff Freeman could wait, his chameleon battle-suits regulated the wearer's body temperature.

"Please advise your Princess that representatives of the Sicherheitsdienst require an immediate meeting with her."

Staff Freeman paused, just long enough to give them the impression that he had received orders, then smiled. "You are granted an audience."

Kat glanced around Captain Gillan's office, checking there was nothing sensitive on view. There was no throne either, and she need to change her clothes. Kat knew that getting the 'power flow' going her way for this meeting was not going to be easy.

"Staff, take the long way, I need more time to prepare," she told Freeman via her comm-link into his earpiece. She didn't wait for his reply. "Anna, bring my Number Two, Parade and Barack, Dress uniform. Full size medals, and attach the Legion d'Honneur too." That was the European Union's highest honour, so *might* make them pause and rethink their intentions.

"On my way," Anna confirmed.

Kat glanced around again. No way to make the table disappear. But . . . "Captain Gillan, I want all the chairs out of here. Lower the lighting. Mike, I want you at my side. Number Two Dress, with leather and metal, if you please."

"Only if Staff Freeman includes a tour of the propulsion spaces," he said, but already moving towards the cabin's door.

"Make it faster," she called after him.

Captain Gillan disappeared. Crewmen got busy making chairs disappear. Anna arrived, and Kat stood to help her Equerry get her changed. A crewman went to take away Kat's vacated chair. "No, that one stays," Kat growled.

Now, if she had just enough time to get this circus show set up, one obnoxious military security operative, Fregattenkapitän Kaltenbrun would find himself in a very interesting situation.

Mike returned, still buttoning up his jacket.

Captain Gillan appeared . . . in the same uniform as Mike, but with the embellishments and differences that went with the rank of Commander. Kat took in his medals. They showed the usual Long Service and Good Conduct you'd expect from 'peace time' military service, but a couple showed he'd seen action too. How had he managed that? Then again, she'd earned all of hers during 'peace time' too. Maybe the last thirty odd years hadn't been as peaceful as the history files suggested!

"I currently have the status of a Reservist, just like the science team, but I did see a bit of Active Duty in my misspent youth," he explained with his trademark grin.

"Consider yourself on "Active Duty" again, at least for the next hour or two, and we evidently need to talk."

Anna was next. Kat had never seen Anna in a uniform that showed her true military rank and accomplishments, and Anna had baulked at wearing it when Kat had suggested she did so whilst on their way back from Nu Britannia several months past. If ever there was a time, then this was it. Unlike Kat, Mike and Captain Gillan, Anna's uniform was the light olive colour of the Land Forces, rather than the dark grey of the Fleet.

They quickly arrayed themselves on either side of Kat, who now sat. Gillan stood on her left, Mike to the right, and Anna behind. At the door Grace watched.

"Sorry Grace, not today, please go to your cabin. Safi, arrange a video feed to her monitor screen."

"Yes ma'am," Safi confirmed.

"Yes, your Highness," the girl said politely. Thankfully she hadn't objected.

The measured tread of multiple boots approaching could be heard from the corridor outside. Kat's gaze went to the door. The lights dimmed.

The Fregattenkapitän entered, his face was difficult to read. An Oberleutnant sur Zee followed, then their assault rifle toting escort of four. Kapitän sur Zee Sörensen followed, a bemused look on his face as he took in Kat's side of the compartment. Fähnrich von Welf followed her Kapitän and edged herself over to put her back against the bulkhead and assumed a very stiff parade rest/stand easy position. From where she stood, she could see everything, including the looks on everyone's faces as associated body postures.

From outside, Staff Freeman's voice came clearly as he positioned his armoured Troopers at the hatchway.

Kaltenbrun eyed Kat through narrow, calculating slits. Kat gave him an open, wide-eyed face, as innocent as any she had ever managed, but said nothing.

Finally, the Fregattenkapitän broke eye contact with Kat to take in those around her. Kat couldn't tell which of her colleagues caused it, but she saw his eyes widen and nostrils flare.

Suddenly, Kat had a strong suspicion that Kaltenbrun knew more about her team than perhaps Kat did. Kat only just stopped her own frown. She was already getting tired of Kalternbrun's presence.

"You wanted to see me Commander," she said deliberately using his equivalent rank in the ABCANZ Fleet, rather than his own. Her voice was suitably un-confrontational, appropriate for a junior officer addressing her senior.

The Intelligence and Security Agency Operative pulled his gaze away from Kat's entourage and focused onto Kat. "I am told you have information about a plot against the life of our esteemed citizen, Ernst-Augustus von Welf, the seventh of that name. If so, the Union of European demands that you share it immediately."

"Quite so, and I have already given all that I know to your Captain Sörensen. If you have talked to him, you know as much as I do."

"I am required to hear it from the source, and in the presence of witnesses."

Kat considered making an issue of that, but decided

against it. She was already bored by a man who couldn't hold a normal conversation and had to demand everything! Quickly she gave him a recap, telling him everything she knew.

"That hardly constitutes quality intelligence," Kaltenbrun snapped. "It is no more than an allegation of rumours heard."

"You may take it as you so please, Commander. But I assure you that if your 'esteemed citizen' ends up suddenly dead in the next few days your superiors might not agree with your assessment."

The Fregattenkapitän swallowed hard. "Do you have an image of this 'Morax' individual?"

"The Angels of Light apparently now forbid the making of imagery of themselves and their followers," Kat advised. "I believe that there are thirty-four of them, and I know that they had a few problems when they showed up in Port Blair and wanted onward travel to Puducherry, as that required identity confirmation, but as it's considered an 'internal' transit, a domestic journey from one part of the Indian Union to another, biometric scans facilitated by a local legal company were apparently deemed sufficient."

The Fregattenkapitän paused for only a moment before saying, "This was not their way when we last heard from the 'Angels of Light.'"

"I doubt suicidal terrorism was either, Commander."

Fregattenkapitän Kaltenbrun frowned. Kat suspected the prospect of going back to his bosses with nothing helpful to add to their pot of boiling paranoia did not excite him.

"We might be able to assist though," Kat said.

"How?" the Fregattenkapitän snapped.

"We have the lad's father on-board. I have his image stored, as I have no qualms about what the Angels of Light do or don't permit. My ship, my rules, simple. We have run the father's image though a software program or two to take the years off his face, the grey from his hair. Commander Gillan, if you please."

"Yes, your Highness," he spoke into his comm-link, and a couple of minutes later his navigator and second-in-command, Myra Sato, also in Number Two Dress, sporting the rank of a Fleet Lieutenant, arrived and handed her Captain a file. "As you requested, sir."

Gillan handed it to Kat who opened it. There was an enlarged image of Beelzebub and a similar sized reworked image. It did look like his son, Morax. Kat handed the images to Mike, who passed them to the Fregattenkapitän.

"Commander, I have personally met the young man in question. This reworked image is a good likeness."

"You've actually met him?" A dozen indictments lurked behind those words, starting with 'treason.'

"Only briefly. He accompanied his father when I first visited the island. I did not see him the second time. His father advised that Morax and his friends had already left."

"Yes . . . the father. You will hand him over to me for interrogation immediately." It wasn't quite an order, more of an assumption of someone who had never been told 'no.'

"No, Commander. He is in our care, he is not our prisoner," Kat advised, then switched to the regal 'plural.' "We are satisfied from our own questioning that he knows nothing more than what he has already told us."

"May I remind you that you are now in a European Union protected Overseas Territory."

"You already have, Commander. And, may I remind you that you are on an ANCANZ Federation ship," Kat said, standing up to her full one-point-eight-two metre height and looking down a good five or six centimetres on the Fregattenkapitän. "And you will now depart from said vessel."

At the hatchway, Staff Freeman appeared. "This way, sir, if you please."

The Fregattenkapitän held his ground for a few seconds, then seemed to shrink. "Your Embassy will hear of this. I will go, but I expect to return." He then did a smart about turn and started to march out. Kapitän Sörensen rested a hand on Kaltenbrun's shoulder as he passed by. "I have had dealings with Miss Severn before. I'll stay behind and see what I can do."

"That would be good, Kapitän Sörensen. Try to get the

father into our custody," Kaltenbrun said, then continued his march out.

The others members of the Intelligence and Security Agency followed their boss out. When the sound of their footsteps could no longer be heard, Kat relaxed. "Turn the lights up, it's way too dark in here."

The overhead lighting went to full. Chairs were returned to the room.

Her team, now seated around the conference table found themselves staring at each other. She had a very puzzled team ... than now included Kapitän Sörensen and a von Welf!

Alexandra settled herself into a chair at her Kapitän's right elbow. He'd taken the seat at the far end of the table, opposite to Kat. "Have you really come to save my father's life," Alexandra asked.

"I didn't have much of a choice. If your father is killed any time soon, Morax and his friends will paint my identity all over the plot. Propagandists will demand that I either stand trial in what I believe is known as a 'kangaroo court' here, or we go to war! Since I don't think King James will willingly hand me over for a show trial with a predetermined outcome, it looks like war, or at least some very heavy-calibre sabre rattling will then prevail!

"You don't sound all that sure about your King?" Sörensen said, a knowing smile on this face.

Kat made a face. "Let's just say I don't want to find out. My Grandpa Jim has tossed me into a lot of crap in recent years ... sink or swim. Therefore, I'd prefer not to see how that might pan out in a European Union courtroom.

"I wouldn't want to take my chances in what passes for justice when international politics are in the mix either," Alexandra said, then changed the subject. "How do we stop these people from killing my dad?"

Kapitän Sörensen was shaking his head. "I don't think they have any chance of getting near enough to Herr von Welf."

"I agree," said Kat.

"What? You dragged us our here to stop this plot,"

Mike said. "But now you say they aren't likely to kill anyone? Any chance you'd like to explain yourself?"

Kat just shrugged. Since Kapitän Sörensen made no effort to talk, she explained. "Morax and his North Sentinel crew are 'fish out of water.' They're white skinned, island dwelling hicks with sand between their toes. As soon as they open their mouths they'll be detained, if not actually arrested. There is no way they will get close enough to Mr von Welf to harm, or kill him."

"So, we are therefore here because . . .?" Mike asked, suddenly sounding very tired of Kat's 'games.'

"Because . . ." Kapitän Sörensen began, "they will be captured. Under interrogation they will mention your Highness, here," he continued, pointing at Kat. "If anyone kills Fähnrich von Welf's father, the trail is now set to lead straight back to Katarina Severn. Heads they win, tails, you lose."

Mike settled back into his chair, eyed the overhead bulkhead and muttered a long line of expletives.

Now it was Kat's turn. "Do either of you know what Herr von Welf's itinerary is going to be?"

"He's already here. Arrived yesterday morning. There's a nature reserve about forty kilometres away. He wants to see a tiger in its natural environment. When I was notified that Puducherry was returning to the European Union's protection, I should have had a bet that dad would be here the very next day. He does love his big game hunting."

Kapitän Sörensen nodded in agreement. "True, but nobody in our military headquarters thought it would be quite this quick. We don't have a secure defensive perimeter established yet! This all feels most contrived to me. Someone has to be manipulating us. (1) Your ship's crew conveniently come across someone in Port Blair that just happens to want passage to what is supposedly an uninhabited island. (2) Kat, in good faith, then visits said island, that just happens to be inhabited by a secret colony of religious extremists, if not actual terrorists, and that gets reported up the line to 'someone.' (3) Puducherry is suddenly "persuaded' to become an Overseas Protectorate again, having been a former French outpost a hundred and something years ago. That last part was most certainly not part of my original orders when we deployed to the Indian Ocean, and has required us to pull in considerable assets from our units based on Reunion. (4) Herr von Welf is encouraged by 'someone' to visit Puducherry prematurely, to pursue one of his passions. (5) The young people of North Sentinel are hastily dispatched on a 'suicide mission' to the very same city to harm Herr von Welf, whom they somehow know is going to be in said city! Great Operational Security there don't you think! And, finally (6) under interrogation they will reveal that Kat Severn of the ABCANZ Federation was on their island home only a few weeks ago meeting with the island's leadership who's grasp on reality is highly questionable." He paused for a second or two. "All that is way, way too much of a coincidence for me," Sörensen concluded.

"Me too," agreed Mike.

"I don't believe in coincidences," said Kat. "Never have. You should all know that by know!"

"And me being here?" Alexandra asked.

"Ha, that is probably the only thing amongst all this that is a coincidence!" her Kapitän laughed.

"I'll reserve my judgment on that, if you don't mind," Kat said, "No offence, Alexandra."

"None taken, your Highness. And, please call me 'Lex.' Only my father calls me Alexandra."

"I agree. It is as if we're being set up for something," Captain Gillan said. Then paused. His finger going to his ear. He was listening to something. Then he stood. "Your Highness, I strongly suggest that we continue this conversation up on the bridge. It would seem matters are evolving."

"What's happening?" came from three or four seated around the table.

"It's quicker if we go and see, rather than I try to explain," hung in the air as Gillan rushed towards the hatchway.

Kat and the others were hard on his heels.

*   *   *

A breathless minute later, Kat and her team arranged themselves in front of the bridge's main display screen. A deadly serious Myra Sato explained what they were looking at.

"Thirty minutes ago, one of the Bay of Bengal's pair of ageing Ro-Pax transporter ships, the *MV Varuna Ratnaker* began her approach into this port, as she does every other Saturday. She operates on a fourteen-day clockwise rotation that takes passengers and cargo from Chennai, to Visakhapatnam, Chittagong, Port Blair and Colombo. Her last port call is here, Puducherry, before going back to Chennai to start over again. Except today, she is currently at her top 'laden' speed of twenty-four knots, not bad for a non-military ship of that size, age, and in these deteriorating sea conditions."

Gillan and Sörensen were nodding in agreement.

"And I take it that's a problem?" Mike said.

"A ship of that size should be slowing down to enter port. If anything unexpected occurs she can then manoeuvre without endangering herself, her crew and passengers, other shipping or the port's overall infrastructure. Six or Seven knots would be better, certainly no more than eight," Myra said. "And in this weather," she said, pointing at the torrential rain now lashing into the bridge's windows, "I'd be going even slower! . . . But . . . she's not. Not slowing down at all. She's actually speeding up, her reactor must be close to red-lining. She's put on 3.5 knots in the last thirty minutes."

"No vessel captain or master would deliberately do this, exposing their vessel to such unnecessary risks!" Sörensen concluded.

"Can we therefore assume that this *Varuna Ratnaker* is no longer under her Captain's control or that he or she is no longer of a sane mind? Mike asked.

"The Port Authority is trying to communicate with her now. No response so far. It could be the weather, but unlikely, as they have full comms with several other vessels out in the Bay. Therefore, either her comms kit is damaged, which seems unlikely, as there's more than one way to communicate these days, and she obviously hasn't lost power, so yes, her bridge is potentially compromised." Myra concluded.

"Talk to me, tell me about the *Varuna Ratnaker*" Gillan ordered his Navigator.

Myra complied, bringing up the required schematics and statistics.

"Almost a hundred thousand freakin' tonnes!" Mike said, "Wow . . . up to three and a half thousand passengers, plus several hundred crew, eight hundred cars and fifteen hundred 'lane' metres of trailer cargo" he added. "That's impressive."

"But . . . she's old. Sufficiently old that she has a first-generation reactor," said Gillan studying the display.

"If she maintains that kind of speed, how long before she gets here?" Kat asked. Her voice was cold.

"Assuming she keeps accelerating at the same rate . . . two hours, twenty-eight minutes . . . maybe a few minutes more if she doesn't add any more speed. Then she ploughs one almighty furrow into southern India, and that's assuming her reactor isn't damaged or deliberately sabotaged and goes into meltdown before then!" Myra added.

"Is that likely? Can you even do that?" Mike asked.

"Most definitely Mike. It's certainly not easy, but not exactly difficult either, especially if you know what you're doing," Safi confirmed. "A mid-level HI could easily do this."

"Where's that wildlife reservation my dad's visiting in relation to all this?" Lex asked.

"Too close for my liking," Kapitän Sörensen commented.

"You have plenty of time to get him out. Task a VTOL aircraft from one of your ships to go in and get him," Kat suggested.

"Unlikely they'll do that," said Gillan who was studying another screen. There's a big old storm coming in, just to make things interesting!"

"Monsoon officially season finished last month," said Sato.

"I know . . . and I'm no meteorologist, but that is a significant storm front coming our way. It will heavily restrict all air and sea operations," said Gillan pointing at the display on the navigator's board.

"The civilian airports all along the south-east seaboard, Chennai, Puducherry, Tiruchirapalli, Thanjavur and Trincomalee are already closed as a precaution," Sato said.

Kat frowned. "Assassin's luck, or planned?"

Sörensen shrugged. "It's not really the season for it, a few weeks late certainly, but not unheard off.

"So, a hundred and fifty minutes, give or take, How many ships can you get evacuated Kapitän Sörensen? Kat asked.

Sörensen shook his head. "Some of the smaller ones, but unlikely we'd get anything larger than a Frigate back out to sea in time . . . although they must know about this storm coming in and, as I'm sure you know, it's better for a big ship to ride a storm out in open water, rather than get repeatedly smacked into the quayside by the wind and waves, so maybe preparations are already underway. I'll need to check with my Flag Officer's staff."

"Have we all been stitched up?" Mike asked. "The EU's military too?"

Captain Gillan cleared his throat, "With all due respect, there is one vessel that can definitely get underway."

"Which one?" Sörensen demanded.

"This one . . . the *Bella*," Gillan said with a sly smile.

The European Union naval Kapitän frowned. Then his eyes grew wide for a moment. "How?"

"The *Fires of Beltane* was rigged for such an eventuality during her refit and repair earlier this year . . . whilst you were all having fun in Emirates City. As we are a 'ship of exploration,' there is no telling what our needs . . . what err . . . misfortune might befall us out in these rarely frequented waters."

"It's impossible. How?" Sörensen asked again.

"No, not when it's done with modern power couplings and the very latest offerings from the science and technology boffins in the Lennox Group's Hampton Road's shipyard." Gillan shot back.

"Captain Gillan please enlighten us as to how you can restart our reactors within the next hundred and fifty minutes." Kat ordered.

"No offence to Kapitän Sörensen, Miss von Welf or to yourself, your Highness, but are you sure you want me do openly discuss this in front of them."

"This isn't the time for such games, Jensen, thousands of lives might be in danger, please enlighten us on what you're proposing."

"I'll spare you the history lesson, but to make a rail-gun a realistic weapon system that's small enough to actually mount into a ship, the power supply needed to be significantly reduced in size from the landside test and evaluation sites. So, they modified the compact Thorium salt reactors used in the Fast Intercept Boats, or FIBs that I know you are intimately familiar with, your Highness. Our rail-gun has two such reactors, one to power each rail. They're not even classified as a reactor, as their power output is under 10Megawatts. We can rewire one of them into our auxiliary power generators. That will be sufficient to get the magnetic containment field back up on one of the *Bella*'s main reactors. We then deliberately overheat the other rail gun reactor, using the generated heat to get a deuterium fuel cell up to its optimum operating temperature a bit faster than usual. And that, should be enough to effectively 'jump-start' the 'tokamak' before the safety plug of the rail gun reactor melts and puts an end to that," he said, grinning as proudly as the cat who ate the canary! "Only down side . . . we'll lose the rain gun, as it obviously can't fire without her reactors to power the rails, so you'll have to make do with ASMs for any offensive action you might be considering."

"Is your *Fenrir* rigged with anything similar, Kapitän Sörensen?" Kat asked.

"Absolutely not. Is that even legal? I've not heard of our Atomic Energy Agency approving anything of this nature recently. Since the *Cardinal Richelieu* incident towards the end of the war with China they've been very reluctant to try anything original, usually waiting for others to prove its reliability first. Thousands died in that accident you know."

Kat walked away from the two captains. One offered a solution, that was probably super dangerous and if it went wrong would kill hundreds, if not thousands of people. The other offered no solution . . . but suggested that the other not do what was being offered, it being too dangerous to even try. Kat found herself staring at a very pale Alexandra von Welf.

"Lex, what do you think?"

"I don't know what to think, your Highness."

"Talk to me, Lex. I need to know what you're thinking."

"Okay," the young woman said, and took a deep breath. "I want to save my dad. Other people may hate him, but he's my dad. Maybe not the best dad around, and he's often made my life miserable, but he's the only dad I have. What do we need to do?"

There it was. A plea from a younger von Welf to save the elder. A plea made by a von Welf to a Severn. Capulet to Montague. *Do I accept it?* Kat asked herself. *Stupid question. My head is in the same noose!*

If she let that Ro-Pax vessel smash into the port then there'd be rocks and wreckage all over the place, and several thousand people on board might be lost. There was then the risk her reactor would go critical and rupture, which was obviously the intended plan. If it did, several thousand deaths suddenly became tens of thousands instead, and one of those would most likely be Lex's father. And, the hierarchy of the EUs Intelligence and Security Agency who would be 'oh so certain' that Kat was behind it all!

With a sigh, Kat winked at Lex. *Watch and Learn*, she thought then turned to face both Captains.

"Kapitän Sörensen, how long would it take to get a warship with enough offensive capability to disable that Ro-Pax, underway?"

"Four or five hours, maybe a bit more. This port isn't

the best you know. Some could undoubtedly sail sooner, but many of the crews are now assigned to duties ashore, as part of the city's consolidation force. So yes . . . we could get away sooner, but then have problems sailing and engaging, being so under-crewed. We've been set up."

"Agreed, we all have," Kat told him. "In the next hundred and fifty minutes, give or take, a rather large ship is going to crash headlong into this facility, killing thousands, both on-board and ashore, and that's before her reactor potentially goes into meltdown and . . . . well, we all know how that ends . . . and amongst the casualties, will be her father," she pointed at Lex. "Ernst-Augustus von Welf suddenly gets very dead indeed." Kat stopped speaking and looked slowly as those around her on the bridge. There was a long silence. They all said nothing. They just looked right back at her. "Out of curiosity, does your young Fähnrich here get a 'field promotion' to whatever title her father currently goes by?"

Alexandra's eyes suddenly got every wide.

And Kapitän Sörensen became very interested in the polished toe-caps of his boots. "I have no idea. It's unlikely, as we have the Salic laws of inheritance, that gives priority to the male line. Naturally I am very aware of this, having multiple daughters and no sons . . . but I suppose it's not impossible. But don't you think that whoever is behind this will have considered that possibility?" He turned to face Alexandra. "It is my duty to protect you, Fähnrich von Welf . . . to my dying breath."

"I don't want your dying breath," Lex snapped back at him, "Save my father!"

Sörensen's shoulders slumped. "We can launch strike weapons from here against that Ro-Pax. Everyone on-board will die, and any intelligence they might have also dies with them. Some may even consider that to be convenient. Unless you want to try something different, your Highness, that is the most likely outcome, and certainly the course of action my people will advocate."

"Someone in the ABCANZ Fleet is willing to try to intercept . . . disable, rather than destroy that ship," Lex growled, "And a freakin' Severn at that!"

"That's if she doesn't kill us all with this reactor re-start nonsense."

"All things considered, and as you think my life to potentially be under threat as well, I'd rather we did all we can to save my father. He has the resources immediately at hand to hunt the perpetrators down. I, however do not, and would have to run . . . hide . . . live to fight another day. Right now, we need to save my father. Herr Kapitän, if our own navy's assets are unable to assist, then I implore you to help these people try."

"And if they fail?" Sörensen asked her.

"If they fail, we can still order a strike against the Ro-Pax."

For a long moment Kapitän Sörensen continued to shake his head, before turning to Kat. "Your Highness, what can I do to help?"

Kat already knew that it was highly unlikely that she'd get any legal authorization to fire on a civilian ship. The Indian Authorities would still be discussing the situation several weeks from now, and that was only after they'd got their heads around the immediate and wider 'big picture' implications! Prompt, decisive decision making and resultant action was not their known forte!

This was certainly one of those occasions when it was going to be prudent to get on with it and ask for forgiveness, rather than wait for permission to be given.

Kat turned to Captain Gillan, "Get the *Bella* underway as quickly as you can."

"Aye, ma'am. I'll have them begin preparations for getting the magnetic containment field back up. It hopefully shouldn't take too long."

"As soon as its back up, we'll overheat the safety plug and 'jump-start' the fusion process," Sato advised.

"No," came from around Kat's neck. "The magnetic containment field that keeps the hydrogen plasma in a torus needs to be carefully balanced and aligned," Safi said. "That is a critical path, as without that, nothing can proceed."

"Captain?" Kat said, raising an eyebrow.

"We'll do it Safi's way," he ordered.

"Are there any of our science team that can assist with this?" Kat asked her HI.

"A few. I've already alerted them to get down to engineering. There are specific conditions, environments if you prefer, within the reactor that need to be created before we can introduce any fissile material."

"All yours, Safi." Kat said, confident that the technical side of things was in safe 'hands.' She turned back to Kapitän Sörensen. "We'll obviously need to advise the Port Authority and your people that we're getting under way."

"Even a blind man would notice what we're attempting."

"So, when do we need to inform them?"

The Kapitän considered her question for a few seconds. "I think it better to ask forgiveness than permission," he replied.

"That's becoming a bit of a habit around here today!" Kat said. "But, I don't think so . . . the security paranoia currently operating could result in us drawing some very immediate and violent attention!"

"Fair point," Sörensen conceded. "Let me talk with our Intelligence and Security Agency." He pressed a few buttons on his personal comm unit. Nothing happened for several seconds, leaving the Kapitän frowning at the device. "What call can he possibly be on that has a higher priority than mine?"

Sörensen was still frowning when a flustered voice came on. "My apologies, Herr Kapitän, I have Konteradmiral Voss on the line, sir. I think it appropriate that you join the call." It wasn't a question.

Kapitän Sörensen turned very pale indeed. Behind him Lex smiled, "Uncle Otto, he'll help us."

Those two, very different reactions, told Kat all she needed to know about the new person 'joining the party.'

"Put the call on the main screen," Kat ordered.

She found herself facing a thin-faced man. His uniform was pristine. Kat immediately checked out the medal ribbons on his left breast . . . they told her very little.

She made a mental note to herself to save the call. When had Commodore Finklemeyer last had a visual of his opposite number?

That however, somewhat assumed that she would survive the currently evolving situation.

"Konteradmiral Voss, I am Lieutenant Severn, Princess Katarina of the ABCANZ Federation. I and my staff have been examining the behaviour of the Ro-Pax vessel *Varuna Ratnaker*. It is our opinion that she is on a suicide mission to destroy Puducherry's port, with the intent on triggering a nuclear 'incident' using the said vessel's old 'first gen' reactor, and thereby destroying the adjacent city, surrounding area, and I believe the life of your most prominent citizen, Herr von Welf. The *Varuna Ratnaker* needs to be stopped."

Kat paused. She was getting no reaction from the man on the screen. No reaction at all. *You'd think that announcing a plot was afoot to kill his political master, if not his actual direct military superior, would get something!* Not from Voss.

"Go on," was all he said.

"May I ask what conclusions the Konteradmiral and his staff have deduced from the behaviour of the identified Ro-Pax vessel? *This is a two-way conversation, mister! I talk, then you talk. It's not all one-way, whatever you might think or want!*

The Konteradmiral finally blinked. "The Ro-Pax's behaviour is unusual. However, the evolution that your vessel is currently undertaking is also irregular. This makes us wonder if you are not intent on some kind of suicide mission too." His words were as cold as ice.

"I find two faults in your deduction, Herr Konteradmiral."

"Would you care to enumerate my apparent errors?"

Kat raised a finger, not giving in to the temptation to make it her middle one. "First, you should already know that during all the attempts made on my life that there isn't a suicidal bone in my body. I very much like being alive and will fight to my last breath to stay that way."

"So it would seem. However, that might have changed. High objectives sometimes demand a high price."

"Not is my book they don't. And, secondly, your 'most prominent' citizen is some forty kilometres away from this port. The Ro-Pax crashing in will hardly ruffle a hair on his head, it's the vessel's reactor meltdown that will achieve the desired effect, and hence you requiring all non-EU vessels to flood their reactors. A very wise and sensible safety precaution."

"Perhaps you are trading? A queen for a queen? No? You do, after all have Miss von Welf on-board your vessel."

Again, the same cold calculations. Kat had had enough. "That does not even qualify as a joke, Herr Konteradmiral. No offence to Miss von Welf, but I am a fully-fledged 'queen' in the 'game' the likes of you and my Intelligence Director insist on playing. Fähnrich von Welf here, is at best, a pawn. Maybe someday to become a queen, but certainly not today."

"No offence taken," Lex said. "Now, Uncle Otto, are we going to sit here arguing who *might* be doing something while not actually *doing anything* to help my father? Are the rumours true that you're with the faction who would quite like to see him dead? Is that why you sit there jabbering while time ticks away from the one ship that could maybe save his life?"

Before Kat had considered the Konteradmiral as stiff as a board. Under Lex's chastising, he became solid stone. "It was necessary for me to assure myself that a treacherous Severn was not playing us for fools. They've done it often enough!"

"That is why I am on-board. I have satisfied myself that this ship can undertake this difficult task, where others, either because of their duties ashore or mechanical status cannot, or due to the rapidly deteriorating weather, a suitable aircraft cannot operate. Do we perhaps have a submarine or some other craft in the vicinity that could intercede instead?" Lex shot back.

"No, no submarine, or other suitable military craft, is within range, given the time parameters we are up against.

I concur that . . . err . . . harvesting the intelligence from those perpetrating this crime, identifying who might be the entity truly orchestrating it, would be most beneficial. Not to mention, save the crew and passenger's lives," he added as an afterthought. "Your mission is authorised to proceed. We will monitor your progress and destroy the Ro-Pax vessel if you are unsuccessful in trying to disable her. I therefore think it prudent for the Intelligence and Security Agency to commandeer Severn's vessel."

"Otto, when I need your people to supress a demonstration of several hundred unarmed civilians, I'll call for you. Right now, I need *this* ship to sail, and a civilian ship neutralized. Let's leave that to a crew who knows how to do exactly that."

"Yes, Citizen Alexandra," The Konteradmiral said, almost bowing to her. "May I send a security team to assure your own personal safety?"

"If you feel you must, but make it a small team, with orders to keep out of the way. Oh, and don't send Kaltenbrun again," the Fähnrich snapped at the Konteradmiral.

"Yes, Citizen Alexandra. If you will excuse me, I will see to it that these things are taken care of."

"One more thing. I believe this ship needs a significant boost of power, so please order the port to give it a direct, high-voltage feed." She turned to Captain Gillan. "Do you need plasma too?"

"Yes, deuterium if they have it. Electricity to get the magnetic containment field back up is our priority. We can do the rest ourselves, but it will certainly help, save us some time."

"I'm on it," the Conteradmiral responded and ended the call.

"Will this mean we don't lose the rail gun?" Kat asked Gillan once the call light went red.

"I wish, ma'am, but unfortunately, no. It saves us using one of the reactors for sufficient power to get an EM containment field up, but we still need the extreme temperatures from over loading the other."

The silence that followed on the bridge was broken only by the usual sounds of an operational ship. A report notification, a flashing button. Nobody spoke.

Kapitän Sörensen remained as white as an arctic snow blizzard. Kat suspected that Lex's next lesson was going to have to come from her. "You may have been a little bit direct with the Konteradmiral, Fähnrich."

Lex pursed her full lips, "You think so? Whenever he came to our house, he was always so friendly. Almost sycophantic . . . fawning to please my father. Dad saw right through it, of course. He'd call him 'two-faced.' That comment about supressing unarmed civilians was one of dads."

"But did your father ever say it to his face?" Kat asked.

Lex thought for a moment, then looked embarrassed. "Yes, you're right, I don't recall him actually saying it to him."

"So, you might want to warn your father when you next see him that that particular cat is out of the bag," Kapitän Sörensen added.

"We're getting a high-voltage power cable from the port," Sato advised. "Connecting it now . . . coupling engaged, connection is secure . . . Routing HV feed to Engineering."

"Well. He's carrying out his orders," Captain Gillan said. "Now let's see how huge Princess Lex's security detail is going to be!"

"I am not a Princess," Alexandra snapped, "But I take your point, my dad operates like he's some kind of unelected 'Emperor,' or 'First Citizen,' so I guess that might make me *something* by association."

"From my experience, that 'something' is actually a *'target'*" Kat observed.

Five minutes later, a squad of ten Sicherheitsdienst troopers double-timed it up the accessway to the *Bella's* quarterdeck. Despite the heavy rain, Staff Freeman and Sergeant Varko intercepted them with a similarly sized and equipped team and formerly 'invited' them to come aboard.

"I know that Korvettenkapitän," Lex said as they

watched the exchange from the rear facing windows of the *Bella*'s bridge. "He's trouble."

"We'll see," Kat said tapping her comm-link. "Staff, please advise the Korvettenkapitän that this ship will be doing in excess of forty knots once we get underway to make contact with the *Varuna Ratnaker*. Spare seats with the appropriate restraints are not in abundance. There is a space for him, should he wish to join Kapitän Sörensen and Fähnrich von Welf up here on the bridge, but you'll need to find somewhere for his people to secure themselves."

In silence, they watched the exchange between Freeman and the Korvettenkapitän. The Korvettenkapitän turned to one of his subordinates, who listened, saluted, pointed at some of the squad and shouted some orders, then led his team away under Sergeant Varko's ever-watchful eye.

That went smoothly enough," Lex said.

"Captain Gillan," Kat said, "Do we have enough restraint rigged chairs up here for all our guests?"

"We're working on it. What station do you want, your Highness?" Gillan replied, aware that he might need to relinquish the Captain's chair to keep up the required appearances to their 'guests.'

"Warfare systems, Captain." Most likely, someone would be taking a couple of shots at that Ro-Pax vessel and the several thousand souls aboard. Fast shots, as the *Varuna Ratnaker* and the *Fires of Beltane* passed each other at a combined speed exceeding sixty, perhaps seventy knots. That was not something Kat was about to delegate.

"Lieutenant Sato," Kat said, as she reached the bridge hatch, "Please send me everything we have on the *Varuna Ratnaker*. I'll be in the Captain's office."

"Yes, ma'am."

"Safi, I appreciate you're busy, but if you have any spare processing capacity, could you please search for additional data on the *Varuna Ratnaker* too."

"Yes, ma'am," came back in a basic computer voice. Safi was evidently very busy indeed.

"Let me check with the Sicherheitsdienst," Kapitän Sörensen said. "They may have information that's not in the public domain."

The Intelligence and Security Agency operative on the other end of Sörensen's comm-link did indeed have additional information but flatly refused to send it to an ABCANZ Federation ship. Sörensen tried hard to reason with him, and was on the verge of losing his temper when Fähnrich von Welf interceded.

"This is Citizen Alexandra von Welf, only daughter of Ernst Augustus von Welf, then seventh of that name." Her tone was hard enough to cut solid granite. "His life, and that of many others, is in immediate danger. Is it your intent to deliberately hinder the attempts being made to save these lives?"

"No, ma'am," came back in a stutter.

"Then see to it that those files are transmitted here immediately. Do this or I will personally come to you . . . to witness your execution. Do I make myself clear?"

"Yes, ma'am. The files are on their way."

Lex turned to Sörensen. "I'm sorry, Herr Kapitän. I know that is not how you taught me to lead. However, that is the style I learned at my father's knee. I am now starting to learn that there is a time to do things your way . . . and a time to do things dad's way."

"That's not an easy lesson to learn," Kat said.

Lex seemed to reflect. "You are right, Kat. It is not at all easy. Was it like this for you?"

"I think you may find it somewhat harder. I get the impression that there is a bigger gap between the way your Navy and your father go about their business, than the way my father and our Fleet do theirs."

"That is something I hope we can talk more about," Lex responded.

"Do you think we could perhaps save your dad first," Kat said with a wry smirk.

SIX : EIGHTEEN

Although Captain Gillan's office had now become Kat's 'OpsCen,' or Operations Centre, it was actually unchanged from their stampede to get to the bridge. Her improvised 'throne' was still on its side on the floor.

The main screen showed a schematic of the *Varuna Ratnaker*. The secondary display was covered in open files. A third, rarely used display screen, now showed a number of concentric circles each rotating clockwise, then anti-clockwise. The outer rings changed from red to amber, then back to red. Beside it was a list of 'file not found' and associated error messages.

At the table Anna was already working, with numerous tablets and data-pads being plugged into the table and some into each other. She looked up at Kat. "You should see the crap were getting from the Sicherheitsdienst. If I didn't know better, I'd say they were trying to take down the *Bella*'s main-frame."

"They had better not be," Lex said. "Try this . . ." She then rattled off a long string of voice identifying challenges, encryption overrides, and authorization identifiers.

The screen of concentric circles blinked red, all turned anti-clockwise, then went amber, turned clockwise, then went green, before changing to a schematic of the *Varuna Ratnaker* not immediately very different from that on the main screen.

"My apologies," Lex said. "It was all password encrypted. I didn't expect the files to be sent through so fast."

"I'm no expert, but I'd imagine that threatening to execute someone usually has that effect," Kat pointed out.

"I certainly does, but I still thought it would take them

a bit longer to collate, encrypt and compress all the information before transmission."

"Evidently our Intelligence and Security Agency has protocols for 'do it now or I'll shoot you!'" Kapitän Sörensen said.

Kat hoped he was joking, but she really wasn't sure. The nod he got from Alexandra von Welf looked far too '*of course we do*,' for Kat's comfort.

How do they operate in this way? Kat mussed briefly before focusing on the display of the *Varuna Ratnaker*.

Where warships like the *Osprey* were built small, slim and fast, to offer the absolute minimum targeting opportunity, the *Varuna Ratnaker* was huge and built like a brick to maximise cabin and cargo space, giving each of the premium cabins on the upper decks its own external view. The most expensive suits had double-aspect views ahead and to the side.

"Before we start planning the detail, I want to give a brief overview summary," Kat began. "The easiest, and safest option, is for an EU warship to launch and all-weather anti-ship-missile or something similar, at the Ro-Pax and destroy it. The downside of that, is that everyone on-board will either be killed by the strike, or be in an escape-pod, life-raft or some other such device. Better than being dead, but only just in these weather conditions. Roger, so far?"

There were nods from those present, mixed with the occasional "yes, ma'am."

Kat continued her summary. "Rather conveniently, no EU warship can recall her crew from 'occupation' duties ashore and effect an interception of the Ro-Pax, with the intent of disabling, rather than destroying, her, in the time remaining. However, the *Fires of Beltane* can, and will, make an attempt to do exactly that."

"And be a convenient 'scapegoat' if our efforts are unsuccessful," added Mike.

Kat didn't comment, just continued. "Finally, given that we don't know who is ultimately behind all this . . . who's actually pulling the strings, getting the Angels of Light to do their 'dirty work' . . . Lex will stay on-board the *Fires of Beltane* for her own protection, rather than go ashore, as it's not completely clear who can be trusted. Although her presence on-board may prevent the *Bella* from becoming a target, it may actually be the exact opposite, i.e. 'two birds with one stone!" She let that sink in for a few seconds. "Any Questions?"

There were none. "So, do we target the *Varuna Ratnaker*'s bridge?" Kat asked, half to herself, half to those around her. Captain Gillan had stayed on his own bridge to oversee the powering-up process, but Kat still had a Destroyer's captain with her. Sörensen was shaking his head.

"I don't think the bridge will get you anything. There's a back-up control room well aft, just before the Engineering spaces," he said. On the schematic behind Kat a space glowed blue just forward of where she expected the propulsion spaces to begin. "These Ro-Pax vessels were designed to be easily converted into troop transports, or R&R, Replenish and Repair units, with logistical supply, equipment and vehicle repair and surgical hospital facilities."

"Is that why your Intel and Security people were so reluctant to share this with us?" Anna asked.

Kapitän Sörensen gently cleared his throat. "You do know, your Highness, that your Equerry, who is now apparently a Special Operations Officer, regularly publishes information about what you get up to?"

"Oh," Kat said. "Is that why Fregattenkapitän Kaltenbrun looked about fit to burst. He was meeting Anna face-to-face and couldn't process how to operate with a known spy being amongst my staff?"

Anna for her part, and despite being seated, managed something between a bow and a curtsey.

"You don't sound surprised," Sörensen said.

"Anna, what's it worth, not to have your cover blown?" Kat asked over her shoulder.

"Hey, that's not fair. You agreed to pay me for early copies of my reports and slightly modified versions that you can include in your own submissions." Anna sounded annoyed.

"I did indeed, but It's not me you need to bribe. It looks like you might have to buy the good Kapitän's silence."

"Mine too," Lex added. "I always need a new party dress!"

"What bribe?" was the low growl coming from the hatchway as the Intelligence and Security Agency Korvettenkapitän followed Staff Freeman in.

"A bit of levity," Kat growled right back at him, "to lighten the burden of figuring out how to damage a Ro-Pax with several thousand souls aboard."

"Why damage it?" The Korvettenkapitän said. "Just sink it."

That brought a strained silence.

"Kat," Lex said in a low voice, "That's my angle too, it's my dad's life we're talking about here."

"Your dad's life and thousands more in the port, the city, the surrounding countryside," Kat agreed. "But, it's not as easy as that. Has anyone calculated the destruction each of our weapon systems might cause on such a vessel?" Normally Kat would have asked Safi to do it, but the low hum across her collar bone told her that her HI was fully occupied.

"I have something similar" Anna said. "The likely damage the *Jarnsaxa* could inflict upon civilian vessels. I did the calculations in preparation for the engagement off Cape Town. I never deleted it."

Beside Kat, Lex swallowed hard at the mention of the battle in which her brother died. She threw Anna a hard glare, as if memorising her face.

Anna looked back, just as hard.

Lex started to open her mouth.

Kat cut her off. "Enough, ladies. A lot of people are hurting from a lot of things that might have been better if not done at all. Today we have today's problems. Kapitän Sörensen, can you tell us something about the thickness of the Ro-Pax's hull? The deck configuration, her strengths and weaknesses."

"That is classified information," the Intelligence and

Security Agency Korvettenkapitän informed them.

"Then keep your 'state secrets' and start recruiting for a new 'First Citizen' or whatever title he goes by. Works for me. Or, you can tell us and just maybe it will help me save his life. Your call Fregattenkapitän, or should I have Fähnrich von Welf here contact Konteradmiral Voss? I'm easy, whatever works for you," Kat snapped at the Korvettenkapitän.

The Sicherheitsdienst Korvettenkapitän looked like he had swallowed something very bitter, but he nodded at Kapitän Sörensen, who promptly gave them his best guess, based on the data available.

Anna fed them into her postulations, then paused for a moment before announcing. "Not good. Lower cargo decks are huge. Water ingress would take her down, and quickly. Upper decks are mostly passenger and crew cabins. Highly unlikely to sink her, but the casualty numbers will be very much higher."

"Can we go somewhere in between? The cargo spaces above the water-line, but below the cabins?

Anna consulted her assembled screens. "Unless that's going to change her course, or reduce her speed, it will still have the same outcome when she reaches the port. A big, bada, boom! . . . This only works if we do something to her propulsion drives to stop, or reduce her speed. We could target her rudders. Jam or destroy them and she'll miss this port, but may still run aground elsewhere and then assuming her reactor goes into meltdown . . . essentially, it's the same overall effect.

"I would have thought, it was rather *obvious*," the Korvettenkapitän said. "Target her reactor. Either damage the containment field sufficiently for it to collapse, or disable the cooling tracts thereby effecting core meltdown. Either way, no more ship, no more terrorists, no more problem."

"Kat . . ." Lex said, not quite pleading.

"That is certainly an option," Kat said slowly. "But it is my last option. I did not put on this uniform to kill several thousand innocent people, their only crime being to purchase a ticket for passage, or the vessel's crew simply undertaking their jobs. Do you understand me, Korvettenkapitän?"

Kat locked eyes with the Sicherheitsdienst's Korvettenkapitän. He glared right back at her.

"My duty is to the State, the European Union, our Leaders and its citizens."

"I understand that, and although you seem very quick to go for the most decisive and destructive option, you have overlooked the small fact that the reactor is heavily shielded. This is *obviously* to protect the crew and the passengers from the radiation, but also makes it incredibly hard to penetrate with conventional weaponry."

"Enough . . . both of you!" Lex shouted. "If you don't want to hit the reactor, Kat, what . . . where . . . do you intend to target?"

Kat ran her fingers along the schematic on the screen. "The bridge, the living spaces, they have no value to us. The Korvettenkapitän is right, we do need to target the propulsion spaces," she said, her finger coming to a stop on the display. "The question is, how do we cripple the ship, drive her in a direction away from the Indian mainland, back out to sea, but in such a way that she can't be put back on course." She glanced over at the Sicherheitsdienst Korvettenkapitän, "But not blown apart."

"The turbines," Anna and Sörensen said together.

"Will someone please rotate this image for me?" Kat asked, not wanting to disturb Safi. And, for once, her HI did not cut in with some snide remark about being quite able to bake a cake and do quantum mathematics at the same time. Safi was very busy indeed.

"Tell me when to stop," said Anna as the schematic of the Ro-Pax vessel started to turn.

Kat found herself facing a three-quarter view of the aft end of the *Varuna Ratnaker*. Two large bronze propellers turned, forcing the water against and around the rudders.

"Rudders only? No thrusters? How do they steer?"

"Very carefully," Kapitän Sörensen said dryly. "Assuming a speed of ten knots or less, there are thrusters at the bow, amidships and stern that make her as maneuverable as a ballet dancer. At their current speed, I doubt they'd have much overall effect. Certainly not an option if you want to get them going in circles that they'll never regain control off."

"How much time will we have to get the Harlequins away?" Kat asked.

Anna consulted her numerous devices. "Somewhere between ten and thirteen seconds. I can't be more accurate as I'm not completely sure what our acceleration will be as we close on them."

"Captain Gillan said around thirty knots," Kat advised, "Perhaps a bit more."

"This merchant freighter is capable of such speeds?" the Sicherheitsdienst Korvettenkapitän was suddenly very interested. "So, this is the much-vaunted ABCANZ Fleet, your so-called 'Royal' Navy, that I have heard so much about."

Kat wasn't sure if he was mocking or admiring.

"Whose only 'in-theatre' ship is preparing to get underway and try something, whilst our numerous vessels are conveniently tied up at the quayside like beached whales," Lex shot back at him.

The Korvettenkapitän sensibly chose to remain silent.

"Anna, give me the broadside view again," Kat said. The display reverted. "Where are the electrical generators?"

Kapitän Sörensen quickly referenced another display, then indicated and area in-between the turbines and the reactors on the main screen.

Kat recalled her time at the Fleet's Officer Training Academy (OTA(F)) in Annapolis, Nu New England. In the Midshipman's second term the various branches of service within the Fleet all presented the career options. Expounding what their particular branch could offer, to entice the new officers currently undergoing training to join them. Once selected, the third term concentrated in their chosen specialization. Kat had chosen Warfare Systems and trained accordingly on the systems that acquired, fixed and targeted the various weapon platforms on-board. Mechanical Engineering hadn't been her chosen career, but she could just about recall enough about how the various iterations of nuclear reactors worked.

Although their designs were constantly under review and numerous upgrades were always being applied, the basic fundamentals of 'first generation' fusion tech had remained the same for decades. The reactor was fueled with an incredibly radioactive substance, usually enriched uranium. When the reactor was first started, plasma, a super-heated, electrically conductive gas of ions and unbound charged particles, was introduced. Powerful electro-magnets were then required to control and contain the plasma. Neutrons within the plasma bombarded the uranium atoms. When the uranium atoms divided or achieved 'fission,' releasing their energy, they freed even more neutrons, that in turn triggered the same process in other, surrounding uranium atoms. Once this chain-reaction was self-sustaining, the reactor was *said to be at 'critical' and generating an enormous amount of heat. Water, under extremely high pressure, to prevent it from boiling, was used to reduce the heat being generated in the reactor core. This water then passed a heat exchanger which contained another circuit of water at a much lower pressure. This second water circuit did boil, creating steam, and hence why it was sometimes referred to as the 'teapot.' This steam turned turbines, and the turbines generated the electrical power the ship required to operate. This was the type of reactor installed on the* Varuna Ratnaker. *It was old tech, and was slowly being phased out. And . . . it may have been why this ship was specifically selected rather than a random coincidence.*

'Second generation' fusion tech, such as that on the Fires of Beltane, *and most other, more modern vessels, utilised the much cleaner and safer 'Tokamak' reactor for deuterium– tritium fusion. The process still generated heat, and that produced steam. The steam still turned turbines and generated electricity, but it was the way the heat was generated that was fundamentally different.*

In a 'tokamak' reactor the charged particles of the plasma were shaped, controlled and contained by massive toroidal magnetic coils placed around the reactor vessel.

Inside, gaseous hydrogen fuel (also known as heavy hydrogen or deuterium), was subjected to extreme heat and pressure, transitioning into plasma. The reactor walls were lined with a 'blanket' made of lithium and when exposed to the super-hot deuterium plasma, they produced radioactive tritium.

Fusing atoms together in this way was four times more efficient, at equal mass, than a first generation reactor. It was also sustainable, as deuterium cells were widely available and nearly inexhaustible, being distilled from all forms of water. And whilst terrestrial reserves of lithium were only sufficient for several hundred, maybe a thousand more years, known sub-sea reserves could fulfil needs for several million.

And, there was no carbon dioxide or other 'greenhouse gas' emission into the atmosphere, the only significant by-product of the fusion being helium, an inert, non-toxic gas. There was no long-term radioactive waste either, as any exposed materials could be recycled or reused within a hundred years.

The risk of rogue proliferation was limited, as it didn't employ any enriched fissile materials such as uranium and plutonium that could be exploited to make nuclear weapons. Radioactive tritium simply wasn't a fissionable material.

In addition to all these other positives, there was no risk of meltdown. An 'accident' simply wasn't possible in a tokamak fusion device. It is sufficiently difficult to reach and then maintain the precise conditions necessary for fusion, so if a 'disturbance' did then occur, the plasma cooled within seconds and the reaction process stopped. The quantity of deuterium fuel present in the vessel at any one time was so small that there was no risk of a chain reaction, theoretically anyway . . . but the safety record statistics of the last two or three decades factually supported that theory.

"If I target the turbines, what might happen?" Kat asked.

"Everything, or nothing," Sörensen said.

Kat nodded. "The round could punch through one side and out the other, or it could cut through a plasma conduit or water pipe and spew super-hot gas or water all through the propulsion spaces. The reactor would then overheat, or the plasma containment would deteriorate. Same result . . . a first gen reactor will likely then go 'boom.'"

"And all on board will die," Mike reminded them.

"Any further forward . . . or further aft," Kat said, "it's pretty much the same outcome."

"But if you don't disable that ship, my dad and thousands of others ashore die as well as those on-board. Surely that's the lesser of two bad options?"

"Yes," Kat whispered softly.

"Could you cut her in half?" Kapitän Sörensen asked.

"Why?" Mike responded, saying what others were thinking.

"That ship is huge, and the cargo decks must have pressurized internal safety doors that act as watertight bulkheads. It's part of maritime law that they have are constructed with them. Has been for years. She's old, but not that old!"

"Doesn't mean they use them though, as they take up valuable . . . chargeable . . . cargo space. The operators make more money if they're left open." Anna suggested.

"Except they can't be," Kapitän Sörensen advised. "Since a number of 'accidents' in the late twentieth and early twenty-first centuries, they have built-in safety features that prevent the vessel from leaving port if the internal watertight bulkhead doors aren't closed and pressurized."

"So, there would be enough air trapped in these spaces to keep the vessel afloat, even if I put a couple of holes into the engineering spaces to disable her propulsion. Where is the turbine generated power stored?" Kat now understood where Kapitän Sörensen was going with his hypothesis.

"It's usually held in large batteries," he said, referencing the schematic again.

"And what happens if I target those batteries? How long would her propulsion drives continue at their current speed if the batteries were taken out?" Kat continued. "Approximately how much stored energy would the *Varuna Ratnaker* have on-board at this stage of her voyage? Could we really damage her enough to make this a viable targeting option?"

The European Union Navy Kapitän shook his head. "I simply don't know."

"And assuming we destroy or cause these batteries to discharge their stored energy what effect would that have to the people on-board?" Kat asked him.

"If we do manage to isolate the front half, or two thirds of the vessel from the aft sections," Anna pointed out,

"There'll be chaos as different sections and decks loose power. Her accumulated momentum will still be driving them forward, as least for a bit. Kat you must remember what it was like when the *Osprey* was hit . . . to be trapped on a disabled ship?"

Once again, the room fell silent.

Kat ran her fingers along the displayed engineering spaces searching for the target that she and Safi would be targeting. "So that only leaves the propulsion units."

"Are the magnetic fields that contain the plasma powered from those batteries too, or do they have a different power source?" Kapitän Sörensen said.

"I have no idea, but I do know that we are the ABCANZ Fleet, not mass murders." Kat told him.

"If your softheartedness causes Herr von Welf to die, there will be a lot to talk about," the Sicherheitsdienst Korvettenkapitän remined them.

"Enough," Lex half shouted. She joined Kat at the display, running her fingers across the passenger cabins, then down through the vehicle and cargo decks, to the engineering spaces and the reactor.

"These batteries seem quite big. Are you sure it's not the best option?"

"Maybe," Kat agreed. "At the speed we'd be coming in at, it's a huge gamble. We could probably punch several holes in her sides, aft, below the water-line, flood the engineering spaces and hope there's enough air trapped in the forward sections to prevent her sinking, but she may still have accumulated enough momentum to finish their suicidal attack." Kat paused for a single breath. "So yes, Lex, it may be out best option, but it's far from being a good one."

"I've never understood power plants. I've walked through a few. They make a lot of noise and have huge things spinning and endless runs of pipework, and lots of spaces marked 'Do Not Enter," so I will have to take your and Kapitän Sörensen's professional evaluation that this is the best way to proceed."

"I would much prefer we simply blew her up," the Sicherheitsdienst Korvettenkapitän repeated.

"Don't be tiresome, Herr Korvettenkapitän," Lex snapped at him. "It is the crew taskings ordered by the State's Intelligence and Security Agency that have left my own Kapitän's ship, and those of our colleagues, as nothing but beached observers of this fiasco. Has someone perhaps chosen to take advantage of circumstances that your supposed 'security measures' have created? Or perhaps the Sicherheitsdienst's orders were an integral part of the plan right from the outset?"

The Sicherheitsdienst's Korvettenkapitän opened his mouth several times before words actually came out. "Don't be absurd, that's ridiculous. Of course not. How can you even think such things," he finally got out.

"Oh, but I can, and I think my dad will too, if he lives." Lex turned. "Kapitän Sörensen, may I have a word with you? In private."

The Midshipman led her Captain out into the passageway. The Korvettenkapitän went to follow.

At a nod from Kat, Staff Sergeant Freeman impeded the Sicherheitsdienst Officer's progress, blocking his way and nearly stomping on the polished toe-caps of his boots.

"Excuse me, sir," Freeman said, and by the time the Korvettenkapitän recovered his composure, Mike was at his side, shortly followed by Anna on the other.

Kat looked at the main display one more time. "I am finished here, Ensign Steiger. I'll be on the bridge, setting up the targeting options with Safi as soon as she becomes available. Please inform Fähnrich von Welf that she is welcome to join me with her associates when she is ready."

Kat passed the Fähnrich and her Kapitän in the passageway, their heads together in whispers. *So this is what a 'palace coup' looks like*, she briefly thought. *I hope it doesn't come down to that. Lex deserves a better chance of survival that she'll get today with that Korvettenkapitän on-board. Give her a few years, who knows what she might become?"*

Hopefully, it would be someone who liked the Severns more than most of the von Welfs ever did!

*　　*　　*

"We have a containment field up and holding that complies with minimum safety standards on our forward main reactor, prepare to overheat the 'RG' Starboard-side reactor," Captain Gillan said as Kat entered the bridge. Silently she sat in her normal place at the warfare systems station and signed-in on the board in front of her.

"Captain, we have a drop in the power we're drawing from the port," Sato suddenly advised. "Containment is weakening."

"Stop the material heating," Gillan ordered.

"Comms, get me the Port Master," Kat ordered.

Before the man who appeared on the image could speak Kat informed him, "This is Princess Katarina. We were promised power. We are at a critical stage, why has it been cut?" Whoever ordered this is now considered a criminal and enemy of the European Union. Do I need to talk with Konteradmiral Voss again?"

"No, no ma'am. I promise you it's just a glitch. We currently have a lot of ships making requests for power, and our relays were not designed with this volume or capacity in mind."

"Get my ship power," Kat demanded. "Do it now."

"Yes, ma'am," the main said and cut the link.

"Should I use our own auxiliary power?" Gillan asked. "I wanted to save it, use it to jump-start our second reactor, to get us out of here a bit faster."

"Keep our auxiliary power back for the moment, see if we can initiate the second reactor using the port's power."

"Port supplied energy is back up," Sato advised.

"Engineering, stand by to begin overheating the RG reactor on the starboard side. Confirm safety tracts are ready to receive matter if the plugs melt."

"Confirmed. Engineering are ready in all respects, sir."

"Everything is ready," Safi advised in her normal voice.

"Any questions or concerns?" Kat asked.

"I think we need to re-write the procedures on how to do this," Safi announced. "Nothing our science team and I couldn't handle, but I wouldn't want someone else to try this without our new, first-hand knowledge."

"Safi, I need you to work on a targeting solution for me as soon as this is complete."

"I thought you might. Let me get this done first, please." There was a short pause. "Heat transfer is underway . . . deuterium is heating. It will take a few minutes to increase heat and pressure now. I will confirm when plasma is being generated and contained . . . we should then be able to introduce it to the reactor. In maybe twenty minutes, we might be ready to proceed."

"We have fission," Captain Gillan announced sooner than Kat had expected. "Once we have enough power stored to get another containment field working, we'll initiate the aft main reactor. I'd rather do that in port than out at sea, ma'am."

"Understood Captain."

"Should be able to begin operations in another thirty minutes, maybe a bit more."

"You've done it? And so quickly?" Kapitän Sörensen said, as he escorted Fähnrich von Welf onto the bridge.

"Yes, but I'm sure you'll understand, I don't particularly want to discuss the finer details, Captain to Captain. Well not right now, anyway." Gillan took the comms-mike from the overhead bulkhead. "All Hands, this the Captain. Prepare to get underway in three-zero. I say again, All-Hands, stations for departure, figures three zero."

Throughout the ship came the noise of the crew moving to their appointed stations.

"I understand we are heading into a new engagement," Professor Brooks said, following Sörensen and Lex onto the bridge.

"Do you want to get off?" Kat asked him.

"If I wanted off this tub, I would have left before the mad scientists amongst us attempted to 'jump-start' a nuclear reactor. So, no, I'm not leaving, but do we really have to be confined to our cabins?"

"I'm afraid so," Gillan cut in. "What we're about to attempt is almost as crazy as what we've just done with the reactors. I need all crewmembers not directly involved in the operation of this vessel to keep out of the way."

Brooks scowled. "Can't we at least see what's going on?"

"There really won't be very much to see, but we'll pipe a feed from here into all cabins," Gillan said. "Now, Professor, if you'll please excuse me, that includes you too."

With quick efficiency, the *Fires of Beltane* prepared to get under way. Today, some things were different. Kat's station had a second chair alongside her own. Lex could see, if not touch, everything Kat could.

Kapitän Sörensen settled into a chair that had been positioned to the left of Captain Gillan's own. The Intelligence and Security Agency Officer was 'parked' at the rear of the bridge, where he could see everything, but like Lex, touch nothing. He had Staff Freeman as his 'chaperone.'

Mike took up a position somewhat further away from Kat than he normally did, so he could keep an eye on all their 'visitors.' There was a glint in his eye, a purpose in his gait, that Kat hadn't seen in a while.

Right on time, exactly when Captain Gillan had said, the auto-tie-downs retracted and the *Bella* maneuvered smartly away from the quayside.

"Safi, start a countdown, time to intercept," Kat ordered. A clock appeared on her board and began to count down. They had just over an hour!

"Stand by for high-speed operations in five minutes," Captain Gillan announced as soon as the *Fires of Beltane* was clear of the port's entrance buoys. "If you need more than five, shout out, but don't expect to get it!"

Kat had already added a couple of extra displays from the numerous radar, sonar, laser and other data gathering equipment they had aboard into her usual Warfare Systems display board. If the *Varuna Ratnaker* did anything even slightly outside of 'normal' Kat wanted to know.

"I have noticed you are very courteous with your crew," Lex said, a strange look on her face. "Does it work?"

"When you already have the best people, who are more than able to think for themselves, showing that you respect them for whatever specialisation they bring to the team is far more effective that a baseball bat!"

Lex said nothing, neither agreeing with Kat or otherwise, but she now had a very thoughtful look on her face.

"Captain Gillan, do we gain anything by closing at a speed exceeding thirty knots?" Kat asked her Captain.

"Myra, run the numbers for two intercept courses, one at thirty and the other at forty knots," he ordered his Navigator.

Two lines appeared on the display, both culminating in the same encounter. "If we go slower, then we'll intercept them a bit nearer to the land, but they'd then have less time to repair any damage we inflict and correct their course back onto their original target. A faster course means we'll intercept them further out, which means they have more time to effect repairs, but if gives us the opportunity to try something different if the first pass isn't successful."

Kat studied the approach vectors, then referenced the firing tables. Ten knots didn't actually seem to make very much difference, and she didn't want to push their own reactors given what they'd just done to them!

"Captain, your ship, your call, but taking her over thirty knots doesn't seem to gain us very much."

"A second shot, not that I'm suggesting you'll need it ma'am. Thirty knots it is." There might have been the slightest hint of a sigh behind his words, but Kat had already moved on to her next question.

"Captain, do we gain any advantage by still being under acceleration when we close on the *Varuna Ratnaker*.

"Sorry ma'm, you'll have to help me out here, I'm not sure I follow you?" Gillan replied.

"You know as well as I do, that despite what they portray in the movies, firing a weapon at a moving target from another moving target, despite all the clever tech at our disposal, is one of the best ways I know to waste ammunition. Therefore, and given these sea conditions, what if we came to as near to a 'full stop' as we could, so we only had to compensate for the pitch and yaw created by the weather and sea conditions? Missing the aim-point, but still hitting the vessel could have catastrophic consequences for those on-board her."

The Captain was nodding before Kat had finished speaking. "Myra, if we cut power, went to a full stop, from say, thirty knots, do you think it's even achievable in the time we have?"

"Theoretically, it obviously is, but in these sea conditions, I'd like to practice it at least once before we did it for real."

"How long would you need to make this ship a steady firing platform once coming to a stop."

"It will never be totally steady, not with these wave heights, but two, more like three, minutes, if I use all of our thrusters to try and compensate."

"Sounds good to me," Gillan said.

"One more thing," Kat continued.

"Aren't you just full of questions today, your Highness," Gillan said, but his eyes were on the screens, monitoring the *Bella*'s departure from Pudacherry at a full ten knots.

"Anna calculates that I'd have about ten, maybe twelve or thirteen seconds to track, get missile lock and fire on the *Varuna Ratnaker*. Does what we've just discussed have any impact on this?"

"Yes," Safi said. "With the *Bella* slowing down its approach, and with a near stationary firing platform, you'll gain approximately another twenty-eight seconds within which you'll need to get the missiles away."

"Captain Gillan, assuming our approach is offset, enabling the Harlequin launcher to traverse a few degrees between each missile release, will there be enough exposure time to get all eight missiles away?

"Theoretically yes, but only just. You'll be lucky to get

300 mils left and right of 'center of traverse' as the target tracks past. That's one ASM away every five seconds and eighty-five mils. That will require around forty seconds. Do you need to get all eight missiles away, ma'am. Isn't that a bit excessive against a single target?

Before Kat could answer, Safi interjected again. "Yes, Captain Gillan, I agree, it is. However, the Princess is correct, as we need to compensate for the other vessel's size and for this storm. I calculate we will require three confirmed hits out if the eight missiles on the launcher beams to disable the targeted vessel.

"Increasing speed to twenty knots in one minute," the crewman at the Helm position announced, and that conveniently curtailed any further discussion.

"Bridge crew, to your stations," Sato ordered.

Kat turned back to her board. "Safi, show me the energy storage battery's location on the *Varuna Ratnaker* schematic again." They appeared on her display. "Assuming that I get the first ASM away at three-hundred mils from 'centre of traverse' and another missile every eighty-five mils, every five seconds in a ripple thereafter, at what kind of vectors will the missile's approach be at?" A translucent red masked off some parts of the display, not unlike the 'safety arcs' that prevented the launcher releasing a missile into their own superstructure.

"Is that the optimum firing solution?" Kat asked.

"Yes, Safi confirmed. "We'll need a lot of luck to pull that off though. The odds are of success are not good."

Beside Kat, Lexy raised an eyebrow.

"Safi has been reading classic fiction for several years now. It makes her easier to talk to."

"It makes you easier to understand," the HI shot back primly.

"Assuming I get two ASMs away as soon as we're stationary and steady, what's the flight time? I'd rather not release another pair until the damage of the first pair can be assessed."

"I'm not sure you'll have that luxury," Safi replied. "By the time you've assessed the first two, you may lose the targeting window for any follow up salvos," Safi advised.

"And that's assuming we get that unobtainable pot of luck!" Lex said.

"Exactly," Kat agreed.

"Is it always like this?" Lex asked.

"Always like what?"

"Your planning process. You start with one plan, thrash it about amongst your command team, refine it, then invite others to critique it, and all the time it keeps getting better."

Kat thought for a moment. "It was certainly like this in the days before the attack at Nu Hawaii." Then Kat remembered her current 'audience' and stopped herself giving a longer explanation. "In Cape Town, your brother didn't give us a lot of time to brain-storm and evolve a plan."

"Do you think he'd still be alive if he had?" It came across as an honest question.

"Honestly Lex, I really don't know. I tried to talk him down. He had a good Kapitän with him, just as you do now, but Gus had the rank, he was the Kommodore, and I understand that Kapitän Langer spent the first half of the battle in his own brig!"

"Poor planning on my brother's part."

"And the reason why you are a Fähnrich."

"That's the story of my life, doing penance for my brother's errors. What about in Emirates City? Did you have a plan for that?"

"Not for any of the things you threw my way. Those were most definitely 'run-and-shoot, shoot-and-run affairs.'"

"I didn't do any planning," Lex admitted, shaking her head thoughtfully. "I just hired whoever I could find available. Very poor planning on my part."

"I hope you're not thinking of having me plan your next assassination attempt on myself?" Kat said, trying to make it sound like a joke, if not a very good one.

"No, I'm sorry Kat. I'm not ever planning another attack on you." But left unsaid whom she might be planning them for.

And, somehow Kat doubted that Lex's promise of a truce between the two of them would have any substance or credibility in a court of law.

SIX : NINETEEN

The *Fires of Beltane* was making steady progress along STR CO-04 in the direction of Colombo, with about ten minutes to go before their attempt at intercepting the *Varuna Ratnaker* would begin, when one of the science team called up to the bridge.

"Are you aware that the target vessel is swaying and yawing badly?"

"No, we weren't," Kat said.

"Kind of hard to tell in these sea conditions, but I wouldn't want to be a passenger on-board her."

"Send me your data," Kat said. "It's very likely to impact on my targeting."

"On its way, Miss Severn."

Lex gave Kat a look. "Miss Severn?"

"It's pretty unusual to have a uniformed science team on-board. Their much closer to being mad scientists that naval personnel, so some of their forms of address, whilst usually respectful, can be a bit, err . . . creative. I never know what they're going to call me from one day to the next. My father made cuts to some ONR budgets last year, so some of them aren't talking to me at all!"

"So, your ABCANZ Federation is no utopia."

"I never said that it was."

"I don't know if the *Varuna Ratnaker* is having trouble keeping up its acceleration," Safi said, "Or, if our science team can provide better data, but it appears their acceleration is falling."

"What about their pitch, yaw and sway?" Kat asked.

"Difficult to be conclusive in these sea conditions, but there may be an increase in all three."

"Which may suggest that one of her propulsion units

has problems," Gillan suggested. "Her propulsion management system is trying to compensate, but the power being used to rotate her propellers in now unbalanced."

Kat knew that roll, pitch and yaw were all terms used to describe the rotation of a vessel about its three-axes due to wave action upon the vessel. Heave, sway and surge were the terms to describe the linear motions of a ship, also due to wave action.

"Will that effect your targeting?" Lex asked. "If she sways over more than you expected?"

"Almost certainly, but I'm sure they teach Von Clausewitz at Das Mürwik . . . 'No plan survives contact,' and all that. If we had more time, we'd go through a lot more contingency planning. The 'what if' *this* happens or 'what if' *that* happens.

The von Welf heir looked lost in thought . . . again.

With a sign, Kat said, "Let's see if our last ace can give us anything." She tapped at her comm-link.

"Mr Beelzebub, we seem to have located the vessel with your son on-board."

The former resident of North Sentential Island came up on part of her board. Behind him, she could see he was in one to the science team's modular accommodation units.

"What are they doing?" the man asked.

"Sailing a fully laden Ro-Pax at her maximum speed, headlong into the Indian port-city of Puducherry," Kat told him. "She's old, so when she hits, it's very likely her reactor will go into meltdown and explode. Killing tens of thousands, if not immediately, then in the years to come from radiation exposure."

The old man said something that might have been a prayer, but given the language used in the scriptures of those 'devoted' to the 'Angels of Light,' it could just as easily of been a curse of damnation. "What can I do?" he asked Kat.

"In in next few minutes I will try to target the power-storage batteries of that ship. Could you say something to him that would make him reconsider his actions, slow the ship and turn it away from Pudacherry?"

"I will certainly try."

Kat turned the man over to the *Bella*'s comms-tech, an older man who Kat knew had children of a similar age to Beelezebub, so would hopefully have some empathy. Five minutes later a message for Morax was being transmitted to the *Varuna Ratnaker*.

A few minutes more and a reply came back. There was no chance of any misinterpretation. It was laced with curses. "You have shown your true self, as a traitor standing in defiance of the teachings of the Angels of Light. You are no better that a nonbeliever. Your eyeballs will boil like those of all the heretics who have gone before."

Full of negativity and defiance the message did however provide the much-needed confirmation that Morax and his colleagues had taken control of the Ro-Pax vessel. How they had done this wasn't clear, as weapon ownership for those outside of law enforcement and the military was restricted in the Indian Union. Only those who needed it for their job, the likes of farmers, park wardens and licenced private security, could legally possess a firearm. And yet, like anywhere, if you wanted one badly enough, and paid the right amount of rupees you could undoubtedly obtain one. Official Indian figures indicated that about seven people in a hundred had an authorised weapon, but there were also as many as one-hundred million unauthorised guns in circulation.

"Should I pass this message on to the father?" the comms-chief asked Kat.

Kat shook her head. "The man is hurting enough, why make it any worse. If he asks, tell him we're still waiting."

At Kat's elbow, Lex commented, "So Severn's do lie."

Kat swivelled her chair around to directly face Lex. "Yes, sometimes, when it's appropriate. I'd rather lie to this old man than tell him the truth. That I can't save his son, because his son doesn't want to be saved! Next time you're economical with the truth, see if it does as much good as mine just did."

Lex said nothing in reply.

The countdown timer on Kat's board pinged, showing only a few minutes remained. The target was now within visual range.

"Sixty seconds to optimum launch window," Safi advised.

The *Bella* went from a speed exceeding thirty knots to a 'full stop' and Lex reached for her 'barf-bag.' She held it clamped to her mouth for most of the next minute, eventually putting it aside, but was still looking decidedly 'green.'

The Sicherheitsdienst Korvettenkapitän noisy filled his own bag and Staff Freeman handed him a second. That was half-filled before he'd finished.

Kat took in these occurrences out of the corner of her eye. Her main focus concentrated on the reports she was getting on the *Bella*'s dwindling inertia and growing stability.

"Sea conditions permitting, we are steady," Sato advised.

"All hands," Gillan announced. "This is the Captain. Wherever you currently are, you will stay. Do not even think of moving. Gillan out."

The display on Sato's board was replicated on Kat's. Despite the pitching sea outside the bridge windows, the ship's systems did their very best to compensate.

"Stand by for ASM launch," Kast ordered. The Harlequin launcher traversed itself to the pre-programmed position for the first missile release. As soon as Kat had the required green light on her board she ordered, "Fire," then checked her board. "Missile away." The launcher immediately adjusted its directional bearing and elevation. A second green light and a second missile away, less that ten seconds between them.

This was almost happening too fast for human participation. Kat, Safi and Lex had gone over and over the firing plans. The solutions and inevitable adjustments were being handled by Safi. When the time had come to execute, only Safi could manage the firing of the second and any subsequent missiles. She would fire two in close succession, then a gap between the second pair being released, so a brief damage assessment could be made and further adjustments applied. Humans may have decided the course of action, but it would be Safi who'd execute it.

Except that Kat had an 'override' button under her palm. At the first sign that their plan was going awry, Kat would hit the button, and Safi would no longer be able to execute anything . . . probably. Safi would theoretically not even remember the plan . . . but with Safi you could never tell.

Kat however would remember that there had been a plan, and that for some reason, she had aborted it. Or had tried to abort it. Could something really pass from her eye to her brain, to her hand, to the red button in the time required?

She'd find out soon enough.

The *Varuna Ratnaker* tracked past at a frightening pace for such a large vessel in the churning waves. She showed no discernible evidence of slowing down.

Kat stopped breathing.

"Firing," Safi advised. A third and fourth missile streaked away.

Was the *Varuna Ratnaker* beginning to slow? Her hull sides perhaps looked as though they were buckling? Difficult to tell in wind and the rain.

Kat blinked, but refused to close her eyes.

The *Bella*'s own thrusters worked overtime to hold her steady.

"Launch window is closing if you want to fire a third salvo," Safi advised. "Ten seconds, nine . . .

Still the *Varuna Ratnaker* raced on, maybe slightly slower than before, maybe not, essentially untouched by the ASMs impacts.

Kat's eyes widened. "Stand by . . ."

A spark, like a bolt of lightning shot from inside the Ro-Pax's hull, then a second, the ship seemed to be twisting itself apart.

Then, in the blink of an eye there was nothing left of the Ro-Pax or the three thousand people aboard.

"Holy shit," someone whispered on the bridge.

Kat just sat there.

"It obviously wasn't a reactor meltdown, as we're still here, but . . . what just happened?" Sato asked nobody in particular.

"Well, I'm glad that's over," came from the position that the Sicherheitsdienst Korvettenkapitän occupied.

From Kat's collarbone, a little girl's voice asked, "Kat, did we just kill several thousand innocent people?"

What could Kat tell her HI?

"I'm sorry Kat," Lex said, reaching out to touch Kat's forearm. "It's not your fault. You did everything you could to prevent this happening."

"Did I?" Kat said, then keyed her comm-link. "Everyone who's been following this last evolution, save all your data. There will be an official enquiry."

"By who?" Lex asked.

"Initially me," Kat snapped, "But I daresay the Indian Union, your people, mine, and anyone else with a vested interest, will want their day in court! Captain Gillan, do a slow circuit of the area, check for any survivors and or wreckage."

"Myra, slow circuit of the immediate vicinity, scan for wreckage and or survivors, if you please."

Kat stood from her bridge station. "Captain Gillan, Kapitän Sörensen, Ensign Steiger," she looked around and found faces missing. She tapped her comm-link. "Major Melnik, Captain Sykes, please report to my OpsCen. Professor Brooks, you too."

"Yes, ma'am" and "As you wish," answered her request.

"Why?" Gillan said.

"Because I am sick and tired of hearing that a 'Severn did this' or a 'Severn did that.' I am so tired of not know knowing the true facts of who did what to whom. This time . . . I want to know exactly what happened. And, if the Sicherheitsdienst wants to say one thing and ABCANZ Security Services concoct something altogether different, both suiting their own agendas and objectives, well at least I . . . we . . . will know the truth! Do you understand where I'm coming from?"

It was Kapitän Sörensen's turn to step forward and face the fire burning in Kat's eyes. "That assumes that, using the data we have, we can actually tell you what happened."

That took a little of the firestorm out of Kat's sails, but not much. "We have some of the best instrumentation of any ship at sea. Between what Captain Gillan has 'acquired' from his previous activities, whatever my resident science team have installed, pulled from the very best universities back home, as well as the equipment that the shipyard installed during the *Bella*'s last refit and repair period, you must have something! And, yes . . . maybe you can't tell me what I did or how it happened that more than three thousand people are no longer alive, but I want you to face me and tell me that with the best information available, collectively you cannot establish what happened. Do you all understand?"

"Yes, I hear you," said Mike, stepping forward. "You've got a lot of people on this board of enquiry. I understand having Captain Gillan and Kapitän Sörensen for their seafaring and offensive action experience, Melnik too, to an extent, as he is non-aligned to any of the parties involved, but me . . . Anna?"

"You were a trained operative of our security services. Although your current assignment is my personal security, you're a trained investigator, Mike."

He couldn't disagree with what she'd just said, and nodded. "As you wish, your Highness."

"Now, if you will excuse me," Kat said, "I need to talk to a father who pleaded for me to save his son's life. Somewhere I've got to find the words to explain why I just killed his boy."

"Kat, that's just cruel," Mike cut in. "Don't do it."

"Until someone gives you a rank, either military or royal, that makes you more senior to my own, shut the hell up . . . please."

The bridge crew stood aside as Kat made her way out.

The silence from Safi was suffocating as Kat made her way through the passageways and stairwells of the *Bella*, trying to locate the cabin that had been assigned to Beelzebub.

When Kat asked Safi which cabin had been allocated, her HI told her, but the directions that would have normally accompanied her answer were omitted. Safi's voice was normal, but clearly her HI was deep in calculating something. Examining something. Deciding something.

That, or maybe the Safi that Kat had previously known was gone.

Kat located the cabin, but it was locked.

Nobody answered when she knocked, when she called out. She asked a passing scientist to confirm she had the correct location. And, yes, the strange man from North Sentinel was indeed assigned to that cabin. Two off-duty Troopers passed by, both paying her the required compliments. Kat tasked them with getting the cabin's door open.

Rather predictably, Staff Freeman conveniently arrived before they succeeded. The shoulders of his wide 'Y' shaped torso blocked most of her view inside.

"You don't need to see this ma'am," he told her. "I know you've seen plenty of death, but he's hung himself and must have had some kind of destructive bio-harness implanted, as this is over and above a normal hanging."

"I thought our med-tech had checked him out?" Kat replied.

"He did, and there was nothing to suggest a bio-harness or cardio-integrated trigger mechanism. This may have been inserted decades ago. Convenient way to keep everyone under your control don't you think?"

Kat backed off. The Staff Sergeant tuned to face her. "Ma'am, may I suggest we re-visit the message this individual sent to those on the Ro-Pax ship, and what was sent in return. Was there anything, a code word or phrase, hidden in amongst all their twisted scripture nonsense. Some kind of suicide-pack activator? Might be a long shot, but worth another look." The Staff Sergeant put his arm around Kat's shoulder and turned her gently around.

Kat had seen men do that to their grown sons and daughters. Her own father had never done that to her.

"I know this will be hard for you, ma'am, but maybe

give Captain Gillan and the others time to review all the data. Let them work this through, let them give you what truth they can about this day."

Kat stared back at the Staff Sergeant, but said nothing.

"Kat, I cannot figure this out," Safi suddenly said into her ear.

"Figure what out, Safi?" Kat said, a finger going to her earpiece.

"We did everything correctly, but we still managed to kill all of those people. I killed all of those people."

"It's we, Safi, you and I. I told you what to do, you did it. You were only following my orders."

"You do know that's not a valid defense," the HI responded.

"I know, but you have to understand, that sometimes, even when you do everything right, it still goes wrong," Kat said, walking away from the assembled Land Force personnel.

"That does not compute. A, plus B, is supposed to equal C. And if A and B are good, how can C be bad? . . . Is it like the use of a double negative in grammar? They cancel each other out and reverse the meaning? 'I ain't got none,' therefore, if you haven't got none, you must have some."

"Safi, I really don't know. I know it doesn't seem right. It isn't fair, but sometimes, it just the way it is. You act with good intentions, wanting the very best for everyone, and it still blows up in your face."

"That cannot be correct. I tried to factor all of that in, to calculate all the possible variables, and it's just not possible. I have to conclude there is something wrong with my programming or circuitry."

"No Safi, there is nothing wrong with you, and probably nothing wrong with me either. It's just something us humans have found out."

"I think I have read about this phenomena."

"What phenomena is that?

"That sometimes shit happens," her HI said.

"Yes, Safi, sometimes, no matter how hard you try, it does."

Kat climbed a flight of steps, that the Fleet referred to as a 'companionway,' calling out the obligatory "Up Ladder" advisory, notifying other crew members that the steps were in use. She found herself in the passageway to Captain Gillan's office, now her improvised OpsCen. Down that corridor, behind that door, were the men and women she'd given the job of measuring her soul, her conscience.

And yet, now that she and Safi had had their little talk, Kat didn't feel so in need of anyone else's approval. Somehow, in facing Safi's first pangs of conscience, she'd found her own measure of right and wrong.

Did she really want to hear what these people had to say?

She went back to her own cabin to await their summons.

What would Grandpa Jim do? Kat suddenly thought. How would her Grandpa Jim feel about the death of several thousand people? *It had probably prevented a war that someone else was trying very hard to start, and that was good.*

General Voss and the Sicherheitsdienst certainly thought it was.

But . . . that path was potentially the route to insanity, the easy justification of truly awful occurrences. It was a path she'd rather not travel. Or at least not frequently!

She had urged her Grandpa Jim to accept the constitutional kingship of a restored monarchy. Asked him to help, to guide her generation through the tough times ahead. He had suggested that it was time for them to make their own way, and mistakes, by way of reply.

Had he really been dodging the crown for another reason? Did he know how burned and blackened his soul was? Had he chased away the easy decisions as deep as he wanted to go, hoping to retire to some quiet life that demanded nothing more from him than choosing whether to go for a round of golf or perhaps take a day's sailing up and around Long Island Sound.

What had she done? She'd started the day trying to save Lex's dad's life and potentially avoid starting a war.

That had taken her to demanding to know why over three thousand innocents should die for that one life.

Now she was pondering if her grandfather really had his head on sufficiently straight to continue being the titular figurehead of the ABCANZ Federation.

All Kat wanted to do right now was go to bed, pull the cover over her head and hide away. Instead, she showered, changed into a fresh ship-suit and marched back down to Captain Gillan's office to face her panel of 'judges.'

She slipped into Gillan's office and settled herself silently into the seat closest to the door, at the end of the table. Heads turned as she came in, acknowledged her choice of seating, and went back to talking over what they were studying. Perhaps their voices were now lower, perhaps not. Maybe they turned away from her, maybe they didn't. Nobody talked to her. Was this what it felt like to be ghost in attendance at your own funeral?

Kat wasn't about to let the situation get out of hand. "Safi, have you analyzed at the imagery recorded by all the ship's systems? Begun your own evaluation?" Kat whispered to her HI.

"No, I am unable to do so. Lieutenant Sato deliberately downloaded everything to a stand-alone secure system. This was primarily to prevent the Sicherheitsdienst from cloning an unauthorized copy, but it also prevents me from accessing it too. It is that stand-alone system they are now using to review the data."

They would no doubt argue that it was in Kat's best interests. Would her being deliberately excluded hold up in an international court of law?

I might not have an actual magistrate on-board, like I originally wanted, but I certainly have a court, and people around me who want to ensure I get a full and honest hearing, if not an actual trial . . . Not yet anyway.

Kat folded her hands and wished Jack had been in her life long enough to teach her how to pray. When she had gotten them into 'another croc of crap' as he'd so often put it, praying seemed to help him get through it, praying and cursing the 'little people' whoever or whatever they might actually be!

Mike glanced over at her. "You said we had an hour or two to review all this. In a normal investigation we'd have several months."

"I know, but today you only have a few hours," Kat told him.

"Any chance we could go and talk with that passenger from North Sentinel?" Major Melnik asked.

"Not without a clairvoyant. He hanged himself."

"Oh, sorry. I didn't know," the Major said.

The assembled team in the OpsCen continued their deliberations for almost another hour, hunched over screens, or data-tables and reports. Several 'hard-copy' print-outs too, which Gillan requested via a comm-link with Sato.

Finally, Major Melnik stood and stepped away from the table. He stretched, then pointed at the main screen. "That image pretty much settles it for me. What about you?"

There were nods from several of the others.

Major Melnik turned formally to Kat. "Lieutenant Severn, if you'd like to reposition yourself so you can see the main screen," he said, indicating several seats nearer the middle of the table.

Once Kat had moved, the Major sat beside her. Captain Gillan then moved to sit on her other side, with Kapitän Sörensen moving to be beside Melnik. Mike and Anna took chairs next to Gillan.

Kapitän Sörensen cleared his throat. "Although Major Melnik's time as a commissioned officer is slightly longer than my own, I Kapitän Kurt Sörensen of the European Union's Naval Forces, as the holder of the highest rank amongst us, will assume the role and duties of this Board of Enquiry's presiding officer. Whilst our findings have been greatly expedited, it is the opinion of this Enquiry that additional time would not result in a different outcome, an outcome that would leave our findings open to accusations of data manipulation. I want that entered into the record of these proceedings as a challenge to anyone who attempts to reopen this matter and review our decision."

For a naval officer, Sörensen seems in full control of the wider implications of this situation, Kat thought, but said nothing, keeping her face neutral.

"For the purpose of this investigation, this Enquiry has relied heavily on the Ultra-High-Density Optical Imagery of the scientific community on-board the *Fires of Beltane*, as recorded by their Ultra High Speed visual spectrum recorder.

Sörensen paused and studied some of his handwritten notes in front of him. "At this point, I wish to ask a question of your own HI, Lieutenant. Can your Heuristic Intellect bear witness?"

"I believe so. Safi, you understand that you must tell the truth as you see it. The whole truth, and nothing but the truth."

"I understand the oath, your Highness, Kapitän Sörensen, and I promise that I will do so."

Kat wasn't surprised that Safi had been called upon to bear witness.

"Safi, if I may refer to you by that appellation?" Sörensen said, "Were you aware of the UHS visual spectrum recording equipment being on-board, and did you review any of its data during the engagement with the Ro-Pax vessel *Varuna Ratnaker*?"

There was only a slight pause before Safi spoke. "I have a full inventory of *everything* aboard the *Fires of Beltane*, and therefore I knew about this equipment, along with everything else on-board. It is listed by name only, with no additional information about its use or capability, and I have no information about its installation or of any data it acquired. Neither the *Fires of Beltane*'s central computer nor Kat's warfare systems board had feed or data integration from it, and I had no access, from or to it, either. To put it another, simpler way, Kapitän Sörensen, I knew this equipment was on-board. I did not know it was active, and I have not received any output from it, either during or after the events involving the *Varuna Ratnaker*."

"Thank you, Safi," the Kapitän said. "With that

resolved, there is only one matter left unanswered for this Board of Enquiry. Therefore, Lieutenant Severn, may I direct your attention to the main screen."

Kat turned her attention to the large display on the wall opposite. She found herself staring at a view of the *Varuna Ratnaker*. It filled the display in spectacular detail.

"This is frame 217-430-105 of the imagery provided to this Enquiry," Sörensen said.

Kat could see the range displayed across the bottom at being a fraction over two kilometers.

"The imagery before this frame only shows the closure with the Ro-Pax vessel. It is either blurred or providing nothing conclusive due to the rather appalling weather conditions. It is only when the *Fires of Beltane* came to a 'full stop' that the imagery stabilized. This is the first image that is of interest to this Enquiry. Lieutenant, could you describe, in your own words, what you see, based upon your plan of attack to disable the Ro-Pax vessel whilst causing minimum damage to her passengers and crew."

Kat wanted to come back with *'Not fair. You've had an hour or so to look at this image. And besides, you cannot make me be my own prosecutor!*

Instead, she let the image draw her in. She studied it, knowing exactly what she was seeing.

The undamaged propulsion units drove the vessel forward. The first missile missed, as did the second. Despite being only a second or two behind the first, the speed of the *Varuna Ratnaker*, combined with a multitude of other factors, weather, air-pressure, the pitch, roll and yaw of both vessels took the missiles astray.

Kat described this to the enquiry.

"Obviously this is not what you'd intended?" Kapitän Sörensen asked her.

"No, sir. I'd hoped to disable the propulsion units, reducing or if possible, cutting all power to slow or stop her. I didn't know that both missiles had missed, but because of the rapid evolution of events, the window of opportunity to get additional missiles away was closing fast. The integrated equipment displayed on the Warfare Systems board on the bridge of the *Fires of Beltane* gave me no indication that the first salvo had achieved the course change or speed reduction of the *Varuna Ratnaker* desired, so my HI released a second pair as we'd planned.

"Do you see anything else?" Captain Gillan asked her.

"I don't think so. Safi, do you see anything?"

"It is hard to be certain from a single image, Kat, but I note the roll and sway are extreme, especially for a vessel of that size and shape. I would need further images to confirm."

"This is three seconds later, image 228-430-105, and the next," Sörensen said. The range had increased slightly. It showed the same damage-free view as the first had. It was hard to confirm exactly how extreme the pitch and roll of the vessel was.

Image 260-467-199," the image jumped ahead at regular, three frame intervals.

It was still hard for Kat to decide if the ship was swaying and rolling over or it was just camera-angle from the movement on the *Bella*.

"Safi, did you have any additional data feed, other than those integrated within the warfare systems board. Feed over and above those that Lieutenant Severn was using?" Kapitän Sörensen asked.

"No Kapitän Sörensen, the integrated visual imagery I was using was running at around a million frames a second, nothing like the speeds of the UHS imagery now being displayed. Does the board have that imagery?"

"Yes, we do," Sörensen said. On one of the smaller, secondary screens, the same view of the *Varuna Ratnaker* appeared. The difference in detail was considerable.

"You had no way of knowing the first two ASMs had missed, as the intensified yawing of the ship let you to deduce some damage had been inflicted by the first salvo."

"That is correct, Kapitän," Safi said. In that instant, I was operating on the assumption that our first two missiles were the cause of the vessels increased instability, but it was potentially insufficient to make any discernable difference to her speed and course, and the window for releasing a second salvo was rapidly closing."

"Thank you, Safi," Kapitän Sörensen said. "Lieutenant Severn, did you have similar assumptions?"

"Kapitän Sörensen, I had no assumptions at that time. It was all happening too fast for me to observe, review or make a revision to anything I'd planned."

"That does not surprise me. Let's see the next image. 372-521-851. This is the point that the third missile should have impacted."

There was nothing. No evidence that the third ASM had impacted.

"Advance to the fourth," Sörensen said.

The *Varuna Ratnaker* was already tearing herself apart.

"Here we can see that although the fourth ASM did not miss," Captain Gillan took over the narrative, as a circle superimposed itself onto the screen, indicating the impact and instantaneous detonation of the warhead amongst an already developing background explosion. "It slammed in to a hull that was already tearing itself apart from the inside. Meeting little resistance, it penetrated an unidentifiable component of the vessel's propulsion spaces. Evidence would suggest that whatever sequence of events was occurring within the *Varuna Ratnaker*, the impact of the fourth ASM made little, if any, contribution to the ultimate outcome that was already occurring."

"Yes," Kat whispered. On her collarbone, Safi did the same.

"I have personally gone over the records of installation and maintenance on the Harlequin launcher and the manufacturers test and acceptance certification for the four missiles fired. There were no anomalies or concerns and all were exactly as they should be," Gillan told them.

Major Melnik and Kapitän Sörensen nodded in agreement.

"The first three missiles fired, due to the extreme weather conditions, all missed their intended target. The fourth missile did not, but the occurrence that brought about the catastrophic destruction of the *Varuna Ratnaker* was already in motion and not a result of the missile's impact."

Now it was Kat's turn to nod.

"There is one further matter," Major Melnik said. "Safi, I am going to send you these images that are currently displayed as evidence. Will you please overlay them and determine if the *Varuna Ratnaker* was indeed rolling so badly, far in excess of what the naval architects ever intended, that perhaps her reactor, plasma tracts or some other element of her propulsion system had become irrevocably misaligned, thereby causing a catastrophic failure."

For much longer that Kat would have expected, Safi was silent, then the main display screen changed. "As you can see from the cloud formation that became occluded between the first and third frames of imagery under consideration, the hull of the Ro-Pax vessel is indeed swaying heavily over to the right, far exceeding the angle of what would be considered normal, or safe. Combined with her doing a speed far in excess of those documented during her original sea trials, and the high-energy of the tropical storm, I conclude that the vessel is out-of-control."

"Our analysis agrees," Major Melnik said, "But, we are not able to calculate exactly what level of internal damage this excessive swaying and yawing from side to side might be doing. It is not unlike the 'loose cannon' analogy from history when untethered cannon, some weighing several tonnes, would roll from side to side as the ship also rolled from side to side in heavy seas, doing far more damage internally than any enemy shot had. Something inside that Ro-Pax had broken loose and was rocking, rolling or propelling itself from side to side and taking out the interior of the propulsion spaces as it moved back and forth."

"She was never designed to operate and such speeds in those weather conditions. The centre of mass is too high in the water," Safi added.

"Yes, we know. Every computer on-board the *Fires of Beltane* has declined this problem, apparently there are too many variables. Do you think you can attempt it?" Sörensen asked Safi.

"I will try."

Kat glanced at the clock on the bulkhead. "Note the time these calculations were started, please."

"Baffles?" Safi suddenly said. "Did the *Varuna Ratnaker*'s plasma tracks have baffle plates fitted to reduce surging?"

"Yes," Captain Gillan said, "But, they were all arranged to prevent surging from side to side, not fore-to-aft, at the same time, nor for any significant heaving of the vessel."

"Oh," said Safi. "That is not good."

"No, not at that speed," Sörensen agreed.

Safi went back to her calculations and contemplation.

Kat glanced around the room. Unnoticed by Kat, Lex had come in and made herself small in a chair against the wall behind Anna. Lex looked at Kat, as if expecting to be asked to leave, but her eyes pleaded for the opportunity to stay.

Kat gave her something that might have resembled a smile, but it might have been closer to a grimace. Whatever it was, Lex settled back, relieved that she could stay.

Kat's brain spun. She was hungry to force a conclusion from the data displayed before them, but wanted to wait until they had explored every option. She felt sick.

With a deep breath, she forced herself to relax. Fingers, fists, arms, breathing, stomach. For a brief moment she swayed. If she hadn't been seated, she might have fallen, then she regained her composure.

"My calculations are complete." Safi suddenly advised almost an hour later. "It is not a simple answer . . . but I think I now have one." A side view schematic and then an aft view of the *Varuna Ratnaker* appeared on the screen. The seconds ticked by as the ship in the schematic heeled over to port, then to starboard, then back again . . . and again. Not only had something broken free inside, spewing hot plasma about the propulsion spaces, but the pendulum-like swing of the ship from side to side was weakening the hull structure, putting a 'twist' into her frame, or ribs. Within her plasma-tanks a tsunami of plasma was sloshing from one side of the tank to another. When whatever it was that had already broken loose inside the propulsion space eventually collided with the tank . . . boom. For two or three seconds, the explosion ripped the ship apart, until finally the freed wave of plasma, outside of its normal environment, caused the magnetic containment fields to malfunction, and that was the end of the *Varuna Ratnaker.*

Kat let out a deep sign, she felt drained. Exhausted.

"I should of recalculated my firing solutions," Safi said, "As soon as the scientists advised the ship had excessive yaw."

"I did not tell you to. I didn't think of it," Kat admitted.

"None of us did," Captain Gillan said.

"None of us wanted to admit what that meant," Lex added. "And anyway, whatever had happened, people were going to die," she added. "At least my dad didn't, and that means we're not on a countdown to war."

Lex got up. She walked over to stand by Kat. "Once the Ro-Pax operators let the . . . sorry, I struggle to think of them as 'angels' . . . those deluded individuals . . . board the ship in Port Blair, every outcome involved multiple deaths."

"Please don't let Conteradmiral Voss hear you say that," Kapitän Sörensen commented to nobody in particular.

SIX : TWENTY

The *Fires of Beltane* returned to Puducherry at a sedate ten knots using the same STR as it had on the way out. That allowed plenty of time for matters to evolve ashore. The tropical storm eventually made landfall, hitting the Kalrayan and Gingee Hills south west of Chennai hard. The poorer inland habitations of the Tamil Nadu region would take years to recover.

More than one plot to eliminate a certain prominent citizen of the European Union, who coincidently also happened to be visiting that very same region, were also uncovered by Conteradmiral Voss's 'associates.' Some of those detained talked whilst under interrogation, leading to even more arrests. Others, who had survived the devastation of the storm, then perished, when they refused to give answers during some rather intensive questioning.

Kat wondered what new leads had died with them.

Alexandra von Welf sent several coded messages to her father, and received several replies. Kat personally made sure that all record of this was deleted from the *Bella*'s comms log. Kat could justify it as a 'professional courtesy,' from one 'princess' to another.

Kat seemed to be getting along remarkably well with the scion of the von Welf dynasty. Exactly how good was quickly put to the test.

No sooner had the last auto-tie-down activated and pulled the *Fires of Beltane* tight onto the fenders of the designated berth, than the Sicherheitsdienst Korvettenkapitän demanded to see Kat up on the *Bella*'s bridge. He wanted to see her and had his escorting detail with him, providing back-up.

"Ignore him," Lex said.

The look on Kapitän Sörensen's face and the slow shake of his head, suggested that he did not think that was a good idea.

"It is critical that you contact your father," Kat told Lex. "Kapitän Sörensen, can you get a security detail from your own ship over here?"

He tapped away at his own comm-link, then shook his head again. "No . . . I'm being jammed."

"So are we," Captain Gillan said, answering Kat's question before she'd even asked it.

Kat reached for the European Union Midshipman, gently holding her arm. "Lex, if something happens to you, I won't stand a chance, they'll pin the *Varuna Ratnake*'s loss on me, regardless of the true facts." She turned, looking for Mike.

"Kat, I'm *your* security chief . . . not Miss von Welf's," he told her.

"I am acutely aware of that fact, Mike," Kat replied, "But my safety now depends on her liberty, if not her life. See that she gets safely back to the *Fenrir*. I don't care if it takes Staff Freeman and every able-bodied Trooper on this boat, get Lex home safe."

There was a noise at Gillan's office door. Kat had just enough time to organize a bland face for herself, before the Korvettenkapitän of the Sicherheitsdienst marched in.

More of a confident prance than a march.

"Severn, you will accompany me," he demanded.

Kat considered open defiance and the bloodshed that would likely accompany it, and decided that probably wasn't the best option. The *Bella* was secured against the quayside. Breaking free would take time, and potentially damage the ship. However, they had not received a request to flood their reactor this time, so maybe there might be 'maneuvering room' for a little drama. Kat decided he was going to have to earn his pay.

"And just why, exactly, should I accompany you?" Kat asked him.

"Shall we start with the murder of several thousand innocent passengers, some of whom will be the residents of

Puducherry, and therefore newly sequestered citizens of the European Union, not to mention the destruction of a multi-million Euro Ro-Pax vessel."

Lex began to open her mouth, but a far from gentle elbow in the ribs from Sörensen shut her up.

The Korvettenkapitän ignored the Fähnrich. Why did Kat suspect that was going to be a life-ending error!

"You attitude intrigues us," Kat said, rather regally. "It pleases us to accompany you. If I comply, can this vessel depart unhindered?"

"It may, and the sooner the better," the Korvettenkapitän said, playing right into Kat's hands.

She turned to Gillan. "Commander, if I am not back on-board within three hours, make best speed to ROSP 4-Foxtrot-6. Get Anna to update Commodore Finklemeyer and ask him to contact both of my grandfathers. I think my Grandpa Jim might rather enjoy it here."

"As you wish, your Highness. I think you should take this," he handed Kat a large, padded envelope.

"And this is?"

"The conclusion reached by the Board of Enquiry, and all supporting documentation and data. And I'd prefer it if Miss Safi stayed with us."

"Agreed," said Kat, unzipping her shipsuit and unclipping Safi from her collarbone. "Although I don't think the truth will be of much concern where I'm going," she added, handing Safi over to Gillan in exchange for the envelope.

"We're stalling for time, right?" Gillan whispered.

Kat gave a single nod. She then turned and conceded to the Korvettenkapitän's request and permitted the Sicherheitsdienst Officer to escort her from her ship. The Bella's corridors and companionways were devoid of any crew nor any of their Land Force detachment. Both groups were noticeably conspicuous by their absence.

The scientists however, had other ideas. Some, who had never talked to Kat before said, "Hi." Others, walking three abreast, deliberately slowed the Sicherheitsdiensts progress. The third time she spotted the same scientist it became clear to her exactly what they were doing.

There was nothing high-tech about what the boffins were up to. The scientists all knew the layout of the *Bella* intimately. The Sicherheitsdienst did not. No sooner had Kat said an emotional goodbye to one, then he or she would move away, and once out of sight, run around to another point on the ship, then wait to shout 'good luck' and begin the farewell 'ritual' all over again.

It took the Korvettenkapitän a good ten minutes, perhaps a bit longer, to figure out what was happening. Predictably, he told Kat in a rather loud voice that if he saw another well-wisher for a second time he would have them shot in the leg. A third time would be in the head.

Professor Brooks sensibly took the hint, and Kat's progress to the accessway became much faster. She finally left the *Bella* to shouts of "See you soon," "Good Luck," and "Stay Safe."

Once clear of the accessway the Korvettenkapitän and their Sicherheitsdienst escort moved Kat towards a waiting 4x4 utility vehicle. Military spec, but with black paint, blackened windows. Like most stereotyping, there was usually some foundation in truth, and those relating to the Sicherheitsdienst never disappointed!

But they didn't prepare Kat for her arrival alongside one of the largest aircraft carriers she had ever been in the vicinity of. The 'R' prefix of the hull's pennant identifier confirmed it was indeed an aircraft carrier, but she couldn't recall the name of the vessel from the numerical suffix, but as the European navy didn't have multiple carriers like the ABCANZ Fleet, it could only be the *Jeanne d'Arc* or the *Holtzendorf.* The vast expanse of quayside and the almost vertical access way, leading from the quayside to a hatch halfway up the side of the carrier's hull, were deserted. Kat recalled that apparently most of the EU navy ships in the port had their crews ashore, consumed by duties relating to the city's 'false flag' occupation, but this suggested absolutely everyone was ashore. With more than a dozen large warships in the port, Kat was quite taken aback at the sheer lack of people . . . of any activity at all. It was almost eerie. The Korvettenkapitän seemed to sense that too, and urged his men on. With heads swivelling to identify incoming threats from every direction they escorted their 'prize' up, into the carrier.

What frightens men whom everyone else is supposed to be scared of? Kat wondered, as she was marched through the empty ship, head high and eyes straight ahead.

Deep in the bowels of this vast ship they eventually reached their destination. The Korvettenkapitän piled his men into a large freight elevator, spoke a word, maybe two, into his comm-link and it moved down. After a far longer time than Kat had expected, it stopped.

The door slammed open, and the Korvettenkapitän found himself facing Fregattenkapitän Kaltenbrun. "What took you so long?" Kaltenbrun demanded.

"The Severn girl did everything she could to delay us."

"And you permitted this?" The Fregattenkapitän sneered. Behind him, several men with machine pistols stood at the ready. It would not have surprised Kat if she'd been gunned down right there, along will everyone else. The bobbing Adam's apples around her suggested that her former escorts had the same uneasy feeling.

Instead, Kaltenbrun waved Kat out of the elevator, the Korvettenkapitän to stay within. He barked something and the doors closed. Kat now had a new escort! At least her old one remained alive.

For now.

Without a single word spoken, this new, larger escort of Sicherheitsdienst personnel formed around Kat, then marched off. Her file must attribute true ferociousness to her if it was felt that an escort of such magnitude was needed to get her from one location within this ship to another. She considered attacking the guard next to her, or maybe rolling to the floor, perhaps foaming at the mouth, but their obvious lack of humor, or any other emotion, convinced her that neither option was wise.

She marched along with them. "At least there's no media," she remarked.

"This isn't the ABCANZ Federation," the Fregattenkapitän snapped back at her.

"My apologies . . . you see the last time I got arrested . . . well unfortunately the media attended," Kat said, recalling the events in Nu Hawaii and her encounter with the loathsome Mindy Malcovitch.

"You will soon see . . . we do things very differently," he growled at her in his clipped, accented English. "We are much more efficient, but I doubt you will find us as easy to manipulate as your biased media."

Kat certainly hadn't found Mindy at all easy to manipulate, but held her own council.

She and her Sicherheitsdienst escort put on quite a parade, not that anyone saw it. The ship seemed totally empty. They stopped outside a hatch that was unmarked, less the usual hatch and bulkhead identifiers, and really quite unremarkable.

"Please go inside, Severn," the Fregattenkapitän Kaltenbrun ordered, swinging the hatchway open for her.

Kat moved, quickly enough not to get shoved, slow enough not to be mistaken for a threat, through the hatch. Kaltenbrun followed her into an outer office, empty except for two more guards, one either side of a second hatch.

"That way, is for you," he said, but made no effort to lead her inside.

Kat moved across the compartment to the hatch, squaring her shoulders. At the hatchway in the bulk-head she paused for a few seconds. Kaltenbrun briefly chuckled.

She opened the hatch and entered.

The room was dark. Kat closed the hatchway behind her and felt for a light switch. There was nothing. "Lights on," she said.

The lights came on to reveal a large, and well-appointed office finished in a décor that was most definitely not 'warship.' There was a heavy wood, or synthetic wood-effect desk, with a large, padded leather-upholstered chair behind it. There was only one other chair in the room, and that was against the wall with the hatch in it.

Deciding that it was highly probably she'd soon be

talking with someone seated behind that desk, Kat moved the chair from against the bulkhead to in-front of the desk. Then she took a minute, taking in the other furnishings, or lack of them. No shelves, no documents, nothing. This was an 'interrogation' space.

There were two pictures. One showed a sunset, a sunset behind an ancient gibbet, with corpses hanging in the evening light. The crows had already started feasting. The other picture Kat was pretty sure was a biblical reference, but she wasn't exactly sure who the tormented figure was, but the man's body was twisted and broken. Both images sent a clear message.

The hatch opened and Conteradmiral Voss entered. 'You are early," he said.

"You are late," Kat replied. She kept her words light.

"No, I think not. Admirals are always on time. Whereas Lieutenants . . . they are either early or late."

Kat smiled. "I do believe, that a 'Princess' trumps an 'Admiral,'" she told him. Kat wondered how long she could keep up the banter with a man who probably considered it a 'light' day if he hadn't ordered several deaths before taking his breakfast!

"We shall see how well you continue this time wasting when you are wearing a detention collar," the Conteradmiral said, pulling one from a draw in the desk. He tossed it at her. "Put in on."

Kat had never held such a device before, but she recalled Safi briefing her on such things. Valaam island in Lake Ladoga near Nu Peter, that now served as a maximum-security prison used such devices. It stopped the inmates trying to escape in the winter months when the lake's waters froze. Stray more than a few kilometers from the island's centre and the explosive charge initiated an severed the wearer's neck, usually detaching their head in the process. Safi had covered all of this in her briefing when Kat had visited a sailing regatta on Ladoga. Like today, the events on that day hadn't turned out at all as she'd expected either.

"It's really not the fashion in the ABCANZ Federation to wear such things, so I'd rather not. I thought this was more of a Russian thing?"

"I have asked you to put it on. Please do so, or I will have it fitted by force."

"I think you'll find our respective chains-of-command go in divergent directions, Conteradmiral."

"Then maybe your delicate ABCANZ sensibilities would be less offended if I told you that it is the perfect fashion statement for a mass murderer." He pinned her with his eyes, challenged her to deny her guilt.

Maybe yesterday she would have accepted his accusations, but not today! She had been cleared by a Board of Enquiry staffed by senior officers. "Sorry, I believe you have the wrong Princess."

"Really? I am advised it was your ship that fired upon the *Varuna Ratnaker*? Are *you* therefore not responsible for the actions of your vessel's weapons officer?" He smiled at her, sure of his entrapment.

"Conteradmiral. I *was* the Warfare Systems Officer."

"You personally killed over three thousand innocent people. Impressive, even for a Severn."

Kat leaned forward, first placing the padded envelope and then resting her hands on the desk, until she was eye-to-eye with Voss. "Yes, I did fire on that vessel."

"Oh," he said, then settled back into his chair. He eyed Kat. He'd expected her denial, her excuses, not her confirmation. Was she trying to get the upper hand? "My field agents may have misjudged your appetite for killing."

That was unlikely, but Kat knew this wasn't the time to enlighten this man about her apparent taste for blood with facts, rather than third-party speculation. "Your field agents may have misjudged me in many ways. It would be interesting to see how much is factually accurate in this file I keep hearing so much about."

That brought a laugh from the Conteradmiral. "No, Miss Severn. You are in my domain, not the other way around. And no. I have no intentions of playing such games with you. Did your mother not teach you how to play nicely?"

"No, I'm afraid not, I think she might have told me not

to bite people, but I can't remember, I rarely listened to her."

"Words. Just words," he said, reaching into his desk and removing a service-issue pistol. "Put on the collar."

Without any thought, Kat had put on the Kevlar-titanium weave body suit that Anna had laid out for her. Just another day in the life of a Princess. If the Conteradmiral shot her in the chest, he might be surprised at the outcome.

Then again, if he shot her in the face, she'd be dead.

It was hard to tell exactly where he was aiming.

If she dropped to the floor, she might get facedown below the desk before he shot her where she wasn't protected. Kat went through her options. Options that she knew were being simultaneously evaluated by Voss.

His comm-link went off.

"Put on the collar," the Conteradmiral demanded.

The comm-link continued to beep.

"You need to take that call," Kat told him, sitting down for the first time.

"Put the collar on, or I will shoot you." His words were harsh demanding. Kat ignored them.

"You masters want to talk to you," can told him, lightly, almost taunting him.

"You could be dead before they utter a single word."

Kat was very aware of that fact. "That is true," she conceded. "But if I die before you take that call . . . you'll be dead by the end of the day."

"Really? You think so?"

"Why don't you take the call and find out?" Kat suggested.

His comm-link continued to beep whilst they debated their respective fates.

The Conteradmiral eventually accepted the call, but his pistol remained trained on Kat.

Kat didn't move. This call would decide if she won or lost. Lived of died.

If she lost, she'd go down fighting. Do her very best to take Voss down too.

"Hallo," the Conteradmiral said. "Hallo, mein Meister," he snapped immediately to attention his hand with the weapon was no longer pointed at Kat.

"Du lebst und es geht dir gut, mein Meister," was followed by a long pause as the Conteradmiral listened."

Kat didn't speak what she took to be German and didn't have Safi to translate.

"Ja, mein Meister, das Severn-Mädchen ist bei mir sicher. I was examining options for her final disposition," he finished, switching into English.

So Kat was now a 'person of interest' to Ernst-Augustus von Welf! So, was he now thinking about the son that she was supposed to have killed . . . or the three thousand plus, that she'd allegedly just killed . . . or the fact that she'd just saved his own life?

"Yes, Herr von Welf . . . it will be so, sir . . . and a long life to you too, sir." The Conteradmiral said, then the link terminated.

"You are a very lucky lady," he told Kat.

"Those who survive have to be," Kat said, standing up.

"You are free to go. Your ship may leave as soon as you return to it." His voice was stripped of all emotion.

"And how will I find my way back to my ship?"

"However you so wish. Our navy does not have 'spare' personnel to act as escort details to every young lady with pretentions of importance."

Kat wasn't about to turn her back on the Conteradmiral. He reached out. "The collar, if you please."

Kat wanted to hurl it at him, but instead she placed it on top of the padded envelope. "You can warn your goons to be careful, I'm no easy takedown."

"I will tell my men whatever I so choose," the Conteradmiral, said but did not raise his pistol.

Kat backed her way towards the hatch, careful not to turn her back on Voss. The Conterdamital didn't move, his pistol stayed down. "See you around," she told him.

"I hope not," he said.

Kat was through the hatch in a second, slamming it hard behind her. The two guards jumped. Why they jumped was unclear, but Kat doubted that many people who went through that hatchway came out again unassisted.

Kat had covered the distance to the second hatch before they'd recovered.

She slammed that hatchway door, too. That helped release the anger inside her gut. She resisted the temptation to run for the elevator, but when she got there, there were no visible controls, no obvious way to summon the elevator or part the doors. Safi could have no doubt done so, but Kat was on her own.

She looked for a companionway. The bulkhead marking told her she was on -7, or seven decks below the flight deck.

By the time she'd climbed to -4, two men in what appeared to be the uniform of the Sicherheitsdienst were following her.

Kat continued to climb. At the next landing she stopped briefly to rest. One more level and she'd be in the hanger, directly below the flight deck, and that wasn't somewhere she needed to be. A hatch suddenly opened and an out-of-breath European Union Matrosenoberfeldwebel partly stepped through and beckoned to her. "This way, your Highness."

"And why exactly should I do that," Kat said, but was already in moving in his direction.

"Kapitän Sörensen sent me, said you might need assistance getting back to your ship."

Kat looked at the name tag on his uniform 'Lamprecht' and instantly made the connection, this was the same Chief Petty Officer she'd first met in the incidents in and around Cape Town and her own command of ROSP 3-Alpha-9.

"You're on the *Fenrir* too?" Kat asked him as she followed him back through the hatch.

"Yes, the Kapitän requested about thirty of us from the *Jarnsaxa* when he got his own ship. Not all his requests were granted obviously, but there's probably around a dozen of us serving on the *Fenrir* that had previously served together on the *Jarnsaxa*." He stopped, checked the bulkhead reference, then led her on, through a maze of grey-painted corridors, the walls of which were covered in multiple runs of pipes and conduits. He pointed at another companionway.

"Up or down?" she asked him.

"Down."

Kat began descending, he followed. Quickly there was no more down.

Two crewman with assault rifles guarded an open hatchway. The metal grating immediately outside the hatch had been lowered to create small platform and from that another, near-vertical gantry of metal steps went down to the quayside.

"Ready?" he asked her.

"As I'll ever be."

"Escorting a guest ashore," Lamprecht told the two sentries as they approached. He didn't wait for their response and followed Kat out and down the accessway before they could be challenged.

When they eventually reached the bottom of the steps Kat asked, "Now what?"

"We run."

Kat started jogging. And continued jogging. After nearly three hundred meters they were no longer over-shadowed by the bulk of the carrier, but an almost-as-large littoral warfare ships, the *Donitz* was the next vessel on the quay.

After clearing the bulk of that ship, the quayside came to a 'T' within another fifty metres.

"Left or Right?" she asked him.

"Right," he told her. Kat gave three approaching sailors a smile.

After another four or five hundred metres they came to an accessway. The end resting on the quayside was blocked by a pair of men in the uniform that Kat had always considered the European Union's equivalent to the ABCANZ Land Forces. Probably some kind of Marine force?

Although some of the original constituent forces of the EU military had a long tradition of soldiers trained in amphibious operations, not unlike that of the ABCANZ Military with their US Marines and Royal Marines, most of the European units did not have the same historical reputation. France had contributed all two thousand men of its 'Fusiliers Marins' and the Spanish, some elements of its 'Infanteria de Marina,' but only those based in Bilbao. Italy had provided its battalion sized 'Lagunari,' but their 'San Marco Brigade' had been transferred to the Senyara States of the Southern European Alliance, although many of the personnel had transferred between the two units as their personal circumstances necessitated prior to the Italian nation dividing. The Dutch had provided the largest and most capable contribution with the 'Netherlands Marine Corps' and 'Korps Commandotroepen' exceeding three thousand personnel. The German contribution had been minimal and was focused on fleet asset protection rather than expeditionary littoral warfare.

The name of this ship, often displayed on a banner running the length of the accessway, was missing.

As she and Lamprecht approached the marines parted and allowed first the Matrosenoberfeldwebel, and then Kat access.

The climb was short compared to that on and off the carrier. The accessway ended on the warship's main deck. Kat stopped, straightened her uniform as much as a shipsuit ever allowed, then turned ninety degrees. The Matrosenoberfeldwebel escorted Kat towards the quarterdeck, saluting the blue, star emblazoned flag and requesting 'permission to come aboard.' Kat followed his lead and did the same. A Junior Watch Officer acknowledged her request and asked Kat to follow her to the *Fenrir*'s Operations Centre.

A very busy Operations Centre. A schematic of the port covered the main display, detailing the ships at each berth. A map displaying the port and the surrounding city filled another screen. Kapitän Sörensen and a Fregattenkapitän studied them for a moment more after Kat entered, then with a single word, all the displays went blank.

"Keeping secrets?" Kat asked.

"As I'm sure you can appreciate Lieutenant, our navy's internal matters must remain exclusively ours," Kapitän Sörensen said. "Let them stay that way, for now at least. I'm sure your Commodore Finklemeyer will provide you with his assessment of the situation in the next day or two. He may jump to the wrong conclusions. Apparently, he often does, or so Conteradmiral Voss would have me believe. Hopefully that won't lead to him sending you off on another ill-conceived mission. Quite remarkable that you've stayed alive so long, once you combine his efforts with those of Fähnrich von Welf!"

"I think I've given you a pretty up-close and honest example of how I've managed to survive during the last few days, Kapitän Sörensen" Kat said evenly.

"Yes, you did," Fähnrich von Welf added as she entered the Operations Centre, "But you can't tell me that my dad using his influence with Voss to get you released wasn't just a little bit helpful?"

"You managed to talk with your father?"

"Yes. Despite the Sicherheitsdienst's best efforts to jam all communications, I did manage a little chat with him. Dad is grateful, and says he'll reconsider his attitude towards the Severns."

"Can I have that in writing?" Kat asked.

"Unlikely. I think it probably best that you get away from here as quickly as you can."

"How will I get back to the *Fires of Bertlane*? Another jog around the quayside, past that carrier again?" Kat asked them all.

Sörensen allowed himself a very small smile. "You can return to the *Fires of Beltane* the same way we came back to the *Fenrir*. One of your RIBs is waiting alongside. It's rather beaten up, but its operational. Just about."

Lex insisted on doing the honors, but their walk through the Fenrir was mostly in silence, at least until they got to the ladder running down the hull-side to the RIB.

"I'm really pleased I didn't succeed in killing you in Emirates City," Lex said.

"So am I," Kat agreed.

"I'm really sorry I involved your aunt in things. I never knew my grandmothers, aunts, or anyone older. Didn't really know my mother that well either."

"I guess life hasn't been easy for either of us," Kat offered, "despite what most people think."

"Have you ever had a real friend?" Lex asked.

"Yes, but he was killed in the fighting off Hawaii," Kat told her.

Lex opened her arms, and gave Kat an honest hug. "Maybe one day we can get together when nobody's life is on the line. Someday when we can just talk girl stuff."

"That would be nice," Kat agreed. "I'm not sure I've ever done that."

"Not sure I have either, but the movies make it seem a nice thing to do."

Kat wasn't sure why, but she was reluctant to break from the hug, but she knew she had to. She needed to get the *Bella* out of port and away before all hell broke loose. "I'll see you around," she said, not really knowing what else to say.

"I'll look forward to it," Alexandra von Welf said.

And with that they went their separate ways. Kat climbed down to the waiting RIB, its crew genuinely pleased to see her.

As soon as Kat reached the RIB and it moved away from the hull of the *Fenrir*, Lex turned away, returning to the internal affairs of the European Union and her miserable life as a Fähnrich.

"Hang on," the crewman at the helm said, barely giving Kat a moment to sit down and secure herself.

* * *

The run back to the *Fires of Beltane* through the assembled European Fleet concentrated within Puducherry's port was made at the RIBs maximum speed, with plenty of zig-zagging in an attempt to confuse and tracking of weapon targeting.

Fortunately, no ship fired at them.

Kat wasn't out of the recovered RIB before the *Bella* was releasing her auto-tiedowns and moving away from her allocated berth. The clanking of their retraction warned Kat not to release her harness within the RIB for a few more seconds. Eventually Captain Gillan announced that they were underway, but only making five knots until they were clear of the port's restrictions. Quickly, Kat was out of the RIB and making for the *Bella*'s bridge.

It was Anna who grabbed her first, giving her another genuine hug. "We were so worried," she said.

Mike looked like he wanted to hug her too, but limited his greetings to, "Very pleased to have you back on-board, your Highness."

Even Professor Brooks was there, although his welcome was exactly what she'd expected. "Can we do some real science now?"

"I'll see what I can do," was Kat's rather lame response.

"Where to, ma'am?" Captain Gillan asked her.

"Not sure, but get us away from here.

Gillan nodded, as did Sato at the helm and Kat felt the surge beneath her feet as the *Bella*'s speed steadily increased. Kat briefly wondered how many days it would be before someone tried to kill her again.

It had only been six hours from leaving Puducherry, when Anna was gently waking her.

"I'm sorry, Kat. It's The Fink. Apparently, it won't wait. There's a briefing in ten minutes.

With a deep sigh Kat sat up, rolled out of her bunk, ignored the robe being offered by Anna and disappeared into the adjoining bathroom, or 'heads' as the Fleet insisted on calling it.

Bladder empty and teeth cleaned, she scrapped her hair back and tied it in place. She couldn't walk the corridors of the ship in a dressing gown, that just wasn't appropriate, so pulled on a new shipsuit and made her way to Captain Gillan's office.

When she entered, the main screen was already up and Commodore Finklemeyer's head and upper body filled the screen. "Sorry to wake you, Lieutenant, but this can't wait."

Kat nodded in acknowledgement and simply said "Commodore," by way of reply.

"Your specific mission objective is simple: Ideally extract, or if not, neutralise any electronic data, intelligence or individual from the subterranean complex on North Sentinel Island, and do it before any other foreign intelligence agency can do the same. We need to know who these people really are. These 'Disciples' of the Angels of Light must be more than the brain-washed, drug-induced delusionists that they appear to be. I want to know who or what is really 'pulling their strings.' Is that clear Lieutenant? Nobody in the senior hierarchy of our military or our civilian intelligence communities believes that the 'Angels of Light' are a stand-alone, self-orchestrated entity."

"I agree, sir." Kat told him. "It does seem unlikely."

"Whoever is behind them, they represent the latest incarnation of non-state sponsored terrorism. I need to know if these 'Angels of Light' are really backed by extremely rich and religiously motivated leaders, or if it's all an elaborate deception . . . a front? Do they really have an intense hatred of Ernest Augustus the Seventh, the European states, the ANCANZ Federation, democracy . . . whatever it is, I need to know"

No political system was perfect, and Kat had studied numerous different models during her university years, and had grown up in an in a house and family that lived, ate, slept, breathed . . . crapped politics.

The ABCANZ Federation was essentially a 'Democratic Capitalist state. That was defined as being 'an economic system that combines robust competitiveness with sustainable entrepreneurship, with the aim of innovation and providing opportunities for economic prosperity to all citizens.' Or, a 'dynamic complex of economic, political, moral-cultural, ideological, and institutional forces', which serve to maximize social welfare within a free market economy.' Its opponents always cited it as being a selfish, immoral and greed driven culture, all of which was certainly true, and the unfortunate by-product of having a relatively liberal culture and a market-driven economy. And, that was before dissenters added in a religious perspective, or their loathing of its 'imperialistic' past!

But, all factors duly considered, she believed theirs to be one of the better models, or at least it would do, for now, until it could evolve.

For Kat it was simple, whoever was behind the recently evolving world events . . . they . . . it . . . he or her . . . needed to be stopped. Ernst August von Welf, the seventh of that name, was suspected by Commodore Finklemeyer as being a main player, although never publicly, but would he really initiate an assassination attempt on the scale of the *Varuna Ratnaker* incident against himself? Was he really a 'wannabe world emperor' or just one of somebody else's 'generals?' The von Welf's did have a reputation for dancing to someone else's tune. Or perhaps the tracks of their own agendas and 'grand plans' of others simply used the same, or parallel 'tracks,' from time to time?

"The insertion plan is therefore as follows, Lieutenant. You are to make 'best speed" . . . but appropriate for a civilian merchant vessel, to ROSP 4-Foxtrot-6. Once there, the Platform's helicopter will be embarked, using the *Bella*'s forward hold top-hatches, as an improvised flight deck."

Both the forward and rear hold hatch covers had been reinforced for exactly this scenario during her last refit. The fact that the front hold was being used was simply because the Platform's 'Vulture' VTOL copter wouldn't safely fit onto the rear, at least not in the current sea conditions, when the pitch and roll of the flight deck was a significant factor.

"Once the VTOL is safely embarked, the *Fires of Beltane* will continue on towards North Sentinel Island. As soon as the island was within the aircraft's range, as it obviously needs to get there and back on a single fuel cell, it will launch. Flying fast and low it will skim the waves until it reaches the island and will insert you, along with Captain Sykes and Sergeant Varko by 'helocasting.'"

This was military jargon for dropping them into the ocean near the beach and swimming ashore.

Helocasting is a technique used by small sized special operations teams to insert into an area near a coastline, lake or other body of water. The small unit is flown, by VTOL aircraft, to a maritime insertion point. Once there, the aircraft hovers at an altitude just above the water's surface at an airspeed not exceeding ten knots. Team members then exit the aircraft and enter the water.

In some circumstances, depending upon the mission parameters and the aircraft being used, personnel may be inserted with an inflatable boat for 'over-the-horizon' operations when the close proximity of the aircraft to the objective would compromise the mission.

"The fourth member of your insertion team will be a 'specialist' on fundamentalist religious groups, Lieutenant. My 'green slime' colleagues have insisted that they accompany you, apparently to oversee the recovery and extraction of anything, or anyone, deemed 'useful.' They are being flow out to ROSP 4-Foxtrot-6 as we speak, and will be on-board by the time you arrive. They will be transferred to the *Fires of Beltane* at the same time as the VTOL aircraft. I am also inserting a four-man Forward Reconnaissance Team, the precise details of whom, when and how . . . you don't need to know. They will undertake a CTR of the island

and the subterranean complex, as detailed in Captain Sykes's Intel report, well before you arrive and then advise on the best method of mission execution and extraction."

"Understood, sir."

"I'm quite sure that Ensign Steiger will object at not being included in the insertion team, but he's a PQO and this is most definitely outside of his specialist skill set. Captain Sykes will therefore assume his responsibilities with regard to your continued longevity on this mission. That is not negotiable."

"Yes, Commodore, I understand."

"Good. That's about it, Lieutenant. Get in there, extract what you can, or if you can't get it out . . . destroy it, so that others don't get it instead. Any questions?"

Kat knew that in a hours' time she'd probably have at least a dozen, but right now, "No, sir. No questions."

"Good luck, Lieutenant," the Commodore said, then cut the transmission.

SIX : TWENTY ONE

Despite the legendary reputation of the Indian Union's politicians and bureaucrats for protracted discussion and debate, its military were the exact opposite, notorious for 'shooting first and asking questions later.' If an unidentified aircraft ever violated their airspace, within minutes of crossing into their territory, said aircraft would be intercepted by a pair of Indian fighters flying sufficiently close that waving at the pilots became possible. Rather predictably, they wouldn't wave back! They had come to get visual identification, and if they didn't like what they saw, they'd quickly introduce you to the business end a couple of air-to-air missiles, or so the numerous Intel reports suggested.

So with that nugget of Intel carefully considered, Kat and her team were secured within the rear compartment of a UH-27 Vulture utility helicopter.

The 'Vulture' had a 'dual-role' designation. The medium-sized VTOL aircraft, with its three-man flight crew, could provide limited personnel or equipment transportation, but also had a 'ground-attack' capability fitted onto the forward stubs.

Right now, the craft was flying fast and low, only metres above the wave tops. Hopefully keeping itself and its occupants below any kind of tracking or surveillance radar that might be operating.

Kat hadn't asked Safi to check the serial numbers, but this VTOL copter must be the identical twin-sister to the one she and Mike had hitched a ride into the desert hinterlands surrounding Emirates City in, only a few months back. It even had the same armoured enhancement of the rear compartment and the same 'improvised' seating arrangements. The Vulture had radar and light absorbing paint and heat dissipating exhausts as standard. The rotor blades were enclosed, one on each side of the fuselage that could modulate their spacing to significantly reduce the blade-vortex-interaction and therefore the noise they generated. It also had a dampened propulsion unit and transmission, and an enclosed tail-rotor. This all helped to reduce their noise signature.

Kat twisted in the improvised web seating, trying to get herself comfortable.

Sergeant Varko sat beside her. His head covered by a knitted hat. Anna sat beside him. She looked to be asleep.

Kat glanced across at the fourth member of her team. The supposed 'specialist' on fundamentalist religious groups, that their 'green slime' and 'grey slime' bosses had insisted accompany them, apparently to oversee the recovery and extraction of anything, or anyone, deemed 'useful.'

The last Intel Kat had on said 'specialist,' provided by Colonel Leo Wood when in Cape Town nine months ago, was that Captain Harriet Stryder was 'currently in a permanent desk job somewhere, pending further investigation,' and yet evidently that wasn't the case . . . as somehow . . . she was sitting here with them!

The Colonel had voiced his concerns about her, as had Anna, who had also briefly encountered Harriet Stryder several years before.

Seated to Kat's right in the semi darkness, and even in the reduced red lighting of the cargo bay, Kat could see that Stryder really didn't look very happy. She probably didn't like flying without complimentary champagne and the pyjamas of Business Class! Or maybe it was encountering Kat and Anna again. Last time they had tried to share a VTOL aircraft, Stryder had had her nose broken by Colonel Wood's well-placed boot smashing into her face.

Stryder hadn't exchanged more than a dozen words with Kat or Anna since being reacquainted. 'Frosty' did not describe her demeanour adequately enough. 'Frozen' if not actually hostile, was a much more suitable metaphor.

It was about a year since Kat had last seen Stryder. She'd left the Frigate *Tenacity* a few days after the events in Lunda-Luba, when they'd reached the 'Wideawake' facilities on Ascension. Kat struggled hard to hide her surprise at seeing Stryder attached to this mission. But, despite all the misgivings that Kat and Anna had privately shared after being reacquainted, Kat had chosen not to challenge Stryder about her presence on this mission. Not yet.

The only thing that had physically changed was Stryder's hair. It was still straight, but used to go down a centimetre or two past her shoulders. Now it was cut into a short bob with a fringe. She still had the same strong, well-defined features. High cheekbones and large eyes. Her mouth was full, her grin wide, although she almost always looked way too serious. Stryder certainly wasn't going to be troubled in her old age by 'laughter lines.' Despite the broken nose, she was still a very good-looking woman. Maybe too good looking? Stryder, at around thirty years of age, had learned how to use her looks to her advantage, manipulating others, especially men, to get her own way. To many, especially female colleagues, that made her less than popular.

They had been on the aircraft for over two hours and Kat's body was starting to ache. She turned onto her left side. She could only just see Anna. She looked over towards Stryder, who was rubbing her eyes with her fists like a sleepy child.

Kat tried hard to follow Anna's example and dose off again, and twenty minutes later she was still kidding herself she was asleep when she got a tap on the back of her legs.

Kat opened her eyes and peered into the semi darkness. The load-master was moving around with small, red-filtered flashlights fitted to both sides of his helmet so as not to destroy anyone's night-vision. He looked at her and held up his hands, showing all ten fingers, informing her they were ten minutes out.

Kat unzipped the sleeping bag she'd wriggled herself into, and despite being enclosed within a dry-suit, immediately felt the cold of the Vulture's uninsulated cargo hold.

She folded her sleeping bag in half, leaving the 'piddle pack' she'd filled inside. Battery operated, the Bladder Relive Device' used a shaped 'cup' that looked more like a child-sized oxygen mask, to detect urine and rapidly pump it away, through a one-way valve and into a plastic bag.

Following Anna and Sergeant Varko's example, she released her assault rifle from its bulkhead restraints. It was one of the pirate's weapons, 'liberated' from the crew of the *Storm Cloud V*. Rather conveniently, the an AK21, was also the most likely weapon of choice for anybody they'd encounter on the ground. Kat had the 'K' or 'korotkiy' model, which quite literally translated as 'short.' This was the folding stock and reduced barrel length variant. The barrel was around two hundred millimetres shorter than the standard version. Although this made it considerably more convenient, especially on a covert insertion, accuracy against anything over a hundred and fifty metres away was compromised. The suppresser that Sergeant Varko had fitted onto the end of the barrel added almost the same length back on.

She cocked the weapon, chambering the first round, then checked the safety before fitting the trigger and parts of the lower receiver into the pre-formed section of a specialized waterproof bag, that then partially inflated. It was a simple precaution that prevented the salt-water of the ocean from damaging it when it became immersed, added buoyancy, and could still be fired if needed, as the trigger area was still accessible. She clipped her coiled lanyard into an eyelet in the bag, to ensure they didn't become separated when she entered the water.

Then she un-zipped the dry-suit's horizontal fastener than ran across her hips. First, she pushed her hand down her right leg, checking that the 9mm pistol, that was in a leg holster against the outside of her thigh, was still secure. Then she removed the cup and piping of a second Bladder Relief Device from inside her underwear.

After Kat had zipped herself back up, she pulled a pair of goggles from her pack and fitted them securely over her face. The lenses were tinted, making her eyes no longer visible.

Kat pressed the stud on the side of her goggles and checked the feed of her real-time satellite imagery, but it continued to show nothing new, nothing more than what she already knew from her previous visits onto North Sentinel.

Checks complete, there was nothing to do for the next two minutes but daydream or get scared. Each of them was lost in their own thoughts, their own little worlds. Now and again Kat could see reflections from the red-filtered flashlights in their goggles. Anna was staring at her boots, Varko straight ahead. Maybe thinking about family, or perhaps what they were going to do after this, or maybe even wondering what or why they were here in the first place! That was most certainly Kat's preference.

She watched the load-master begin packing loose equipment away, placing it into a large aluminium container. Once they had exited the VTOL aircraft and the rear hatch had been closed again, he would stow any other mission related equipment into it, then dispose of it when the aircraft returned to the safety of the *Fires of Beltane* or ROSP *4-Foxtrot-6*.

He started a final sweep with his flashlights to make sure nothing was loose which would be sucked out as soon as the rear hatch was opened. Nothing must compromise the mission.

Land Force Captain Harriet Stryder was standing slightly in-front of Sergeant Varko. She was tethered to him on a two-metre length of 40mm web strap.

Stryder was supposedly an Intelligence Branch operative. Mid-ranking officers in that food-chain usually spent significant parts of their careers attached to Embassies, posing as diplomatic assistants to various attachés, attending the never-ending circuit of diplomatic receptions. Always on the look-out to recruit potential new intelligence sources through the mediums of cocktails and small-talk, if not pillow-talk.

Nocturnal clandestine VTOL insertions were certainly

not part of their usual day-to-day modus-operandi, although thankfully it was covered somewhere within their training.

Kat knew that Stryder had once been exactly that, attached to the ABCANZ Fed's Embassy in Lunda-Luba as an assistant to its then Defence Attaché, Colonel Leo Wood, another 'green slime' operator who wasn't at the top of Kat's 'Yuletide Greetings' list by any stretch of the imagination.

Stryder somehow looked supremely confident about the impending helocast, as though she'd done it a thousand times before. She hadn't, and that was why she was tethered to Sergeant Varko. Kat knew Stryder always took her job seriously, sometimes too seriously, so had probably read and watched fifty different vid-files on the do's and don'ts of helocasting and thereby knew more facts and figures that the rest of them combined.

Despite her copious research, she was still regarded as a 'strap-hanger,' by Anna and Sergeant Varko. In the Special Operations world, any mission augmentee, be that scientist, linguist, Intel analyst, anyone who didn't wear the winging dagger of Special Operations on their right shoulder, was considered a 'strap hanger,' and were 'just along for the ride!' Kat smiled inwardly. Stryder now had the physical strap of the tether to confirm her status!

This was to prevent her getting separated from the team whilst in the water.

Kat however, also technically a 'strap-hanger,' had been a champion skiff racer during her university years and had undertaken a slack handful of high-speed emergency immersions during that time. Granted, they were never using military kit, or from an aircraft, but when Sergeant Varko had asked her dozens and dozens of questions about it, and then more on 'what if this happens' or 'that happens,' her answers had obviously been sufficient that she wasn't being tethered to Anna as a safety precaution too.

Stryder turned and looked at Kat. They made eye contact and Kat gave her an 'everything is okay' nod.

The Load Master then motioned them towards the rear hatch. Their back-packs, that each containing about twenty kilograms of equipment, were suspended from a pair of harnesses in front of their legs. They waddled forward like a family of ducks putting weight on each foot in turn. Kat was thankful that their back-packs didn't need to be fully laden. If everything went to plan, they'd only be on the island for a few hours.

There was a pause of about ten seconds as the load master spoke into his mike to the VTOL aircraft's flight crew, confirming their direction, air-speed and altitude.

Conversation over, he moved to the rear ramp's controls. The ramp itself was about two metres in width and the same in height. After pulling out both of the safety override leavers, then twisting them anticlockwise, he hit the controls that killed the rear compartment's limited internal red lighting. Then he pressed the button that powered the ramp down.

Kat could feel the massive inrush of frigid air, thrashing at her dry-suit. Where the ramp had previously been there was now an open square of cold, black nothing. The plethora of coloured tags within the rear compartment fluttered frantically. The cold air stung at her face. Kat gripped the airframe for support, keeping herself upright as the aircraft banked, adjusting its overall direction of flight.

When the aircraft levelled out, the island and potentially hostile territory, now lay directly behind the aircraft and was getting further away with each passing second. Kat could just about make out the island against the dark sky and even darker sea. They all did their final checks. Right now, Kat wanted nothing more than to get this insertion out of the way . . . get the job done ashore . . . and be back on-board the *Bella* for coffee and toast by early tomorrow morning.

They got closer to each other. The roar of the wind, combined with the VTOL aircraft's engines, now rotated to enable the aircraft to hover, was so loud Kat could hardly think. At last came the hand-held red light from the Load Master. They all joined in, acknowledging with "Red on!" None of them could hear each other, so it was pretty pointless, but apparently it was the procedure that was always followed.

His light changed to green and he shouted "Green on." Then he moved back, out of the way.

"Ready." The team called, then moved forward.

"Go."

Out they spilled, stepping off of the ramp. Four people jumping into the waters of the ocean only a few metres below. Anna went first, then side-by-side, Sergeant Varko and Stryder, and finally Kat. She counted to herself, then jumped at the prescribed interval, after the others. Too quickly and you risked landing on top of them. Too slowly, and they'd be too much of a gap between them in the water, risking unrecoverable separation.

As she jumped, she remembered Sergeant Varko's instructions and crossed her arms across her chest, her hands up by her shoulders and clamped her knees and ankles tight together.

Kat knew the impact of the water would be hard and cold, but she wasn't ready for just how hard and how cold. The sudden impact of the water made her cry out, only to have water cascade into her open mouth as she went under.

Several seconds went by, then after what seemed like an eternity her head broke the water's surface and air raced back into the lungs. Gasping, coughing, choking, spluttering, she trod water whilst she composed herself and got her bearings back.

Their insertion point was on the south-western corner of the island, not via the small inlet that the *Bella* had used on their two previous visits. Offshore from of this corner of the island was the strongest of the nearby ocean currents, moving directly towards the island. Apparently caused by local winds combined with equatorial 'Kelvin' waves, this would greatly assist them in their swim ashore. The staff of the Tactical Operations Centre, the specialist personnel who had transferred onto the *Bella* with Stryder and the Vulture VTOL and who now ran this insertion, had certainly done their 'homework.' It was they who had determined that a helocast was the most appropriate method of insertion, rather than the VTOL putting them down directly onto the island. Apparently, there were too many 'unknowns' in their threat assessment to sensibly pursue that option.

A minute after hitting the water, Kat was reliving her time in the waters of the Pacific off Whangarei, New Zealand. Even in calm waters, the swell, the rise and fall of the waves was far greater that it ever seemed when viewed from on-board a boat or an aircraft. One moment she was up on a peak, searching for her colleagues, the next she was down in a trough and could see nothing but a black wall of water on all four sides.

Kat continued to tread water until her breathing stabilised, then she studied the device attached to her left wrist. The watch-like unit was essentially a glorified compass with a built-in GPS and tracking capability. Kat had to locate her colleagues and move in the general direction of the shore.

On the peak of the next wave, she looked around. She looked left then right, trying to see where her team might be. She could maybe see something on her left side, but she couldn't tell who it was.

All she felt the push of the current against her body, taking her naturally towards the island's shore. The harness that ran around her waist kept her pack suspended directly beneath her helped to give her a lower profile in the water. It bumped against her legs as she continued to tread water.

She checked the display of her wrist unit again and began swimming in the direction it indicated.

Kat wasn't worried where everyone else was in the ocean, both Anna and Sergeant Varko were professionals, she just needed to concentrate on sorting herself out.

On the next wave peak she had another look around, to locate and then orientate herself in relation to the others. She glimpsed Stryder and Varko and moved herself towards them.

In a minute, maybe two, Kat was with them. Stryder, still tethered to the Sergeant, looked scared, like a small child.

Kat checked her wrist unit again. It looked exactly as she'd hoped. Everything was running to plan.

For the next fifteen minutes they made their way towards the island's nearest beach. Kat thought that maybe she was seeing the occasional light on the shoreline.

Anna was ahead of them and was now moving through the waves breaking onto the beach. The waves were much bigger than they looked, and knocked her over. A figure ran forward and helped her up. Kat's goggles were in their 'infra-red,' mode rather than night-vision, so she couldn't see who it was providing assistance.

Kat scanned along the shoreline, looking for the tell-tale infra-red flash of the other team. It was similar to the light used on the top of tall buildings to warm aircraft, but instead of being constantly lit, it threw out a brilliant, but quick, flash of light, but was only visible through an IR filter. She kept looking out into the darkness.

Suddenly she saw it. On the beach, slightly to her right.

Kat was almost at the beach. She stopped swimming, put her feet down and felt for something solid beneath her. The waves were continually pushing her forwards. Her feet contacted the sand and she was running forward, through the surf. The breaking waves were big, powerful, and just like Anna, Kat was knocked flat by a torrent of white water connecting with her back.

A body appeared beside her hauling her back onto her feet. The four personnel of a Special Operations Forward Operating Team had been on North Sentinel conducting a Close Target Reconnaissance, or CTR for the previous twenty-four hours, initially gathering intel and now two of them manned the beach insertion point. The Tactical Operations staff back on the *Bella* had not briefed Kat as to exactly how this Forward Operating Team had been inserted, but she knew enough of how this clandestine world operated that she wasn't about to ask. Kat suspected in would have likely been a high-altitude, high opening (HAHO) parachute jump or perhaps a swim-in from an appropriately equipped submarine, but she wasn't about to speculate as whatever she said, it would be neither be confirmed nor denied.

"You okay, ma'am?"

Kat immediately recognised the voice. Veronica Perry, had been a Lance Corporal in the Embassy Protection Detachment in Emirates City, but since gaining a very recent promotion to full Corporal, she'd returned to her 'Special Operations' roots in the elite ranks of the covert insertion Forward Operating Teams.

"Yes, I'm fine . . . thank you. It's good to see you."

Within seconds of leaving the water their waterproof 'weapon bags' were opened and they moved silently towards another figure providing 'over-watch,' twenty metres away. This figure and Perry were both wearing night-vision-goggles.

Dry-suits tugged off, the large rubber neck seal being particularly uncomfortable when tugged over the wearers face, then stowed away into their back-packs, they were soon all making their way through the sand at the rear of the beach, apparently heading towards the location previously identified as being the Great Hall.

All of team were dressed the same, in olive green one-piece overalls, not unlike the Fleet-issue ship-suits. Not as tight fitting, as they all had civilian clothes underneath as part of their 'escape and evasion' contingency plan if the mission went 'pear-shaped' and they had to deceive the Indian authorities by pretending to be misguided tourists. They all had a belt kit or chest rig of magazine pouches, water bottle and other essential, mission critical, kit. They wore boots of their own choice, a civilian brand and style available on any local high street and not something that had a restricted geographical retail market, or exclusively military usage that could be traced.

For the last twenty-four hours this Forward Operating Team had initially been reconnoitring the subterranean structures at the heart of island, identifying how they were powered, then preparing and placing an explosive attack that was going to close down any identified power supplies whilst the target area was infiltrated.

*   *   *

"This is the Emergency RV," Perry said in a low whisper. "If it all goes 'tits-up' we RV back here."

Kat motioned for Stryder, ensuring they both stayed out of the way as Anna, Varko, Perry and the other Special Operations team member, Trooper Carter, got themselves prepared. Kat and Stryder got down in-between the large root fingers of a nearby banyan tree, a species abundant right across the island. Through the canopy twenty metres above their heads, the stars gave them just enough light to move by without tripping over their own feet. It was something that Kat had always loved about sparsely populated places, uncontaminated by city lights . . . the night sky, the stars. It felt as if you could see the entire universe.

The night air seemed warm and humid after the coldness of their VTOL ride and subsequent immersion into the ocean.

Kat glanced at Stryder and she nodded. Stryder had a much smaller back-pack than Kat's, containing her trauma kit, and anything else she might need. Once mission critical kit was packed, Kat knew that whatever else went in was down to her own personal choice, after all, she was the one who had to carry it, nobody else.

Corporal Perry joined them with a cheerful, "You ladies, okay?" As if she felt he needed to counter Stryder's miserable demeanour.

Stryder looked at her blankly and said, "Let's get on with this shall we?"

There was a pause as Perry let the tone of her reply sink in. She didn't like it. "Okay, let's do it." Perry pointed at Stryder. "You, behind me. Then you, your Highness" she pointed at Kat, "behind her. Okay?"

On a track between the two clumps of banyan trees Kat could see Sergeant Varko moving into a single-filed patrol formation. Perry stood to follow, then Stryder and Kat. Trooper Carter would follow them, covering their rear.

Kat's secondary function on this mission was to protect Stryder. They hadn't told Perry that if there was a drama, they were to go, leave the rest of the team and try to get away, faking it as a pair of clueless western tourists, lost whilst on vacation. Kat wasn't at all happy about it, but her orders clearly stated that she was to leave them, protect Stryder, and let the others get on with it. And, if that meant the team got killed, well . . . that apparently was okay, and not her problem!

They inserted themselves into the patrol formation as Perry had instructed, then moved silently into the shadows, weapons at the ready. Kat's rifle butt was tight into her shoulder, her index finger across the trigger guard, her thumb on the safety catch. Stryder only had a pistol, and like the team's assault rifles, it wasn't the model usually issued to the ABCANZ military. She only had it for her personal self-defence. Kat and the Forward Operating Team were there to facilitate everything else for her.

For another ten minutes they moved through a terrain dominated by large banyan trees and the grass-like grain crop being cultivated between them. When they finally stopped, all Kat could only hear was the incessant clicking and buzzing of unseen insects, and the wind in the tree canopy above their heads. Ahead of them was the target, although just as before, when visiting the Great Hall with Zeebub, nothing was visible above ground level.

As they drew nearer, the access steps down to the tunnel became more evident, despite the shadows cast by the moon shining through the moving canopy of tree branches.

Their designated Ground Commander was a Land Force Captain, Nick Maddox. He came silently up alongside Kat, smiled, then introduced himself. He was about ten years older than she was, and needed a shave. Sergeant Varko knew of him by reputation, if nothing else, and considered him to be 'one of the good guys.' Undoubtedly in love with his wife and kids, in love with his job, and his car, house and probably his dog too!

"This is the Final RV," he told them. "The target . . . if you look down the steps and into the tunnel, is through a pair of doors, about fifty metres inside."

They were both looking where the Captain had indicated.

Kat nodded, she'd been down that tunnel before.

"Once the power is out, the doors will be breached. We'll get inside and move along the corridor. Then into the space your Intel referred to as the Great Barn. We'll drop into the floor recess and then locate that concealed door and whatever lies beyond. That's where we think they are, or at least where they were all heading last night. We've had this access point under surveillance all day, so unless there's another entrance we've not located and they snuck out . . . or perhaps they've decided to go all suicidal like that other fellow . . . *this* is where they're going to be."

"You've found their power supply?" Kat asked him.

"Yes, took a while. It's an underwater turbine, turned by the ocean currents of the north side of the island."

"But we looked there! We looked everywhere. Did multiple scans, with every bit of tech we had," Kat told him, almost indignant.

"You didn't miss it. Its deep, fixed just above the seabed. Japanese tech, a turbine that converts the ocean currents into electricity. It's deliberately placed deep, a hundred metres or more, so it's not effected by wave motion or creates a navigation hazard to shipping. No scanners or clever tech would have ever picked it up that deep down. We only identified it from the cables bring the power ashore, and they were shielded and concealed. Really clever tech, even 'Tracy Island' would be envious," Maddox told her.

Kat had no idea what the 'Tracy Island,' reference meant and let the Captain's comment slide.

"And, we found an advanced Link Twenty-Two half-wave dipole antenna concealed within one of these trees. That's serious kit for receiving or transmitting something."

Kat nodded in acknowledgement and filed the information away. She had no idea how that fitted into the ever-expanding puzzle she was now trying to solve, but maybe Anna or Safi would make something of it when this was all over.

She leant back against a tree root as the rest of the team continued pulling kit slowly out of back-packs, thereby reducing overall noise. There was no light from anywhere other than the moon and the starts above.

Sergeant Varko and Corporal Perry checked in with Captain Maddox and after a brief conversation, they moved off. Maddox then pulled out the telescopic aerial on a device about the size of an oversized comm-unit and began pressing buttons. Kat didn't have a clue what the device was called, but she knew what it did. A red pea light came up, then began flashing, first red then amber. Finally, it went green and stopped flashing. That confirmed he had comms with whatever explosive devices were rigged around the electric cables which supplied the power into this complex. Kat didn't know for sure, but presumed they'd be using a number of small, stand-off penetration charges. Something about the size of a soda can to cut through the thick metal core of the cables.

Stryder suddenly wanted additional information about the target profile and questioned Maddox. "Are you sure this is the right complex? Are you certain that they're in there?"

He wasn't used to be quizzed during a mission and told her politely that whilst they might both hold the rank of Captain, *he* was the designated commander on the ground so he'd very much appreciate it she'd shut up and let him do his job.

Maddox then made his final assessment on the target through his binoculars and confirmed his final orders with the rest of the team. There were no changes to their plan. He looked at Stryder, "Ready?"

She nodded back at him. "You may proceed."

"Okay everybody, here we go." Maddox pushed up the protective safety cap of his control box for the explosive charges and pulled up the aerial its last few centimetres. "Standby . . . standby."

Kat heard the deliberate, stiff mechanical click of a button being pressed in. There was a delay of maybe a second, perhaps two, then a bright flash in the distance, beyond the trees. Then, after twenty, maybe thirty seconds total darkness returned.

Maddox was back to enjoying life, despite Styrder's irritating presence. He checked a second hand-held device. "Power's down . . . okay people . . . let's do this."

They moved off at a slow jogging pace through the cultivated cereal crop towards the steps

The double-doors, down within the tunnel were predictably locked, which meant they'd have to blow the lock, and perhaps the hinges too. Perry had already pulled pre-prepared charges and detonators from her belt kit. Kat recalled she had seen Mike prepare a door in Nu Piter using an explosive paste that cured hard after a few minutes of being in contact with air, but could initially be squirted into locks and alike. They didn't have time to wait for that tonight.

Perry worked silently, methodically, unwinding the explosive-filled det-cord. Kat had seen that before too, in the hold of the merchant freighter she'd help apprehend off Cape Town, linking the charges that had been rigged to punch holes in the ship's hull and send her to the bottom of the sea.

At a signal from Perry they all turned away to preserve their night-vision whilst the second, much smaller, explosive charge, detonated.

Kat and Stryder quickly followed the others down the steps and moved into the tunnel and past Anna and Corporal Perry who were holding then remnants of the shattered wooden doors aside.

It was exactly as Kat remembered it, traditional materials but framed within a very modern construct.

They moved at a fast, walking pace along the tunnel, as fast as searching ahead through a weapon's sighting aperture whilst wearing goggles with a night-vision filter applied ever permitted. At the ninety-degree intersection with another tunnel Trooper Carter and Sergeant Varko already knelt, their weapons pointing into the darkness of the adjoining tunnels. There was the occasional outburst of hollering and calling from somewhere ahead. It wasn't

English. Kat guessed it was probably Afrikaans. It wasn't frantic, the voice simply sounded annoyed that the power had failed.

Eventually they reached the end of the tunnel and got down on either side, against the walls. Anna and Corporal Perry moved forwards together and pushed at another pair of doors. This time they weren't locked and parted easily.

They moved directly through the now open doors and into the Great Hall.

Suddenly voices were shouting again, although the team couldn't see from where they originated.

The voices got closer and Kat could hear the sound of flip-flops slapping against feet. Two middle-aged men entered the Hall from an adjacent tunnel. A tunnel that Kat didn't recall seeing previously. Both were wearing the same worn fatigues she'd seen previously on those working in the fields. They were talking very loudly, highly animated about something.

Troopers Carter and Friel pounced and almost immediately Kat heard a distinctive buzz and crackle. The two men were getting 'tasered' and then being dragged out of sight. Electroshock, stun-gun and taser are all variations on a glorified cattle-prod . . . but for humans. As the fixed electrodes or projected wires touch the body, and the trigger is depressed, a high voltage, low energy electric pulse is delivered into the target. Kat watched. She'd never seen them used by the military before, only by law enforcement agencies on numerous media reports, usually criticizing the Justice Department for using excessive force. She didn't know that you could hold the victim at the same time as administering the electrical charge, without getting fried by the current yourself. *Interesting.*

Voluntary muscular function temporarily disrupted, Friel and Carter got the two men down onto the floor. Kat waited until the moaning and groaning under the hands that now covered their mouths ceased.

Captain Maddox looked back at Kat to confirm all was still okay, then following his lead, they collectively moved towards the central recess, or pit, in the hall's floor.

When Kat reached the recess, Sergeant Varko was already down on the lower level, and as soon as Corporal Perry had joined him, they both went into overwatch as first Stryder, then Kat, were lowered down.

Next to drop was Anna, followed by Maddox. Troopers Carter and Friel would stay at the higher level, moving into a back-to-back kneeling overwatch of their colleagues.

Corporal Perry began searching for the concealed doorway in the pit's opposite wall.

Inside the Great Hall, including down inside the recess, everything remained dark and silent. In a loud whisper Maddox said, "Stay sharp," as they waited for Perry to locate the concealed entrance. Their night-vision filters give them all imagery like a green photographic negative.

Kat became aware of a slight smell of burning. A different variety of mind-control gas? The Great Hall was climate controlled to a very acceptable ambient temperature without the natural humidity of the region, yet there was no evidence of any air-conditioning or similar artificial climate regulation.

Finally, Perry had the concealed doorway located and opening.

After a short distance inside, little more than the likely thickness of the walls, the newly revealed passage stopped and another, at ninety degrees to the first, started.

At the junction they all stopped. Maddox had stopped on the left-side, Stryder was close behind him. Kat came up level to Maddox on the right. She wasn't too sure which way they were now heading, but was confident the Ground Force's Captain would soon tell her. Yes, he was indicating that she should move left.

Kat went in the direction indicated, moved forward three or four metres then stopped. She waited, knowing that Maddox would be clearing in the other direction.

As Maddox cleared any rooms off the passageway in the opposite direction to Kat, Anna now moved silently towards, then past Kat. Styder still had her pistol holstered and was sensibly keeping very close to both of them. The passage's floor was hard, a laminate, maybe tiles or perhaps rock or concrete. Whatever it was, it made the rubber roles of their boots squeak.

Anna stopped and pointed at a door, then took her weapon out of her shoulder. Back against the wall, she reached for the door handle.

Sergeant Varko moved to the opposite side of the door, his weapon still up in the shoulder, ready to make the entry.

Anna nodded.

The Sergeant thumbed off the safety of his weapon as Anna turned the handle and he moved quickly inside, pushing the door with him.

He was blinded. The night-vision filter of his goggles totally whited out. It was as if someone had let off a signal flare right in front of his face.

Anna shouted, "The freakin' lights are back up.'

Varko instinctively fell to his knees, presenting a smaller target and pulled off the googles, blinking hard as he tried to get back some normal vision. This would never have happened in the new 'full face' visor of the updated 'Chameleon' battle suits, which could analyse and adjust to such changes in a fraction of a second. But that wasn't an option on this mission, as it would have instantly identified them as being ABCANZ Fed operatives.

As his vision partially returned, the Sergeant could make out movement against the back wall of the room and rolled to the left, trying to make himself into a smaller, harder target to get a fix on. As his eyes adjusted, he saw another middle-aged man, this time dressed all in white, his head was bald apart from wiry side hair. He was curled up on a sofa against the far wall. His hands protecting his face. He was panicking even more than Varko, Anna or anyone else in the team had been a few moments before.

The 'Disciples' obviously had their own back-up batteries or super-capacitors, perhaps a mini uninterruptable-power-supply or UPS that would provide near-instantaneous emergency protection from primary or mains power failure. Such kit was very expensive, so was usually utilized to protect servers in data-centres, telecommunication equipment and in facilities where an unexpected power disruption could cause injuries, fatalities, loss of fusion containment, serious business disruption or data loss.

Electronic equipment filled every corner and wall of the room. Banks of computer displays and associated processors and servers. The connecting cabling snaked everywhere.

Anna pointed at the man, then immediately called for Stryder.

The Intel Branch operative entered and confirmed, "Yes, that's him." She spoke to him in his own language and he immediately did as he was told, sitting up on the sofa, staying well away from the desk with all the equipment on it. He didn't dare move. His eyes were wide, trying to work out just what was happening, whilst listening to Stryder at the same time.

From her own back-pack Kat pulled out six thermite incendiary grenades. All she needed to do was pull the safety-pins and they could be out of there.

However, Stryder evidently had other ideas and pulled a datapad and some leads from her own back-pack and started connecting them into the computers on the desk whilst still talking to the man. She made reference to the script displayed on the two largest display screens. He talked fast. He was being fully compliant, evidently doing his very best to stay alive.

Kat was confused. This definitely wasn't part of the mission brief. She tried to keep her voice calm. "Harriet, what are you doing? It's time to go."

Captain Maddox was back with them, sticking his head into the room to see what was happening, but stayed outside in the passageway, providing them with much needed overwatch protection.

Kat wasn't an expert in such operations but she knew enough to know that Maddox would now want to get away as quickly as possible. After all, they now had what they had come for. "Harriet, how long is this going to take?"

She was still scrolling through the screens.

Kat didn't like being ignored. She was a 'Princess,' a Severn. People didn't routinely ignore her. This wasn't what they were supposed to be here for.

"No idea, just do your job. Keep everyone else back." Stryder snapped at her.

Kat evidently needed to reiterate the problem they faced. "This has the potential to get nasty Harriet, and quickly. Let's grab him and go."

Stryder wasn't even looking at Kat, she was concentrating on the screens and keyboards.

The man remained seated, looking almost as confused as Kat now felt.

Captain Maddox was starting to get agitated. He stuck his head back into the room. "How much longer ladies?"

Stryder said, "What is it with you people. Freakin' wait out." She seemed fixated by the information that was now displayed before her.

Kat walked over, trying to be diplomatic. "Harriet, we really do need to go. If not, we're in a whole world of crap." She grabbed her arm, but Stryder yanked it away and glared back at Kat.

"I don't understand," Kat continued. "We have one of their 'Elders' in custody, so let's restrain him and go."

They were only a few centimetres apart, so close Kat could feel Stryder's breath on her face when she spoke. Stryder was tall, but was still several centimetres shorter than Kat.

"There is more to do, Severn. It's that simple," she said, slowly, deliberately. "You don't have the full brief."

Kat felt the anger in her start to surge. Once again, Commodore Finklemeyer had got her doing stuff with only half the available Intel. She had only been shown one piece of a much bigger puzzle. Situation freakin' normal! The green and grey slime types would dismiss any protests she made, justifying their actions with predictable phrases of 'need to know or 'operational security.'

Just as Kat took a step back the silence was suddenly broken by shouting, then the distinctive signature of an automatic weapon firing.

"Shit . . . don't move, stay put," Maddox shouted into the room. They had 'gone noisy,' and that wasn't good. He ran back down the corridor and Kat closed the door.

SIX : TWENTY TWO

Kat could hear the sound of several assault rifles returning fire, and lots of shouting from both sides. It didn't matter that their adversaries could hear them shouting in English, there was so much gunfire and confusion that it was irrelevant. Clear command, control and communication between the team members was now far more important. Basic field-craft that might keep them alive!

Kat tried to calm her anger. "Harriet, it really is time to go!"

Stryder ignored Kat and continue working. Their new 'best friend' on the sofa appeared to be getting more and more agitated. There was another exchange of automatic weapon fire out in the corridor.

"Harriet, I really can't put this in any simpler terms . . . we need to get out of here . . . and do it now!"

Stryder spun around, her face taught with anger. "No, what don't you understand? Not yet." She almost spat the words, then jabbed a finger in the direction of the firing as another volley of weapon fire was exchanged. "That is what they get paid for. So let them get on with it. Your job is to stay with me, so do it."

Maddox was now at the right end of the passageway, shouting at the top of his voice. "Get them out Severn, get them out now!"

Kat moved across the room towards the man on the sofa. He had curled himself up into a ball, like a terrified child. She grabbed him by the arm and started to pull him off the sofa. She hadn't put the restraints onto his wrists yet. "Harriet, Let's go."

Stryder turned, and as she did, Kat realised that she was drawing her pistol. She aimed it directly at Kat's chest, then took a step back, so that to there was enough distance between them to prevent Kat from making a lunge for the weapon.

Their 'new friend' didn't want anything to do with this new development. He just stood next to Kat, his arm still half elevated by her hand, gently and calmly mumbling. Praying to himself, as he waited for the inevitable. To die.

Stryder had had enough. "Sit him down," she told Kat, then snapped at him something in Afrikaans that must have been the equivalent of "Sit down and shut up."

He sat down, silently onto the sofa.

Stryder turned to Kat. "I'm staying here. This," she said pointing with her pistol at the screens, "Is super important. It's not going out to a server in another location, it's all here. Understood?"

Kat had no idea what Stryder's revised agenda was, nor did she particularly care. If Stryder deemed it to be important, who was Kat to contradict her?

Stryder tuned back towards the table, holstered her pistol and went back to work, tapping away at the keyboard of the computer and the screen of her own datapad.

Kat made one last attempt. "Can't we just take some of this with us?"

Stryder didn't even look up. "No, it has to be done this way. Extracting him only gave us access to what is in his head, what he can remember or reconstruct, but this . . ." she indicated the equipment on the bench, in the room "This is a gold mine. It gives us all their files, all their planning, their resources, assets. I need to copy it before you fry it."

Kat immediately understood what she was being told, and was still formulating their best way to procced when she heard voices outside in the corridor. Considerable shouting in Arikanns. Where was Captain Maddox?

The best way for Kat to protect Stryder whilst she worked was to go out of the room and neutralise this new threat. And, do it quickly, before it came screaming in to get them. "I'm going out," Kat said in an urgent whisper. "Don't go anywhere until I get back. Do *you* understand me?" She checked the magazine was tight on her weapon.

Stryder briefly looked up from her datapad and gave the briefest of acknowledgements.

Kat put her AK21 into the crook of her elbow, and holding it at the 'port arms' position, opened the door with her left hand.

The lights were back on in the passageway and although the sound of voices was lounder to her right, near Maddox's position, her more immediate concern was the noises coming from their unprotected left. She decided to move down to the next intersection, that way there would be a weapon at each end of the passageway, protecting Stryder in the middle.

Kat closed the door behind her and started to run. After seven or eight paces, as she moved past another internal door, it suddenly opened outwards. The thud as it impacted into her was hard and fast, as if she'd walked into a moving vehicle, flinging Kat against the opposite wall. Momentarily stunned, her weapon was ripped out of her grip. It clattered against the wall, but was prevented from hitting the floor by its coiled lanyard.

There was yelling from both sides, from Kat, as she recovered her breath and composure and from her assailant. Before she could recover the assault rifle, he grabbed her and they fought like a scene from a fifth-grade playground. She tried to get her pistol out on her right thigh, but he had her in a solid hold, a bear hug, around her armpits. She was pinioned with her arms out at ninety degrees.

She tried to kick and buck herself free, then to head-butt him. He was doing the same. Both of them were shouting.

Her assailant stank. He had a week's stubble on his face and it was rough against Kat's face and neck as he squeezed and squeezed. He closed his eyes, snorting through his nose and he shouted out for help. He was a big man, middle-aged, solid. Strong from years of manual labour in the cultivation of the island.

Kat needed help too and called out for Stryder, but there was no response.

Kat wasn't entirely sure what the man was trying to

do. Did he want to kill her, or was he fighting to protect himself?

Kat called out again, "Harriet . . . Stryder!"

He responded by shifting his weight slightly and screaming at her even louder. That gave Kat a brief opportunity and she head-butted him again, trying to make contact with wherever she could. He responded by doing the same and Kat felt a sharp stinging in her right ear. His teeth were sinking into it. He was biting harder and harder. Her earlobe was in his mouth and he was starting to pull his head back.

She felt the blood immediately, warm and wet, splashing against the side of her cheek. He was in a frenzy, growling at her through the teeth clenched onto her ear, through blood, snot and saliva.

She managed to get her legs around his waist and tried to squeeze, but she could only just get her feet together. She felt the snorting from his nose move away from her face slightly, and the pain in the earlobe intensified, it was like a blowtorch being applied to the side of her head.

He stopped trying to bite off her ear. As his head moved back Kat managed to get her hands onto his head. She could see her own blood on his face, the mucus running from his nose and he fought to breathe through his blood and saliva filled mouth. He spat at her to empty it, trying to improve his own breathing. When her fingers reached his eyes, he squeezed her even harder, shaking his head and screaming as Kat began to get a good hold of his face and dig deeper with her thumbs. Now he tried to bite her fingers. Kat moved her right hand so she had her palm under his chin, then switched her left to just below the crown of his head and grabbed a fistful of his hair.

She tightened her legs around him, trying to keep him in one place, then managed to get her boots interlocked. At last, she could squeeze and push down with her legs at the same time as twisting up with her arms as hard as she could. She kept on turning as they both screamed at each other. He evidently didn't like it. He knew what she was trying to do, but fortunately for Kat, he wasn't able to do very much about it.

His neck finally went, though without the tell-tale crack. His grip released and he slumped down. There wasn't any noise coming from him now, no body jerking or spasms. He just went very still. Kat's hands were covered in blood, snot and saliva.

Her weapon was still attached to her via its lanyard. She picked it up and checked the magazine was still securely fitted, then started to move back towards Stryder's location. She stopped. She could hear firing again, and people screaming and shouting, in both English and what she still took to be Afrikaans or a locally evolved derivative. It was close, probably twenty, no more than thirty metres away.

Her hand went to her chewed ear. She didn't try to stop the bleeding, it would sort itself out. Kat remembered the mess Colonel Wood's boot had made of Stryder's nose back in Lunda-Luba, but you'd never know that now, as the cosmetic surgeons had worked their magic and restored her oh-so-beautiful features to their former glory. Kat was confident they would do the same for her ear. Having a VDM or visual-distinguishing-mark, really wasn't something she wanted to entertain. She recalled the instructors at OTA(F) advising against tattoos, body piercings, and other visible modifications, if the young Midshipmen didn't already have them, as some avenues of Fleet activity were not open to anyone with a VDM. Ironically most of those 'activities' involved the self-same clandestine crap that Kat hated and swore she'd never get involved with ever again, or at least not until the next time Commodore Finklemeyer manipulated her and secured her unwilling participation once again. Exactly like now!

But, more importantly, she simply didn't want a masticated ear! She also recalled some of the Senior NCO Instructors at OTA(F) who wore their battle scares like a badge of honour. That wasn't something Kat ever wanted either. Yes, she was proud of what she did as a career, but didn't need a cybernetic optical enhancement, a scarred cheek or forehead, nor a mangled ear to prove it!

She went back to the room with Stryder working

within. She tapped on the door. "Harriet, it's me. I'm coming in."

Maddox was still at the other end of the passage. When he heard Kat's voice he shouted "Come on, hurry up. Drag her freakin' arse out if you have to, we need to get out of here!"

He was right. If they didn't go soon, chances were, they would all end up dead.

Kat pushed the door open and Stryder was still standing over one of the laptop computers with her own datapad plugged into it and some other tech stuff. She looked over at the man on the sofa. He was sitting in exactly the same position she'd left him in, as if he was watching the two screens.

A small amount of blood was trickling from a hole in the front of his shirt, but it was the bullet-hole in his forehead that left her in no doubt. Blood was oozing from it. His head lolled back against the sofa. It had ballooned-out slightly, but the skin was keeping all the fragmented skull and brain in place. He definitely wouldn't be online ever again.

Without looking up at Kat, Stryder tapped frantically away at the keyboard. She said. "He tried to attack me, but he is happy now. The Angels of Light have given him tranquillity."

Kat looked at him again. He hadn't moved from where he'd been when she had left the room and there was certainly no look of tranquillity on his face. He hadn't attacked her. She had executed him!

Kat didn't know what she thought. *That certainly isn't part of the original plan, but do I actually care? It's probably part of that exclusive 'alternative brief' that only Stryder is apparently privy to.* Another burst of automatic weapons fire focused Kat back into the real world.

"Come on, we need to go. Now Harriet!"

"No," she shook her head. "I need a few more minutes."

The incendiary grenades were still on the table. One of Kat's mission tasks, unless Stryder was about to tell her that they had changed too, was to destroy anything that couldn't be recovered so hostile intelligence agencies didn't recover it instead.

Stryder stopped tapping away at the keyboard. "Okay, we can go," she said suddenly and immediately started to pack her tech away.

Kat went over to the sofa and pulled the body forward, letting him roll onto the floor. Picking up one end of the now empty sofa, she dragged it across the room, to lean it against the table of computers. Then she got the recyk waste bin, scattering its contents of mostly plastic and foil food wrappers across the table, before adding the rug from the floor, then a couple of chairs. She wanted anything and everything flammable to be near the incendiary grenades.

"Are you quite sure you're ready now?" Kat asked.

It was the first time the Intel Branch operative had looked up since Kat had returned to the room. She briefly studied the bloody mess on the side of Kat's head, then nodded her affirmation, "Yes, we can go."

Kat pulled the pin on the first device and positioned it on the table amongst the multiple display screens. Its red banding colour and INCEN stencilling clearly advising exactly what it did. When Kat removed her hand, the lever flew off and by the time the third one was placed the previous two were burning fiercely. Kat could feel the intense heat of the burning thermite on her face and through her clothes. She removed her back-pack and threw that onto the fire too. There was nothing in it she now needed, everything essential was on her belt or in her pockets. The room was quickly filling with the noxious black fumes of burning plastic and the sofa's cushioning foam.

Kat first, then Stryder, who already had her own backpack onto her shoulders, headed for the door. Kat opened it a few centimetres and called to Maddox. "Coming through, coming through."

He yelled back. "Shut up and run! Just freakin' run!"

Kat didn't look left or right, she ran for the opening that would take them back to the Great Hall.

Within a minute or two they were being helped out of

the recessed pit in the Great Hall's floor by Troopers Carter and Friel and by the time that three, maybe four, minutes had passed, they were nearing the mangled remains of the passageway's entrance doors. The steps up to the surface were only a few metres beyond.

Kat's eyes searched frantically for anyone blocking their way. She ran in a low stoop, trying to make as small a target as possible. Just before they reached the broken doors Kat slowed, allowing Stryder to get ahead of her.

She caught a brief glimpse of Maddox behind them, and another figure, possibly Corporal Perry, even further back. Bullets ricocheted of the chromed steel and neat stonework, or embedded themselves into the wooden planking. The 'Disciples' of the Angels of Light were firing on automatic, expending far too many rounds in a single burst, so making it difficult to control their aim.

Anna reached the doors and pushed the twisted metal frame aside. Stryder slid through it like a baseball player going for a base, not at all what Kat had expected from her.

Kat pushed through, so as not to block the gap for the others coming through behind her.

Nothing happened. Nobody followed.

Anna had already seen the reason why. "Man down, man down," she called.

Kat could see a shape on the ground about twenty metres back. Perry had already stopped beside Maddox and had her hand in his 'loop' and was trying to drag him down the passageway towards the doors. All of them wore a casualty recovery harness, a purpose made arrangement in padded nylon webbing that ran around the body and culminated in a loop between the shoulders by which a downed body could be dragged or hooked up to a VTOL copter's winch for a quick extraction. "Stay here. Don't move," Kat told Stryder. She could see from Intel Branch operative's expression that for once she was going to do exactly as she was told.

Sergeant Varko was now with Perry. Between them they hauled the Captain along. He was moaning and groaning like a drunk. "Shit, I'm down. I'm freakin' down.

No way."

A good sign. If he was talking, he was breathing.

Kat could see that the legs of his overalls were already sheened with blood, but that would have to wait for later. Number one priority was to get him, and the rest of the team out of this tunnel.

Stryder continued to remain silent. Her part of the mission was now effectively complete.

Finally, they were all at the foot of the stairs leading up to the surface, less Anna, who remained to cover their withdrawal.

Carter and Friel had already ascended the stairs and were now in position, amongst the large root 'fingers' of another banyan tree, only a short distance from the top of the steps, ready to provide covering fire as the others came up and out.

Kat was aware that they all needed to conserve ammunition, they most certainly didn't have the 'everlasting' magazines used in the movies and video games.

Varko had effortlessly assumed 'field command' of the operation and was busy issuing orders to Perry and the rest of the team via his comm-link. "Move back, get back to the Final RV." He then bent and pulled Maddox onto his shoulders, making the Captain give out a truly horrible half-scream, half-choking sound.

Trooper Carter in the first fire team and Sergeant Varko in the second, both carried combat stretchers, essentially a big nylon sheet with eight loop handles, four down each side, as part of their kit. As soon as Carter had reached the top of the steps he'd quickly pulled it out of his belt order and laid it out on the ground. Varko, who was now at the top of the steps and despite the added weight of Maddox, knelt and the Captain was gently rolled off of the Sergeant's shoulders and onto the sheet. Kat took Maddox's back-pack and chest rig that Perry silently passed to her.

Maddox was being secured onto the stretcher. Somehow, he was still conscious, but Kat knew he would soon go into shock.

They were about to lift him and move into better cover

when Perry said, 'Wait.'

She'd heard the ominous slurping noise in time with Maddox's breathing, meaning he probably had a sucking wound to his chest. Air was being sucked inside his chest cavity instead of going in through his nose and mouth. That would need sorting out quickly, otherwise he'd die. Kat was no med-tech but she knew there wasn't enough time to do that immediately. If they attempted it now, it was likely they'd all become casualties. It would have to wait until they got back to the relative cover of the Final RV.

Taking Maddox's hand, she placed it firmly on his chest. "Direct pressure, Nick" she told him. "You need to plug it up."

He remained sufficiently conscious and coherent to understand what he needed to do. Kat remembered the casualty treatment drills of her annual military refresher training and knew that they couldn't administer morphine to a chest wound, so he was going to have to take the pain. Morphine sulphate had remained the pain relief of choice for battlefield trauma for decades, but wasn't routinely administered for chest wounds as it caused instability in blood-flow and hypoventilation of the respiratory system. Trials with nebulised morphine in a battlefield environment were still ongoing, but none of them had the kit or the training for that right now.

As soon as Anna was up the steps and in position to provide covering fire, Perry extended the telescopic tubular poles to give the stretcher rigidity. With Perry at the front, Kat at the rear, they stood and started to move with Maddox as quickly as they could. Stryder, who now had her pistol drawn, followed along at Kat's heels, facing back towards the steps down to the Great Hall. Kat didn't look at what was going on behind her.

They reached a nearby cluster of banyan trees. Maddox's moans had been distorted by the jolting as they moved as quickly as a stretcher casualty ever permitted. They carried him further into the grove, finding cover behind several older trees with large, gnarled trunks. Somehow Maddox remained conscious, but was breathing noisily as they put the stretcher down.

Bright 'chemical' flames and billowing smoke were now ravaging the access tunnel, illuminating the area where the steps came up to ground level. It gave off more than enough light for Kat to see her own hands as they worked on saving Maddox. There was no need to worry about clearing his airway, but his hand had fallen from his chest. Kat put her own hand over the wound to form a seal. Hopefully, with his chest now airtight, normal breathing would return. Kat could see the anguish in his eyes. His throat spluttered blood as he coughed, fighting away the pain.

"What's it like? How bad is it? What's it like?" he mumbled. The Captain screwed up his face even more when Corporal Perry moved him. That was a good sign. He could still feel it, his senses hadn't given up. Not yet.

Perry finished checking him over. "No exit would."

Therefore, their priority was to plug the leaks, then to replace the fluid that had been lost. Kat watched as the Corporal grabbed the field dressing from Maddox's own belt kit and ribbed it open. Kat knew that you always used the casualties' own dressings, as you might need your own later. The outer packing was unmarked, so couldn't be traced back to any particular origin, be that manufacturer or nation state. The field-dressing itself was essentially a large, absorbent gauze pad, impregnated with a haemostatic power to help the blood coagulate, with a bandage and a pair of pins attached for holding it in-place. Its function was to block up the wound and stop the bleeding by the application of direct pressure. It hadn't really changed very much, less the chemical composition of the haemostatic powder, since its initial introduction and inclusion in a soldier's kit in the early twentieth century.

Another round had ripped through the muscle mass on Maddox's right thigh, like a butcher's blade slicing into a side of beef. He was losing blood fast. Perry started to cavity pack his wound.

The Captain was still breathing. Over and over he groaned, 'What's it like? How bad am I hit? What's it like?"

Kat looked down at him. He was covered in sweat.

Dust and sand were caked onto his face. "Don't worry, Nick," Kat said lightly, "It's nothing we can't fix." In training they were repeatedly told to never let a casualty see or hear your concern, 'always reassure the patient.'

Stryder was several paces away from Kat, watching the route they had just taken, her weapon out, held in a two handed-stance, pointing at the ground.

Kat half whispered, half shouted, "Harriet, come here."

She moved towards Kat.

"Put the heel of your hand over this hole when I take mine off. Okay?" Kat told her

Maddox was rapidly losing consciousness. Kat put her mouth close to his ear and said, "It's okay Nick, you can speak to me." There was no response. "Come on Nick, talk to me," she said again.

Perry pulled up Maddox's left sleeve to expose a fifteen-centimetre tubular bandage on his forearm. Underneath that was the cannula, already inserted into a vein before they had deployed onto the island. A bit of anti-coagulant was added into the cannula to stop the blood from clotting and that usually lasted for approximately twenty-four hours. The arm was a bit sore afterwards, but Kat knew it could save your life. She and Mike had seriously considered pre-mission cannulisation before their operation to extract Olga Stukanova from Nya Svealand, but had decided against it, essentially because it was a known 'special ops' identifier and that mission had needed to be totally deniable and untraceable. It made a lot of sense to pre-cannulate, as it was hard to find a vein to insert a cannula into when you've already starting to lose fluids, and especially when under enemy fire and in the dark!

Corporal Perry had finished packing out his thigh wound. Just covering that injury would have done little, as the muscle underneath would continue to bleed. By packing out the cavity the bullet had made, and thereby keeping direct pressure on the wound, it would now hopefully stop the bleeding. With that completed, he now needed fluid.

Maddox's breathing was becoming rapid and shallow,

which wasn't a good sign. Kat felt the pulse in his neck. Same problem, his heart was working overtime to circulate what fluid was remaining, around his body.

Occasional shots continued to be fired in their general direction, and at a range of no more than a hundred metres away, but all of Kat's attention was now focused on Maddox.

Perry spoke to Stryder. "Watch him, and tell me if his breathing starts to slow down. Got it?"

Stryder nodded.

Kat located the SLS canister from within Maddox's back pack, a clear plastic half-litre container. Sodium lactate solution boosted plasma-volume by increasing osmotic pressure. She ripped it from its plastic wrapper, then bit off the protective cap to expose the membrane beneath. Hygiene was a secondary issue. Infection could be sorted out in hospital. Keeping him alive to get to a hospital was now their priority.

Pulling out the IV set, she attached it to the canister. Kat inserted the connector into the self-sealing membrane in the neck of the plastic SLS canister, then released the screw clamp. She took off the sterile end-cap and watched as gravity ran the fluid down the line. It splashed out onto Maddox's face. He didn't react. Not a good sign. Kat closed the screw clamp to stop the flow. A few air bubbles in the line really wasn't ideal, but it wasn't critical either. Getting the fluid into him was.

There was another burst of small-arms fire from the vicinity of the steps. And, for the first time, their team who were now all amongst the surrounding trees, returned the fire.

Kat could hear Sergeant Varko giving orders. He had remained several metres away, waiting whilst they sorted Maddox out. "Roni, sitrep. How much longer until we can get out of here?" he asked Perry.

"Two or three minutes. I need everyone's SLS canister," the Corporal said, getting to her feet. "Connect him up, ma'am."

As Perry moved away to collect the medical supplies, Kat removed the end cap of the cannula in Maddox's arm and connected the IV set into it.

Stryder was still covering the chest wound. Kat could hear her breathing quickly in her ear as she leant over Maddox. 'Severn, listen to me. Leave them to it. We don't have time for any of this crap, we need to go."

Kat ignored Stryder and carried on working on the Captain, gently squeezing the canister to get the fluid into him.

Stryder whispered again, a bit more urgently 'Come on, we need to go now. Remember, they're all expendable . . . this is what they get paid for."

Maddox had to be dangerously low on fluids, but somehow he still remained conscious.

"Harriet, give me your SLS canister, quick," Kat said.

Stryder used her free hand to slip her back-pack straps off her shoulders to get to it.

The first fluid canister was already empty. Kat turned off the IV line with its screw clamp. Stryder had the new canister in her hand.

"Open it," Kat instructed.

She heard her ripping of plastic, as Stryder tore apart the sterile outer bag as Kat disconnected the empty canister. Stryder handed over the new one.

There was another exchange of automatic weapon-fire that seemed to be closer than before.

Corporal Perry, now with several fluid canisters pushed down the front of her shipsuit, was panting hard as she collapsed down on the floor next to Kat, Stryder and Maddox. Kat continued to connected the new SLS canister Stryder had provided into the IV set and opened up the screw clamp.

Perry got onto her knees and was studying Maddox. All of a sudden she shouted, "No. For fucks sake!" and leaned over, grabbing Struder's hand and lifting it.

There was a hiss, like a rush of air escaping from the valve of a car tyre and a fine geyser of blood sprayed in all directions. One of the bullets must have pierced his lung, so as he breathed in, the oxygen was escaping from his lungs and going into the chest cavity. The pressure had built up so much in his chest that his lungs hadn't been able to expand and his heart wasn't functioning properly. That was why Stryder had to 'watch and listen,' because the pressure on his heart and lungs would make him breathe much slower that he now needed to.

Perry was instantly angry. She was still gripping the back of Stryder's hand.

"You need to freakin' watch him!" Perry told her again.

Stryder said nothing as the air-hiss and blood spray subsided. Then, very calmly she reminded Perry who was the boss. "Let go of my arm, Corporal. You do your job. And, let me do mine."

Perry placed Stryder's hand back over the chest wound. Somehow, Maddox was still conscious, but losing blood internally. The Corporal got right up to his face. "Show me you can hear me Nick, anything, show me." There was no reply. "We're going to move you. Hang in there. Not long before we'll be out of here."

All she got was a low moan by way of reply, but it was better than nothing.

Perry turned him partially over, then checked the thigh dressing. Blood had started to ooze from the wound and through the dressing.

Styder looked directly at Kat. Her annoyance of their situation, if not necessarily any particular individual, was plain to see.

The other team members were starting to gather around them. All were out of breath, perhaps confused as to what had happened.

"Is everyone here?" Sergeant Varko asked aloud, then had them number off. "Is he ready to go?"

Corporal Perry, still checking the casualty over, said "I think we're about to find out." Using a surgical clip from her medical kit she fixed Maddox's tongue to his bottom lip. The Captain was out of it and couldn't feel anything. The danger was that in his semi-unconscious state, his tongue might roll back and block his airway.

Kat turned to Stryder as the team quickly sorted out

their own kit out for the next phase, then policed their immediate location for any discarded medical wrappings and empty canisters. She whispered into her ear. "Our best chance is to stay with this team. If you want to go it alone, that's your call, your prerogative, but leave all your nonessential kit with them, they can take it back."

The look on Stryder's face said she already knew they had no realistic alternative, despite her brave words. Stryder wasn't about to go anywhere alone, she didn't have the necessary skill-set. She needed Kat, if not the rest of the team, as back-up.

Perry moved Stryder's hand, then placed one of the opened plastic-backed dressing wrappers over the chest wound to get a better seal and instructed Stryder, "Keep your hand firmly on that . . . ma'am. Continue to check his breathing"

The team then picked up the casualty on the stretcher. Perry and Trooper Friel were in the rear positions. Perry kept the canister of fluids elevated for it to run freely by holding its suspension loop in her teeth.

This certainly wasn't going to be anything like a 'tactical' move to the extraction, it was simply a case of getting there as fast as they possibly could with a stretcher casualty. Kat didn't know what was going on behind them at the subterranean complex and honestly didn't actually care, she just wanted to be away from here as quickly as possible.

They moved off, and Kat pushed the butt of her weapon into her shoulder, then look up a position approximately ten metres out from the stretcher party, in a patrolling over-watch that covered their right flank. Sergeant Varko was out doing the same on their left.

After fifteen minutes of moving through the cultivated cereal crop and more tall trees, they paused to momentarily rest. Trooper Carter moved forward, covered by Friel, to drag a tarpaulin from something ahead.

Kat moved nearer to take a closer look at what had been concealed. She immediately recognised it. It was the open-topped utility vehicle that she'd originally seen

Beelzebub and Morax arrive in during their first visit to the island.

"Where'd you find this?" she asked one of the Troopers.

"This afternoon, when we were looking for the island's power supply. It was down in its own underground parking garage. It's a bit underpowered, but certainly better than walking," Friel told her with a grin.

Kat went back to Maddox. Perry was attending him again and had told Stryder she could remove her hand. Kat motioned for Stryder to step away, to give Perry more space.

When Stryder got nearer, she said "We need to get going," almost hissing at Kat through clenched teeth,

Kat pointed at the utility vehicle. The tail gate was fully open and they were frantically folding away the rear seats and loading up equipment to make a suitable space for their Captain. Looking back, Kat noticed that the rest of the island remained dark. The main power supply was still out, the flames in the access tunnel were no longer visible and it looked like they hadn't been pursued by anyone.

Friel motioned for Kat and Stryder to get into the vehicle. Sergeant Varko got into the front, passenger side, next to Anna who was getting herself comfy behind the wheel.

Varko turned in his seat, "As soon as Perry is ready, we'll move to the Extraction RV on the beach," he told Kat and Stryder. "Unless you'd like to get out and walk home, ma'am?" The comment was directed firmly at Styder, not at Kat.

As they sat waiting in the darkness, Anna pulled down her goggles from atop her head, selecting the night-vision application on the function stud. She moved her head from side-to-side, letting her eyes adjust to wearing them. There was a tension in the air. They all knew that they needed to get moving.

Kat didn't talk to Stryder. After a wait of several minutes, and Stryder's ever growing and obvious impatience, Perry and Carter lifted Maddox on-board and closed up the trail-gate. Anna then put the vehicle into 'drive' and manoeuvred it across the island, trying to keep to existing tracks and trails.

Progress was slow and Stryder took that as being her cue to get the datapad out. To an observer the datapad's screen was inactive, but with the right application in her own goggles, Stryder could see everything she needed. After a few seconds she was typing away again on the display screen. Despite the obvious concentration, being sweaty, dirty and having had her nose broken, she still somehow managed to look glamorous.

Kat accessed the same function in her own googles and the datapad display showed her maps, diagrams and text. It was in something other than usual Latin alphabetical characters of most European languages and meant nothing to her. Stryder's well-manicured nails were furiously tapping away at it.

They drove slowly, the vehicle's six oversized wheels lumbering across the sandy soil. Although decidedly underpowered for its size, it was much better than being on foot. On foot, and hauling a stretcher laden with an unconscious casualty. Eventually they stopped.

Although the vehicle's propulsion unit was idling, the only discernible noises were from Stryder's nails continuously tapping away on the datapad's display, her mumblings in whatever language it was that she was translating, and the waves rolling in on the nearby beach.

A beeping noise unexpectedly came from Stryder's datapad.

"Damn it," she muttered, maybe the battery was running low.

Then there was suddenly a commotion coming from the rear of the vehicle. Perry began working hard on Maddox, yelling at him, trying to get a response. Silence was obviously no longer an option, not now, as she fought to keep him alive.

Sergeant Varko looked at his watch. After about five minutes of waiting he nodded to Carter. The Trooper stood, then activated an IR Firefly, sticking it to the top of the vehicle's roll-bar with its integral magnet. It emitted an infra-red strobe that was invisible to the naked human eye, but wouldn't be to someone with the right filter selected within their helmet's visor. Someone like an 'on-station' VTOL copter pilot.

Almost instantly Kat started to hear a deep throbbing noise far away in the distance, but less than a minute later the sky was filled with the steady, ponderous beat of the incoming UH-11 Albatross, the largest VTOL aircraft in the Fleet's inventory, their equivalent of the Land Force's Condor. From where it had come from Kat didn't know. Commodore Finklemeyer had somehow pulled multiple strings to get an Albatross equipped asset into their vicinity so quickly. Perhaps the storm had conveniently necessitated an unscheduled port-call of just such an asset.

The differences between and Albatross and a Condor was minimal, and apart from the obvious paint finish, folding sections to reduce its overall size when packed into an assault carrier's hanger deck and undercarriage to accommodate the ever-changing roll and pitch of a ship's flight deck, there weren't many other easily discernible variances.

The noise became deafening as the pilot swung the aircraft through one-eighty-degree arc right in front of them, before setting it down, orientating the aircraft so the vehicle could drive straight up its rear ramp. Sand and shell fragments clattered against the windscreen, bodywork and occupants of the vehicle as it rocked under the downwash of the Albatross's ducted turbo fans. The pilot would be using a FLiR filter (a) to see the IR Firefly's strobe beacon, and (b) to enable him to see through all the swirling dust and sand that the turbo-fans were throwing up.

A few seconds later a figure loomed out of the dust storm, bent double. He, or she, flashed a green light twice at them and Anna commented, 'That's it, let's go."

The vehicle edged forward. They drove for several metres, into the maelstrom of swirling sand, before things started to calm down. Blue cylume sticks glowed around the open ramp and the interior of the cargo bay was bathed in red light.

The Load Master, wearing non-descript, non-standard body-armour and goggles, was beckoning the vehicle urgently forward him with cylume sticks held aloft in both his hands. They didn't need any encouragement!

The six-wheeled utility vehicle bumped up and onto the VTOL copter's ramp as if they were driving onto a ferry. Another crewmember then signalled for them to stop.

As soon as the rear of the vehicle had cleared the ramp, Kat felt the aircraft lift off its hydraulic suspension. Moments later they were in a low hover.

The Albatross swayed to the left and right as the pilot adjusted for the increase in load-weight whilst the Load Master lashed down the vehicle with purpose-made clamps that tightened quickly around each wheel of the vehicle.

Hovering no more than twenty metres off the beach, Kat felt the nose of the Albatross dip down as they started to move forward, then bank hard over to the right as they gained speed.

Total mayhem had already erupted inside the aircraft's cargo bay. The team spilled from the vehicle, shouting at the Load Master to give them 'white light.' He gave the activation command and it was instantaneously like being on a floodlit sports pitch.

Kat hadn't studied the aircraft's exterior, but her quick assessment of the now illuminated cargo-bay, and therefore presumably the rest of the aircraft, established it was devoid of anything that identified it as belonging to the ABCANZ Federation. Even the flight-gear of the crew was devoid of the usual name, rank and aviation branch identifiers.

In the 'white light,' the rear space of the appropriated utility vehicle now looked like the interior of a medieval slaughterhouse. The Captain was still on his back and Perry had cut-away more of his clothing to expose a very messy chest wound. His blood was just about everywhere.

Anna ran over to the Load Master who was now up by

the copter's rear ramp, doing his checks to confirm that it was securely closed. She shouted as loudly as she could and pointed at the rear vehicle. "Trauma pack. We need the trauma pack!"

The Load Master took one look towards the vehicle, saw the blood splatter and spoke rapidly into the voice pick-up of his earpiece.

Everyone had a job to do. Kat's was simply to stay out of the way. She left Stryder sitting in the back of the vehicle, still consumed by the datapad's display. Kat moved towards the front of the VTOL copter. She knew where the rations and drinks should normally be stowed, so if nothing else, she could act as the resident 'tea lady!'

As she moved towards the front of the cargo bay, she met another member of the Albatross's crew, bringing a pair of oversized black holdall bags. Kat stepped aside to let him pass, then watched as Perry helped him open the first bag and begin removing the contents.

Stryder suddenly appeared next to Kat, her precious datapad and its power cable clutched in her hands. She was shouting at the crewman "Power. I need power." She was trying to get his attention over the noise of the aircraft's engines.

He went to push her aside, yelling, "Not now, keep out of the freakin' way!"

"No," she shook her head angrily and put her hand on him. "I need power!"

He shouted something back at her. Kat didn't know what because he was now facing away from her, but he was pointing towards the front of the cargo bay.

Stryder nodded, then moved quickly past Kat towards the cockpit, fully focused on nothing but her continued analysis of the recovered data. Kat followed, also heading for the bulkhead behind the cockpit.

Releasing one of the secured flasks, Kat untwisted the cap. Coffee had never smelt so good.

As Kat walked back, past the vehicle, coffee flask in hand, she could hear them, even above the noise of the aircraft, shouting with frustration. Two new drip lines were being held up and a circle of sweaty, dusty and bloodstained faces were frantically working on stabilising Maddox.

Corporal Perry looked as if she was in full control, as usual. She was holding Maddox's jaw open, breathing into his mouth. The 'safety pin' on the unpacked defibrillation kit was still in place. Kat was now close enough to see Maddox's chest rise. Trooper Friel had his hands over the chest wound, ready to depressurise. Once Perry had finished inflating his lungs a few times she shouted. "Go!" and Friel started cardiac compressions. "One and two and three."

There was obviously no pulse and Maddox wasn't breathing. He was technically dead. They were filling him up with oxygen by breathing into his mouth, then pumping his heart for him, whilst simultaneously trying to make sure no more fluid escaped from any of the numerous holes that he had in him.

They were all way too busy to drink coffee. Acutely aware she had nothing useful to contribute Kat pulled up her left sleeve and peeled back the tubular bandage. Carefully she removed the surgical-tape holding the cannula in place, then pulled it out, pressing down on the puncture wound with her thumb until it clotted.

She looked around for Styder. The Intelligence Branch operative was now sitting near to where the coffee flasks were stowed. She'd found the cargo bay's bank of power points and had plugged the universal power cord in. Her fingers were now dancing frantically back over the datapad's display again.

Turning away, Kat looked at the small, fuselage-mounted display screen. The location map showed that they were heading west, out into the Bay of Bengal, but the external image feed added nothing, showing only a black sky and sea.

There was a bank of several wheeled 'booster battery' packs secured right across the first third of the cargo bay, extending the aircraft's range. This was evidently a 'direct flight,' but to where exactly . . . that remained unclear.

Despite the recent reinforcing to the *Bella*'s front hold hatches, she couldn't take an aircraft of this size and weight, and anyway the UH-27 Vulture that had inserted them onto the island was likely occupying that space already. Kat's best guess was that this Albatross was heading directly for ROSP 4-Foxtrot-6, which most certainly could accommodate her. They could then wait. Wait until the *Fires of Beltane* arrived, to return the platform's own VTOL aircraft, exchanging it for Kat, Anna and Sergeant Varko.

Kat took a sip from her coffee. Although she stared at the small display screen, she didn't actually register any of the displayed data on altitude, speed or direction of travel. Her mind had started to wander, she began to doze, only to be suddenly pulled from her daydreams by a despairing shout.

"For fuck's sake!" The Trooper who had been administering cardiac compressions to Maddox's prone body was leaning back, telling Kat everything she needed know.

Kat went back to staring at the display. This time she processed the displayed data. They were flying low and fast over the water. The visual still didn't show anything other than 'black' in any direction. Her ear was throbbing. Kat reached up to it and touched the mangled lobe. The pain made her wince. Hopefully they'd be able to tidy it up, but it really didn't matter. Hardly a priority right now. She was alive and that was all that mattered.

"He's dead," Kat told Stryder.

Nothing.

"Harriet, Maddox is dead," Kat repeated.

She carried on tapping at the display. She didn't even look up to see Kat offering her the flask of coffee.

Kat tapped Stryder's foot with her own boot. "Harriet . . . Captain Maddox is dead."

Stryder finally turned her eyes towards Kat and said, "Oh, okay," then looked straight back down and carried on with her work.

Kat looked down at the dark, dried blood covering Stryder's hands. Maddox's blood. Stryder didn't seem to notice or care.

If it hadn't been for Stryder's deception, not telling them what the full extent of her mission really was, then maybe Maddox would still be alive?

Corporal Perry and the rest of the team were now sitting in solemn silence, either lost in their own thoughts or busy opening flasks and Individual Field Rations. Their Captain hadn't been moved.

The only exception was Stryder, who remained completely oblivious to her surrounding and carried on, relentlessly scrolling through, then frantically tapping away, at the screen of her datapad.

They were all doing what they got paid for. This wasn't like the movies . . . Special Operations didn't always go to plan . . . as Kat knew only too well.

She sat down again, put her feet up and took another sip of the coffee, content to let her mind wander.

Eventually Kat watched the outline of ROSP 4-Foxtrot-6 draw nearer in the dawn sky on the flight-status's display monitor. She'd been angrily reflecting on just what exactly it was that she was doing. *Why am I here? Why I am I playing these ridiculous 'games' again. Commodore Finklemeyer, Colonel Wood, Harriet Stryder, just how exactly do they all sleep at night? How do they remember all the multiple lies they tell, the complex web of deceit and deception they all spin? How? Who? Why? They can keep it, this duplicitous world of subterfuge. My life is already complicated enough, I certainly don't need to add the clandestine antics that you green and grey-slime operatives so evidently get some kind of thrill from!* Kat remembered when 'The Fink' had asked her to join his team, several years back, when she'd still been a lowly Ensign, during her first year out of OTA(F). Her answer remained the same now as it had been back then. A most definite, categorical 'no way, not then, not now!'

*   *   *

Showered, and wearing a new shipsuit, that still showed the fold lines from being in its original packaging, and devoid of any rank, name or branch identifier, Kat now sat in the ROSP Commander's day cabin. The 'waiting for call to begin' screen, incorporating the logo depicting the 'all seeing eye and sword' insignia and purple branch colour of the Fleet's intelligence directorate, suddenly changed to show Commodore Finkelmeyer seated in an office. An office Kat had often wished she wasn't so familiar with for someone of such a lowly rank.

"Good morning, Commodore,' Kat said, paying the required respects, trying not to show any frustration, anger or any other emotion to her superior.

"And to you Lieutenant," he said, looking up from the multitude of documents arrayed across the desk. "Although it is still evening here. Shall we get this over with? Be advised, copies of this communication are not permissible under any circumstances and I need you to confirm your HI is not operating. I know this it is an ELFI transmission, Lieutenant, but this communication is to be considered *Top Secret* and is intended for your ears and eyes only. Is that completely clear?"

"Yes, sir," Kat said. "I confirm my HI is not present or operating. What should I tell my team?" Kat asked him.

"Nothing. You tell them nothing. I will be speaking with each of them, individually, immediately after this call, and under the same security classification, and also using Encrypted Life-Feed Imagery. You will therefore, not interact with any of them, in any way, until I have spoken with Captain Sykes, and then with Commander Gillan and Ensign Steiger, when they arrive later today. Is that clear Lieutenant?"

"Yes, sir. Crystal."

"Obviously, I have now spoken with my European Union counterpart, Konteradmiral Voss, and we have reached an agreement. This is the official narrative: The *Fires of Beltane* is a merchant vessel, that although contracted to ABCANZ Federation's Fleet Command, has been undertaking scientific research in the Indian Ocean.

Jensen Gillan is her documented civilian master and commander. Yes, there are a small number of ABCANZ Military personnel currently on-board her, acting as Liaison Officers, but you Lieutenant, are not listed as being amongst them. Are you with me so far?"

"Yes sir," Kat said. No surprises there, he was just reiterating the previously issued 'official' line, although her omission from the list of Fleet personnel was a new bit of detail.

"Very few individuals within the European Union's naval assets have had any interaction with the merchant vessel known as the *Fires of Beltane*, and those that have will be briefed that she was conducting scientific research, as per the detail within her official contract with our own military," Finkelmeyer continued talking. "Even fewer of their personnel, probably not more than a dozen, know that you are actually on-board and it will remain that way. Those individuals who do know will be 'spoken to' by the Konteradmiral's senior staff, if not the Admiral himself, being duly advised that discussing any element of what has transpired in the last seventy-two hours will be considered a career, if not life, terminating transgression."

Kat nodded, confirming her understanding of what the Commodore was now telling her.

"The unfortunate events regarding the loss the Ro-Pax vessel known as the *Varuna Ratnaker*, including her crew and passengers, will be put down as a tragic accident, caused by an unusually high-energy tropical storm. A storm that has sunk several other vessels, albeit much smaller, but has also done considerable damage ashore. The Indian authorities have found no survivors from the *Varuna Ratnaker* and due to the abnormal atmospheric conditions created by the tropical storm, no satellite or mobile communication were possible, and therefore no civilian calls were made from or to said ship, advising the wider world she had been taken over by extremists. I know from reading your most comprehensive 'After Action Review' that the *Fires of Beltane*'s bridge team had a brief exchange with the *Varuna Ratnaker* using VHF communications at short range, but apart from the *Fire of Beltane*'s signal log, which will be 'modified,' there are no other records of any communication to or from the said vessel."

Kat continued to say nothing. Her conscience was clear, she wasn't responsible for the thousands of souls lost on the *Varuna Ratnaker*, that fact had been established, but using the storm as a 'cover-story' somehow didn't sit right with her.

"I am sure there will be an official search, and no doubt numerous maritime salvage experts will speculate as to what might have happened when the wreck is eventually located and surveyed, but as that is likely to be years away, any involvement by the *Fires of Beltane*, or you, Lieutenant, is fully deniable."

"Yes, sir," Kat said, not really knowing what else to respond with.

"Intelligence recovered from the recent sortie onto North Sentinel is still being analysed, but as the island settlement was illegal, any survivors that may surface have got rather a lot of explaining to do on that front before any accusations they might want level at others will be given credibility. And, they need to tread very carefully, as whatever they say will likely incriminate them, thereby adding 'terrorism' to the charges already stacked against them. A crime that has a 'capital' sentence in that part of the world, I do believe."

"I understand, sir."

"Good. Not one hundred percent tidy, but probably as good as it's going to get for now. I'll get my people working on tidying up any loose ends."

"Yes, sir."

"I don't think there's anything else Lieutenant. I believe you have some leave coming up . . . although you've only been away a few months, and you might want to get that ear sorted out . . . and then I think we need to get yourself onto a Principal Warfare Officers' course. Your Warfare Systems Branch training has held you in good stead so far, when commanding small patrol ships, but you can't command anything bigger, like a corvette or a frigate, until you have that course under your belt, and even General Hanna can't bend the rules on this occasion. Your Fleet career can't develop until that's completed."

"I understand, sir . . . and thank you, sir. Did you see my comments about Captain Maddox's unfortunate death and Captain Stryder's conduct when on North Sentinel in my AAR too, sir?" Kat asked the Director of Fleet Intelligence.

"I did indeed, and Maddox's death is most unfortunate. He was an accomplished and decorated Special Operations soldier. As for Stryder, once again, her conduct causes me much concern. However, if I challenge her, or escalate it to others, then the North Sentinel mission becomes known to a wider audience. For now, I choose not to do anything about Stryder, as I want to *minimise* who knows about our involvement in these events, not expand. However, that does not mean it will always stay like that, but it will, for now at least."

Closing pleasantries exchanged. the Commodore ended the call and the display screen when black.

Fleet Lieutenant Kat Severn sat silently in the partial darkness of the Commander's Day Cabin of ROSP 4-Foxtrot-6 and reflected on what the Commodore had just told her. He'd cleaned up her mess . . . again . . . and yet he evidently wanted her around, as she apparently still had a career in the Fleet, subject to her completing the right career and promotion courses. No obvious evidence of General Hanna or her Grandpa Jim manipulating events from the sidelines this time, but Kat wasn't naive anymore. She couldn't recall a previous encounter when those three weren't secretly colluding and conspiring with each other over her future in the Fleet.

So . . . what now . . . where next?

GLOSSARY OF TERMS

1st Fleet — The ABCANZ Fleet that operates in the waters of the North Atlantic, including the Caribbean.

2nd Fleet — The ABCANZ Fleet that operates in the waters of the North Pacific.

3rd Fleet — The ABCANZ Fleet that operates in the waters of the South Atlantic.

4th Fleet — The ABCANZ Fleet that operates in the waters of the Indian Ocean.

5th Fleet — The ABCANZ Fleet that operates in the 'European' waters of the Baltic, Black, Mediterranean, North and Norwegian Seas.

6th Fleet — The ABCANZ Fleet that operates in the waters of the South Pacific.

127mm — The standard calibre of the guns mounted on most ABCANZ Fleet vessels, usually turret mounted, firing a 21kg shell over 25 kilometres.

AAR — After Action Review.

ABCANZ Federation — The Federal alliance formed by the United States, Britain, Canada, Australia and New Zealand in the latter years of the war.

ABCANZ Fleet — The Maritime (Navy) component of the ABCANZ military.

ABCANZ Land Forces — The Land (Army) component of the ABCANZ military.

Administration Branch (L) — Both the British and the US Army had appointed Paymaster Generals during times of conflict, but it was not until 1816 that the US Army appointed permanent military pay staff to each battalion. (The British continued to use civilian pay staff until the establishment of the Army Pay Corps in 1878). The appointment of Adjutant Generals followed a similar path, but their original duties have little resemblance to the modern, unit-level personnel administration. Their insignia is a pair of crossed feather quill pens, over which is the elongated diamond of US Army Finance. The branch colour is light green. 'Defendere et Ministrare' (Defend and Serve)

The Land Force's Chaplains Branch (a sub-branch of the Administration Branch) traces its origins back to 1791 and the appointment of the first US Army chaplain by Congress. (British regiments had traditionally appointed civilian chaplains and it was not formalised as a military position until a Royal Warrant dated 1796). The Chaplain's insignia is an open book of scripture resting on a pair of olive branches, over which is placed a shepherd's crook, signifying the 'tending of their flock.' The branch identifying colour is violet. 'Potentia Vera Didei' (The Power of True Faith)

Administration Branch (F)   The ABCANZ Fleet's Administration Branch, often know as clerks or 'writers,' from a time when most seamen were not literate, are responsible for the pay, welfare and career management of their assigned Officers and Enlisted personnel. Their origin goes back to the earliest days of the Royal Navy, with senior administration personnel being referred to as captain's clerk, the bursar, the purser and the paymaster. (The US Navy formalised this provision for administrative 'yeoman' in 1794). The Fleet's Administration branch insignia, motto and colour is the same as the Administration branch of the Land Forces.

The Fleet's Chaplains Branch (a sub-branch of the Administration Branch) of the ABCANZ Fleet traces its origins back to 1626 when King Charles I ordered that Chaplains should sail on all ships of his naval fleet, with public worship being made mandatory in 1653. (The US Navy Chaplain's Corps was established in 1775). The Fleet's Chaplain's Branch insignia, motto and identifying colour is the same as the Land Forces Chaplain's Branch.

Admiralty Staff / Command (F) The Fleet's Admiralty Staff traces its origins back to 1916 with the establishment of the US Navy's Office of the Chief of Naval Operations in Washington DC. This became the senior command, operational planning, policy and strategy department within the US Navy. This was emulated a year later by the Royal Navy. The Fleet's Admiralty Staff branch insignia, motto and colour is the same as the General Staff branch of the Land Forces. The same insignia is also worn by all Fleet officers assuming a 'command' appointment, be that of a ship, a flotilla, a fleet, or a shore establishment.

Afrikaner — A South African ethnic group descended from predominantly Dutch settlers first arriving at the Cape of Good Hope in the 17th and 18th centuries

Agri-farmers — Agricultural (crop growing) farms and their associated work force.

Ahab — An Anti-Ship Missile. Small and relatively cheap. More commonly used for defensive purposes than offensive. Often seen on defensively equipped merchant ships, but rarely used by legitimate naval forces due to its short range.

AK12 — An old Russian Assault Rifle. The 3rd Generation of the ubiquitous 1947 'AK47' Kalashnikov, ungraded in 1974 as the AK74, the AK12 was the 2012 enhanced model. Although old, hundreds of thousands were manufactured during the war and are still in abundance, especially in Africa and Asia.

AK21 — Later version of AK12

AMAP — Advanced Modular Armour Protection. Utilising bonded layers of high-hardened steel, white titanium, aluminium-titanium alloy and nano-crystalline ceramic to provide relatively lightweight armour with impressive ballistic protection.

Andaman Islands — An island archipelago in the north-eastern Indian Ocean about 130 km southwest of the coast of Myanmar's Ayeyarwady Region.

Andrac — An EU based manufacturer of high-quality, tech-enabled, armoured battle suits.

Annapolis — A prosperous maritime city district of Nu New England situated on Chesapeake Bay. Home of the Fleet's Officer Training Academy OTA(F) and the National Security Agency (NSA). Located in the former state of Maryland. Population of half a million. 72% are white, 15% black and 6% Hispanic.

APFSDS — Armour-piercing fin-stabilized discarding sabot, long dart penetrator, or simply dart ammunition, is a type of kinetic energy penetrator ammunition.

Arab League — Also known as LAS, or the League of Arab States. A large, post war Muslim state extending across North Africa and the Middle East. From the former countries of Morocco in the west, to Oman in the East. Remains heavily contaminated in the Suez, Palestine and Kuwait Bay regions.

Armoured Branch (L) — The Land Force's Armoured Branch, traces its origins back to 1658 and the establishment of the 1st (His Majesty's Own) Troop of Horse Guards, formed from the followers of King Charles II whilst he was in exile in the Netherlands. (The first US Cavalry formation was authorised by Congress in 1776). The Armoured insignia is a pair of crossed swords, each held by an armoured gauntlet, representing their knightly and subsequently cavalry origins. Behind the swords is a modern weapon sight. The branch identifying colour is yellow. 'Vires et Honores' (Strength and Honour)

Artillery Branch (L) — The Land Force's Artillery Branch traces its origins back to 1716 and the establishment of the Royal Regiment of Artillery at Woolwich, near London. (The first US Artillery formations were authorised by congress in 1775). The Artillery insignia is a pair of traditional crossed cannons over which is a single, more modern, missile. The branch identifying colour is red. The motto refers to their duty to be in action wherever needed. Quo Fas et Gloria Ducunt' (Where right (sacred duty) and glory lead)

ASM — Anti-Ship-Missile.

Aviation Branch (L) — The Land Force's Aviation Branch traces its origins back to 1912 and the establishment of the Royal Flying Corps at Farnborough, England. This would become the Royal Air Force in 1918. (The US Army established their Army Air Service in 1918). The Aviation Branch insignia is a pair of wings with a Roman Gladius sword between. The sword points down, signifying the strike is delivered from above. The branch identifying colour is sky blue. 'Per Ardua ad Astra' (Through Adversity to the Stars)

Aviation Branch (F)   The Fleet's Aviation Branch traces its origins back to 1910, when the Royal Navy and the US Navy both begin experimenting with aircraft. The Royal Navy Air Service was established in 1914 and the first dedicated US Navy Aviation facility opened in 1917. The Fleet's Aviation branch insignia, motto and colour is the same as the Aviation branch of the Land Forces.

baht   The official currency of Thailand.

Bali   Is one of the many islands that make up the Pancasila Republic, with Java to the west and Lombok to the east. Beginning in the 1960 and 70s, tourism has continued to grow, making it one of south-east Asia/Australia's most popular tourist destinations.

barf-bag   A small bag commonly provided to passengers on board airplanes and boats to collect and contain vomit in the event of motion sickness.

Banyan Tree   A member of the fig family with extensive exposed roots. National tree of India. Common throughout India and southeast Asia.

Beltane   An ancient festival held halfway between the spring equinox and the summer solstice. Special bonfires were lit and their flames, smoke and ashes were deemed to have protective powers.

Berserker   A Viking warrior. The name of a Fast-Attack Corvette (K101) in the ABCANZ 1st (North Atlantic) Fleet.

Biome   A distinct bio-geographical zone, with distinct vegetation, climate, weather and animal life,

Black Swan City   The name given to the expansion of the Perth metropolitan area in Western Australia along the Swan Coastal Plain and inland along the Swan River. Population of three million.

Branch-of-Service   Both Fleet and Land Forces are broken down into fifteen separate departments or branches.

Fleet	Land Force	Identifier
Administration	Administration	Light Green
Aviation	Aviation	Sky Blue
CBRN	CBRN	Cinnamon Brown
Chaplains	Chaplains	Violet
Command Appointment	General Staff	Crimson
Communications	Communications	Dark Blue

Electrical and Mechanical	Electrical and Mechanical	Pewter Grey
Fleet Intelligence	Intelligence	Purple
Legal & Justice	Legal and Justice	Orange
Logistics	Logistics	Cobalt Blue
Medical	Medical	Raspberry
Musicians	Musicians	White
Port Services	Combat Engineering	Black
Science and Tech	Science and Tech	Dark Teal
Special Operations	Infantry	Dark Green
Veterinary	Veterinary	Chartreuse Yellow
Warfare Systems	Armour	Yellow
Weapon Systems	Artillery	Red

Branch Identifier Flash   With rank insignia being displayed only on the right upper arm, and the branch of service coloured identifier stripe adorning the left, it was necessary to be able to identify an officer from and enlisted serviceman if approaching from the left side, so the correct compliments could be paid. The adopted stripes, with just the 'diamond jack' on the left upper arm are used on combat armour, but are displayed on both upper arms of Number 1, Ceremonial and Mess dress, with the rank and branch insignia embroidered onto them centrally. They are also continued along the outside seams of the white breeches of Number 1 dress. On Number 2 dress a coloured lanyard in the branch colour is used around the left shoulder. On shipsuits the same concept as combat armour is used.

Enlisted   Officer   Flag / General

Campbell Bay   Also known as Tenlaa, is the largest conurbation on the island of Great Nicobar. (Population of 5,000)

Cape Town   Capital city of the Western Cape, located on the South Atlantic coast. The only intensive urban habitation of Western Cape, with a population of about 10.5 million. Population is about 40% white, 20% black, with the remainder being of mixed race or other ethnic groups.

Capulet and Montague — The two feuding families in the play, Romeo & Juliet, by William Shakespeare.

Cat out of the bag — A colloquialism meaning to reveal facts previously hidden. The derivation of the phrase is unclear. The most common suggestion is that the phrase refers to the punishment of flogging, administered on Royal Navy ships in the 18th and 19th centuries by the Bosun's Mate using a braided and knotted whip called a cat o' nine tails. The "cat" was kept in a leather or baize bag. It was considered bad news indeed when the cat was 'let out of the bag.'

CBRN Branch (L) — The Land Force's Chemical, Biological, Radiation and Nuclear Branch, traces its origins back to 1916 and the establishment of the War Department's Experimental Station near Salisbury, England. Their remit was the of researching and development of chemical weapons. (The US Army formed its own Chemical Warfare Service in 1918). The CBRN branch insignia combines the established symbology of chemical, biohazard and radioactive placed over each other. The branch identifying colour is cinnamon brown. 'Quaerere et Defendatis' (Search and Defend)

CBRN Branch (F) — The Fleet's CBRN Branch of the ABCANZ Land Force traces its origins back to 1964 and the expansion of existing NBC facilities to include the Royal Navy (Like the Royal Navy, the US Navy was content to let its respective Land Force take the lead in CBRN matters, using existing Army establishments to facilitate their own CBRN training and research. The Fleet's CBRN branch insignia, motto and colour is the same as the CBRN branch of the Land Forces.

Century City — A residential development in the Ysterplaat district of Cape Town. Multiple bars, restaurants and shops in the Canal Walk retail facility, (once the largest in Africa) also comprehensive sport and leisure opportunities. Several hotels, some with roof-top pools and casinos.

Cetus — An advanced, effective, but expensive short range anti-ship-missile, manufactured in the European Union by Thales Naval Systems.

CGD — Combustible Gas Detector

Chaplains Department   See <u>Administration Branch</u>

Chief   Chief Petty Officer (see <u>Enlisted Ranks</u>).

civvies   Military slang for 'civilians' and for wearing civilian clothing instead of uniform.

Clausewitz   Carl von Clausewitz (1780-1831), an early nineteenth century Prussian General and military theorist.

clip   Slang term for a weapon's magazine.

close protection   A type of security guard or government agent who protects a person or people (usually public, wealthy, or politically important) from danger: generally assault, kidnapping, assassination, harassment or other criminal offences.

coir fibre   A natural fibre extracted from the outer husk of coconuts.

Comanche   A fierce Native American tribe of the Southern Plains of the United States. The first 'upgraded' Fast Attack Corvette being developed for the <u>ABCANZ Fleet</u>.

Combat Engineering Branch (L)   The Land Force's Combat Engineering Branch traces its origins back to 1716 and the establishment of the Corps of Engineers at Woolwich, near London, before moving to Chatham in 1856. (The first US Army Engineering formations date from 1802). The Combat Engineering insignia is a pair of crossed pioneer axes, above which is a tower, representing their long tradition of fortification construction. Below the axes is an anchor, representing their role in bridging and river-based conveyance. The branch identifying colour is black. 'Construere est Vincereo' (To build is to win)

Command and Staff College   An academic facility that Land Force Officers attend at various stages to advance their careers through promotion. Located in the Quantico district of Nu New England.

Communications Branch (L)   The Land Force's Communications Branch traces its origins back to 1854 the established of a Telegraph Troop by the Royal Engineers. They would lay some 21km of cable during the Crimean conflict. In 1920, they would become a separate entity, The Royal Corps of Signals. (Congress established a permanent Signals

Corps within the US Army in 1863) The Communications branch insignia combines the traditional crossed flags with crossed electrical bolts of radio communication with a centrally placed globe with orbiting satellites. The branch identifying colour is dark blue. 'Certa Cito' (Swift and Sure)

Communications Branch (F) The Communications Branch of the ABCANZ Fleet traces its origins back to 1799 and as the issue of a standardized signal code system for the entire Royal Navy. Prior to this, flag signalling had been an ad-hoc and primarily a one-way system, whereby individual Admirals issued their own instructions. (US Navy was devising its own flag signalling protocols about the same time) The Fleet's Communications branch insignia, motto and colour is the same as the Communications branch of the Land Forces.

Co-ord   Coordination.

Corvette   A warship, smaller than a Frigate, but larger than a Patrol ship.

Darwin   Although small (population of 200,000) it is the largest conurbation in the region, and the capital of Australia's Northern Territory.

Dewa Ruci   A spiritual text that puts into consideration the fact that there is no code for doing the right thing since everything can be explained subjectively depending on people's deep spiritual morals. The moral of this story is that the highest point of enlightenment is to be found deep inside an individual.

Diamond Jack   The diamond shaped representation of the ABCANZ Federation flag, worn on most uniforms on the upper left sleeve, over (not above) the vertical 'branch' identifying coloured stripe(s). Sometimes referred to as 'The Jack.' Approximately 40mm x 40mm.

Diego Garcia   An island of the Indian Ocean Territory, an overseas territory of the ABCANZ Federation. It is a militarized atoll just south of the equator in the central Indian Ocean, the largest of 60 islands comprising the Chagos Archipelago. Settled by the French in the 1790s and transferred to British rule in 1814.

discharging — Maritime terminology for the unloading of cargo.

DO — Duty Officer. A temporary position assigned to a junior military officer in a shift or watch system. The Duty Officer is charged with responsibility for a military unit and acts as the Commanding Officer's representative. The Duty Officer attends to menial tasks for the Commanding Officer such as being at the scene of an incident and being 'on call' during the night. This duty is in addition to the officer's normal duties. The Duty Officer's tour is generally 24 hours, but may be reduced to 12 hours if 'combat operations' are in effect. Large commands or vessels may also have a JDO (Junior Duty Officer) to assist the DO.

Dolos — An advanced, encrypted UHF radio system used by the ABCANZ Land Forces. Unlike mobile/cell phone technology, the location of the sender can be concealed. Uses integrated IFF handshake protocols as standard.

double-time — Military terminology for moving at a jogging pace. Twice as fast as a normal marching pace, hence 'double time.'

DTG — Date-Time-Group. A standardised sequence that gives the date, time and time zone of an occurrence or event.

EAP — Evasive Assault Pattern.

ECM — Electronic Counter-Measure is an electrical or electronic device designed to trick or deceive radar, sonar or other detection systems, like infrared or lasers. It may be used both offensively and defensively to deny targeting information to an enemy. The system may make many separate targets appear to the enemy, or make the real target appear to disappear or move about randomly.

Elec and Mech Engineering Branch (L) — The Land Force's Electrical and Mechanical Engineering Branch, traces its origins back to 1914 and the formation and deployment of Mobile Workshops by the Army Ordnance Corps into France, as the reliance on horses diminished and the use of mechanical transport and equipment increased. The equipment repair function would separate into its own corps (the REME) in 1942. (The US Army introduced a similar system when it joined the hostilities in 1917) The Electrical and Mechanical Engineering insignia is a mechanical cog pierced by a pair of electrical bolts. The branch identifying colour is pewter grey. 'Arte et Marte' (Skill and Initiative)

Elec and Mech Engineering Branch (F)   The Fleet's Electrical and Mechanical Engineering Branch its origins back to 1835. Originally this included engines, motors, pumps and other mechanical devices, but today's engineers are responsible for both mechanical and electronic systems including radar, sonar and the vessel's fusion reactor. (The Mechanical Engineering Department in the US Navy traces its roots back to 1840, when steam propulsion first came into service). The Fleet's Electrical and Mechanical branch insignia, motto and colour is the same as the Electrical and Mechanical branch of the Land Forces.

Electrical Resistivity Tomography   A geophysical technique for imaging sub-surface structures from electrical resistivity measurements taken at or above the surface.

ELFI   Encrypted Live-Feed Imagery, the Fleet's latest secure video communications systems.

Elmendorf Base   The small ABCANZ Federation military base in Anchorage, Alaska. A former USAF facility.

EM   Electro-Magnet, or Electro-Magnetic.

Emirates City   A coastal city of the Arab League in the Persian Gulf. Incorporating all the former cities/Emirates of Abu Dhabi, Dubai and those further eastwards along the coast such as Sharjah.

Enlisted Ranks   Fleet   Land Forces

Fleet Chief Petty Officer.........Sergeant Major
Chief Petty Officer..................Staff Sergeant
Petty Officer............................ Sergeant
Master Crewman....................Corporal
Leading Crewman...................Lance Corporal
Crewman................................Trooper

Note that within the rank of Sergeant Major / Fleet Petty Officer, there are three levels, and three different rank insignia, identifying the holder as being either a Company, Battery or Squadron Sergeant Major, or a Battalion or Regimental Sergeant Major, with the highest level being a Garrison or Branch of Service Sergeant Major. As a Fleet Chief, the levels are for a single, larger vessel, a shore-establishment or Flotila, with the most senior being the most senior enlisted seaman in one of the six established Fleets and usually on the commanding Admiral's staff.

Equerry   A personal attendant appointed to a member of the Royal Family.

EPD   Embassy Protection Detachment. A Land Force Infantry Formation, of approximately Troop size, augmented by other branches of service, such as a med-tech, VTOL flight crew and ground support team, Heavy Weapons squad and other specialists required by mission parameters.

ERB   Emergency Ration Bar.

ERT   See Electro-Magnetic Tomography.

European Union   The most powerful of the post-war European states. Much smaller than the original 'EU' but consisting of the former states of Germany, France, Belgium, The Netherlands, Luxembourg, and Ireland with the northern, industrial regions of both Spain and Italy. Joint Capital cities: Nu Paris and Rhinestadt.

FAC   Fast Attack Corvette

Fähnrich   The European Union's equivalent of a 'Midshipman,' or an Officer Cadet, still in his or her training to become a commissioned military Officer.

Falkland Islands   The ABCANZ Federation Dependency in the South Atlantic. There is only one city, Fitzroy, which encompasses the former habitations of Stanley and Mount Pleasant and is the main operating base of the ABCANZ's 3rd (South Atlantic) Fleet.

False Flag   Originating from the 16th century, when a warship entered a hostile or neutral port flying a flag other than their own nationality to gain entry under false pretences. In modern times, used to describe a hostile act whereby one nation acts against another, citing a reason that actually of the perpetrators own manufacture, as justification for their actions.

Feldwebel — A rank of the European Union's military, of German origin, equivalent to a Sergeant. The literal translation is field-usher.

fender — A barrier, usually rubber, foam or plastic used to absorb the kinetic energy of a ship bumping against a quayside wall, jetty or other vessel, preventing hull damage.

Fenrir — A wolf, a son of Loki and the giantess Angrboða in Norse Mythology. He is foretold to kill the god Odin during the events of Ragnarök but will in turn be killed by Odin's son Víðarr.

FIB — Fast Intercept Boat. Small, very fast patrol ships.

Filibuster — An action such as a prolonged speech that obstructs progress in a legislative assembly while not technically contravening the required procedures.

Fitzroy — The small, and only city in the Falkland Islands. Encompasses the former settlements of Stanley and Mount Pleasant. Population of half a million people, although as much as 40% are transient, being ABCANZ military or oil and gas industry employees.

Flag Ranked Officers — Admirals and Commodores are considered to be of "Flag Rank." From the earliest days of the Navy, the Admiral in command of a fleet would fly an identifying flag from the mast of his "flag" ship.

Fleet Base Facility — An ABCANZ Fleet base that has ships permanently based at it.

Fleet Command — The overall authority on all matters appertaining to the ABCANZ Fleet (Navy)

Fleet Support Facility — An ABCANZ Fleet base that had no ships permanently based from it, but provides re-supply to any Fleet assets that require replenishment.

Fox Hole — See Shell Scrape.

Fregattenkapitän — A European naval rank, the equivalent of a Commander. Usually depicted with three full-size cuff rings and a narrow ring between the top and second full-size ring.

FRS   Short range "Family Radio Services' comprising of twenty-two short range, two-way voice communication radio channels used for walkie-talkies, baby monitors and children's toys.

FSF   Fleet Support Facility.

Furchtlos   German adjective, translates as fearless. *Das Furchtlos* is therefore *The Fearless*.

G58 Assault Rifle   A 5.56mm assault rifle manufactured in the EU by H&K and is the evolution/upgrade of their successful HK33 and HK53 models.

Galeries Lafayette   A Nu Paris headquartered luxury department store chain.

galley   Accepted naval/maritime terminology for a kitchen aboard a ship.

Gardiners Island   A 10km x 5km island in Gardiners Bay, at the eastern end of Long Island, Nu New England.

General Staff Branch (L)   The Land Force's General Staff Branch traces its origins back to 1903 and the establishment of a General Staff in Washington DC to assist senior officers in battlespace management. (The British Army followed, establishing their own in 1905, rotating its officers between command (non-staff) and staff appointments). Most officers serving in Staff positions retain their original branch insignia to make their speciality easily identifiable. Only the Brigade (or higher) formation's Commander, Deputy Commander and Chief of Staff replace their original branch insignia with that of the General Staff. The insignia is a stylised compass and compass ring. The branch identifying colour is dark crimson. 'Ducens ad Vicoriam' (Leading to Victory)

Geneva Convention   A series of international laws that regulates the conduct of armed conflict, seeking to limit its overall effect.

GPS   Global Positioning System.

Great Nicobar   The southernmost and largest of the Nicobar Islands. The island covers 921 km² and is sparsely inhabited, with a population of under 10,000. Largely covered by rainforest, it has a unique and diverse wildlife.

green slime   The derogatory term used within the military for Land Force Intelligence. 'Grey slime' is the Fleet equivalent.

grey slime
The derogatory term used within the military for Fleet Intelligence. 'Green slime' is the Land Force equivalent.

Gyre
There are five major global gyres, which are large systems of rotating ocean currents.

HAHO
High Altitude – High Opening. A type of clandestine parachute insertion technique utilizing a high-altitude jump, above radar detection heights for the jump, and a high-opening, enabling them to come in slowly. Usually undertaken at night and with oxygen to assist breathing.

Hai Private Security
A large, Bangkok headquartered, Private Security Contractor (PSC), providing standard and bespoke law enforcement, close quarter and VIP security services to governments and private individuals within south-east Asia.

Hampton
A maritime city district of Nu New England, in the former US State of Virginia.

Hampton Roads
The largest ABCANZ Fleet Base. Home of 1st Fleet as well as many other Fleet and Land Force training, educational, research, evaluation and intelligence facilities.

Harlequin
A highly effective short range, ship or aircraft mounted anti-shipping missile used by the ABCANZ Fleet.

HI
Heuristic Intellect. A computer that modifies itself as it learns.

High Command
The supreme military headquarters that sits above Fleet Command and Land Command in the ABCANZ military.

HV
high-voltage

IDent
The standard biometric identity data used throughout the ABCANZ Federation that accesses stored records of fingerprints, retina scanning and facial recognition to confirm an individual's identity.

IFF
'Identification, Friend or Foe' is an identification system designed for command and control. It uses a transponder that listens for the required 'interrogation' signal and then sends an appropriate response that identifies

the broadcaster. IFF systems often use radio or radar frequencies, but other electromagnetic frequencies, or infrared transmissions may be used.

Infantry Branch (L) — The Land Force's Infantry Branch traces its origins back to 1650 and the establishment of the Coldstream Guards, the oldest continuously serving regular formation of the British Army, at Coldstream, Scotland. (The first US Infantry formations was authorised by Congress in 1775). The Infantry insignia is the flaming grenade of the Grenadier Guards, a devise also synonymous with many infantry formations right across the world. Over this is placed a Roman gladius sword. The branch identifying colour is dark green. 'Quicquid Capit' (Whatever it Takes)

Intelligence Branch (L) — The Land Force's Intelligence Branch traces its origins back to 1873 and the establishment of an Intelligence Branch within the London War Office. (The US formed their own Military Information Division in 1885). The Intelligence insignia uses the 'all seeing eye' within a triangle and the rays of the sun, (referencing the all-seeing, all-hearing Greek god Helios) pieced by a Roman Gladius sword. This was considered a more obvious depiction of the Branch's function than the rose and some other devices used historically. The branch identifying colour is dark purple. 'Victoria ex Scientia' (Victory from Knowledge)

Intelligence Branch (F) — The ABCANZ Fleet's Intelligence Branch traces its origins back to 1882 with the Royal Navy establishing its Foreign Intelligence Committee, and the Office of Naval Intelligence of the US Navy being formed within in the same year. The Fleet's Intelligence branch insignia, motto and colour is the same as the Intelligence branch of the Land Forces.

IPB — Intelligence Preparation of the Battlefield.

IV — Intra-Venous. Term used to describe the administration of fluids and medicines directly into the blood, rather than by ingestion or absorption.

Jarawa Base — A large naval base and airfield of the Indian Armed Forces located in Port Blair. It provides logistical and administrative support to Indian navy ships deployed to East Asia and the Pacific

Ocean. Base is commanded by a 3-star general or equivalent.

Jarnsaxa | In ancient Norse mythology a sea goddess and the girlfriend of Thor.

JDO | See DO

Jessi Mauboy | An Australian singer, magician, songwriter, and actress. Born and raised in Darwin, Australia in the first half of the 21st century.

Kalmar Union | The post-war European state that encompasses the former nations of Denmark, Norway, Sweden, Finland, Iceland, Greenland and their former territories in and around the Norwegian Sea. Capital City: Kalmar City. The name is taken from the previous union of these nations between 1397 and 1523.

Kapten | An officer rank of the Thai military. equivalent to an army Captain.

Kapitän zur See | A naval rank used in Europe. Higher than a Kommander and lower than a Kommodore. Usual rank insignia is four rings on the cuff.

Katchal | Katchal Island, previously known as Tihanyu, is not easily accessible and even Indian nationals need a special pass to visit the island. Due to the remote location and lack of exposure with the rest of the world, the islanders were exploited until 1957, when Indian government legislation prohibited non-islanders from visiting. After the atomic war of the 21st century, several new micro-settlements were established illegally. Their continued existence continues to be debated.

klicks | A slang term for kilometres.

knot | A unit of speed used by shipping and aircraft, equivalent to one nautical mile (1.852 km) per hour.

Kommodore | A rank currently used in some navies and previously used in others. Higher than a Captain, but lower than an Admiral.

Koperal | A junior NCO rank in the Thai military.

Korvettenkapitän | A European naval rank, the equivalent of a Lieutenant Commander, but often using three rings on the cuff.

Kresty Noya — A Russian maximum-security prison located on Valaam Island on Lake Ladoga. Sometimes referred to as 'The Monastery,' (the previous resident of the island), as it too had 'cells.' Inmates wear a collar that contains an explosive charge that detonates if inmate is more than 7km from the centre of the island to prevent inmates trying to escape by swimming, or when the lake freezes over during the winter months.

Kwashaka — The megalomaniac dictator of South Africa during the war years. Changed allegiances several times depending on who was offering him the most money and influence. Authority maintained by his extensive and brutal military regime. Eventually eliminated by the ABCANZ Fed in the final year of the conflict.

Lake Ladoga — A freshwater lake to the east of Nu Piter. Largest lake in Europe, at 219km long x 83km wide.

Land Command — The overall authority over all matters appertaining to the ABCANZ Land Forces (Army).

L Band — The range of frequencies in the radio spectrum from 1 to 2 gigahertz (GHz). This is at the top end of the ultra-high frequency (UHF) band, at the lower end of the microwave range. It is used by various applications such as radars, global positioning systems (GPS), radio, telecommunications, aircraft surveillance and missile guidance.

Legal and Justice Branch (L) — The Land Force's Legal and Justice Branch traces its origin to 1855 and the permanent establishment of the Military Mounted Police in Aldershot, England. Prior to this, there had been units formed "to keep discipline and deal with an excess of criminality and desertion" from 1813, but they were disbanded at the end of hostilities. (The US Army did not formally establish a Military Police corps until 1941). The Legal and Justice insignia is the bowls and balance arm of the 'scales of justice' with the central support or fulcrum being replaced by a Roman gladius sword. Behind this is an eight pointed 'police' star and the letters MP. The branch identifying colour is orange. 'Fiat Justitias' (Let Justice be Done)

Legal and Justice Branch (F) — The ABCANZ Fleet's Force Legal and Justice Branch, traces its origins back to 1699 and the establishment of the 'Master at Arms' position on-board every ship. Maintaining order and discipline became the responsibility of the Regulating Branch, when shore-establishments were added to their remit in 1944. (The US Navy established its own 'Master at Arms' position by act of Congress in 1797 with the 'Shore Patrol' being established in 1942). The Fleet's Justice and Legal branch insignia, motto and colour is the same as the Legal and Justice branch of the Land Forces.

Leftenan_____A junior officer rank in the Thai armed forces equivalent to a Lieutenant.

Legion d'Honneur_____The highest award given by the European Union for 'most excellent conduct or service.' There is no military or civil distinction. It is a hybrid of the old French Legion d'Honneur and the early 20th century meritorious award of Germany known as the 'Blue Max.'

Lennox Group_____An ABCANZ Federation engineering conglomerate. Global headquarters located in Nu New England. The company has four main business sectors: Industrial, Energy, Military and Healthcare.

less leather and metal_____An unofficial term used with Number 1 or Number 2 Dress uniforms to indicate that swords, scabbards, sword belts, full size medals and headdress are not to be worn (usually because it is a social event), in which case a waist sash and miniature medals are worn in lieu.

Leutnant zur See_____Usually just referred to as a Leutnant, the lowest rank of Officer in the European Union's navy. Equivalent to an Ensign in the ABCANZ Fleet.

LiDaR_____Laser imaging, Detection, and Ranging. It uses ultraviolet, visible, and/or near infrared light to image objects by targeting an object with a laser and measuring the time for the reflected light to return to the receiver.

Little Andaman_____The fourth largest of the Andaman Islands with an area of 707 km^2. It is 88 km south of Port Blair.

Logistics Branch (L)_____The Land Force's Logistics Branch traces its origins back to 1888 and the establishment of the Land Transport Corps in Bristol, England. Before this, military logistics was an unsatisfactory affair using the services of numerous civilian contractors. (The US Army did not establish a Transportation Corps until 1942). The Logistics insignia shows a vehicle steering wheel to represent transport, from the top of which are three ears of wheat to symbolise food distribution. Over this are two crossed keys of the Quartermaster's stores, representing the storage and distribution of the resources required to conduct operations, including munitions, as symbolised by the stack of six cannon balls. The Branch identifying colour is cobalt blue.'Sustindum Victoriam' (Sustaining Victory)

Logistics Branch (L)
The Fleet's Logistics Branch traces its origins back to 1550 and the appointment of a Surveyor-General of Victuals by the Navy Board. The reforms of 1832, saw the Admiralty's replace that position with a Comptroller *of Victualling and Transport Services. (The US Navy's Supply Corps* considers as its establishment date as 1795, when the first Purveyor of Public Supplies, was appointed by President Washington). The Fleet's Logistics branch insignia, motto and colour is the same as the Logistics branch of the Land Forces.

M37 Assault Rifle
Standard issue, 5.56mm assault rifle of the ABCANZ Military. 40 round magazine. Effective range of 400 metres.

M85
A thirty-five millimetre grenade launcher, used by the ABCANZ Land Force Infantry, fed from a ten round carousel magazine.

M214
Multiple rotating barrelled, 5.56mm standard Squad Support Weapon used by the ABCANZ Land Force Infantry. Ammunition carried in an armoured belt from the auto-feeding backpack. Can use both MPT-SD or a more conventional ball-tracer mix.

M504 Halberd
Standard anti-armour, anti-bunker and anti-aircraft capability missile used by the ABCANZ Land Forces. Usually fired from a twin-tubed shoulder launcher, Known as the 'jackhammer' by the Infantry because of its 'double-tap' capability. Firing a ten-kilo tandem shaped charge up to three kilometres. Vehicle mounted pods and launcher racks with multiple missiles are also utilized.

Maana
Or Maan, the Hindi word for mum or mother.

Mahaapaur — A Hindi word roughly equivalent to a town mayor.

Marion Island — See Prince Edward Islands.

Marlin torpedo — Mk67 Marlin. The standard sub-surface anti-ship missile used by the ships of the ABCANZ Fleet.

masked palm civet — A nocturnal cat-like creature endemic to south-east Asia.

Matrosenfeldwebel — Also known as a *Maitre*, the European Union's equivalent rank title for a Petty Officer.

Matrosenoberfeldwebel — The European Union's rank title for a senior Petty Officer.

Matrosenstabsfeldwebel — The European Union's equivalent rank title for a Chief Petty Officer.

Matrosenoberstabsfeldwebel — The European Union's equivalent rank title for a Fleet Chief Petty Officer.

Med Centre — Medical Centre.

Medical Branch (L) — The Land Force's Medical Branch, traces its origins back to 1855 and the establishment of the Medical Staff Corps in Chatham, England, formalising the previous arrangements of the Army Medical Department and Hospital Conveyance Corps. (The US Army's 1775 provision for medical services were not formalised by Congress until 1908). The Medical insignia is the outline of a small-arm cross over which is a snake entwined sword, a variation on the Rod of Asclepius, the Greek deity associated with healing and medicine. The branch identifying colour is raspberry shade of pinkish red. 'In Arduis Fidelis' (Faith in Adversity)

The Land Force's Veterinary Branch, (a sub-branch of the Medical Branch) traces its origins to 1859 and the establishment of the Veterinary Medical Department at Woolwich, near London. This brought together all the earlier strands of horse care, some of which formed in 1796, but were usually civilian appointments made by individual regiments. (The US Army has a similar situation, with early provision not being formalised by Congress until 1916). Their insignia is the outline of a small-arm cross, over which is a stylised horse head facing right and a dog head facing left, the two animals that are still used by the military. The branch identifying colour is chartreuse yellow.

Medical Branch (F)   The ABCANZ Fleet's Medical Branch, traces its origins back to 1692 when treatment for sick and wounded Royal Navy personnel was administered by the Commissioners of the Sick and Hurt Board. (The US Navy used civilian contracted physicians until 1871 when the Medical Corps of the United States Navy was established). The Fleet's Medical branch insignia, motto and colour is the same as the Medical branch of the Land Forces.

The ABCANZ Fleet's Veterinary Branch, (a very small sub-branch of the Medical Branch) provides a veterinary service to the drug and explosive sniffer dogs used by the Legal and Justice branch. (Their seniority date is 1916). The Fleet's Veterinary branch insignia, motto and colour is the same as the Veterinary branch of the Land Forces.

MPT-SD   Multi-Purpose Tracer - Self Destruct. The 20mm M940 round combines a light armour and high-explosive capability into a single round. The self-destruct feature engages at 2,300 metres and destroys the round, preventing it from falling back to earth and inflicting collateral damage.

Mürwik   The main training establishment for all German (since 1910) and then EU Naval Officers. It is located in a costal district of the European Union's most northern conurbation, Schleswig.

Musicians Branch (L)   The Land Force's Musicians Branch traces its official origin back to the establishment of the Royal Military School of Music in 1857. A great many bands of varying standards had existed prior to this date, formed at the discretion and purse of individual regimental Colonels. (A similar situation existed within the US Army and the United States Army Band, also known as 'Pershing's Own,' was not officially established until 1922.) The Musicians insignia is a five stringed lyre within a laurel wreath. The branch identifying colour is white. 'Nulli Secundus' (Second to None)

Musicians Branch (F)   The Fleet's Musicians Branch traces its origins back to 1767 when Royal Marine Bands were formed in Plymouth, Portsmouth, Deal and Chatham, along England's southern coast at existing Royal Navy facilities. Music on-board RN ship often consisted of a seaman who could play the fiddle or accordion. A more proficient, larger ensemble, at the discretion of and funded by, the Captain could also be retained. (The United States Marine Corps band consisting of 34 musicians was established by Congress in 1784). The Musician Branch insignia, motto and identifying colour is the same as the Land Forces Musician's Branch.

MV   Merchant Vessel.

Nancowry and Trinkat   Islands in the Nancowry subgroup, about 58 km north of the Great Nicobar.

narra tree   Also known as asana, padauk, mukwa, Burmese rosewood, or Andaman redwood, a genus of timber trees of the pea family, native to Asia and Africa.

NATO   North Atlantic Treaty Organisation. A collective defence treaty, formed in 1949. Responsibly expanded beyond military remit when United Nations disbanded in late 21st Century.

NCO   Non-Commissioned-Officer.

NGO   Non-Governmental-Organisation. Providers of specialized technical products, knowledge or services to support development or relief activities implemented on the ground by other organizations.

Nicobar Islands   An island archipelago in the eastern Indian Ocean, 150 km north of Banda Aceh on Sumatra, and separated from Thailand to the east by the Andaman Sea. Located 1,300 km southeast of the Indian subcontinent, across the Bay of Bengal, forming part of the Indian Union Territory of Andaman and Nicobar Islands.

Nitrous Oxide   Also known as 'Laughing Gas' can cause euphoria and/or mild hallucinations.

Nordsafe   Headquartered in the Kalmar Union, Nordsafe are a leading global manufacturer of marine life-saving systems, including lifeboats, rescue boats, davits and survival pods, integrated into a total safety solution for the military, merchant and offshore markets.

Northrop-Sperry   Northrop Sperry Marine is part of Northrop Grumman Mission Systems. Created by various mergers in the 20th and 21st centuries of smaller marine engineering companies, headquartered in Nu Britannia, with global offices and manufacturing facilities.

North Sentinel   One of the Andaman Islands. Home to the Sentinelese, an indigenous people in voluntary isolation who have defended, often by force, their protected isolation from the outside world. Since 1956 the Protection of Aboriginal Tribes Act prohibits travel to the island.

Nu Hawaii   A small ABCANZ city in the Pacific Ocean spread around the apron of the three still active volcanoes on Big Island, Hawaii.

Number One Dress   The reference given to the uniform worn for formal Ceremonial and Mess occasions by the ABCANZ Military. The same tunic, breeches and boots are worn for both, but the 'accessories' are tailored to suit. (See less leather and metal).

Number Two Dress   The reference given to the uniform worn for parade and barrack duties. Resembling a civilian suit of jacket (tunic) and trousers (or skirt) and worn with a shirt/blouse, tie and peaked cap. It is dark grey for Fleet and dark olive for Land Forces. It can be augmented with leather belt, gloves, sword and full size medals for parade occasions, The tunic and tie are often omitted for office-based barrack duties in the summer or hotter climates.

Number Eight Dress   The reference given to the camouflaged combat uniform worn for everyday 'in-barrack' use by enlisted ranks and by all personnel when operationally deployed. This is standard 'temperate climate 'splinter' pattern' camouflage on general issue to all personnel. Specific, non-standard camouflage patterns, such as those for desert, tropical or arctic environments are only issued as required and also have their own reference numbers.

Number Twelve Dress   The reference given to the dark grey one-piece suit, not unlike a military aviator's flight-suit, worn by all ABCANZ Fleet personnel for normal, day-to-day activities, when another uniform is not deemed more appropriate.

Nu New England   The vast, principal metropolis of the ABCANZ

Federation, encompassing most of the original 13 States of the USA, the States south of the Great Lakes, and the southern parts Ontario and Quebec Provinces of Canada.

Nu Paris — The joint-capital city of the European Union. Built post-war, slightly farther south than the old city of Paris, covering significant parts of the former regions of Bourgogne, Centre and the northern Auvergne. Population of 40 million.

Nya Svealand — The second city of the Kalmar Union. Home to 10 million people, covering all of the former Swedish city and county of Stockholm.

Officer Ranks

Fleet	Land Forces
Admiral	General
Commodore	Brigadier
Captain	Colonel
Commander	Major
Lieutenant	Captain
Ensign	Lieutenant

Note that within the rank of Admiral and General, there are four levels, with different rank insignia, identifying the holder as being a higher formation commander or holding an equivalent appointment at some training institutions and or headquarters and commands.

ONR — Office of Naval Research. A department within Fleet Command that coordinates, executes and promotes the science and technology programs of the ABCANZ Fleet.

OpsCen — Operations Centre. A facility, usually on a warship, manned 24 hours a day, where all incoming communications, reports and information are received, logged, analysed and processed.

op-sec — Operational Security

Osprey — A large, fish-eating bird of prey. A fast intercept Patrol ship of the ABCANZ 2nd Fleet.

OTA(F) — Officer Training Academy (Fleet)

OTA(L) — Officer Training Academy (Land)

Padang — The capital and largest city of the of Pancasila Republic region of West Sumatra. (Population of 1 million) padauk — An endemic tree in the Andaman and Nicobar Islands but is also native to India. It grows in deciduous and semi-moist forests up to 100m tall.

Pancasila Republic — Formerly known as Indonesia. Name changed after the war to formerly recognise the principal philosophy on which the state of Indonesia was re-formed after the partial Chinese occupation.

Paramagnetic — An electro-magnetic treatment/coating applied to clothing and equipment to enable a small electric charge to increase or decrease the spacing of the particles, thereby effecting a colour change.

Parley — A meeting between opposing sides in a dispute, especially a discussion of terms for an armistice.

Peconic — The bay of water between the North Fork and South Fork at the tip of Long Island, in Nu New England. Popular for sailing.

Pennant — Abbreviated reference to 'Pennant Number,' the visual flag referencing system originally used to identify warships in 18th and 19th century. Duly replaced by numbers painted onto the hull in the 20th and later centuries.

Port Blair — The capital city of the Andaman and Nicobar Islands. (Population of 200,000)

Port Facilities Branch (F) — The Fleet's Port Facilities Branch traces its origins back to 1546 and the founding of the Royal Navy, as it inherits the linage of the Shipwrights. Its modern function is to provide all dockyard and port facilities not specifically provided by another branch, including expeditionary port enhancement. (The US Navy established its Naval Construction Force in 1942) The branch uses the same insignia, motto and identification colour of the Land Force's Combat Engineering Branch.

Port Salish — An ABCANZ city on the Pacific coast of North America, encompassing parts of the former Washington State around Seattle and the parts of British Columbia around Vancouver and Victoria.

PQO — Professionally Qualified Officer.

Prince Edward Islands — Two small islands in the sub-Antarctic Indian Ocean. A Dependency of Western Cape. Both

Marion Island and Prince Edward Island have been declared Special Nature Reserves and activities on the islands are restricted to research and conservation management.

PSC — Private Security Contractor

Rail-Gun — A linear motor device, typically designed as a weapon, that uses electromagnetic force to launch high velocity projectiles. The projectile does not contain explosives, instead relying on the projectile's high speed, mass, and kinetic energy to inflict damage.

Recyk — Brand name of multi-national waste recycling organisation, Recyk Inc. Becoming synonymous with any recycling activity and is often used as a verb.

Reunion — An island dependency of the European Union in the Indian Ocean, east of Madagascar. Population of about 1 million. The EU maintains an enhanced Airmobile Brigade and significant naval facilities on the island.

revetment — A barrier of sandbags and/or corrugated-tin, providing protection from blast and preventing trench walls from caving-in.

RF — Radio Frequency

RG — Rail Gun

Rhinestadt — The joint-capital of the European Union, situated to the east of the River Rhine encompassing the entire former German region of North Rhine-Westphalia.

RIB — Rigid Inflatable Boat

ROSP — Remote Operational Support Platform. An oil-rig like structure positioned by the ABCANZ Fleet into areas where no friendly land based facilities exist to give operational support to deployed Fleet assets. Providing limited quantities of fuel, food, armaments and limited hospital and repair faculties.

RPG — Rocket Propelled Grenade.

rounds — Military terminology for ammunition. From bullets in a rifle, to shells in an artillery system, all are referred to as 'rounds.'

RPG — Rocket Propelled Grenade.

RV Point — A rendezvous point. A series of locations used by ground troops when on a mission or patrol. They can be pre-planned or improvised. Final RV, Emergency RV or numbered 1stRV.

Ryazan Academy — A military educational institute of the Russian military. Since 1947 the official military academy and advanced training centre of Russian Airborne Forces.

Safe-Transit-Routing — An internationally agreed navigational routing used by shipping to avoid wrecks and contamination. Categorised Green, Amber, Red and Black, depending on how 'safe' the route is.

Saigon Mói — Formerly Ho-Chi-Minh City, the largest city in Vietnam, situated in the southeastern region, the city follows the Saigon River delta and lines both banks inland for over a 100km. (Population of 10 million)

San Angeles — The second largest city in the North American territory of the ABCANZ Federation. Encompasses most of the former state of California.

sAPPHIre — s-ADVANCED PERSONAL PROCESSING HEURISTIC INTELECT-re. Shortened to 'Safi.'

Sarjan — A senior NCO rank in the Thai military roughly equivalent to a sergeant.

Science and Technology (L) — The Science and Technology Group is not part of the Land Force, but a civilian agency funded by Land Command to provide professional scientists and technical support to military operations. Field deployments are not uncommon and therefore a pseudo branch identity was required. Its origins date from 1907 and the formation of what was to become the Armament Research and Development Establishment. (The US Army's civilian Science and Tech agencies did not get established as a single entity until 1991). The Science and Tech insignia consists of mechanical gears retaining atomic arcs that in turn surround a bubbling chemical flask from which a biological construct propagates. The flask sits above a stylised circuit board. The branch identifying colour is dark teal. 'Imagina Invetio Inspiro' (Imagine . Invent . Inspire)

Science and Technology (F) The Science and Technology Branch is not part of the Fleet, but a civilian agency funded by Fleet Command through the ONR (<u>Office of Naval Research</u>) to provide professional scientists and technical support to Fleet operations. Ship deployments by its personnel are not uncommon and therefore a pseudo branch identity was required. Its origins date back to 1872 and the establishment of the Admiralty Experiment Works in Torquay, England. (The US Navy's ONR was established in 1946) The Fleet's Science and Technology insignia, motto and colour is the same as the S&T personnel supporting the Land Forces.

SCIF A small, sub-surface craft used by the military for covert beach insertions from larger vessels. The abbreviated form of Scuba Craft Insertion – Fast.

Screw Sloop A propeller-driven sloop-of-war. In the 19th century, during the introduction of the steam-driven ships, 'screw' was used to differentiate from those driven by paddlewheels. Other propeller-driven warships included screw frigates and screw corvettes.

Scopolamine A natural drug that renders the receiver susceptible to suggestion, (mind control). combined with short-term memory loss.

Section An <u>ABCANZ Land Forces</u> formation of four men, sometimes referred to as a 'fire team.'

Sekhmet The warrior goddess of Upper Egypt.

Senior NCO Senior Non-Commissioned-Officer. The group of ranks above 'Junior Ranks' and below 'Commissioned Officers.'

Sharjah A semi-autonomous District of Emirates City. Large free port and industrial activity. Traditionally more conservative than some other districts. Alcohol is unavailable and modesty codes on dress for men and women are still enforced. Population of 2 million.

shell scrape A shell scrape, also known as a fox hole, is a shallow depression often quickly hand-dug to accommodate one or two soldiers but offering little protection unless occupant(s) is prone.

shipsuit See <u>Number Twelve Dress</u>.

sit-rep   Situation Report. An update on the current situation.

skiff   A civilian corruption of SCIF. The smaller, faster, civilian version of the military Scuba Craft Insertion - Fast.

SLS   Sodium Lactate Solution. A mixture, usually administered intra-venously, of sodium-chloride, sodium-lactate, potassium-chloride, and calcium-chloride in water. It is used for replacing fluids and electrolytes in those who have low blood volume or low blood pressure following trauma.

snoopers   A low tech camera and sound recording mini-UAV platform used extensively by the tabloid media.

South Anderman   The southernmost island of the Great An daman group and home to most of the population of the Andaman Islands.

Southern European Alliance   A post-war European nation, also known as 'The Pigs.' (Portugal, Italy (southern half), Greece and Spain (southern half). The original 'break-away' states of the old European Union with less robust economies. Also included are the islands of Malta, Cyprus, Sardinia, Sicily and the Balearics for geographic, economic and historic ties. Capital city: Barcelona. Many of these regions had previously been united under the 'Crown of Aragon' from 1344 to 1713. Sometimes referred to as the 'SEnyerA States.'

Special Operations Branch (F)   The Fleet's Special Operations Branch traces its origins back to 1940 and the formation of the Commandos, who were established to carry out covert amphibious raids against German occupied Europe. (The US military formed a joint Army/Marine amphibious reconnaissance unit the following year in preparation for operations on the beaches of North Africa). All personnel permanently supporting Special Operations belong to this branch, with the actual operators also displaying the winged dagger badge (below). The branch insignia, motto and identifying colour is the same as that used by the Land Force Infantry Branch.

Special Operator   Fleet and Land Force personnel who have passed Special Operations Training. Subsequently becoming part of a deployable, elite Special Operations formation. The insignia of a winged commando dagger is worn on right upper arm, above any rank and branch identifier.

Squad	An ANCANZ Land Forces formation of eight men, usually in two sections or 'fire-teams,' each of four men.
stag	Military slang for a rotational guard duty. Either being 'on stag,' or to be 'stagging on.'
Staff Officer	A military officer employed in a headquarters with an administrative, planning or intelligence analysis function.
Stern Chase	When the pursuing craft follows directly in the wake of the vessel being chased.
STR	Safe-Transit-Routing. A navigational route used by shipping to avoid wrecks and contamination. Categorised Green, Amber, Red and Black, depending on how 'safe' the route is.
Suez	The canal linking the Mediterranean with the Red Sea. Due to strategic location, it was extensively bombed with Atomic, Biological and Chemical munitions during the war. Returned to operational status within ten years of hostilities ending, but region remains heavily contaminated and the Red Sea is infested with pirates.
TDT	Tactical Data Tablet. An A5 sized 'ruggedized' computer, used by military commanders. Known universally as a 'battle-board.'
Teapot	Slang and derogatory term for the nuclear reactor on a ship, as the rection process boils water.
Texas City	The third largest of the Federation's five North American mainland conurbations. Includes the old cities of Dallas, Fort Worth, Austin, Houston and Galveston.
The Residency	The official residence of the Prime Minister of the ABCANZ Federation. Located in 'The Capital' district of Nu New England.

Thunder Cove   The British and United States military have used <u>Diego Garcia</u> since at least the mid-1960s. The island has port facilities and an airstrip capable of handling large aircraft. Approximately 2,000 military personnel in residence. The base serves as a support facility for both surface ships and submarines. It also houses sophisticated radar, space tracking and communication installations.

Tokamak   A type of fusion reactor. The word is actually a Russian acronym that stands for "toroidal chamber with magnetic coils."

torus   A revolving, geometric shape resembling a ringed donut.

Tracy Island   The tech-heavy secret headquarters of the fictional International Rescue organisation in the late 1960s British children's TV series *Thunderbirds*. The Series has been resurrected and reinvented numerous times (approximately every 15 years) throughout the 20th and 21st centuries. and has seen adaptations into movies, animations, and other media platforms based on the original TV. In the original series, the tech-heavy, heavily-camouflaged island is located in the South Pacific Ocean and is home to the Tracy family.

Tribune   In the Roman period, young men of noble birth who served as officers in the Legion. Below the overall command of the Legate, but above the experienced war-fighting Centurions. Deemed a very necessary 'stepping-stone' to a future career serving in the Imperial Senate.

Troop   A Land Forces formation comprising of 3 'fighting' Squads and a command/support Squad. Usually 32 men strong, commanded by a Lieutenant.

tsunami   A large wave (or series of waves) generated by the displacement of water by an event, above or below the water, such as an earthquake, a volcanic eruption, an underwater landslide, a glacier calving and a meteorite impact.

UAV   Unmanned Aerial Vehicle.

UHF   Ultra-High-Frequency radio frequencies.

Unteroffizier   A junior NCO rank of the European Union's military, of German origins, equivalent to a

Corporal.

Valaam Island
A remote island in the northeast of <u>Lake Ladoga</u>. Home to a monastery for more than 600 years. Now the location of the <u>Kresty Noya</u> maximum security prison.

VDM
Visual Distinguishing Mark. A mole, scar, tattoo, birthmark or any other permanent mark on someone's (face, hands and arms) which can be seen without removing their clothes.

VHF
Very High Radio Frequencies

VTOL
Vertical Take-Off and Landing.

Warfare Systems Branch (F)
The Fleet's Warfare Systems Branch operate the radar, sonar and other sensor and target acquisition systems operated by the Fleet and trace their origins back to 1918 when R-Class Royal Navy submarines were first fitted with hydro-phonic equipment, the forerunner of Sonar. (The US Navy received ASDIC equipment from the British in 1940) However, because the Navigation and Helm functions are also grouped under Warfare Systems, their establishment and seniority date is pushed back to 1546 and the founding of the Royal Navy. The branch insignia, motto and identification colour are the same as that used by the Land Force Armoured Branch.

Weapon Systems Branch (F)
The Fleet's Weapon Systems Branch traces its origins back to 1546 when King Henry VIII established a permanent and armed fleet of ships, the Royal Navy. (The US Navy's equivalent establishment date is 1775). Responsible for the crewing and operation of all weapon systems onboard ship, their insignia, motto and identification colour are the same as that used by the Land Force Artillery Branch.

Western Cape
Originally a province in the south-west of South Africa. It broke away from being ruled from Pretoria during the war. Now an independent nation thanks to <u>ABCANZ Federation</u> intervention. Principal city: Cape Town. Closely allied to, but not a member of the ABCANZ Federation.

XO
Executive Officer. The appointment of 'second-in-command' on an ABCANZ Fleet ship, shore facility or military formation.

Yuletide _____ The late December, end-of-year festival adopted by the ABCANZ states to replace the Christmas celebrations with a pre-Christian, non-religious festival, running from the Winter Solstice to the New Year.

MENTION IN DESPATCHES

My continued gratitude to Geoff Bargus who once again went through the evolving drafts and corrected my frequent errors.

My former colleague Kershaw Scoines must have special mention for giving me just enough information on missile operating and guidance systems to make my writing factually accurate, whilst not getting either of us into 'hot water' with breaches of the Official Secrets Act. Most appreciated Mr S, thank you.

Josie Hall for once more so effortlessly personifying Kat on the front cover, and Nathan Alti who took the images of Josie and then somehow crafted them into a Nicobari beach at sunrise. And, to Megan Jade Houlahan for Josie's hair and make-up.

Unlike all of Kat's previous adventures, that were written at numerous locations around the world, due to the travel restrictions of Covid 19, *Ardent Warrior* was exclusively written at home in southern England.

And finally, to my dear mum, Audrey Mason, nee Dunning, who sadly passed away whilst I was writing this adventure. A lady who unconditionally gave me so much, she is very much missed and so totally irreplaceable.